Porcupine County

All proceeds from the sale of this book will be donated to

Friends of the Porkies
www.porkies.org

The Friends of the Porkies is a non-profit organization aiding the Porcupine Mountains Wilderness State Park in Ontonagon County (prototype of Porcupine County) in the Upper Peninsula of Michigan. Among the Friends' many activities are cleaning up highways and trails in the park, organizing the yearly Porcupine Mountains Music Festival, running a folk school, sponsoring an artist-in-residence program, and providing volunteers for park-related community events.

PORCUPINE COUNTY

Also by Henry Kisor

Other Steve Martinez Mysteries

Hang Fire, 2013
Tracking the Beast, 2015
The Riddle of Billy Gibbs, forthcoming

Nonfiction

What's That Pig Outdoors: A Memoir of Deafness, 1990
Zephyr: Tracking a Dream Across America, 1994
Flight of the Gin Fizz: Midlife at 4,500 Feet, 1997

Contents

Season's Revenge

First published in hardcover by Forge Books, 2003
First published in paperback by Forge Books, 2004
First published as an e-book, 2011

For Vicki

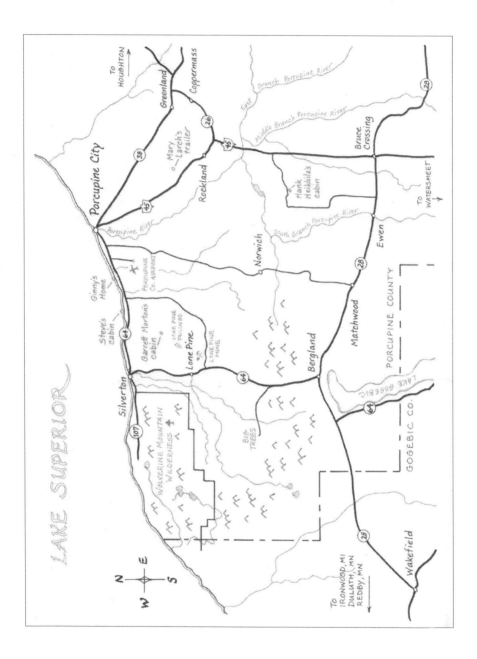

ONE

The people to whom I was born had lived here before fiercer tribes from the East chased them onto the Great Plains. From time to time they, too, must have stopped to take in the view. Framed in oak, it would have rivaled the photographic landscapes sold in the hopeful little gift shops that crop up in every dying small town in the Upper Peninsula of Michigan. This one was a panoramic shot of a stand of tall virgin white pine that crowned a rocky escarpment submarining upward from a deep green sea of pine and hemlock, birch and aspen. Just below the escarpment, a lily pond sparkled in the freshening sun. At dawn a light rain had misted the forest, raising the loamy aroma of damp woods. It was a still, cloudless morning in August, the loveliest time of the year.

Blood stained the foreground. Deep claw marks raked the victim's grizzled chest and bearded face, twisted in the rictus of sudden and painful death. His right arm jutted rigidly from the torn sleeping bag in the tatters of his tent, the shoulder deeply punctured, shreds of muscle and sinew dangling from the bone. Under the ruined ripstop nylon, blood puddled in a grisly pudding. Dozens of bear tracks — some of them streaked with crimson, bits of tissue clinging to grooves dug by claws — crisscrossed the moist ground around the campsite.

I looked up and sighed, trying to make sense of what I saw. From the bow of the escarpment jutted a lone wolf pine a hundred feet tall, its windward side limbless from decades of tacking into winter storms howling off Lake Superior. In the second-growth forests of westernmost Upper Michigan, wolf pines — aged, once-lordly white pines that had escaped the logger's ax because they were just out of easy reach — are symbols of flinty endurance to the people who hang on in this rugged wilderness country where livings are hard to make.

The Finns who settled here a century ago called that quality "sisu" — perseverance, fortitude, steadfastness. That morning I didn't know I was going to need it in the weeks to come.

Far from the well-trod hiking paths, Big Trees is a favorite retreat of veteran woodsmen who know the most remote crannies of Porcupine County. I'd been there once myself, as the companion of a local hunter. The place lay a rugged three-hour trek through clouds of mosquitoes and biting flies along a rocky, barely visible footpath — little more than a deer trail — branching southwest from an axle-snapping old loggers' track. The latter led into the Ottawa National Forest from a narrow paved road serving as the southern boundary of Wolverine Mountain Wilderness State Park, largest of its kind in all Michigan.

Still sweating from the hike, I stepped back from the tent, squashed a mosquito, and hitched up my gun belt, from which hung a .357 Combat Magnum in a tooled leather holster. No yuppie 9mm Berettas for me, I had vowed when I took the job with the sheriff's department. In the woods, I had reasoned, a man wants a heavy slug carrying lots of foot-pounds of energy. Large animals, especially charging ones, are harder to stop than gangbangers carrying Glocks. Aren't they?

It was not long until I discovered people don't need firearms of any kind in the woods, not unless they're hunting, either for game or for a dangerous felon. The people who live here walk in the forest all the time without weapons, except maybe a four-inch Buck knife, the woodsman's favorite tool, far handier than a cell phone is to a stockbroker. They feel comfortable in their surroundings, and they know the woods intimately. If one should encounter a large animal, both parties to the meeting usually take their respective leaves with as much dignity and alacrity as they can muster. And felons? They're in short supply here in the north woods. There's little to kill for, and less to steal. People here don't have a lot.

In the seven years I'd been a Porcupine County deputy, I hadn't had to draw my weapon except to dispatch an injured deer or wounded dog after a highway encounter. But I hung on to the heavy, old-fashioned .357 anyway, out of either fondness or sheer stubbornness, maybe, or just to be different. Nobody else in the sheriff's department carries a revolver.

Normally a deputy wouldn't be called in for ordinary bear incidents in either the park or the national forest — local rangers and conservation officers take care of matters — but this was a human death, the first bear-related fatality in the county in more than a decade. And the bloodied victim was no hapless tourist but a wealthy eminence of Porcupine County and one of its most celebrated woodsmen.

TWO

When I was a brand-new deputy, a big-bellied and elderly but strong and rangy man in sportsman's khakis and old-fashioned high-laced boots had paid a visit to my boss, Eli Garrow, the epitome of the good-old-boy country sheriff, more politician than peace officer. As I watched from my desk in the squad room, they met behind closed doors, and when they emerged half an hour later, Garrow looked as if he had swallowed something unpleasant.

I shot a quizzical glance at Joe Koski, the chubby, deceptively cherubic head dispatcher, chief corrections officer, and foremost gossip of the Porcupine County Sheriff's Department. Joe nodded and put a finger to his lips.

"Who's that?" I asked when the principals had disappeared.

"Paul Passoja," Joe said. "He is *the* big cheese of Porcupine County, bigger even than the sheriff or the prosecutor or all the commissioners rolled together — and, Steve, don't you ever forget it, if you want to keep your job."

Passoja, Joe continued, was the retired founder and president of a big Minnesota paper company who had grown up in Porcupine City, son and heir of Einar Passoja, the county's biggest lumberman and landowner. Like so many who call themselves Porkies, Paul had left his birthplace to make his fortune, adding a large pile of his own to his considerable inheritance. When he retired, he built a huge, showy summer home just east of Porcupine City on prime lakefront land that had been in the family for generations. In it he had installed a succession of young trophy wives — four or five, Joe wasn't sure how many.

Unlike most Upper Michigan timber barons, Einar had not abandoned all the forest land he owned to the taxman once it had been clear-cut, but hung on to prime acreage, including some along the lakeshore. In their monumental log mansion on one of the lots, the Passojas had long spent May through November, wintering at an equally luxurious pile in La Jolla.

Paul Passoja's public face was that of an amiable, unpretentious old-timer. Everybody liked him instantly on first meeting, and so did I. The teenage boys of the county loved him, because for decades he generously taught them the skills of survival in the woods, often taking half-a-dozen hikers at a time deep into the forest for several days' camping. In the last quarter century he had included members of the local Girl Scout troop as well, for he could change with the times.

But beneath that Santa Claus avuncularity, Joe had warned me, lay an iron will that brooked no impudence, especially in the affairs of Porcupine County. Paul Passoja was the wealthiest man in the county, maybe even the whole U.P., and held strong and conservative opinions about its welfare. No politician, not even the U.S. congressman who represented the entire Upper Peninsula, made a move that might affect Porcupine County in the smallest way without first consulting Passoja.

Often deals were struck during one of the all-male retreats he hosted during deer season at Nonesuch, his hunting camp just south of the Wolverine Mountains Wilderness State Park in the western end of the county, close to Big Trees. An invitation to Nonesuch meant you were a man of parts, that you had arrived, for the most powerful person in the county had noticed you. It was a kind of rite of passage in Porcupine County and one I had never undergone, being a lowly deputy sheriff as well as a relative newcomer.

Passoja's campaign contributions were just too hefty for politicians to ignore, and while he exercised his power in an unseen and largely benevolent manner, he also had a way of subtly turning people against those who had offended him with either their actions or their ideas. One soft word and a county commissioner too adventurous with his opinions would find himself isolated, the lamest of lame ducks until the next election turned him out.

Once a year Passoja would hike alone into the most remote corners of the forest and camp, often under the Big Trees he had loved so much in his youth, just to keep up his celebrated forest skills. Out of these trips came captivating stories and pictures of his adventures with wildlife, both as a hunter and as an accomplished amateur photographer. It seemed that he had met just about every inquisitive bear in the park and national forest. Only one man in the county, it seemed, knew more about bears than Paul Passoja did. That was Stan Maki, the Michigan Department of Natural Resources conservation officer who had arrived on the scene shortly after the hikers who discovered the body radioed their grisly discovery to him on their truck's CB.

THREE

Though he had been officially retired for years — he was in his late seventies, like Passoja — Stan was an unofficial part-timer who almost always was called in whenever a bear became a nuisance. Nobody in the Upper Peninsula was better at handling them than this small, bald, leathery, whipcord-strong and ageless man, so tanned by years in the outdoors that his skin never faded, even in the winter.

He was accompanied by a tall — six-seven, at least — and broad-shouldered lad of nineteen or so, also clad in DNR uniform. "Garrett Morton," Stan said by way of introduction. "Summer ranger. Plays basketball for Kalamazoo."

I shook hands with the blond giant. I'm not a small man, but Garrett towered over me by nearly a head. "Nice to meet you, Garrett," I said. He grinned, his dewy cheeks dimpling, and bobbed his head like an oversized puppy, cheerful and eager to please despite the grim circumstances of the morning. Still a kid, and probably not overly well-upholstered with brains.

Neither of the two middle-aged brothers who had found the body were strangers to me. Like the victim, Frank Metrovich and his younger brother, Bill, both short, squat, solid, hard-working, and public-spirited paper-mill hands, were "good men in the woods," the quiet and rare accolade Upper Peninsula natives give those who know the wilderness intimately. They stood uncertainly to the side of the small clearing, drawn and white, looking ready to part with their breakfasts.

"How'd you come to find him?" I asked the brothers.

"Paul told us in Merle's Café yesterday that he was going to Big Trees," Frank said. "The weather's so great we thought we'd hike in and say hello."

Bill nodded in assent, then sighed. "You know, Steve,"

he said, "Paul had seemed a little out of it lately. He's getting on to his eighties now and sometimes he gets forgetful. In the space of half an hour he told us three times he was going to Big Trees. Frankly, we were a little worried and wanted to check up on him."

By this time another hiker had trudged up the trail to join the scene. The place was becoming a regular Grand Central.

The newcomer was Hank Heikkila, a slight but immensely strong hermit in his fifties with a long, flowing, untrimmed beard like a Lubavitch Hasid rabbi and the same sour, untrusting view of his fellow man that a Lubavitcher has for the *goyim*. Hank lived in a rude shack deep in the forest on land he sometimes claimed was handed down from his grandfather and sometimes said belonged to a private party who let him live there in exchange for watching the place.

Many of us suspect the shack illegally lay on state forest land, but because Hank led a tough life—a manic-depressive, an off-again, on-again mental patient, from time to time he washed up at a halfway house in Porcupine City—we let him be to make his meager living among the "voices" he said he heard. He called himself a trapper, but—legal fur-bearing mammals being rare in this country and the trapping season quite short—he really scratched a few dollars together now and then as a woodsy jack-of-all-trades, as did so many people in this land of high unemployment. Now and then Hank cut a little aspen pulp wood from the national forest to sell to the mill. Once in a while he carpentered a shed for a landowner. I suspected he grew a little pot, too, mainly for himself.

In his cups he often claimed to be descended not only from Finns but also *voyageurs* from Quebec who in the seventeenth century left their long canoes on the beach, settled in this country and intermarried with the local Ojibwa. He spoke only when spoken to, and always in an almost inaudible growl. His neighbors, however, did not fear him. Frightening as he seemed to the uninitiated, he never turned violent. Though we suspected him of poaching, he took a deer quite legally every season—the resident license fee is only thirteen dollars—with a .45-70 Springfield, a heavy, long, cumbersome single-shot Army rifle with a trapdoor breech that was obsolete before the Spanish-American War. His transportation was a 1960s-vintage Ford pickup so rusty the only place solid enough to hold the license plate was the rear window.

"Hi, Hank," I said.

Grunt.

"How'd you hear about this?"

Mutter.

"Hank, I'm talking to you!"

"Scanner," he said finally.

Yes—the rural jungle telegraph. Porcupine County lay way too far out in the boonies for reliable cell-phone coverage. Some people owned CBs, but everybody had a radio scanner. I did, too. We listened to the road commission, especially in winter, when we wondered where the plows were and when they'd arrive to free us from our snowy prisons. We eavesdropped on PorTran, the state-subsidized commission that sent buses all over the county to pick up riders on demand. We listened to ambulance runs, to lake freighters and pleasure boats calling the Porcupine River swing-bridge tender, and to the operations at the sprawling paper mill. Everybody listened in as Joe Koski dispatched deputies everywhere. Hank, I suspected, owned a scanner just to keep one ear on the doings of the law while he performed the duties of the lawless.

Stan broke the mood. "This campsite is set up good and proper," he observed in a crisply professional tone that drew us all back to earth. "Tent well away from the cook site. Food pack hanging in the air."

Passoja had pitched his nylon backpacker's tent a good

twenty yards from the bare flat rock where he had prepared his last meal. His food cache dangled fifteen feet in the air, suspended on a rope between two tall aspens. But tracks and claw marks from a large black bear—"a mature one, at least four hundred pounds," Stan estimated—lay scattered around the tent, not the cooking area or under the food pack.

"Why'd the bear go after the tent instead?" Stan asked, echoing the thoughts of everyone present. "That's not how they behave. They go for the food."

"No weapon?" I asked, already knowing the answer. Like most people in these parts, Passoja never carried a firearm—unless he was hunting.

"None," Stan said.

It didn't look like a crime scene, but I am a cop, and cops always process scenes of violent death as if they were homicides. Nobody knows what really happened until all the facts are in.

So I did what cops do. I donned latex gloves and scanned the scene for clues. Dozens of them—platter-sized and claw-tipped—stared back at me.

Stan beckoned. "Look here, Steve," he said, crouching over the damp loam. "See those? The slash across them?" A faint raised diagonal line crossed the indentations made by the bear's left front paw. "An old scar, probably from a trap. That'll identify the bear when we catch him."

With a Polaroid camera I snapped pictures of the tracks, the body, and the tent, carefully peeling back the nylon shreds after taking each photo, until Passoja's ruined corpse lay fully exposed. Then I saw a few dark quarter-sized spots on the nylon, one a splatter, near a corner of the tent by the entry flap. I sniffed. Bacon grease.

"Hey, Stan," I said. He squatted and nodded as he saw the spots. I photographed them.

A tiny gray lump lay almost hidden in the dust by the tent entry. I picked it up. A shred of bacon.

It figured. "Nothing like coffee and bacon on a cold evening in the woods," Passoja often had said. He was an old-fashioned woodsman—none of that high-tech freeze-dried adventure-backpackers' stuff for him, although, out of respect for the danger of forest fires, he carried a modern one-burner butane stove. He always packed a small iron skillet and a rasher into the woods, and anybody fortunate enough to camp with him would spend the evening wreathed in the world's most delicious aroma.

I placed the scrap of bacon into a tiny flat-lidded tin that had once held a dozen cough drops—I save little containers like Sucrets tins and photo film cans, intending to use them to hold small things like fish hooks and screws, but never seem to get around to it. They pile up on my workbench, in my glove compartment, in my kitchen drawer, the detritus of good intentions and poor follow-through. I slid the tin into my shirt pocket.

"Looks like Paul might have carried his supper to the tent while he got something else and accidentally spilled some," Stan said soberly. "Maybe he wasn't even aware of it. But the odor would have attracted the bear during the night, and it would have tried to rip into the tent after more food. Probably Paul woke up and struggled to escape from his sleeping bag, and the surprised bear did what comes natural, defending itself. This isn't the first time something like this has happened."

I nodded. I am a great believer in Occam's razor, the adage that the simplest explanation for an event is most likely the true one.

By then another deputy had arrived with a litter. She was Mary Larch, the department's sole female sworn officer, a rookie with less than a year's experience behind a star. She and I worked the same eight-to-five shift. I covered the north and west of the county while she patrolled the east and south. We encountered each other frequently, both in the office and on patrol, especially when one of us needed backup.

Mary was a native of Porcupine County, a determined late bloomer in her mid-thirties, and studied criminal justice part-time at the university in Hancock. She was small but rugged, pretty, and very ambitious, and I was sure she'd go on to bigger and better things in larger departments. I admired her.

"Need help, Steve?" she asked brightly, always ready to pitch in in whatever way she could. "Joe thought you might. I brought a four-wheeler, but it's about a mile from here—I couldn't get it any farther in than Mills Creek."

The sheriff's department kept a powerful four-wheel-drive all-terrain vehicle in the bed of a pickup truck to get around in the boonies, but the faint track from the creek to Big Trees was too steep and rocky even for it.

"Nope, we're done here," I said. "We're ready to zip him up."

Stan and Garrett rolled Passoja into a body bag and levered him onto the litter. Even with Mary and Hank helping the big basketball player, it would be a laborious hike through the forest to the four-wheeler for the half hour's ride to Porcupine County Memorial Hospital. There Fred Miller, one of the county's two physicians and its elected coroner, would pronounce the death.

"I'll take the tent," Stan said, "for the dogs."

I nodded. He'd hire a local farmer and his brace of bloodhounds to hunt down the bear, and he needed the tent to establish a working scent of both bear aura—those animals stink mightily—and Passoja's blood.

Stan gathered the gory mess into a large wad and stuffed it inside a plastic supermarket bag. When he returned to headquarters, he'd arrange transport of the dogs and their handler to Big Trees to start the search.

"You'll come?" Stan asked.

"Sure thing," I said. It was my case, after all, and I always enjoyed hikes in the woods for any reason, any reason at all. Wilderness is a purgative. Every time I return from a walk in the woods I feel clean, all the poison scoured out of my system.

When I finally emerged from the rocky brush and returned to the department's Explorer, I radioed ahead to Joe Koski, asking him to tell the hospital that the body was on its way.

FOUR

At noon I left the sheriff's department and drove down
to the DNR office near Lake Gogebic in Gogebic County, well
outside my jurisdiction, to meet Stan and the rest of the search
party. Though I was still in uniform, I was now technically a
volunteer civilian, not a law officer. Mary Larch had driven
back to Porcupine City to break the news to Marjorie Passoja,
Paul's gorgeous young wife, that she was a widow. I knew
Mary would be gentle and caring. She and Marj were good
friends.

As I pulled into the parking lot, I saw that the news of
Passoja's death had spread rapidly across the western Upper
Peninsula. Fifty or sixty men of all ages milled about, their
faces shining with eagerness, some sprawled on the benches
in front of the office and some lounging in the beds of their
pickup trucks. All were armed with high-velocity rifles, some
of them with huge scopes. Clearly they were out after big
game.

Stan whistled from the office doorway. "Your attention,
please, guys!" he shouted. After the men had swiftly gathered
about him like kindergartners around a teacher, he laid down
the law in softly reasonable but firm tones.

"Thank you for coming here to volunteer," he said,
"but the truth is everything is under control. The dogs have
found the trail and the rangers are closing in. A crowd's not a
good idea during a rogue-bear hunt. We appreciate your
concern, but please go home."

Actually, Stan told me after the disappointed
volunteers had pulled out of the lot, only two men — the dogs'
handler and an armed park ranger — were in hot pursuit of the
bear, or at least as hot a pursuit as can be mounted after a
swift quarry in thick woods. They had started from Big Trees

late in the morning and, reporting their positions by radio, were moving swiftly southwestward in the direction of Matchwood, a small town nine miles from the wild place where Paul Passoja had died. The trail, they said, was hot and the dogs spirited.

"You don't want all those untrained fellows with rifles crashing through brush scaring the bear and maybe shooting each other," he said. I nodded. Pounding the woods after dangerous quarry is not a job for people without experience at it.

"All we need is four who know what they're doing to help the trackers once they locate the bear and to take it down. And that's you, me, Garrett, and that Commando for Christ over there." Stan pointed across the parking lot at a short, muscular blond fellow, dressed in faded desert fatigues and bearing a heavy scoped rifle.

"Ah." In southern Porcupine County lay a large training camp for missionaries operated by a religious organization that was nondenominational but so fundamentalist that mainstream evangelicals raised their eyebrows at it. It trained young men (women need not apply) in the arts of wilderness survival, using rigorous techniques borrowed from the Army Rangers and Navy SEALs, even teaching the campers to fly and to fix their own aircraft at the jet-capable concrete airstrip in the middle of the camp. Graduates could go anywhere in the world, win souls for Christ, and emerge alive. I had no doubt that they could break Satan's neck if they had to. We called them "Commandos for Christ" behind their backs, and the sobriquet wasn't far wrong.

I'd met a few of the polite, well-scrubbed missionary cadets, who asked almost immediately whether my soul had been saved but did not press the issue when I changed the subject. They impressed me. If anybody had the physical and emotional endurance needed to run down a rogue bear, they did. Single-mindedness can be an asset. No wonder Stan had called the camp and asked for its best man with a rifle.

I introduced myself. "Gary Keefe," he said, his sky-blue eyes gazing directly into my dark brown ones. He shook my hand with a grasp as gentle as his smile. I was grateful for that. His palm felt like boulders. He looked to be in his late twenties and carried himself with ramrod military bearing, his blond hair clipped into a brush cut with whitewalls.

"Let's saddle up," said Stan. "Get your weapons."

From the Explorer I fished not a rifle but a police riot gun—a short-barreled 12-gauge pump shotgun—and a box of deer slugs. The powerful rifle Keefe carried would be deadly at a distance, but a riot gun with its slow but heavy slug was unbeatable at close-in work. You could knock down a wall with it. Stan and Garrett both were armed with tranquilizer dart rifles and huge .44 Magnum revolvers on their hips. We bundled our arsenal into the back of a wrinkled green DNR Suburban, and departed the parking lot, Stan and Garrett in front, Keefe and I in the back.

"Do we know anything about the bear besides it's a big one and has a scar on its paw?" I asked Stan as we pulled onto the highway.

"There's a fair possibility it's one of the dozens of adult bears in the Wolverines and that it drifted outside the park," Stan said, "although it could also have wandered in from elsewhere. If we can, we'll try to put it down with a dart and look over its fur and claws. 'Course, if it comes at us, we'll have to kill it. We will anyway if we find human blood or tissue. Can't relocate a bear that has tasted human blood."

The radio on the Suburban's dash came alive. "Fred to Stan," said the disembodied voice of Fred Mitchell, the chief DNR ranger at Gogebic. "We're on M-28 four miles west of Matchwood. The bear's crossed the highway and gone into the state forest. Trail's still hot. We're not far behind, but he's moving fast."

Stan stopped the Suburban, pulled out a topographical

map from the glove compartment, and spread it on the dash. At the point on the state highway where the trackers had reported in, I saw, the state forest is only half a mile wide before it ends in a vast expanse of scrubland, huge stump fields denuded of their trees nearly a century ago. Old logging roads crisscross the scrub.

"We'll cut around here on that track and park at that clearing south of that copse, get out, and wait for them to come to us," Stan said, pointing to a spot on the map just a mile and a half south of the highway. "If the bear changes its bearing" — if he noticed the inadvertent pun, he didn't show it — "we can move quickly in either direction."

Stan would have made a great tactical general, I thought as the Suburban turned off the road and bounced down a barely passable logging track. The Patton at the wheel drove hell-for-leather after the enemy as if the Suburban were an armored personnel carrier, his vehicle creaking and groaning as it jounced and jolted. Actually we were doing less than twenty miles an hour, probably ten too fast for sensibility. The Suburban wasn't built for that kind of abuse, but Stan was retired and didn't have to answer to DNR headquarters in Lansing for damage to official equipment.

"Jesus!" I said as the Suburban jarred across a deep rut, the seat belt saving me from bashing my head on the roof.

That was Gary's cue. "Have you met Christ?" he asked solicitously, as if we were sitting in a parsonage drinking tea instead of bouncing around the backwoods. I almost laughed, but won the fight with my face.

"Gary, this isn't the time or place!" Stan said, chuckling, as he wrestled the wheel, the Suburban's right front wheel scraping a boulder by the side of the track. Had the vehicle had any hubcaps at the start of this hunt, it would have lost them long ago.

Keefe did not press the question but stared ahead serenely.

"Jesus comes to all who seek," he said. "We'll talk

about it later, okay?"

I ducked instinctively as the Suburban crashed through a thick tangle of alder branches hanging across the track.

"What's a man of the cloth doing bearing arms?" I asked, just to be provocative. Keefe's question had irked me a little. I don't care for religiosity displayed on the sleeve in public. One's faith, I felt, ought to be practiced privately, like sex, or at least in church where it wouldn't offend nonbelievers.

"God gave us dominion," Keefe said, fervent certainty edging his quiet voice with steel. Passion like that scares me sometimes.

"Stan to Fred," the old bear ranger said into the mike. "Where are you?"

The tracker gave his map coordinates.

"You're just half a mile north of us," Stan said. "What's the bear's heading?"

"Directly at you, it looks like," Fred said.

"We'll be ready. Keep your heads down." Stan didn't want the trackers caught in a cross fire. "Out."

Stan stopped the truck at the edge of a large clearing and opened the door. "Let's roll!"

"Isn't that what we've been doing since Gogebic?" I asked as I stepped out.

"You know what I mean. Move over there, please."

We spread out just off the track in the waist-high brush in a skirmish line not more than twenty yards wide, Stan and Garrett at the edges with their dart rifles, Keefe and I in the middle, directly across from a wide promontory of trees jutting from the woods about fifty yards away. I crouched slightly in front of Keefe, ready to fire down the bear's throat if it came out of the tree line directly ahead. Keefe stood erect, rifle at his shoulder, arm through the sling ready to pivot in either direction.

Not five minutes passed before we heard the

bloodhounds, their faint baying masked by the forest. "Stan to Fred," the ranger said quietly into his handheld radio. "We hear you now."

"Fred to Stan. If you're where we think you are, the bear's gonna be upon you in less than a minute."

Now we could hear it crashing through the brush, the crackling of branches growing louder with each passing second. I stared straight ahead, the shotgun held loosely in my hands. Where would the bear emerge? The promontory of trees that jutted from the forest was about two hundred yards long from edge to edge. If it came out of the woods directly in front of me, I'd have a clear shot, but not much time to get it off. A bear can cover a lot of ground in a second or two.

I could feel Keefe behind me, breathing softly but regularly, coiled like a rattler ready to strike. At the left end of the skirmish line Stan crouched in tall grass, his dart gun poised, his holster unbuckled. To the right Garrett stood nervously behind a small aspen, dart rifle in his left hand, revolver in his right, its muzzle pointing forward. He was taking no chances.

"There it is!" Stan cried.

The bear erupted from the woods far to the left at the base of the promontory a good seventy-five yards distant, well out of dart-gun and deer-slug range, heading slightly away from us, aiming at full gallop for another patch of woods to our left. In the space of a tenth of a second I took in these things: First, the bear was big, almost grizzly-sized. Second, it was half hidden by brush and tall grass. Third, even for an expert rifleman it was going to be an almost impossible full-deflection shot, through patches of saplings and brush that would knock any bullet from its path.

"Stay down!" Keefe shouted just above me, rifle butt in his shoulder and eye at the scope as he swiveled smoothly from the waist, leading the bear with his crosshairs. The crack of the heavy cartridge stunned me, but not so much that I could not see the bear leap, then tumble end over end through the grass, fetching up in a twitching heap.

Stan, Garrett, and I stood up and plunged through the brush to the bear. It lay motionless. After a sensible interval, no more than two minutes, Stan approached the animal, revolver trained upon its massive head. "Dead," he said, just as the bloodhounds emerged at full bay from the tree line, Fred Mitchell and the farmer who owned the dogs close behind. The latter yanked back the hounds and spoke sharply to them. They sat, quivering with excitement, their eyes fixed on the carcass.

Stan picked up the bear's left front paw and turned it over. "It's our boy, sure enough," he said. "Look at that scar."

The dirty scarlet sheen on the bear's jaws and chest, I thought, doubtless would prove to be Paul Passoja's blood.

For a moment we all contemplated the bear. Then I said, "Keefe, where did you learn to shoot like that?"

"Marines," he said. "Discharged last winter."

"Afghanistan?" I asked.

"Yeah. First Marine Expeditionary Force. Recon."

I whistled. Gary Keefe had been one of the elite, a highly trained killer, probably a sniper. I wondered how this man had come to discover Christ and become a missionary.

"Semper Fi," said Stan quietly, extending his hand to Keefe. Stan had been a Marine in Korea.

"Semper Fi," Keefe replied.

After a moment Stan said, "This bear has to be a known bear. It wore a radio collar some time ago—see this groove in the fur? They often rub the collars off after a while. No ear tags, though. This bear's never worn any. Feel the ears."

I rubbed an ear between thumb and finger, searching for ridges of scar tissue left by staples.

"Weird," said Stan. "Researchers almost always tag the bears for easier ID when they collar them."

"Where could it have come from?"

"Wisconsin, probably, or even Minnesota. Rogues often

travel long distances."

Garrett, who had barely been heard from during the entire operation, stood slack-jawed, gazing alternately at the bear and at Keefe. A mixture of terror and elation crossed his face, enlivening the dull expression he had worn all day. Still a boy, I thought.

Nobody said anything more as we dragged the smelly carcass to the Suburban, and hoisted it in with the help of a block and tackle.

Just before getting into the truck I spotted a small bear sitting on its butt like a little Buddha in the middle of a thimbleberry patch, unconcernedly munching the sweet fruit while watching us intently. The cinnamon fur that marked the typical black bear's muzzle extended over his face past his eyes and almost to his ears, giving him the look of a wise and worldly chimpanzee. The bear gazed at me steadily, not at all frightened or wary, as if it were the most natural thing in the world to share this small space in the forest with human beings. I nudged Stan and pointed.

He chuckled. "About sixteen months old. Momma probably kicked him out of the nest last week. Not too bright, is he? That shot should have scared him all the way into Ironwood County."

The little bear watched steadily as we climbed into the Suburban. As Stan wheeled the truck, clanking under its new burden, around the ruts and headed back to headquarters, I looked back. The bear had disappeared into the woods.

Later, on my way back to Porcupine City in the Explorer, the radio crackled.

"Steve?" said Koski. "We just heard from Doc Miller. He says he doesn't think Passoja's wounds killed him. He's sending the body to Baraga for an autopsy." Dr. Miller was an internist, and questionable deaths were sent fifty-three miles east to be investigated by Dr. John Oakes, a certified pathologist and the medical examiner of Baraga County.

The shadows were growing long when I arrived at my

cabin on the lakeshore. I patted my shirt pocket and found the tin with the bacon shard. I had forgotten to turn it in at the sheriff's office with the photographs of the scene that morning, but I could do that the next day. I popped it into the freezer between a couple of frozen trout I had caught in a mountain stream a few weeks before, and fell wearily into bed.

FIVE

The next morning Dr. Oakes faxed his report to the sheriff's office. A massive heart attack had killed Paul Passoja. His seventy-nine-year-old arteries had been clogged from a lifetime of steak and potatoes. It had just been a matter of time before sudden stress did him in. He probably was dead before the bear's teeth and claws ripped into him.

What's more, Dr. Oakes said, he had found in Passoja's brain scattered gray plaques that were unmistakable evidence of encroaching Alzheimer's disease. This aging man definitely had not been in full ownership of his faculties. The Metrovich brothers had been right.

Eli Garrow nodded expressionlessly as he slipped the fax into the Passoja case file, salting away the whole in a cabinet. Without a doubt, I thought, Passoja's death had relieved him of a huge political pain in the ass.

Eli, the second most powerful politician in Porcupine County—only Garner Armstrong, the county prosecutor, outranks him—is a short, bald, and bullet-headed man with a luxurious iron-gray handlebar mustache, so broad-shouldered and big-bellied that two of him could span a barn door with room to spare. While all his deputies wear solid brown uniforms, Eli stands out in a blindingly white shirt and gold braid as befits the boss. "The Target," we call him behind his back, for he'd be the first one the bad guys would try to take out during a firefight—if we were ever to have one.

Still, as country officeholders go, Eli is popular with the voters—so popular that he barely has to break a sweat running for re-election. He is surprisingly honest and upright for a career politician, though over the years what passes for scandal in the Upper Peninsula has slightly tarnished his reputation. When Eli hired his own wife as jail matron and took on a nephew as a deputy, the Republican candidate gave him a run for his money in the next election. Another time Eli used a brand-new departmental four-wheeler for deer hunting, thinking it was a perk of the job, but the county board roasted him over the coals for that. As a deputy in his forties, he had been a notorious womanizer, but now, close to retirement age, he rested on the laurels of that reputation, even poking fun at it.

A born campaigner with a folksy manner, he calls women of all ages "young lady" and greets men with "my fine man" or "young man" as he pumps their hands, one meaty paw on their shoulders. But nobody mistakes his cheeriness for insincerity. For all his commodious ego, Eli loves being a politician. Most people can't help liking a man who enjoys his job so. Small children and dogs adore him.

As for me, he is sometimes irritating, but I feel benign tolerance toward him as long as he stays out of my way, which he does, mostly. He's rarely in the office, preferring to cruise the county pressing flesh, and he believes in the chain of command, dealing with his troops mainly through Gil O'Brien, the undersheriff.

Gil is the real boss of the department. Tall and rangy, he is a former Army drill instructor and a dour martinet who, unlike his hail-fellow-well-met boss, thinks the department should be run like the military. He is very good at his job and is highly respected by fellow law enforcement officers all over the state. He is also brilliant at writing grants to wrest funds out of state coffers for departmental equipment—grants Eli, ever the beamish pol, tends to claim credit for. And Gil is a by-the-book stickler. Thanks to his meticulousness, judges and juries rarely find fault with the Porcupine County Sheriff's Department. I'm very careful around him.

"There you go," Gil said. "It's cut and dried—Passoja had a heart attack during the struggle with the bear, which happened because he got old and demented, and Doc Miller's going to rule it death by misadventure. Case closed."

I nodded. Anyone with an ounce of sense would agree with that conclusion. Not being of sound mind, the victim forgot his own teachings, carried his dinner to his tent and spilled bacon on it. Bear smelled the grease, bear came to get it, there was a confrontation, and a man died. Very simple.

Or too simple? A small cloud began to shadow my thoughts.

"At least Passoja died doing something he loved," Gil suddenly added. "Be nice if that happened to us, too."

I forgot my doubt and winced inwardly. This banal sentiment always turns my stomach. How can anyone declare what goes through another man's mind when he meets violent death? Did Passoja feel joy at struggling against the sharp claws and teeth of a huge animal with halitosis? Did he exult when pain tore through his heart? I kept this thought to myself. For all his brisk competence the stern undersheriff was not an empathetic man, and my observation would have been lost on him.

Not for many days would my reservation about Passoja's death again work its way into the sunlight.

SIX

At two o'clock in the afternoon on the fifth day after Paul Passoja was found dead, Porcupine City buried him. It seemed that not only the entire county but also the whole Upper Peninsula turned out for the funeral, and the full complement of the sheriff's department was called in to handle the hundreds of cars from in and out of town that arrived at Holy Redeemer Lutheran Church, the county's largest and wealthiest place of worship. I pulled duty at the entry to the parking lot.

When Eli Garrow arrived in his chief's cruiser — the department's newest, never used on patrol and kept shiny and waxed by the jail trusties — I waved him to a VIP slot close to the lot's entrance. Though the lot was nearly as large as the asphalt meadow in front of the town's supermarket, it was filling up fast and we'd have to direct cars to the city's Little League field next to the church.

He emerged puffing from the cruiser resplendent in dress uniform and all the decorations he had gathered in a lifetime. I could have sworn he wore his Boy Scout medals among the gaudy ribbons and brass gongs bestowed upon him by sovereign bodies ranging from the Chamber of Commerce to the Elks. He clanked when he walked.

"Look at all these cars," Eli marveled. "Bet half the people have come to say good-bye to Paul and the other half just to make sure he's dead."

I chuckled dutifully at the boss's joke.

Then I had to hasten as two long black limos pulled in, full of politicians from Lansing as well as the Upper Peninsula congressman, Geoffrey Armstrong. A cynical thought fleeted across my mind: they were there to make sure Paul Passoja stayed buried.

In a few minutes Marjorie Passoja arrived in her gray Mercedes sedan—no ride in a common undertaker's limo for her—with Mary Larch at the wheel. I saluted respectfully and directed the Mercedes to the place of honor in front of the pathway to the church. I opened the curbside door for Marjorie and whispered, "My condolences, ma'am," as she emerged.

"Thank you, deputy," she said in a tiny voice, dry-eyed, her face composed, touching my sleeve gently. She looked straight ahead, almost rigidly, as if trying to control her emotions.

She wore a tailored black jacket and sheath that could not subdue her exuberant curves. Marjorie Keenan Passoja was a classic Southern California beauty in her mid-thirties, and she always dressed like one, in smart designer clothes that would not have looked out of place in a Maryland mall. For this reason alone she stood out in Porcupine County like a swan among mallards. For this reason, too, people in these parts were a little wary of her, just as they watched themselves around her husband.

But she never struck me as putting on airs among the peasants. Unlike many of the wealthy women who summered on Lake Superior—especially the tanned and wrinkled matrons who had married money and who couldn't go out of the house unless they were decorated with at least ten pounds of gold and diamonds—she never wore jewelry, not even a wedding ring. Nor was she wreathed in clouds of expensive but cloying perfume; up close, I am sure, she would have smelled simply of soap.

Whenever I encountered her, either during official duties or not, she often just seemed painfully shy. At social events, I noticed, the Passojas arrived as a couple but did not mix as one. Marjorie gravitated toward the women while her husband peeled off to talk to the men. Only at the end of the evening would they get together again—to depart. That certainly was not unusual, of course, in a social milieu that still believed in old-fashioned gender roles. Porcupine County is nothing if not conservative.

As she walked into the church, Mary supported Marjorie's left elbow gently, and nodded to me as they passed. I didn't think it odd, as some did, that a local working-class girl like Mary would mix with out-of-town gentry like Marjorie.

Marjorie was Porcupine County's Lady Bountiful. It seemed that her main task as Paul Passoja's consort was to bestow their charity on the most deserving institutions in the county. And that they did. But a string came with each boon: A large brass plaque bearing the legend GIFT OF PAUL AND MARJORIE PASSOJA — Paul's name always preceded hers — had to be affixed somewhere visible. Sometimes the thing had to be named for them: The new wing on the county's nursing home. The MRI scanner room in the county hospital. The gorgeous stained-glass window bearing the image of Christ on the cross in the nave of the church. Their gifts had to be large, imposing, and enduring. They were generous people and they wanted everyone to know it.

I knew, however, that one of Marjorie's pet projects was the Andie Davis Home, the county's only battered women's shelter. She had given a considerable pile of money — I suspected it was her own, not her husband's — to buy and fix up an old motel in a hamlet in the eastern part of the county, but had not insisted that it carry the Passoja name. Indeed, Marjorie had not mentioned that at all, according to Mary, who volunteered there during her off hours and had befriended the reticent Californian.

Soon the flood of arriving cars slowed to a trickle, then stopped. While another deputy kept watch upon the lot, I sneaked into the sanctuary of the crowded church just in time for the eulogy. Geoffrey Armstrong, Paul Passoja's man in Washington, did the honors, and he pulled out all the stops. Passoja's generosity was prominently mentioned, and so was his probity, his courage, his saintliness, and so on. It was a nauseating performance even for a beholden politician, and the congregation stirred restlessly.

So did I, standing in the doorway of an anteroom just off the sanctuary. As Armstrong droned on, filling the air with a fog of insincerity, I looked about the room and directly into Joseph's eyes. This was a wooden Joseph, a full-sized effigy hewn from white pine a century ago by an immigrant Finnish logger who had created the figures for the Christmas crèche placed out front in the snow every December since then. The flat, oblique planes of Joseph's face, stained a deep walnut, bespoke a folk artist of genuine talent who had carved it as a labor of love. So did the faces of the Magi, whose gentle expressions, molded by the dim shadows inside the anteroom, appeared sour and nauseated as Armstrong phumphered away. I took comfort in their rustic honesty as I sneaked a look at Marjorie and Mary, sitting alone in a front pew before the casket, all of the elect occupying rows behind them. They gazed stonily, unmoving, at the altar.

It was almost with simultaneous sighs of relief that the pastor launched the crowd into a hymn and I slipped out the door to take up my station.

An hour later, one of the last vehicles in the departing trickle was a newish but muddy brown Ford van, PORCUPINE COUNTY HISTORICAL SOCIETY emblazoned on its front doors.

"Hi, Ginny!" I said as the driver paused on the way out.

"Steve," Ginny Fitzgerald replied with a brilliant smile. I couldn't think of a thing to say.

"See you tomorrow night," Ginny said. "Bring a good appetite."

I nodded dumbly, a silly grin on my face. She drove away.

"You bet," I finally said as the van turned at the corner and disappeared.

SEVEN

Virginia Anttila Fitzgerald is a sturdy, striking green-eyed redhead in her late thirties, all legs and bosom in snug jeans and loose flannel lumberjack shirts, with the kind of scrubbed, freckled beauty that is insulted by makeup. She is almost a ringer for Maureen O'Hara, the gorgeous film star of the 1940s and 1950s, and every time *Miracle on 34th Street* airs on late-night TV during the holidays, I am startled by the resemblance.

Ginny is by profession a historian and the director — indeed, the only paid employee — of the Porcupine County Historical Society. She had grown up in Porcupine City, a third-generation Finnish-American, daughter of a mining engineer. In her early teens the Lone Pine Mine, the last working copper mine and smelter in Michigan, suffered one of its periodic shutdowns, and she moved with her family to Arizona. When she turned eighteen, her father sent her east to college, and there she met her husband. Not long after she was widowed in her early thirties, she returned childless to the county of her birth to start life again.

These scant facts I had heard from Joe Koski. "She hasn't been home but a year, Steve, and she already knows everything about everybody in Porcupine County," said Joe when I inquired about the pretty redhead in charge of the benefit supper I had attended at the Historical Society. "Tell her your name, and if you're from here, she'll rattle off your family tree all the way back to Adam. But I hear she's a grieving widow still and a hard nut to crack — a lot of local men have asked her out, but she always says no. Don't break your back trying to get to first base."

That exchange had occurred when I had been a Porcupine County deputy only three months. I had spoken briefly with Ginny at the supper, attendance at which seemed a good way for a greenhorn law-enforcement officer to learn something about his jurisdiction. I was fresh out of the army and starting a new life myself.

From time to time I had run into her at official functions as well as the society's museum, a cavernous former supermarket in Porcupine City whose donated purple paint, slathered on by volunteers, made it leap out from the weathered, whitewashed wood of the rest of downtown. Later, when I had at last sunk formal roots into the county by buying a little four-room cabin on the lakeshore eight miles west of Porcupine City, she plucked its history out of the air one afternoon.

"Built in 1946 by August Kokkanen, a first-generation Finn, out of the last cedars logged from what is now the state park," she said briskly, unconsciously curling a loose strand of hair behind her right ear. That habit, I would soon learn, meant she wanted to change the subject, to be sharp and businesslike. But at that moment the gesture was immediately endearing, and it caused my heart to do a somersault.

"Kokkanen floated the logs down the shore to the property and let them season for two years before constructing the cabin for Milton Browne, a businessman from Stevens Point, Wisconsin. Browne summered there on the lakeshore with his family for half a century. The cabin was originally rustic, with no running water and only an outhouse, but over the years he improved the place, putting in a well, plumbing, and electricity. When Browne died, having outlived his wife, the family put the cabin up for sale, and it was vacant for a year before you bought it.

"You've got a good place—they don't build them like that anymore, especially that beautiful stone fireplace. It'll last at least another fifty years."

"How did you know all that?" I marveled.

"It's my job," she said, with a brilliant eye-crinkling

smile that reduced me to awkward shyness. At that moment I vowed to break through her reserve if I could.

Hers was a subtle aloofness. Ginny really was a friendly, generous soul, openhearted with everybody who came to her cluttered office at the Historical Society. But whenever I—or anyone else—tried to get her to talk about herself, let alone ask for a date, she changed the subject with a warm smile, a gentle but firm hand and a quick tuck of hair behind her ear.

But I had all the time in the world. After carefully managing just to happen upon Ginny at Merle's Café at the same hour half a dozen Sunday mornings in a row and having breakfast at her table, ostensibly to absorb a few more details about Porcupine County history, I suggested that the following Friday evening we try the venison at a new restaurant specializing in wild game that had just opened outside town. "Why not?" she had said after hesitating only a moment. "It'll be good research for me."

That was the camel's nose under the tent, and slowly I had shoved it farther in. Our "dates"—if you can call them that—had been both informal and impromptu, little more than two people agreeing to share the same space at the same time—but at last she had invited me home for dinner.

EIGHT

After the funeral I returned to the sheriff's department to attack my never-ending paperwork, then after quitting time stopped at Hobbs' Bar, Grill and Northwoods Museum for a six-pack.

Hobbs' is a cavernous two-story Main Street storefront right across the parking lot from the Historical Society. Its splintery pine walls are festooned with old skis, snowshoes, beaver hides, and rusty nineteenth-century firearms, none of which seem to have much value except to yuppie lounge designers in Chicago, who always are trying — unsuccessfully — to buy them. Nonetheless, Hobbs' is a favorite of the townsfolk, primarily because of its two pool tables and skeeball range. They provide amusement during the long Lake Superior winters when there is nothing else to do except move snow from one place to another, tear through woods and across fields on snowmobiles and four-wheelers, drink, and make love.

Like all such places, Hobbs' has seen its share of disputes. Few escalate to the point where deputies need to be summoned. For the most part the joint is downright peaceable, thanks to its proprietor and barkeep, Ted Lindsay, a Porcupine County native who had spent his professional life downstate as a Detroit patrolman. Though graying and long retired in his seventies, Ted was still burly, agile, and skilled at the uses of a police baton and kept one behind the bar instead of a baseball bat.

On the way home from the sheriff's department after work I passed Hobbs' almost every day and often stopped in for a six-pack and because I liked talking to Ted, not just because he used to be on the job but also because he judges a man by what he does in life, not where he's from or what he looks like.

Three big Harleys squatted in the parking lot as I swung through the doors, dressed in after-work denims, police gear locked away in the Explorer. That was neither surprising nor dismaying—bikers from Wisconsin and Minnesota often passed through Porcupine City on the way to camp in the Wolverines. For the most part they belonged to respectable cycle clubs and, though they sometimes liked to frighten the timid by mimicking Marlon Brando in *The Wild One* with leathers and red bandannas, they usually minded their own business and said "Yessir" and "Ma'am" to old folks. Once in a while, however, an outlaw biker—or a wannabe outlaw—caused trouble.

"A six-pack of Heineken," I told Ted, "and pop a Pepsi, will you? I'm driving."

Ted opened a bottle and placed it on the counter. I took a stool while Ted disappeared into the back for my six-pack.

"Hey, chief?" came a damp voice from nearby.

I blinked but didn't respond.

"I'm talking to ya, Injun!" the same voice said in a slur that suggested a long afternoon with the bottle. I *hate* gratuitous references to my biological ethnicity. I am tall for an Indian—six feet three, two hundred ten pounds—but the color of my skin is reddish-brown, almost mahogany in the summer sun, and I have high cheekbones and a hook nose, the very stereotype of the warrior on the old buffalo nickel.

Sheriff Garrow sometimes calls me "Tonto" when he wants to be funny. "You look like Crazy Horse!" well-meaning people often exclaim, unaware that no likeness of that great war chief ever was made during his lifetime. How would they know what Crazy Horse looked like? The odd thing is that he could have been my great-grandfather, but that's another story.

"Ain't drinkin', are ya?" I shook my head slightly, without looking back.

"Whoever heard of a sober Injun?"

This time I glanced behind me. At one of the pool tables glared a man mountain in cycle leathers and studded fingerless gloves. Burly, sweating, red-faced, and rheumy-eyed, he stood at least six-six and carried an overhanging belly, a heavily creased neck wider than his close-cropped head, and forearms like sixteen-pound hams. At least three hundred pounds, maybe more. Two almost equally large leather-clad comrades flanked him in truculent support.

Ted refuses to serve obvious drunks, so the biker must have concealed a snootful when he rolled in the door.

I picked up the Pepsi and moved down the bar. Sometimes ignoring a challenge will make it go away. Not this time.

"I said I'm talkin' to ya, chief!"

I could smell him as he stepped up close behind me. He reeked of days-old sweat as well as booze.

"What can I do for you?" I said politely as I turned. I took a step back, enlarging the personal space the biker had invaded.

"Bet you know where I can find some squaw pussy around here!" he hissed. "Bet you got a sister! Ten bucks for a blow job?" He leaned menacingly toward me.

By this time Ted had returned. He refuses to allow race-baiting in his establishment, and if people who voice ugly sentiments ignore his invitation to depart, he will encourage them with an expert display of his nightstick. If, however, actual physical force is required, he will call the sheriff's department just three blocks away. "It's their job," he says simply, and he's absolutely correct.

"That's it, asshole!" Ted growled, pure cop in his voice. "Take your attitude outside—right now!"

"Fuck you!" bellowed the biker, kicking a stool aside.

I shook my head slightly, throwing Ted a subtle let's-do-this-by-the-book glance. "Now please calm down, sir," I said to the biker, showing him my palms in peace. "There's really no need for that." Gentle methods first. Especially since my antagonist outweighed me by nearly a hundred pounds.

"Bet you like white pussy!" the biker snarled, clamping an enormous fist on my left forearm, the one toward him. He had reached the point of no return. He was spoiling for a fight, trying to provoke me into throwing the first punch. He was wide open for a short and sweet right to the solar plexus, and I was tempted.

Instead I whispered, without moving, "That's assault."

Ted reached under the beer taps, fished out his baton and slid it down the bar toward my right hand. Now was the time for me to announce that I was a deputy and take matters from there, perhaps with an expert application of the nightstick. But I did not want to allow a racial taunt to result in the use of force. That, I felt, would diminish me in the eyes of the dozen citizens of Porcupine County who looked on in dead silence, their eyes glittering with the prurience of country boys at a gentlemen's club.

Briefly I weighed the scales of justice. An arrest for simple assault and disorderly conduct would result in a night in jail, a couple of meals paid for by the county, more paperwork for Joe Koski, and extra court time for me. If I could just get the oaf out of the county, the hassle would be over.

Besides, the biker had the advantage not only of weight but also a foot of reach, and I was not sure the nightstick would equalize the difference. I wished I had the .357, but it was locked in the Explorer.

The biker hesitated. I quickly took the advantage it presented. "Come over here and let's talk," I said in a reasonable tone, stepping away from the bar and around it, away from the rest of the patrons. He followed stumbling, clumsily knocking aside another stool.

In the corner I took out my star and gave the biker a long eyeful. "I am a police officer," I said slowly and carefully, making sure he understood. "We can do this the easy way or we can do this the hard way." That's a hackneyed but eternally useful offer for a cop to make. "I can either take you down right now for assault and disorderly conduct, or you can step back from me and walk out that door, take your friends with you, and never show your face in here again. Your call."

The biker swayed, considering the unexpected choice. Enough function remained in his sodden brain cells for a simple thought to take root. But just as his piggish eyes began to show a glimmer of intelligence, four grimy hands appeared on his shoulders and made the decision for him.

"We're outta here," said the other two bikers simultaneously, hustling their comrade toward the door. "C'mon."

The air suddenly went out of the oaf.

"Very sensible of you," I said to the smaller bikers.

But I wasn't through.

"Friends don't let friends drive drunk," I said, keeping my voice prim. "There's a motel across the street. Rent a room, let him sleep it off tonight, then get on your bikes and be on your way."

I watched as the two bikers carefully placed one foot in front of the other across the pavement, delicately steering their big comrade between them, and disappeared into the motel. They left their bikes in Hobbs' parking lot.

I turned back to the tavern. The citizens had resumed their chatter, the nightstick had disappeared, and Ted stood by the bar, unconcernedly scrubbing beer glasses.

He looked up at me. "One on the house?" That was a rare show of generosity for this tightfisted barkeep, and I knew I had earned his approval.

"Nope, Ted," I said. "Your backup was enough. Thanks for that."

As I made my way out the door, six-pack under my arm, a grizzled old woman turned from her table, smiled toothlessly and gave me a thumbs-up.

I was grinning as I drove away. "Happy trails," I told the world at large. Sometimes Tonto was worth a quote.

NINE

The next morning, as I peered outside the bathroom window of my snug little cabin tucked under a thick stand of birch and balsam just yards from the beach, a family of loons cut the mirror-smooth surface of the water. A golden coin on the eastern horizon heralded sunrise. Before long a small flotilla of Canada geese slowly paddled by in line astern, a feathered naval squadron on maneuvers from its anchorage up nearby Quarterline Creek. Just down the shore a doe and her fawn drank daintily from the lake.

The air tinkled with muffled calls from the geese and loons, with accompaniment from lovesick frogs in the nearby swamp. In the lulls, soft winds sighed through the leaves.

Who could have asked for more?

I loved that little cabin, bare and rustic as she was, furnished in what my mother once called Hopeless Bachelor. She would have been right about the four bare pine planks, separated by unpainted bricks liberated from a demolition site, that made up my overflowing bookcase, and she would have been right about the badly cracked but still comfortable mahogany leather sofa I'd bought for a song at the estate sale of a deceased lawyer. I preferred to think of the decor as Country Eclectic, and I was even proud of some of the pieces, like the brass double bed I'd found in a junkyard and restored to shiny newness with Brasso and elbow grease. Someday I was going to brush a dozen coats of finish, carefully polishing them between each application, on a maple rolltop desk I'd built from plans during long lonely weekends. The place was simple, it was comfortable, and it was all mine. I paid no installments and owed no mortgage.

I felt even more benevolence toward the world when, driving into Porcupine City, I timed the bikers at fifty miles per hour, five under the limit, as they rode their Harleys carefully out of town—heading west, I hoped, for Hurley in Wisconsin, a rough town full of gentlemen's clubs and biker's bars that is well out of my jurisdiction. Identical pairs of green Ray-Bans shaded their eyes, doubtlessly yellowed and bloodshot, like egg yolks kept too long. Not too smugly, I hoped, I congratulated myself on serving as the engine of their departure.

It was a promising start to a day that ended the same way. As the sun lowered into the horizon, I dined with Virginia Fitzgerald at her home on the shore in the woods a few miles east of mine on the highway to Porcupine City. It was the first real evening we had spent together in our slowly—*very* slowly—unfolding relationship.

When she opened the heavy oak door, its leaded glass glinting in the firelight, was that a touch of blush and a dab of eyeliner I saw? Was that very slight scent a hint of Vol de Nuit? Were her jeans a little snugger, her lumberjack shirt slightly smaller?

"My one extravagance," Ginny said as I admired the interior of her efficiently designed log home. She had had it built the previous year by a local craftsman on property her family had owned for generations. Outside, it looked like one of the many small vacation homes owned by modestly well-to-do summer people who came up from Chicago and Milwaukee. These homes dotted the shoreline twelve miles west from Porcupine City to the mountainous, heavily forested state park that anchored the county's western end.

Inside, Ginny's furniture was understated but expensive, I saw with my cop's eye, a mixture of antique Arts and Crafts pieces and contemporary items well-constructed from solid quarter-sawn oak in mission style. Brightly colored cushions helped the oak pieces stand out from the logs of the exterior walls, and other decorations were not the customary rows of bleached driftwood and ranks of kitschy-fussy gift-shop figurines found in most Upper Midwest log homes, but rich tapestries, platters, vases, and urns from the Middle East. This was a woman who had traveled and who knew what to collect.

"Yemeni silver?" I asked.

Her eyes widened in surprise. "How would a north woods cop know that?" she demanded. Then she colored as she realized what she had said. "I'm sorry," she added quickly. "It just seems so unlikely that anyone else up here would know where those things came from."

"I spent time in the Middle East myself," I replied, "as a military policeman in the army. And in college I took a little art history. But I've never seen anything like this."

I peered down at a foot-high balsam fir, seemingly spun from pure silver, gracing a low oaken cabinet. A simple cross crowned its top and garlands wreathed its lacy branches, "Look at that exquisite tracery. That's obviously Yemeni. But a Christmas tree's not the sort of thing you find in a Middle Eastern tourist market full of Jewish artisans from Muslim countries. Where did it come from?"

"Jerusalem," Ginny replied. "My late husband had it specially made by a Yemeni and gave it to me one Christmas. It's so beautiful I never put it away after the holidays. It reminds me of my husband, and it provides me a little bit of Christmas all year."

She blushed, as if embarrassed at being caught in an unguarded expression of sentimentality. But I thought it was a lovely thing to say.

Suddenly she pulled out a chair from the massive oak dining table. "Sit down, Steve Martinez," she said. "I want to hear all about you. Where are you from and how did you arrive in this wild and lonely corner of Upper Michigan?"

"There isn't that much to tell," I said, opening a pricey California merlot I had been saving for just such an occasion. "I'm from Troy, a small city in upper New York State. I went to Cornell on an army ROTC scholarship, then studied criminal justice at CUNY, and when I got out of the service, I wanted to start my career in a place I'd never been. Porcupine County was hiring, and so here I am." That was accurate enough, but incomplete. Some details, I had long thought, were best left unvolunteered.

"New York?" she said. "With your name, your black hair, and your brown skin I'd have pegged you for border Texas, but you don't sound like a Texan at all. You do speak Spanish, don't you?"

"No. I'm not Tex-Mex," I said. "I'm Indian . . . , er, Native American." I dislike using the politically correct term. Indians did not invent it. Well-meaning white academics did. Most American Indians call themselves Indian, or use the names of their tribes. Creation myths notwithstanding, the ancestors of Indians probably were no more native to this hemisphere than the Europeans who followed them, most likely having emigrated from Asia via the Bering Strait.

Not knowing how Ginny felt about the issue, and being the kind of fellow who doesn't like to offend needlessly, I employed both terms. If we had been north of the border, I'd have used the Canadians' clever and inoffensive "first citizens."

She drew her chair closer, her eyes sparkling with interest. "'What tribe? Oneida? Seneca?" It surprised me that she'd know about the Iroquoian tribes of New York State.

My origins were something I rarely talked about, but I could not resist this woman's unsettling directness.

"Neither of those, but Lakota, I was told, or Sioux as most people say. Full-blooded as far as I know."

"From Pine Ridge?" she asked. Many Lakota — especially the Oglala band to which I was born — live on that infamous reservation. I nodded.

"How'd you get from there to New York State?"

I sighed, and opened up. "I was adopted as a baby from the reservation orphanage. My adoptive parents are Caucasian. Or, rather, were — they died long ago in an auto accident. They were evangelical missionaries. My adoptive father was descended from Spanish settlers in Florida, and that's where the family name came from. All the Hispanic tradition had been leached out of them over generations of intermarriage.

"When they went back East after the adoption, they brought me up the best way they knew how, as a good white Christian they'd saved from the Indian witch doctors. In those days that was the thing to do with poor Indian kids—the idea was they were better off in white communities than with their own tribes. The only part of my Lakota heritage they kept for me was the name the orphanage gave to me when I was born, Stevie Two Crow. That's my middle name now, Two Crow.

"I was only ten when they died, too young to start asking questions about my birth parents. I don't know a thing about the Lakota other than what I've read."

"That can't have been easy," she said with a suddenly soft voice. You're Indian outside, but white inside."

"For some of us it was pretty tough, but not so much for me," I said with a laugh. "Well . . ." And suddenly the rusty floodgates creaked open.

"Look, when you don't fit people's ideas of what you should be, they get confused and disappointed. It's not their fault, they think—it's yours for not being the person they had in their minds. Sometimes it makes them hostile, sometimes it makes them afraid. It's human nature."

Ginny nodded. "What can you do about it?"

"Not a hell of a lot," I said, adding a rueful chuckle. "It takes effort to reach some of these folks. Sometimes you have to meet them more than halfway. Sometimes I'll work real hard to win people over—and sometimes they turn out not to be worth the sweat."

Ginny lifted an eyebrow wickedly. "And am I worth the trouble to get to know?" she said.

"Oh, absolutely not," I said, trying to keep a poker face.

She giggled, then did the thing with her hair.

"Tell me about your childhood," she said.

"My adoptive parents loved me," I said. "They were good people who thought they were doing the right thing, and, really, they grounded me pretty well in their sense of values, and so did the uncle who raised me after their deaths. They truly believed in Christian brotherhood, in people being decent to each other. I have no complaints about that."

Troy was a largely white but in some neighborhoods a fairly diverse small city, I added, spotted with blacks, Asians, and Hispanics, and as a kid I was just another brown face in a multicolored working-class school crowd. Quite a few of the youngsters were deaf kids who spoke sign language, and they gave me the name sign that all my friends, hearing ones included, used when they spoke of me—hand held to the back of the head, palm facing forward, like a single eagle feather.

The odd thing was that all my white friends nevertheless considered me white because my parents were white. To them I just had a very good tan. But my black friends knew better. They thought of me as a minority just like them, casually using the word *honkies* when chatting with me about our white friends. At that preadolescent age we didn't take racial matters seriously.

But when early teenage insecurities brought out cruelty, some of the white kids made fun of my appearance.

"Once a kid called me a 'dirty Indian,'" I said. "I called him back 'a fat white four-eyed slob' because that's what he was, and he burst into tears. I didn't feel very good about that.

"But I was good at sports, and that more than anything else gets a kid accepted despite looking different from the others. Football, basketball, baseball—I was on all the teams in high school.

"When I started dating, some parents weren't too happy about their daughters seeing a boy with dark skin, but they weren't openly hostile about it, at least in front of me. There weren't a lot of incidents, but I remember all of them."

"Is it too painful to talk about them?" Ginny asked softly.

"Not really," I said. "Some of them are kind of funny in a pitiful sort of way."

Once, in college, I had gone home for Thanksgiving with a well-to-do Virginia girl who lived just outside Richmond. Her parents at first treated me with the elaborate politeness of southern gentry uncomfortable with onrushing social change. But they asked me if I'd take dinner in the kitchen to spare two unreconstructed elderly maiden aunts who, they said, "are not kindly disposed to people who are not like them. We know you understand."

I did. I thanked them as graciously as I could for their hospitality, and on the spot left for Cornell.

The very next weekend, I continued, I was the unofficial guest of honor at a faculty cocktail party. The school was just beginning a drive for scholarship funds to diversify its student body, and it paraded me before a host of wealthy alumni like a football team mascot. "Did I ever feel like the Indian in a cigar-store window!" I laughed.

"What was most annoying about that party were the well-meaning people who learned my story and thought I should 'discover my Native American self.' "

"And did you?" Ginny said.

"One summer I did visit Pine Ridge. But I had no more in common with anyone there than you would have. I asked at the orphanage about my natural parents, but the records had been poorly kept, and anyway, they told me, I was probably better off not knowing. Many of those Lakota led pretty dismal lives, full of alcohol and poverty. They often died young. I'm sure my natural parents did, too."

Ginny looked directly into my eyes. "Upper Michigan is a strange place to find a college-educated white Sioux cop named Martinez. Why, really, did you come here?"

"I ran away," I admitted. "Not from the law but from—

from — oh, hell, a broken romance. It sounds so stupid now. Before I went to Saudi Arabia, I was going to marry my high school sweetheart. She was such a darling, Scots-Irish and perky, an All-American sort of girl. She was six months pregnant when I shipped out, but we weren't in a hurry to get married. We were going to tie the knot properly, with a big wedding, when I got back."

Her letter had arrived during the height of Desert Storm, when my MP unit was herding freshly captured Iraqi prisoners of war into barbed-wire enclosures. No barb could have been sharper than the news that the baby was blond and blue-eyed, and that the father was not me but my best friend. She had married him in a quiet little ceremony and hoped I could find it in my heart to forgive.

"I was devastated," I said, carefully maintaining an expressionless face. Ginny rested a cool and sympathetic palm lightly on my forearm. "All I could think about was that I couldn't go home. I thought I had to escape somewhere far away, completely different from the place where I had grown up. When I got back to the States, I jumped at the first law enforcement job offered me, and the one in Porcupine County was it."

Ginny patted my hand. "I am so very sorry," she said. After a discreet beat, she added, "In a way, though, I'm glad."

My heart did a small jig. "No regrets either," I said. "The pay is low but my needs are few. This country suits me."

TEN

Suits me? "Don't go to work in a small town," my army comrades had warned. The pinched narrowness of outlook and experience these city slickers saw as typical of both cops and civilians in rural America, they said, would have me in no time at all pounding hungrily on the front door of a big-city police station looking for a job.

In some ways they were right. Many natives of Upper Michigan, like the rest of backwoods America, vote Democratic but think Republican; they rely on government handouts for their survival but see that same government as also threatening their right to bear arms and teaching science that challenges the biblical account of creation. The same people also tend to display a neighborly solicitousness nearly unheard of in the cities. They may recoil at your ideas, but they care about your humanity. They're the ones who show up on your doorstep with casseroles when there's a death in the family. They're the ones who drop by to make sure you're okay when illness has kept you out of circulation for more than a few days. They're the ones who bring Christmas to shut-ins.

Many of them harbor surprising secrets, most old and even obscure, but some percolating dangerously just under the surface, like hidden sulphur springs looking for a crack in the rock to burst through. If and when they emerge, things often become interesting for law enforcement officers. People are not always what they seem, and that keeps things lively. That's true in the cities, too, but out here in the wilderness where folks are few and far between, you notice it more.

In other ways the naysayers had no idea, absolutely no idea. There's nothing tiresome about police work in a rural Upper Michigan sheriff's department. Sure, much of it is routine—property theft and damage investigations, bar brawls, assaults, drug offenses, domestic abuse, process serving, and every once in a very long while a homicide. Plus, of course, traffic stops upon traffic stops. In twenty years there had been only three murders in Porcupine County. In the last one, seven years before, a farmer who wanted to get rid of his domineering wife dispatched her with a revolver—but forgot to lose the murder weapon, with which even a little boonies cop shop and a local prosecutor could win an easy conviction.

The Porcupine County department numbers only a dozen employees—besides Eli Garrow and Gil O'Brien, five sworn regular deputies, including me, and five dispatchers who also serve as jailers. All of us have taken the three-month law enforcement officer's course at the Michigan Police Academy in Lansing.

I'm the only outsider. The rest are homegrown Porkies who know every nook and cranny of the county, as well as just about everyone who lives there. I'd been hired because at the time of the vacancy no natives of the county had applied.

In the beginning my Indian features raised some of the residents' hackles. Porkies are 99 percent white—only three residents are African American and a handful Hispanic—and are largely descended from the Irish, Cornish, and Croatian miners and trappers who settled the county in the last half of the nineteenth century as well as the Finnish farmers and woodsmen who flooded in during the first decades of the twentieth.

They are no more and no less bigoted toward people who look different from them than the eastern urban whites I had grown up among, but some particularly resent the Ojibwa who live on the reservation in Baraga County to the east. The Indians, they growl, have things both ways while the whites have to struggle to make a living. Rents on the reservation are low, Bureau of Indian Affairs handouts plentiful. The Ojibwa, they say, love to torment the whites by exercising their treaty rights to take fish with nets and spears—something the whites can't do — while at the same time raking in dough from their gambling casinos. I doubt that the casinos do a Las Vegas sort of business, though — they are too far off the beaten path to attract high rollers from Chicago, Minneapolis, and Detroit.

Even though my Lakota ancestors had been driven out onto the Plains centuries ago by the invading Ojibwa, themselves under pressure from white expansion in the East, I don't begrudge casino Indians their success at double-dipping, if that is what it is — God knows the white man screwed them for three hundred years. And they almost never complain. Indians hate complaining, a fatal trait in a nation in which the squeakiest wheels get the most grease.

But once they heard my name the Porkies figured me for Hispanic, as Ginny had, and except for a few louts the reserve they showed toward me was the same they display toward any unfamiliar outsider — and toward any law enforcement officer.

We keep the peace with just five official road vehicles, only two of which are the usual expensively beefed-up, specially manufactured Ford police cruisers with powerful engines that can chase and capture anything on the highway. They are getting long in the tooth, with more than two hundred thousand miles on their much-patched chassis.

Two of the cars are retrofitted Crown Victoria sedans from a local dealer, used mostly for local investigations. One is a four-wheel-drive Explorer, my usual mount — and one I sometimes park at home with the department's blessing because of all the deputies I live closest to the Wolverines and often find myself representing the law deep in the woods on rough gravel tracks. Off-duty I drive a rusty old Jeep Wrangler.

Sometimes I fly the department's thirty-year-old Cessna 172, a high-winged four-seater kept in a ramshackle hangar at the Porcupine County Airport hard by the lake. It's one of the undersheriff's grant-writing trophies, purchased with state funds when he discovered I had earned a pilot's certificate in the army during the weekends. We don't use the airplane very often, except for occasional low-level sweeps looking for missing elderly people, some of them suffering from Alzheimer's, or boats in distress on Lake Superior. We also use the plane to hunt drug shacks and marijuana fields in the woods or on cutover land, and now and then we'll transport a prisoner to a penitentiary in Lower Michigan.

For the rare forays into the lake or up the Porcupine River, the department also keeps a sixteen-foot outboard boat on a trailer next to the lockup, which consists of eight cells. Four are for general-population cons doing short sentences for misdemeanors, one is a detox cell for drunks and would-be suicides, one is for females, one is a max security cell for dangerous prisoners, and one is a holding tank for fresh arrestees. Few cells are occupied at any one time. Porcupine County is not a hotbed of felony, and we deputies are not overworked crime fighters.

Every fall, however, we stomp around in the woods for a few days in the annual permutation of Operation HEMP (Help Eradicate Marijuana Planting), in which local deputies, village constables, state cops, and Drug Enforcement Agency zealots play Green Berets in the jungle, sniffing out and destroying marijuana patches planted on fallow farms and in forests, often by locals but sometimes out-of-staters.

More often we serve not as antidrug commandos but impromptu social workers, refereeing domestic disputes and rescuing people from themselves. Life in Porcupine County is too rugged for most eccentrics to survive, but we do have a few.

Just a few days before, I had had to help the county authorities find an institution to take a mentally disturbed old man who lived in terrible squalor in the woods in a filthy shack with more than three hundred cats. He shared their bulk cat food and, when found, had not changed his clothes in six months. The place stank to high heaven, and I did not envy the county's animal control officer his job dealing with all those orphaned and semi-feral cats.

The job all of us hated the most was dealing with child sexual abuse. There wasn't a lot of it, but we remembered every case. In July there had been one involving a predatory Minneapolis high school teacher who had hooked up in an Internet chat room the year before with a thirteen-year-old girl from Chicago. She and her parents spent a month every year at a lakeside resort just outside Porcupine City, and the previous summer the creep had rented a cabin half a mile down the lakeshore. The parents had thought their daughter spent hours every sunny day walking the beach searching for agates.

During the spring the girl had boasted to her classmates about her special friend, and one of them told her own parents, who contacted the authorities, who tipped Eli Garrow and Garner Armstrong. When the Chicago family and the Minneapolis predator arrived on almost the same day, almost the entire department was ready and waiting in the bushes outside the creep's cabin.

He was short and balding, doughy and almost apologetic, protesting gently as we recited his Miranda rights that he was not a criminal but suffered from a sickness. I could not understand how a precocious thirteen-year-old girl out for a lark could find him attractive at all.

Mary Larch in particular was so enraged that she clapped her cuffs on the guy much too hard, and when we thrust him, whimpering, into the lockup cage his hands had turned blue.

"Easy, Mary," I told her. "Even sons of bitches have rights. What's gotten into you?"

"I've been there," she replied, and that is all she would say.

ELEVEN

"Now," I told Ginny, "you know everything there is to know about me. Your turn. You haven't told me a scrap about yourself."

In answer she tucked back a strand of hair and stood up from her chair. "All in good time," she said with that crinkly smile, at once endearing and irritating because it was so effective at deflecting questions. "Tomorrow is a working day for both of us. It's time for you to head for your cabin and a good night's sleep."

At the door I said hopefully, "Next Friday, maybe?"

"Sure thing," she replied. And just before she closed the door, she stood on the tips of her toes and graced my cheek with a feathery kiss. "Goodnight, Steve."

At home, reaching into the freezer for a pint of ice cream, I saw the little tin again. A vague feeling that something was not quite right with the Passoja case had been building up in me ever since the day the medical examiner called in his report. Alzheimer's or no Alzheimer's, would a man who had spent all his life in the woods really have fallen out of ingrained habit so easily? Did Passoja really spill his supper on his tent? And if not, how did that bacon grease get on it?

TWELVE

For the next three days, as Labor Day came and went, the more mundane tasks of an Upper Peninsula sheriff's deputy pushed the matter of Paul Passoja to the back of my mind. Most of them had to do with — surprise! — traffic stops. Tourists in Expeditions and Grand Cherokees from Chicago casually did eighty on U.S. 45 from the south and on M-64, the state highway bordering the lake, as is their habit on the interstates in northern Illinois. They are genuinely surprised when I tell them that twenty-five miles per hour over the limit is not a "gimme" in these parts.

Frequently they aren't wearing their seat belts, an automatic forty-dollar fine on top of the speeding citation, when I approach their cars.

"But I took it off to get my wallet and driver's license out of my back pocket!" many of them protest.

"Sorry, sir," I say politely. "I didn't see you do that. All I can see is that you're not wearing your belt."

Sometimes, if a driver seems genuinely contrite over having broken the limit, I'll give him a break and issue just a warning on the speeding violation — but not for the seat-belt violation. Paying that forty bucks ensures that he won't forget to keep his belt fastened, not if his brain has more than two memory cells.

Summer residents who study the sheriff's reports in the local weekly newspaper often observe that few Porcupine County residents are ever fined for traffic offenses. Almost all the convictions are of out-of-staters. More than once I've been asked if we cut breaks for locals.

Though I'd never officially admit it, we do. When we see the people we stop on the highway every weekend in the hardware store, the supermarket, or in neighboring church pews, when our children go to the same schools as theirs do, when we know they barely make enough money to survive, let alone pay traffic fines, we will give them a pass. Rather than hand them a citation, we will administer a thorough roadside chewing out. Indeed, repeated offenses will result in an expensive ticket, but most Porkies have too much sense to risk that.

But there is one violation for which I will never be lenient: driving while intoxicated. That morning I stopped a Caddy that had been weaving in its lane, and when I smelled the bourbon on the driver's breath, I immediately radioed Mary Larch, asking her to drive over from her patrol area for backup. If sexual abuse brought out Mary's dark side, drunken drivers bring out the worst in me, for one had killed my adoptive parents.

Mary's presence kept me from stepping over the line into rough justice. I stood aside, smoldering, as she administered the simple tests — asking the driver to walk a straight line heel to toe, stand on one foot, followed by a request to touch his nose with a finger with his eyes closed. When he nearly poked himself in the eye, she made a face and helped the staggering driver into the backseat of her cruiser for the trip to the department and the breath test.

But I tried hard to be gentle when I informed a summer visitor that there wasn't much the department could do about the bite she had suffered from a German shepherd that attacked her as she waded on the beach past its owner's lakeshore cabin. No, the dog was neither registered nor immunized — we were keeping an eye on it for signs of rabies, uncommon in this part of the state — but legally the visitor had been trespassing, even though everybody walks along the beach for miles without encountering a NO TRESPASSING sign. What's more, no country judge would find for a well-to-do outsider against a resident who was an impoverished old woman whose dog was her only protection. Sometimes the victims have no rights, I agreed soberly. Let the matter drop.

Twice that summer I rousted high school kids partying in boarded-up hunting camps, ignoring the sweet smell of marijuana while looking for harder drugs and checking ages. Young people in Porcupine County haven't much to do on weekends except drink, smoke dope, and have sex. The county does provide a teen hangout for them in town, but few use the Ping-Pong tables simply because, in the way of young people everywhere, they refuse to let adults tell them what to do.

But we deputies are sworn to uphold the law, so uphold the law we do—we chase them out of the camps, first checking to see if they've trashed the place, then making sure someone's sober enough to drive home. If a girl is below the age of consent, we'll take her home and tell her parents where she has been. Such matters ordinarily are decided in the family—exactly how varies from family to family, but it's rarely gentle.

With teenagers we're sometimes faced with a dilemma. We might pick up a youngster for a minor misdemeanor, but if the kid's father is an abusive one—many desperately poor men brutally take out their frustrations on their families—we have to decide whether to book the kid, inform the parents, or just let the kid go after a lecture. Once you've seen a pretty teenage girl with new bruises on her face a day or two after you've turned her in to her folks, you're not likely to rat on her to Daddy again.

Only on prom night do we let the youngsters mostly alone—it's better that at the most booze- and hormone-ridden time of the year we keep them within manageable bounds—but we'll bust anybody dumb enough to drink and drive. Judge Rantala always hands first-time DWIs a day in jail and a $340 fine, a lot of money up here where jobs are few and unemployment is high. He believes in early intervention, even if he wouldn't use such a social worker's term—he calls it "nipping sin in the bud," like the conservative Christian evangelical he is. To the judge, the greatest sin in the world is carelessly endangering someone else's life. I'll go along with that.

As the sun reached its apex, I put aside these thoughts and backed the Explorer into a disused gravel driveway, just out of sight of M-64 but within radar range, and focused the beam on the highway. Time to catch some speeders, but first a little lunch. I fished a sandwich and a Pepsi from my cooler and flicked on the radar.

I ignored the traffic doing sixty and sixty-five miles per hour, five and ten miles per hour over the limit, and winced at the elderly men nursing their decrepit pickups down the highway at forty and forty five—they were accidents waiting to happen at the hands of aggressive drivers. The fines for doing five and ten over the fifty-five-miles-per-hour limit did bring the county some revenue, but breaking the law at seventy or better meant real money. I decided to wait for bigger fish while I finished my sandwich.

The radar readout flashed 60, 66, 64. At 69 I was tempted, but kept chewing. Four bites in, a large black sport-ute sped by. Seventy-four! A big one! I tossed the remainder of the sandwich to unseen critters in the brush, flicked on the flashers and siren, and fishtailed out onto the highway, the Explorer's tires throwing gravel. Though the sport-ute was more than three hundred yards ahead, almost immediately its brake lights blinked on and it pulled off the road onto the verge. Knows he's been caught red-handed, I thought as I maneuvered the Explorer close behind.

Almost immediately I recognized the vehicle. It was Paul Passoja's Navigator. And the driver, I saw, was Marjorie Passoja. I radioed Joe Koski to inform him of the stop and its location and ask for information on the Navigator's license plate. My Explorer didn't have the wireless computer linked into the State of Michigan vehicle registry that the department's cruisers boasted. "It's Marjorie," I told Joe.

"I'm sorry," she said, contrition coloring her voice, as I

approached the driver's door. She was wearing her seat belt. "How fast was I going?"

"Seventy-four."

"Damn," she said quietly. "I've been distracted, but that's no excuse."

"I know, Mrs. Passoja," I said, trying to be gentle. My heart went out to her. But I was still a cop with a job to do. "May I have your registration and license, please?"

She fished in her purse and gave them to me, her beautiful face barely suppressing an expression of anguish.

"Wait here," I said. "I'll be right back."

"Joe?" I said into the radio. "Anything for me?"

"Nothing on the plates except it's Passoja's Navigator, all right. License is current."

I gave him Marjorie's driver's license number. The click of computer keys, then Joe's voice again. "No priors," he said. "She's clean."

"Okay," I said. "That's all."

I made a decision.

"Mrs. Passoja," I said, "nineteen miles an hour over the speed limit could cost you several hundred dollars. But considering all that's happened, as well as your clean driving record, and the fact that you admit you made a mistake, I'm just going to give you a warning."

She slumped in relief and sighed. "Thank you, deputy. I promise to be more careful."

"Thank you for that, Mrs. Passoja," I said. "Please take it easy."

"I will," she said.

At that moment I looked up as Mary Larch's cruiser, its lights flashing but siren silent, sped toward us. Swiftly she U-turned, pulled up behind my Explorer, and got out. Striding right past me to the Navigator, she peered in at Marjorie, and said, "You all right?"

"Yes," Marjorie replied in a wavering voice. "Deputy

Martinez just gave me a warning for speeding. My mind was elsewhere." The two locked gazes for a moment, then both glanced back at me.

"Marj, why don't you go home and take it easy?" Mary said, patting her on the arm. Marjorie nodded.

"Off with you, then." The Navigator drove away.

"Thanks, Steve," Mary said. "I worry about her."

"I guess you do," I said. "But I think she'll be all right. She didn't give me any crap but owned up to the violation right away. No point in lumbering her with a citation."

"You're a good guy, Steve," Mary said.

I thought about asking her why she was so concerned about Marjorie, but figured it was none of my business. One doesn't casually intrude on relationships in Porcupine County.

With a brisk nod and a thin smile Mary returned east to her patrol area, I went to mine, wishing I hadn't tossed that sandwich away. For the rest of the afternoon I pinched speeders, even those doing only sixty-one miles per hour, figuring that a bunch of small fish would make up for the big one I had thrown back.

THIRTEEN

Before I went home there was one more task that day: taking the sheriff's Cessna into the sky for a maintenance flight. At least once a week I flew the airplane for an hour or so, just to exercise the engine. Disused airplane engines rust inside, shortening their lives, and that is why you see so many weekend pilots going nowhere, just lollygagging around their airports and boring expensive holes in the sky. They're keeping their engines limber and lubricated for the times when they really have to go somewhere.

I could use official departmental time for this job, but the sheriff pays for it anyway, and flying on somebody else's dime is a rare treat. So I perform the task on off-hours, usually in the early evenings when the rising thermals have settled down and the air is at its smoothest and most velvety. Flying low and slow at times like that gives a small-plane pilot a ringside seat on the glories of creation.

The airport lies three miles west of Porcupine City and is almost always deserted, except for the dispatcher and the director of the PorTran bus service, headquartered in the little three-room airport office building. Often I see Doc Miller in his hangar working on his little "warbird," a Korean War-era Bird Dog spotter plane he keeps in pristine condition, looking as if it had just been delivered to the army. He looked old enough to have flown her over Inchon, but I knew that he had served in Vietnam as a navy doctor.

Next to the Bird Dog the faded paint on the sheriff's Cessna looks sadly tattered, like an ancient movie queen who doesn't realize the ton of makeup she puts on every morning cannot hide the ravages of age. But the decades-old airplane is in excellent mechanical condition, stoutly airworthy, its engine freshly overhauled.

I patted her flank as I began the preflight tasks, checking the hinges on the ailerons, flaps, elevator and rudder, wiggling the control surfaces, draining a sample of fuel from both tanks to make sure water had not gotten into them, marking the oil level, examining the propeller for nicks, the nosewheel strut, the tires, the brakes. This pilot's ritual, I sometimes thought, was little different from that of a Lakota war chief, a shaman who spread out and read the contents of his medicine bag before going into battle. The ceremony comforted both of us, for it meant that we were leaving nothing to chance, that we were preparing ourselves to the last detail for what lay ahead.

Yes, I often think about being an Indian. How can I not? It's what I am, even though any Indian-ness I have comes from occasional reading forays into Indian history, not from living it.

When the Cessna lifted off the runway and I banked east over the lake, a bald eagle suddenly joined me in formation, fifty yards off my left wingtip. Up, up, up we rose together in a sweeping circle, soaring wing to wing.

To the Lakota the bald eagle symbolized the spirit of war and hunting, and was a messenger from God. For a brief moment the adrenaline rush coursing through my veins filled me with the powerful medicine of invincibility, as if I were riding with Crazy Horse. "*Hoka hey!*" I yelled, as the Lakota had when they fell upon their enemies. "It's a good day to die!"

At a thousand feet the eagle suddenly folded its wings and stooped. As I banked the Cessna to watch, he plummeted downward, a feathered heat-seeking missile, and slammed into a passing mallard in a cloud of down. Leveling off, he headed inland below me, quarry clamped in his talons.

It was a violent spectacle, but I rejoiced nevertheless. I felt as if the sight — a rare one — had been a gift. Eagles usually snatch fish feeding near the surface of the water, only occasionally going after waterfowl, large and elusive therefore more difficult targets, but always taking whatever fate proffers them. This eagle had lived up to what nature had designed him to do—indeed, it was as if by taking a duck he was counting coup with all creation as his audience—and I felt rapture in his victory.

A Lakota mystic probably would have patted me on the back and informed me that I had just had a vision. Having grown up as I did, however, I hardheadedly realized that my woolgathering was just a fantasy, the product of an imagination overwhelmed by the joy of flight. *Hoka hey,* indeed. "A good day to die!" is hardly the sentiment of a thoughtful and careful pilot. I was glad nobody had heard me shout it.

I pointed the Cessna's nose inland also, peering down at the land below. As long as I was up here doing an official job, I might as well stretch the sheriff's dollars and search for wrongdoing.

Every year during Operation HEMP I had dipped low over the tailings, looking for one of the DEA's Official (and somewhat redundant) Warning Signs of Illegal Marijuana Growing: "Unusual amounts of traffic on and off the property (usually at night); use of tents, campers, or other recreational vehicles on wooded property with no evidence of recreational activity taking place; unusual purchases of fertilizer, garden hose, plastic PVC pipe, chicken wire, lumber, machetes, camouflage netting, and clothing; large amount of PVC pipe or irrigation hose in heavily wooded areas; and heavily patrolled or guarded woods, swamps, and other remote areas."

I think druggie-hunting is a waste of time and effort— booze, in my view, is far more dangerous than pot—but cops in the north woods sometimes like to play Green Berets just for something else to do besides pinch speeders, even though we know that the American antidrug army has about as much effect on the trade as King Canute had on the ocean. And I go along, usually in the Cessna. I have to; it's my job, and the law is the law.

For miles and miles I flew along searching, the engine thrumming smoothly five hundred feet above the forest canopy and the clear-cut, stump-strewn open lands, from time to time circling rustic shacks used by the locals as deer camps and sometimes as cat labs.

Cat, short for methcathinone, was first made and peddled in the Upper Peninsula in the early 1990s, later spreading all over the Midwest. It's a designer drug closely related to khat, the mildly narcotic weed chewed all day long in Yemen, and is a cheap substitute for methamphetamine. Cat is sold as a white crystalline powder made from easily obtainable ephedrine or pseudoephedrine—common over-the-counter nasal remedies—mixed with a witches' brew of battery acid, Drano, lye, and paint thinner.

Cat, also called goob, Jeff, bathtub speed, and Cadillac Express, is highly toxic and highly addictive. Abusers suffer paranoia, delusions, and hallucinations, sometimes a complete psychotic crash.

It's bad shit, all right. When we bust a cat lab—they still crop up in Porcupine County from time to time—we have to call in the state hazmat people to haul away the dangerous evidence.

This time I saw nothing, nor did I expect to see anything. Most drug entrepreneurs are smart enough to camouflage their paraphernalia from air searches, though once in a while a large crop of marijuana will stand out from the surrounding vegetation, inviting later investigation on foot.

I checked my watch. Nearly sixty minutes had passed since takeoff, and it was time to get the airplane back on the ground. I wanted to soar on eagle's wings until the sun went down, but aviation fuel is expensive and Gil O'Brien, that tightfisted undersheriff, would demand I justify wasting the department's money.

As I closed the hangar door I felt relaxed and mellow, as I always do after a good flight. One of these days I was going to ask Ginny if she would like to go for a ride in a rental aircraft from Ironwood or Land o' Lakes—I wasn't about to use departmental equipment for pleasure flights with civilians. I hadn't yet asked her, because I didn't yet know how she felt about flying in small airplanes.

The only person who had gone up with me in that Cessna was Mary Larch, as an extra pair of eyes during an official search for a missing boat and once during an Operation HEMP flight. She had no fear of flying, but neither did she take much joy in it. To her it was just part of the job, not a particularly noteworthy event. Not liking to fly certainly does not mean a character defect, but I was disappointed nonetheless.

FOURTEEN

I was not, however, displeased with Mary either as a person or as a colleague. Late in September I learned something new about her, a rare occurrence indeed, for her armor was nearly impossible to breach.

None of us knew what had happened in her youth that would have explained why she was so hard-nosed toward child molesters. I asked once, and she replied with quiet steeliness, "Let's not go there."

That was her answer whenever anybody asked her anything about herself. She was as private a person as Ginny. But Ginny, who was a master at subtly and painlessly deflecting unwanted questions, Mary simply threw up a brick wall. She wasn't rude about it. She didn't say, "None of your business!" but we all knew what she meant. Sometimes, when someone became insistent, she'd level a granite gaze at her interlocutor and say, "Please back off. I don't want to talk about that."

But there was nothing sullen about Mary. She was not terminally bright and bubbly, as are so many impossibly perky small women, but strode into the office every day with a simple smile, wave, and quiet hello for everyone. In the sheriff's department we all had grown fond of her, and as she gained experience as a cop we came to respect her as well, even though we all expected she'd outrank us someday, so determined was she to earn an advanced degree in criminal justice.

Her parents had died when she was still in her late teens and she had struggled to get where she was, waiting tables and digging ditches with the road commission while going to college. On her off-hours she not only volunteered at the Andie Davis Home, the shelter she and Marjorie Passoja had together turned into a sanctuary for abused wives, but also coached the peewee hockey team. She had an easy sense of humor, calling herself "Ms. Bulletproof Boobs" whenever she wore a Kevlar vest on duty.

Best of all, she believed in the same law enforcement philosophy I did: Whenever possible, solve problems with patient reason, not swift force. Unlike many young and inexperienced female cops, she never voiced any kind of macho toughness in a misguided attempt to get along with her male counterparts. I admire calm reticence in both sexes and have never subscribed to the idea that a cop should automatically carry an intimidating presence. There are times to be tough and times to be gentle, and the good cop knows the difference. Most of the time, anyway.

Mary was getting very good at talking overwrought subjects down from the limbs of rage they had climbed out upon, and her relaxed curbside demeanor in a traffic stop was actually a pleasure for a fellow cop to behold. So gentle and polite was she with speeders that they almost took their citations with gratitude.

Except for one thing — her sexuality — Mary was not an off-duty mystery, but a familiar part of the community. She was a regular at civic functions, often flipping pancakes at the annual firemen's open house breakfast. Her powerful throwing arm won her the left field spot on the Hobbs' Tavern softball team. She was as good with the bat as she was with the glove.

And, though she hated drawing her pistol on duty, she was a crack shot. I'm skilled enough with firearms, though no world-beater, but at departmental target practice Mary always outscored me and often beat Joe Koski, a former army weapons instructor and an expert with all kinds of firearms, short and long.

Her petite blue-eyed brunette beauty — she had sharp but delicate features accentuated by the ponytail she always wore, and her male-cut uniform could not conceal a shapely figure—caused plenty of local men, even a couple of deputies, to ask her out. I would have gotten in line myself, had I not already set my hat for Ginny. And, I am sure, I would have been politely but firmly refused, just as everyone else had been.

Out of uniform Mary looked like a typical "Yooper woman." Up here in the Upper Peninsula where the seasons are "winter, winter, winter and blackflies," as the droll U.P.er saying goes, everybody, male or female, wears sensible jeans and flannel or woolen shirts, often with a well-worn, comfortable pair of hiking boots. Dress-up is a new sweatshirt with flowers on the front. Ginny dressed similarly, too, but always wore something bright and colorful—a scarf, a headband, a kaleidoscopic ski parka. Mary never did that—I could not imagine her in hose and heels, let alone blush and lipstick. "I wish I could give her a complete makeover," Ginny once said. She recognized quality raw material when she saw it.

Because of Mary's sexual aloofness as well as athletic skills, some men thought she must be a lesbian. I didn't—I thought she was simply asexual, perhaps because of what must have happened to her as a child. But it was none of my business.

Mary and I were sitting in Merle's Café on a coffee break near quitting time when the radio call came from Joe Koski. "Nancy Houlihan needs a deputy out at the airport," he said. "You decide who goes."

"On my way," I said. The airport, just west of town, is properly in my patrol territory.

Nancy is the director of PorTran, and my first thought was that there might have been a fender bender of some kind, but Joe hadn't said why Nancy wanted us. That meant she had asked him to be discreet so that every Tom, Dick, and Einar eavesdropping on the sheriff's frequency wouldn't know about it.

The call piqued Mary's curiosity, too. "I'll go along,"

she said.

When we arrived, Nancy and the driver stood by the door of his bus with sober and concerned expressions. The bus stood empty except for a teenaged girl sitting in the back.

"Problem kid," Nancy said. "I didn't want to call her parents. She needs a talking-to from someone in authority." That was a familiar role for us deputies.

Jennie Brady was a troubled youngster who on her way home from her part-time job bagging groceries had started acting out, cursing the driver and passengers, kicking the backs of the seats and refusing to get off. The driver had dropped off his other passengers and returned to base at the airport to deal with his young problem.

I knew Jennie. I'd picked her up a couple of times at beer parties and delivered her home. I knew, as Nancy did, that she had a father who in his cups disciplined his children with his fists. She was a good kid, but sometimes a difficult one, as teenagers with family grievances can be.

"Steve, let me handle this?" Mary said.

"Okay," I said, standing back. I had worked with her long enough to know that she had a soft and reassuring touch with youngsters, and they responded to her big-sister approach more readily than they did to my clumsy pseudo-avuncularity. Like most male deputies, I had little finesse with teenagers.

She climbed aboard the bus, where Jennie huddled in back, clasping her knees to her chest, head down, motionless. I stood in the door as Mary sat down next to her.

"What happened, Jennie?" Mary said gently.

The girl did not answer.

"Jennie, we're not arresting you. You didn't break anything. We just want to know why you did this. Maybe we can do something."

Jennie snuffled, then began weeping softly. "It's Daddy. He's drinking. He hit me." She looked up and I saw the fresh welt on her cheekbone.

"Jennie, I'm sorry," Mary said, putting her arm around the girl's shoulders. "But you can't let that make you strike out at other people. The people on the bus didn't do anything to you, did they?"

"I'm sorry," Jennie said. "I won't do it again."

"I know," Mary said. "Come on down off the bus now."

"Please don't take me home," Jennie said.

Nancy and I looked at each other. We both knew what would happen if Jennie went home to her drunken father.

"Jennie, you're coming home with me," Mary said firmly. "We'll have hamburgers and potato chips and watch TV. You can sleep over and go home tomorrow."

The girl looked up. "You sure?"

"I'm sure," Mary said, taking Jennie's hand. "I'll call your mom. Just a sec."

Mary had spotted the glance of uncertainty on my face. We walked around behind my Explorer out of earshot.

"Not the Andie Davis Home?" I asked quietly.

"No. She's underage. My house."

"Is this a good thing to do, Mary? You're a cop, not a social worker. You shouldn't get this involved with a subject."

"You got a better idea?" she countered. It would take days, maybe weeks, before the child protection agencies could act, unless the child was in clear and present danger. Harsh discipline is a gray area.

"Not really," I said after a beat or two.

"Before I take Jennie home tomorrow," she said, "Brady will have slept off the drunk. I'm going to go there and tell him that if he raises a hand to her again I'll beat the shit out of him." In her voice I could hear the sickening thunk of a nightstick against a skull.

I blinked. That was the first time I had ever heard Mary speak in favor of rough justice. I had no doubt she could do what she threatened, too. Small as she was, she had the strength and the skills. Of course, administering impromptu justice is unprofessional and illegal and properly called police brutality. In Porcupine County we never "tune up" bad guys the way cops do in the big cities. Not very often, anyway.

"All right," I said.

"One more thing, Steve."

"Yes?"

"Don't tell Gil." She wasn't going to put her humanitarian act on her report, for the undersheriff would take out his official disapproval at the top of his lungs.

"My lips are sealed."

"Thanks."

Then she did a most uncharacteristic thing. She stood on tiptoe, raised her palm and touched me on the cheek. So surprised was I that I almost forgot the fists and knuckles in her threat against Brady.

FIFTEEN

On patrol at the beginning of October I saw a large knot of cars and tourists outside a fried-chicken-and-soft-ice-cream emporium that had been a constant source of worry to the authorities of the Upper Peninsula, and not just because of the cholesterol bombs it served to hordes of grease-loving campers so obese I often suspected their rusty vans and pickups strained the state gross vehicle weight limits. The Cackle Shack was one of several roadside restaurants struggling for the skimpy tourist business, and its biggest attraction was not fatty drumsticks but garbage bears.

Most restaurants' Dumpsters lay behind high cyclone fences topped by barbed wire, but this one stood unprotected out in the trash-strewn open. Two small bears, little more than yearlings, nosed through plastic bags while the rump of a full-grown sow, its fur stained with mayonnaise, protruded from inside the open Dumpster. Scores of goggling tourists huddled worrisomely close to the scene, snapping photographs and scooting laughingly back to their cars or into the restaurant whenever one of the bears took a step toward them.

The scene was not illegal — backwoods cafés are not required by local law to protect their Dumpsters in enclosures, and many of them encourage the bears with careless storage of their garbage.

"I can't afford no fence," the Cackle Shack operator often said, tongue firmly in cheek. "I clean up the place every morning but the bears just won't stay away."

Not that he cared — clearly the bears were good for business, and more than once I'd seen him toss garbage from the kitchen right into the lap of a begging bear — but they were also an invitation to trouble. Someday somebody was going to get hurt, especially one of the unwashed trailer-park yahoos seeking to impress his buddies by getting close to a bear. Repeatedly the proprietor had been warned about liability and a lawsuit, but he scoffed, "Who's gonna sue *me*? I ain't got nothin' but this restaurant, and it's worthless without a little attraction out back, if you know what I mean. Besides, I allus call in the bear wranglers before things go too far."

But the problem was getting worse. In past years one and sometimes two bears had taken up residence in the woods just behind the Cackle Shack, but now as many as half a dozen came to supper every evening, some of the bolder ones appearing under the bright sun of mid-afternoon. The population explosion of black bears in Upper Michigan had intensified during the last few years, and the wilderness could sustain only a limited number. The pressure to find food was turning more and more of them into garbage bears, venturing out of the woods and down the shore looking for goodies.

I had seen more than one outside my cabin window snuffling around the heavy lumber enclosure that once sheltered my garbage can. After it had been smashed to flinders once too often — those animals are incredibly powerful and single-minded — I had taken to keeping the garbage can in my kitchen and putting it out on the highway once a week for the scavenger service.

In the middle of the restaurant tableau I spotted a familiar green DNR Suburban, trailing a long, cylindrical bear transporter on wheels. I parked the Explorer and hailed Stan and Garrett. Both stood by the transporter.

"Seems to me I'm seeing a lot of you guys lately," I said. "What's the problem here?"

"That bear in the Dumpster has been charging the crowd," Stan replied. "Time to knock her out and relocate her to another part of the forest before she gets up too close and personal."

Garrett nodded eagerly, as if Stan's words were an enormous revelation.

'"What are the chances she'll be able to make it in the wild?" I said, knowing the answer but asking the question to educate the goggling tourists.

"Not good. Once a bear learns about garbage, it's unlikely ever to forage in the wild again. Chances are it'll find its way back in a few weeks. Then we'll probably have to shoot it before it hurts somebody stupid enough to get in its way."

Garrett nodded again.

"The young ones?" I asked.

"They're old enough to fend for themselves," Stan said. "We'll just chase them into the woods."

Nuisance bears, I had learned early in my Porcupine County apprenticeship, came in several varieties. Most were harmless, even amusing, especially those in the Wolverines. Black bears are not ordinarily potential killers, like the much bigger grizzlies of the West. Only about thirty-five deaths from black bear maulings were reported in the United States during the entire twentieth century, and the last bear-related death in Upper Michigan — before Paul Passoja's — occurred in the 1980s when a hiker in the Wolverines climbed a tree, pack on his back, to get away from a persistent sow. He slipped on a mossy branch and fell out of the tree to his death on the rocks below. Statistically, one is ninety thousand times likelier to die in a homicide than from the teeth and claws of bears.

Everybody in bear country will tell you that the animals are always unpredictable. Mothers will protect their cubs, but most will flee from human contact. When cornered a bear will often charge, but stop at the last minute, whoofing loudly and stamping aggressively, then disappear into the forest. Sometimes it'll take a quick swipe at the air with its sharp claws, like a shadowboxing heavyweight, before skedaddling.

Some bears learn that suddenly popping up from a bush next to a trail causes passing hikers to drop their backpacks and slowly withdraw — as the rangers suggest is the safest course whenever a bear is encountered — allowing the bears to sample the contents at their leisure. These bears aim for food, not people.

One that took up residence near the Wolverine Park's drive-in campground would simply amble into a campsite and squat patiently on its haunches, softly huffing like a furry teakettle, a few yards away from a family at a picnic table. Sooner or later the diners would uneasily rise and move away from the table, and the bear would lumber in for the feast.

Bears like these often can be relocated, if not reeducated. But bears that make a habit of gorging on garbage are almost always hopeless cases, and sometimes they get mean. Those have to be destroyed before they hurt somebody. The trick is determining when to relocate and when to destroy.

"Garrett!" Stan growled. "Stop thinking with your dick! Did you shut your head in the truck door?"

The blond giant, who had been gaping with wet lips at an overendowed teenage girl in a tight T-shirt, blinked and turned to us.

"Get the popgun," Stan said. "Be quick about it."

As Garrett strode to the truck Stan said to me, "He's missing a few slats under his mattress, he is. Hard worker, though."

When Garrett returned with the air rifle, Stan slipped a tranquilizer dart into its muzzle.

"Back me up?" he asked. "I could use some crowd control."

I nodded and shooed the gawkers well back from the clearing. With a heavy rifle held loosely in his hands Garrett rode shotgun beside Stan as the older man crept up toward the Dumpster, squatted and waited patiently for the sow to emerge. In a few moments, sated, she threw herself over the edge of the Dumpster and waddled slowly toward the crowd. She bore a large spot on her chest, a slash of cinnamon-colored fur. Stan sidled behind her with the rifle.

"*Thut!*" The dart struck the bear in one large haunch. Irritatedly she peered back at Stan. She took a step toward the forest, then sat down to consider the new development. Soon she began to sway, then slowly toppled in a stupor. Quickly Stan slipped a muzzle over her massive head, then with Garrett's help dragged her to the transporter and shoved her inside. It was not an easy job—she weighed a good three hundred pounds or more.

"She'll be released in the forest on the other side of Lake Gogebic," Stan said. "That's a good twenty miles away, well past a bear's usual range. Let's hope she won't be back." The dour expression on his face suggested that he believed otherwise.

SIXTEEN

Afterward, on my way into town to drop off some daily reports, I saw Mary sitting in her cruiser on a side road off the highway, head back, eyes closed, taking a break from chasing speeders. I slid the Explorer next to her vehicle and rolled down my window as she awoke sleepily.

"How's it going?" she said.

I told her about the events at the Cackle Shack.

Quickly she sat up. "Hmm," she said. "Where'd they take the bear?"

"Out beyond Gogebic, they said. It'll be back."

"Ya think?"

We fell silent for a moment. "How'd it go with Brady?" I asked.

"All right," she said. "He had a big head this morning and said he was very sorry. He said he wouldn't do it again. I believed him when he said he was sorry, but I also believe he'll do it again sooner or later. They always do."

"Did you tell him you'd beat the shit out of him?"

"Yes."

"What'd he say?"

"He said he'd complain to the sheriff."

"And?"

"I said, 'Do you think the sheriff will believe a woman half your size could wipe up your backyard with you?' "

"And?"

"He didn't respond. He knows I can."

"But will you?"

"If I have to."

"Let's hope not."

She nodded slowly

"Jenny?"

"I took her there later. She was glad to get home. She loves her father. When he isn't drinking, he's good to her and to her mom. I hope it lasts for a while."

For a moment we sat silently, door to door. I couldn't speak for Mary, but I couldn't help thinking that rogue humans aren't much different from rogue bears. They're unable to stop the behavior that gets them in trouble in the first place.

SEVENTEEN

It had been nearly two months since Paul Passoja was found dead when I went to Doc Miller for my annual physical.

"How'd you get that?" said Doc Miller, probing a small indentation in my skull behind the left temple, hidden under my thick black hair. "Tomahawk?"

He chuckled. I didn't.

"Golf club," I said, trying to keep the resignation out of my voice. "I stepped into somebody's backswing when I was fourteen."

"Ouch," he said.

Doc Miller is a sixtyish man with a rubbery bloodhound face like Walter Matthau's. He put the same questions to me at every annual physical. At first I was annoyed. I was sure he remembered the answers from year to year, but Fred Miller is a decent and caring man and it's not worth carrying a grudge over a tasteless question meant in gentle humor.

"Knife fight?" he asked, finger running gently across a jagged scar on my chest.

"Bamboo tomato stake," I said with a sigh. "It broke when I was shoving it in the ground."

"Ouch. More than one sexual partner?"

"None of your business."

"I'm your doctor, for Chrissake. Not your mother."

"No." The real answer was "Lately, none at all," but I wasn't going to confess that. From time to time I think about answering "Yes," just to hear Doc Miller's celebrated lecture about AIDS, condoms, and needle-sharing. Before he came to Porcupine County Hospital, he ran an inner-city clinic on Chicago's South Side. There was a story in his escape to the north woods, I thought, and someday I'd like to find it out.

"You're a disappointment, Steve," he said with mock lugubriousness, as he does every year. "Otherwise you're in excellent health."

"I've got a question," I said, shrugging into my shirt. The question had been building up inside me for a while, waiting for an opportune moment to be asked, and here was as good a time as any.

"Shoot."

"How can you tell if somebody's got Alzheimer's?"

He looked at me sadly. "Relative?"

"Uh-huh." Despite myself I glanced aside, a sure giveaway that I was dissembling. I kicked myself mentally. Look Doc in the eye!

"We can't tell absolutely for sure until an autopsy, if the family requests it, and if we find amyloid—that's a gummy protein that accumulates in the brains of Alzheimer victims—in two or more brain regions. If the hippocampal and cortical tissue of, say, an eighty-year-old demented patient contains fifteen or more amyloid plaques per square millimeter, it's usually clear evidence of Alzheimer's, as is a hippocampus overrun by plaques."

I got his drift. Doc Miller, I thought, must have lectured in medical school sometime during his long career. "Well, yeah, but—" I said.

"Yes, but what good is a postmortem diagnosis to a patient?" he finished the question. "Still, we can make a pretty good guess while the patient is living."

According to the textbook, said Doc Miller, still sounding like one, the symptoms of Alzheimer's "include losses in four principal abilities: memory, orientation, judgment, and reasoning.

"The failing mind loses the ability to find words and converse, to write a note, to read a book, to identify by touch a leaf or a blade of grass, to recognize orange juice by its taste, or realize that a passing object overhead is an airplane, not a bird. In other words, the patient loses the ability to make connections, and this invites delusions. He might not recognize himself in the mirror. His synapses might make the wrong connections so he thinks he's the devil. But he's not aware of what's happening to him."

"You mean if my Aunt Trudy" — I had plucked the name out of the air — "complains that she's always forgetting things, she doesn't have Alzheimer's?"

"Probably not. It's those who forget things and don't complain who tend to have it."

"How about if Aunt Trudy goes on and on in great detail all the time about the years in which she taught chemistry, yet talks about her dead husband as if he's still alive?"

Dr. Miller glanced up. "You're looking right into the heart of the disease," he said. "In the Alzheimer's literature there's a classic story. There was an eighty-four-year-old woman in a nursing home who had been a concert pianist and a piano teacher all her life. Every afternoon she would sit down at the Baldwin and hammer out show tunes from the forties. Can you imagine what that took? Her brain had to recall millions of rapid, highly nuanced finger movements with exact timing, sequences, pressures. She never missed a note. But she often forgot that she'd played a song and might start it all over again, playing it several times, like an old record with a skip, until somebody tapped her on the shoulder and started her in on a new tune. In other words, Alzheimer's victims usually retain their long-term memory while their short-term memory goes all to hell."

"Ah," I said. Then I had a brilliant idea. "If Aunt Trudy's been a cook all her life, would Alzheimer's make her forget she'd picked up a pot of boiling water to pour into the sink, then carry it into the living room when the phone rang instead of setting it back down on the stove? She spilled the water on the coffee table, ruining the inlaid wood. At least that's what we think happened. She says she doesn't know how the coffee table got soaked."

"Not necessarily," Doc Miller said. "Even with Alzheimer's, a woman who has spent so much of her life in the kitchen isn't likely to lose her long-term memory of the rules of cooking. She'd almost always set the pot back down on the stove before going into the living room."

"But how'd the coffee table get ruined?"

"Who knows?" Doc Miller shrugged. "You can't diagnose Alzheimer's from a single incident. It could've been anything. Maybe a tiny stroke. Maybe she just forgot—that happens, you know. Maybe somebody else ruined that table."

I sighed. "Well, thanks, Doc," I said. "See you next year . . . if I remember."

"You will," he said, raising a skeptical eyebrow over my lame attempt at gallows humor. As I turned to open the door, he looked at me with a grave expression I thought contained suspicion among the sympathy. "I hope everything's okay with your aunt—what was her name again?"

"Trudy," I said, thanking my stars I remembered. "Trudy."

"Uh-huh," I said, and departed.

EIGHTEEN

Ninety-nine percent of the time, Ginny Fitzgerald is a lovely person whose easy agreeableness lifts the spirits of everybody who encounters her. Her honest interest in other people always flatters them. When she speaks to you, you get the distinct impression that at that moment you are the most important person in her life.

But God help you if she finds you ridiculous.

Ginny possesses an extraordinarily disconcerting laugh. It is neither a ladylike titter nor a mannish barroom guffaw, but a rich, double-barreled cataract of a contralto. It begins with a throaty chortle, dips to the diaphragm where it gathers power and volume, then bursts out of her ample chest in a crescendo that rattles the silverware. She often throws her head back, teeth flashing, tears running down her cheeks. This is a laugh to beat all laughs.

If the occasion warrants, her laugh can be so infectious and irresistible that I have seen perfect strangers rise from their tables, walk over, and inquire timidly, "What's so funny?"

And if the occasion also warrants, her laugh can be so derisive it makes the victim feel smaller than a pebble on a shingle beach. More than once I've seen her knock the emotional props out from under honest, well-meaning, and innocent people this way. It's not deliberate. She just can't see what she's doing.

It took me a while to figure it out, but her booming ridicule is also a means for her to warn people off, to say "Don't mess with me." But I'm getting ahead of that part of the story.

That evening, as I told Ginny at a steak house unsurprisingly named the Sirloin about that day's encounter with the doctor and the earlier morning with the body of Paul Passoja, I had confessed a doubt that slowly had been building.

"Something's not quite right," I said, "but damned if I can put a finger on it. Seems to me Passoja was just too much of a woodsman to have made such a greenhorn mistake as spilling his supper on his tent, even with Alzheimer's. He was still in the early stages of it, anyway, the medical examiner said."

In that equally disconcerting way she has of cutting to the quick, Ginny said, "You mean you think Paul Passoja died as a result of foul play? With a *bear*?"

"Well . . . ," I said, hesitating. There it was finally, out in the open, that ridiculous idea I'd been turning over in my brain ever since the coroner's announcement.

That was all she needed. I sat back glumly as the concert of laughter began and other diners' heads rose in amazement. There was nothing to do except wait until Ginny had died down to a snuffling gasp.

"What are you saying?" she asked, wiping away tears, but speaking softly so the other diners couldn't hear. "Maybe somebody might have a good reason for killing Passoja, but a bear makes the world's worst murder weapon. Sure, maybe if you tie the victim to a tree and throw a gallon of chicken fat on him, then let the bear have his way. . . ?"

Her voice again rose to fill the room. "Oh, Steve!" And she started up again.

Ginny was right, I thought, as I grinned in blushing embarrassment. Everybody knows that bears are too unpredictable.

Just like the present company, I might have added. Suddenly Ginny did that thing with her hair, as if her spectacular outburst had never happened. She may not be a police officer, but as a historian she has a good eye for unexpected possibilities. "But that doesn't mean someone wouldn't have had a grudge against Paul," she said, again in a whisper, leaning toward me.

"What do you mean by that?" I asked. "I knew about his power in this part of the state, but I'm not aware that he had mortal enemies."

"It doesn't take much to piss somebody off in Porcupine County," she said, "Relationships up here go way back, and there aren't many of us. Most of us haven't much money, so all we can hold on to are memories of the way other people have treated us. If somebody does you dirty, you remember it a long, long time. Grudges just fester, like a splinter in your fingernail."

"Well, how would Passoja have angered somebody enough to want him dead? How would one find that out?"

"I don't really know," she said, "but if I were a cop, I'd start with his land deals. Over the years he sold a lot of his family's property, and that was how he touched the lives of many people here."

I had been unable to nail down the means. Maybe a motive would be easier to uncover, if there was one, and it would lead to the weapon—and the killer, if there was one. Without telling my colleagues—their reaction to the worries I had confided to Ginny would have been just as loudly scornful but without her empathy—I set out on an unofficial and unacknowledged investigation into the death of Paul Passoja. As somebody wiser than me once said, "Sometimes you've got to back out of the driveway with your lights off."

Of course I had to do everything discreetly and in between my regular deputy's duties, and the "investigation"—if I can call it that—proceeded agonizingly slowly.

94

NINETEEN

A few days later, on my day off, I visited the Department of Records and Deeds in the courthouse. There I told Laura Stillman, deputy recorder of deeds, that I was interested in buying some land and needed to research the history of several parcels. Cheerfully she led me to racks of ledgers in the records room.

"First you have to look up the parties to the sales in these indexes," she said brightly. I am from a part of the country where civil servants like to be uncivil, doing their best to make patrons feel guilty about taking up their valuable time. Public servants in Porcupine County, however, seem to be so delighted to have good jobs in an impoverished economy that they don't jeopardize their income with crotchety behavior.

Nor was Laura at all surprised that I wanted to go through the records. At any one time there are only three or four lawyers in all of Porcupine County, and they are constantly busy, so careful and thrifty property buyers and sellers often do their own paralegal legwork among the titles and deeds. They copy the pertinent records and take them to the attorneys for their professional once-over and approval, saving both time and fees.

"See, there are two sets of indexes," Laura said. One lists the names of the grantors first, in alphabetical order, and by chronology. Grantors are the sellers. The other index lists the names of the grantees — the buyers — first. See, each listing contains the page number of a third volume — the deed volume — where copies of the actual deeds are kept."

She pulled down a deed volume and opened it at random. "Right here on each deed is a full description of the property — its dimensions and all that stuff," she said. "All set now? I'll leave you alone with these, and if you need to copy a page, just call me. Each copy is a dollar."

For hours I sat at a long table sifting through dusty old ledgers, looking for transactions between Paul Passoja or the Passoja Land Trust and other parties. I do not have a trained lawyer's eye, but as a cop I have seen enough official records to distinguish unusual things amid the boilerplate, and I know how to read fine print over and over again until I can understand it.

Since the end of the Second World War, Passoja had sold many parcels of land, some of them to locals whose names I immediately recognized. Sheriff Eli Garrow was among them. So were a host of local merchants and bankers and miners, woodsmen and people from Wisconsin, Illinois, and Minnesota, including the late Milton Browne, who had once owned my lakeshore lot.

Out of a sense of proprietorship I carefully examined the Browne deed and the subdeeds attached to it. According to the 1946 deed, Browne's land, three hundred feet of lakeshore frontage, extended only from the beach four hundred feet inland to a point fifty feet from the gravel road that Highway M-64 had been then. Passoja had retained the frontage land along the highway, giving Browne access rights over a dirt track to get to his property.

The frontage clause was clear enough, but it also was buried near the bottom of the description, couched in careful legal language that might have been bafflegab to the layman. In another volume I found a deed dated 1983 in which Passoja had sold the fifty-foot frontage to Browne for far more than the latter had paid for the entire lakeshore property in 1946.

That looked familiar, and I riffled back through the deeds and sub-deeds of other lakefront properties Passoja had sold over the years. Sure enough, starting during 1944 and extending well into the 1970s, nearly all these deeds had retained for Passoja a 50- to 100-foot-wide frontage all along the highway. Since then he had sold the frontages to many of the parties to the original deeds.

"There's no mystery about that," Ginny said at her kitchen table that afternoon. "After the Second World War and the founding of the state park a lot of people thought that the lake shore had a lot of commercial potential, especially when M-64 was at last paved in the early 1960s. Many of the families who owned the forest land along the highway worried that it might become an ugly commercial tourist strip. Keeping ownership of that fifty-foot frontage made sure the highway would never become a commercial eyesore."

Lovely as it was, the place never became overrun with tourists, even when summer hikers and campers visited the huge Wolverine Mountains Wilderness State Park, or when skiers and snowmobilers flocked to the park and the remote trails of the national forest next door. The Wolverines are hundreds of miles from the nearest big city, just too far for a weekend jaunt.

"When the years rolled on," Ginny continued, "and everybody realized that tourism would never come to Porcupine County in a big way, those frontages slowly were offered for sale to the other landowners."

"Especially when the frontage owners realized they'd never get rich from selling to commercial developers," I observed cynically. "The prices at which they sold the frontages were hardly token. They were out to get what they could."

Ginny nodded. "They were and are businessmen."

I wondered, I told her, if some of those early buyers may have been unaware that their property lines hadn't extended to the highway. They might just have assumed it, trusting in the fairness of the sellers' lawyers who drew up the land contracts. And since they had easy access between their property and the highway, they may never have suspected a thing for a long time.

And then I remembered something I'd encountered in the courthouse: In the 1960s the Metrovich brothers — the two woodsmen who had found Passoja's body—had bought a lakefront parcel from him. Later that afternoon I stopped at the records and deeds office and had another look. Sure enough, that clause about the highway frontage existed on their deed. And there was no later subdeed giving them possession of the frontage. At the time of his death, Paul Passoja still owned that land.

This, I realized, did not mean the Metroviches had had anything to do with his death, but any homicide investigator will tell you that the first thing in building a list of suspects is to check out the person—or persons—who found the body, as well as those present at the scene, and anyone who might have profited financially from a murder.

I laid them out on the blackboard of my mind.

The first was Marjorie Passoja, who, as far as I knew, inherited everything Paul owned, though the probate attorneys hadn't yet done their stuff. I doubted she was the culprit. She already enjoyed all the things Passoja's money could buy, and nobody had ever whispered a thing about clandestine boy toys. Beautiful as she was, she seemed too shy, too withdrawn, to take up with young hunks, even as a widow. I wouldn't write her off until all the facts were in, but so far I could see no reason to make her a suspect.

Stan Maki? Highly unlikely. He was originally from Wisconsin, had no apparent history with Passoja, and in any event had been playing in an amateur golf tournament at Land o' Lakes for two days before we found Passoja's body. He had taken the third-place trophy. I knew from the chatter at Merle's Café that he had returned to Porcupine City late the night before Passoja's body was found and had had drinks at Hobbs' to show off his prize.

Hank Heikkila? A distinct possibility, but churlishness isn't a crime, and I hadn't seen anything that connected him to Passoja.

Mary Larch? A colleague, an officer of the law. No

apparent connection, either.

Garrett Morton? An utter simpleton.

I drummed my fingers. Of the people who had been at Big Trees that morning, the Metroviches seemed the likeliest candidates, for there was a paper connection between them and Paul Passoja. There was a possible motive in those deeds.

TWENTY

I had to plan my confrontation with the brothers carefully. This was not yet — if ever it was going to be — an official investigation, and I didn't want to tip either the department or the Metroviches to my suspicions. I respected them too much to risk the genuine friendship we had built over the years. Cops in big cities early on develop a cynical attitude toward the people they supposedly serve and protect, because they usually see only their bad sides. But Porkies like the Metroviches are easy to like and admire.

All their lives the brothers had survived hard times, doing what they had to do in order to put food on the table. They had been born to an old lumbering family that had turned to mining early in the twentieth century when Porcupine County's timber was cut over. In the last two decades of the century, the Lone Pine Mine near Silverton had faltered and closed, its copper ore no longer profitable enough to wrest from the earth. Fortunately the paper mill, the county's last remaining industry, found the brothers' multiple skills as woodsmen in the second-growth pulpwood forest valuable enough to add them to the fewer than five hundred workers it employed, most of them part-time.

Frank, the elder by half a dozen years, had raised Bill almost single-handedly after their mother's death from pneumonia, and the younger man as a result was utterly devoted to his brother. Separately, I thought, they might not have been able to remain in such a country of high unemployment, but together they made ends meet.

And in doing so they helped others do the same. Their pickup had a detachable plow that helped them earn a little extra money in classic Upper Peninsula fashion by clearing the snow from people's driveways. When some of their customers were too broke to pay, the brothers cleared the driveways anyway. And they had been known to drop off a free cord or two of firewood at the houses of old folks who couldn't afford to stay warm in the winter.

Someday the favors were likely to be returned, if only in the form of a cherry pie, a bottle of wine or, more often, a few hours of labor. Once an elderly woman press-ganged her daughters into cleaning the Metroviches' house—a typical bachelor sty—from top to bottom while the brothers were gone for a few days in the woods, and they had returned not only to a sparkling home but also fresh-cut wildflowers on the kitchen table. They were amazed that anybody would go to all that trouble.

But these acts are not simply noble selflessness. People up here try to help others not only out of good-heartedness but also because they can't make it without neighbors to watch over them, too. It's the quid pro quo of survival. Like so many Porkies, the Metroviches may not be rich and sophisticated, but they straightforwardly, even courageously, make the most of what they have—and from some points of view it is a surprising lot.

And that is why I hoped fervently that the brothers weren't the guilty parties. But I am a cop, and I could not look the other way.

Over the next few days I made sure I casually ran into the Metroviches at Merle's or the hardware store and exchanged a few pleasantries. At any time I enjoy talking with them, not least because they speak a soft, almost pure "Yooper"—lots of "dis, dese, dem, dose" and the frequent "eh?" at the end of a declarative sentence that sounds almost Canadian. The genuine accent is slowly disappearing from the Upper Peninsula, thanks to the flattening of regional speech by radio, TV, and the Internet, and most Yooperspeak one hears these days is slathered on like stage Irish by merchants for the benefit of tourists.

Neither brother showed the slightest sign of guilt, and

I have long considered them simple and guileless men. I confronted them subtly at breakfast one morning at Merle's in early November, while the proprietor of the same name stood on a stepladder replacing the Halloween decorations with pine boughs, wreaths, and Christmas lights.

"Getting a jump start on the holidays, eh?" I said. This was rare. Unlike the big cities, where the Christmas commercial push begins not long after Labor Day, Porcupine County still considers Thanksgiving the start of the holiday season.

"Yep," Merle said. "Way the economy's going, I can use all the help I can get."

Shaking my head sympathetically, I slid into a booth behind the Metroviches and turned to face them. "Times are getting tougher, aren't they?" I asked.

"Not so's we've noticed," Frank said for them both. "They're always tough."

"It's been a hard year," I agreed, seguing into reminiscence about that unhappy day at the Big Trees.

"Paul Passoja was quite a fellow, but what kind of a guy was he personally?" I asked casually. "You ever have any dealings with him?"

I gazed out into the street but watched the brothers' reflection in the window for their reactions.

"We bought our property from him away back in 1963," Bill volunteered forthrightly. "Never had any trouble, eh? He treated us like everybody else. We did a lot of hiking in da woods with him, cleared some land for him and even worked on his cribs."

Frank nodded in quiet assent. "He paid well, and he wasn't afraid of workin' with his hands. He'd often shuck his coat and work right along with us, eh?"

Cribs were the low log-and-stone semi-jetties many lakefront landowners had built, or had had built for them, to fight wave-borne erosion of their beaches before the government put a halt to it in the 1970s as environmentally unsound. Milton Browne had himself constructed two cribs on the beach of the property I had bought from his estate, and they still stood after forty years of battering from the waves. They needed repair, however, and the next summer I was going to have to spend part of my vacation sawing logs, hauling rock, and driving spikes. "Yes," I said, "maybe you can give me some advice on my cribs. The lake is beating them all to hell."

"No sweat," Frank said amiably. "We'll give you a hand."

I decided to take the plunge. "When you bought your land from Paul in '63," I asked, "I guess he must have kept fifty feet of frontage along the highway, like he did with Milt Browne, who owned my cabin. Did you ever buy that frontage from Paul?"

"No, indeed," said Bill without hesitation. "He offered, but we didn't have the money. He wanted five thousand bucks. It wouldn't have been worth it anyway—it wouldn't have made any difference to us except to tidy things up nice and legal, eh?"

"I've had the idea that a lot of people who bought beach land from Paul didn't know for a long time that they didn't own their land clear up to the edge of the highway," I said neutrally. "Was that so with you?"

"It sure was," Frank said without rancor, but his expression betrayed a tinge of irritation over the memory. Nobody likes to be had.

"We learned about it only when the electric company started running a new line of poles along the highway, down the part of the property we thought was ours. They never contacted us, and when we asked about it we learned that it was Passoja's land they were using."

"Didn't that frost your cheeks?" I asked.

"Well, sure, for a while," Bill said. "We did feel kind of cheated. We didn't know how to read a land deed. But lots of

others were in the same boat. That was just how Paul Passoja
was. He was a smart fellow. He wasn't mean, just a little
sneaky, like his daddy before him—now there was an
operator—and like all those sharp fellas who ran the mills and
the mines. And in the long run it made no never mind."

It just did not seem that the Metroviches were lying,
although I still felt uneasy. I put them on the back burner of
my mind, and for a while my unofficial investigation lost
much of its energy.

TWENTY-ONE

My courtship of Ginny Fitzgerald, however, gathered steam, and in more ways than one. As the nip of oncoming winter chilled the first weekend of November, I found myself at her dinner table again, a cheery blaze crackling in the hearth, the branches of the lovely silver Christmas tree from Jerusalem twinkling in the firelight. Partly because as an assimilated Indian I have no special heritage of my own, the national customs of other people have always attracted me, as if hanging out with them might give me a greater sense of belonging.

So it is with the Finns of Upper Michigan. Even though they have been thoroughly absorbed into American life for many decades — almost all of their old people are at least second-generation Americans — and they have intermarried widely, they have nevertheless hung on to many traditional ways. I'm not talking about folk dances or cooking (although I have grown a soft spot for the sweet holiday bread called *nisu*), but something deeper. I often envy Finns their rootedness, I told Ginny, and I love the gentle satiric humor they are able to poke at their own culture because they feel so comfortable in it.

"You mean like St. Urho?" Ginny said with a twinkle.

"Who's that?" I asked.

"Every March sixteenth," she said, "just before everybody in Chicago turns into an Irishman and drinks green beer on St. Patrick's Day, everybody up here turns into a Finlander and drinks purple schnapps to celebrate St. Urho's Day."

I chuckled.

"And don't forget the Heikki Lunta."

"What's that?"

"It's a snow dance we do, like you Indians with the

rain dance."

I looked at her sharply, then relaxed. Casual remarks about my being Indian or, more often these days, Native American raised my hackles sometimes. I hated being shoved into pigeonholes where I didn't belong. But Ginny went on unconcernedly, as if she had just stated a harmless commonplace. Indeed she had, I suddenly realized. I look Indian, and there's nothing I can do about that, or anybody else. She just accepted it for what it was.

"The ritual is very specific and demanding," Ginny said in mock seriousness, "but there are minor regional differences. Here in Porcupine County we put on our red long-handled underwear, our swampers and chooks—what you call rubber-bottomed boots and toques—and plunk some polka music on the stereo, good and loud. If we are truly lucky we'll find an accordion player. We'll dance around the yard imploring Heikki Lunta—that's Hank Snow in English, and he's the god of the white stuff—to let 'er rip.

"The performance is best conducted with ample amounts of brandy. Some folks prefer beer, and others feel Mogen David is acceptable. If the dance is done with sincerity and in true faith, Heikki will bless us with a hearty storm. If the dance is halfhearted, though, it invalidates the process, and another performance is required. True fact."

Ginny's expression was so mock solemn and schoolmarmish that I burst out laughing.

"I understand that the famous Finnish sauna is giving way to the California hot tub," I said. "Just last week Tina Hokkanen told me she and her husband had discovered that while they were out of town their high school boy invited the whole senior class to a hot tub party in their basement. They cut class the day afterward and went over to clean up after themselves very carefully, and they would've gotten away with it, Tina said, if she and Toivo hadn't come home the next day to find the house spic-and-span but the dryer running, still full of towels."

Ginny chuckled. "Never let it be said that Finns aren't adaptable. A good soak in a hot tub is great after a long afternoon snowmobiling. And just because some of us have become spa people doesn't mean we aren't hairy-chested Finns. Only our sauna-enhanced blood can handle the water when it's at a full rolling boil."

All the same, she added, saunas still survived all over the Upper Peninsula. "Younger folks are building electric saunas in their basements now," she said, "but real Finns still do it the old way — with wood fires in little outdoor buildings, log ones preferred. We don't flail each other with birch branches anymore, but the tougher ones among us do run straight from the sauna into the lake."

I shuddered. Lake Superior is cold, even in the summer, although in recent years, as the water level has dropped owing to sparser snowfall and warmer winter temperatures, it can be almost bearable. I've been in a few times in August when the inshore water has warmed to just over seventy degrees.

"How do people sauna in groups?" I asked. "Do you wear bathing suits or do you just go coed naked like California hot tubbers?"

"Finlanders do sauna in the nude," replied Ginny expressionlessly, "but we are very modest people. The sexes take their saunas separately, except for families with very small children. And, of course, married couples and lovers."

I could have sworn she eyed me speculatively.

"Have you ever taken a sauna, Steve?"

"Nope," I said. "Milt Browne didn't build one on his property and nobody's ever asked me."

"Well, now, Steve Martinez, it's time to change that. I'll go start the fire." She pointed out the window at a small, low log structure at the edge of her beach. I'd thought it was a woodshed. Only then did I notice the stovepipe at one end.

"Uh," I said, "I didn't bring a swimsuit."

"Don't need one," Ginny said. "We're adults. We know what boys and girls look like. Besides, you're a sworn officer of the law. I can trust you."

"You're going to sauna, too?"

"Why not?"

"Well . . ."

"Don't tell me you're a prude!"

TWENTY-TWO

I am not ashamed to admit that the distinct possibility of getting lucky that evening entered my mind. There had been a desultory relationship with a young lawyer after the army, and a one-night stand with an unattached female cop during a law enforcement seminar in Lansing the previous year, but other than that I had led a regrettably celibate life.

There had been opportunities. Middle-aged widows and divorcées who live alone in the countryside sometimes call in handsome younger deputies to obtain services not ordinarily provided on a police department's menu. Unlike one or two of my brother cops, however, I always extricated myself as gently and as firmly as I could from such situations. If it is unseemly for merchants to sleep with their customers, I thought, so it is indiscreet for cops to serve and protect in that particular fashion, especially in a county so sparsely populated that everybody knows everybody else. We might have to arrest a former paramour someday. And, in the worst case, how can you shoot someone you've shared a bed with? I will admit, however, that I often felt tempted—and, boy, at that moment, was I ever.

I resolved not to push matters—Ginny, I thought, was worth whatever patience it took to reach her heart. Nonetheless, when an hour later she beckoned from the low door of the sauna and I trotted over from the house, I was goose-bumpy not only from the evening chill but also anticipation. It had been a *long* time.

Through the door I saw Ginny sitting on a high bench in the cedar-lined cabin, swathed like me in an oversized white terry-cloth robe. "C'mon in," she said, a cheery smile on her face.

It was, I thought, like stepping into a dry oven, and I gasped as the cedar-scented heat hit me. A large thermometer on the wall proclaimed 110 degrees Fahrenheit.

"Close the door and sit down here," said Ginny, spreading a towel on a low bench, almost painfully hot to the touch. I sat.

She climbed back on the high bench. "Okay, you can take off your robe now," she said, "but please keep your eyes out the window."

I obeyed. Then, as I heard her robe slither behind me to the bench, the short hairs on my arms and legs prickled.

But the heat, steadily building up in the room as if it were a wooden pressure vessel, had begun to wilt my impure thoughts. And when Ginny, beautiful naked Ginny unseen behind me, suddenly poured a ladleful of water onto the heated rocks at the side of the room, the sexual tension in the room expired in a flash of steam. It was like being thrown alive into an autoclave. Every sweat gland in my skin suddenly erupted. I began to pant like a beached fish.

"Good, huh?" asked Ginny. "More steam?"

"This takes getting used to," I gasped.

"We'll go easy on you the first time," she chuckled.

Ten minutes passed. I closed my eyes, seeing only red from the window light as the rising steam insinuated its way into my being through every pore I owned. I tried to breathe shallowly in order not to sear my lungs. From time to time Ginny dipped another ladleful of water onto the rocks, further boiling me in my own juices.

I felt agonizingly well-done when Ginny suddenly said, "Time to go! Head for the lake."

The moon had risen over Lake Superior as I burst out of the sauna in a dead run, robe forgotten on the bench, thundered across the beach and plunged into the water. The lake couldn't have been much colder than about fifty-five degrees—the unseasonably warm fall had kept the water comparatively warm inshore into November—but the effect was like leaping from a deep fryer into a bucket of supercooled ice. Electricity — I can call it only that — rocketed through my body as my pores slammed shut, every one of my nerves protesting the double insult to their harmony.

"*WhooooOOOO!*" I surfaced with a glorious bellow, triumphant that I had survived. I caught a flash of red hair and naked breast as Ginny herself erupted from the water in the moonlight twenty yards away, her delighted laugh echoing from the woods. I dove in again and sprinted a good seventy-five yards out into the lake, turned, and sprinted back.

I was puffing as I staggered over the rocky inshore out of the water. Again in her robe, Ginny leaned on a crib, gazing away from me to the west down the lake, watching the moon dip behind a bank of clouds. My robe lay on the crib where she had put it, and I donned it, marveling at how so very splendid I felt.

Ginny turned to me. "Now you can introduce yourself as a full-blooded Finlander at the next St. Urho's," she said with a chuckle.

After we dressed — in separate rooms — it felt only natural to say good night. Anything else, I thought, would have ruined a wonderful evening.

At the door Ginny's kiss and embrace were warm, the warmest ever. Her eyes shone as she waved good-bye and I walked out to the Explorer, feeling about as agreeable as I had felt in many, many years.

With flying colors I had passed a test, although exactly what kind I wasn't quite sure.

TWENTY-THREE

By the time I got home, the moon had dipped below the horizon and the stars sparkled in the night sky, diamonds scattered on jeweler's velvet. Up here in the north, away from the lights and pollution of the cities, night is extraordinarily dark and clear, a perfect background for stargazing. I strode down to the water's edge and searched for a constellation I had loved ever since my boyhood.

"The Big Dipper," I could hear my Uncle Fred saying. "The Romans called it Ursa Major, the Great Bear." Fred, who took me under his wing when my adoptive parents died, was an amateur astronomer as well as a salty front-stoop storyteller. One night we peered at the northern sky through his big reflector telescope.

"The Romans had this knockout of a huntress called Callisto," Uncle Fred said. "Jupiter, the boss god, had the hots for her. He took on the shape of Diana, the goddess of hunters, so he could nail Callisto. Afterward she bore him a son called Arcas. But Juno, Jupiter's wife, heard about the rape, got jealous, and turned Callisto into the Great Bear.

"One day Arcas was out hunting, saw the bear and was about to kill it, but Jupiter stopped him and changed him into a bear, too — that's Ursa Minor, the Little Bear, just to the right and below Ursa Major.

"And now the Great Bear and the Little Bear forever rotate around the northern sky without ever setting, just to remind Jupiter of what he'd done."

As I studied the constellation through the telescope, Uncle Fred grasped my shoulder. "There's something even cooler," he said. "American Indians also saw a bear in those stars."

Some tribes told a story about three warriors chasing a

huge bear through the forest for many days, many nights, and many narrow escapes. Finally, exhausted, the bear jumped into the sky, but the resolute Indians leaped after it. Now, all year round, the hunters pursue the bear across the northern sky.

What's more, Uncle Fred said, "in the autumn Ursa Major has turned upside down, with the bear flat on its back. That means the Indians have caught it and killed it, and its blood is falling from the sky and coloring the leaves of the trees. In the winter, when they cook the bear, its fat drips and turns the land white. As the moons pass and the sky once more moves towards spring, the bear slowly gets back on its feet and the chase starts all over again."

If two vastly different civilizations could see the same animal in the constellation, I thought decades after my introduction to the magic of the stars, perhaps the Great Bear was a kind of bridge between cultures. Or maybe not. The classical story, full of sex and revenge, clearly reflected an accurate view of human nature. But I liked the Indian tale better, for there was grandeur in its union of the stars with the seasons. And I could relate to the doggedness of those warriors.

I am not ordinarily a spiritual fellow, despite — or maybe because of — my upbringing by Christian missionaries. All the same, as I stood on the shore of Lake Superior staring into the night and recalling Uncle Fred's stories, it seemed as if the eternal Great Bear were beckoning, inviting me into the cosmos, gathering me into the great chain of being where I had so long struggled to find my place.

It suddenly reminded me of a worldlier event — what had happened to Paul Passoja at the claws of a black bear — and that darkened the almost mystical cloud of contentment I had been wrapped in since that sauna with Ginny.

And then, in the cabin, I opened the freezer for a couple of ice cubes. There, in a corner, sat the little Sucrets tin covered with hoarfrost, its gray shard of bacon invisible inside. With a start I thought guiltily, "That's evidence in a murder investigation and I'm concealing it."

But then common sense won out. There was no murder investigation, just a few loose doubts rattling around in my brain. What really had happened to Paul Passoja, the consummate woodsman? Did a malign disease of old age kill him, or did something else? Why? Who? How? And did anyone care?

I sighed and turned in, sleeping fitfully all night, dreaming of chasing the Great Bear around and around the timeless sky.

TWENTY-FOUR

A week later, before going on duty I played Saturday-morning dodgem with housewives hell-bent on vehicular homicide in the produce aisle at Frank's Supermarket as carols boomed out from speakers scattered around the store. I winced. Every holiday season Frank's elderly manager always turned the music up a couple of notches too high. I suspected that was because he was going deaf. Or maybe the music was making him deaf. I wished I had brought earplugs.

Navigating around a stack of canned cranberries and past a rack of Christmas cards, I nearly cannoned my cart into a tiny, stooped, gray-haired woman squeezing the grapefruit and leaning conspiratorially toward what looked like her twin sister. It was then that I heard the name for the first time.

"It was Karelia," the first woman whispered to the other. "Reino was never the same after." I looked at them blankly as I attempted to squeeze by.

The other noticed my glance and nudged her friend. "Shh," she whispered sharply.

I chuckled inwardly and sniffed a cantaloupe. Whoever Karelia was, she must have been quite a temptress, I thought, if Reino had never recovered from her. The women still gazed at me guardedly as I turned the corner into the frozen foods section.

TWENTY-FIVE

As I pulled the Explorer into Ginny's driveway just before lunch, a waxed black Lincoln only a year or two old loomed in the parkway next to her muddy Toyota 4-Runner. Michigan plates, I noticed automatically, always the alert and suspicious cop.

A small Detroit Lions sticker sat in a corner of the Lincoln's rear window — a dead giveaway that this was a Lower Michigan car, because the western Upper Peninsula is culturally part of Wisconsin and Minnesota, and people here root for either the Packers or the Vikings. What's more, U.P. vehicles are usually muddy and dusty — keeping a car clean in the north woods is both useless and an extravagance — but the Lincoln's paint was spotless and shiny, except for the bug-spattered hood and windshield, which bore a Grosse Pointe municipal sticker.

An out-of-town car that had come all the way up from Detroit, probably over the Mackinac Bridge, I deduced brilliantly. I should have been a detective.

The front door opened and two men walked out to the Lincoln, where I still stood. Both were middle-aged, balding, and dressed in nearly identical dark suits, expensive by the look of their cut. One of the men was portly and the other wore French cuffs. When you see suits like that in the U.P., somebody is about to be killed, buried, or foreclosed upon. I was prepared to dislike these two men.

"Good morning, deputy," said Portly in a gentle, cultured voice. "I hope nothing's wrong?"

"Nope, this is just a social visit," I said. "Mrs. Fitzgerald home?"

"Yes, she is," said French Cuffs with an amiable grin, like a Lions Club vice president. "The coffee's very good this morning, too."

A slightly awkward moment of silence followed. "Well, we'd best be getting back home," Portly said. "Long drive ahead."

"Nice to make your acquaintance," said French Cuffs.

I nodded and stood aside. The Lincoln drove off slowly, as if in law-abiding acknowledgment of the presence of authority in this part of the world.

Ginny stood in the door, a worried expression on her face and a blue power suit on her frame. It was strictly businesslike, yet smartly cut to accentuate her womanliness. "Donna Karan" came to mind for some odd reason; I am hardly knowledgeable about women's fashion, yet designers' names are part of the worldly flotsam that has stuck in odd corners of my brain. A simple strand of pearls lay on the ruffled blouse that peeked from her jacket. Neutral hose clad her legs—it was the first time I'd ever seen them outside Levi's, and they were shapely—atop alligator-leather pumps. Ferragamos, I thought blindly. Then I noticed the makeup— tastefully understated eye shadow, blush, and lipstick. This astonishingly elegant woman wouldn't look out of place in a corporate boardroom in Manhattan.

"What's wrong?" I said. "Did those men threaten you?"

"No," she said, relaxing only slightly. "Far from it."

"Who are they?"

For a moment she gazed at me speculatively. Then she touched her hair.

"Come in and I'll tell you," she said. "You're going to have to know sometime and I guess it's now."

A shapely seven-foot balsam, not yet trimmed, stood in its stand by the glowing fireplace of her great room, a huge combined kitchen and living room. A splendid aroma of newly cut balsam, burning maple logs, and Colombian coffee enveloped us.

We sat at the kitchen table. French Cuffs was right. The coffee was good.

"Steve," Ginny said, "I know I can trust you never to repeat to anyone what I'm about to tell you."

"Providing it doesn't break a law," I said.

Ginny snorted. "Those men," she said, "are my attorney and the director of my foundation. We meet once or twice a year to sign papers."

"Foundation?" I said dumbly.

"Yes," Ginny said. "I am a wealthy woman. Filthy rich, in fact."

It had been obvious to me that Ginny had some sort of outside income — her home and its furnishings were evidence of that — but I had simply thought her husband had left her reasonably well provided for before his death.

"When John died," Ginny said — it was the first time she had used his name — "he left the whole thing to me. And it was a rather big thing."

He had inherited his father's prosperous electrical parts company and in a few years quadrupled its capital. Upon his death Ginny took over the president's chair, and in a year the company had nearly doubled its income, thanks to John's judicious choice of management, including a whip-smart chief executive officer.

"But I'm a historian," Ginny said, "not a businesswoman. Although the company was thriving, there really was nothing for me to do except chair stockholders' meetings, and I held nearly all the stock. Two years after John died, a bigger company made a very generous merger offer, and I took it with the blessing of his management."

All those millions and nowhere to spend it — and no inclination to, for that matter. Ginny was simply uninterested in money, except for the good things it could do, and with the help of Portly and French Cuffs — who had been her husband's legal and financial advisers — she set up several foundations to distribute her income to worthy causes.

I would have to find out the real names of Portly and

French Cuffs someday, I thought — no point in referring to upright, law-abiding citizens as if they were Mafiosi.

"I really wanted to come home and study the history of this place," Ginny said. "And maybe help out a little, where I could, with the foundations."

Within a year her volunteer work at the Historical Society had led to its poorly paid directorship. But no one in Porcupine County — indeed, no one outside the law offices of Portly and French Cuffs and the Internal Revenue Service — knew that she was the head of the foundations that put a new roof on the museum building, that provided much of the money for the restoration of the 150-year-old lighthouse at the mouth of the harbor, that paid for the new recovery room at the county hospital, that bought new uniforms for the peewee hockey team Mary Larch coached, that put the St. Nicholas Project's Christmas fund drive over the top. All that was just the tip of the iceberg,.

"No wonder you're so successful at writing grants," I said with a chuckle. "You fund them yourself."

"Money changes the way people look at you," Ginny said. "I don't want anyone here ever to know that I have it, like Marjorie Passoja. I love this place and I want to be an ordinary part of it. I want to be accepted for who I am, not what life has given me."

"I know," I said. "I do, too."

"You'll never tell?" she said.

"Never," I said. "Not unless you finance a revolution or hire a hit man."

She hugged me across the kitchen table, her eyes moist.

"Thank you, Steve Martinez," she said.

At that moment I loved her mightily and would easily have been swept away, my deputy's duties for the day forgotten, had she just beckoned. But she gazed distractedly out the kitchen window onto the calm and windless lake beyond, watching a fleet of mergansers dive for their breakfasts, popping up hither and yon, a pack of feathered submarines. I had been entrusted and I was not going to jeopardize that trust with a clumsy pass. There would be another moment, I was sure.

I broke the silence. "Speaking of hit men," I said. "In a way I was almost one this morning."

TWENTY-SIX

As Ginny changed behind her bedroom door, I told her about my odd encounter in the supermarket that morning.

"This Karelia sounds like quite a gal. Who was she?"

Ginny chuckled as she swept back into the living room in her everyday Levi's-and-Woolrich outfit, still in makeup. She was achingly lovely in anything she wore.

"Karelia wasn't a woman," Ginny said, unconsciously switching into historian's lecturing mode. "She was what used to be the eastern region of Finland. But she did cut quite a swath through the Upper Peninsula once."

"Clue me in," I said, consciously switching into detective's listening mode.

Back in the early 1930s, Ginny said, the government of the Karelian Autonomous Soviet Socialist Republic sent agents to upper Michigan, Minnesota, and Canada. They sought to recruit skilled and talented Finnish-American farmers and industrial workers for a better life of opportunity in the worker's paradise of Karelia, a province of largely Finnish-speaking inhabitants that over the centuries had changed hands several times between Finland and Russia. The Karelian commissars, nationalist to the core, thought importing American and Canadian Finns would prevent Moscow from packing the sparsely populated region with ethnic Russians.

"Karelia fever" captured many Upper Peninsula Finns. "We have always been highly political and intensely devoted to our community," Ginny said, "and in the old country we had all been Evangelical Lutherans. That was a stern and authoritarian state church, and we all did as it told us to. But over here, as you'd expect, many younger immigrants and second-generation Finnish-Americans had broken away from the old ways. It was the Depression, after all, and many had become radicalized. Some of them were looking for a whole new religion, and Marxism offered a glimpse of heaven."

The traditional churchly Finns, she added, had no illusions about godless communism and railed against the Karelian agents and their "Red dupes." Fistfights broke out at political rallies the recruiters held in halls all over Finnish immigrant territory. Families split, many fathers disowning their radical sons, some of whom had joined the Communist Party, and friendships crumbled as idealistic Finnish-American "pioneers" signed up and departed for Karelia to put their agricultural and industrial skills to work in the brave new world.

Like Americans elsewhere during the Depression, Finns were on the move. Thousands participated in the reverse migration to Karelia, Ginny said, their numbers swelling to more than ten thousand as the Depression deepened.

"Some of them of course were Communists," she said, "but many more were just naíve, terribly poor people seeking a better life. The Upper Peninsula had been hard hit by the Depression, and there was a lot of poverty here."

But when the pioneers arrived, things weren't as they expected. They had to go where the commissars told them to, in jobs that rarely fit their talents. Skilled artisans were put to work digging ditches. They couldn't travel without official permission and were denied access to Western newspapers. The promised land was a prison.

By 1935 Karelia fever had subsided. Stalin decided at last to move more Russians into the region instead of importing capitalism-tainted Finns from North America. The Karelian officials who had dreamed up the reverse-migration scheme were demoted, and when the great Soviet purges began in 1937, they were executed. The Finnish language was banned in Karelia, and when war between Finland and the Soviet Union loomed in 1938, the Soviets clapped into labor camps many of the immigrants from America as potentially disloyal elements. Some died in the camps and others were brutally liquidated. Few survived the Stalinist holocaust to return to freedom in the West.

"That's a horrible story," I said when Ginny finished. "How come I've never heard about it?"

"Simple," she said. "We're ashamed of it. We were suckered. It's a closed subject, even in my own family. A couple of great-uncles took their whole families to Karelia, and only one of them came back—alone. A cousin still lives in a cabin in Baraga County. We never talked about Karelia, partly out of respect for him, because he never brought up the subject—it was just too painful for him. His wife left him, and took the children with her when he couldn't send money back from Karelia. And he lost all his land in America to the banks that grabbed the land for nickels on the dollar at tax auctions. When he came back, the new owner of his home just laughed at him and said he'd made his own bed and had to lie in it. It happened time and again, and many people who haven't shoved the whole Karelian episode under the bed still hold grudges about it."

"Even now?" I asked. "The people who remember Karelia fever have to be in their eighties and nineties."

"Yes, but their children and grandchildren remember, too, because in so many cases they lost their birthrights. There are still people in their sixties and seventies who don't talk to each other even today. Watch them at church and in public places. They may be neighbors, but they don't speak. They don't kill each other in bar shootings anymore, as happened a few times long ago, but they don't speak. It's as if the Hatfields and McCoys decided to hang up their weapons but just can't forget."

"Hmm," I said. Then the obvious conclusion occurred to me. "This could be a motive for murder. In the late thirties Paul Passoja was the right age—in his late teens—and as the son of a big landowner came from the right background."

Ginny looked up. "Still riding that horse, are you,

Steve?"

"I'm afraid so," I said with a deep sigh. "It just won't let go."

"Like Karelia," Ginny said.

TWENTY-SEVEN

The first time I laid eyes on the Porcupine Township Library I was delighted. I'd never thought such a small town in the middle of nowhere could have such a well-stocked library complete with a couple of Internet computers. As I learned more about Porcupine County, however, I understood.

The county's population, once in the healthy five figures, had dwindled to less than eight thousand — the fewest in the state — as its young people left to find jobs in Milwaukee, Detroit, and Chicago. At the same time, more and more exiles who'd made their pile were returning home to live on their pensions.

And why not? In many ways Porcupine County was Michigan's prettiest retirement community. Second-growth forest was restoring the countryside to much of its original wilderness. Except for the vast fields of tailings north of Lone Pine Mine, the wounds the copper mines had carved in the woods — now the Ottawa National Forest — had largely been hidden by scrub, brush, and young aspen and birch. The wildlife had roared back to the point where some species, like whitetail deer and black bears, had become nuisances. Timber wolves had returned to the most remote outback more than a century after they had been wiped out. There were even rumors of mountain lions. Most years the stream and lake fishing was as good as the hunting, and so was the snowmobiling and skiing.

Porkies who leave tend to get an education and then good jobs and more than a smattering of culture, and when they come home to retire they want to stay in touch with the outside world. Despite — and maybe because of — their isolation they demand books, magazines, and newspapers. If the library doesn't own a certain book, the state interlibrary loan system will provide it.

Millie Toole, the small, blue-haired dynamo of a librarian, is like so many people in the county a master at writing grants, and while many city libraries languish because their budgets are cut to hold the line on taxes, Millie's collection grows and grows. It's getting so big that she's negotiating for more space in the township building where the library occupies most of the ground floor.

As I walked in on my next day off, I spotted the Metrovich brothers sitting in overstuffed chairs across a low table from each other in front of the library's picture window, bedecked with pine boughs, holly, and a mock-Gothic *Season's Greetings* painstakingly lettered in tempera. Their noses were buried in the daily newspapers, Frank's in the *Duluth Mining Gazette* and Bill's in the *Detroit Free Press*. Like most Porkies, the brothers must husband every cent they have, and they often spend their spare moments catching up with the news in the free papers at the library. I shot them a hello, and they waved back. I looked at them closely. Way too laid-back to be killers, I thought.

"Hi, Steve," Millie said from her desk. As a mystery novel addict I'm one of her better customers, but she's jaunty and cheerful to everybody. "What can I get for you today?"

"I'm on a history kick," I said. "I'd like to rummage around in old newspapers from the area. Got any?"

"Yep. The entire archive of the *Porcupine County Herald*, all the way back to 1890, is on microfilm."

"Could I see the films beginning January 1, 1931?" I asked.

"Sure," she said, and in the shake of a squirrel's tail I was sitting behind a microfilm reader. Millie showed me how to insert a roll of film—I remembered from my college days, but there is always pleasure in watching an expert do things—and adjusted the focus.

"Yell when you need more," she said. I smiled. Millie

was not a shusher. Like so many gatekeepers to small-town libraries, she was proud that hers was bright and bustling, not gloomy and hushed.

Rolling through scratched old microfilmed newspapers is a slow job but a fascinating one. It's like peeking into the diary of a departed time. Old stories about people meeting untimely ends always demand full reading. The ads, with their ridiculously low prices — five hundred dollars for a new Chevrolet, eighty-eight cents for a house dress — captivated. The personals, full of pleas for work, implied sad stories, while the "Help Wanted" listings were pitifully meager. As months rolled by, the numbers of official public notices headed "NOTICE OF MORTGAGE FORECLOSURE SALE" grew in number until, in early 1932, the *Tribune* printed almost an entire page of them. Notices of auctions of tax-delinquent lands escalated, too. The Depression had well and truly hooked Porcupine County.

All the while I scanned the stories for the words *Karelia, socialist, emigrate, Finland,* and *workers needed* — as well as the names of anybody I might connect to Paul Passoja. All through 1930 and most of 1931 there was nothing about Karelia, although there were plenty of stories about socialist workers' organizations and Communist hall meetings, most of them slanted in disapproving language.

One was headlined *Help for Karelia Sought.* A representative from the Karelian Technical Aid Society in New York was to speak at a workers' hall one weekend in October 1931. There was, said the story — clearly retyped from a press handout — a great need in Soviet Karelia for skilled lumbermen with tools and machines to harvest the vast forests in exchange for badly needed foreign currency. Preference would be given those who spoke Finnish. Those who agreed to go would be assisted in their passage.

I would have expected the *Tribune* to print an occasional story announcing that another party of Finns was heading for the Soviet Union, but it was silent on the matter.

Finally, in the issue dated October 24, 1932, I saw this item:

"SIX FINNISH PEOPLE LEAVE FOR RUSSIA. Mr. and Mrs. Simon Talikka, Mr. Arthur Weser and sons Arthur Jr. and Elmer, and Henrikki Heikkila, who have lived at Greenfield for several years, left Thursday for Kontupohja, United Social Soviet Russia.

"A farewell party was given for them at the Farmers' Hall at Greenfield Monday evening."

That gave me pause, not only because of the creative rendering of the name of the Union of Soviet Socialist Republics, nor the fact that my cabin lies just a mile west from Greenfield, halfway between Porcupine City and the Wolverines. That name *Heikkila* jumped out at me. The diminutive for the Finnish *Henrikki* is "Heikki," and "Hank" is the English equivalent of *Heikki*. Hank Heikkila had been at Big Trees the morning Paul Passoja was found dead. Could it be?

TWENTY-EIGHT

Indeed it was.

"Hank Heikkila?" said Ginny, that gorgeous human card catalog, while we feasted on lake trout at my cabin. "Yes, he's the grandson and namesake of Henrikki, who went to Karelia and disappeared into the Gulag. I'm not certain, but I think you will find that the taxes on Henrikki's farm went delinquent when he stopped sending money back from Karelia—if he ever sent a cent—and that somebody, maybe Einar Passoja, bought it at a tax auction. Quite a few well-connected Porcupine County businessmen turned into tax title sharks in those days."

"What happened to Hank's father?" I asked.

"Urho Heikkila was a teenager when Henrikki left for Karelia," she replied. "Urho was about the same age as Paul. They must have known each other. Urho's family probably went on relief. We do know that Urho joined the army in the Second World War and came back to work in the mines. He died fairly young, not long after his son was born, from alcoholism."

"It's not really relevant," I said, "but what about the grandson's claim that he's also descended from the voyageurs?"

"It's possible," Ginny said. "I think Urho was the one who started the story. It's a historical fact that voyageurs settled in this area and intermarried with Indians—you'll find that some Ojibwa on the reservation near Baraga have French surnames. But a lot of the poorer people in the county like to give themselves a little dignity by dressing up their genealogy and making it more interesting than it really is. Rich people do that, too. We all want to be descended from kings."

TWENTY-NINE

Sure enough, Ginny was right. The next day it took only an hour at the courthouse to find the records: Henrikki Heikkila's land had been sold at tax auction to none other than Einar Passoja in 1934, barely two years after Henrikki had left for Karelia. In 1940 Einar sold the property for four times the price he had paid.

This time, I thought, I was not going to beat around the bush. Hank Heikkila was so crazy-man-of-the-woods reclusive that he was probably the last person who'd share with his nearest neighbor the details of an encounter with a deputy sheriff. As one of Porcupine County's more notorious bottom feeders, he wouldn't want to call attention to himself in the slightest way.

I knew where Hank's shack was, deep in the tall spruce and balsam second growth in the southern quarter of the county at the end of an old logging trail, but he was not visible when I arrived in my ancient Jeep, trailing a cloud of dust. It was my day off, and I was wearing civilian clothes. This was not an official visit from a sheriff's deputy. Nonetheless, I tucked the .357 into my belt at the small of my back.

Amid a score of traps in various stages of disrepair a dozen fisher pelts hung drying in the sun on a board leaning against the front of the shack. That was grounds for a bust right there—the season limit for fisher is three per person. I knew, however, that the threat of arrest might prove a useful lever to get Hank talking, for Molly Schultz, the DNR's Porcupine County conservation officer and Stan Maki's boss, would be highly interested. Molly is tough and always pushes for the maximum penalty for poaching.

The door to the shack was open. I peered inside from the doorway. Hank's big Springfield rifle rested against a badly cracked pine table piebald with remnants of red and white paint, and the few other sticks of furniture — two rusty gray metal folding chairs and a peeling brown cardboard wardrobe — suggested that no one in this room had ever uttered the word *houseproud*. Animal hair and dried mud lay scattered in the corners, as if chased there by desultory swipes with a broom.

On a nearby bureau missing half its drawers sat a .38 revolver — an old Smith and Wesson Police Special, cylinder open and empty. In Michigan, handguns must be registered, and I doubted that one was, for Hank Heikkila was not the kind to respect the niceties of the law. But I was after something more important than proper paperwork.

I checked the .357 at my back. Though he had never been known to be violent, Hank was the sort of woodsman who could quietly trail someone through the forest for hours, remaining just out of sight and sometimes just a few feet away, like a preternaturally patient Indian waiting for the best spot to attack. Everyone in the county suspected he often did, just to show himself that there was something he could do better than anybody else. It would not have surprised me if from time to time during the stalk he trained the sights of his old Springfield on his unsuspecting quarry, a kind of counting coup over a powerful enemy, perhaps even gently touching the trigger at the moment of greatest glory. If he indeed did that, it was a dangerous game.

"Hank!" I shouted. He had to be close by. He was too smart to go off somewhere for a few days and leave stuff like those pelts and the .38 out in the open.

No answer.

"Hank, where are you?"

No answer.

"You want me to tell Molly about those pelts?"

"Gahhhhhhhh-*dammit!*"

Hank stepped out from behind a fat oak, and my nostrils wrinkled as I smelled him. I was yards away, but directly downwind. It had been a while since he had bathed, and he was sweating. I was sure he had followed me as I drove in, cutting on foot through the woods to keep up with the Jeep.

"You're not gonna bust me and tell her, are you?"

"That depends," I said, I relaxed. Hank was unarmed, and his hands were out in the open. He knew the fine points of dealing with the cops. He'd been pinched often enough.

"On what?"

"On what you can tell me about Paul Passoja."

"I ain't telling you a fucking thing," he said, defiance smoldering in his reedy voice.

"Those pelts?"

He glanced at them guiltily. With his record of poaching convictions, they were good for at least a few months in the slammer and a heavy fine, and Molly would demand the max.

"What do you wanna know?"

"How you felt about him."

"He was a shit."

"Why do you say that?"

"You know."

"Know what?"

"What his daddy did to my grandpa. Everybody knows."

"But that was a long time ago."

"Yeah."

"Why are you so pissed off about it?"

"What's it to you?"

"Just curious."

"Like hell."

This conversation was going nowhere. I decided to take a chance.

"Are you happy Paul's dead?"

"Sure. Just like a lot of other people."

"Like who?"

Hank swept his arm around as if to include the whole forest and every living creature in it.

"Did you kill him?"

Hank's eyes smoldered. "A bear did. You know that."

I blinked. Maybe Hank was unaware of the coroner's conclusion.

"Did you help the bear?"

"Oh, sure," Hank said. "I led the bear right up to the tent by the paw and said, 'There he is. Eat.' Who are you kidding?"

I tried another tack. "Why did you hate Paul so when it was his father who took your grandfather's land?"

Hank cracked open the door to his anger. "He never let me forget it. When I was still a kid he would laugh and say, 'Your grandpa was a Red and got what he deserved.'"

That was an unusually long sentence from Hank, I suspect the longest he had uttered in many years.

"And after that?"

"He'd say stuff like 'I was on your grandpa's old farm the other day. Too bad your family couldn't keep hold of it.' He liked to bring it up, to rub it in. He was like that. He liked to be cruel when there was no call for it."

For Hank Heikkila, that was a Johnstown Flood of words.

"Sounds like a lot of people might have had it in for Paul Passoja," I said.

"You better believe it."

"Who?"

"I told you."

Hank had purged his tanks and was going to say no more.

"All right," I said. I strode away from the doorway, got into the Jeep and rolled down the window.

"Hank."

"Yeah?"

"We never had this conversation. And I never saw those fisher pelts. Or that .38."

He looked at me, his eyes glowing like coals over the underbrush of his beard. It was just a slight nod, but it was enough.

Hank, I was certain, knew something he wasn't telling. In a place where there are so few people everyone knows everyone else's business, secrets are valuable, for someday they might come in handy — for money or for something else. But what Hank's secret was I had no idea. Nor did I have any idea just then how to go about finding it out. I'd have to file the notion in the cluttered "unsolved cases" drawer of my mind until a better opportunity presented itself — maybe a return visit to his cabin.

My spirits, however, lifted as I drove down the track away from Hank's cabin. Not a hundred yards away a small clearing appeared by the road, and in it was a small bear digging up roots. Quietly I stopped the Jeep to watch. There is something about wildlife of any kind that touches my soul, and these little interludes in the woods often make my day. This one did.

For the little bear was the same one I had seen the afternoon of the day Paul Passoja died, when we tracked down the big one that had given him a heart attack. He looked a little larger than before, but his broad cinnamon face was unmistakable. I wasn't surprised that he was there; the spot where we had killed the rogue bear lay scarcely five miles southwest.

"Hello, buddy," I whispered.

The bear instantly looked up and locked eyes with me. I could have sworn he nodded at me. Some kind of acknowledgment passed between us, but I couldn't for the life of me explain it. All I can say is that it felt almost as if he were saying, "Nice to see you again, friend."

Presently he gave the ground one last swipe of his paw,

glanced at me once more, then ambled slowly into the trees and disappeared.

I drove on, smiling.

THIRTY

Standing at the kitchen sink, Ginny reached behind her and tucked in the shirttail of her sheer silken blouse with the unconscious candor that comes from living alone, a frankness that outlined her generous breasts against the light from the bright November moon in the kitchen window. The sight brought an involuntary catch to my throat.

I stood up, folded my arms around her, and kissed her graceful neck. She giggled and squirmed against me. I felt my blood rising. It had been soaring all evening and was about to trip the safety valve.

"Bring your toothbrush," she had said that morning.

We had set the Thanksgiving table together and prepared a small turkey, I ministering to the wild rice as best as I could. At the meal we said little, for we were as shy as teenagers preparing to say farewell to their virginity. A delicious tension built slowly but firmly as we savored every bite, every moment, speaking desultorily about nothing at all, looking into each other's eyes and glancing away demurely. By dessert I was as ready as I'd ever be. Ginny's face was flushed, her eyes shining, but she sweetly prolonged the wait, insisting that we wash the dishes.

Then she put her hand in mine. "Come, Steve," she said, gazing into my face with what seemed a mixture of adoration and unabashed lust. We climbed the stairs to her bedroom in the loft overlooking the great room. Her eyes fixed on mine, she drew back the eiderdown comforter covering her huge oaken bed, seemingly four feet off the floor.

"Close your eyes, Steve," she said. I did. Fabric rustled softly.

"Steve."

She stood by the window, its filmy white drapes softly

billowing, the reddening autumn light dancing through wind-rustled branches on the joyously ripe body of a woman at the height of her sexuality. I had never seen anything so beautiful, and I gasped.

She smiled. "Come here," she said, and began to undo the buttons on my shirt.

In bed, when I began to draw her close to me, she suddenly stiffened, pushing me away, and burst into tears.

"I can't, Steve," she said. "I can't."

"What . . . Why . . ?" I said, startled.

"Steve, don't! Just hold me, will you?"

In a welter of disappointment, confusion, and frustration I wrapped my arms around her, and after what seemed like hours of silent wakefulness we fell asleep, snuggling like spoons in a drawer.

Some time before three in the morning she stirred and reached for me. This time there was no hesitation, no reluctance, and just as dawn reddened the eastern sky, we slept once more, exhausted.

THIRTY-ONE

It was after nine when I smelled the wonderful odor of coffee and fresh nisu, the braided Finnish holiday bread made with cardamom. As I stumbled into the kitchen buttoning my jeans, Ginny turned from the stove in her nightgown and embraced me as if she never wanted to let go.

"Sit down, Stephen Two Crow Martinez," she said. "After you eat, I have something to tell you."

She watched every forkful as it went in. Then she did the thing with her hair.

"Ready?"

I nodded.

"It's about last night," she said. "I'm sorry how it began."

"I'm not sorry how it ended," I said.

"You deserve an explanation, though."

"Okay."

"About a year after John died," she said, "I met a man who hurt me very badly."

I placed my hand on hers and waited.

"He was the most incredibly charming man I had ever met, and one of the most fascinating, too. Malcolm was the director of a Baptist refugee agency and told me the most heartrending and hair-raising stories about saving lives in the Gaza Strip and the Balkans. You wouldn't believe the danger he put himself into in places like that.

"The cliché is true—Malcolm swept me off my feet. I'd rather not go into the details, but after a few months we became engaged. He started living with me most of the time, secretly of course because, he said, his church wouldn't have approved. Oh, Steve, I was so bubble-headed, so naive about it all.

"My best friend, Sheila, who is a lawyer, demanded that she draw up a prenuptial agreement for us. Malcolm was *insulted*. I was, too. 'He's a hero!' I said. 'We don't need one!' But she insisted.

"I was so *stupid*. I didn't notice when Malcolm's lawyer—by now he had hired one—proposed that half of John's company stock go to him in the prenup.

"It was the classic story, Steve. I was a lonely widow and Malcolm paid me the kind of attention no man ever had, not even John, who was absolutely devoted to me.

"I might have married Malcolm if he hadn't made a stupid mistake. After my accountants delivered my income tax return for my signature, Malcolm so very kindly offered to take it to the post office. Later that day he came back seemingly very upset. He had put down his jacket to play pickup basketball in a park, and it had been stolen. Naturally the tax return was still in it.

"I was unconcerned. Oh, all the accountants had to do was run off another copy on the printer, and I'd sign it. No harm done.

"But a couple of weeks later I went to Malcolm's house on an errand. I needed a pencil to leave him a note, and I opened his desk drawer looking for one. There was my tax return. It had been opened. And there was yellow highlighter across the names of the stocks Malcolm had suggested for his half of the prenup settlement.

"I went to Sheila and told her about what I had found. She didn't say anything. She just handed me a folder. It was from a private investigator she had hired to check on Malcolm. He had not been married just once, as he had told me, but five times. All his wives had been wealthy, and he had taken them for every cent he could. He loved being a hero, but he didn't mind being a son of a bitch, too."

I looked up at Ginny. A single tear coursed down her cheek. I reached up and wiped it away.

"It took me so very long to learn to trust completely

again," she said. "Until last night."

I chuckled softly. "And is that the real reason you came back to Porcupine County? You ran away. Just like me."

"Part of it, yes," she said, smiling. "But not all. And *now*, Steve, you know all my secrets."

I wasn't sure about that, but in response I swept her into my arms. She snuggled her head between my neck and my shoulder as I carried her up to the loft. We didn't wake again until almost noon.

THIRTY-TWO

I had just ticketed the teenage driver of a dilapidated old Chevy that had proved it still could get its speedometer needle to ninety when Mary Larch's voice crackled on the open radio.

"Car twelve-oh to dispatcher," she said. "I'm at Hank Heikkila's cabin. Bring the camera, will you? And send the ambulance, but tell them not to hurry."

By "camera" Mary meant for Joe to send the sheriff's department's evidence kit. By "not to hurry" Mary meant someone was dead. I grimaced. Three weeks before Christmas this wasn't what I wanted to hear on the radio.

"This is Steve," I broke in. "I'm on M-64 near Silverton. Want help?" Like most of the other deputies, I never bother with the protocol of identifying myself by car number. We all recognize each other's voices anyway. Being young and gung-ho, Mary, however, believed in the rules. Gil O'Brien often asked the rest of us why we couldn't follow them.

"Yeah," said Joe. "Mary, Steve's on his way."

Half an hour later I bounced down the logging track and pulled up at Hank's shack. Mary had cordoned off the place with crime-scene tape, although I doubted a rubbernecking crowd would form this deep in the woods.

"Steve," Mary said soberly.

I didn't say anything. Not even "What do we got?" — that hackneyed expression beloved of television detectives. I just raised my eyebrows wordlessly.

"Come look."

I stepped into the shack. On the floor Hank sprawled supine, missing most of his head above the eyebrows. It was spattered low on the wall behind him, a stew of blood, brain matter, and bone shards still dripping slowly to the floor. His Springfield rested on his stomach, muzzle pointing toward his mouth. Powder burns blackened his lips. He was fully dressed except for bare feet.

"Whatever happened to holly and mistletoe?" I asked nobody in particular. "Just what we wanted to see at this time of year."

A sheriff's deputy is bound to encounter violent death from time to time, especially on the highway. A car wreck does terrible things to the human body. Cops develop a protective emotional carapace against such sights.

But suicide has always been hard for me to keep at arm's length, because my first thought is to wonder what inner demons could have driven a fellow human being to such a despairing act, to wall himself off with such finality from society. Donne was right: "Ask not for whom the bell tolls; it tolls for thee."

Mary evidently heard the tolling, too. She looked drawn and white. I suspected that she had lost her lunch while I was on the way. I doubted that she had ever seen a gunshot death, though she had encountered plenty of traffic victims.

"Looks like he put the barrel in his mouth and used a toe to press the trigger," Mary said, as if I needed to be told the obvious. She was not brazen about it, but she sometimes subtly treated her brother deputies as if we were not as quick off the mark as she was. It didn't matter. Smart young people tend to be smart-ass, too. I used to be that way myself. We grow out of it.

"Find anything else?" I asked.

"This note," Mary said, pointing to a table. "I haven't touched it."

"That's good, Mary," I said.

She bristled slightly.

"I'm not being sarcastic," I said. "You'd be surprised at how many country cops would disturb a possible homicide scene without realizing it. We just don't get that much

142

experience."

I looked at the note, face up on the table. It contained three words in crude block printing: **LIFE IS SHIT**.

Next to it was a half-empty fifth of Jim Beam, the cap beside the bottle.

In the wilderness, suicide is not uncommon. Up here many people use alcohol to pacify the resentments of poverty, loneliness, and hard winters. Booze easily triggers depression, and every year two or three people in Porcupine County decide they've had enough. Mix despondency with a few drinks, and a quick bullet sounds good. It happens in the cities, too. And Hank already had been halfway there. Some people might say he had heard voices from the beyond, beckoning him to join them. Others might declare he only had needed his medication adjusted. In either case I would have been sorry.

"Anything else?"

"No."

New seeds of doubt sprouted in my mind. Where was that .38 I'd seen a few days earlier? Why hadn't Hank used it instead of the clumsy Springfield? True, a .38 slug is much lighter than that of a big .45-70, but in the fashion Hank had apparently chosen for his exit, it would have been just as effective—and a lot easier.

The revolver was nowhere to be found among Hank's mess, and I did not mention it to Mary. I had filed no report of my unofficial and unauthorized visit to Hank's shack, and I was not about to tell my superiors about my equally unofficial and unauthorized quasi-investigation—if you could call it that—of a case that had been closed.

But someone, I was certain, had taken that Smith and Wesson, and I was equally sure that its disappearance had something to do with what Hank Heikkila had not wanted to tell me. I prowled around outside. The fisher pelts I'd seen were gone, and so were all of Hank's traps. Perhaps he'd sold the pelts and left the traps in the woods, but a few traps always sit in pieces around a trapper's shack, awaiting repair. "No traps," I told Mary. "That's odd."

She caught on quickly. "Possible robbery-homicide. That's enough to call the blues, isn't it?"

Rural sheriff's departments don't have the resources for any but the most elementary criminal investigations. The state troopers do have the goods, and when we know we're out of our depth we call them in. Often they take over a case entirely, usually with the swift agreement of the sheriff. One fewer headache for him.

I radioed Joe, who spoke to Gil, who authorized him to call the Michigan State Police post at Wakefield, fifty miles southwest of Porcupine City. The thirteen-trooper post there includes an evidence-gathering team of uniformed technicians all too happy to drop their daily routine of traffic stops on U.S. 2 and fight crime instead.

Soon two troopers arrived, siren blaring and blue lights flashing. The drive up from Wakefield had taken them just forty minutes. They'd kept the pyrotechnics on even while bouncing down the narrow logging track in the middle of nowhere. At least the siren drowned out the sound of their big highway cruiser's undercarriage thumping on the ridges of the deep ruts. State cops like to make an entrance. Deputy sheriffs would, too, if they knew how.

I told them what I thought. They shrugged.

"Anything could have happened to those traps," said one after carefully examining the scene. "Trappers trap, after all. They're probably out on the line. Look, here's a bit of cash in a drawer. The place doesn't look as if it's been tossed."

"Looks like suicide," said the other trooper. "Open . . ."

"And shut," said the first.

"No shit?" I said. Though I knew their real names, I privately called them Monoghan and Monroe, the dirty-mouthed wiseguy detectives who always are first at the opening murder scene of a cop novel by Ed McBain, whose books I had devoured in high school.

I kept the skepticism out of my voice. We have to get along with these folks, who, like state cops everywhere, tend to look upon country deputies as a bunch of dimbulb clodhoppers who can't write a legible traffic ticket. Sometimes, though, even their smart evidence guys — and these two, for all their airiness, were really quite competent — quickly reach a conclusion and only then find the facts to back it up, missing a detail that might cast a little doubt. They're only human.

And they didn't know about that .38.

"Mary," I said.

"Steve?"

"What brought you out here in the first place? This isn't part of your regular patrol run."

She shook her head. "I got bored and decided to extend it a little. Besides, any reason to go into the woods."

She loved them as much as I did.

"Makes sense."

I nodded, then climbed into the Explorer and keyed the mike. "Joe?" I said. "Steve. Returning to patrol now."

"Ten-five," Joe said.

"Ten-*five*?"

"I get tired of saying 'Ten-four' all the time," he replied.

Despite my mood I laughed. Joe *never* says "Ten-four."

But I felt glum again as I drove back down the track. I hadn't said a word to my superiors about that bacon shard in the freezer, I hadn't said a word about my suspicions about the death of Paul Passoja, and I hadn't said a word about my earlier visit to Hank or that old .38 on his table. This was not acceptable behavior for a sworn police officer, and I knew I was digging an awfully deep hole for myself if ever the department found out.

THIRTY-THREE

"Anything could have happened to that .38 in the three days since I saw Hank," I told Ginny at her kitchen table that evening. She had confided her secrets to me, and now I was returning the compliment — which, when you think about it, is more of an intimacy than the sharing of a bed. "Maybe he sold the gun. Or lost it in the woods somewhere. Or maybe somebody came along and saw it and stole it. Maybe it *was* suicide. Damn, I wish I'd had the presence of mind to write down its serial number. Maybe it *was* suicide."

Ginny folded her arms and gazed out the kitchen window. "But you don't think so," she said.

"No."

"Why?"

"I don't know. Intuition, I guess. Cops sometimes get hunches for no good reason at all. When they pan out, we're geniuses. When they don't, we're dummies."

"And you men make fun of women's intuition." Her smile, however, was sympathetic. "Now what are you going to do?"

"Maybe I've been making a mistake trying to find an obvious motive for killing Paul Passoja," I said. "Maybe I'm barking up the wrong tree. Maybe I should be looking at the means instead."

"The bear?" Ginny sounded doubtful. "How? Tracing a bear isn't like tracing the ownership of a gun. People don't register bears. They belong to the woods."

I nodded. The carcass of the bear that killed Paul Passoja — or, rather, frightened him to death — had long been buried beneath tons of garbage in a landfill. The rangers had been unable to discover where the bear had come from. Wisconsin wasn't missing one. Neither was Minnesota. The university biology departments had drawn a blank, too. It looked as if the bear had never been counted and tagged, although it had once worn a radio collar. That was odd — researchers who collar bears almost always tag them on one or both ears for easy identification.

It looked as if all leads to this murder weapon, if it indeed was that, had simply vanished as effectively as if it had been tossed off a ship crossing the deepest trench in the Pacific.

"Maybe not *the* bear," I said, "but *a* bear."

"Hmm?" Ginny said.

"If I can prove that *a* bear can be induced to kill somebody, maybe that will lead somewhere."

"And how do you propose to do that?"

"I've got an idea."

THIRTY-FOUR

The next morning I pulled up before a red-brick university building in Marquette and looked up Dr. William Ursuline on the register. I had called ahead to his secretary, asking for an appointment, and at the elected hour his office door swept open.

I must have gaped. Before me stood the most bearlike man I had ever encountered. He was not tall, perhaps five-seven, but thick, muscular, broad-shouldered and, except for his pink pate, astonishingly *hairy*. Curls of dark fur peeked above his collar and around his cuffs, and a magnificent full black beard adorned his strong chin.

"Ursuline," I thought. That must come from *ursa*, the Latin for "bear."

The human bear smiled and held out a paw. "Bill Ursuline," he said with twinkling good humor. "It's not true what you're thinking."

Was I that obvious? I blushed.

"People may grow to resemble their dogs," he said, "but biologists don't necessarily look like the animals they study. Jane Goodall hardly looks like a chimp, does she?"

Dr. Ursuline, however, resembled his lissome and celebrated fellow field biologist in at least one way: for years he had studied his subjects intimately, living with them and becoming an accepted part of their world. He spent weeks and even months in the woods following the animals, chronicling their every waking movement and publishing his findings regularly after he got home and washed away the smell of bear.

At first people thought he was crazy, but as the fame of the "Bear Man" spread far and wide, he soon became acknowledged as the leading scholar in his field. Huge universities proffered lucrative professorial chairs, but he refused them—he wanted to stay close to his bears in case he took the yen to spend a weekend with one. Next to Dr. Ursuline, a state bear wrangler like Stan Maki was a kindergartner.

"Well, Deputy Martinez, what can I do for you?" he said.

I started in surprise. I had not identified myself as a law enforcement officer when leaving the message on Dr. Ursuline's answering machine asking for an appointment. All I said was that I was a concerned citizen with a bit of information the biologist might be interested in.

Dr. Ursuline smiled shrewdly. "You don't think I'd check up on strangers who want to come see me?" he said with a chuckle, "All it took was a call to the Porcupine County sheriff's department. A fellow named Joe Koski assured me you weren't a lunatic or a Jehovah's Witness."

It stood to reason that before heading into the wilderness, the biologist would make sure law enforcement all over Upper Michigan knew what an apparent wild man in the woods was up to, and would know whom to talk to in every cop shop.

But I was unhappy that Joe knew I'd contacted a bear expert in Marquette. Maybe I could minimize the damage.

"Well, yes, I guess so," I said. "But I'd really rather you didn't talk about my coming, if you don't mind."

"You're investigating a crime?" Dr. Ursuline said forthrightly.

"Not exactly," I said. "Not officially, anyway. Just tidying up some loose ends." That was perfectly true.

He leaned back in his chair and studied me frankly. "This has to do with Paul Passoja, doesn't it?"

"How the hell did you know?" must have been written all over my face.

"Elementary, my dear Martinez," said Dr. Ursuline with a laugh, not waiting for me to respond. "What would a cop want to see a bear man about, except something having to do with an unfortunate event, such as the demise of a very important Upper Michigan personage?"

I shook my head. "That case has been closed," I said truthfully.

"As for the case I'm unofficially working on," I added, lying only by omission, "I'm sorry, but for legal reasons I cannot share the details with you. I know you probably will wonder why, but I can only ask you questions—I cannot answer any of yours. If ever there comes a time when I can talk about this with you, I will. That's a promise.

"And I am going to ask for full confidentiality about our meeting. I hope very much you won't even tell other people that we met."

Dr. Ursuline didn't hesitate for a moment, but looked me straight in the eye. "Yes, of course," he declared. "It won't leave this office. You have my word."

I sighed in relief.

"Now," he said briskly, "how *can* I help you?"

"What I came here to find out is whether a bear could be trained secretly to attack a human being, and if so, what it would take to make sure it would really do the job."

Dr. Ursuline's eyes widened. He shook his head slowly, but leaned back in his chair, lost in thought.

"They're too unpredictable, aren't they?" I asked after a moment.

"Not necessarily," he said. "There are a lot of myths about bears. For instance, there's never been a documented instance of a mother black bear defending her cubs by attacking a human being.

"Unpredictability is largely a myth, too. Bears are creatures of habit, just as we are. And like us they're individuals. Every bear lives by a set of habits that are both similar to but also appreciably different from those of any other bear. If you know a bear well, you can generally predict what it will do at any old time. It's the bear you don't know that's unpredictable."

I waited. "Bears are easily conditioned," Dr. Ursuline said. "It doesn't take much to turn one into a garbage bear—just two or three encounters with food waste will do. They're pretty smart about that. They're smart enough to understand that where humans are, there will be easy food. And you know that if humans get between them and their lunch, that's when they can turn dangerous.

"If a bear wants food and you won't hand it over, it's likely to forget its natural fear of humans and go for you in anger. It wouldn't be hard to figure out how to piss off a bear. Stake one to a tree, or hold it in a cage, and starve it for a bit while dangling wonderfully smelly food just out of reach. Now where could this be done? Let's say a remote place deep in the forest where nobody goes except once in a long while. Perhaps a week, perhaps two weeks, and you'd have a large and ugly killing machine that needs only to be baited."

"Could you be absolutely sure a particular bear would kill in a given situation?" I asked.

"Could you be absolutely sure a particular *human* would kill in a given situation?" he replied, quickly adding. "I'm sorry, I'm not supposed to be asking the questions."

I laughed. "I can answer that one. No, of course not. But given certain facts, the odds would be in favor of that happening. You just need the right opportunity."

"There you go," said Dr. Ursuline with a brilliant smile. "Same with bears."

I stood up. "That's all for now," I said. "Thanks. You've been very helpful."

"If it's possible," said the bear man, "I'd like very much someday to know exactly how."

"I promise," I said, and took my leave.

On the drive back to Porcupine City I felt as if I had achieved a major step forward in the case. Maybe I didn't yet have motive, but I very likely had nailed down the means.

With a little help, a bear could make an excellent murder weapon—one, if things went as expected, that could disappear into the woods under its own power, as this one had.

Yes, Paul Passoja had been killed by a heart attack, but if the hand of a human being had been behind the bear assault that ended in his demise, I had a good case for homicide—maybe even murder one.

I just wished Joe Koski, Porcupine County's biggest gossip, didn't know I'd gone to Marquette.

THIRTY-FIVE

Swish-*clunk*. Swish-*clunk*. Swish-*clunk*. Though my breath hung visibly on the cold air, I had fallen into a soothing, sweat-oiled rhythm at the chopping block in my backyard, the broadax rising and falling in graceful arcs upon maple bitts, splitting them into manageable chunks for the cast-iron wood stove with which I heated my cabin. The hickory handle felt hard and dry inside my tingling hands. It was a chore I looked forward to every day.

Half an hour a morning at the woodpile provides me with enough fuel for the long cold season, October through April, and the exercise keeps my wrists, arms, and shoulders supple, limber, and fit while relaxing the tensions of life. Chopping wood salves the body and calms the mind.

Like most Upper Peninsulans who live along Lake Superior, I keep a small propane tank and furnace in reserve for the times when I can't be in residence, but a pile of wood the size of a couple of Buicks—mostly maple and oak that has escaped the pulp logger's chainsaw—is the most economical way, as well as the healthiest, to stay warm in the winter.

The shore of Lake Superior in winter is as windswept and desolate as any Arctic coast, but in the warmth of summer and fall it teems with wildlife—bear, deer, otter, fishers, bald eagles, Canada geese, canvasbacks, mallards, mergansers, and loons.

And garrulous little chickadees. Constantly they talk to one another, "*chick . . . chick . . . chick a dee, dee,*" over and over, keeping in touch with one another, a close-knit community brimful with belonging. "*Chick a dee, dee, dee,*" I called, immediately answered by a "*dee?*" in the big maple above me.

You could carry on entire conversations with these birds, and I often did, to Ginny's considerable amusement. But she understood my feelings: in our "chats" these little birds gathered me into their fellowship of the woods, as they must have some long-ago ancestor of mine. At times like these I felt almost as if I had come home.

I was not surprised to hear the sudden rising beat of large wings, gathering power as they drew closer. I looked up just as a loose formation of a dozen Canada geese flashed past just offshore, scarcely a foot off the water, honking frantically as they bore in like feathered torpedo bombers for my closest neighbor's crib three hundred yards east on the beach. Following close aboard were scores — no, *hundreds* — of honkers. The sky darkened as they swooped by and splashed down into a bobbing flotilla around the crib. In an ordinary year they would have been long gone to southern climes for the winter, but the extraordinarily warm autumn — and the lack of violent storms that signaled the time to depart — had delayed their migration.

I looked at my watch and smiled. Four-thirty, feeding time. You could set your clock by Sheila Carnahan, a wide-bodied widow who, every day at that hour, spring through autumn, waddles out from her house with twenty pounds of cracked corn and spreads it along the shore. The geese wade through the shallows and up the sand as if it were Omaha Beach, honking and hissing, bobbing and nodding like humans at a dinner party. As the geese pecked for their dinner, frantic gulls dove and darted in to contest possession. The noise was deafening.

These days naturalists advise us not to feed wild birds or animals, for that, they say, upsets the normal routines of nature. That makes sense, but Sheila is all by herself a normal routine of nature, and I can't see that her indulgence of geese affects their lives, except perhaps to make them a little cushier while they hang around.

I returned to my task. Swish-*clunk*. Swish-*clunk*. Swish-*craaack!*

A maple limb twelve feet away at the level of my head

exploded in splinters, followed an instant later by the heavy report of a powerful rifle. I dove into an untidy heap behind the woodpile toward the lake, rolling in the sand, my elbow bouncing off a boulder as I reached for a revolver that wasn't there but in its holster on the kitchen table. That damned sidearm! Never there when I needed it! For several seconds I lay still, nuzzling a man-sized pine log, sand gritting my teeth, a pain shooting up from my abused elbow. No sound except the sigh of the breeze and the echo of honks from down the beach.

"Who's there?" I called at last, raising my head cautiously above the woodpile.

No answer.

"Show yourself!"

No answer.

I took a deep breath and gathered my wits. Judging from the brief but definite interval between the smashing of the branch and the sound and location of the shot, the shooter must have been three or four hundred yards away through heavy scrub—hardly a distance at which a man deliberately tries to kill another, not unless he's using artillery. Most likely it was just a random shot from an overeager hunter keeping his eye sharp at target practice. But bear season had ended a month ago, firearms deer season the week before—except for antique muzzle-loaders, and that shot hadn't come with the heavy whump of a black-powder weapon. This wasn't a time to hear the crack of modern big-bore rifles. Somebody was getting careless.

I stood up, rubbing my sore elbow, and strode back to the cabin, counting the charges I'd file against the trigger-happy idiot if I ever caught him.

THIRTY-SIX

In the early afternoon, as I drove to the sheriff's office, that familiar feeling of uneasiness wrapped itself around my entrails. And it settled in to stay as Joe Koski gave me the big hello through the lumpily decorated little Douglas fir that obscured the top of the dispatcher's desk.

"Steve," he boomed cheerily, all heads in the squadroom rising as one. "What are you doing, getting ready for next year's bear season? Did the Bear Man tell you the best places to find 'em?"

Joe's jocularity told me he didn't suspect the real reason for my visit to Dr. Ursuline, but now I was sure everybody and his grandmother in Porcupine County knew about it. I kept my voice light as I responded, "I'm thinking about changing jobs and learning how to live with bears. It might pay better than this one."

Everyone laughed and returned to work. Porcupine County deputies hardly drew excessive salaries and they were often the subject of bitter humor. I hoped the joke had deflected their curiosity.

The phone rang, and Joe answered it. His expression turned somber. "Steve," he said, "that call was from Union Bay campground. An eighteen-foot outboard boat that was launched from the ramp there hasn't been heard from since last night. Four people aboard. Time to hit the air. I'll have Mary cover your patrol area."

I nodded. From time to time, even on a perfectly pleasant day like this one, Lake Superior can change its mood almost without warning. Small boats launched from the public ramp near the campground at the Wolverines park sometimes get into trouble with high waves or stiff winds, and the warm autumn meant more campers had extended the fishing season long past a sensible time.

The nearest Coast Guard helicopter station is at Traverse City in lower Michigan, 230 miles to the southeast. It takes the Guard's speedy Dolphin helicopters almost two hours to make the flight to Porcupine City, so when somebody gets in trouble off Porcupine County, the sheriff's department usually is the first called to mount an air search. Small planes flown by Civil Air Patrol volunteers from nearby airports also help, as does the Gogebic County sheriff's department just west of Porcupine County.

At the airport I rolled the Cessna out of its hangar, quickly did the preflight chores, and ten minutes later rose from the runway, heading for the lake. Since small boats often are driven onshore by bad weather—and the waves the previous night had pounded the beach from the north—I decided to start the search along the lakeshore. Maybe the boat had gone aground somewhere along the thirty miles of park shoreline, uninhabited except for summer and fall hikers who used a couple of rustic cabins near the beach.

Banking west two hundred feet out from the shore, I held the Cessna's altitude at three hundred feet above the waves and carefully watched the sand and tree line for signs of life. All I saw for nine miles was the occasional agate hunter out on the stony beach, then civilization disappeared as the Union Bay campground passed beneath my left wing. Mile after mile passed, the only visible living creature an occasional deer that spooked and dashed into the tree line as the roaring aluminum eagle swooped close overhead.

After crossing the mouth of the Presque Isle River, the westernmost boundary of the park and my jurisdiction, I keyed the radio on the departmental frequency. "Porcupine Sheriff six-eight-six-Papa-Quebec from Presque Isle," I said, giving the airplane's registration number, 686PQ. "No joy on the shoreline. Starting grid search of the lake now." In the air I followed radio etiquette. The Feds demanded it.

"Charlie-Alpha-Papa-seven-five-niner-Sierra-Echo

from Ironwood to Porcupine sheriff's aircraft," my receiver crackled in response. It was a Civil Air Patrol volunteer. "Copy. No joy either west of Presque Isle."

Climbing to two thousand feet, I began a steady sweep farther out from the shoreline, extending the pattern half a mile with every reciprocal change in course. The waves grew choppier and choppier the farther out I flew. Two miles, then three, then four. At six miles from shore, almost directly north of Union Bay, I spotted the overturned white hull of the boat, bobbing wildly in the surf. First I marked the location on my handheld global positioning satellite receiver, a little electronic instrument that reads signals from man-made birds orbiting in space and locates my exact spot on earth with an accuracy of three feet. Then I wrote down the coordinates and called them in to the sheriff's department and Coast Guard helicopter, still a hundred miles to the southeast.

Dipping down to a scant hundred feet above the waves, I circled repeatedly, looking for survivors. I could see none. No one who had gone into the fifty-degree water the previous day was likely to have lived more than a few hours before dying of hypothermia — unless they'd had the sense to dress in waterproof thermal "dry suits," which few sport boaters owned. It was going to be a search for bodies now, and that was a job for the Dolphin from Traverse City as well as the Coast Guard cutter from Houghton fifty miles to the east and the smaller sport boats from the Guard auxiliary in Porcupine City.

When it arrived — it was still a good half-hour away — the Dolphin would use the overturned boat as a reference point for its search, flying two ever-increasing circles in a bow-tie shape, using the boat as the "knot." The boats would sail a course much as I had flown, running parallel to the shore for five miles, then turning ninety degrees out from shore half a mile and sailing the reciprocal course until reaching a point five miles offshore. They'd repeat the pattern farther down the shore until they either encountered survivors, bodies, or nightfall. Once darkness came they'd almost certainly give up all hope, trusting to currents and waves to wash the bodies onto the beach within days or weeks.

Sadly I banked the 172 away from the boat, my job done, heading for base. I did not fly southeast straight to Porcupine County Airport, but directly south toward the shore of Union Bay, where I'd turn east toward my destination. Flying over open water in a single-engine airplane makes me nervous, as it does most sensible pilots — we often hear imaginary misses and catches from the engine — and I will go miles out of my way to get "feet dry" as soon as possible.

Before turning toward the airport, I decided on a low flyby over the Lone Pine Mine tailings fields, a desolate moonscape of sterile, rocky leftovers from processed copper ore, a wasteland speckled with ponds of poisoned water three miles wide by five miles long left by nearly a century of mining and smelting. Until very recently, astronauts could have used the tailings to train for landings on inhospitable planets. Now environmental laws had frog-marched the mine company into seeding the area with fast-growing ground cover from the air, hoping to heal decades of industrial rapine. That would, I thought, take many generations.

For years, however, the fertile forest floor had slowly crept over the outer edges of the tailings, and that, the sheriff thought, might be a likely place for criminal entrepreneurs to grow small crops of marijuana. I throttled back to seventy knots and dropped to three hundred feet above the tailings, gazing into the narrow verge of dry brush and brown grass between the tree line and the moonscape.

Almost immediately I saw a large dun patch, maybe a hundred feet by seventy-five feet, standing out from the evergreens around it. Even this late in the year, enough leaves remained to reveal regular borders, almost squared off.

Crapped-out sheriff's aircraft don't boast night-vision devices and high-tech thermal-imaging gadgets that allow DEA and state police aircraft, usually helicopters, to spot the heat emitted by pot farming, from indoor grow lamps to moving bodies and disturbed earth, from thousands of feet in the dead of night—but at low altitudes in daylight in any season the old Mark One Eyeball still has its uses.

In summer and early fall the color of marijuana is unique, an almost iridescent green with such a bold hint of blue that novice spotters sometimes confuse it with blue spruce, among which it is often grown to camouflage it from the air. From low altitude pot—which can be anywhere from a couple of inches high to eighteen feet tall, with three-inch trunks—looks spiky, like a prehistoric shrub. Growers plant it just about everywhere, from cornfields and swamps to backyards and gardens. Often perps who think they're being clever will scatter clumps around the inside rows of a huge cornfield, trusting the tall stalks to hide the pot from prying eyes at the verges of the field. From the air, however, the bushes stand out like zits on a teenage beauty.

Porcupine County is too far north, its growing season too short and its soil too clayey, for commercial corn farming. If a warm summer is forecast, however, dairymen and gardeners sometimes will plant corn on the southern sides of tree-lined roadways, protected from north winds, mostly for cattle silage and a little for sweet eating, and once in a while pot entrepreneurs will try to hide their handiwork among the rows. In Porcupine County we airborne pot-spotters more commonly find our quarry in small clearings and along forest edges, usually close to natural water sources like ponds, streams, or swamps. Water buckets, plastic fencing, trails, and vehicle tracks are also clues.

I circled over the patch, snapping photographs with the old Minolta and two hundred millimeter lens that was part of the plane's law enforcement tool kit. Maybe it was nothing, just an illusion, but the dried-up patch ought to be investigated, and despite the lateness of the season and my antipathy for drug laws I decided to report what I'd seen; a few of us might have to follow up the next day on the ground just to see if any clues remained. I marked the position on the GPS.

Thunk! Something—a small bird?—struck the right wing. I leveled the Cessna and eyeballed everything I could see. The instruments reported nothing out of the ordinary and the controls behaved as they should. All the same, I decided to break off the search and return to base immediately to check out things. I hoped the leading edge of the wing hadn't taken on a big dent; that might require a trip to the mechanic at Land o' Lakes some forty miles south for expensive aluminum reskinning. The plane had suffered bird strikes several times; such are the perils of low-level searches over wilderness.

After taxiing up to the hangar and swinging around the tail, I stepped down from the plane, walked around to the right wing, and immediately saw the two holes. One—.30 caliber, by the look of it—punctured the underside of the leading edge not much more than a foot inboard of the wingtip, and the second had butterflied out through the aluminum skin on top. Fortunately, the bullet had struck no ribs or spar, and a simple riveted patch would make the fix. A few inches of duct tape could serve as a temporary repair.

I picked up the mike to radio the department and call out the troops for an armed search of the woods near the tailings for the shooter, who likely was the cultivator of the pot crop—if that is what it was. Second thoughts, however, won out.

This was the second time that day I had been shot at. Fool me once, shame on you; fool me twice, shame on me. Thanks to Joe Koski, that one-man loudspeaker system, the whole town—including whoever set up Paul Passoja—by now knew I had an unusual interest in bears.

But was that someone really trying to kill me, or just

send me a message? If the shooter who blasted the maple branch while I was chopping wood was the same person who holed my wing, he didn't seem to be trying very hard. Furthermore, there are much better ways to ambush somebody. It would have been child's play for a halfway decent marksman with a scoped rifle to pick me off from the brush on the short walk from my cabin to the Jeep in the driveway, or to put a bullet into the slow-flying Cessna's fuselage right under the pilot's seat.

How serious a target was I, really? Did the other guy know I was on to him, or was he just trying to draw me out, toying with me until something cracked?

I sighed. Going to the undersheriff meant I would also have to report my suspicions about a closed case without a shred of solid evidence. That wasn't likely to result in anything but derisive laughter in front of everybody else and a full-bore drill-sergeant chewing out behind closed doors, maybe even suspension without pay. Things may be different on TV cop shows, but law enforcement brass does not like lone-wolf officers, regarding them as loose cannons on their tight ships. A cop's first duty if he wants to keep his job is to keep his superiors informed.

Sure, reporting the bullet strike on the airplane would bring everybody out to hunt the shooter by the tailings, but he likely would have disappeared. If he had anything to do with Paul Passoja's death, a raid would just cause him to go to ground for a good long time.

And there was no point in giving that good-hearted blabbermouth, Joe Koski, something else to gossip about.

I was going to have to do this alone.

THIRTY-SEVEN

But I did not feel lonely. Not with Ginny Fitzgerald by my side: my sounding board, my sidekick, my Sancho Panza, my love. For a long time now we had been an Item for the town gossips from Joe Koski on down, and now everybody thought of us as a couple, even though we did not yet live together. "Bring that fine young deputy of yours with you," people automatically would say while inviting Ginny to dinner.

Before then, few of them would have thought of inviting me alone, sometimes because I was the law, sometimes because I was not a white man, and sometimes because I tended, consciously and unconsciously, to keep people at arm's length.

Increasingly I realized that the protective standoffishness in which I had wrapped myself for years did me more harm than good. As a biological Indian and a cultural white I often felt part of two worlds, but not completely at home in either. When I was exceptionally far gone in self-pity—thankfully a rare event—I thought of myself as a restless misfit endlessly sailing the oceans looking for a safe harbor.

Sometimes I failed to recognize an offer of friendship, thinking instead that it was a patronizing gesture toward my Indian-ness, or maybe a calculated act of manipulation because I was a police officer. Sometimes I could be my own worst enemy.

In some things, I was beginning to see, Ginny was very much like me. And we were both slow learners.

At her invitation I had moved in my toothbrush, but that was it. Sometimes I'd spend the night, especially if I was off-duty the next day; sometimes she'd spend the night. Every day I saw her at least once, if only fleetingly, and we had dinner together several times a week. Our relationship settled into a comfortable routine, ripening slowly, neither of us making demands on the other.

In different ways we both had been hurt by circumstance—I by being wrested from my biological heritage and she by loss and betrayal—and, mutually, silently, we had agreed to heal slowly so that our cures would be complete. We had all the time in the world.

THIRTY-EIGHT

On the tenth day of December I stopped at Merle's for breakfast. Even before the sun came up holiday lights twinkled in the storefronts all up and down Main Street, *Merry Christmas* and *Happy Holidays* blazing from shop windows. Inside Merle's the faces, however, looked as dark as the predawn chill outside. "Who died?" I asked as I sat down at the counter next to Joe Koski.

"Maybe all of Porcupine County," Joe said gloomily. "We've just been watching the Weather Channel, and the forecasters predicted no precipitation for the next three weeks. You know what that means."

"Ouch," I said. The Upper Peninsula of Michigan—indeed, the entire northern reaches of the Western Hemisphere—had been experiencing its third consecutive unseasonably warm autumn. We hadn't seen even the usual three-day October blow out of the northwest off Lake Superior, a vicious forty-knot wind that slams shutters like pistol shots and chases the last summer people south. In the papers, Alaskans had complained that the permafrost that served as their basement was melting, their roads rolling and cracking in mush underneath, and engineers worried that the oil pipeline south from Prudhoe Bay would crack and spill black stuff all over the landscape. For the southern shore of Lake Superior, the warming trend meant no snow, except for a light dusting, might fall until after the New Year.

I had no idea whether the culprit was global warming thanks to greenhouse gases or just one of nature's mood swings, but whatever it was, the consequences could be disastrous to Porcupine County's economy. Last year the first heavy snow didn't fall until December 28, meaning the ski slopes at the state park and the snowmobile trails didn't have enough pack until it was too late to attract the Christmas and

New Year's skiers and snowmobilers from Chicago and
Minneapolis. Several restaurants and motels, dependent on
the holiday trade to stay alive, went under. A second
consecutive snow drought could mean curtains for the county
as a viable economy. "Porcupine County needs white stuff to
make green stuff," people often said.

I shook my head feelingly. I am not a fan of
snowmobiles, even though I own one just to be able to get into
the woods over unplowed tracks when going by cross-country
skis just takes too long. Snowmobiles are noisy, smelly beasts,
and they often awaken me on Sunday mornings when stoked-
up snowmobilers roar past my cabin at blinding speeds along
the frozen berms beyond the beach. Snowmobiles and booze
seem to go together like fish and water, and every winter I
have to clean up after messy accidents. In Porcupine County
at least three or four snowmobile fatalities occur every
winter — usually involving a drunk zooming off-trail into a
barbed-wire fence or to the bottom of a lake whose ice is too
thin to support the weight of a speeding machine. When I
carry on about snowmobiles, however, it is always when I am
alone with Ginny, who has the insouciance to remind
hypocritical old me that I like to drive annoyingly noisy,
smelly beasts, too — those with wings and a propeller.

But I'd never knock snowmobiles in public. Porcupine
County's merchants depend on the money visiting
snowmobilers spend, and many volunteers belonging to the
Wolverines Snowmobile Club devote hours to grooming
snowmobile trails leased from local landowners.

"There's something else, though," said Joe. "Yesterday
Gail Sheehan came up with the idea of having a Christmas
parade, with floats and fireworks and everything, on the
twenty-third." Gail was the operator of the local day-care
center and a civic-minded lady.

The café's patrons visibly brightened at Joe's words.

"It's a great idea," said Merle, smiling for maybe the

first time in weeks.

It was. I could see that getting people together for a public celebration of the birth of Christ, or the winter solstice, or just generally the holidays, depending on one's religious belief, was a way of drawing wagons into a circle against adversity. Even if the first big snow was too late, a Fourth of July-style festival might help folks' resolve to tough it out— and possibly could bring in visitors from outside the county, visitors who might spend a little money.

"What are the rules?" I asked.

"There's only one rule," Joe said. "Only one Santa for the entire parade, and he's to ride on the fire engine. No use confusing the kiddies, Gail said."

"Makes sense."

I paid for the eggs and toast and left, the gloom in Merle's having lifted at the prospect of a parade.

THIRTY-NINE

"Be careful, Steve," Ginny muttered sleepily as I slipped from her bed well before dawn the next morning. I didn't have the luxury of time. I had to nail the killer of Paul Passoja before he nailed me.

And so, at cold daybreak on my next day off, two days after the Cessna took the bullet, I jounced in my Jeep southward up a rocky track through the forest leading to the western edge of the mine tailings. When I was still half a mile away, I pulled off into the brush, backed the Jeep out of sight, and concealed the tire tracks with evergreen boughs and twigs. I would hoof it the rest of the way.

Around my neck dangled the Minolta and telephoto, which looked like a standard woods photographer's equipage. If I should encounter anyone — unlikely at this hour and in this place — I was merely indulging in my notorious new hobby of bear-watching, and had they seen any that hadn't yet gone to ground, hibernating for the winter? My .357 nestled behind quick-release Velcro tabs in a fanny pack, ready for action. To blend in with the brush as well as protect myself against the thirty-degree chill I wore a camouflaged canvas hunter's jacket over a warm down inner coat and a similarly colored Elmer Fudd hat with earflaps — a typical nature shutterbug's outfit.

For half an hour I threaded my way through the trees, avoiding footpaths, treading softly on the balls of my feet, not the heels, silent as an . . . an . . . an *Indian,* grinning to myself at the irony. The dead brown grass was so dry that my boots kicked up dust as I moved diagonally through the tree line. Even this late in the year a careless spark could start a wildfire.

I tiptoed past a large field of stumps arranged in neat

rows, fat ones and thin ones, like a company of soldiers lined up according to size. It was a freshly harvested Christmas tree plantation, one of scores in Porcupine County, and though its produce had long been wrapped in netting and trucked south to Milwaukee and Chicago, the sharp sweet smell of pine sap still hung in the air.

Presently, through the edge of the forest the desolate, bare tailings loomed high above me, green-stained copper-bearing rocks mixed with crystalline slag from the old smelter. I pulled out the GPS and took my bearings. The suspicious patch I had spotted two days before still stood three-quarters of a mile away.

I had full confidence in the device, although they'd led us deputies on some merry chases. A few years before, when handheld hikers' GPS receivers first came on the market, a local merchant became the first Porky to buy one. He was an unpopular man who frequently abused his wife. She often called us in mid-beating, but never would press charges.

Shortly after the merchant boasted about it to everybody one day in Merle's Café, he disappeared into the mountains. When he didn't come home by the next morning, his wife called the sheriff, and we had to mount a six-hour search-and-rescue operation before we found him deep in the hinterlands, thoroughly lost.

Worse, the following weekend, having declared that he *really* had learned how to use the GPS, he vanished into the woods again. And again we had to tramp around for hours to find his sorry ass. "I'll never know why Sylvia ever bothered to call him in missing," Koski said afterward. "I'd just have let the bears eat the idiot."

Thanks to my aviation experience with the GPS, I wasn't likely to get lost in the woods. Carefully staying out of sight within the tree line, I trudged slowly southward, picking my way over log falls and boulders and skirting thick copses, until the GPS had led me almost to the spot I had marked in the air. It was a wide low expanse of dry, spiky brush eight feet high, harvested many weeks ago. Peering carefully in all directions, I bent down, plucked a withered brown leaf from the ground, crumbled it between thumb and forefinger, and sniffed. *Cannabis sativa*, sure enough, and probably of high quality as well. After bagging several leaves for evidence, I turned back to the woods, glad to get out of sight again.

Instead of retracing my route along the edge of the forest, I plunged directly east, hoping to find evidence of cultivation — tools, irrigation pipes, empty fertilizer bags. I saw none, but a hundred yards away through the brush, half a mile east of the tailings, the outlines of a rough cabin and outbuildings took shape. I saw wood smoke curling from a chimney at the same time I smelled it. Someone was around.

Drawing upon all the woods lore I had learned in the army and from the *Boy Scout Handbook*, I tiptoed toward the cabin, hiding behind spruces and pines, breathing shallowly, making not a sound, waiting after each step to see if I had been discovered. My .357 hung heavy in its fanny pack. I briefly considered drawing it, but decided that I did not yet have sufficient evidence of wrongdoing.

Then I saw him as he emerged from the cabin. It was Garrett Morton, the hulking and not overbright summer ranger who had arrived at Big Trees with Stan Maki the morning Paul Passoja had been found dead. This was a surprise. What was Garrett doing here in the backwoods of the Upper Peninsula in early December instead of playing forward for Kalamazoo College's basketball team? I had not seen him since he and Stan had captured that bear at the Cackle Shack, and assumed he'd gone back to school.

I stayed hidden, mulling over this new discovery. Garrett wore jeans and a bright blue down parka, was unarmed, carried only a heavy rucksack, and did not seem a present threat to my safety or anyone else's. Quickly I decided not to make myself known. Other than the presence of the cabin half a mile east of the tailings, there was nothing to connect Garrett to the marijuana patch or to the shot fired at my airplane. Better be sure before moving in on him.

By himself Garrett didn't behave like an overeager puppy, but he still stumbled about like a clumsy suburban kid who didn't quite fit into the woods. He shouldered aside saplings and shuffled noisily through fallen leaves and twigs as he strode to a low outbuilding. He wrenched open a ramshackle door, its hinges creaking in protest, and in a moment drove out in an ancient, rusty yellow Scout, its loose tailpipe rattling as it bounced onto the track and then northward toward M-64, three miles away. I waited, still as a Sioux scouting an enemy, until I could no longer hear the rattle.

Before I could move toward the cabin, a lone doe nearby snorted, causing me nearly to jump out of my skin. When deer think there's something they should be seeing, they often blow, or snort, to see if they can't startle it into moving. They always nailed me.

I had no warrant to search the place and doubted if I could get one, even if I was on an official investigation. I was tempted to go ahead on my unofficial own, but didn't want to taint a possible legal case. I could, however, look as much as I wanted so long as I didn't touch any doors or enter any buildings. I peered in a window past a rough burlap curtain.

A table, chairs, bed, cabinets no doubt holding canned and dried food, and water jugs — the typical layout of a hunting cabin, which this one obviously was. Clothes lay draped over the folding metal screen standing to the left of the fireplace, where smoke rose still. Not very smart — an ember could pop into the room and start a blaze. This was not a seasoned woodsman who lived here, or even a tenderfoot with half a brain. Nor was this anybody who planned to celebrate Christmas here — there wasn't a wreath or ornament of any kind.

Eureka! In a corner lay two large bags of fertilizer with a roll of flexible PVC irrigation pipe. There was the link to the marijuana patch.

Double eureka! In another corner was propped a well-worn bolt-action Winchester Model 70 with a powerful scope. I would have bet everything in my wallet that the rifle was a .30-'06 and the same weapon that not only scared the daylights out of me while I was chopping wood but also ventilated the right wing of my Cessna.

I had my man, I was certain. But I couldn't go blundering in just yet. I needed more evidence — evidence I could use in court — and a solid motive as well.

Still, I now had the advantage: I knew exactly who my quarry was.

Wishing mightily that I could break into and search the outbuildings, I started back through the forest, paralleling the track to the highway but remaining well clear of it, out of sight and out of earshot. Within an hour I reached my concealed Jeep and was on my way back to civilization, smiling to myself for having stolen through the woods unseen and unheard until I had encountered my prey and, in a modest sort of way, counted coup. Crazy Horse would have been proud.

FORTY

"Who the hell is Garrett Morton, anyway?" I asked Ginny at her kitchen table that noon while the strains of Pavarotti's "Adeste Fideles" wafted from the speakers by the fireplace. "What do you know about him?"

"Zip," she replied. "He's not from around here, after all. Where did you say he played basketball?"

"Kalamazoo, I was told when I met him at Big Trees," I said.

"I've got a friend in the Kalamazoo Historical Society," she said. "Let me give her a call and see what she can turn up in the local papers."

I blinked. "I've got an acquaintance down there, too," I said. "Cop who went through the state training program at the same time I did. I'll drop a dime on him. May I use your phone?" I didn't want to make the call from the department where I might be overheard.

Just ten minutes passed before Sergeant Ted Conover of the Kalamazoo Police returned my call. "Steve," he said, "been a while. What can I do for you?"

I took a deep breath and decided to trust Ted. "I'm involved in a very unofficial homicide investigation," I said, "and I'd appreciate it if you kept this under the rug."

"Sure," Ted replied. "Who do you like for the deed?"

"Nobody just yet—I'm still sifting a list of possible suspects. One of them is a young man from Kalamazoo College named Garrett Morton. Basketball player."

"Know him sure enough," Ted said. "Big palooka, quite a forward on the freshman team last year, the varsity's best hope this year. Let me punch him up on the computer."

In a moment Ted was back. "No real record," he said. "I busted him once last year, for possession of small amounts of pot at a wild frat party with a bunch of others. His rich and connected daddy, who's a big auto company executive, got the case dismissed.

"Before then he got into a bar fight and laid out a couple of kids pretty good, but they wouldn't press charges. I think Daddy bought 'em off, too. But he doesn't sound like a hardened felon to me, just a kid too big and strong for his own good and not too bright besides. That's all I got for you."

I thanked Ted, hung up and headed into town to start the day's work, meeting Mary Larch to consult with the fire chief, Dudley Richardson, on the origin of a blaze at Gitche Gumee Tractors and Implements on the east side of town. A transformer in a shed had shorted and caught fire, gutting the shop. It wouldn't ordinarily have been considered suspicious, but Jack Pillanpaa, the proprietor, was such an incorrigible, much-disliked jerk that arson had to be ruled out.

I'd had a run-in with Jack when I was a young deputy and stopped by to rent a chainsaw. He refused, saying he didn't have any available — though half-a-dozen well-used McCullochs sat on his counter — and I chalked that up to anti-Indian prejudice.

Dudley sounded disappointed when he told me the fire had been started by ancient and frayed electrical wiring. "Ought to have been fixed years ago, but Jack is such a cheap bastard he wouldn't have spent the ten bucks for new wire."

Mary laughed. "He wouldn't have spent *five* bucks," she said. "I can't stand him. He screws people every way he can, including himself. Oh, I could tell you about the run-ins I've had with him."

Joe Koski, who had stopped by on his way to work, cut in. "You're telling me," he said. "Years ago he wouldn't sell me a new carb for my lawn tractor because I didn't buy the tractor from him."

People, I suddenly realized, are often the way they are because of what they are, not because of who *you* are. In fact, an unpleasant encounter with Jack Pillanpaa was a kind of initiation into Porcupine County society. This place, like everywhere else, was bound to have its share of disagreeable human beings. Nothing to do with me.

Mary broke my reverie. "You okay, Steve?" she said, eyeing me closely.

"Oh, yes, thanks."

"You seemed far away."

"I get that way sometimes. Don't you?"

"Nothing's happened?"

"Not a thing."

"Okay." She didn't sound as if she believed it. "Take care."

She climbed into her cruiser and drove away.

At the end of the shift I decided to bask in the presence of an extremely agreeable personage, the exact opposite of Jack Pillanpaa. I stopped in at the Historical Society, and spotted Ginny sitting in her office at the back of the cavernous room, packed floor to ceiling with displays of artifacts in glass cases. A life-sized diorama of a Finnish Christmas of 1900 occupied one corner, a bewigged mannequin in lumberjack dress handing a gift to a small child in front of a potbellied woodstove. The gift-shop counters groaned under their burden of holiday sweetmeats, some of them Finnish, some of them Croatian, some of them Cornish.

Ginny waved as she saw me, pulled me into her office and closed the door.

"I have something good for you, Steve," she breathed sexily as she melted her body against mine and planted a thorough and lingering kiss on my lips.

"Not here!" I protested when we came up for breath. "There are people out there!"

"I didn't mean *that*," she said, giggling, doing the thing with her hair, "although you could be a little more adventurous, you big stick-in-the-mud. Sit down."

I sat, puffing slightly.

"I got through to my friend in Kalamazoo, and she

came up with some interesting stuff about Garrett Morton. There were a couple of columns in the newspaper there about why he hadn't returned this fall to play basketball. He was that big a star on the freshman team. It was a huge disappointment to the whole college that he didn't return.

"One of the stories said that his grade-point average his freshman year was so low he might not be eligible for sports that season, not without a lot of remedial courses. He could have taken them and played, but he chose not to return — the columnist speculated that like so many student athletes he just wasn't college material, even for a basketball factory like Michigan, let alone a small school like Kalamazoo.

"The second column — are you ready for this, Steve? — reported that Morton had told a friend he wasn't coming back because he'd found a girl in Upper Michigan. It offered no further details."

I rubbed my jaw thoughtfully. "Who the hell could that be?" I said. "Up here everybody knows everybody else and who's doing what with whom. But I haven't heard a thing about Garrett Morton and any locals. Have you? And what possible reason could he have for wishing Paul Passoja dead?"

Ginny shook her head. "I think when you find out who the girl is, Steve, you'll have the solution to that mystery right in your lap."

She's beautiful, smart, and encyclopedic, my Ginny. And, let me add, remarkably prescient.

"What do you plan to do now, Steve?" Ginny asked with concern.

"Nothing much," I said, "Just a little breaking and entering."

FORTY-ONE

I was going to have to swallow my legal pride and break into Garrett Morton's cabin if I was to get to the bottom of this business, but any information I gathered illegally could never be used in a court of law. All the same, I figured, blindly poking a stick into a hornet's nest seems reasonable when you are the target of a man who may or may not have homicide on his mind, and maybe an unlawful act or two would shake out enough independent evidence to convict. I didn't have much choice.

And so shortly after dawn on my next day off, I took the long way around the tailings, driving west to nearly the entrance to Wolverine Park and then south to the old mining town of Lone Pine. There I entered the mine property, waving to the lone watchman at the gate who was unsurprised that a deputy might have business there. County officials come and go all the time. I took a rough track eastward past the southern edge of the tailings and into the forest, where I parked the Jeep in the bushes again. This time I would approach Garrett's cabin from the south just in case he had the presence of mind to watch the road from the north.

On the fourth day of December no snow had fallen. Even so I could see no trail through the thick second-growth forest, clotted with dry thimbleberry bushes and grasping brush, even with my Indian's eyes, so I used white man's medicine — the handheld GPS — to find my way. For three miles and two hours I trudged due north, walking slowly not only to make as little noise as possible but also to keep my footing on the rough, stumpy ground. These were the low hills leading into the Wolverines, full of bare escarpments that bore visible traces of the copper that had attracted men by the thousands during the nineteenth century.

The going was slow, often almost straight up and down

and sometimes through muskeg swamp, and as the bright sun rose into a cloudless sky I was thankful for the crisp, chilly air. Hiking in this place during the height of summer, as I sometimes have to in order to fulfill my professional duties, can be an exercise in navigating the seventh circle of hell, fighting off swarms of blackflies — tiny winged demons brandishing fiery pitchforks.

So intent was I on walking an accurate track that I tended to keep my head down, eyes on the GPS, that from time to time I collided with a tree or stumbled over a stump, swearing softly. I was looking down when I heard the low whimper through the brush to my right. I looked up and immediately spotted the rusty steel cage ten yards away, half hidden by tall grass. Inside it was a brown furry shape. Stepping over, I saw that it was a small bear, and then it looked up. It was my little acquaintance, the one with the cinnamon face.

"Hello, friend," I said. It was odd, I thought, to see a bear up and awake that late in the fall. Nearly all Upper Peninsula bears turn in for the winter by the end of November. But the unusually warm autumn had delayed hibernation for many.

In response the little bear gave a soft rolling growl and examined me quizzically, seemingly unperturbed at either my presence or its entrapment in the cage, about eight feet wide by ten feet long. A bag of dog chow and a nearly full tub of water sat in a corner by a large, straw-lined rustic cedar doghouse, the kind lumberyards up here sell ready-built to summer people for their Labs and golden retrievers. The bear was being carefully cared for, that much I was sure about — the doghouse doubtless was intended as an artificial den for the winter's hibernation — but I doubted that whoever had captured and caged the bear had complied with the necessary legal paperwork.

The little bear's calm was unsettling. No wild animal I

had encountered showed such apparent trust in human beings. By rights it should have been pacing nervously, snarling, trying to reach me through the steel mesh, protesting against its imprisonment.

The brush suddenly rustled behind me and I caught a whiff of a heavy rank odor. I whirled, and my bowels melted when in the next instant I saw a massive dark shape through the dry saplings, stamping and whoofing angrily, getting ready to charge. It was a full-grown black bear, and it was furious.

As I reached around for my .357, fumbling with the Velcro tabs, the bear crashed forward, bellowing and slavering, yellow teeth bared to bite into my neck. Involuntarily I shut my eyes and scrabbled at the fanny pack, hoping to get the Magnum out and bring it around in the second before the animal struck.

Twaaaaaaaaannnnggggg! Scarcely six feet away the bear suddenly lifted and crashed into the ground, rolling, scrambling to regain its feet, knifelike claws tossing up clods of dirt. It charged again, and the heavy chain that bound it to a tree twenty feet away once more brought it up short. Like a dog fastened to an outdoor stake, the bear stood on its hind legs scything its forepaws, still trying to get at me, flashing a crescent-shaped splash of white fur on its broad black chest.

Were it not for the chain, I realized, the bear could have slashed me to bits before I wrapped my finger around the trigger of the .357, and even so powerful a handgun slug might not have worked. The bear was a tall and mature specimen, skinnier than it should have been for the hibernating season but still weighing about 250 pounds. Only a well-placed shot through the mouth to the brain might have stopped it. And at the best of times I am only an average marksman.

On hands and knees, my heart thumping, I scratched my way well clear of the bear, now sitting on the ground, its huffing subsiding only slightly. It sat right in the middle of the path I had trod through the tall dry grass. The little bear's whimper had drawn me outside the range of the chain. Suddenly I realized that I owed my life to that animal.

It did not take the acumen of a Dr. Bill Ursuline to figure out that someone had chained the large bear to the tree for a purpose — no doubt to turn it into a lean, mean killing machine.

Squatting in the brush, I considered the situation. The bear's charge had made a lot of noise, and anyone within half a mile would have heard the ruckus. I withdrew behind a tree and waited silent and still, counting off thirty minutes on my watch. No one came.

Carefully I stood up and sidled around the tree to which the bear was chained, keeping well out of harm's way even though the animal, seemingly having lost interest in me, was now snoozing in a patch of sun.

It didn't take long to find the Tupperware container that had held the bacon grease, and it didn't take much longer to find drying grease splattered on saplings in a wide circle just a couple of feet outside the bear's reach. The frantic animal had trampled the grass into an almost perfect circle trying to get to the saplings.

It had not been completely starved. Not far from the Tupperware lay a rancid sheet of butcher paper still sodden with the juices of raw meat, probably hamburger, judging from the shreds that stuck to it. Whoever was tuning up the bear knew just how far he could go and how much food he needed to keep it going. And when a few yards away I found the sharpened, spearlike eight-foot-long sticks, tufts of fur sticking to their tips, I realized that the bear had been physically tormented as well, no doubt to keep it furious and focused on human beings.

How long the bear had been made to suffer I didn't know, but I guessed at least a couple of months, judging from the deep grooves rubbed in the stout maple to which the bear's chain was padlocked. There was no doghouse or lean-to for a winter den. Somebody had plans for this bear and they didn't include hibernation.

Twaaaaaanggggggg! The bear had awakened and lunged at me through the grass again, and even though I was a good ten feet out of its reach I still leaped clumsily into a low berry patch, barking my shin on something hard and metallic.

Groaning softly, I rubbed my shin, drew aside the curtain of brush and saw an ancient bear transporter, decades old by the look of it. Careful not to disturb the brush or the ground, I examined the long cylinder. Orange rust crept over its faded green paint and dried leaves filled both ends, the heavy mesh doors lying open. Its tires were nearly bald. But the wheel bearings had been recently greased and the door hinges oiled.

I looked upslope through the trees and in the brown sedge grass saw the double tracks the transporter and whatever vehicle pulled it had made. Following the tread marks a few yards, I saw that they emerged onto a rough, stony road that would have tested even my tough little Jeep. The road pointed toward Garrett's cabin just under a mile northward through the forest.

I am not a gambling man, but I would have happily laid ten to one that the transporter had spent some time recently up near Big Trees. That the bear was the one Stan Maki and Garrett Morton had tranquilized and hauled away from the Cackle Shack a month before. That it was being starved and harassed to anger it into an assault on someone, that someone quite possibly—make that probably—being me. And that the person who was doing the deed was none else but Garrett Morton.

I felt certain that Morton planned to load the bear into the transporter and in the dead of night release it at a spot very close to my cabin. Did he really aim for the bear to kill me? I still doubted it—I could think of at least a dozen smarter ways to dispatch, or perhaps just divert, a nuisance cop who was coming uncomfortably close to the truth. Maybe Garrett was playing some kind of weird game toying with his quarry.

But he didn't seem bright enough for that—he was, so far as I could see, a dim sort of fellow who charged ahead blindly without regard for nuance or consequence. And, maybe, I suddenly realized, he was also the kind of fellow who was happiest doing what he was told. Maybe by whatever girl he had taken up with.

Suddenly the notion of breaking into his cabin didn't seem like such a good idea, at least not just yet. That could wait, now that I had some idea of Garrett's plans. I was now certain that he was the shooter who had put a bullet into my airplane and another into a tree limb while I was chopping wood, and I was also now certain that he wasn't trying to dispatch me by gunfire.

Instead of going to him, I thought, the best thing to do was let him come to me—and to be ready. For a moment I considered freeing the little bear from its cage, but that would have revealed my presence. Anyway, he had enough chow and water for several days, and Garrett likely would keep him fed and watered.

"I'll be back," I whispered to the little bear. He gazed at me with unearthly calm.

Slowly and quietly I withdrew, backtracking along my original route, taking pains to steer clear of the large bear and carefully rearranging the disturbed brush behind me to conceal my presence.

Back home that evening I went to the gun cabinet and withdrew my prize Browning twelve-gauge over-and-under shotgun, an heirloom bequeathed me by Uncle Fred and with which I occasionally hunt pheasant and grouse. I oiled its action, loaded both barrels with deer-slug shells, switched on the safety and propped it by the door. At close range and put into the proper place, those slugs could stop anything, two-footed or four-footed.

FORTY-TWO

As I shaved the next morning, the phone rang. "Steve?" It was Joe Koski. "Eli wants you to come into the shop as soon as possible."

"The sheriff wants to talk to *me*?" I replied. That was rare. Usually Garrow dealt with deputies through the undersheriff. Laid-back as he was in personal and political habits, he believed in the chain of command.

"Yes," Joe said, "and he doesn't look happy."

Had the sheriff somehow put together what I was up to?

On the drive into town I turned over a number of scenarios in my mind, and the curtain in each fell with me handing in my star and sidearm and stalking in disgrace out the door, my career in law enforcement forever stained.

But when I walked into the squadroom the deputies waved casual hellos from their desk, and Undersheriff O'Brien barely looked up from his. "Hiya, Steve," said Joe from behind the holiday tree at his counter, his tone unconcerned. "Sheriff's in his office."

I knocked.

"Come in," Eli boomed.

I barely suppressed a sharp intake of breath as I saw Garner Armstrong sitting next to the sheriff's desk with a sour expression. The county prosecutor is a good one and an upright man, although highly ambitious — it's clear to everyone that he looks forward to a long and fruitful career in Congress.

"We've got a problem, Steve," Eli said. I steeled myself.

"It's my aunt," Garner said. "Cordelia."

I looked up in surprise. "What's happened now?"

Cordelia Armstrong, sister to Garner's uncle, Congressman Armstrong, was another singular Porcupine

County eccentric, a Vassar-educated former New York bank officer who'd had a nervous breakdown after hitting the glass ceiling, come home to recuperate, and never left. Now aging and almost toothless, Cord lived alone amid rusting automobiles, broken farm machinery, and assorted trash on the old family farm on clear-cut land deep in the southern part of the county.

Rumor had it that when her cow barn burned down during the coldest weeks of winter she had sheltered the beasts inside her rotting old farmhouse, and when the manure rose too high, moved into a single-wide trailer she'd found in an auto graveyard. According to the story, she vehemently denied that she had a soft heart for animals. Those cows, she said, represented money in the bank.

Few people visited Cord, an exceptionally cantankerous sort who often threatened to shoot any passerby who trespassed upon her property, often brandishing a rifle to make her point. She loudly included state police, sheriff's deputies, and, indeed, any government official among her potential targets, and none of us looked forward to what seemed an inevitable confrontation with this crazy old lady.

She was not a recluse, but she drank so much you could have garnished martinis with her eyeballs. She had been bounced from every bar in town, except Hobbs'. Ted Lindsay refused to overserve her, which was why she didn't go in there much, except to start a binge. When she did that, Ted always made sure that when she left she was not armed. He had yet to find a weapon on her, but there was always a first time.

Cord was most notorious for her long-running feud with Ettie Lahti, her neighbor, whose house lies just a couple of hundred feet from Cord's. The war had started years before when a few dozen of the hundreds of rabbits Ettie raises and sells for meat escaped from their pen, squirted through the wire fence separating the two farms, and went to work on

Cord's lettuce. Instead of complaining to Ettie and asking restitution, Cord took out her shotgun and blasted the rabbits — and what remained of her lettuce crop — to kingdom come. Ettie took offense and threatened to sue, and that was the beginning of the county's most notorious border dispute.

Garner had paid Ettie for the loss of her rabbits out of his own pocket, although she didn't have much of a legal case against Cord. All the same, little by little Cord had escalated the hostilities, once knocking down Ettie's mailbox with her tractor and scattering its contents over the windy meadow. Now, every time Ettie drove by on her way to town, Cordelia would burst out of her house, fling a loud hail of four-letter words in her rival's direction, and give her the finger.

What's more, Cord had screwed a phony security camera to a fence post, pointing it directly at Ettie's house a hundred feet away. First Ettie had bought thick new shades and drapes for the windows in the side of the house facing Cord's, then had an eight-foot-high, sixty-foot-long cedar board fence erected along the property line. Two days after the fence went up, the word **ASSHOLE** appeared on Ettie's side of the fence in three-foot-high barn-red letters.

What could we deputies do? "It coulda been anybody," Cord said defiantly, and she was right. Everybody in the country has a can of barn red paint in the garage.

Ettie had complained often and bitterly to the sheriff, but, mindful of the miscreant's relationship with the prosecutor and the congressman, Eli did nothing. Garner, to his credit, often tried to defuse the situation. But neither sweet reason nor outright threat moved Cordelia, who never missed an opportunity to berate Ettie whenever and wherever they met, in town as well as the woods and fields.

"Now it's gone too far," Garner said. "The other day Ettie and Cord ran into each other at the checkout line in Frank's Grocery and in front of God and everybody and a lot of small children, Cordelia called her a cunt."

"It gets worse," Eli said. "Ettie has lawyered up with a

downstate attorney and he's threatening to expose us for nonfeasance if we don't do something. You remember that case a couple years ago in Standish when a young fellow was convicted of public obscenity? You know, the one who said 'fuck' in front of a bunch of kindergartners and their teacher watching from a bridge when his canoe flipped over? The lawyer says he's gonna cite Garner and me for not upholding the law."

That case made the papers nationwide. The young canoeist had been convicted under an obscure 1897 law that prohibited cursing in front of women and children. The judge declared the "women" part of the statute unconstitutional, but upheld the "children." The canoeist protested that the river was freezing and anyway he had cussed only a couple of times, but the jury believed the witnesses, who said he had spread the F-word hither and yon at the top of his lungs at least ninety times by their count. That water must have been *cold*.

He could have been sentenced to ninety days in the pokey and a hundred-dollar fine, but the judge, mindful that the American Civil Liberties Union would appeal in the name of free speech, slapped his hand with four days of community service and a seventy-five-dollar fine. The ACLU was right. On appeal the law was declared unconstitutional and the conviction thrown out. Garner and Eli well knew that the most Cordelia could be hit with were charges of personal harassment and disorderly conduct, a catch-all that almost never went to trial. But those were legitimate beefs Ettie's lawyer could claim the Armstrongs had failed to follow through on.

"Worst of all," Garner cut in, "that lawyer's threatening to tip the Detroit papers to the story. And the election is next year."

It didn't take a brilliant scholar of journalism to behold the comic possibilities in the great back-fence feud of a couple of rubes, one of them politically connected, in a far north wilderness county. And Geoffrey and Garner Armstrong, for all their virtues, have no sense of humor about political matters.

"So you want me to bring her in?" I said.

"Yup," said Eli, Garner, and Gil simultaneously. The undersheriff had wandered into the boss's office in the meantime.

"Why me?"

"She's said she respects you," Garner said. "She told me she'd seen you toss a bunch of drunken bikers out of Hobbs' without drawing your weapon, using just words."

Now I remembered. Cordelia was the old woman who had flashed me the thumbs-up as I left Hobbs'. She *did* favor digital communication, I thought, concealing a smile.

"She likes that kind of thing," Garner said, "and you know she never says anything good about anybody. I think she'll come with you without any trouble. If anybody else goes out to arrest her, she'll just barricade herself in her trailer with those guns and who knows how many boxes of ammunition."

He handed me the warrant.

"Okay," I said. "I'm on my way. Anything else?"

"Take Larch for backup," O'Brien said as I departed the sheriff's office. I hoped the sheriff, undersheriff, and prosecutor could not see the expression of relief on my face.

FORTY-THREE

Mary slipped into the right seat of the Explorer. "I hope this isn't going to be fun," she said, pulling a face as we pulled out of the lot. "I don't love it when people point guns at each other."

I chuckled.

We drove silently for a while, enjoying the crisp and sunny morning. Feeling amiable, partly because the prosecutor had paid me a compliment, partly because the sheriff had not confronted me with my unofficial investigation, and partly because a pretty colleague I liked rode in my presence, I opened up a bit.

"How much longer do you have to go to get your sheepskin?" I asked Mary, forgetting that she didn't like personal questions.

"Just a year," she replied, gazing out the window at the passing forest, I realized what I had said, and looked over at her. Her expression—almost always grave, alert, and professional—softened, and her eyes sparkled.

"And after that?"

"Oh, I don't know. But since you asked"—she turned and looked at me directly—"I'll tell you the possibilities."

In a couple of years, she said, she might apply for a job in a small city, like Muskegon or Grand Rapids, and work her way up, maybe eventually going to Lansing or Detroit. But lately she was thinking about trying for a scholarship to law school, having done well in academics as a part-time undergraduate.

"After that, who knows, maybe the FBI?" she said. My already warm opinion of her ratcheted up a notch. I approve of dreams.

"What about marriage and a family?" I asked, swiftly

wishing I hadn't.

Surprisingly, she laughed. "I could ask you the same question. We're all wondering about you and Ginny."

I glanced out the driver's window, trying to hide the blush, and was almost glad to see the carcass of the deer in the middle of the road ahead.

I stopped the Explorer and Mary and I got out. The deer, a mature doe, was dead, but the blood around it was not fully dried. It had probably been struck not an hour before. I wondered if the driver had called in the accident. Many of them don't bother, especially those who don't carry collision insurance on their old trucks and automobiles. It's mostly those with newer cars and full insurance who report deer strikes in order to collect on their policies.

It didn't annoy me that the driver hadn't attempted to move the deer off the road, as most will. Probably it was a senior citizen without the strength to drag a 120-pound animal across the pavement. I sighed. Dead deer on the road are a problem in the Upper Peninsula, not only because there are so many of them but also because nobody wants the responsibility for hauling them away.

The county road crews say that belongs to the DNR, for it is notorious for telling people that the deer belong to the state and that you have to pay the state for them. But the DNR doesn't have enough rangers to do the cleanup job. At one time the sheriff's department decided to take on the job itself, because deer carcasses on the road are a safety hazard. We deputies were ordered to stop and pick them up, toss them in the trunk and haul them away to the dump.

That policy was short-lived. There's nothing like a rotting carcass and a deputy with a dry-clean-only uniform staring at it in disgust. Then, too, the smell of decomposing meat as the temperature climbs and the sun bakes the trunk can be too much to take.

In the summer, local residents will do the job themselves, dragging the corpses into the woods away from their property.

Mary and I had no choice. We each donned latex crime-scene gloves and in each hand grasped a leg, hauling the creature to the side of the road.

"Let's get it to the tree line," I said. "That'll protect the eagles."

Bald eagles, those symbols of tribes and nations, may be glorious to behold on the wing, but on the ground their feeding habits are less than pleasant. They're opportunistic scavengers some ornithologists think are more closely related to vultures than hawks. They will eat carrion, especially in the winter when the rivers and much of the lakeshore are frozen, and they often feast on roadkill.

Eagles need about twenty feet of "runway" to take off and climb above the danger zone of an oncoming car, and sometimes they get hit. Sometimes they gorge so much that they can't get into the air at all, and have to walk around on their talons for hours until they've worked off enough ballast to get airborne.

A partridge inside the tree line loudly drummed its wings, annoyed at our intrusion, startling us.

"Don't you just love the sights and sounds of nature?" I said. Mary and I grinned at each other. Then she gave me an odd glance, as if she were sizing me up. For a moment I wondered if I had made a breakthrough—if she was on the verge of allowing me into a deeper friendship, the kind in which the parties share things they don't tell other people. Then Mary looked away, and the moment disappeared.

The job done, we drove off, and within half an hour pulled up by Cordelia Armstrong's junkyard of a homestead.

"Maybe you'd better stay in the vehicle until we know what she's going to do," I said. "But be ready to back me up if I need it."

"Gotcha," Mary said, unclipping the strap on her holster.

PORCUPINE COUNTY

I walked the few yards to Cord's door and knocked.

"Yeah?" came an irritated voice from inside.

"Steve Martinez here," I said. "Sheriff's department business."

"Okay, just a minute," Cord said almost meekly. "Be right with you."

In such a situation, some cops would draw their sidearms. Sensing that Cord would cooperate, I didn't. The sight of a .357 in my hand, I figured, might trigger an alarm in her disturbed mind.

The door opened and Cordelia stood in it, her hands empty.

"What can I do for you?"

"I think you know why we're here, Cord."

She looked past me, saw Mary, and nodded.

"Ettie's stirring up trouble again, eh?"

"I'm afraid so," I said. "She's filed a complaint of harassment and disorderly conduct, and I've got a warrant. I'll have to take you in and book you, but Garner will make bail right away. Somebody will drive you home. It'll take only a couple of hours."

"All right," Cord said. "But one thing."

"Yes?"

"Do you have to handcuff me?"

"It's the regulation," I said. "But I won't put them on till we get to the department."

She thought a moment. "Fair enough," she said. "Let me get my teeth."

She got her purse as well, climbed into the back of the Explorer, and we were off.

For much of the way we drove in silence.

"Is that your camera on the dash?" Cordelia suddenly said.

"Yup." I had taken to carrying the Minolta, its long telephoto attached, everywhere on duty and off, just in case someone asked about my interest in bears. And Cord

191

naturally had heard the gossip.

"For bears?"

"Yup."

"See many?" Mary interjected.

I glanced at her. "They're never around when you're looking for them. Mostly just the ones at the Cackle Shack." That was perfectly truthful.

She chuckled.

"Why are you so interested in them?" she said.

I had prepared a little speech just in case. "They're fascinating animals," I said. "Do you know that they have individual personalities? Some of them are laid-back, some of them are timid, some of them are vicious, some of them are just cranky . . ."

"Like me," said Cord in a rare flash of humor. Sometimes she could be almost rational.

"Have you ever had any personal experiences with bears?" Mary cut in, her expression intent.

Before I could go on, we arrived at the sheriff's department. I was almost sorry; my little speech was quite truthful. I had grown interested in bears for their own sake, not just because of the jam I was in, and I could have gone on for a while.

We got out of the Explorer, Cordelia meekly presented her wrists for the cuffs, and Mary and I escorted her to the women's lockup. Within an hour the judge met with Cord and her court-appointed lawyer for the arraignment, after which Garner paid the hundred-dollar bail. At her court date next month, everyone agreed, she'd plead guilty to disorderly conduct and pay a fifty-dollar fine, and, everyone hoped, that would end the matter.

I had my doubts. Cord Armstrong wasn't the kind of person who'd easily let go of a satisfying mad. She ate, slept, and breathed anger at the world.

Another deputy drove Cordelia home, and that was my

day. I felt it had been a productive one, full of good police work. The safety of the public had been upheld and the wheels of justice had been set in motion without anyone getting hurt or having to raise their voices. I'd even done a little bonding with a colleague. I'd almost, but not quite, forgotten my predicament.

FORTY-FOUR

Shortly after midnight two days later I was returning in my Jeep from a holiday poker evening with colleagues in the Gogebic County department at a café in Watersmeet, an hour south of Porcupine City, when my high beams glinted off a vehicle hidden in the brush around a curve of U.S. 45. Probably nothing, I thought, an old junker abandoned off the highway, but habit called—on duty or not, cops just have to check out unusual sights. I slowed the Jeep, then returned to the spot where I'd seen the vehicle. I alighted, a big four-cell Maglite in hand, and panned it across the dry brush by the side of the road. In a moment the beam skipped across yellow metal screened by a thick grove of bare aspen shoots.

I stepped off the road, grumbling softly as my spit-shined, tooled Western boots—one of my few sartorial extravagances—sank into unfrozen muck. I'd missed the nearby track, rough but high and dry, leading off the highway and into the aspen grove. Not fifty yards inside it sat a rusty yellow Scout. I felt its hood. Still warm; it had been parked within the hour. Only one person in all of Porcupine County drove a yellow Scout, so far as I knew, and that was Garrett Morton. But he was nowhere to be seen. What could he be doing this late at night and why was his Scout parked like that?

Emerging from the grove, I took my bearings. The moon had risen, softly illuminating the landscape. The aspen rose hard by a creek that led across a meadow to an abandoned farmhouse and tumbledown barn I knew well, having rousted partying teenagers there more than once. That reminded me that one of my fellow deputies lived not two hundred yards away on the other side of the grove. Mary Larch. Just a year before she had leased a bit of land, parked a used double-wide house trailer on it, and had a well dug.

Was Garrett Morton stalking her?

Swiftly I returned to my Jeep and fished the Magnum from the glove compartment. I returned to the grove, .357 in one hand and a smaller, pocket-sized pilot's Maglite with a red lens in the other, and found the track through the dead grass Garrett had trampled. It led toward Mary's trailer.

Carefully shielding the Maglite to conceal my presence — its red beam did not harm night vision — I slowly followed the path across the meadow to Mary's double-wide, soundless as a Shawnee, stopping at every tiny scrabble of pebble and rustle of twig to make sure I had not been seen or heard.

A dim light burned from within the double-wide. I squatted in the shadows a few yards away and listened. Bing Crosby was singing "White Christmas" on a tape deck somewhere in the trailer, and a soft murmur — Mary's voice — wafted intermittently through the window. She did not sound troubled. But then I heard another low voice, harsher, more masculine. Garrett? I couldn't tell. But then there was a soft gasp, followed by a sharper one, then a moan. Was she being attacked?

I crept forward to the trailer. A curtain in the rear, I saw, had not been completely closed. I stood up, holding the .357 before me, and peered into the window.

The room was dark, but inside it the light from the new December moon outlined a Scotch pine festooned with tinsel and stockings hanging from an impromptu mantel nailed to the flimsy interior wall. Three large boxes trimmed in Christmas wrap sat before the tree. But the inhabitants of the double-wide weren't snug in their kerchiefs dreaming of sugarplums.

Through the open door on the far side I could see Mary.

Her back was to me. She was nude, straddling a supine and equally naked man whose face I could not see, on her double bed. Her pelvis rose and ground in abandon, her back arching as her gasps softly increased in volume and frequency.

Inwardly I blushed. I am not a prude, but neither am I a voyeur, and I hate to intrude on other people's intimate moments. I had started to draw back from the window when the man's head rose into my view.

It was Garrett.

"What the —?" I muttered to myself as I squatted back out of sight. Mary Larch and *Garrett Morton*? Mary Larch and *anybody*?

Unbelievingly I stood up again to make sure I had seen what I thought I had seen. What I then saw shocked me to the core.

A naked blond woman, shapely breasts swinging, walked into view. A concupiscent leer wreathed her face as she sat on the edge of the bed and kissed Mary with an open mouth. It was Marjorie Passoja.

"My God," I thought.

Swiftly I considered what I had seen. A ménage à trois is none of my business, either personal or professional. But Mary and Garrett, Mary and Marjorie? My mind raced, my thoughts tripping over one another.

Both women are fully a decade older than he, and a lot smarter and more ambitious besides. Maybe I was wrong that Mary was repressed and asexual. Maybe she was merely a single woman in her full ripeness using a brainless young stud for pleasure. That must be it. But Marjorie? Yes. She and Mary were lesbian lovers. It fit. Their connection was a battered women's shelter. They had been friends, then had become more than friends. Maybe Marjorie had introduced Mary to the joys of bisexuality and had suggested they find a suitable boy toy to share.

Then it hit me. If those two women were involved amorously with Garrett, they could be — no, make that probably, even very likely — involved in other things with him. Such as conspiring to thwart and maybe hurt, even bump off, a curious deputy sheriff who wouldn't let go of the Paul Passoja case.

Mary? I couldn't believe it — didn't want to believe it. But there it was.

Quietly, crouching low in the grass and stopping frequently to make sure I had not been made, I retraced my steps to the aspen grove, then the highway where I had parked the Jeep. Keeping the lights off for half a mile and driving slowly so that my brake lights wouldn't flash and reveal my presence, I returned to Porcupine City, stewing all the way.

FORTY-FIVE

"What can you tell me about Mary Larch?" I demanded the next morning as Ginny came down for breakfast. I'd waited hungrily for her, for the previous evening she'd made prune-filled Finnish Christmas tarts, one of my favorites, and the scent of fresh butter pastry still filled the air.

"Aren't you going to kiss me good morning first?" she said. I hung my head in mock guilt and chuckled. Even bundled in green quilted robe and matching flip-flops, red hair askew and eyes heavy-lidded with sleep—or maybe because of it—Ginny looked extraordinarily desirable.

"Sorry," I said, and complied thoroughly with her request. So thoroughly that when she came up for air, Ginny said through her gasps, "Mmm. Let's go back upstairs." So thoroughly that I forgot all about Mary Larch and Marjorie Passoja and Garrett Morton.

An hour later Ginny awakened, poked me, and said, "Now what about Mary?"

I told her what I had seen the previous night.

At first Ginny started to snuffle with suppressed mirth, the rolling teakettle building up pressure for one of her patented spells of hilarity. I steeled myself.

"*Mary Larch*?" she said. "Mary Larch and *Marjorie Passoja*? Mary Larch and *Garrett Morton*?"

But almost instantly Ginny's bubbling subsided. Her eyes widened and her grin faded. "A three-way?" she said. "Maybe it's not so surprising about Marjorie. She does come from that anything-goes Southern California background. Three-ways wouldn't have been uncommon among bored young people in Beverly Hills and Brentwood. And when you're widowed and lonely you grasp at straws. You do odd things just to connect with others. Sometimes it involves sexual identities you didn't know you had."

"But Mary? Not only doesn't she seem the type, Garrett doesn't seem her type either," she said. "Or Marjorie's, for that matter. I have to agree with you about that."

"So it's just sex, you think?" I replied.

"No. Think about it," Ginny said. "Would a female sworn officer of the law, an intelligent and promising one like Mary, take up with a much younger and not very bright lout, let alone a lesbian relationship with a woman as prominent as Marjorie? This is a big county with a small population, and that kind of activity is bound to be discovered sooner or later. Not that there's anything immoral about it — none of the principals is married — but it's exactly the kind of thing people like to gossip about."

"So there's got to be more to it?"

"There must."

"But what?"

Ginny lay back on the pillow thoughtfully. "I don't know," she said. "Let's put Marjorie aside for the moment and consider Mary. She was born and grew up here, like her parents. Her mother was from a Finnish family, her father an English one. He was a storekeeper in town, one who like so many of them up here just made ends meet. After he retired they sold their house in town and lived in an old farmhouse on cutover land out near Ewen. They died about a dozen years ago."

"You think Mary's father abused her?"

"We never heard anything like that," Ginny said. "I think that would have gotten around."

"And they had no link to Paul Passoja?"

"I'm sure they knew Passoja and his family, as everyone else did, but I don't know of any harder connection."

"I don't, either," I said. "I can't remember seeing the name Larch in any of the Passoja land records I turned up last month."

Ginny lay silent for a moment. "Maybe there never was a land sale," she said. "Maybe they rented their house from Passoja. Maybe something went on there."

I nodded. "It'll be easy to find out who owns that land, and who owned it before."

Without a word we lay together for a minute. Then the comforter rustled downily.

"You're such a wanton," I said.

"Aren't I?" she said.

Joyously we wasted — if you want to call it wasted — the rest of that Sunday morning.

FORTY-SIX

Ten minutes at the courthouse and I had my answer: Paul Passoja had owned the land Rudy and Tillie Larch rented and still lived on at the time of their deaths a little more than a decade ago, she first and he a few weeks later. But what was the connection between Passoja and Mary Larch—if there was one beyond her parents?

That was what I had to find out now. But how? I couldn't go brace Mary and demand to know, nor could I throw Garrett up against a wall. The scant evidence I had was purely circumstantial, much too weak to overcome the trouble I was bound to get into if the sheriff's department learned about my rogue investigation.

For the next couple of days I either ran into Mary at the department or waved to her as she passed by in her cruiser. She waved back pleasantly with an unconcerned expression. Either she did not know I knew—or did, and didn't care.

Late the evening of the second day I stayed at the office after everyone except the night dispatcher had gone home, on the pretext of having to catch up with my paperwork. When the dispatcher left to make his rounds of the cells, I quickly fished Paul Passoja's file out of the drawer containing closed cases. Except for the stuff having to do with his death, there was nothing in the file except a single sheet reporting that at age twenty-two he had pleaded no contest to a disorderly conduct charge as a result of a drunken brawl in a town bar. That told me nothing. Half the men in Porcupine City must have at one time or another in their lives thrown a sodden punch at the wrong guy.

But the coroner's report contained Passoja's address in La Jolla as well as Porcupine City. That gave me an idea. I'd call the police in La Jolla. If Passoja had spent winters in California for many decades, maybe he had a record there.

Clearing off my desk, I bade the dispatcher good evening and went home to make the call, because I'd be hard-pressed to explain a long-distance item on the sheriff's dime to Gil O'Brien, who kept a suspicious eye on the phone logs in case a deputy tried to hang a personal call on the county. A sheriff's department in a poor rural county has a very, very tight budget, and every pencil, pen, and Post-It must be accounted for, let alone every gallon of aviation gasoline.

"Deputy Steve Martinez, sheriff's department, Porcupine County, Michigan," I told La Jolla's chief of detectives, giving him my star number. "I'm calling in connection with a homicide investigation here. Can you tell me if you have a sheet on a fellow called Paul Passoja, P-A-S-S-O-J-A, address 1382 Camino Real del Norte, La Jolla?"

A few minutes later the chief returned to the phone, having checked out both the files and my bona fides. "Yup," he said. "There's one. I'll fax it to your department."

"I'm going to ask a favor, Chief," I said. "I'm calling from home, and time's a-wasting. Can you just read me the highlights?"

"Sure. There isn't much, just one arrest and charge of statutory rape fifteen years ago. It was pleaded down to misdemeanor disorderly conduct in exchange for psychiatric counseling and a five-hundred-dollar fine. That's all."

"How old was the girl?"

"Fourteen. Guy said she looked eighteen. They all say that."

"Thanks."

I put down the phone and sat in a puddle of sudden understanding. Paul Passoja had been the fellow who assaulted Mary Larch when she was a girl.

I hopped into the Jeep and rolled down to Ginny's. She was still awake, having a cup of tea in the kitchen. I told her what I'd discovered.

Her eyebrows rose. "Mary was a Girl Scout at the time

202

Passoja started taking them on overnight hikes," she said. "Five gets you ten she went on one of them."

"Do you think he might have done something?"

"If what you said happened in La Jolla is true, it's not just possible — it's almost certain."

"Ever hear of him doing anything like that here?"

"Nope. If he had been caught, we'd all know about it. This is a small town. But La Jolla's a pretty good-sized place, full of rich people with both the knowledge and the money to keep things quiet."

I drummed my fingers on Ginny's kitchen table.

"And Marjorie?" I said.

We spoke at the same time. "The Andie Davis battered women's home!"

"That has to be it," I said. "Paul abused Marjorie in some way. Maybe not physically. Maybe she found out about his habits and he threatened her. Maybe he didn't beat her but abused her emotionally. It's logical that she would find something more in a women's shelter than just a place to donate her money. She'd find someone to tell her story to. And that probably was Mary. And having exchanged secrets about Paul Passoja, they'd work up enough anger to seek revenge."

Ginny nodded silently.

"But abuse doesn't change a victim's sexual orientation, does it?" I said.

"No. That's innate. Mary and Marjorie's relationship is probably just happenstance. It was their histories that led them to meet. Probably once they discovered the same man had abused them, they decided to strike back."

"Now what?" I said.

"Now what, indeed?" she said.

I looked at her. "I've got means, and now I've got motive. But I still haven't got a stick of evidence except some very circumstantial stuff."

She nodded again. Clearly she found the scenario hard

to believe, but there it was right in front of her.

"Looks like I'll have to take a stick to that hornet's nest again at Garrett's cabin. Maybe this'll be third time lucky."

But I wasn't in a rush. I could wait for him — and Mary, if indeed she was connected — to deal the next hand. If there was anything I had inherited from the genes of my Indian ancestors, it was patience.

FORTY-SEVEN

In the middle of that week Garrett finally rewarded my forbearance. Ginny had come over to my cabin to spend the night, parking her Toyota next to my Jeep and the department's Explorer in the driveway, so that I could roast a leg of lamb on the grill for us. I was still in bed the next morning when I heard her gasp and shout from outside, then the back door slam, followed by a thump that shook the cabin.

"Steve!" Ginny called from downstairs. "We've got a bear on the deck! And it's a big one!"

I scrambled into my jeans and thundered into the living room barefooted.

"Where?"

Another huge thump against the back door.

I pulled back the curtain. The bear, foam on its lips, scrabbled and slashed the screen door, ripping the metal screening into shreds. It already had made short work of the grill on which I had cooked the lamb. I doubted that it could get past the sturdy maple inner door, though it could easily burst through the glass windows if it had enough intelligence to figure them out.

Ginny squatted well out of sight, breathing fast but not panicky. "This one's a rogue, Steve," she said. "I was out in the backyard gathering boughs and cones for the kitchen table when it charged me. I made it into the cabin just in time. It's not going to go off into the woods after a while."

With a splintering sound the bear tore the screen door from its hinges.

I nodded. "I'll call Stan."

Maki answered on the first ring. "Mean bear in my backyard," I said. "It's got us trapped. Can you bring the bear kit?"

Within fifteen minutes Stan, who lives just five miles

west at Silverton, arrived in his pickup, transporter jouncing behind, and parked it behind our vehicles. Almost immediately the bear turned from destroying the deck and charged the pickup, covering the twenty yards before Stan could get out of the vehicle. With a mighty crash it collided with the driver's door, denting the metal and starring the glass.

By then I was out on the deck, shotgun cocked, trying to avoid stepping in my bare feet on the sharp metal shards from the back door screening and the wicked splinters from the door frame. Behind the bear scrabbling to get into the pickup, Stan, trapped in the driver's seat, saw me. He nodded, raised his hand, cocked his thumb and pulled an imaginary trigger.

I whistled.

In one swift motion the bear whirled, saw me, and leaped. I fell to one knee and aimed carefully at the crescent-shaped white patch on the charging animal's chest. At a range of ten yards the shotgun boomed and the bear stopped. Another shot and it dropped. Quickly I broke open the Browning and reloaded. But the bear lay motionless in a furry brown heap.

"Put another in its head," Stan said anyway. Unable to wrest open the sprung driver's door, he had emerged from the passenger door, rifle in hand.

I administered the coup de grace and stood back, panting, as Ginny walked up behind me, my .357 in her hand. "We won't need that," I said. She nodded and removed her finger from the trigger. Gently I took the revolver from her.

Stan squatted by the carcass. "I've seen this bear before," he said. "It's a big one, but it ought to be a lot heavier for this time of year. It's past the normal denning time, you know."

Ginny cut in. "I'd wondered about that, but the warm season has delayed things, hasn't it?"

"Yeah," Stan said. "See this mark?" he added, pointing to a ring in the fur circling the bear's neck. "Radio collar."

I knew what that mark really meant and where that bear had been and who had put it in my backyard, but it wasn't yet time to let Stan in on the truth.

"Maybe it's a roadside zoo bear," I said. "Owners closed up the place, brought it up here and dumped it in the forest?" That was a possibility. Northern Wisconsin is full of highway tourist traps of that kind.

"Yeah," Stan said. "But I think that bear's been starved."

Then it dawned on him. "Hey, that's the bear Garrett and I took down at the Cackle Shack when you were there. See the blaze on its chest?"

"Yep," I said.

"Not surprised it came back from where I had Garrett drop it. Twenty miles isn't much for an adult bear to cover once it's made up its mind."

"You didn't go with Garrett to let it loose?"

"Naw, it doesn't usually take two of us to release a bear, or even many brains. He dropped me off at my house on the way."

We contemplated the carcass in silence.

"Better get it out of here," Stan said. "I'll take it to the DNR station. We'll have the vet look at it."

I helped Stan winch the carcass onto the bed of his pickup and waved as he drove off.

Once he was out of sight, I said to Ginny, "I bet I know where Morton set that bear loose."

We strode west across the backyard and a hundred yards into the woods to a small lakeside clearing on the next property. A sandy road led from the clearing to M-64 another hundred yards away. The damp sand revealed two sets of fresh tire tracks, one pair clearly made by a heavy vehicle, the other obviously made by a lighter one with nearly bald tires. Three large imprints of bear paws in the sand, pointed toward my cabin, clinched it.

"Time to pay an official visit to Mr. Garrett Morton," I told Ginny.

At the cabin I dressed in my deputy's uniform, strapped on the Magnum and reloaded the Browning with buckshot, stuffing extra shells into my shirt pocket. I'd left the riot gun at the sheriff's department so a gunsmith could install a new firing pin, for the old one had bent during the last monthly target practice. The two-shot Browning and the .357 would have to do.

This time, I had probable cause: the presumption that Morton had assaulted Ginny with a bear. I wouldn't need a warrant to get into his cabin legally, although I still would have plenty of explaining to do: how I had first seen that bear with the white crescent on its chest chained in the woods and why I had not reported it to the DNR, let alone the department.

Most of all, I would have to justify not calling in for backup. No intelligent cop goes after an armed felon without at least one fellow officer riding shotgun, preferably the entire department. But the only other deputy on duty at that hour of the day was Mary Larch.

And Garrett Morton was the most dangerous kind of bad guy: a stupid one who'd act—no, react—without considering the consequences.

I sighed. No more scouting, no more parleying. It was time to put aside patience and ride against the enemy.

"Be careful, Steve," Ginny called as I strode out to the Explorer in full deputy's uniform. This was going to be official.

"*You* be careful," I retorted.

"I will, Steve," she said, adding almost under her breath, "but I've got your back."

I was too preoccupied to ask what she meant.

FORTY-EIGHT

This time I drove all the way up the track to Morton's cabin, parking the Explorer directly behind his Scout and trapping it against the tumbledown outbuilding. He might break out on foot, but he wasn't going to escape on wheels.

No one was in sight. I alighted, shotgun in hand, the Explorer's broad bulk screening me from the cabin thirty or so yards away. "Garrett!" I shouted, taking care to keep the Explorer between me and his front door. "Sheriff's department!"

No answer.

"Garrett! Where are you?"

The curtains in a front window twitched as a sash shot up. A rifle muzzle emerged, and I ducked below the Explorer's hood, behind the heavy engine. Not a lot of armor, but it would have to do.

"Show yourself, Garrett!"

The rifle answered with a heavy bark and the police radio antenna atop the Explorer sailed into the woods end over end.

A .30-'06 for sure. Now calling for backup, whether it was Mary or not, was utterly out of the question. It was going to be *mano a mano*, Morton against me, alone in the woods until one of us either was hit or ran out of ammunition — or both.

I held my fire. No point in wasting the few rounds of buckshot I had, and a .357 with a four-inch barrel wasn't accurate beyond fifteen yards or so. I had to get closer, where the Magnum slug and double-ought could do their best work.

I peeked around the front of the Explorer, spotted the glint of the heavy scope under the sash and quickly ducked back as the rifle coughed again, the bullet splintering the plastic bumper cover.

"That's damage of public property!" I shouted. "You're just adding on to the charges against you, Garrett!"

"Yeah?" he answered from the window. "What are they?"

It's a small psychological breakthrough when the subject shows a little curiosity. Maybe I could work on that a little, perhaps weaken his resolve, at least distract him some.

"Cultivating marijuana!" I said. "Resisting arrest! Assault! And, most of all, murder!"

Morton wasn't a bad shot, and at any good distance that scope would help. But up close it would make the rifle clumsy to swing and hard to sight.

An ancient oak with a six-foot-thick trunk stood to the right of the Explorer, six or eight yards closer to the cabin. I safetied the shotgun, cradled it loosely, and erupted into a crouching sprint around the rear bumper. Within an instant I hit the ground by the tree and rolled up against the trunk, flicking off the safety, the shotgun ready for action. At least half a second too late Morton's rifle barked, the bullet kicking up a clod of dirt a good six feet behind me. A big Winchester with a powerful scope was no close-quarters weapon.

Morton had fired three times. A Winchester Model 70 chambered for the .30-'06 cartridge carries four loads in its magazine and one in the chamber. Two left, unless he had reloaded, and I doubted that he had either time or presence of mind. It was a good moment for me to deliberately draw fire.

I unsheathed the Magnum and checked its load. Taking a deep breath, I quickly dodged into view around the right side of the tree, keeping my body behind the trunk, and hastily squeezed off a bullet that shattered the window two feet above the rifle muzzle I aimed for. As I ducked back the muzzle swung and coughed, Morton's bullet splintering the bark a good eighteen inches above where my head had been.

One left.

Morton's small woodpile, scarcely three feet high and

six feet across, lay five yards closer to the cabin, just to the left on a line from my oak to his front door. It would partly screen me from his view if I took the chance and ran for it. I did, and Morton's last bullet—if indeed it was that—thunked into the soft ground in front of the woodpile a nanosecond after I fetched up against it with a heavy thump. At almost the same instant I shrieked in mock pain, and let a long moan trail off.

This time I lay motionless, shotgun at the ready, .357 in its holster with the strap undone. Though the window was out of sight I could see a sliver of the front door through the haphazardly piled logs. Five minutes passed.

And another five.

Morton lost patience. "Martinez!" he yelled.

I did not answer.

"Martinez!"

I lay silent. Then the door swung slowly open. Two more minutes passed before Morton's head and shoulders sidled into view a good six feet behind the door. I waited. He waited. Then he emerged into full view, rifle at his shoulder, its muzzle pointed toward the woodpile, his eyes scanning the forest behind me.

I stood up suddenly, Browning at my shoulder. Just before I loosed both barrels, one after the other, I heard his Winchester's firing pin click on an empty chamber.

The first charge of buckshot missed, splintering the door frame, but the second caught him in the left leg, spinning him out of sight inside the cabin and sending the Winchester skittering across the floor.

Quickly I dropped the empty shotgun and hurdled the woodpile, .357 at the ready, and burst through the door.

FORTY-NINE

Morton lay slumped against the wall in a heap, tears streaming down his face.

"You've killed me!" he sobbed as he cradled his bloody thigh.

With a double-handed grip I kept the .357 trained on him.

"I'm gonna die!" he whimpered.

Nineteen-year-old infant or not, he had to be searched. Swiftly slapping his hands away from his leg, I said, "Garrett, put your hands on top of your head."

Still crying, he did so. Within seconds I'd rolled him over and tossed his clothes. Nothing except a penknife that I slipped into my hip pocket.

"Get me the ambulance!" he shrieked.

"It'll take a while for that," I said. "You shot off my antenna, remember? And there's no phone here."

Morton keened and rocked like an old woman at a Greek funeral, grasping his thigh above the wound.

"Shut up and let me take a look," I said.

I ripped open his trousers and examined his leg. Flesh lay exposed and torn and blood oozed copiously, but the heavy buckshot had not hit an important sinew or artery. The wound looked a lot worse than it really was. He'd recover, though he'd limp for a good while.

I didn't tell him that.

I tore apart a bedsheet and bound the wound. The bleeding had dwindled to an ooze. Often people in pain and shock will spill the beans easily, and I decided to work on Morton while I could, before he regathered whatever wits he had.

"Before I get the ambulance," I said, "let's have a little

talk, Garrett."

"I'm dying! There isn't time!"

"I'll get you to the hospital faster if you tell me a few things first."

"You greaser shit!"

I might have been a shit, but that "greaser" offended me—all racial and ethnic slurs do. I am a minority, after all, even if I'm also a honky by adoption. I decided to be even more of a shit.

"Greaser, Garrett?" I said in my best bad-cop voice. "I'm an Indian, not a Mexican. That's much worse for you. Do you know what we used to do to captives? We liked to stake them out on the ground naked in the hot sun and let the fire ants eat their privates. Then we'd take their scalps. Slowly."

He shrieked.

"Oh, Jesus," I said. "You baby!"

I sighed, holstered the Magnum, settled into a rocking chair, then drew the little laminated Miranda card from my shirt pocket.

"You are under arrest, Garrett Morton. You have the right . . ." I recited.

"Do you understand?" I finished.

"Yeah, yeah, hurry up, damn it!" he whined.

"Why did you kill him?"

Morton panted as sweat coursed down his face.

"He found the bear," he said. "He came in here and said he knew what Mary and I had done."

"Who?"

"Hank."

"Hank Heikkila?" I said, surprised. It was Paul Passoja I had had in mind.

"Yeah. He said he was going to find you and tell you."

"Mmm."

I settled deeper into the chair. That must have been the secret Hank had nursed. He must have encountered the bear with the blaze on its chest some time before our conversation at his shack, afterward putting two and two together and figuring that Morton had planted the first bear near Big Trees. But would Hank, who has absolutely no respect for authority, have come to me with that information?

Maybe. Hank, for all the torment in his mind, was an intelligent fellow. He probably figured that telling me what he'd found would buy him some much-needed goodwill. It's too bad, I thought, that he hadn't reached that conclusion during my visit to his cabin. If he had, he might still be alive.

"For God's sake, let's go!" Morton whimpered.

"You put that Springfield into Hank's mouth and pulled the trigger, didn't you? And then you arranged the body to make it look like suicide?"

"Uh . ... Mary told me to."

A lock clicked into place in my brain.

"Was she there at Hank's?"

"No."

"Where was she?"

"I don't know. Out somewhere at work, I guess."

"What did you do with his .38?"

The tears stopped briefly and he looked directly at me. "You know about that?"

I nodded.

"It's in the bottom drawer there. Hurry up, for God's sake."

I strode over to a cracked old bureau, pulled open the drawer and fished out the revolver, careful to thread a pencil through the trigger guard to protect the prints. If Morton's prints were mixed on top of Hank's, that was pretty good evidence. And so were the fisher pelts crammed underneath. The forensics guys could easily tie those to Hank. Then there was all the pot-growing paraphernalia in the corners — as well as the game traps. I had Garrett Morton nailed six ways from Sunday. Sure, I'd still be in deep shit for my lone-wolf investigation, but I had the goods, and that was what counted.

"Now, Garrett," I said, as if talking to a child would keep him acting like one, "it's almost time to go. But first you tell me about Paul Passoja."

"We weren't planning to kill him," Morton said.

"*Shut up!*" a female voice barked from the doorway.

I turned and gazed right into the wicked little muzzle of a nine-millimeter Beretta. Directly behind it stood Mary Larch, trimly pretty in her deputy's uniform, with a fierce expression on her face. I had seen it only once before, the day we picked up the child molester, and I was very sorry that it was aimed at me along with the pistol.

FIFTY

"Take your piece out of the holster with your fingertips and slide it to me," Mary ordered. I did so as gingerly as I could. Quickly she thrust the Beretta into her belt and trained my .357 on me, then strode over to Morton, still whimpering on the floor. "You'll live, blabbermouth," she said with icy contempt.

She turned to me. "I'm sorry, Steve," she said.

Regret tinged the steel in her expression.

"Just doing my job," I said, trying to keep my tone reasonable.

"I know."

"What are you going to do now, Mary?"

She didn't answer immediately but gazed at Morton thoughtfully.

"I don't know just yet," she said, "but I'll think of something. You stay right there and don't move."

Doubt. When subjects show doubt, work on it, keep them talking — maybe they'll talk themselves into surrendering. That's what we were taught in the hostage situations class at cop school. Of course, now I was the hostage. But still . . .

"Mary, can I ask you something?" I spoke in a friendly voice, trying to make her think I was on her side.

"What?"

"How did you know I'd come out here this morning?"

"Heard Stan on the CB talking about the bear in your backyard."

I decided on a frontal assault. "What did Passoja do to you?"

She looked at me in surprise.

"How did you know he did anything to me?"

"Just police work, Mary. Why don't you tell me?"

Her face clouded, that twisted expression of hatred returning to mar her pretty features. "The son of a bitch."

"Yes," I said. "It must have been awful."

"I was thirteen," she said, her emotional dam bursting in slow motion, like a levee giving way to floodwaters. Maybe she was planning to kill me, but I am sure she wanted me to understand why she had done what she did, as if my knowing the truth would somehow ease and even justify my death. Or maybe she was getting ready to do something else. I'm no psychologist.

"He'd taken five of us Girl Scouts camping in the woods for two days. On the morning of the second day he asked me to go to a spring with him a mile away to fill the canteens, and when we got there he told me I was very pretty and that he wanted me to do something special for him."

Her jaw trembled. It was hard for her to revisit the memory.

"He made me take my jeans down, and he touched me. Then he opened his pants, and . . ."

Involuntarily I reached a hand to her. For a moment she turned toward it, then away.

"It was awful. I can still remember the taste."

She shut her eyes tightly, then opened them quickly, keeping the Magnum trained on my chest. They were dry. Whatever grief she had shed for her innocence had been shed long ago.

"I am so very sorry, Mary," I said, honestly meaning it. For the briefest instant I *was* on her side, no longer the cop, feeling deep down that Paul Passoja had gotten what he deserved.

"Then he said if I ever told, he'd throw my family off his land. He said he knew we had no money and had nowhere to go."

She was telling the truth.

"The bastard," I said with feeling. "Where in the woods

did this happen?"

"Big Trees."

My eyes widened.

"Later on, when I was old enough," Mary continued, "I found four other women he did the same thing to when they were girls. I tried to talk them into bringing charges, but they were too scared of him and his power. He could have destroyed them if he wanted.

"And it was only my word against his. Who would have believed me?"

I nodded. "You were in a terrible jam, Mary," I said. Agree with her. Build up the mitigating factors. Build up hope that she might escape the worst consequences for her acts. It was an old trick, and I doubted it would work with a cop as smart as she, but there was nothing else to do.

"From time to time, even after I became a cop, I'd run into him, and once when we were alone I told him I would get him some day. He laughed and said, 'You just try.'

"From then on, every time he saw me he would chuckle and shake his head. That man was not just evil, he was contemptible."

Just as Hank Heikkila had said. Men rape to achieve power over their victims, and strengthen their hold by tormenting the victims afterward. What Passoja had done to Hank was also a kind of rape, a rape of the soul.

"What about Marjorie?" I asked.

Her jaw dropped. "How did you know about that, too?"

I told her. She had the grace to blush.

"Last year," she said, "Marj and I got to talking, and she told me that she'd discovered Paul in their bedroom in La Jolla, having sex with an underage girl. He threatened to kill her if she ever told, but he couldn't leave it at that. He kept telling her that she was too old, she wasn't as good in bed as the young stuff and that she loved his money too much to leave him. He broke her spirit."

Mary told Marjorie about her youthful experience with Passoja, and the shared anger drew them closer together. They fell in love.

"It was Marjorie's idea to use Garrett, but together we figured out a plan."

Calmly Mary told the story. Early in the summer she had met Garrett Morton on one of his bear-catching jobs with Stan Maki. With a young jock's blind cockiness he had come on to the pretty deputy, and in the beginning Mary swiftly discouraged the much younger man. She told Marjorie how Garrett had hit on her, and Marjorie suggested that Morton, for all his denseness, had had enough intelligence to absorb a bit of knowledge from Stan. The women began to hatch a plan. They'd entice him the best way Marjorie knew how and use him to do the dirty work.

It was not hard to figure out why Mary had rowed back across that river of pain that Passoja had thrown her into at such an early age. Rape is about control, and its victims sometimes try to retake control of their lives in the same way they were victimized. The same thing went for Marjorie, but in a different way. That desire for control also explained why the women would try to get back at Passoja in the woods, on his own territory.

"Passoja boasted so much about camping without a gun and knowing what to do with bears. But we didn't really expect the bear to kill him. We thought he'd just be chewed up a little and the whole thing would embarrass the hell out of him."

Whatever their intent, a human death had resulted, and the charge — if I could get Mary to surrender — still would be murder. Maybe in the second degree, but still murder. Maybe a good attorney could plead it down to aggravated manslaughter, but there was the matter of that second bear, the one Garrett had sent after me.

"Think of it, Steve," she said. "A bear as a weapon? So

unlikely! Who could ever think somebody would do that? And how could it possibly be traced?"

"But aren't bears unpredictable?" I said. "What made you think you could train one well enough to go after somebody?"

She smiled ironically. "Same way you figured that out, Steve," she said. "You went to see Professor Ursuline. In the library at Houghton, between cop classes, I read one of his monographs on the behavior of bears and the regularity of their habits."

I realized I could have done the same thing and avoided a lot of publicity. I kicked myself mentally.

"Keep your hands in your lap, Steve," Mary said. "I'm telling you this because I think you have a right to know, before . . ."

She let the sentence trail off, doubt in her eyes. She was thinking, I was certain, that she would have to kill me, but was not sure if she really wanted to.

"Yes, Mary," I said. Keep her talking. "Go on. What happened then?"

After she and Marjorie had finally hooked up with Morton, Mary continued, they had persuaded him with little difficulty to buy an old bear transporter at a junkyard in Wisconsin and drive it at night to the empty hunting camp where we now sat, hiding it in the copse where I had found it. The bear they planted on Passoja was a woods itinerant Morton had baited and shot with a tranquilizer gun borrowed surreptitiously from the DNR and returned before anyone missed it. He had done the same thing with it that he did with the bear that had surprised me near his cabin, chaining it to a tree with a heavy leather collar.

"It took just two weeks to starve it, teasing it with bacon grease, until it was ready. When I heard Passoja tell the Metroviches at Merle's that he was going into Big Trees, I had Garrett take the bear into the woods that day and let it loose as close as possible. That turned out to be only about a mile, right at Mills Creek."

I looked at Morton, staring sulkily at Mary but saying nothing.

"What did you do then, Garrett?" I said.

He had emerged from shock and slowly picked up on her unspoken thought that I was being honorably informed before the disposal.

"Sneaked up on him while he was cooking and baited the tent with grease. Then I left and went home. Nothing more to do."

I nodded. "Pretty easy to figure out what happened then."

Then I remembered Heikkila.

"What about Hank?" I asked. "We were talking about him a while ago."

"Mary told me to kill him."

"I did no such thing, you idiot!" Mary said. "I told you we'd take care of him later."

She turned to me. "He hears what he wants to hear."

"But I thought . . . ," Morton protested. Now he turned to me.

"It was an accident," he said. "We wrestled with the rifle and it went off. I didn't know what to do and tried to make it look like suicide."

Morton was changing his story, trying to make things look better for himself, even though Mary had the drop on me and presumably was going to kill me before long. That meant doubt had fogged whatever remained of his resolve, or maybe it was just loss of blood.

"You said Hank found the bear," I said. "Which one was that? The one you planted on Paul or the one you planted on me?"

"On you," Morton said.

"Why me?"

"You were too close," Mary said. "We had to do

something. And if a bear worked once, it might work again. We were hoping it would hurt you badly enough so you would have to quit and go somewhere else."

"You didn't want it to kill me?"

"Not really."

I wanted to believe that. Maybe it was true.

"I don't know whether to be disappointed or pleased," I said.

"You're a nice guy, Steve. You're just in over your head."

The room fell silent. There seemed to be nothing more to say.

A pickup door slammed loudly outside.

Mary turned to the door, the muzzle of the .357 in her hand following her eyes. That was a mistake.

FIFTY-ONE

I leaped, aiming my head at her lower right rib cage as I reached for the Magnum with my left hand. Whether by design or by blind luck, my aim—and my timing—was perfect. The collision scattered furniture in a clatter across the room. The wind whooshed out of Mary as I tore the revolver from her hand just as she bounced against the wall and collapsed, struggling for air. Before she hit the floor I had wrested the Beretta from her belt.

I am not that fast. I will always believe that something good, something honorable, rose from her heart and told her to slow down, to allow me the advantage, to end it.

"Steve! Are you all right?"

Bright sunlight diffused Ginny's trim form in the doorway, but there was no mistaking the sharp outline of the saddle carbine at her shoulder, eye steady on the sights and the muzzle locked on Mary. Behind her loomed Stan Maki, his big-bore rifle on Morton.

"What did you hear?" I said, puffing, still winded from my exertions.

"Plenty," said Stan.

"How long were you out there?"

"No more than five minutes," Ginny said, "but enough to know what happened at Big Trees last month and twenty years ago."

"Smart move, slamming that door."

"Stan's idea," Ginny said.

I shot her a "what the hell do you think you're doing?" look.

She smiled back sweetly.

Mary's breathing had returned to regularity, but she was sobbing. I helped her, tears streaming down her face, into a chair.

"There's a hard way, and there's an easy way, Mary.

You're a cop. You know that." I kept my tone as gentle and sympathetic as I could. "Despite what you've done, there was a reason, and I think that reason may help you. If you cooperate, I'll do my best with the prosecutor."

"My life is over anyway," she said.

"Maybe not," I said.

"Okay." She nodded.

Stan harrumphed.

"What got into you, Garrett?" he said disgustedly. "I trusted you."

Morton gazed dumbly at his boss from the floor. His bleeding had long stopped and so had his whimpering, replaced by an expression of confused incredulity. He didn't answer.

"It's time to go in and get that leg taken care of," I said. "Ginny, would you call the department on the CB and get the ambulance and some backup out here? Oh, never mind. I'll do it."

I reached Koski. "This is Steve," I said. "Put Gil on."

The undersheriff's voice crackled over the radio. "What's going on?"

I took a deep breath and told O'Brien where I was. "There's been a firefight and a shooting, and it also involves two murders."

"Of whom?"

"Paul Passoja and Hank Heikkila."

"Who're the killers?"

"Garrett Morton. And Marjorie Passoja. And" — I hesitated for a moment — "Deputy Larch."

"Holy shit!"

There was a moment of shocked silence, then Gil said, "I'm going to take a chance and believe you, Steve."

"Thanks," I replied. "I'll explain the whole thing when I get back. Now send somebody out to bring in Marjorie Passoja, will you?"

"I'll go myself."

The radio clicked off. I hoped Gil would reach Marjorie before the whole eavesdropping county showed up to watch the arrest.

Thirty minutes after I made the call, two squad cars carrying the department's three remaining deputies — swiftly called in from their off-duty pursuits — and the Porcupine County ambulance arrived.

Quickly I filled in the deputies, and they gently but firmly placed Mary, docile and handcuffed, into the backseat of a squad for the trip to town.

"I'm really very sorry, Mary," I said before the door closed on her. "Up to this you were a good cop." She nodded stonily.

"How did you find out, Steve?" she said.

"It was that piece of bacon I found by the tent," I said. "I didn't think Passoja was so far gone in Alzheimer's that he'd forget old habits that easily."

"Bacon?" Morton cut in from the stretcher as the paramedics carried him by. "I dripped a few spots of grease on the tent, but there weren't no pieces of bacon in it." He was too dense to understand he was digging his hole even deeper.

Ginny and I stared at each other. Paul Passoja *had* helped do himself in. Fogged by dementia, he had spilled his supper on his tent. Life is full of little ironies.

FIFTY-TWO

As usual, Eli Garrow cheerfully tried to take as much credit as he could. Honeyed "we," "my deputy," and "my department" dripped from his lips as he held forth to the press from all over Michigan, Minnesota, and Wisconsin, crowded into the sheriff's tiny squadroom. He had dressed the place for the occasion. A fat little spruce, ten times the size of the one on Joe Koski's desk, squatted in the corner and a huge cardboard cutout MERRY CHRISTMAS had magically appeared on a wall. Eli the old pol was at work, and the reporters looked about and jotted in their notebooks what they saw.

At "we dug out the cancer in our midst" I tuned him out. Sooner or later the reporters would work it out for themselves.

Gil O'Brien wasn't fooled. After I had handed in my report, Mary had signed her confession and both Marjorie and Morton had lawyered up, the former with a nationally famous criminal defender and the latter with a high-powered Detroit attorney — thanks to the fast footwork of his well-connected father — the undersheriff shot me an "I'll deal with you later" look.

But both he and I knew I wasn't in for more than a pro forma tongue-lashing in his office. Nothing neutralizes the consequences for what we might call "procedural irregularities" like solid results.

And the outcome was not in doubt. Shortly after the news broke, spreading like a shockwave across Porcupine City thanks to the CB conversation I had had with Gil, one of Mary's sister Girl Scouts came forward, saying she'd testify that she'd been molested by Passoja, too, now that death had muffled was power to hurt anyone. Garner Armstrong, visibly moved by her story and those of Mary and Marjorie, hinted broadly that he'd plea-bargain the charges against the women, maybe to aggravated manslaughter, especially if they cooperated in the case against Morton. The women would have to do time, but with good behavior they'd be paroled in a few years. There would be no further career in law enforcement for Mary, but I thought that with her drive and intelligence she'd succeed somewhere. I hoped Marjorie and her lawyer would see the light and take a plea, too.

Morton, however, was lucky that Michigan did not have the death penalty. He was looking at life without parole for murder one for the Heikkila killing as well as long sentences for murder two in the Passoja death and attempted murder on the deck of my cabin. Almost as an afterthought there was that marijuana patch. His goose was well and thoroughly cooked.

As for Ginny, in midafternoon she and I drove out of Porcupine City, the first few miles in silence. Then I couldn't stand it anymore.

"Whatever possessed you to come out to Morton's cabin?" I demanded. "You're not a trained cop! You could've been killed!"

"Is that a thank-you?" Ginny replied. "If so, you're welcome."

"I'm sorry," I said. "I just can't stand the idea of you getting hurt."

"Oh, Steve," she said, as if I were a small boy. "I shot my first deer when I was fourteen. Dressed it, too. I've seen blood, and I've spilled it."

Ginny placed her hand on mine. "I'm not stupid, though. When I saw Mary driving hell-for-leather west on M-64 this morning, I guessed where she was heading, and I figured you needed the cavalry. I called Stan and filled him in on the way. He never doubted me, not for a moment."

At that I had to chuckle. "Cavalry. The cavalry rescuing the Sioux."

"You'd have been up that famous creek without a paddle, just like Custer at the Little Bighorn."

I sighed and inclined my head toward her. "Yes. Thank you."

"You're welcome again."

My mind drifted to the twenty-fifth of June in the year 1876, and to Crazy Horse, Sitting Bull, Two Moon, and Gall, the Lakota allies who had waited patiently for the Seventh U.S. Cavalry to blunder into the trap they had laid.

"My people called it the Battle of the Greasy Grass."

Ginny glanced at me. "Your people?"

"Yes. At the moment I'm feeling like a victorious warrior. But ask me again tomorrow."

Then I started. "Hey! We're forgetting something!"

"What?"

I told her about the little bear in the cage out at Morton's cabin. I'd forgotten all about it during the excitement of the morning. "We've got to go out and let it loose."

"Yep."

FIFTY-THREE

"It's so darling," Ginny said as we contemplated the little bear. It sat in a corner of the cage, seemingly contemplating us in the same way.

"Stand aside and I'll open the door," I said.

Then I had second thoughts. "This bear has been around people a lot," I said. "What do you think will happen to it?"

"A hunter will kill it next season, probably. Or, if it's lucky, it'll become a garbage bear and get killed the year after that."

"I don't want that to happen."

"Why?"

"I owe it my life."

"You do?"

I explained. "We could relocate it."

"Where?" she said dubiously. "There isn't really anyplace in Upper Michigan where hunters don't go."

"How about the Boundary Waters Wilderness?" That's the back country of northeastern Minnesota, just around the western corner of Lake Superior.

"Hunter's paradise."

"Hmm."

"Steve, I've got an idea. Ever hear of the Red Lake Reservation?"

"That's in northern Minnesota, isn't it?"

"Yes. The Ojibwa who own it don't hunt bear there, I know that for sure. It's a big place, more than eight hundred thousand acres of woods and swamp. This little guy would have a better-than-even chance of growing up to be a big bear there."

"We'd never get the permits." We'd need one from the State of Michigan to remove the bear, one from Wisconsin to transport it across the state, one from Minnesota to accept it, as well as veterinary documents and God knows what else.

"Somehow, Steve, I don't think that'll stop you." She was right. I wasn't a stickler for proper procedure. I'd gotten away with it once and I'd get away with it again, or so I hoped.

"Or you."

"I'm in," she said, and hugged me. "Now I've got to make a call. I've got a friend on the reservation."

Luckily Morton's camp stood on a rise high enough to be within cell phone range. The connection was weak, but good enough.

Ginny turned off the phone. "She knows exactly where to let the bear go."

"She?"

"Old college friend."

"Is there anybody you don't know?"

"Probably not."

"How long does it take to get there?"

"It's three hundred fifty miles. About eight hours."

"But how are we going to smuggle the bear all that distance cross-country? My Jeep isn't big enough."

"We'll use my van," she said. "I've got a traveling cage big enough for two or three dogs. The bear will fit into it with room to spare."

"Hope we don't get caught," I said. I didn't relish the thought of tangling with Gil O'Brien, let alone the natural resources departments of three states.

"You leave that to me."

Within an hour I'd dropped off the Jeep at my cabin, called Joe Koski to tell him I'd be out of touch for a while, and returned with Ginny in the Historical Society's van. We'd removed the two rear seats from it to fit in the rusting dog cage, one of the society's enormous pile of useless gifts donated by people who thought they had value just because they were old.

"You don't think the society will mind?" I asked. "Isn't it supposed to be in the Christmas parade tomorrow?"

"It won't know a thing," Ginny replied. "With luck we'll be back in time. Besides, I gave it the van."

"Do you have a dog tranquilizer in that mighty kit bag of yours?" I asked. "How are we going to get him into the cage without getting an arm or two ripped off?"

Out of a paper bag Ginny pulled a bottle of Dramamine and a baggie of raw hamburger. "My dad used this to sedate his Labs for long car trips," she said. "Puts them right to sleep for a few hours. We'll give it a fifty milligram pill, the same standard human adult dose Dad used on his dogs."

I was dubious, but she was right. Within fifteen minutes after we dosed him, we'd coaxed the woozy little bear from its enclosure into the smaller cage and lifted it with two mighty grunts into the rear of the van. Small as the animal was, it was round and fully packed, ready for hibernation, and had to weigh at least 150 pounds. Fortunately it was cooperative, moving when we wanted it to, and once the cage was manhandled into the van it settled down and fell soundly asleep.

"That bear really is trusting," Ginny said.

"Yeah. See what I mean?"

"One more thing," Ginny said, disappearing behind a tree. I went back to the enclosure, scooped up a bucket of dog chow and a bucket of water, and placed them inside the cage, covering it with a ratty old army blanket. The little bear didn't stir.

Ginny returned and we gingerly shut the van's rear doors, careful not to wake up our cargo.

"Let's go," she said, glancing at her watch. "It's four o'clock. If we don't stop except for gas, we should be there by midnight."

FIFTY-FOUR

For the first four hours we made good time on U.S. 2, the northernmost national highway. I carefully stayed at or slightly below the speed limit, hoping not to provoke police curiosity. Underneath the army blanket the bear slept quietly, now and then stirring and huffing gently, like a teakettle on low heat. It sounded to me as if he was just trying to be companionable.

Early into the trip a rank smell wafted up from the rear of the van, and I turned up the fan and cracked the driver's window to the cold air outside.

"That little bear speaks softly and carries a big stink, doesn't he?" I observed.

Ginny chuckled throatily. I didn't envy her the job of cleaning up the van once we had returned. We'd spread a plastic tarp over the floor of the van and shoveled in sawdust from my woodpile, but that smell was the kind that penetrates and hangs around for weeks.

Night had just fallen as we were rolling out of Duluth at eight o'clock, the town's Christmas lights fading in the distance, when a siren screamed and blue beams flashed in the rearview mirrors. I checked the speedometer. Forty-eight miles per hour, and we were in a fifty-mile-per-hour zone.

"Shit," I said. "Driving While Indian." Many cops in states with large reservations profile Indian drivers, especially after dark, partly because of widespread alcoholism and drunken driving and partly because they don't like Indians in general. Several times since my boyhood I'd been stopped just because a cop took exception to my looks.

I pulled over and the Minnesota trooper nosed his cruiser behind the van.

"License and registration, please," he said.

232

I handed them over and showed my star.

"On the job, deputy?"

"Not really."

He chuckled, but it was a friendly sound. "Bit out of your jurisdiction, eh?"

I relaxed. I wasn't going to be asked to step out of the van and walk a straight line.

"I was wondering what a commercial van with Michigan plates was doing in Minnesota, that's all," the trooper said.

Sure.

"What's in there, anyway?" Brother officer or not, he was still doing his job.

Damn.

"A bear," Ginny piped up. "We're transporting a young bear to Redby."

I shot her an "I hope you know what you're doing" glance.

"No kidding?" The trooper peered into the back. "Can I have a look?"

Legally we weren't obligated to open the van, but if we refused, the trooper would interpret that as a suspicious act and keep us there until another brought a warrant.

I got out, opened the rear doors, and pulled aside the army blanket. The bear, having been awakened by the small commotion, stuck a wet nose through the bars and wiggled it quizzically.

"Cute little guy, even if he kinda smells," said the trooper. "I suppose you got papers."

Busted! I thought.

"Right," said Ginny. "You want to see 'em?"

I tried not to gape at her.

"Why not?" the trooper said.

"Just a sec." She rummaged in the back of the van and returned with a large plastic Ziploc bag containing a thick, brown-spattered manila envelope. She opened the bag. The odor that had followed as all across Michigan and Wisconsin suddenly billowed into an unbearably intense cloud. My eyes watered. The trooper took a step backward as if stunned.

"What the hell is that?"

"I'm sorry," Ginny said. "I accidentally dropped the papers into poop when we were putting him into the van. They're pretty gross, aren't they?" She opened the flap of the envelope.

"Never mind, never mind," said the trooper, hand to his mouth. He took several steps to the side of the road and breathed deeply. "I don't know what that bear's been eating, but he's not fit for polite company."

"I'm sorry," Ginny said again, a winsome expression on her face.

"Have a good trip," said the trooper suddenly, spinning on his heel and returning to his cruiser with as much dignity as he could muster. Then he laughed.

"I hope you make it before that stink kills you."

"So do I," I said. I wasn't sure we would get there. My knees had grown weak.

The cruiser's blue lights snapped off and the trooper wheeled around in a U-turn, unnecessarily tossing gravel, heading back to Duluth.

Ginny tossed the noisome mess back into the plastic bag and zipped it shut.

"Get rid of that," I suggested.

"No. We might need it again," she said.

"That's not bear crap, is it?"

"No. It's liquid hog manure. There was a jar of it at Garrett's place. He'd been using it to fertilize the marijuana."

"You're brilliant."

"Aren't I?" she said. "Now move over. I'll drive the rest of the way."

FIFTY-FIVE

Just before midnight we arrived in Redby, the largest village in the reservation belonging to the Red Lake Band of the Ojibwa Nation. I'd returned to the wheel an hour before when Ginny began to nod.

"Pull up at that filling station," she said. "We're being met there."

A strikingly good-looking, brown-skinned woman in denims, long dark hair pulled into Indian braids, stood in the light of the doorway. NOEL winked in neon above it. "Ginny?" she called.

"Sheila!" The two women embraced, laughing. "It's been years!"

"This is Steve Martinez," Ginny said. "Sheila Prudhomme. My college roommate."

Sheila extended a graceful hand. "I've heard a lot about you," she said. "You're Stevie Two Crow. My Ojibwa name is Standing Deer, but they call me Runs With Scissors."

Ginny laughed. "Sheila's a kindergarten teacher in the reservation schools. It was a joke but it just stuck."

"Let's have a look at the bear," Sheila said.

I opened the rear doors and pulled back the blanket. Sheila bent close and whispered something in Ojibwa. The bear chuckled happily and stood up. I quailed as she extended her fingers through the steel mesh and wiggled them. That's a good way to lose a pinky. Bears, after all, are wild animals. But he just licked Sheila's fingers.

She saw my concerned glance. "I wouldn't do this with just any bear," she said. "But it's okay with this one. My people and I have a special relationship with bears."

She didn't explain, but shined a penlight into the bear's eyes and examined them intently.

"That's a cute face," she said. "He looks healthy. Tell

235

me about him."

I did, keeping the story as brief as I could.

Sheila nodded slowly. "A very good reason to let him go free here. It's important to us."

"Why?"

"I'll explain on the way."

We climbed into the front seat of the van, Ginny in the middle and Sheila on the right. Immediately Sheila pulled a U.S. Geodetic Survey topographic map from her jacket and switched on the dome light.

"See, this dirt road goes to the northwestern corner of the reservation. That's where we take problem bears when they get too close to people. It's far enough away so that they don't often return. We'll let him go there." She pointed at a spot near a small lake.

I nosed the van onto the gravel track.

"Now, Steve," Sheila said as the van nosed through the night, brilliant light from its headlamps boring under the canopy of leafless branches over the road, "there are seven clans in the Red Lake Band, each named for an animal indigenous to the reservation. My family is a member of the Bear Clan. It is against our belief for any member of the Bear Clan to hunt, kill, or eat bear. We save them whenever we can. That, according to our tradition, is a holy deed. They trust us, and we trust them. Most of the time, anyway. There are exceptions sometimes."

For an instant I heard an echo from Professor Bill Ursuline's office.

"What about the other clans?" I asked. "Are they bound not to hunt bears?"

"No," Sheila said. "But in practice we all respect each other's clan animals. It's part of how we get along. This is a very poor reservation, and we need to keep our ties with each other to survive. Yes, there are casinos on the rez, but we're a long way from the interstate highways, so they don't produce a lot of money."

I was silent for a while, absorbing the information. Then I nudged Ginny. "No wonder you suggested this place."

It was two in the morning when we arrived at the spot on the map. Swiftly the three of us pulled the cage from the van and set it on the ground by the side of the track. We looked at each other and nodded.

"Let me," Sheila said. She opened the cage door. Calmly the little bear emerged, walking unhurriedly to the tree line. The Dramamine had worn off hours before. It stopped and peered around.

Softly Sheila began chanting in Ojibwa. The bear watched her intently, and when she was finished it glanced at Ginny, then me, and swiftly disappeared into the brush.

"It's way past time for him to den," Sheila said. "Not far from here there's a ridge with a lot of downed pines. He'll find a warm spot to hibernate in one of the deep root holes."

I looked up at the sky. The new December moon shone brilliantly and the stars twinkled. In the north I found Ursa Major and watched as the dark veil of an oncoming front from the northwest that extended from horizon to horizon slowly extinguished its starlight.

"A snowstorm's on the way," Sheila said, shivering.

"I hope so," Ginny said.

FIFTY-SIX

Within an hour we had returned to Redby. "Come on in," Sheila said as we arrived at the filling station, "and have some coffee before hitting the road."

We entered and Sheila opened a door to a back room. Inside, under a grimy wall festooned with greasy gas station girlie calendars, sat four Ojibwa, three men of middle age and one an ancient, playing penny-ante poker around a cracked oaken table so decrepit that it looked as if it must have arrived on the reservation with fur traders two centuries before. Perry Como was singing a Christmas medley from a boom box atop a stack of old tires.

"My brother Jack," she said, introducing the biggest. "He owns this place." Jack stood politely. Like me, he was tall for an Indian, with yard-wide shoulders, and he wore his hair like his sister, in braids.

"Mike and George and Grandfather," Sheila added. "Meet Stevie Two Crow. He's Lakota."

Mike and George nodded gravely, but Grandfather stood, muttered something sternly in Ojibwa, gestured at the roof, and stalked out of the room.

"What did he say?" I asked.

"He said, 'Don't let the Lakota leave this room alive,' " Jack said, his expression stony.

"Jack!" Sheila punched her brother in the shoulder. "Stop that!"

Jack threw back his head and laughed gleefully. "He actually said, 'I'm going to bed. Don't wake me before noon.' " The big Ojibwa extended his hand. "We're honored to have you. Have a cupper."

Mike and George made room, shoving aside stacks of bald tires, and we all sat. Sheila told the others what we had been doing that night.

"Well," Jack said, "that bear sounds like a peace offering."

I looked at him quizzically.

"Did you know, Steve, that in the year 1765 just a few miles from here at the mouth of the Sandy River, the Ojibwa and the Sioux fought their last battle, and you guys left these parts for the Dakotas and became horse Indians?"

"I admit I wondered how you'd feel about a Lakota coming onto the Rez."

"Oh, all that happened a long time ago," said Jack. "Now we Indians have to stick together against the whites." He winked at Ginny. "Present company excepted, naturally."

"It's after three," Ginny said presently. "Time to go. If we keep driving, we'll make the Christmas parade."

We all stood. Jack laid an enormous hand on my shoulder.

"Stevie Two Crow, on behalf of the Red Lake Band of the Ojibwa Nation, I appoint you an honorary member of the Bear Clan." There was no levity in his voice, only gravity.

"Hear, hear," said Mike and George, thumping the table. Sheila clapped.

"I mean it," Jack said. "*Mii-gwech*. That's Ojibwa for 'Thank you.' "

Sheila hugged Ginny and me warmly, as if she had known us all her life, and we set off into the night.

FIFTY-SEVEN

A blinding light, then a clearing in the forest. In it a gigantic bear, a good thirty feet tall, sat on its haunches.

"Stevie Two Crow," it said benevolently.

I gaped. The bear spoke in a rolling, sonorous voice that sounded as if it had come out of Harlem by way of an Italian opera. I could think of nothing but De Lawd in *The Green Pastures*, Marc Connelly's once beloved but now hopelessly dated Negro spiritual play from the 1930s.

"Thank you, bro, for bringing Little Bear back to us."

"You're welcome."

"That was a very Indian thing to do, you know," the bear said.

"But I'm not really that much of an Indian."

"Oh, you are, more than you know."

"How?"

"It's hard to explain. Indian-ness is a state of mind more than it is a state of being, if you get my drift."

"I'm confused. People think I'm Indian but I was brought up white. I think white, even when I want to be an Indian."

"*You're* confused? I'm a bear but I think like a human. Talk about fish out of water, excuse the metaphor."

"What am I supposed to do?"

The bear shrugged. "Who knows? You'll find a way. Maybe you've found it and don't know it yet."

"You're not sure?"

"I'm only a bear. I'm not God, or even a shrink."

"I thought maybe you were one of those."

"See? We're never what others expect us to be."

"Yeah, but . . ."

"Look. You just solved a mystery and brought three

criminals to justice. Doesn't that count for something? Makes you a pretty good deputy sheriff, in my opinion."

"Thank you. But that's only part of me."

"Feeling fragmented, are we?"

"Yes. I'd like to be more of a Lakota than I am."

"Then you'll have to consult a Lakota spiritual advisor. I'm not licensed in that department. I'm only a paramedic, so to speak."

"Why did you call me into your presence, then?"

"Who says I did?" said the bear. "It's *your* dream. You conjured me, not the other way around."

He was right.

"What am I doing here, anyway?" I asked plaintively.

"Finding your way, of course. It's a process, not a phenomenon."

"You do sound like a shrink."

"Now, now. Just think of me as a guide."

"What's your advice? If you have any."

"Just this: You're doing fine. Go home and carry on. And cherish that Ginny. She's a keeper."

"That she is, that's for sure."

The bear elaborately consulted a pocket watch with a face the size of a kitchen clock.

"I've got a dinner date," the bear said, "with three of your kind. I never look forward to it, but tomorrow is always another day. Ta-ta."

Just before the bright light again flooded my eyes, the bear said: "*Mii-gwech*, Stevie Two Crow."

FIFTY-EIGHT

"Did you know that you talk in your sleep?" said Ginny from behind the wheel as I came awake. Day had broken and the van's headlights punched weakly through heavy, driving snow. A good six inches had fallen, and more was on the way. Through the thick white veil I could make out a line of taillights, some of them on snowmobile trailers and some of them on SUVs bearing skis on their roofs.

"Where are we? What time is it? What did I say?"

"We've just entered Michigan, and it's almost noon," Ginny said. "You've been sleeping for six hours, and you didn't make much sense."

"I just had the weirdest dream," I said. "I was talking to an enormous bear that sounded like James Earl Jones."

"What happened?"

"I don't know exactly," I said, "but it wasn't a nightmare at all. In fact, I feel pretty good."

"I know. You were grinning in your sleep."

"Somebody's been doing the Heikki Lunta," I said with a chuckle. "The gods have been listening. Looks like this is going to be a big snow."

With a start I realized that from a certain point of view, what I had been doing the last twelve hours was itself a kind of propitiation, unconscious as it may have been. I kicked myself mentally. What a preposterous notion. But then it started to grow on me. Who can explain spirituality, anyway?

"Hey, slow down!" The snow tumbled down so thickly we could see barely fifty yards ahead. Ginny braked gently, keeping the van in its lane.

"We'll just make the parade," she said.

We didn't stop at our respective cabins, but kept on into Porcupine City, where at the river bridge late in the afternoon the first marchers and floats of the Christmas

PORCUPINE COUNTY

parade were about to step off for the quarter-mile-long trek down Main Street. Right in front of our van Santa sat atop the cab of the town's big yellow pumper, PORCUPINE COUNTY VOLUNTEER FIRE DEPARTMENT emblazoned on its doors. Through the fake beard I saw the cherubic cheeks of Dudley Richardson, the fire chief. He waved cheerily at us.

"'Bout time you showed up!" said Joe Koski, resplendent in dress uniform, clipboard, and pencil. "We thought you'd run off for the weekend after all that excitement yesterday."

"Something like that," I said.

"Just a sec," said Joe. With duct tape he affixed large cardboard signs to the van's front doors.

"What do they say?"

"Get out and take a look."

HONORARY PARADE MARSHALS, said the sign. MERRY CHRISTMAS FROM STEVE AND GINNY, PORCUPINE COUNTY's WORLD-FAMOUS DETECTIVES.

"Aww," I said. Ginny's eyes glistened.

"I really shouldn't tell you," said Joe, who never in his life had failed to tell anyone anything they shouldn't have been told, "but guess who were going to be the honorary marshals up to yesterday morning?" The Porcupine County parade tradition was for committees to make such announcements on the day of the celebrations.

"No!" said Ginny, "You're putting us on!" She is a lot quicker on the uptake than I am.

"Yep. Larch and Passoja."

My jaw dropped, then closed in a broad grin. That did make sense. The two women had done the county a great good in their work with the Andie Davis Home. And some might say they had done the county an even greater good by relieving it of Paul Passoja, but I was not about to debate, even with myself, such moral relativities. I was enjoying Joe's unexpected irony too much.

"Go say hello to your fans," Joe said, wrinkling his nose

at a sudden whiff of pig poop. *"Where* have you b—"

Ginny drove on before he could finish the question.

As the snow diminished into a few huge flakes parachuting slowly through the air, we drove down Main Street at a stately pace, waving to the crowds under the Christmas lights. The stores stood open, their windows packed with holiday decorations, some of them seasonal and some of them religious. Crowds lined the curbs. I'd never seen so many people at a Porcupine County Fourth of July parade, and this is highly patriotic country.

Christmas hymns filled the downtown air from the chimes in the steeple of the First Methodist Church on the east side of town. Old holiday standards boomed from the exterior speakers on Ulla's Antiques in midtown. Inside the North Woods Bank next door glittered a huge Christmas tree, a six-foot-high pile of gift-wrapped packages before it. I smiled. The St. Nicholas Project was at work. Run by civic-minded folks with assorted affiliations, it placed trees inside the banks of the town. To the trees the St. Nicks affixed paper mittens, each containing the sex and age of a needy child and a suggested gift—and there were hundreds of them—to be plucked by bank patrons and replaced with presents.

In front of the bank a uniformed Salvation Army officer imported from Houghton swung a handbell, smiling and nodding as passersby filled his kettle. Men and women on motorcycles zoomed past, bearing stuffed animals for the Marine Corps toy drive.

A small crèche filled the front window of the village hall as it had every Christmas for more than a hundred years. The sight always brought a grin to my face. During the last few years the Wise Men had smiled down on Baby Jesus from under a Star of David, and a menorah, its electric candles alight, stood prominently in one corner of the window. A crescent hung unobtrusively in the other. There wasn't a Jew or a Muslim in town, but the city fathers knew how to appease the American Civil Liberties Union as well as the Lord. No busybody from the big city could possibly complain. Garner Armstrong, who knew his constitutional law, had seen to it.

Seemingly all of Porcupine County had showed up, and most of Gogebic and Iron Counties as well. They were there to cheer on the snow, they were there to cheer on the holiday season, and they, it seemed, were also there to cheer us on because the Passoja case had put the county on everybody's map.

"Steve! Ginny!" the crowd called delightedly as the van passed. I couldn't speak for her, but an odd feeling suddenly crowded my heart. Was I coming home at last?

Not really, I realized suddenly. The sentiment of the moment simply had overtaken me. Tomorrow I'd be the same confused fellow — 50 percent white, 50 percent Indian, 100 percent dissatisfied.

"Things could be worse," I heard the Great Bear growling from somewhere deep in my head. "Enjoy the moment, numskull. It's a gift. You want it tinsel-wrapped? Take it or leave it."

I took it, and waved to the crowd. A man in clerical collar, scarlet vest, and tartan slacks waved back. He was Father Ted McGillicuddy, rector of St. Matthew's Episcopal Church, Scotland's most prominent contribution to Porcupine County.

"Hey, Steve!" he called. "We haven't had so much fun since the moose got loose on Main Street!"

With that, a salute of Roman candles shot into the sky from the piers on the nearby Porcupine River, followed by bright, sky-filling starbursts. The crowd cheered. Fireworks for Christmas! Only in the Upper Peninsula . . .

Later, when we pulled into the driveway of my cabin, the front had passed south, opening the skies, and a vermilion scrim wreathed the setting sun. Red squirrels chattered and scolded as they chased one another through the trees, and a woodpecker jackhammered a snag overlooking the snowy beach.

"Ooh . . . a pretty end to a hell of a day," Ginny said with considerable feeling.

In the cabin I opened the freezer, hunting for supper. The little Sucrets tin with the shred of bacon winked at me. I opened it, chuckled, and shook my head. I'd have to file it in the evidence room tomorrow — not that it was going to make a lot of difference to the prosecution.

"Let's not waste that sunset," Ginny said. "Grab the peppermint schnapps, and I'll get a couple of glasses."

"Fine idea," I said. "But there's one more thing I've got to do."

"See you in the living room," Ginny said.

I picked up the phone and dialed.

"Merry Christmas, Professor Ursuline," I said when he answered. "Can you spare a few minutes? Got a story to tell you."

A Venture into Murder

First published in hardcover by Forge Books, 2005
First published in Great Britain by Robert Hale Ltd., 2006
First published as an e-book, 2011

For Will

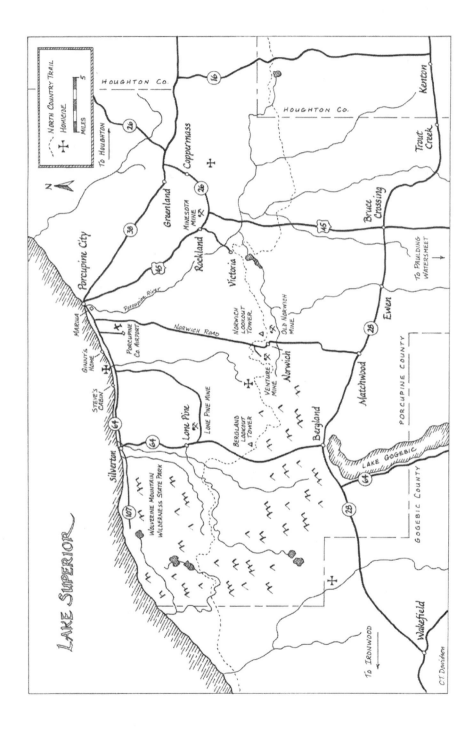

ONE

"Start at the beginning," I said, stepping gingerly away from the corpse in the sand. It had a hole in its chest. But Elmer Knapp had none, and he proceeded at full throttle and with a bottomless fuel tank. Mr. Knapp had found the body.

"Me and the wife are from Bloomville, Wisconsin," the octogenarian said, sweeping off his threadbare fisherman's porkpie and mopping his head, its bald white pate divided neatly from his stubbly cheeks by a deep farmer's tan. Like many vacationing heartland country dwellers of his generation, he dressed not in the Lands' End shirts and stonewashed jeans of midwestern Baby Boomers but in faded military khakis and a flap-pocketed blue chambray work shirt buttoned all the way up, collar gaping around his tanned turkey neck. From his frayed pants cuffs jutted stained, scuffed work boots with lug soles. Dead center on his rawhide string tie lay a bright Navajo turquoise clasp, no doubt a souvenir from a vacation in the Southwest. He looked utterly authentic, and for the most part sounded the same way.

"That's down near Antigo in Langlade County, you know. Last Saturday, that's two days ago, we were going to go to Bayfield—that's out by the Apostle Islands, you know—because Aunt Pearl has been poorly with the arthur-itis, and the wife wanted to get something pretty to cheer her up. But I can't stand that gift-shop junk—you know, Bayfield is becoming touristier and touristier with every passing year, and all it's doing is attracting the wrong kind of people from all over, you know, the ones who throw McDonald's trash all over the highway, and . . ."

By this point most other police officers would have rolled their eyes and said in so many words, "Yes, yes, can we get to the point?" But I believe in letting witnesses rattle on, even elderly ones no longer inclined or even able to distinguish relevant from irrelevant. You never know what might spill out when a witness charges along under a head of steam.

"And?" I said in an encouraging tone.

"And I managed to persuade Elfrieda, that's the wife, that her Aunt Pearl, who loves pretty stones, might like an agate or two from the shore of Lake Superior. So we decided to drive to Porcupine City and rent a cabin for a few days, as we've done a week or so every other year since 1957 or thereabouts, and hunt up some stones on the beach. That was last Friday. No, I said it was Saturday, didn't I? What day is today?"

"Monday," I said.

"Yes, that's right, we have eggs Monday mornings," Mr. Knapp said firmly. "It's definitely Monday. Sunny side up."

"Then what happened?" I said.

"After breakfast we started walking west down on the beach looking for agates. In the morning when the sun is low it's best to keep it at your back so you can see the pretty rocks sparkling ahead of you, you know. It was kind of foggy, though."

I nodded and jotted a word in my notebook. Foggy.

"After about an hour we heard a sport fisherman raise its anchor and start its engines maybe half a mile off the beach. That was probably the *Mary-El*. You know, that's a party boat, takes people fishing."

"Yup." Another jot. *Mary-El*. A thirty-six-footer out of Silverton, just about the only sizable commercial sport fishing vessel along the 150-odd miles of nearly deserted Lake Superior shoreline between Ashland, Wisconsin, and Houghton, Michigan. I'd been aboard her myself a couple of times, on forays for lake trout. "See her?"

"Just barely," Mr. Knapp said.

" 'Bout what time was that?"

"Eight-fourteen. I just happened to check my watch. It's a Timex, you know, the best twenty-dollar watch in the world, never stops running. I got her at a garage sale. You know what I paid?"

He leaned toward me conspiratorially. "*Two bucks.*"

"Wow," I said. "That's a buy."

"Damn right," he said. Another thrifty child of the Depression, the kind who hunts for mail-order and garage-sale bargains, clips coupons, never pays retail, and always buys a used car. I admire those who are careful with their money because they have to be, as I suspected Mr. Knapp was, and pity the tightwads who don't need to scrimp but still boast about their steals at Costco and Sam's Club. The rich man who walks a mile to save a penny is a sad human being indeed.

"Was that Central time or Eastern time?"

"Central. I don't change my watch up here. Makes me late to supper."

Though it lies seventy-two miles farther west than Chicago, Porcupine City, seat of Porcupine County, runs on Eastern time, like the rest of Michigan except the four counties along the Wisconsin state line. Michiganders who live next to Wisconsin just find it easier to live by Central time. In Porcupine County, however, being on Eastern time means late dawns and late sunsets during the summer. Often last light doesn't fade until ten-thirty.

"What happened next?"

"By and by, maybe ten minutes later," he said, "Elfrieda tapped me on the shoulder and said, 'Elmer, that's odd.' I looked up and saw a bunch of crows, half a dozen or so, way up the beach pecking at a log half in and half out of the water. Now crows don't usually do that. They're not shore birds, you know. I said to Elfrieda, I did, 'You're right, that's odd. Let's go have us a look.' "

Elmer sighed. "When we got there, Elfrieda said, 'Elmer, logs don't have arms nor legs.' And I said, 'This one don't have eyes neither.' The crows had been at it a while."

He shuddered and looked back on the beach, where other Porcupine County sheriff's deputies stood over the body, trying not to gag as the sun rose higher in the June sky and accelerated the processes of putrefaction. To my eye the half-naked corpse, a large and burly male lying face up and clad only in jeans and a single sneaker, had not been in the water long, judging from the bluish skin and lack of bloat. The chill of Lake Superior most likely had slowed decomposition.

"And that's when we went to that cabin over there and, you know, asked them to call the arthur-ities."

For a moment I thought Mr. Knapp had said "arthritis." I took a deep breath. One more "you know" and I'd go nuts. Young people have corrupted the everyday language of many of their elders with that useless locution, and "like" isn't far behind it. I was sorry. If it had not been for that I would have been persuaded that Elmer Knapp was an utterly pure and unspoiled old-timer from the midwestern countryside. They're hard to find nowadays, what with television and the Internet turning the speech of too many people between the Hudson River and the Sacramento Valley into that of cookie-cutter Middle Americans of the youthful persuasion.

"Thank you, Mr. Knapp," I said. "You've been very helpful. Now I don't think we'll be needing you any more today. Could you give me your address and telephone number in Bloomville, just in case?" He did so, and I shook his hand gravely. "Maybe you'd better look to Mrs. Knapp. She seems unwell."

Mrs. Knapp sat disconsolately on a log nearby, as if she had suddenly been told that her salmon-colored double-knit pantsuit, set off by a bright yellow chiffon scarf, had been out of fashion for thirty years. It looked almost new, as if she wore it only on special occasions, like vacation days. Probably it was another product of the pinched thriftiness of the lower middle class. But I suspected that what really ailed her was the unexpected sight of an eyeless corpse.

"Who is it, do you think?" Mr. Knapp said. "What happened to him?"

"I don't know," I said. "Maybe a fisherman who fell out of his boat a few days ago."

I didn't tell Mr. Knapp about the dimpled perforation directly under the stiff's left nipple. I'd spotted it when I arrived on the scene an hour earlier. I would have bet good money the hole had been made by a bullet, although it was possible the corpse had been punctured postmortem by a snag as it rolled in the shallows. I'd told the two deputies who followed me on the scene to let the body lie as it was, then called my immediate boss, Gil O'Brien, Porcupine County's undersheriff, and told him the facts. Right away Gil phoned the state police post at Wakefield, a little more than fifty miles southwest of the sheriff's department in Porcupine City. Rural sheriffs rarely have the means or manpower to investigate suspicious human deaths in these semi-wilderness parts and generally let the better-equipped troopers do the job.

I looked out on the beach. Here, not quite halfway along the fifteen miles between Porcupine City and the vast Wolverine Mountains Wilderness State Park in western Upper Michigan, some fifty feet of sand spanned the distance between tree line and water's edge—a fairly wide beach for this stretch. The lake was still this morning, the gentle lap-lap of the waves barely audible in the soft breeze. Heaps of skeletal white driftwood thrown up by spring storms spotted the beach like a bleached wooden boneyard, an ossuary of dead pine and cedar—except along the three hundred or so feet that belonged to the owner of the cabin Mr. Knapp had hailed. Evidently the owner was an anal-retentive sort. Unlike most lake shore property holders, who tended to prefer nature's helter-skelter design and let their beachfronts alone, he had raked the sand clean so that it shone spotlessly white, like Waikiki Beach on Sunday morning. But there was no fringe of stately palms, only a thick line of birch and aspen broken by a few towering white pines left over from the logging days of a century ago.

Through the trees I saw oncoming flashing red, blue and white lights, and checked my watch. It wasn't even an hour since I'd called Gil. The state cops must have covered the fifty miles from Wakefield at ninety miles an hour, even though there was no life to save, only a corpse to investigate. The big Ford cruiser fishtailed to a stop on the access road in a cloud of sand and gravel. Smokeys like to make dramatic entrances, as if to emphasize their exalted status on the law-enforcement food chain, several links higher than their not-too-bright country cousins in the sheriff's department.

"Okay, girls," said a gruff voice as a beanpole in blue blazer and khaki slacks emerged from the passenger side of the cruiser. "It's ours now. Skedaddle."

I laughed. Sergeant Alex Kolehmainen, the smartest state police detective and evidence technician in all of Upper Michigan, loved to play the stage bully with sheriff's deputies. At first he spooked rookies. At a skinny six feet six he was all elbows and knees and Adam's apple, like Tony Perkins in "Psycho." His mock bombast, coupled to fast-growing gray stubble on his cadaverous cheeks, made him look like the Grim Reaper in a coat and tie. Sooner or later, Alex's hamminess tipped off even the greenest probationary deputy that his fierce manner was all a put-on.

Alex, who had grown up in northern Wisconsin and served in the Army after college, like me, had started his law enforcement career as a lowly sheriff's deputy himself, and he showed great respect for the kind of work we did. "You couldn't ever get me to handle a domestic dispute again," he often said of a common task country deputies hated. It's a frustrating scenario: The abusee calls the cops. The cops arrive and attempt to restrain the abuser. The abusee suddenly feels loyal to the abuser, and the cops end up getting hammered by both sides. Occasionally the abusers — and even their mates —

are armed as well as drunk or drugged. "That's worse than wrestling a crocodile," Alex says.

And like me, he had not yet married. Women quickly see past his lanky homeliness and set their sights on him, but Alex is a choosy sort. He likes women but loves the bachelor life more. Women invite him to dinner and sometimes he spends the night, but he's always gone after breakfast. Still his paramours forgive him, for he is dashing and generous and dumps his ladies so gently and magnanimously that they are barely aware of the end of the relationship. I doubt that Alex has ever been dumped himself. At least that's how it seems. Though he and I are good friends, he has never talked about the women he has known. He likes and respects the ladies too much to tell tales out of the bedroom.

Alex stepped over to the body. "What have we here?" he said, broadly including me and my brother deputies in the pronoun. Not "What do we got?", the hackneyed query of the movie cop. Alex is as careful with his grammar as he is with his tools. "Fill me in."

As the responding officer I did. Alex nodded as I finished my much-edited tale of the Knapps' discovery of the body, then went to work, photographing the corpse from several angles with an Olympus digital camera for quick results and a Nikon thirty-five-millimeter film camera for legal backup. He also gathered samples of sand and measured the water's temperature, leaving no pebble unturned.

"Anything else turn up on the beach?" he asked after an hour of meticulous labor.

"Nothing we could see. We searched it for half a mile in both directions."

"Okay, shall we bag him and drag him?" The Porcupine County Hospital ambulance waited behind the cruiser to transport the body to Houghton forty-eight miles east, where the medical examiner would perform the postmortem. Porcupine County has a coroner, but he's an internist, and all questionable cases needing a pathologist go to Houghton. Suspicious ones often end up at the state police forensics lab in Marquette, the only one in the Upper Peninsula.

Alex stood up. "Most likely a homicide," he said, officially voicing what we on the scene all thought of that hole in the man's chest. "The doc'll decide."

"How long ago, do you think?" I asked.

"Hard to say. Could have been just a few hours, but maybe a couple, three days. I'll have to get a range of water temperatures at this time of year."

From June to mid-September Lake Superior's inshore waters are often warm, sometimes topping seventy degrees Fahrenheit, but a sudden shift of wind can roil the lake, bringing up colder waters from the bottom and dropping the surface temperature into the low fifties in a couple of hours. It often takes hours of studying weather and temperature charts to arrive at just a rough time of death.

Alex stripped off his crime-scene gloves and tossed them into a hazmat container in the trunk of his cruiser. "I'll call you when we know anything," he said. "Probably be at least a couple of days, maybe a week."

I nodded and shook his proffered hand.

"Thanks for keeping a clean scene," Alex said as he shut the door of the cruiser. "That helps a lot. Honest Injun."

He winked at me.

I winced only a little.

TWO

That evening, in civilian attire, I dined alone on lake trout at George's Supper Club in Silverton, five miles west of my log cabin on the shore. George's, the dining room of the big inn that catered to hikers and skiers in the Wolverines state park on its doorstep, was the closest thing to a gourmet restaurant in Porcupine County, and that isn't saying much. Its menu was heavy on deep-fried everything, the favorite of north country natives, but at least the salad-bar veggies were fresh, and George's broiled lake trout was as good as anything I'd had in the seafood emporiums of Boston and Chicago.

That was because Rudy Makinen currently was in residence as executive chef, or whatever George's called its head cook. Though Rudy is not a graduate of the Culinary Institute of America, he had learned his trade in one of the toughest kitchens in the world: the galley of a nuclear submarine, where tight storage space means a simple menu of a few items prepared perfectly.

Every year or so Rudy has a fight with the manager of the inn, usually over accounts. He quits and hangs up his shingle, or skillet, or whatever it is chefs hang up, at O-Kun-de-Kun, the restaurant in the mall at Lone Pine, the old copper mining community six miles south. As soon as the local diners discover Rudy has dumped George's, they emigrate en masse to O-Kun-de-Kun, and George's is left with only the tourists. By and by Rudy has a fight with the owner of O-Kun-de-Kun, quits, and takes his skill back to George's, the local clientele again in tow.

One year Rudy decided to be his own boss and opened the Starlight Inn on the highway in the countryside seven miles east of Porcupine City. For two years his seafood restaurant was the brightest constellation in the Upper Peninsula's dining firmament, for Rudy ranged far and wide for the best and freshest salmon, trout and whitefish he could find. In the summer he'd catch lake trout on his day off Monday and serve it to a few lucky friends Tuesday, and his Friday night fish broils—even the shrimp were broiled, not battered and deep-fried—drew diners from all over the U.P. and northern Wisconsin. A meal at the Starlight was worth a two-hour drive.

But the economics of the restaurant business are always shaky, and they are shakiest of all in the hard-luck boondocks where the clientele is constantly shrinking. The bank foreclosed, and Rudy went back to his shuttling between O-Kun-de-Kun and George's.

And that was why, after a slab of broiled trout exceptional even for Rudy, I was feeling content with the world. Then, as I was just leaving the restaurant, a neighbor placed her hand on my arm.

For the last couple of years Mary Ellen Garrigan, a wealthy and fortyish divorcee who lived in Winnetka, Illinois, an upscale Chicago suburb, had been a summer resident at a huge, brand-new, and expensive six-bedroom beach home built for her by a Wisconsin contractor with imported labor, not Porcupine County carpenters, on the lake shore just half a mile east from my cabin. I had not yet encountered her, for she was not the kind who mixes with locals, who meet and greet each other daily at the town's modest supermarket. She didn't shop there but had gourmet foodstuffs delivered at great expense from chichi stores that served the resorts around Eagle River and Rhinelander two hours south in Wisconsin.

Her meager relations with Porcupine County residents bordered on the imperious. To them she was haughty, rude in the unconsciously and sometimes deliberately belittling manner the very rich often display to those lower on the economic and social ladder. Next to people like her on my scale of annoyance are the self-absorbed second-rate urban intellectuals whose snobbish disdain for rural Americans is born less from ignorance than desperate striving to be superior to somebody — anybody. I had known both kinds of twits in my youth and in college and despised them equally.

Mary Ellen Garrigan's social life at her lakeside mansion was unsurprising for her kind. It consisted of weekend house gatherings with others like her, often attended by much younger hunks in BMWs and Jaguars, college boys with too much money and too little supervision. They were noisy and wild occasions, and rumors of debauched parties were beginning to emerge.

All these things Joe Koski, the sheriff's department's chief dispatcher, one-man intelligence service, and unofficial town crier, had told me. Nothing escapes Joe. He can tell you — and will tell you whether or not you want to know — who's been occupying a bed they shouldn't have, who's visiting their relations in New Mexico and whose dog has just had puppies that need a home. He's a terrible busybody. I wouldn't have been able to tolerate him if he hadn't been a nice guy, a poster child for Officer Friendly. He helps old ladies across the street, kisses children's boo-boos and lends broke deputies a tenner till payday. Everyone knows Joe. With their scanners, as common to a Porcupine County household as a color television, they listen to him all day on the police radio as he sends deputies to accident sites and takes their license and registration queries during traffic stops. The only person they listen to more than Joe is Annie Tollefsen, WPOR's motherly morning personality, who gets half her gossip from the dispatcher anyway.

I didn't need Joe to tell me that Mary Ellen Garrigan stood out wherever she went. She was still a knockout. Her boy-short bottled blonde hair set off a deep tan. Her ears, wrists and neck dripped with diamonds and gold, a rare sight in a place where an embroidered sweatshirt is considered dressing up and jewelry is left mostly to the pierced generation. The few times she appeared in public places like

George's, she wore skimpy spaghetti-strap outfits designed to show her lack of tan lines as well as display a bust that just had to have been surgically augmented. For everyday wear she preferred snug slacks, high-cut shorts and jerseys not from the Wal-Mart at Houghton but from Bergdorf Goodman in New York and Marshall Field's in Chicago. One doesn't often see expensive clothing in Upper Michigan, except for the Timberland boots and top-of-the-line down parkas North Woodsers save up for because the warmest winter garments give them the best chances for survival in deep snow.

Mary Ellen often took the summer sun in the nude on the sand behind her house, barely concealed from the shoreline by a low dune. More than once that summer Sheila Carnahan, the hefty middle-aged widow who was my immediate neighbor to the east, had happened upon Mary Ellen either sunbathing or swimming on the not quite deserted beach in what Sheila delicately called "the altogether." Sheila, who often played hostess to two adolescent nephews from Arizona, had asked Mary Ellen not to go about without clothes when they were visiting, but the reply was succinct and rude.

Now, skinny-dipping is hardly a federal offense. I often indulge in it myself on warm summer days, when Sheila is out of sight in her house and nobody else seems to be on the beach. I suspect Sheila sneaks an occasional peek at me with the big Pentax binoculars she keeps on her kitchen counter for birdwatching. Anyway, she has never complained.

"That woman makes no effort to cover herself!" declared Sheila, who, like so many Upper Michigan women, is deeply modest. I had not felt the urge to investigate, having no law-enforcement reason to do so, but gently suggested to Sheila that she keep that information to herself.

"If it gets out that Mrs. Garrigan likes to go about outside without clothes," I had said, "every horny teenage boy in the county, let alone your nephews, is going to be stomping around on the beach trying for a peek. Let's see if we can avoid that."

Sheila, who is as sensible as she is straitlaced, agreed. So far, so good. The beach remained largely deserted, except for the few residents and occasional out-of-town visitors who liked to hike for miles along it. Mary Ellen had not yet become a celebrated part of the scenery, let alone a familiar one. Sooner or later, however, that was going to happen.

All these things ran through my mind when Mary Ellen's brown and bejeweled hand suddenly grasped my arm in the parking lot just outside George's. No one else was about.

"Hello, Steve Martinez," Mary Ellen said, her eyes shining into mine as she leaned uncertainly toward me. They glittered from the pitcher of martinis she had downed with two other wealthy matrons at a table near mine. I could almost see olives instead of pupils in her eyes. Inside George's she had glanced my way several times, a few of them with bold interest. "You're the Indian deputy, aren't you?"

"Ah, yes, Mrs. Garrigan," I replied, trying to maintain a friendly tone although the unnecessary mention of my ethnicity irritated me. "We're neighbors on the beach. I've meant to introduce myself, but never got around to it."

"You live in that cute little shack to the west, don't you?"

"Shack" is hardly the word for my modest but well-constructed four-room cedar log cabin on the shore, but I let it go. People like Mary Ellen Garrigan just can't help patronizing their neighbors.

"Yes, that's the one."

She belched discreetly and giggled. "Sorry."

She was drunker than I had thought. I suddenly felt as if I had become the quarry of a woodland beast, and said hurriedly, "It's nice to meet you. I'll be seeing you around."

That was a dumb thing to say, considering what I'd been told about her. It gave her the perfect opening.

She leaned even closer to me and whispered conspiratorially, "I don't pussyfoot around. Come on down to the house tonight. You'll see a lot of me."

She hiccupped. "You'll be my first Indian. "

I drew back, pretending I hadn't heard.

"I'm a *very* good lay," she insisted, pressing her considerable cleavage into my arm. "I'll bet you are, too."

For an instant she touched my male vanity, I have to admit, but I've never been interested in winding up as a one-night notch on a predatory female's bedpost—especially in these sparsely populated parts, where everybody's private business tends to get broadcast as soon as it is transacted. Besides, although she didn't know it and probably would never understand why, she had insulted me profoundly. I don't mind being hit on—I enjoy that as much as any other red-blooded American male does—but I just can't stand being thought of as a novelty lay, a piece of exotic meat. Suddenly the well-fed feeling I had carried out of the restaurant dissipated.

"Good night, Mrs. Garrigan," I said as severely as I could, turning on my heel. I did not look back as I walked out to the Explorer.

"Jerk!" she called after me, loud enough to be heard inside the restaurant. "You don't know what you're missing!"

THREE

My full and official title is Deputy Stephen Two Crow Martinez, Sheriff's Department, Porcupine County, Michigan. Genetically I am 100 percent Native American, born to the Lakota nation — one of the Teton Sioux tribes — but culturally and emotionally I am the white-picket-fence Eastern Methodist I used to be. I was adopted as an infant by well-meaning white missionaries from the poverty-stricken and dismal Oglala Lakota reservation at Pine Ridge, South Dakota, and was brought up as a seemingly well-tanned preacher's kid in middle-class Troy in upper New York State, listening to Mötley Crüe in my bedroom when I was not belting out "Battle Hymn of the Republic" in the choir of the church my father pastored. My middle name is the only remnant of Indian heritage my devout parents allowed and my last name is the echo of old Catalan settlers in Florida. Nobody in our family has spoken Spanish for generations. But my dark skin and Spanish name often make people think I'm a Latino.

Red on the outside, white on the inside — that's why I take offense when thoughtless and self-absorbed twits like Mary Ellen Garrigan think they know all about me just because I'm a ringer for the Indian on the buffalo head nickel. If I haven't made myself clear, I *hate* being pegged that way. Of course, decent folks do the same thing out of well-meaning ignorance, and if I want to have any friends I've got to cut them some slack. I spend a lot of time gritting my teeth. Here's what I'd tell them if they showed any interest in my history, and sometimes they do.

At eighteen I attended Cornell on an Army ROTC scholarship, then after graduation studied criminal justice at City University of New York, picking up a good deal of street knowledge from the New York Police Department officers who moonlighted as instructors. After a year at CUNY I

served three years as a lieutenant in the military police and
herded Iraqi POWs into Saudi camps in the aftermath of
Desert Storm. Afterward, on an impulse — and who wouldn't
be impulsive after receiving a Dear John letter at the height of
battle from a girlfriend who said she was pregnant? — I took
the first police job that came my way. It was in the absolute
basement of law enforcement — a low-paid rookie deputy in a
backwoods sheriff's department, a position well beneath my
education and capabilities, or so my horrified Army superiors
said. In a short while, realizing that I'd simply engaged in a
silly exercise of dramatic self-laceration, I'd expected to move
on to a city job after a couple of years.

But this beautiful and isolated part of the country, and
the people who live here and keep it that way, slowly wormed
their way into my soul, and I am still here after almost a
decade.

Part of the reason, I'll have to admit, is what I can
describe only as a spiritual call to the blood. The Lakota and
their kin, the Dakota and Nakota, lived in this place hundreds
of years ago, before the more warlike Ojibwa crowding in
from the East under European colonial pressure forced them
out onto the Great Plains. In sentimental moments, when I'm
feeling most Indian, I sometimes imagine that I've come home
to my nation's ancestral hunting grounds. But that doesn't
happen often.

Nor am I much of a hunter, unlike most Yoopers, as the
people who live in the U.P. jocularly call themselves. I'm still
just too much of an Eastern city boy to be attracted to deer or
bear hunting, though both of those pastimes are ways of life,
often necessities of survival, in the Upper Peninsula. Still,
having inherited a heirloom shotgun — a beautifully engraved
12-gauge Browning over-and-under — from my father, who
loved hunting upland birds with dogs, I do go after partridge
and grouse when they're in season. Not that I've had much
success — I'm just not that good a wing shot. But I cherish the

eternal rhythm of the hunt, the careful preparations, the long walks in the fields and woods with dogs, the cool evenings before a roaring fire with a spot of brandy and a dollop of good fellowship. I often think my Lakota forebears felt the same way as they sat around their council fires celebrating after a long day of harvesting buffalo.

There are other attractions. Upper Michiganders, especially those who live in Porcupine County, tend to take care of each other in ways almost unheard of elsewhere. This is a land of high unemployment, the last copper mine having closed a decade ago and the last tall pines having been logged out almost a century before. Slowly younger people have moved elsewhere in search of jobs, leaving behind mostly the elderly and those who scratch livings in whatever way they can, like cutting second-growth pulpwood from the Ottawa National Forest for the paper mill. After its last count the Census Bureau declared Porcupine County a frontier county, meaning its population had fallen to fewer than seven people per square mile. McDonald's, Wal-Mart, and Starbucks have not seen fit to open stores in Porcupine County — that's how thin we're spread.

People up here may lose more and more of their neighbors every year, but that just seems to make them cherish the remaining ones as best they can. Old folks no longer able to get around easily often wake up to a bag of groceries on the doorstep or a fresh cord of split maple in the woodshed. Middle-aged matrons volunteer to watch their young neighbors' kids so Mom and Dad can spend a couple of days camping in the Wolverines, a cheap and popular date hereabouts.

Not that Porkies, as we call ourselves, are angels. We are no less prone to violence and depravity than those who live in the cities, but since there are so few of us, major felonies just don't happen often. Especially during the long and lonely winters, people do get drunk and take pokes at each other in the town bars. So do husbands and wives at

267

home, and since every household in hunting country contains at least one rifle, one shotgun and lots of ammunition, enforcing the peace can get hairy. Fortunately battling couples are almost always too pie-eyed to hold a steady aim, though we cops of course can't count on that. Our motorists are just as aggressive or inattentive as those anywhere else, and they keep us busy writing tickets. Now and then a citizen gets desperate enough to grow marijuana or set up a cat lab to make methcathinone, or poor man's methamphetamine. Much as I despair over the nation's futile and self-lacerating war on drugs, the law's the law, and I'm paid to enforce it.

Porcupine County is nearly all white, descended mostly from the Irish, Cornish and Croatian miners who arrived in the 1840s and 1850s during the copper boom and from the Finnish woodsmen who came here between the 1870s and the early 1900s when the Upper Peninsula shipped millions of board feet of lumber south to rebuild Chicago after the Great Fire. There is a smattering of Jews and Latinos and, according to the last census, exactly three African Americans. So few blacks are seen in these parts at any time of year that Porkies automatically assume they're tourists from the cities. There also are quite a few Indians, mostly casino-rich Ojibwa who have spilled over into Porcupine County from the reservations at Baraga to the east and Lac Vieux Desert to the south.

At first most Porkies thought I was Mexican because of my name, but when they learned I was Lakota shrugged and figured me for just another odd bird who had washed up on the beach and stayed. They sometimes include me in their grousing about the casino Indians — "you all look alike, you know" — but the few instances of outright hostility I have experienced have come more from my job than my biological origins. People everywhere are just uncomfortable around cops. There's a little larceny in everyone, and they just don't want to be reminded of that.

Slowly, however, over the better part of a decade I've come closer and closer to acceptance as a true Porky. And by none prettier than one Virginia Anttila Fitzgerald, the red-headed director and only paid employee of the Porcupine County Historical Society. Ginny is an extraordinarily wealthy woman, thanks to her late husband, an industrialist, but nobody in Porcupine County except me knows that.

We are naturally an item, and not merely a romantic one. Ginny is both lovely and loving, not to mention shapely, and the gravy is that she owns one of those encyclopedic memories that pops out in conversation like a drawer from a card catalog at the library, and it specializes in everything and everyone in Porcupine County. Ginny is blessed with the ability of almost total recall. Having read a document once, she can forever repeat its contents—a handy talent for a historian and a godsend for a boyfriend who is a low-ranking law enforcement officer needing to find out things about people in a hurry. With Ginny's knowledge and moral support, I have occasionally been able to solve the infrequent mystery that crops up in this cold and lonely land where felons are few and far between.

And that is why I found Mary Ellen Garrigan so easy to turn down. Why should I settle for stew on the road when there's sirloin at home?

That's everything about me worth knowing, and what isn't wouldn't fill a thimble.

FOUR

"I know something you don't," Alex chortled.

I heaved a mock sigh into the phone. "Why do you torment me so?"

"Because it's so *easy*."

His call had come while I was at my desk in the squad room of the sheriff's department gathering my monthly reports, seemingly ninety-nine per cent of which had to do with traffic stops, the usual country deputy's main task. Now, I liked my work, but sometimes its stultifying sameness got me to toying with Alex's idea that I should consider applying for a state trooper's job and moving up the ladder of law enforcement. But though I had the credentials, I hadn't the desire.

Alex chuckled. "That stiff on the beach last week? We've made him."

"Yeah?" I said.

"Just enough skin left on his fingertips for good prints. He is—was—a small-time mob muscle out of Chicago and Las Vegas named Danny Impellitteri. Long rap sheet for extortion and battery. One short stretch in Joliet for aggravated assault, but they never were able to get him on anything else. He was pretty slick. The DEA was looking at him as a drug courier but never made a connection. No relations, no family. The *capos* in Chicago and Vegas naturally say they never heard of him. Nobody to claim the body."

"Do tell." This was interesting. "Go on."

"That hole in his chest was made by a thirty-ought-six." A .30-'06 is a common rifle cartridge—just about everybody of hunting age in the Upper Peninsula owns a weapon chambered for that round. "There was no exit hole. That's rare for a powerful round like that, you know."

"Did the examiner find the bullet?"

"Yes." That meant the law very likely would be able to match the bullet to the rifle that fired it, if it ever could be found. But .30-'06s being as common in Upper Michigan as Frenchmen are in Paris, I doubted that anyone would search hard for the weapon.

"The entry hole was not round but oblong, slightly flattened," Alex continued. "Most of Impellitteri's ribs were shattered and one lung was cut up by the slug and contained blood. Both lungs were full of water. What does that tell you, Junior?"

"An oblong entry hole suggests that the bullet glanced off something, perhaps water, tumbled and lost some of its velocity before hitting the subject," I said in as professorial a tone as I could muster. "That and the broken ribs explain why there was no exit wound — the bullet bounced around in there. Water in the lungs means he lived for a while, then drowned. Considering his — ah — trade, first thing I'd think of is a mob hit. Maybe another hoodlum invited him fishing and carried out a contract."

"You know, Steve," Alex said, frank admiration in his voice, "you should have been a *real* policeman."

"Don't start," I said. "How long was Impellitteri in the water?"

"Coroner thinks from eight hours to three days, maybe a little more."

"Where'd he go into the water?"

"Hard to say. Could have been right off Porcupine City, could have been off the Apostles."

That island archipelago lay more than fifty miles west of the point where the body had washed up.

"But the Keweenaw is full of slow eddies, and he could've floated into one and spun around for a while."

The Keweenaw Current runs west to east from the westernmost tip of Lake Superior near Duluth in Minnesota all the way to the tip of the Keweenaw Peninsula, the thumb that juts out into the lake some sixty miles northeast of Porcupine City. The current meanders along in most places at about five miles per hour, but at certain points offshore can reach eleven miles per hour, a pretty good clip.

"What makes it tougher to pinpoint the site, " Alex continued, "is that the fellow's chest and pants had postmortem abrasions and tears that makes the coroner think the body got caught on a snag in the shallows for a while somewhere before rolling back out into deeper water. Could've been anywhere."

The inshore waters of western Lake Superior are full of rocky shoals, toothy underwater escarpments linked to the copper-bearing ridges inland, as well as scores of old shipwrecks and vast sunken rafts of waterlogged hardwood and white pine lost in storms while being towed to the sawmills at Sault Sainte Marie a century ago.

"Anything else?"

A moment of silence at the other end, then a rustling of papers. "Yes. We found a bag of marijuana in his pants pocket. World-class stuff, too — absolutely loaded with delta-9-trans-tetrahydrocannabinol. About 15 per cent by dry weight, almost unheard of."

I whistled. "That's a lot of THC." Tetrahydrocannabinol is what gives pot its pop.

"Probably doesn't mean anything," Alex said, "except that Impellitteri could afford the best of everything."

"Or was peddling the best of everything."

"Yes. There was a fragment of peyote button in his pocket, too."

That was odd. The use of peyote, a mild psychoactive bud from a cactus, is mostly a Southwestern Indian religious custom followed by members of the Native American Church. Most Upper Michigan Ojibwa are either Catholic or follow the traditional Ojibwa religion. I doubted that there was much of a market for peyote in these parts.

"Maybe he'd been in New Mexico, traded a few ounces of pot for a button, wanted to see what it was like," I said.

"Whatever," Alex said. "There's still more."

"What?"

"*Banisteriopsis caapi.*"

I sighed. "You're going to lecture me, aren't you?"

"You need to complete your education, sonny."

"All right. Slide me down the banister-whatsis, willya?"

"Very well. It's a giant woody vine found in the Amazon rain forest. In Ecuador and Peru they call it the 'vine of the dead,' or in their word, *ayahuasca*. When its crushed leaves are combined with those from another plant, usually one called *chacruna*, or *Psychotria viridis*, the result is the brew also called *ayahuasca*. It's like LSD — it sends you to the moon. The natives of the Amazon valley have used it for millennia as a psychotropic drink for healing, divination and black magic. But it's almost unheard of in North America, except among scientists."

"You're reading from a book, aren't you?"

"How did you know?"

"Cop's intuition."

"Yes, well, bits of the vine of the dead were also caught inside the stiff's pocket seams with the pot and peyote."

"That's odd. Wouldn't they have been washed out when the body was rolled around by the waves?"

"Nope. The forensics guys found weeny grains of the stuff caught inside the stitches. These guys can find microscopic evidence in clothes even after several washings. Anyway, what does all this tell you?"

"Maybe this stiff was a well-traveled courier, a middleman who dealt in a whole drugstore of high-quality happy powder for upper-crust users. Maybe he got into a disagreement with a mob supplier over something, say, quality or price, made a threat he shouldn't have, and got wasted."

273

There was a brief silence, then Alex said, "Works for me, too."

"What are you going to do with the case?"

"Put it in the freezer," Alex said.

"What about the Feebs and the DEA?"

"They don't care." I knew that the FBI had enough on its hands hunting al Qaeda, and that the Drug Enforcement Administration had more to do than investigate another dead small-time Midwestern hood, even if he apparently had been in the drug business, unless the known facts promised to lead to big game.

"Let me know if anything turns up at your end, okay?" Alex added.

"Okay," I said. We both knew that the Porcupine County Sheriff's Department, let alone the Michigan state police, was not about to expend money and manpower on a homicide victim nobody cared about, especially a homicide victim on the wrong side of the law. Such legal triage was not justice, true, but it was common sense. We in law enforcement are stretched thin enough. And so Danny Impellitteri would go into the bulging cold case file, eventually to be forgotten.

Still, Alex was reminding me of something: Although the case was officially a state-police problem, and not a very urgent one at that, he was unofficially inviting me to stay involved as a brother officer if new facts came to light. After all, a corpse *had* washed up in my jurisdiction, and I had been the first to catch the case. Alex was quietly performing a professional courtesy, the unspoken kind that comes from mutual trust and respect.

"But," I said.

Alex's voice perked up. "But?"

"Assuming I'm right and this was a mob hit," I said, "what would a Chicago or Vegas hood be doing aboard a boat in Lake Superior? It's more than seven hundred miles from Chicago up Lake Michigan to the Soo and then out here."

"Flies don't grow on you," Alex said.

"You've checked already."

"The Chicago mob squad says only a couple of hoods own boats big enough to make the trip, and they haven't left harbor for weeks."

I sat silent for a while, contemplating.

"You still there?" Alex said.

"Yes."

"What's on your mind?"

"Doesn't seem that there would be a reason for mob activity way up here in the middle of nowhere," I said. "Nothing to extort. Nothing to steal. The only thing I can think of is it's drug related, especially with that stuff in the stiff's pocket, but that's so unlikely. Especially now."

Upper Michigan, with its long and sparsely inhabited Lake Superior shore, was a hotbed of smuggling during Prohibition, when Canadian rumrunners raced cases of gin and Scotch across the lake in powerful Chris-Crafts from Port Arthur and Fort William under cover of darkness. Lately there has been drug-running from the same places, but much less than a short time ago. Ever since the al Qaeda attacks in 2001, Air Force eyes-in-the-sky have constantly patrolled the Canadian border, watching for unauthorized flights from the north. No longer is Washington Island, just west of Isle Royale in the northern stretches of Lake Superior, a favorite drop zone for small planes carrying loads of marijuana and cocaine to be transferred to pleasure boats and carried to inlets on the U.S. side.

Lately dope smugglers had been stowing their stuff in the noisome cargo of garbage trucks carrying Canadian waste over the border at Sault Sainte Marie to landfills in Upper Michigan. The hazmat scanners and drug-sniffing dogs at Customs can't detect such contraband amid the smelly garbage. Only poking about by hand worked, and the Customs people had to limit their searches to random checks. Lots of cocaine and other hard stuff got through that way, but the politicians south of the border were now demanding that the Canadian authorities check the loads themselves and guarantee their cleanliness.

"Yeah," Alex said. "No point in keeping this case active, is there?"

"Right. Now would you mind going away? I've got paperwork to do."

"Didn't know shitkicker deputies knew how to read and write."

"Screw you," I said, but I couldn't help laughing.

FIVE

That reminded me. I'd forgotten to drop by Silverton to check out the *Mary-El* and see if her skipper, Tom Whiteside, had seen anything while fishing on the morning the corpse of Dan Impellitteri had washed up on the beach. It wasn't important, just a loose end to nail down for the files, really a useless bit of work considering the item would likely be forgotten in the cold case drawer, but I was grateful for any excuse to leave my desk behind on a warm sunny day. Grabbing my garrison cap, I checked out on the board and headed in the department's Explorer thirteen miles west to the small settlement at Silverton.

Silverton is an old mining town named for an undiscovered lode of silver whose existence was suggested only by metal flakes that had drifted down the Iron River during the middle of the nineteenth century. The town consists mostly of a large chain motel with a restaurant — George's, of course — a general store with gas pumps, a bunch of tiny gift shops that cater mostly to summer campers and winter skiers and snowmobilers, and a warren of dented secondhand mobile homes intermixed with small, old miner's houses. Most everybody who lives there just scrapes by. Many of them are former miners at the old Lone Pine copper mine and smelter several miles south.

Tom berths the *Mary-El* at a dock at the mouth of the Iron River, one of the few waterways for hundreds of miles along the Lake Superior shore that doesn't turn into an impassable sandbar after the spring runoff. Even so, the mouth is so shallow that at times of lowest water the good people of Silverton often laid bets on whether the *Mary-El* would ground on the shifting sandbar going out or coming in, requiring Tom to winch her off with a stout steel cable

277

fastened to an onshore oak.

The *Mary-El* was in, and as I strode down the rickety planks of Tom's dock I saw that her big diesel engine lay in pieces next to the boat, its crankcase split open to reveal the innards. Tom lay snoozing in a deck chair, soaking up the sun, but stirred as he heard my tread on the boards.

"Steve!" he called. "What can I do for you?"

"If you guarantee that I'll catch a thirty-pound coho today, I'll hire the *Mary-El*," I said. I'd had pretty good luck aboard her a couple of times in the past, going out for lake trout on county-sponsored outings in the days not so long ago when the county could afford such treats for its workers.

"Sit down, Steve," Tom said. pointing to a ragged deck chair across the dock from his. I sat.

"I can't guarantee you'll catch a thirty-gram minnow," Tom said, "not with that Cummins in the shape she's in." He pointed a wrench at the engine.

"What's wrong?"

"Cracked the crankshaft a couple of weeks ago," he said. "Do you have any idea how goddam long it takes to get a new one? And how much the bastards cost?" This, I knew, would make the difference between black ink and red on Tom's meager balance sheet for the year.

I sighed. "That's tough, Tom," I said. "And not much time, is there?" No matter if his boat returned to the lake by the following week, he couldn't make up the time he had lost. The Lake Superior sportfishing season is short. The tourists don't arrive until after Memorial Day and are mostly gone by Labor Day, except for folks who prefer the quiet silence of the cool early fall in these parts. By the end of October, the autumn storms would begin, locking the *Mary-El* in her berth for the winter.

"You said the engine broke down two weeks ago?"

"That's right."

That was a week before the hoodlum's corpse had

washed ashore.

"You weren't out on the lake a week ago Saturday?"

"In what?"

"The guy who found that body on the beach last week said he'd seen the *Mary-El*, or maybe a boat that looked like her, just offshore the morning that body washed up on the beach. Thought you might've seen something." I didn't need to remind Tom about that day. Everyone in Porcupine City had heard about the corpse and the prevailing theory that it had been a mob hit.

"Sure wasn't the *Mary-El* out there," Tom said, reaching into a grimy file folder and pulling out a copy of a fax from a Milwaukee marine dealer acknowledging a similar communication from the Lumbermen's State Bank of Porcupine County, which kept a fax machine for its customers. The original fax was an order for a new crankshaft, and the reply was stamped with a date five days before the body had washed onshore.

"You're not a suspect in anything, Tom," I said, but I was glad for the proof anyway. Eliminated a possible lead.

"Might as well be one," he said wearily. "Don't have nothing else to do anyway."

"Okay, if we can't find a better perp, we'll let you know so you can apply for the job."

"I could use one," he said.

"Yeah." Off season, Tom kept himself housed, fed and clothed by repairing snowmobiles at the Polaris dealer in Porcupine City. But it would be another two months before enough snow had fallen for steady work there.

"You'll make out," I said. "You always do." I twirled my cap and rose to leave. "But what boat could that witness have seen that morning?"

"Don't know," Tom said, rubbing his stubble. "The *Mary-El*'s the biggest party boat in these parts. Maybe your witness saw another boat with the same shape." The *Mary-El*'s profile was distinctive, with a high flying bridge set closer to the stern than most, lake trout rods stuck vertically into holders at her fantail.

"What could that be?"

"The *Lucky Six* out of Porcupine City is one," he said. "But she's a private forty-footer that belongs to Morrie Weinstein and he says she's been in Lakes Huron and Michigan all summer on charter."

"Um." I knew Weinstein. He was a transplant like me, a wealthy entrepreneur from Chicago, scion of an old Upper Peninsula mining family, who in the last few years invested in all sorts of startup outfits in the area, the *Porcupine County Herald* front-paging every one of them. For a long time, as far as I knew, few if any of his efforts paid dividends, except for one. Three years ago he had opened up an old copper mine that had been in his mother's family for generations and turned it into an underground nursery, raising high-quality flowers and seedlings as well as experimental plants for the pharmaceutical industry. Slowly the enterprise had expanded, and now he employed thirty-odd Porkies and a dozen horticultural specialists from Chicago in two shifts. Everyone considered Weinstein a godsend to the county. Another year or two, and he would be its second biggest employer after the paper mill on the river across from Porcupine City.

I didn't know his motives, but it was not unheard of for independently wealthy people who had fallen in love with Porcupine County to invest in it and its people for reasons other than raw profit. I slept with one of them.

"Who knows?" Tom said. "That boat could have been from anywhere, come inshore that morning in hopes the trout were maybe running in the shallows."

"Could be," I said, "but it's probably not important."

Nevertheless, I jotted a few lines in my pocket notebook. You never can tell.

On my way back to the Explorer I spotted Olga Wennerstrom standing in the doorway of her single-wide across from Tom's dock. I hoped she hadn't seen me, but she had, and I quailed. Olga is an overimaginative old lady who, like so many aged and lonely folks, shows little self-restraint in her conversation and never misses a chance to express herself. To hear her talk, Silverton is a reeking Sodom of crime and sin, and it all washes up the Iron River from Lake Superior. I had no doubt that over the decades Silverton had seen its share of rumrunners and drug couriers from across the water, but today there were easier ways of making a nefarious living. There are a lot of Olgas in Porcupine County, and they are largely harmless, although Olga's habit of writing garrulous, mean-spirited and meandering letters to the editor of the Herald—letters that were printed verbatim, complete with unsubtle remarks about "the homosexuals" and "the colored"—caused me to avoid her when I could. Being a member of a minority group makes me sensitive about the slights others must suffer, and sometimes I can't watch my tongue. I often had to bite it, because in rural America the letters columns in country weeklies often are the only free outlet for citizens to sound off, other than on radio rant shows, where words disappear into the air as soon as they are uttered. Readers often turn to the letters columns as soon as their newspapers arrive in their mailboxes so they can find out who's pissed off this week, often by a letter or two in the previous week's edition. In the countryside the letters-to-the-editor page is the nearest thing people have to a legal dogfight, complete with blood and snarls. Letters columns sell newspapers, too. "They're better than Fox News," Alex once said, "for the crackpots." Alex is a liberal, a rarity among cops, city or country.

"Deputy!" she called. "Steve! Martinez!" I sighed, squared my shoulders, and strode to Olga's trailer.

"Yes'm?"

"You're too late!" she said, her voice ringing with accusation.

"Too late for what?"

"The white slavers!"

"The white slavers?" That was a new one.

"They landed last night, at that very dock there, and they brought in prostitutes, a lot of 'em," she sputtered.

"Who's they, ma'am?" I asked politely, turning to a fresh sheet in my notebook.

"You know, those people. The ones who come in every other day bringing all sorts of evil to good Christians."

"Right, those people," I said, jotting an imaginary note. "Where did they take the, uh, ladies of the night?"

She pointed across the road to Moriarty's, a tumbledown tavern whose closest brush with evil came with the penny-ante poker half a dozen wrinkled retirees played every afternoon. In the course of police work, aiming of course to dredge up possibly important information on slow crime days, I'd sat in on a couple of games—and hadn't arrested the players when they cleaned my pockets of loose change, chortling at having put one over on the law.

"I'll check 'em out," I said. "Thanks for the heads-up."

"Steve!" she called before I'd gone ten yards. "If there's a reward, I want it!"

"Sure thing, Olga."

Tom was standing by his pickup, the vehicle cheek by jowl with the Explorer. "Olga go on about hookers?" he said with a broad grin.

"Uh huh."

"Warm day yesterday, and there were tourists in bikini tops. Some of those tops weren't very big." He rolled his eyes in mock horror.

"Uh huh."

"Moriarty's could use some new scenery."

"I'll say."

SIX

The second corpse turned up in the middle of July, and this time it was not on the beach but deep in the second-growth forest in the southern reaches of Porcupine County. I was wrestling paperwork in the office when the radio call came in from Joe Koski.

"Chad just called," said Joe. Large, rawboned, good-looking, and amiable, young Chad Garrow was the deputy on shift in the southern and eastern half of the county. I liked him although I sometimes couldn't stand him. Chad is a clumsy sprawl of a lad, all knees and elbows, unkempt red hair and loose shirttails, the kind who unconsciously bulls into your personal space even if he may be standing six feet away. Women steer him away from antique chairs and gently take dishes out of his hands so he won't break them. Whenever we go out together in a sheriff's cruiser, Chad drives and I sit in the back seat — it's safer that way.

Chad is the newest hire in the department, and the nephew of Sheriff Eli Garrow. This wasn't quite a case of out-and-out nepotism, although it came close. Chad had been the only Porcupine County resident who applied for the deputy's job when it fell open the previous Christmas season, thanks to the arrest and conviction of its former occupant in a celebrated revenge killing. There had been smarter and more experienced applicants from outside, but Porcupine County prefers to hire its own when possible. Chad had just barely qualified in the other requirements, and as a green deputy he sometimes did not seem the sharpest axe in the woodshed.

We could have done worse. Chad, whose heart always occupied the right place even if his head didn't, tried hard to follow instructions. In his six months in the department, he had not embarrassed us. That gave Eli Garrow a lot of good-old-boy pride even though it caused the rest of us to shrug. When I was partnered with Chad on the same shift, as I was now, I tried, as we all did, to teach him the finer points of police work. The lad always put forth his best efforts, although there were times I wondered if he'd survive his year's probation.

"Body in the woods out back of Coppermass," Joe said. "Looks like it might be Saarinen."

"Out back of Coppermass" is a tangled wilderness where over the decades many people had disappeared without trace, so many that the locals called it "the Yooper Triangle." Frank Saarinen had gone deer hunting there one frigid weekend the previous November and never returned to his wife and four small children, who he had long supported, as so many Porkies did, by scratching out meager odd jobs. Saarinen was a familiar hard-luck case. He was a diligent worker skilled at many trades, but his drinking had cost him good jobs, one at the old Lone Pine Mine, the last Upper Peninsula copper mine to close, and another at the paper mill. Recently he had sobered up enough for Morris Weinstein to take a chance on him and put him to work at the nursery buried deep in the Venture Mine.

Saarinen's disappearance was not an uncommon occurrence in the northern wilderness. Hunters and hikers, even those native to the county, sometimes get lost, suffer heart attacks, and shoot themselves or each other by accident or by design, usually suicide. When bad things happen we find most of the bodies, but now and then one never turns up — or turns up only long afterward. The forest is large, deep, and thick. I had spent three days in the department's battered old Cessna four-seater, exercising the pilot's license I earned in the Army and hunting for Saarinen. I hoped he had found a clearing and possessed the mother-wit to build a smoky fire and wait for rescue. I didn't complain at the assignment. Searching by air is infinitely more pleasant than pounding the ground through snow and bitter cold.

"Here's the Saarinen file, Steve," Joe said. He didn't have to tell me to get going—I was already on my way out the door to the Explorer. Among other things, the file would inform me what Saarinen's wife, Sally, had said he was wearing when he disappeared, helping in the identification of skeletal remains.

Forty minutes later I pulled up behind Chad's cruiser, an ordinary Ford sedan the local dealer had converted into a poor man's police car, on a gravel track four miles off State Highway M-26 and set off into the woods. Chad had called in the coordinates from his hand-held GPS, these days a standard item on a wilderness deputy's equipment belt, but it was easy enough to follow the old deer trail into the forest. I knew exactly where the scene was—on the edge of a cut-over meadow in old mining country, part of the Ottawa National Forest. In fifteen minutes I joined Chad and Tommy Goodkind, the veteran woodsman who had stumbled over the corpse while foraging for downed hickory to cut up for pulpwood to sell to the paper mill.

"No wonder we never found him last year," Chad said unnecessarily. The body lay nearly hidden by the boughs of a fat blue spruce Terry had brushed aside while shouldering his way through a thicket.

"I stopped when I heard the rattle of bones," Terry said, "and there he was."

I squatted and held aside a spruce branch. The body lay face down in matted leaves and spruce needles, almost completely skeletal. Even though the leaves concealed most of it, I could tell that the skull had been shattered. The stock of a rifle protruded from under the body.

"Stop fucking up my crime scene," a familiar voice cut in as a lanky shadow loomed in the sunlight on the spruce. I jumped slightly. For all his love of noisy arrivals, Alex Kolehmainen, a veteran woodsman, knows how to sneak soundlessly through the forest. He'd make a better woodland

Indian than I would.

"Who says it's a crime scene?" I asked mildly as Alex took a pair of latex gloves from his kit bag. I fished a pair from my shirt pocket and handed an extra set to Chad, motioning to him to put them on. It was probably the first time he had ever needed them, and he had not thought to carry a pair with him. I sighed, but I also knew it wouldn't happen again. You had to show Chad only once—thank goodness for that.

"It's always a crime scene until I say it's not," Alex said. "Can't you get that through your thick heads?"

Chad and I grinned at each other.

"Up yours, Sergeant," Chad said affably. Even though he was still a rookie, he had already learned that Alex's fierceness was entirely theatrical.

"There'll be time for that later," said Alex just as amiably. "Let's get to work."

Enough remained of the clothing on the skeleton to match it with what Sally had said her husband was wearing the day he had disappeared. "Green canvas jacket," I said, riffling through the file. "Orange-and-black Pendleton wool shirt. Green cord trousers. Teeth ought to clinch it."

"Maybe not necessary," Alex said as he carefully fished a wallet from the wretched little pile of bones and rags with large tweezers. With latex-gloved hands he opened it. "Driver's license. Frank Saarinen, all right. Hunting license, too. The usual stuff, all in his name. Thirty bucks in tens. Here's a wooden cross, too."

The hand-carved hickory cross, inlaid with copper, matched the list in the folder.

Before touching anything else Alex photographed the scene from all angles with his digital camera, as always taking pains not to disturb the corpse. Macabre his task may have been, but I always admired the professionalism he brought to every case. Fifteen minutes later, satisfied with the prints, he squatted for a closer look. He brushed the leaves from the skull.

"See the hole?" he said, shining a penlight on a clean, slightly puckered indentation on the right temple. The left temple — indeed, most of the skull on that side — was missing, the edges of the bone rough and shattered. Alex reached for the camera.

"Bullet?" said Chad, grasping the obvious.

"Yup," said Alex, who did not suffer fools but showed patience with greenhorns. "Let's turn him over."

That was easier said than done. Bone by bone, sleeve by sleeve, Alex rearranged the skeleton on its back, constantly dictating what he saw into a small tape recorder in his pocket, microphone clipped to his collar.

"Right foot missing. Left ulna missing. Most of left arm gone."

Scavenging animals and birds had carried away parts of the corpse. Bodies discovered in forests are rarely ever complete.

"Where do you suppose the bullet went?" Chad asked.

"Probably hundreds of yards away," Alex said. "If this was a high-velocity deer round, as I suspect it was, it would just have kept going."

We contemplated the corpse for a while.

"One of three things happened here," Alex said presently. "An accident, suicide, or murder." His conclusion, painfully obvious to me, was meant for Chad, although addressed to us both. Consciously or unconsciously Alex was a born teacher, and all the cops and deputies who worked with him benefited from his subtle mentoring. "I don't think he shot himself accidentally."

"Why?" Chad said. He was paying attention.

"Look," said Alex, standing up.

Frank Saarinen — if the body indeed was his, and there was no reason to think it wasn't — had fallen over his rifle. That was clear from the original arrangement of the bones and scraps of clothing.

Alex picked up a stout branch four feet long and pointed it at his right temple, extending his right arm so that his finger rested on an imaginary trigger in the middle of the stick. "If you shot yourself this way," he said, "the recoil would catapult the rifle away from you and the impact of the bullet would drive you in the other direction."

Alex abruptly tossed the branch aside and lurched sidelong, well away from the spruce.

"See? It's unlikely that happened here. Besides, people who commit suicide with rifles almost always shoot themselves in the mouth, often with their toes on the trigger. That's easier than any other method. It shortens the distance between the head and the trigger."

I riffled through the file. "Nothing here that makes me think Frank was despondent," I said. "No obvious reason for suicide. Besides, he had a brand new deer license. You don't need one of those to kill yourself."

Alex nodded and looked at Chad, who was absorbing it all.

Alex picked up the rifle. A year's worth of rust had crept over the blued steel of the Remington .270 and its four-power scope. It had been an expensive rig, especially for a man like Frank, but like so many poor but proud Porkies he had spared no expense on the tools that kept his family alive. Frank, I felt sure, had fed his wife and children with lots of venison, both in season and out.

"This was a valuable rifle," said Alex. "If this had been a murder, the killer most likely would have taken it and Frank's wallet as well."

"Nothing in the file to suggest anybody had it in for Frank," I said. "No orange, either."

Frank had not worn a fluorescent orange vest or hat, as do most sensible, safety-minded hunters, to keep others from mistaking them for game. It's the law in Michigan. Deer are color blind, but some hunters won't take that for granted, and refuse to wear orange. Some don't want to be seen in the woods, perhaps because they're poaching, perhaps because they don't want other hunters to discover their favorite spots, and perhaps because they just don't want the government to tell them what to do. Porkies tend to be fiercely libertarian. They mistrust official bodies of all kinds, especially the Michigan Department of Natural Resources, whose statewide one-size-fits-all policies they consider unsuited to the special needs of dwellers in the remote wilderness, most especially Porcupine County. I was sympathetic. I knew how bureaucracies work, being a member of one myself.

"All right," Alex said. Holding the rifle in front of him, butt against his shoulder and muzzle pointed forward ahead, he took up position by the tree and peered ahead between boughs. "Frank is waiting at the ready for a deer to come by on the trail. Another hunter over here" — Alex pointed to the right across the clearing — "sees Frank's shape against the tree and thinks he's a deer. Bang! Frank's head explodes and he falls forward into the tree with his rifle in front of him.

"The other hunter sees his target fall, runs over, and discovers it isn't a deer. He panics and clears out as fast as he can. A lot of people would. Think about it. Thousands of hunters in Upper Michigan every November and we have no idea where most of them go. The bullet's away in the woods somewhere, and so are lots of other bullets hunters have fired over a hundred years. He didn't mean to kill Frank, but it'll be a terrible mess for him if he calls the cops. It's easier just to run away. 'Course, sooner or later it'll hit him that he killed a human being, maybe one with a wife and family, and he'll have to live with that the rest of his life.

"And it's entirely possible that didn't happen. Deer hunters don't aim for the head. That'd ruin the trophy. They aim for the heart. Maybe the shooter had no idea that he had hit anything and never came over to find out. And of course that bullet could have been just a stray. It happens."

There was nothing more to do except search the area

for a few yards around the tree. Chad turned up two large skull fragments, and Alex found a human finger bone an animal had carried away to gnaw upon. There was no point in hunting for more. We had enough for a burial, anyway.

"We're done here," Alex said after half an hour. "Let's bag the remains. Not enough left for the medical examiner to work on. I'll send them to forensics in Marquette for confirmation. For now it's a hunting accident."

Chad, Terry and I helped carry what remained of Frank Saarinen in a body bag to Alex's cruiser. The bag felt remarkably light.

"Be good, girls," Alex said as he drove away.

I raised Joe Koski on the radio. "It's who we thought, all right," I told him discreetly.

"Steve, stop by the next of kin," the undersheriff cut in. I hate that assignment. None of us like being the bearers of bad news. But it has to be done. I hurried so I could get there before Sally Saarinen heard it on the grapevine. No one should have to learn about the death of a loved one that way.

SEVEN

Sally Saarinen was just thirty-eight years old, but she looked fifty. Like so many single mothers who teeter on the edge of destitution in Upper Michigan, she had suffered from years of just getting by. She had once been an attractive woman, but now her puffy features—and those of her four children, ranging in age from six to fifteen—bespoke the usual fat-loaded, carb-heavy diet of rural food-stamp poverty, mostly day-old bread, a little hamburger and a lot of venison. Their clothes, faded and threadbare, came from the fifty-cent racks at St. Vincent De Paul's, the big charity store the Catholic church operated in downtown Porcupine City.

But the shirts and pants were clean and mended, the shoes freshly resoled. Sally, I knew, scraped up enough money each year to pay the minuscule property taxes on her battered single-wide mobile home and the half acre on which it sat at the edge of the woods on Quarterline Road, eight miles outside Porcupine City. The broad yard around the trailer was carefully swept, the grass trimmed right up to the concrete blocks bearing the junked '79 Ford pickup and '83 Chevy sedan in the back. Only two of the four cars Frank had been stripping for their parts to sell before his disappearance remained. Sally, who knew her way around vehicles—she had been a transcontinental eighteen-wheeler driver when she met Frank—had expertly completed the scavenging, and only the frame of the pickup and rusty shell of the sedan remained. She did what she could to survive. And she kept up appearances. That allowed her retain her pride. Often that was all some Porkies owned, but their neighbors respected them for it.

Sally was out hanging up the wash on a limp cotton clothesline strung between the trailer and a stout oak branch a few yards away, and when I got out of the Explorer she calmly finished pegging a child's jersey to the line before she turned to me, her face set in resignation.

"It's Frank, isn't it?" she said.

"Yes. We found his body this morning in the woods south of Coppermass. Looks like a hunting accident."

She took a deep breath, but her careworn face remained carved in stone, the crow's feet around her eyes deepening but remaining dry. "You'd better come in," she said.

Two children, four and ten years old by the look of them, stood in the doorway. "Take Janie out back to the sandbox, won't you?" Sally said to the older one, and the two skipped down the steps and scooted gaily around the back of the trailer. I was glad they were too young to suspect the reason I had come to their home.

"Okay," said Sally as she sat on a lumpy couch in the tiny living space, I in an equally ratty overstuffed chair. "What did you find?"

I was honest but terse, editing out unnecessary details. "We can identify him by his teeth, of course," I said.

"He never went to a dentist in his life," Sally said. That was unsurprising. Poor rural people often never get physicals or dental care, unless they spend some time in the military or in jail.

"Then at some point we'll need you to come down to identify the clothes. There's a carved wooden cross, too."

She nodded.

"While we're pretty sure it was an accident," I added, "I still have to ask some routine questions. I can come back later if you'd rather."

"No. Let's get it done now."

Over the next twenty minutes I took Sally through the contents of the folder, step by step, reviewing what she had told us a year ago. Her answers remained the same. That impressed me. Memory being chancy at best and unreliable at worst, details change over time. A red sweater becomes a blue one. Brass belt buckles turn into steel. Loafers transmogrify into tennis shoes. Some cops, not understanding these common quirks of the mind, become suspicious that their interviewees are deliberately changing their original stories, and the interviewees wind up as suspects themselves. A lot of time gets wasted sorting out memories and facts. But Sally Saarinen changed nothing. Every detail remained the same.

"I'm sorry, but I've got to ask some personal questions," I said. I hated this part of the interview, especially with people like Sally. They have so little except their privacy. To take that away from them is to strip them of their final belongings. But there was no choice.

Sally shrugged. "Yes?"

"Was everything okay between you and Frank?"

"Yes. When he joined AA almost two years ago, we stopped fighting all the time. We got along pretty good. He was good to the kids. He had a steady paycheck. He came home every night instead of going out to a bar."

"Frank didn't seem depressed or unhappy, did he?"

"Nope. That man loved life. When he drank he often was down and when he sobered up he said he was no good. But he'd been sober for quite a while. He loved that job in the mine growing flowers and plants. He told me they were the first beautiful things ever to come from his hands."

"Then I guess there wasn't anything wrong at work?"

"No," she said, and after a beat, added, "Well . . ."

"Yes?"

"I didn't really think about it at the time. Frank was never one to bring worries home from work. But I think something was bothering him there."

"What could that have been?"

"I don't know. But a couple of weeks before he disappeared in the woods, he said he didn't want to go to the company picnic. I talked him into it, 'cause the kids don't get much chance to go out and have a good time — it's too expensive to go anywhere. We did go, but he didn't want to talk to anybody and played with the kids instead. When I asked afterward, he said nothing was wrong and to forget it."

I waited, but she had nothing to add.

"Probably doesn't mean anything," I said. I suspected it did, but I doubted that she knew why.

"Not anymore, anyway," she said.

I stood up. "Thank you, Mrs. Saarinen," I said. I knew her familiarly as "Sally" — I'm on first-name terms with most law-abiding people in the county — but this was a formal and sober occasion. Now I had to finish the formal and sober questions. "In a week or so we'll release Frank's remains. Do you have a preference for the funeral home?"

"I don't know," she said. "We can't afford one."

"I think something will be done about that." The Evangelical Lutheran church to which the Saarinens belonged most likely would come to the rescue. Devout churchgoers up here are loath to let their brethren depart this world in potter's fields. When accidents happened to the poor, religious charity took care of most of them. There was a lot of that in the Upper Peninsula, for the impulse to do God's work helped hold together the dwindling population.

"Yes. Thank you." Her expression remained calm.

I walked out to the Explorer.

"Deputy." She usually called me Steve.

"Yes?"

"There's one more thing I just remembered."

I waited.

"About a week before Frank disappeared, he held me close in bed and made me promise to take care of the children if anything happened to him."

I stared at her.

"I'm sorry, Deputy," she said. "I didn't think anything of it at the time. I thought he was just having a fight staying sober and had to unload his worries. But now . . ."

I examined her strained face carefully. She was not dissembling. This was not a last-minute panic attack, a clumsy attempt to forestall accusations of concealing evidence. To her this was truly a revelation that had come only with the passage of time and the jogging of memory. Whether it was significant or not was anybody's guess. I made a guess, anyway.

"It's all right," I said. "Knowing that wouldn't have helped us find him, anyway."

"It was an accident, wasn't it?" she said, her cheeks beginning to tremble from the effort of keeping a brave face.

I nodded. "So far as we can tell, it was. Thank you, Mrs. Saarinen."

She closed her door.

Just as I started the Explorer, I heard sobs start up in the trailer. They were deep and ragged, the letting-go kind.

EIGHT

I was in bed with the brains of the outfit when I told her what I had been doing at work that day. For reasons I have never quite been able to divine, our skull sessions often take place after what she archly calls "physical therapy on the fitness bench," her term for happy activities under the coverlet of the oaken four-poster on the second floor of her roomy, exquisitely furnished log house on the shore a few miles east of my snug cabin. With my finger I traced an imaginary line through the perspiration covering the ample curves of Virginia Anttila Fitzgerald's person, fine and firm in its early forties. Still panting lightly, as I was, she let the finger advance on its objective for several inches before she giggled and slapped it.

"So what's the trouble?" she asked. "Sally Saarinen is made of hickory and steel, and if any poor single mother's going to manage to raise her children well, she's one of them. I'm sorry about Frank, I really am, and those children do need a father, but things could be a lot worse for them."

"Yeah. But it was what she said about Frank maybe having trouble at work that makes me wonder."

"What's that got to do with the accident? It's fairly obvious that's what it was. Besides, Steve, everybody has difficulties at work at one time or another. That doesn't necessarily lead to murder."

"Who mentioned murder?" I demanded.

She sighed. "I know how your mind works. You get a pebble in your shoe and it grates on your instep all day. Suddenly it becomes a boulder on your brain. One cross word from somebody's boss in the morning and by midafternoon it's a motive for homicide."

"But what about Frank asking Sally to promise to take

care of the kids if anything happened to him?"

"You've never been a father, Steve," she said. "Every man, in the wee dark hours when scary molehills grow into terrifying mountains, worries about his family's future. Frank probably woke up from a bad dream and looked to Sally for comfort. You've done that more than once yourself."

"All right, all right, ma'am," I said. "You have me there." I began to retrace the alpine route my finger had traveled.

"That tickles. Stop it." She made no move to halt my progress. I stopped anyway.

"But I'm curious," I said.

"Don't stop," she said. "About what?"

"Frank's boss, Morrie Weinstein. Now that we mention it, I don't know anything about him, other than that he lived in Chicago, spent his summers here as a kid, came back a few years ago, tried his hand at a few things and finally opened up that nursery in the old Venture Mine. What do you know about it, Ginny?"

She lifted herself up onto one elbow and turned to me, the sheet dropping from her body. I closed my eyes, hoping to retain on their dark backdrop as long as possible the delicious image of her hip's graceful curve and the shadow beneath.

"Is that a rhetorical question or a serious one?" she asked.

"A serious one." Suddenly the languorous spell broke.

"All right." She sat up and hugged her knees. I could almost hear locks clicking open and drawers sliding out.

"Now then. Weinstein's mother, Edna, was the daughter of Gordon Holderman, the last magnate to operate the Venture Mine. Actually, 'magnate' is too splendid a word for Holderman. By the time he bought the mine from its owners in New York City sometime in the 1920s, it was moribund. Not even the demand for copper to make shells and rifle cartridges during the First World War could bring it back from the dead. There was still copper down there—there still is all over the Keweenaw Range—but it's just not economical to bring up, compared with the ore in those huge open-pit mines in the Southwest."

As Upper Michigan copper mines went, the Venture, founded in 1849 by a consortium of Manhattan investors, was a small one, but bigger than most mining enterprises, which tended to peter out when digging failed to uncover either rich seams of ore or mass copper, almost pure metal scattered in boulder-size chunks throughout the ridges of the Keweenaw.

"The Venture had a single vertical shaft about twelve hundred feet deep, with one skip that served seven drifts."

"Skips? Drifts?"

"A skip is the elevator car that's lifted up and down a mine shaft. A drift is a horizontal tunnel driven into the ore from the vertical shaft. Sometimes several drifts branched out from a single level. Sometimes a drift expanded from a low tunnel into a huge room. It all depended on what the miners found."

"Ah. Go on."

The old Venture owned a stamp mill for crushing ore hoisted up from the drifts where it was carved from the rock, often with the help of explosives, but it had no smelter. Once crushed, the ore was packed into barrels to be drawn by horses to the docks at Porcupine City for shipment by schooner to smelters in lower Michigan. Later in the century it was trundled to a horse-drawn tram line that served several mines along the Keweenaw Range and ended at the bigger and much richer Minesota Mine at Rockland, twelve miles east of the Venture. At the Minesota—that's one *n*, by the way—the ore was smelted and loaded into hopper cars to be hauled by locomotives to the harbor at Porcupine City for transshipment to the Soo and points east. Not Minnesota. Minesota. I wanted to know why there was only one *n*, but I wasn't about to deflect Ginny's head of steam.

"Profits at the Venture were always modest, even

during the wartime booms of 1861 to 1865, 1898 and 1914 to 1918, when the demand for copper wire and shell casings was high, and to protect their investors during the lean decades the owners converted the property to a tribute mine. That means the miners were given no wages but themselves sold the ore they mined and paid the owners one-eighth of their proceeds in tribute. Nobody got rich, but everybody could keep their heads above water that way."

What's more, Ginny said, tribute mining wasn't terribly good for either the mines or the miners. The miners worked only the best rock, shoving the poorer ore aside under the ground — a practice the industry called "gophering" or "mine robbing." They also skipped a lot of safety measures, such as stout timbering of the drift ceilings, endangering themselves. Many tribute miners perished in cave-ins deep underground.

"By the stock market crash in 1929 the mine was all but played out. The owners had sold off the stamp mill machinery, and most of the other equipment — except the steam-driven shaft hoist — when Holderman bought the property for a song. He had been the manager since 1907, running two decades of tribute mining even after the scandalous deaths of several miners under his supervision. At first it seemed that he intended to expand the mine's operations — it was rumored briefly that a large mass of pure copper had been discovered deep at the end of the lowest drift — but he could not find investors. After the Second World War he turned the mine into an operating museum, taking skiploads of tourists down two or three levels. By 1955, however, the tourists had lost interest, so Holderman closed the museum and shuttered the mine. He died a year later at age ninety."

The mine stayed in the family, passing down to Edna Holderman, Gordon's only child. She had married a well-connected Chicago Cadillac dealer, and upon her death, her only son, Morris Weinstein, inherited the deserted property from his mother. Weinstein, who had also been handed down a pile from his father, had founded and sold a string of small businesses in Chicago, then invested the proceeds in a number of Internet start-ups. Presciently he had pulled his considerable fortune out of the stock market just before the technological bubble burst.

"He seems to be the kind of man who in a small way can often spot a sure thing," Ginny said, "and capitalize on it, like Warren Buffett."

A Canadian mining company's promising experiment with growing pharmaceutical plants deep inside the Lone Pine Mine, just south of Silverton and fourteen miles west of the Venture, had piqued Weinstein's interest. Surely, he announced, he could use the Venture to produce high-quality seedlings and flowers for the suburban Chicago market as well as his own pharmaceutical plants for university experimenters, and by the turn of the twenty-first century the Venture Underground Agricultural Company had become a going concern. Every week, summer and winter, an eighteen-wheeler or two pulled out of the Venture property carrying sturdy young plants to the south.

"The mine now employs twenty full-time nursery workers and about the same number of part-timers," Ginny said. "Weinstein has been a lifesaver for Porcupine County."

"How did you know all that?" I said. I am still amazed by the things she comes up with. I sometimes think our relationship is like sharing a bed with a human database. At times that can be very helpful in my profession.

"It's my job, dummy."

I pinched her. She slapped my hand. But not hard.

"Did you know that I love you for your mind, not your body?"

"Do you expect me to believe that?"

"Not really."

"Then show me."

I did.

NINE

"We're ready to call the Saarinen case an accident," Alex said, sneezing into the phone and hurting my ear.

"God bless," I replied. "Yeah, but there's one more thing I have to do before we close it," I said. "I ought to go say hi to Morrie Weinstein and ask the routine questions about Saarinen's work record."

"You do that. It'll give you rare practice in good law-enforcement techniques."

"Screw you," I said, and put the phone down. I dialed headquarters and told Jerry Koski where I was going and why.

"Wrapping up the details," I said.

"Cool," Jerry said.

Gil did not bother to add the usual vexed grunt from his cubicle.

I drove out of town and then south on Norwich Road, a paved but potholed track that led twenty-four miles south to the hamlet of Matchwood. At the fifteenth mile it weaved through the steep forest-clad and copper-bearing escarpments, some of them almost a thousand feet high, that made up the western stretch of the historic Keweenaw Copper Range. The range, which bisects Porcupine County from east to west, runs more than a hundred miles from Fort Wilkins on the eastern end of the Keweenaw Peninsula, a thumb of land jutting out into Lake Superior, to the Wolverine Mountains fourteen miles west of Porcupine City.

After a twenty-minute drive I arrived at the Venture Mine, as everyone in the county still called the place deep in the thick woods. The mine nestled in a hollow hundreds of yards broad. One end of the hollow lay open, a two-lane gravel road running a mile east from the mine to Norwich

Road. A rough Forest Service track climbed the far end of the hollow and headed west through the Ottawa National Forest.

An assortment of single-wide and double-wide mobile homes had replaced the tumbledown wooden structures that had housed miners and their equipment from the turn of the nineteenth century into the twentieth. Ancient stone and brick foundations still protruded, like loose teeth from a skeletal jaw, out of the scrubby brush and grass of the hollow.

Only the tall grey stone hoist house remained from the original mining settlement, and it had been tuck-pointed and refurbished, fallen stones carefully recemented into the walls, and its old steam engine replaced by a huge, modern electric motor. Its whine greeted me as I opened the Explorer's door outside Weinstein's office, occupying one end of a spartan double-wide on concrete blocks next to the hoist house. This was not a fatcat chief executive officer who liked to gild his nest with stockholders' money, although profits seemed to be flowing constantly out of the mine on skids, carried by forklifts from the hoist house to two waiting eighteen-wheelers. Today the skids bore hundreds of flats of low, gnarled plants. A score or more workers scurried busily before my eyes.

"Ginseng," Weinstein said from the door of the mobile home as he followed my eyes to the activity outside. "Bound for China. I think we'll do pretty well with it this year. What can I do for you, Deputy?"

"We've found Frank Saarinen's body," I said. "Tying up all the loose ends."

"I heard," Weinstein said with a sigh tinged by regret. News gets around fast on the north woods' jungle telegraph. Everyone has either a hand-held or table radio that continually scans radio channels, official and unofficial, all over the Upper Peninsula. We don't bother with standard police radio code because everybody knows it anyway.

Weinstein shook his head in mournful commiseration. A tall, burly, handsome man dressed in what Yoopers jocularly called "woods formal" — worn jeans and woolen shirt — he was relaxed, open-faced and friendly. With heavy features, olive skin and dark curly hair, he reminded me of a Mossad agent I had met in Tel Aviv on my way to Riyadh during my Army days. Like that fellow, Weinstein projected an air of amiable but alert watchfulness, as if welcoming you into his presence but remaining ready to act if you, God forbid, turned out to be an enemy.

But Weinstein was the kind of genial, outgoing person who was liked immediately, and I myself had taken a shine to him when we had met at a spaghetti dinner at the volunteer fire department two years before. We had exchanged commonplace pleasantries over a handshake, and I remembered his hearty, unpretentious grasp.

Today we sat in cracked old leather easy chairs in Weinstein's office.

"This is routine," I said, opening the Saarinen file. "Just a few questions, then we'll be able to close the case and send Frank on his way."

"Shoot," Weinstein said, chin in hand, elbow on armrest.

I led him through Saarinen's employment history according to the file, and like Sally Saarinen, Weinstein offered exactly the same answers he had given the deputy who had investigated her husband's disappearance the previous year. Nothing had changed. I was glad. That made things ever so much easier. I closed the file.

"So you'd say he was a good employee?"

"Absolutely," Weinstein said. "He was knowledgeable, hard-working and extremely reliable, especially after . . . Deputy, it's no secret that Frank was in recovery. In the beginning of his employment, when he'd gone off on a toot he'd miss some work, but not since he joined AA. I was very sorry when he vanished. People like him are always difficult to replace."

I nodded. "Mr. Weinstein, Sally Saarinen told me that a few days before Frank disappeared, he'd seemed upset about something at work. He wouldn't tell her what it was. Would you have any idea?"

Thoughtfully Weinstein leaned back in his chair and looked at me directly. "I don't really know," he said, "but from time to time Frank could get into it with his foreman, Roy Schweikert. Another good man lost."

My eyebrows rose. Schweikert, a veteran nurseryman Weinstein had brought up from Chicago shortly after he turned the mine into a hothouse, had drowned the previous winter in a freak accident in neighboring Gogebic County. Like so many who should have known better, he had gone drinking and snowmobiling one weekend. Out on a trail in the deep woods, he missed a curve at sixty miles an hour and plunged with his heavy and powerful machine through the thin ice of a frozen creek, so stupefied by alcohol that he drowned in less than four feet of water. Death by misadventure, the coroner ruled. Every winter in the Upper Peninsula a dozen snowmobilers bite the big one, usually against an unyielding tree but sometimes clotheslining themselves on barbed wire.

"I don't like to speak ill of the dead," Weinstein said. "But Roy and Frank didn't get along very well. They were temperamental opposites. Frank was a careful, meticulous worker, but Roy was a Type-A guy who always wanted folks to move faster. Basically they got along, but from time to time Roy would push Frank just a little too much, and you could almost hear them yelling all the way down in the seventh level of the mine."

"They ever get into fisticuffs? Threaten to knock each other off?"

"No, no, things never got that far. Just pissing matches, over almost as soon as they began. 'Course, things between them would be tense for a while, but sooner or later they simmered down. They were proud men, but they were grown men, too."

"Was there a dispute about the time Frank disappeared? That might explain why Sally thought he was upset."

"I don't know," Weinstein said. "Possibly. I don't remember, really. Those things come and go, you know — forgotten as soon as they're over. Wish I could help there."

I waited a moment, but he had nothing further to say.

"Okay, I guess that does it," I said, standing up to leave. "Thanks for your time, sir."

"Oh, don't be in such a rush," Weinstein said. "It's time for lunch. Have some with me. And don't call me sir. Call me Morrie."

I hesitated, as I always do at such an offer, suspecting the offerer's motives. Currying favor with the law? Patronizing an Indian? Or just being friendly?

Weinstein's smile was direct and guileless.

"Okay," I said. "And thanks. But please don't go to any trouble."

"Won't," Weinstein said. "We've got a little fridge and a kitchen here. Plenty of sandwich makings. What would you like?"

"A ham sandwich would do me," I said. Then I realized what I had said, and added, "I'm sorry. I don't know if you keep kosher."

Weinstein grinned widely, as if I'd walked right into a trap.

"Noooooo," he said slowly, "but there was once a time when I didn't eat meat on Fridays."

"You're not . . ." I said dumbly.

"Not since my paternal great-grandfather, also called Morris, was baptized by an insistent Jesuit sometime in the 1880s. He didn't change his name. He was proud of it. We've been Catholics ever since, although some of us of course are lapsed. Except for the genes I'm no more a Jew than you are a

Sioux." He smiled at his ironic rhyme.

I sat down in mild embarrassment.

"You know about that?"

"It's hard not to," he said, "with your track record here."

Not to be immodest about it, but I've had a few successes as a police officer. Word gets around.

"Thanks," I said.

"So I know a little about what it feels like to be you," Morrie said.

It's rare anybody understands what it means to be one thing but look like another. Morrie did, and in my book that made him an all-right guy.

"*Ess, ess, mein kindt,*" he said, mimicking a Jewish mother, as he spread the sandwich makings, including a well-carved ham. "Eat, eat, my child."

"So you know a little Yiddish."

"Of course," he said. "Just like you know a little Lakota."

"*Hoka hey,*" I said, echoing Crazy Horse's call to battle: "It's a good day to die."

"It's a good day to *eat,*" said Morrie, who needed no translation. "We are who we are."

"No argument there," I said, tucking in. We ate almost silently, now and then pausing for a banality about the weather. Presently, after we had polished off the sandwiches, Morrie said, "Ever been down in the mine?"

"Not yet," I said. From time to time Morrie, proud of his enterprise, invited the public to an open house at the Venture, taking small parties on tours deep into the mine.

"Time to rectify that," he said.

"Why not?"

He led me to a large map, four feet high by seven feet wide, behind his desk. It was a chart, dated 1998, of the entire mine, showing the single vertical shaft and seven long drifts, the dimensions carefully called out in printed legends underneath. On the map were stuck colored push pins, tiny paper tags with handwritten names and dates tied to each pin. There were a lot of pins, so many that they almost obscured the outlines of the drifts.

"Each pin shows what we're growing down there, when it was planted and when it's being harvested," Morrie said. "Now let's go see."

TEN

At a low double-wide next to the hoist house Morrie led me into a locker room that could have served a high school football team. Instead of steel lockers for jerseys and pads, dozens of pristine white coveralls, emblazoned with the word VENTURE in bright red letters, hung from hooks lining one wall. A row of pegs on another wall carried yellow miner's helmets. Cardboard boxes of clear plastic booties stood on the floor. Three washing machines and three dryers, all of them running, lined a third wall. Two long changing benches bisected the room.

Morrie tossed me a pair of coveralls and a couple of booties.

"Suit up over your clothes," he said, "and put these booties on over your shoes."

"Okay. Why?"

"We don't want surface contamination to get into the mine or out of it. The place is not absolutely biosecure, like a biological weapons lab, but we try to keep things as clean as we can. We ask our guys to shower before coming to work, and we ask them to leave their used coveralls here for washing."

I stepped into the voluminous coveralls and took a freshly scrubbed miner's helmet and a pair of dark-lensed goggles from Morrie's hands. He checked my equipage the way an astronaut examines another's, then we stepped out of the locker room into the hoist house proper. A few steps away lay the steel skip, twelve feet by twelve feet and protected on all sides by a twelve-foot-tall mesh cage. A perfect cube, I thought for no reason at all.

"The skip can hold fifteen men or nine four-by-four skids of plants," Morrie said. "More if the plants are low and we can stack the skids on top of each other." He spoke with proprietary pride, as he did during our entire time underground.

With a screech of machinery and a whine of cables the skip descended slowly down the vertical shaft past a long ladder of bare light bulbs, following a line of thick black electrical cables affixed to the roughly carved basalt walls every few feet. The lamps at the top of the skip illuminated frequent glitters of shiny quartz with greenish threading — veins of copper. It was the first time I had ever descended into the bowels of the earth, and the fascination of adventure enveloped me. I felt like a small boy being introduced to a natural wonder.

"How far down are we going?" I asked as we passed first one, then two drifts hacked out of the grey stone, workers inside waving to us as we dropped. A gentle breeze whooshed up the shaft.

"More than a thousand feet, all the way to the seventh level," Morrie said. "That wind you're feeling comes from a two-foot air shaft the original copper miners drilled down from the top of the hill. We've got fans and filters up there. Mine air tends to be full of carbon dioxide. We don't need that, though the plants love it. Photosynthesis, you know."

The air grew warmer as we descended, until about halfway down, when the temperature seemed to stabilize.

"Not going to get any hotter until we hit the molten center of Earth?" I asked.

"Nope. It's a constant seventy degrees throughout the mine," Morrie said. "The grow lights bring up the temperature. Perfect for growing most plants. No cold snaps, no heat waves, just a steady, boring, pleasant temperature. Plants love sameness, just like sheep."

With a small bump we reached the seventh and last level and Morrie swung out the skip's tall steel-mesh door. We stepped onto a pathway of wooden boards laid over the bumpy rock floor. The jagged ceiling of the drift loomed just a few inches above our heads.

"Mind your noggin," Morrie said. "Lots of big rocks jut from the overhead." Those safety helmets aren't for just in case something bad happens. As we walked along, the ceiling rapped my well-protected head despite my best efforts to stay clear of stony perils.

Twenty feet into the drift we fetched up against a heavy wooden door.

"Put on your goggles," Morrie said. "It's bright in there."

He swung open the door into a huge irregular chamber, its ceiling supported by dozens of rock pillars, the lumpy walls spray-painted a blinding white.

"Ninety feet wide by two hundred feet long," Morrie said. "This was the mine's richest seam of copper back in the nineteenth century."

Even with the heavy smoked goggles my eyes hurt. Rows and rows of fluorescent grow lights, hovering over rows and rows of seedlings in flats and tubs, made the place seem as if it nestled next door to the sun. A loud hum from the lights filled the room, several degrees warmer than the passage outside the door.

"Thousand-watters," Morrie said. "We keep the temperature steady with metered air from the shaft. These are mostly tropical plants, so they like a little extra warmth."

I am no gardener, but even with dark goggles I could tell that the seedlings stood a uniform height, about a foot, above their flats. Their thick stems, smooth broad leaves and deep color suggested vigorous health. I recognized hibiscus, roses, basil and other herbs, and a distinctive plant with huge leaves. It looked familiar, but I couldn't think of its name.

"What's this?" I said.

"Tobacco," Morrie replied.

My eyebrows rose.

"This isn't for Philip Morris," Morrie laughed. "They're a special, genetically modified variety we're growing for a drug company that's experimenting with a protein extracted from them. It fights bone cancer. Over there we have some sweet wormwood, *Artemisia annua,* which produces a drug called artemisenin, used as an antidote for malaria. We're experimenting with new varieties of corn to make hepatitis vaccines, and with alfalfa against rabies.

"Just about all the plants in this room have been genetically modified. We call this the biosecure room. Actually, everywhere down here in the earth we're far away from insects and disease and wind and drought."

"Bioengineering protesters, too," I said. A lot of people hate the idea of genetic modification of living things — to some, that's playing God, and to others, it's risky to experiment with Mother Nature. As in every group of protesters, a few can get violent. Some ecoguerrillas have committed spectacular acts of sabotage, torching fields of designer corn and bombing agricultural laboratories.

Morrie nodded.

"True. But it works the other way, too. We don't sell living bioengineered plants. In fact, except for that tobacco — we carefully pack the harvested leaves in plastic for shipping — we don't let them out of here to get loose in the wild and contaminate ordinary plants. For the moment in this room we're just experimenting, seeing what we can do to improve certain species. There's nothing to trouble these babies — we don't even need to use pesticides — and they'll all grow up proud and strong. Because they're so healthy, every successive generation stands prouder and stronger. And they grow fast, because they're given a steady supply of nutrients and they stand under those grow lights eighteen hours a day. See those birches over there?"

Two dozen or so white birch saplings, six feet tall, stood in large plastic pots against the rock wall.

"Those are normal birches, not genetically modified. We started them from seed just one year ago. In the wild it'd take five or six years for them to reach that height."

"How come they grow so fast down here?"

"We don't know all the details yet. Some folks think electromagnetics have something to do with it. Those vary at different depths in the earth. There's still a lot of copper in the rock around us. Copper is known for its conductivity, and that could pump up the electromagnetic fields down here. Last week a biologist told me he thought the slight natural electrical current that copper carries discourages slugs from coming down here and eating the plants. Maybe the slight increase in air pressure from the fans helps increase the rate of photosynthesis. But personally I think the biggest thing is that the highly controlled environment just takes the stress out of growing. These are laid-back plants. They're fat and happy."

I'd not heard much about plant bioengineering. It's not the sort of thing one reads about in the daily papers.

"Why aren't the big drug companies interested in these plants?" I asked.

"Simple. It's hard to patent new drugs made from plants. That's why Abbott and Lilly and Pfizer generally stick to synthetic chemicals."

"Where does the research money come from?"

"Universities, mainly. They farm out their lab work to us, so to speak." He chuckled.

"You must use a lot of electricity," I said presently. "The lights, the hoist."

"The pumps, too," Morrie said. I could hear a low rumble from somewhere deep below. "We've got heavy-duty sump pumps keeping groundwater out of the mine."

"Doesn't all that cost?"

"Yes. It wouldn't be economical to grow ordinary seedlings and vegetables down here. But everything's absolutely top premium quality, and many people are willing to pay premium prices. We're now selling to upmarket greenhouses all over the United States and even foreign countries."

"Looks like a perfect place to grow very, very good pot," I said jokingly. A pioneering Canadian company raised medicinal marijuana, quite legal and government-controlled in that country, in an abandoned copper mine in Manitoba. The company had been in the news recently, for its first results were uneven, either too strong or two weak. The problem, the company said, was that it had to obtain confiscated marijuana seeds of unknown origin from the Royal Canadian Mounted Police. U.S. government sources owned pure strains of pot, but for political reasons—the hard-core drug warriors' influence reached everywhere—refused to share them with the Canadians. And the Canadians, forced by their own laws to obtain seeds only from licit sources, couldn't just buy good stuff from an illegal grower in, say, northern California.

Morrie laughed. "I hear that all the time. Everybody who comes down here looks around for weed. But you won't find it. We're inspected all the time, even by the DEA. Those guys like to look for trouble where there isn't any."

"Amen," I said. I'd been on plenty of useless forays with the feds into the countryside for small-potatoes pot growers and do-it-yourself meth labs. We expend a lot of money and manpower that way. One reason it's hard to alter the scattershot aims of the so-called war on drugs is that the law-enforcement bureaucracy that has grown up around it has become self-perpetuating and fights any attempt to shrink it to reasonable proportions.

"Want to visit the other six drifts?" Morrie asked.

"Are they the same as this?"

"Pretty much."

"Naw, one does me fine," I said. "Time for me to get back on patrol anyway."

"One more thing," Morrie said. "I want to show you something."

I followed him into a short side tunnel, blocked

halfway through by a massive and rusty old iron door. With a key he undid a heavy Yale padlock and pulled the door open, its hinges sighing smoothly. They had been recently oiled. I followed Morrie inside and he shut the door.

"This drift doesn't go in very far—about a hundred yards in, the roof collapsed long ago," he said. "We sometimes use it to store stuff and we sometimes use it to educate folks."

"About what?" I asked.

In response Morrie reached up on the wall and flicked off the light switch.

Think of the blackest black you have ever been in, and multiply it a hundred times. When you can see absolutely nothing, not even the tiniest glow of light—my shirtsleeve blanketed the luminous dial of my watch—you slowly become confused, unable to tell which way is up. In all my life I had experienced that disorientation only once, having flown through thick fog when the airplane's vacuum system failed and the attitude indicator, the artificial horizon on the instrument panel, tumbled crazily. Fortunately the flight instructor who was teaching me instrument flying pointed to the electric turn-and-bank indicator and the altimeter, and by keeping the wings level with the first and the altitude constant with the second I was able to fly the airplane straight and true despite a seat-of-the-pants sensation that falsely told me the plane was diving. Now that clammy, long-forgotten sensation came back to me. Involuntarily I put my hand on the jagged rock wall to recapture my faltering balance.

"Wow," I said. Words always failed me at times like that.

"Yeah," Morrie said with a sly chuckle. "Now think of the millions and millions of tons of rock above your head and what would happen if that tunnel roof failed some more."

I am not ordinarily claustrophobic, but beads of sweat broke out on my forehead and my bowels churned as I contemplated that possibility, which seemed to grow less unlikely by the second. I began to breathe heavily.

Suddenly Morrie flicked on the light. I took in a deep slug of air.

"You're a fairy, it seems," he said.

Despite my discomfort I bristled.

"Relax. Fairies are what a lot of miners in these parts used to call folks who don't like going deep into the earth," Morrie said with a broad grin. "Nothing to do with the other meaning. Fairies live in the trees, you see. Trolls — miners — dwell underground. Those terms go back to the old Cornish miners who used to work the Venture. Pretty apt, huh?"

"Okay, now let's troll right out of here, do you mind?" I said, trying to keep my voice light.

Morrie laughed. "C'mon. But don't be embarrassed. Your reaction's quite normal."

In a few minutes, at the entry to the drift as we waited for the skip to pick us up, I noticed a rubber-clad electrical cable the size of a man's thigh dipping down into the hoist pit below. It looked as if it could handle billions of watts.

And I said so. "What's that thing for?"

"Those sump pumps take a lot of juice," Morrie said. "Gotta overengineer to be absolutely safe."

At almost the same moment the skip ground to a stop, and we climbed aboard, the cable forgotten.

In a few minutes I stepped gratefully out of the hoist house, suffering from what I can describe only as delayed panic, and inhaled a deep breath of fresh fairyland air under the friendly sun. I could never have made a living as a troll.

"Thanks, Morrie," I said as I climbed into the Explorer. "For lunch and for the tour."

"Good to get to know you, Steve," he said. Don't be a stranger."

"Won't," I called back.

"Steve!" Morrie suddenly shouted.

"Yeah?"

"I'm going out in my boat with a couple of friends

tomorrow morning for lake trout. Be delighted if you'd come. Bring a guest. Whattaya say?"

I needed less than a tenth of a second to make the weighty decision. It had been a long time since I'd gone lake fishing. Most of my angling outings are up the rivers and creeks for rainbow trout in the spring, before they've deserted the streams for the cooler water of Lake Superior in the summer, and for walleyes in Lake Gogebic at the southern end of Porcupine County. And Morrie Weinstein's *Lucky Six* was a big, comfortable cruiser, the kind for kicking back under a warm sun.

"Sure! What time?"

"We'll meet at the marina at five-thirty and be out on the lake by six."

Some days end better than others, don't they?

ELEVEN

And that one sure did.

In the evening I told Ginny about my visit to the Venture Mine, my nonkosher lunch with Morrie Weinstein, and his invitation for Saturday. She listened with considerable interest to my description of the interior of the mine and eagerly accepted the rare chance to go fishing. About the lunch with Morrie, however, she was unimpressed.

"That's not so surprising. Morrie's mother was a Catholic, too. All the Holdermans were. For most Jews, except those in the Reform movement, Jewish identity is handed down through the mother, not the father. One wouldn't necessarily have expected Morrie to be a practicing Jew even if his father had been."

"Still," I said, "I can understand how he feels, being one thing while looking like another. He was pretty open about that. It's hard not to like the guy."

Ginny nodded with deep understanding but not a whole lot of sympathy. She'd heard me on the subject all too many times. She thought I should grow up and accept things I couldn't change. She was of course right, but it's sometimes hard to shake a lifetime of resentment at the cards circumstance had dealt.

I sighed and shrugged. "He's quite a fellow," I said "Like you he's put a lot of financial capital as well as emotional investment into Porcupine County."

Ginny, who as the widow of an Eastern industrial magnate had inherited a pile only a little smaller than that at Fort Knox, spreads much of her wealth around the county where she was born without letting anybody know where the money came from. Many, if not most, of the grants she writes for the Historical Society she runs, as well as other needy

Porcupine County institutions — such as the nursing home, the Little League team and the historical society she heads — are sent to her own foundation, headquartered in Detroit. She never wants anyone to judge her by the accident of her wealth and keeps it carefully under wraps. I am probably the only person outside her foundation director and her lawyer who knows the truth about her money, and I have no idea how much she is worth. I am not sure she does, either. Her fortune is the kind that fluctuates by six and sometimes seven figures a day, depending on the mood of the stock market.

"I don't think Morrie makes a lot of money out of that mine," I added. "Maybe not yet. Maybe not ever. Maybe it's just a labor of love."

"That," said Ginny, "is hardly surprising. People up here care."

They do indeed. Porcupine County is not an easy place to make a living, but it is an attractive place to live. The woods, the wildlife, the fishing, the lake, the astonishingly neighborly people who remain here are powerful magnets for someone like me, who has always searched for a welcoming home. As jobs have dwindled so has the population, and perhaps to slow down the exodus, those who remain behind try to take care of each other, even if it's only donating labor for a new roof on a needy family's house or repairing an ancient pickup truck for free. One finds altruism in surprising places, and so it stood to reason that Ginny was not Porcupine County's only wealthy benefactor. Morrie Weinstein was probably a close second. He loved theatrical groups and generously supported the Northwoods Playhouse in Porcupine City.

"Good old Morrie," I said. "Good old Ginny."

She crooked an amused eyebrow. "Thank you. Now let's tuck in."

We sat down to a leg of lamb I'd grilled over charcoal, slathering it with mint jelly Ginny had put up from the herb garden she raised in the sandy soil between her house and the beach. She puts up a lot of jelly each year, for the mint she had planted a few years before had spread like kudzu, even in these cool northern climes. At Christmas seemingly everybody in Porcupine County gets a jar of Ginny's mint jelly with hand-lettered labels. Sometimes I tease her about the jelly, once suggesting she put up a sign where her driveway meets the lakefront highway and selling it to passersby, the way many people who live up here augment their meager incomes by selling eggs to locals and firewood to campers in the Wolverines.

"Experiencing the life of a poorer resident," I once suggested in a moment of blind self-righteousness, "might make you a truer Porky."

"Except I don't have to do it," she replied. "They do. I wouldn't insult them that way."

And she was right. I can be *so* dumb.

Rounding out the feast was a plate of buttered fresh asparagus I'd picked up in Rhinelander and a tureen of wild rice the Ojibwa had harvested from inland lake shallows on their reservation near Baraga fifty miles east of Porcupine County. We washed it all down with a inexpensive and unpretentious but excellent Australian merlot I'd found in an Eagle River liquor store, returning several times to stock up on it. Home cooking in the remote North Woods doesn't get better than mine, I will immodestly admit.

After an hour I said regretfully, "Can't stay the night. Got to get my tackle ready for tomorrow."

"Getting old, eh?" Ginny replied slyly.

"Hey! No fair!"

"Just kidding. We'll need our sleep."

"See you at five-fifteen."

I kissed her good-bye and drove home.

TWELVE

At a quarter to five I arose in pitch dark, quickly donning heavy sweatshirt and sweatpants over T-shirt and cargo shorts against the morning chill, rounding out my wardrobe with a pair of Docksiders. By ten o'clock the sun would warm the day, but this far north even a summer dawn almost always broke in the low fifties. A quick splash of coffee and I was almost ready to go. But first I popped into a knapsack a bag of one of Upper Michigan's best-kept secrets — *korppu,* the flavorsome hard cinnamon toast Finnish loggers once carried into the woods for their midmorning coffee breaks. The most-sought-after *korppu* is also called "Trenary toast" for a celebrated bakery at Trenary, a tiny town in the waist of Upper Michigan between Marquette and Escanaba. Every day the toast is baked fresh and shipped to cafes and supermarkets all over the Upper Peninsula and to mail-order customers, most of them exiled Yoopers, in every state of the nation. *Korppu* looks like overgrown zwieback and amounts to something like the hardtack biscuits sailors used to eat during long voyages, but is much, much tastier. A little *korppu* slathered with butter and softened by hot coffee gives one a jolt of energy that easily lasts until lunch.

I selected a seven-foot medium-action spinning rod — the *Lucky Six* would carry plenty of specialized lake trout gear, but like the true Yooper I wanted to be someday, I preferred familiar old tools — then saddled up the Jeep and in ten minutes was at Ginny's place five miles east on the lakefront highway. Ginny, bless her heart, is a woman who believes in being prompt. I have never had to cool my heels while she pulls herself together to go out, dabbing on lipstick and visiting the bathroom for one last time to brush her teeth. She stood waiting outside her door, rod in one hand, kit bag on a shoulder, and a gorgeous smile on her face, ready to go. My heart, as it always does when I see her for the first time every day, did a little lub-de-bub-dup.

At five-thirty on the dot we arrived at the Porcupine City Municipal Marina a few hundred yards up the Porcupine River from the rock-lined channel to the lake. A dozen or so automobiles, pickups and minivans occupied the large asphalt parking lot, their owners doing boat things under half a dozen powerful floodlights that illuminated the thirty-eight-slip marina. Almost all the boats aft tied up there were sixteen- to twenty-foot runabouts with big outboard motors. Most local yachtsmen are not rich, and Morrie Weinstein's forty-foot *Lucky Six*, moored at the end of the single pier where the water was deepest, the burbling exhausts of its two powerful engines raising foam at the stern, overshadowed all other boats.

I started in surprise. Under a floodlight at the entrance to the slip, holding a duffel in one hand and the elbow of Mary Ellen Garrigan in the other, loomed big Chad Garrow, grinning from ear to ear.

"Hi, Steve!" Chad shouted gaily. "Ready to go for a big one?"

I glanced at Ginny. A small smile played on her lovely countenance, threatening to break out into a huge amused grin, but she won the fight with her face.

"Ginny, this is—," I began.

"We've met," Ginny said, in a friendly way. "Nice to see you, Chad, Mary Ellen."

One of Ginny's talents is something I will never master in a lifetime: the ability to greet people with just-folks ease and a chummy disposition, no matter who they are or what the circumstances. Everybody always feels comfortable entering her presence.

Not necessarily mine. "Hello," I said to my brother officer and his companion. In my consternation that was all I could think of to say.

"Steve!" Mary Ellen called gaily, so loudly that heads snapped up all over the marina. "So good to see you again!" She took a deep breath, her ample chest nearly bursting her thick alpaca turtleneck sweater. She looked me in the eye, as if to declare that our unpleasant little encounter at George's was only the opening skirmish in a patient campaign to get me into her bed. I couldn't see it, but I knew Ginny's left eyebrow was rising in barely concealed amusement. She was comfortable in her own beauty and not the sort to feel threatened by another knockout of a woman. And I had not told her about the scene at George's. It hadn't mattered.

"Mrs. Garrigan," I responded politely.

"Mary Ellen," she said in an insistent tone.

"Okay," I said, although it was not okay.

Chad, who is not much smoother than I am socially, just stood rooted to the spot, like a huge oaf with a thatched red roof and an expanse of teeth that spread from east to west as if he were showing off a record catch on the dock at Key West.

"Hiya," he said brilliantly.

Morrie Weinstein broke the moment with a bellow from *Lucky Six*. "Right on time!" he shouted. "We're ready to go!"

Down the slip we scrambled, then leaped onto the big fiberglass boat, Mary Ellen's shapely round rump, outlined in tight stretch jeans, preceding us aboard. On the boat's broad stern was painted its name in flamboyant white script, FORT LAUDERDALE in smaller Roman capitals underneath. A short and wiry fellow in a hooded blue sweatshirt waved to us from his perch high on the flying bridge, the glow of a cigarette barely lighting his face, obscured by the hood. A long ski-jump nose protruded over the cigarette.

"This is Mike Anderson, the skipper," Morrie said, making introductions all around as he cast off the stern line. As the boat drifted away from the slip in the slight current, Anderson opened the throttles gently and swung the wheel to its starboard stop, swiveling the big boat almost in its own length to enter the Porcupine River from the marina, a rectangular pond carved from the riverbank just west of the village. I knew enough about boats to recognize the maneuver as an expert though unflashy piece of seamanship. Anderson clearly knew his stuff, and I felt better. Lake Superior can be fatally treacherous, a fast-moving squall churning a gentle chop into six-foot whitecaps in just a matter of minutes. This was no Sunday captain of the sort I sometimes had to go searching for out on the lake in the sheriff's Cessna.

As we headed around into the river the skipper loosed a blast from the boat's horn, and a hundred yards away the lights of the low swing bridge over M-64 carved a slow horizontal arc through the night as the highway deck pivoted to open a clear passage for the *Lucky Six*. The span, a much-repaired relic of the Depression and the last operating swing bridge in all of Michigan, required a full-time bridgetender during the boating season. The state highway department had scheduled it to be torn down the following year when M-64 was rerouted just upriver from the marina. A new stationary concrete bridge would go up high above the river, and it would need no human attendant. Another job would be lost to Porcupine County.

On the other hand, sometimes during hot August weather the steel in the old bridge expands and the swiveling span binds shut. Often cold river water has to be hosed onto the rusty, swollen metal to shrink it and free the span. All the same, I was fond of this battered old piece of early-twentieth-century engineering. Steel swing bridges have grown as rare as wooden Kentucky covered bridges and carry the same nostalgic appeal for those who like old machinery.

As *Lucky Six* entered the turning pool just before the two-hundred-yard-long steel-and-stone channel jutting from the shoreline, she lurched slightly to starboard, then port. The lake outside lay almost calm, slow, whale-like swells breaking gently on the beach, but a nasty chop roiled the channel.

Some years before I came to Porcupine City, the Army Corps of Engineers had reinforced the rock riprap that made up the channel breakwaters, in its infinite wisdom lining the channel with huge corrugated steel sheets driven into the bottom. The steel would hold back the lake for a century, the soldiers said, and no doubt it will. But they're army, and they're engineers — they're not sailors. The corps had no idea that instead of breaking up the waves as did the rough rock riprap, the vertical steel walls would magnify them. The rollers ricocheted their way upstream and created a turbulent hazard for small boats. It is not for nothing that Porcupine County natives take a dim view of the munificence of outside government. Federal and state bureaucrats never listen to the advice of the locals.

Mike, however, steered the *Lucky Six* expertly through the turbulence as Ginny and I sat on a bench in the stern, huddled together for warmth and because we just like huddling together. Presently the boat chugged past the lights at the ends of the breakwaters and out into the open lake, the insistent pounding of the hull replaced by gentle rolling. Mary Ellen and Chad sat opposite us, lost in each other as well, his huge arm around her shoulders. Barely half a mile out the eastern sky began to lighten. Ginny and I faced the sun as it slowly rose from the horizon, flooding the sky with light, its rays reddening the high cirrus that floated down from the north and outlining in stark green relief the slowly receding forested shoreline. Fifteen miles to the west we could see rising from the tree line the mountains the Indians who once crossed these waters in war canoes called the Wolverines, after the shape of the animal they saw on the horizon. The huge wilderness state park named for the mountains marked the western boundary of my jurisdiction.

"C'mon up here," called Morrie, who had stood shoulder to shoulder with his skipper on the bridge just above us as Anderson conned the boat out into the lake. I climbed up the half-dozen steps onto the bridge under its canvas awning and looked about. Though I am not a sailor, modern electronic equipment always interests a pilot, and the *Lucky Six* was as well-equipped a sportfisher as I'd ever seen. On one side of the cockpit coaming lay a marine radio set to the distress channel, two big electronic fish locators and a depth finder. A large monitor built into the center of the coaming displayed a rotating green line, the visible return from the radar antenna high above the bridge as it swept the empty lake for miles ahead. Another screen, fed by a global positioning satellite receiver, displayed the *Lucky Six*'s latitude and longitude within half a dozen feet, the numbers slowly changing as the boat churned farther north. An older readout from loran ground radio stations displayed an almost identical position. I approve highly of redundancy in navigational equipment. If we should sink, we'd know exactly where we went down at the very moment we did, as if that were any comfort. But we'd never lose our bearings on the open water far from the sight of land.

Over the windshield a scoped Remington rifle lay cradled in wooden pegs, lashings keeping it secure to the bulkhead. That was odd. Why would a sailor need a deer rifle out on the lake?

"Cool, eh?" Morrie said, breaking my reverie.

"Why the rifle?"

Morrie glanced at it. "Protection, of course."

"Against what?"

"Pirates."

"*Pirates?*"

"Not here on Lake Superior. The Caribbean. In the fall and winter we charter the *Lucky Six* out of Fort Lauderdale, and sometimes outside American territorial waters Colombian crooks lie in wait to snatch charter boats and use them to run drugs up from South America. When they're done with a run they scuttle 'em and go back to hijack some more."

"I'll be damned." I was mollified, although a stray thought struggled unsuccessfully to reach the surface of my brain.

"This sure is a hunk of pleasure boat," I said after a moment. "It must cost an arm and a leg to keep up."

"Yeah," Morrie said. "We charter her a lot to help pay the bills. That's why I've got Mike. He lives aboard and runs the charters. I often go down to Florida in early May to help him bring the boat up the St. Lawrence Seaway and through the Soo. Takes a couple of weeks. Mike's just back from a charter in Lake Huron with half a dozen fellows from Chicago. He cleared the Soo two days ago and got in just last night."

I looked at Anderson, who had pulled back his sweatshirt hood as the sun warmed the day. Under his long-billed sailor's ball cap his beak thrust forward like an old underslung nineteenth century battleship prow, but that was not his most striking feature. He was a fairly young man—mid-thirties, I guessed—but I had never seen anyone so leathery, seams and wrinkles crisscrossing his deep brown face like the hide of an old sea turtle. But this was not just a man who had spent a lifetime at sea. Anderson looked almost reptilian, glittering black eyes sunk under prominent brows, lips pushed forward by prognathous teeth already yellowed by the cigarettes he smoked constantly. It must have been hellish to go through life looking like that. He had barely said a word since we came aboard.

"Where'd you learn about boats?" I asked, just to be polite.

"Navy," he said after a long beat.

"Sailor?"

"Petty officer." His response also took longer than needed.

I had done time in the military, and I knew that the noncommissioned naval rank of petty officer could have covered a thousand specialties in the modern service, from coxswain to nuclear technician. But I didn't press the subject. No point in poking a reticent fellow with a sharp stick. And anyway, he needed to pay attention to his job. All the same, his manner seemed appropriate to his looks. He creeped me out.

Three miles offshore Morrie climbed down from the bridge and shouted "Time to fish!" He had been chatting soliticiously with Ginny, playing the genial host while Chad and Mary Ellen stared hand in hand out over the lake, no doubt anticipating their upcoming evening. Chad glanced at Mary Ellen frequently, almost in disbelief, as if he could not understand why this gorgeous and — at least to him — elegant creature had taken up (if that is the word) with a rough-hewn clodhopper like him. I could have lectured him about notches on bedposts, but young men of his age aren't inclined to listen to the wisdom of their elders. It was none of my business anyway.

"Do you really, really need to catch lake trout today?" Morrie asked nobody in particular. "If so, we can use the high-tech stuff, the fish finders and all, and go out real far and real deep. We do that on charters so that the customers are all but guaranteed to go home with a fish or two. But if you want to give 'em a sporting chance, we can just use basic tackle, a ball downrigger and ten-pound test, and the depth finder."

"Fine by me," said Chad, immediately raising my estimation of him by a notch. It usually takes a young guy much longer to learn that hunting and fishing are not just about the quarry, but also the adventure. He must have spent time with wise men at deer camp in his boyhood.

"Fine by me," I echoed.

"Sure," Ginny said.

"You go right ahead," said Mary Ellen. "I'm going up front to catch some sun."

As Morrie took the helm Mike climbed down and swiftly prepared the starboard downrigger tackle. A simple downrigger is nothing more than a heavy iron ball weighing five to ten pounds, attached to the end of a braided wire line dropped over the stern from a stiff rod, four feet long, jutting over the gunwale. The other end of the line is attached to a winch, the bigger ones driven by an electric motor, as Morrie's were. On the heavy-duty models like those aboard the *Lucky Six*, a dial on the winch tells how far down the iron ball is running as the boat trolls it astern, and a digital readout reveals the water temperature at the ball. Far down on the cable a few feet above the iron ball, a quick-release clasp holds ordinary monofilament fishing line trailed from an ordinary fishing rod. At the end of the monofilament is a standard steel leader to which is affixed the bait.

"Wimps use minnows," Morrie had said. "Real men use spoons." Those are large silvery steel fingerlings, shaped like long, skinny serving spoons, with sharp hooks on the business end. Dragged through the water, a spoon wiggles and flutters sexily and, in theory at least and in practice often enough to keep people using it, is simply irresistible to lake trout. Once a fish strikes, the clasp on the cable releases the monofilament so the fish can be played with the rod and, if the angler is lucky, brought to the surface and taken home for dinner.

"Ladies first," called Morrie from the bridge.

Ginny took up the rod and watched as the iron ball slowly sank below the surface. Swiftly and wordlessly Anderson readied the port side downrigger. He looked up at me. I nodded to Chad. "Youth before age," I said.

The lad didn't even hesitate in deference to a superior, let alone an elder, but eagerly grasped the rod, his thumb on the reel. I chuckled inwardly. That was me once.

"We'll let the rigs down to about eighty feet," Morrie said. The bottom's at ninety all along this stretch, and as we go on it'll fall to about a hundred twenty feet, where the big ones are." Leaving one engine throttled back, he opened up the other slowly, pushing the boat ahead at a bare three or four miles per hour. The downrigger cable hummed insistently, the water strumming it like a huge bass fiddle string.

Time passed, Ginny and Chad at their rods, fingers lightly touching monofilament, feeling for a strike. Onward the *Lucky Six* trolled, Mike paying out downrigger cable as the bottom slowly fell away. An hour went by without a strike. Presently I broke out the coffee and *korppu* – both Ginny and Chad were too absorbed in their quest to accept any. Morrie, the genial host, sat with me, and we munched and chatted about anything and nothing as the boat chugged slowly ahead and the sun rose higher. Just as I thought we'd be skunked – not that that made much difference to me – Ginny shouted. "Got one!"

Her rod bent almost double as the fish struck the spoon and ran to starboard.

"Reel!" Morrie shouted. "Reel it in now!"

Soundlessly as always, Anderson knelt by Ginny, ready to snatch the rod from her if she spooked or tired. She didn't. It was easy to tell that she'd grown up around boats and fishing, just as she'd spent large parts of her youth in hunting camps. She is not a frail little thing, but tall and strong, with wide shoulders and hips, and she carries plenty of well-shaped but lean meat on her bones. She chops her own firewood and shovels her own snow. Now and then she shoots a deer during hunting season and stocks her freezer with venison. For all her wealth and education Ginny Fitzgerald is a true "Yooper Woman," an accolade that is not lightly bestowed.

"This is a good-sized trout," she said unnecessarily. "Not a monster, but it'll feed quite a few people."

"Going to take it home if you get it in?"

"Absolutely. Without a doubt. Now stand back."

To make a long story short, Ginny expertly played the trout for ten minutes, letting it exhaust itself by running out and back, then slowly reeled it in. With a long-handled net

Anderson scooped the fish from the water, letting it flop on the deck as the life leaked out of it. When it was still he removed it and hung it by the gills from a fish scale.

"Nineteen pounds," Morrie said. "Not bad."

All the while Chad had watched with one eye, paying attention to his own rig with the other. He wasn't a greenhorn. He grinned at Ginny, generously happy for her, totally undisappointed in his lack of luck. There's hope for the lad yet, I thought, as I looked at my watch. It was eleven, well past the best feeding time for lake trout, and the sun was nearing its zenith in the sky.

"If we go out farther and deeper, we might get lucky again," said Morrie, himself delighted in his guests' pleasure. "But chances are we won't. What say we go home?"

"Sure," I said.

"Right," Ginny said.

"Okay," Chad said.

Mary Ellen said nothing. We hadn't seen or heard her for the last hour, and simultaneously we all stood and looked toward the bow.

She lay supine atop the forward deck, taking the sun, her head cradled on Chad's big duffel. Cotton balls covered her eyes. A black wisp too skinny to be called a thong covered her womanhood. Nothing covered her breasts. Chad's eyes covered all of her. Before I could avert mine Ginny punched me in the ribs, but she giggled softly. Morrie grinned at me from the bridge. Next to him Anderson stared stonily astern, as if he had seen it all before, more often than he cared to count. Charter-boat skippers are like the old Pullman porters of a hundred years ago — faceless servants that are just part of the furniture with which a luxury traveling conveyance is equipped. Aboard trains and boats many adventurous and conscienceless passengers indulge in indiscretions they'd never commit at home, confident that they'll never see the crew again.

Most of the way home I stared astern too, chatting

casually with Ginny while Chad sat up forward beside his girl friend, at least fifteen and maybe twenty years older than he, enjoying the view. Morrie and Anderson stood on the bridge, their heads together, talking quietly, paying no attention to the flesh-colored scenery on the deck a few feet in front of them. From time to time Ginny glanced at me and giggled.

Just before we entered the channel Morrie dropped down from the bridge.

"Ginny," he said, "has anybody volunteered to fund the new wing?"

The previous year the Historical Museum had hired an architect— paid for, of course, by a foundation Ginny secretly funded with her widow's wealth—to design a new wing devoted to Porcupine County's mining history. The museum owned a great deal of old mining equipment donated over the decades, including huge winches, hoists, skips and tram cars, but was unable to display most of it for lack of room inside the old former supermarket building downtown. The architect had suggested taking up part of the parking lot, never half filled by vehicles even at the museum's busiest times, for the extension. A specialist would be hired from Eastern Michigan University to sift through the relics and design an authentic historical display. But the total cost would approach six figures, and Ginny hesitated to write herself another grant, for fear the size might attract attention.

"Not yet," she said.

"I've been thinking about it," Morrie said. "The Venture's begun to do well enough so that we can put some money back into the county. How much do you need?"

Ginny told him. Morrie's expression didn't change.

"I think we can cover that," he said. "How about I come down to the museum sometime soon and talk about it?"

Ginny nodded, delighted. "That's very generous of you, Morrie. Of course we could name it for you."

"No. How about the Gordon Holderman Wing? My

grandpa would have loved that."

"It's a deal."

At Ginny's house that night, as we ate the trout— slathered with lemon and butter and broiled over charcoal— Ginny did not mention Mary Ellen. Many women would have, some of them shrilly, until they had discussed, criticized, dismantled and condemned every physical and moral defect of their subject. Not Ginny, whose self-confidence had grown boundlessly during our months together. She was a hell of a woman and she knew it. Much later that night, she let me know she knew.

Afterward, just before falling asleep, I thought about Morrie Weinstein, my new friend and fishing companion, and his understanding, his generosity, his geniality, and his all-around good-eggedness. "Too good to be true," I told myself quietly as sleep began to enfold me, but I also thought I was just being Steve Martinez, Lakota off the reservation, fish out of water, a stranger in a strange land, unable to appreciate a gift freely offered.

THIRTEEN

On the southern shore of Lake Superior in upper Michigan, the shank of an August evening is the best time of year to sit out on the beach in a folding lawn chair, feet up on a big old log, and contemplate one's world. Often the lowering sun reddens the sky through a scrim of high cirrus into subtle shades of vermilion. The onshore wind that kicked up a chirp of wavelets on the beach all day usually has settled into a slight breeze just enough to shoo the mosquitoes inside the tree line. The sigh of grass on the sand is interrupted now and then by squawks of geese and calls from loons. From time to time an eagle that often perches on a snag just down the beach will soar low over the water, hoping to snatch a minnow feeding close to the surface in the shallows. If I'm lucky a doe and her fawn, or perhaps a small black bear, might emerge from the woods by Quarterline Creek a hundred yards or so up the beach to the west and take a sip from the lake.

I could investigate many more interesting cases and make a lot more money as a detective in Duluth or Wausau or any of the small cities half a day's drive from Porcupine County, but the boondocks routine and subsistence salary of a country deputy does me just fine for now. I don't miss the crash and yammer, the snarl and snipe of daily combat on urban battlegrounds. Been there, done that, thank you. Of course sometimes I need better brain food than rustic life can provide, but though the Joffrey Ballet and the Chicago Symphony never come to town, we've still got itinerant musicians, community theater, arts colonies, PBS, Minnesota Public Radio, C-SPAN, and the Internet. We're not exactly isolated from the rest of American cultural life, although sometimes it can seem that way when a racist yahoo shatters a beer bottle in a roadside bar and threatens a dark-skinned visitor. But that happens in the big cities, too.

If one has enough food and shelter, the comfortable routine of the North Woods can be gratifying and by no means boring. For the unexpected sometimes happens in Porcupine County.

In the far distance toward the east I saw a figure walking down the beach in my direction and, figuring him to be a local looking for agates, glanced away and lost myself again in my reverie.

"Hello," said a soft and cultivated voice.

I peered upward. A small, slight and brown-skinned man about my age stood on the sand, squinting into the sun. He wore faded jeans — the genuine old-fashioned kind, not the artificial stone-washed stuff beloved of mall marketers — and a cast-off military khaki shirt, its flap pockets bulging. A lumpy blanket bedroll hung from one shoulder on a rope that bound both edges, in the old frontier style. Modern moccasins with rubber soles clad his feet. He wore his rich black hair long, in double braids resting on his chest in traditional Indian fashion. A leather medicine pouch dangled from his neck. His face was broad, his eyes sparkling and intelligent, and a gentle smile played upon his lips.

"Hi," I replied. "What can I do for you?"

"Sir, I need something to eat and a place to sleep," he said casually, as if remarking upon the weather. His relaxed manner suggested that if I said no, he would simply nod politely and say, "Just asking," and continue on up the beach. And if I said yes, he would simply nod politely and say, "Thank you."

"Well," I said noncommittally, "who are you and where are you bound?"

The lake shore is mostly lonely and deserted, except on summer days when residents sun themselves and take dips, sometimes exercising by walking a mile or two in either direction and back. Once in a long while a long-distance hiker with backpack and bedroll will break the routine, returning my wave from the cabin if I'm at home. Now and then one tarries a bit for a chat and, if he or she seems interesting, I will offer a cup of coffee.

One Sunday, shortly after I had settled into the cabin and long before I met Ginny, a beautiful blonde graduate student in sociology from Helsinki who had been visiting her American kin in Porcupine City had stopped by. I offered her lunch and, to make a long and complicated but sweet story short, we hit it off. On the last morning before she returned to Finland I woke up to find her pillow next to mine empty, but with a lovely good-bye note and a fresh daisy plucked from the roadside. Itinerants like these, I knew, were only temporary visitors to the wilderness. They had homes and careers to go back to.

Instantly I knew that the man standing in front of me was no stranger to the Upper Peninsula.

"I'm Anishinabe," he said, using the Ojibwa word for Ojibwa—it means "Original People," and some Anishinabe include all Native Americans in the term—and holding out his hand. His grasp was strong. "My name's Edmund Sixkiller, I'm a medicine man, or shaman as some say, and I'm heading for the reservation at the Lake in the Woods. Call me Ed."

"I'm Steve Martinez. Wow, that's a long way. What is it, about three hundred miles?"

"Something like that."

"We don't get too many folks like you on this beach," I said. "Most everybody else is a local just going up and down for a bit."

"Men and women must take long journeys," Ed said "Otherwise, what's the point? You haven't found truth unless your feet hurt." He grinned, sat on the log and faced me.

"Medicine man, eh?" I said. "Tell me about your job."

"It's not really a job," he said. "It's a calling, like the ministry or the priesthood. It chooses you, you don't choose it."

"Exactly what does an Anishinabe medicine man do?"

"Depends. Some of us are full-service healers that will take care of your body as well as your soul, but let's face it, the calling has changed and modernized for all tribes and nations. Many of us are specialists now. The specialty I'm working toward is helping troubled souls become grounded with Mother Earth again."

He cocked his head and gazed at me with the same narrow-eyed, professionally interested expression Doc Miller has when he's giving me a physical at Porcupine County Hospital.

"Do I look troubled to you?" I said, only half seriously.

"Everybody's troubled. It's the times."

I chuckled. "What's your diagnosis?"

"My guess is that you were born Indian and brought up white." His eyes twinkled, but he did not laugh.

"Now how would you know that? I've never seen you before!"

"Sheriff, everybody in this small part of the world knows about you. Even we Anishinabe take notice of a Lakota cousin who has made his mark on the world."

"Well, I'll be —"

The medicine man grinned widely.

"And I'm a deputy, not a sheriff."

"If you say so."

I changed the subject and made a decision. "All right. Stay for supper. You can sleep on the couch."

"Thank you." Ed said casually, as if his request was rarely turned down.

"Anishinabe medicine men don't ordinarily depend on charity, do they?" I asked.

"This one does. But I've had a lot of practice at being a mendicant. I used to be a Franciscan friar."

"Really?"

"Yes. I grew up on the Baraga reservation and was

educated by the Black Robes—that's what we called the Jesuits long ago—and I thought I had found my calling as a monk. But one morning not too long ago I woke up and decided the Catholics didn't have all the answers, at least for me. So I decided to return to the blood and become a traditional Anishinabe."

"That must have been difficult, given your Jesuit education."

"All belief systems and creation myths are based on revealed truth. One man's religion is no more outlandish than another's."

"But the Franciscans must have given you something," I said.

"Indeed they did. Among other things, their vows of poverty taught me how to live without owning anything except what I can carry on my back. What you see is what I've got. That's a mark of the traditional Anishinabe, by the way. We believe that people should own nothing. Traveling light allows a medicine man to bear heavy spiritual burdens, his own as well as those of others. And you never have to worry about feeding the Internal Revenue Service."

"Hmm."

"Sheriff, I don't mean to be rude," Ed said, "but I'm hungry."

"Deputy," I said again. "So am I."

We dined in my cabin on broiled whitefish and new potatoes sprinkled with basil and parsley. I had a little shiraz, but Ed declined the wine. "It's not that we're just denying ourselves something pleasant," he said. "Anishinabe religious tradition holds that alcohol causes people to lose control of themselves. And that is what has happened to Anishinabeg everywhere. Whites, too, of course."

"Do you think alcohol should be banned on the reservations?"

"It is in many places, but prohibition never works.

Anishinabeg who want to drink will find liquor. What we need to do is teach Anishinabeg to disdain alcohol, to find solace and self-control in our religion. It must come from within, not without."

On into the night we talked about that and about the Ghost Dance, the mystical nineteenth century revival that had brought together Indian tribes from all over North America and badly frightened the whites. We talked about the central belief of Indian religions — the sanctity of Mother Earth — and the latter-day Native American Church. We also talked about the casinos — Ed hated them, for he believed gambling as dangerous as alcohol to an Indian's sense of self — and about a million other social problems facing the Native American in "the twenty-first century of the Common Era," as Ed put it. We talked about the Packers (Ed favored them) and the Vikings (I'm a fan) and the Lions (both of us disdained them). We talked about the best places to buy genuine hand-picked Ojibwa wild rice.

And we talked about the *midewewin*, the Grand Medicine Society of the Anishinabeg that Ed hoped to be invited to join someday. "It practices a strict code of ethics," Ed said. "It has eight stages, or degrees, on the road to spiritual knowledge, and I'm just what you would call a postulant. My first language, like yours, was English, and I'm still learning *Ojibwemowin*, as we call our tongue. I have a long way to go."

We also talked about the Venture Mine. I told Ed about my visit and my delight that an old copper mine was being used to grow plants to benefit humanity as well as provide jobs for half a hundred Porkies.

"Did you know that traditional Indians believe modern mining rapes the earth?" he asked. "Drilling deep violates its sanctity, and wresting precious metal from its ribs robs it of nourishment."

"But Indians also mined copper in the old days, didn't they?"

"Yes, but they merely scratched a small bit from the surface, knowing that Mother Earth would eventually heal the scars in her skin. That was considerably different from the white man's drilling, crushing and refining ore and scattering the tailings over acres and acres, poisoning the water table. And America has used most of its copper not to make bowls to feed people and decorations to delight them but for munitions of war to kill other human beings."

I nodded. "But now, perhaps, growing medicinal plants in the mines can change that view?" The Ojibwa are famous for their knowledge of such plants.

"I don't know. Great harm has been done to Mother Earth for a long time. Can a small good heal it? I have my doubts."

It was well past midnight when we hit the sack, I in my bedroom and Ed on the old leather couch. He refused my offer of a coverlet, preferring his woolen blanket. "Hudson's Bay," he said, "woven by Indians. Tight and warm, and it also makes a good shelter from the rain."

Just before he lay down he patted my laptop computer, sitting on a small desk next to the couch. "*Wiindibaanens*. That translates literally as 'little brain machine.' *Ojibwemowin* is a wonderfully supple language. It evolves with the times."

I expected him to disappear before dawn, as that Finnish student had done years ago, maybe leaving a pleasant little bread-and-butter note behind. But shortly after sunup I awoke to a soft sound from the beach. Ed sat cross-legged on the sand, chanting not in *Ojibwemowin* but in some other language over the glassy lake toward the rising sun.

As I approached I heard these words:

"*Pater noster qui in caelis es, sanctificetur nomen tuum. Adveniat regnum tuum, fiat voluntas tua sicut in caelo et in terra.*"

I remembered enough Latin from my schoolboy classes to recognize the Lord's Prayer. "Matins?" I asked in open-mouthed astonishment.

"Lauds, actually," Ed said. "Matins are sung at three in

the morning, lauds at dawn."

"Why? I thought you'd become a traditionalist Ojibwa."

"You can take the boy out of the Franciscans," Ed said with a chuckle, "but you can't take the Franciscans out of the boy. Don't look so surprised, Sheriff."

"Deputy. It was just the notion of an Ojibwa medicine man reciting a Catholic prayer that startled me."

"No religion, no tradition, is pure and unchanging," Ed said. "Early Christianity was greatly influenced by the pagans it overwhelmed. Indian beliefs changed when Christianity swept the Americas, and I daresay American Christianity has been and is being influenced by Indian spirituality, too. Remember, I was educated in the Western tradition, as you were. It is a strong and appealing intellectual heritage, but North American Indian wisdom is also powerful. Western culture engages the mind, but Indian spirituality touches the heart. They need not war against each other, as perhaps they are inside you, Sheriff. You can accept them both. I have, and I am the more content for it."

To that I had no response, although Ed's words made sense to me. We went inside for breakfast—juice, eggs, *korppu* and coffee.

"Where did you get this swill?" Ed demanded, tapping the coffee pot.

"Hey, that's good French roast from Starbuck's." I'd bought several bags there on my last foray to Rhinelander.

"Nonsense. You want pure Colombian. And not from a designer chain but the grocery store."

"Opinionated, are we?" I said with a laugh.

Ed laughed, too. "About some things. Like everybody else."

After breakfast he stood up and said formally, "Thank you. Now I must bless your house for the charity it has given me."

He took the medicine bag from his neck and opened

the pouch, shaking a few bits of tobacco into his palm. Into the four corners of my living room he tossed a few grains, chanting softly in Ojibwa as he did so.

"An offering to the *manitou*, the spirit, of the house," he said. "It's analogous to the sprinkling of holy water and the wafting of incense. It may make good things happen here."

"I hope so," I said.

He peered into the pouch. "Have any cigarettes?"

"I don't smoke."

"I'm getting short of tobacco. I'll have to ask as I go down the beach."

"You use cigarette tobacco for medicine?"

"Sure. Priests make holy water of ordinary water by sanctifying it with a blessing. We medicine men don't exactly sanctify tobacco, though. The spirits like it just as it is. Of course, aromatic pipe tobacco is the best kind, but that's because it smells so good in the medicine pouch. When we can't get it we'll field-strip cigarettes."

Swiftly Ed bound his extra clothes into his blanket bedroll, tied it with the rope and slung it over his shoulder. I followed him out on the beach.

"Any parting advice for me?" I said.

He drew himself straight and peered out over the lake.

"Sheriff, the central belief of any Indian tradition is to look at yourself as not what circumstance has made you but what you have done with your life," he said. "The songs in your memory will celebrate what you leave behind." After a beat, he added: "The Christian Bible has something to say about that, too. 'What good is it, my brothers, if a man claims to have faith but has no deeds?' That's James, chapter two, verse fourteen."

After a moment of shared silence I said, "I guess this is good-bye."

"Anishinabeg don't say good-bye. That's too abrupt, too final. We say '*Gigaa-wabamin,*' which means 'I'll see you again.'" He thrust out his hand in farewell. "*Gigaa-wabamin,* sheriff."

I didn't bother to correct him, but watched him shrink into the distance as he strode down the beach and finally disappeared around a rocky promontory.

FOURTEEN

Ginny eats slowly and daintily, like the cultivated Wellesley graduate she is. For no good reason I tend to bolt my food like a starving dog. I always have, despite my adoptive mother's efforts to rein in my headlong appetite. My adoptive father was no help. All his life he had too many things to do and too many people to see to regard the dining table as anything other than a brief and necessary fuel stop. Much as I love the taste of good food, I was sadly influenced, and boyhood habits are hard to break once they've become ingrained. Lectures about slowing down to enjoy the taste make good sense, but about eating I have never been sensible.

Ginny and I finally reached a truce after several months of hissing at each other across the tablecloth: "It's not a race!" and "You're the president of the Slow Eaters of America!" And so I sat patiently waiting for her to finish her lamb chop in an upscale lodge restaurant in Eagle River, where we'd escaped for a little midweek rest and recreation. It was late and the place was nearly empty, but we spoke in hushed tones, as if the walls hung on every word we said.

Almost immediately after I told her about the visit from the Ojibwa medicine man, Ginny quietly dropped the bomb she had carried all the way down from Porcupine City.

"I'd like a child," she said casually, as if she were telling me what she'd prefer for dessert.

An iceberg of panic suddenly calved from the walls of my stomach. Only once before had that glacial feeling enveloped me. It happened the night my childhood sweetheart told me she was pregnant.

"You would?"

"Yes."

Thank God I didn't say "Why?" But consternation must

have been written all over my face, for Ginny took my hand in hers and gazed calmly into my eyes.

"I'm not getting any younger," she said, "and neither are you."

"I don't know if I — "

For a couple of years now Ginny and I had been keeping company, as the old-timers still called relationships like ours. We still lived in our own cabins several miles apart on the lake shore, but had settled into a comfortable routine of weekends at each other's places, content to enjoy the present without dwelling on the future. I could have gone on for years more, basking in the love of a beautiful woman while making her happy in small, everyday ways. Sooner or later, I knew somewhere in the unvisited nooks and crannies of my mind, things would have to change. It was the natural order of life. But I was hardly ready for that, even though, like Ginny, I had reached my early forties.

"But aren't you — "

"Too old?" she said. "Yes, for a natural child. I know the risk is small these days, but I don't want to take it. I want to adopt."

Her use of the first person startled me. "You?" I said dumbly.

She arched a pretty eyebrow and gazed at me steadily.

"Don't you mean we?" I said.

"Perhaps." Her eyes fastened on mine like lasers.

"I — "

"Stevie Two Crow, you are having trouble finishing your sentences."

"This is so — "

"Sudden?" she said after a long beat.

I nodded and looked at the table, then the far wall, then the ceiling, anywhere but into her eyes.

"I need time to get used to the idea," I stammered.

"Obviously." Ginny's smile was warm and amused, but maybe not as warm and amused as it could have been.

For a few moments we sat silent. Then she rolled another grenade down the aisle.

"I'd like to adopt an Indian child."

My jaw dropped as a rush of memories blindsided me.

The Reverend Carl Martinez, the white Methodist missionary who with his wife had adopted me, loved me. In the manner of so many public men, however, he was incapable of showing it with those closest to him, though he was generous and demonstrative with God's love for his flock. To an immature lad like me it seemed that to me he could express only anger, infrequent but often accompanied by a slap or whack of limber birch. I loved and hated him at the same time, as sons will. I learned the truth about Dad's feelings only long after he and Mother were killed at the hands of a drunken driver. He was proud of the child he had rescued from the pagans to bring up as a highly achieving, although brown-skinned, Christian schoolboy and athlete. Deep down I had always known Dad cared, but by then it was too late. I had left his church. Not for me his piously selfish certainty that Jesus was the only true path to salvation.

I was glad, however, that he was not around to learn that my girlfriend had become pregnant. I doubted that the generosity of his Christian forgiveness would have extended that far. He just would have been too disappointed that the youth in whose bright future he had expended so much hope and energy had turned out to be like everyone else, tasting forbidden fruit before marriage—even though we had planned to wed as soon as I returned from Desert Storm. I doubted that Dad would have thought to console me after I learned one dark night in Iraq that my sweetheart was pregnant not by me but by the close friend who had been part of our inseparable neighborhood triumvirate when we were growing up in Troy. Nor would he have approved of the impulsive, self-lacerating leap I then made, resigning my lieutenant's commission as soon as I could and running away to hide as an ill-paid deputy in an obscure Upper Michigan backwoods sheriff's department. Of course I had come to believe that that hasty act was the smartest thing I had ever done, for it had led eventually into the heart and arms of Virginia Anttila Fitzgerald as well as roots in a part of the country I had also fallen in love with.

But now I began to resist Ginny's plan. "You know it's not necessarily a good idea for whites to adopt nonwhite children," I said. "I know something about that, after all."

"Indeed?" said Ginny. "And what if there aren't enough good Indian homes for Indian orphans? Should they be left to grow up in pinched and crowded orphanages with only meager bits of love from overworked caregivers?"

"No, but—"

"But?"

She had me there, and I couldn't argue with what she said next.

"Steve, times have changed since your adoption. No matter what minority a kid belongs to, the thinking today is that his adoptive parents, whatever they are, should ground him solidly in the culture of his birth parents. Everybody recognizes that the problem you had—and you *still* have—is a problem and has to be dealt with."

And then she drove home the lance. "Besides, Steve, what better adoptive parent could an Indian child have than you?"

Involuntarily I sucked in my breath. The word "marriage" had never been mentioned in our relationship. Someday, sure, I had thought many times, Ginny and I might marry, but "someday" seemed to be a vague time a long way ahead. But did "parent" mean, to Ginny, "husband" or "partner" or "lover" or something else?

"You're thinking Lakota?" I said to cover my confusion.

"Why not Ojibwa?" she said. "The tribespeople of Upper Michigan almost all belong to that nation."

"I don't know much about being an Ojibwa," I protested.

"Do you know much about being a Lakota?" Ginny countered.

During the 1870s, I knew, the Lakota sent a spearhead of warriors farther west to Wyoming to win glory with Sitting Bull and Crazy Horse and their Cheyenne allies at the Battle of the Little Bighorn. Like a fifth-generation Boston Irishman singing the praises of Cuchulainn, I was proud of the Indians' victory over Custer and his men and would often relive their brilliant military tactics over the dinner table, but that didn't make me a cultural Lakota, only a genetic one. What could I say? Everything I knew about my native people—which wasn't much—came from books and from a brief and unsuccessful visit to Pine Ridge when I was in college to see if I could locate my birth parents. And from yesterday's visit from an Ojibwa medicine man.

"No," I admitted, trying to keep the grudging edge out of my voice.

"It would be a new journey for you, Steve, learning how to be an Indian at the same time you're teaching your son how to be one." Ginny, like me, preferred the old word to "Native American," a term invented by a bureaucrat in the United States Department of the Interior and instantly adopted by white professors. I think "Native American" smacks of academic condescension, though I won't argue with anybody who uses it. Many Indians do, though others simply want to be known by the names of their tribes. Identity politics is complicated and more shape-shifting than a Navajo skinwalker.

"I'm just—" I couldn't think of anything more. I stared dumbly out the window into the night, hoping the stars would tell me what to say.

"Not ready to commit," Ginny finished.

I shrugged mutely. Maybe I was and maybe I wasn't.

Damn it, a man needs time to get used to a new idea. It's in our nature. Some of us take longer to come around than others, and I am one of the slowpokes. Deep down I knew that I wanted to be a father someday, and deep down I knew that I would love an adopted child as much as a natural one. But I didn't know it yet.

Silently Ginny slid the bill toward me. We usually went Dutch. I couldn't afford fancy restaurant meals for two on a deputy's salary, but Ginny refused to rub my nose in my poverty by offering to pick up the checks. Tonight, I knew, I had disappointed her with my lack of enthusiasm, and she was making me pay for it.

We drove back to Porcupine City in silence, both of Ginny's hands in her lap rather than one on my leg provocatively. At her house she did not invite me inside, as I had eagerly anticipated earlier in the evening, but instead gave me a cool kiss on the cheek and a pat on the shoulder.

"Good night, Steve," she said. "Think on it a bit."

"I will," I said, and drove home to my cabin and a lonely bed.

FIFTEEN

By noon the next day I was feeling better, having spent a long morning in the shallows repairing one of my two cribs, twenty-four-foot-long, eight-foot-wide log-and-stone jetties jutting into the lake like beached wooden bargeloads of rocks the size of basketballs. Well into the nineteen-sixties, owners of beachfront property on Lake Superior constructed the cribs to protect their shorelines from savage winter tempests, but the truth was that they mostly just caused sand to pile up on one side of the crib or the other, depending on the direction of the waves. Whether or not storms ate away a sandy beach depended more on the fluctuating levels of Lake Superior than on any human intervention. Mother Nature was more powerful than any but the most aggressive concrete fortifications thrown up by the Army Corps of Engineers, and the soldiers had to spend considerable time, as I did, to keep their structures in good repair. And now new cribs were forbidden because they upset the natural course of the currents, or so the feds claimed. They were probably right, although no true Porky would admit such a thing.

I suspected that many cribs were originally cobbled together not only to protect the shoreline but also to give their wealthy out-of-town owners something to occupy their time during the summer in a place that has no theme parks or shopping malls. Out of a perhaps misguided sense of respect for the late Milton Browne, a Wisconsin businessman who had a Finnish craftsman build my four-room cedar log cabin and its cribs shortly after World War II, I kept both in good repair. Log structures are as high-maintenance as Victoria's Secret models and a good deal less exciting to look at. Winters are hard on wooden edifices in Upper Michigan, and to keep ahead of rack and ruin people must spend many days, even weeks, fixing them. Over the decade since I'd bought the cabin from Browne's estate shortly after my arrival in Porcupine County, I'd replaced the roof and several windows, re-chinked the logs and fought rot with hammer, chisel and epoxy wood filler. The summer before, I'd had to have a decayed bottom log in the cabin replaced with masonry, a job I left to the Metrovich brothers, skilled mill hands and bachelor woodsmen who live on their own lakefront land near Porcupine City. They hadn't charged much, just what I could afford with a small bank loan.

I could probably have let the lake slowly pound away the cribs — it would take decades, so solidly built were they — without jeopardizing my beachfront, but inasmuch as the cabin lay dangerously close to the water right on the tree line, I wanted to take no chances, feds or no feds. Hence I spend several weekends each summer repairing storm damage that is usually slight but if ignored will eat away the cribs bit by bit. Mostly I have to wrestle massive stones, hurled by huge waves, back into the log-enclosed structures, sometimes needing block and tackle for a hundred-pound boulder, now and then shoring a broken side log with concrete. Every couple of years a big log needs replacing, and for that I enlist the help of the Metrovichs. We find twenty-foot white pines uprooted by winter storms floating close to shore, trim off the branches, notch the ends and nail things home with yard-long steel spikes and heavy iron sledges. I love watching the Metroviches work. They both are chainsaw sculptors who can scoop out log ends solely by eye, without measuring, and drop them into place over their neighbors for a perfect fit.

Repairing cribs not only helps keep me in shape, but the sweat lubricates my mind, helping me deal with problems that have nothing to do with property maintenance. Each stone heaved back into the crib is a step closer to truth. And so, rock by rock, I was coming to terms with Ginny's dream. Yes, it was time, time to settle down, marry her and start a family. That's not exactly an unexpected milestone for a man, but sometimes a guy has to be blindsided into facing it head on. We give up our carefree old lives only grudgingly. If this was what it took to keep the heart of a treasure like Ginny, so be it. She was right. Marriage and an instant family would be a challenge, but today I felt quite up to it. And so I was going to tell her that evening, for she hadn't broken our supper date at her house.

I had been working in the shallow water bare-chested in soaked jeans and neoprene canoer's shoes to protect my feet from sharp stones. A gentle onshore breeze was clearing the beach of sand flies and mosquitoes, allowing me to work shirtless. Suddenly I felt a familiar yen. My beachfront is isolated, and Sheila Carnahan, I knew, had gone away for the weekend. So had the couple from Arizona who occupy the beach house to the west. And the temperature of the inshore water had crept well into the seventies under the summer sun.

Yes, Lake Superior is cold — fishermen often chill their beer over the gunwales of their boats — but by mid-July the inshore water temperature can climb into the upper sixties, warm enough for comfortable swimming once one gets over the initial shock of immersion. Later in the month and all through August and the middle of September, gentle onshore winds often blow warmer surface water into the shallows, sometimes raising the temperature into the low seventies. Today was one of those days, and it would have been a crime not to glory in it.

Shucking my jeans, briefs and canoe shoes and laying them atop the crib, I dove naked into the water, stroking briskly over the pebbly bottom to a sandbar seventy-five yards out. There the water was shoulder-high, and I could feel a colder layer below my knees. I began swimming laps parallel to the shore, counting two hundred strokes each way and navigating with the edge of the sandbar below through the glass-clear water. Rounded stones lay scattered in piles among the smooth, clean sand, and now and then a minnow darted away in panic as I splashed by. As I swam I exulted quietly in the unfettered stream of water past my flanks, the truest glory of skinnydipping. This must be what it feels like to be a dolphin. I am not a naturist — there are few in Upper Michigan, because of the intense fogs of mosquitoes and blackflies the only sizable American region that has no commercial nudist camps — but I can still appreciate unclad closeness to nature.

Especially in the splendid isolation of these parts. The low growl of an outboard carried over the water from half a mile away, and the only other sign of life was a sail far in the distance, hull below the horizon. Probably a yacht harbored at the Porcupine City marina. Floating on my back in waist-deep water, I let the warm swells rock me gently as the sun flushed my face and belly. In a minute or so I had been lulled into a semi-doze of sensual contentment, and my thoughts drifted to Ginny. She would, I felt sure, be happy about the decision I had made, and would reward me not only with a splendid dinner but also a lovely — ah — dessert far into the night. That mental image, helped along by the warm kiss of the sun, stirred the center of my being. There I felt twitches of anticipation that slowly grew firmer as I lost myself in lustful thoughts. And then a strange hand grasped me.

I looked up into the eyes of Mary Ellen Garrigan.

"God *damn!*" I bellowed. She was as naked as I.

"Thought I'd surprise you, Steve," she said, laughing, her face colored by a concupiscent leer, the kind often seen on the faces of people to whom sex is a contact sport.

I backed away from her in consternation, eyes fixed on her body. It was impossible not to look. Even without her usual encrustation of gold and diamonds she was a traffic-stopper, her tanned flanks doubtless sculpted by hours of work at the Nautilus as well as nips, tucks and shoves by a distinguished and very expensive plastic surgeon. As I'd seen aboard the *Lucky Six*, her boob job looked almost natural instead of resembling hard grapefruits tucked under the skin, and if her breasts had swayed a little more I'd have been fooled. She'd had a butt tuck, too, I was certain. And she was shaven. A wet dream for porn addicts.

Despite my deepening anger at the woman's arrogance—I am, goddamnit, just too proud to allow my Indian identity to be used for cheap thrills—I am a healthy male with a normal autonomous nervous system and normal physiological reactions, and my body was now fully awakened. Despite that I stood and strode furiously through the now knee-deep water across the pebbled bottom toward the beach, ignoring the painful crunch of rough stones under the soles of my feet.

"Let's!" Mary Ellen called breathily. "Right here in the water! Nobody will see!"

I stopped and turned to her, fighting to keep my composure. "I'm not interested, Mrs. Garrigan," I said from between clenched teeth.

"What a sorry, sorry asshole you are!" she replied as I strode onto the beach next to the crib. She followed me out of the water, lunging and reaching for me, laughing. I quickly stepped back out of range.

"You want me, Martinez, but you're a coward!" Scorn stained the leer on her face.

I glanced down at myself, dismayed by my still-attentive state, and hid it with my jeans. "Please go home, Mrs. Garrigan," I said. "You are on my property, and I do not want you here." It took all my willpower not to call the scheming bitch a scheming bitch.

Just as she turned and strode to the pile of clothes she had left on the beach, a car door slammed. I peered into the woods. The brown Ford van belonging to the Historical Society that Ginny drove every day fishtailed violently, throwing gravel, as it sped away up my dirt driveway to the highway beyond the forest. My heart sank, and so did the rest of me.

SIXTEEN

Long before we met and shortly before she returned to Porcupine County, Ginny, then a young widow in Manhattan, had very nearly lost her heart—and her considerable portfolio—to an unscrupulous, much-married fortune hunter who had also betrayed many other wealthy women in order to fund the charitable enterprise that had made him famous. She discovered his treachery in time, but her recovery from the betrayal took many years and a change of scenery from glittering New York City to rustic Porcupine County, where she had grown up, daughter of a mining engineer who sent her to Wellesley. I'd been recovering from the shock of my sweetheart's perfidy, too, and Ginny and I had slowly healed our wounds together. Now she thought I had turned on her. Her newfound, hard-earned confidence was probably shattered. Persuading her otherwise was going to be difficult. Very difficult. She had seen what she had seen, and the truth would just sound lame.

I pulled on my jeans and shirt and, not bothering to comb my hair, leaped into my Jeep and tore after her. But when I knocked on her door, she called out the kitchen window, "Please go. I don't want to talk to you."

"But, Ginny—" I said, ashamed of the pleading I could not keep out of my voice.

"Go."

I left. What else could I do?

I wrested the Jeep back onto the highway and drove home, flooring the accelerator, the rusty old heap's transmission protesting as it slowly crept up to its top speed, seventy-five miles an hour. There would be no cop to run me down, for I was the cop who caught speeders on Highway M-64 along the lake shore.

On my way to work the next morning I pulled up at the

Historical Society, an old supermarket building in Porcupine City slathered with donated purple paint, and strode inside.

"She called twenty minutes ago," said Nancy Aho, the sweet blue-haired docent in charge, "and said she had to go away for a while, but that she'd be in touch. Is anything wrong?"

"No," I said, ashamed of the lie, trying to keep my voice normal. "Just checking."

"I'm sorry, Steve," Nancy said. "But I'm sure everything will be all right. Is this your first fight?"

Shit. It's impossible to conceal a secret of the heart from the good ladies of Porcupine County. They generally don't make other people's sex lives their business, but they're extraordinarily observant about them. And, there not being a lot else to occupy their minds besides hunting, fishing, moving snow and making love, as the old Yooper joke has it, they gossip. A lot. Before nightfall every woman in the county and many in the neighboring ones would know that the Lakota deputy and his sweetheart were on the outs. And so, by the time supper was done, would the men.

I tried Ginny's cell phone from the Jeep without result. But she either wasn't answering or was out of range, for few places in the Upper Peninsula are hospitable to wireless calls. With a sinking heart I guessed where she had gone. She was on her way to Detroit and the comfort and counsel of her lawyer and accountant. It would take her almost eleven hours to get there, for she had to drive due east to the Mackinac Bridge, then south by southeast down the middle of Lower Michigan.

I knew the number of her lawyer — she had entrusted me with it just in case something untoward happened to her — but knew that he would take his client's side against mine. That's a lawyer's job. It was pointless to call.

I drove back to Ginny's cabin and scrawled a note.

"Dearest," it said, "it's not what you think. Please call.

My deepest love. Steve."

Banal as these words are, they were all I could think of, and I knew they would not move her.

But I slipped the note inside an envelope and left it inside her screen door, hoping it would be the first thing she saw when she returned.

SEVENTEEN

Before I had finished dressing the next morning, my heart a cast-iron lump in my chest, the radio on my kitchen table crackled. It was Joe Koski.

"Steve?"

"Here. Still at home." As I listened I buckled on my gunbelt, from which dangled a tooled leather holster cradling a well-oiled .357 Combat Magnum, an old-fashioned six-shot revolver the other deputies, who carried up-to-date 9mm Beretta semi-automatics, liked to make fun of. But I preferred tried-and-true old tools. Though it was unlikely, a high-tech nine-shot Beretta still could jam. A revolver never would.

"It's Sam Williamson and Steve Turner," Joe said.

"Oh no," I said. I knew what that meant.

"Yes," Joe said. "Steve is in the woods outside Sam's place and they're shooting at each other," he said. "With hunting rifles. Neighbor heard the gunfire and said he saw Steve behind a tree shooting cedar shakes off Sam's house."

"Jeez."

Williamson and Turner, two elderly and fierce Porkies, occupied opposing sides of an issue that recently had inflamed the more politically engaged segments of the county: the return of timber wolves to the western Upper Peninsula. The wolf had been eradicated from the state early in the twentieth century along with the passenger pigeon, grayling trout, caribou, fisher, wolverine and moose. Over the last few years a couple of wolf packs from Canada had traveled south and east around Lake Superior through Canada and upper Wisconsin, seeking *lebensraum* — room to live — and food. Wilderness had returned to the old cut-over logging and mining lands where the population of deer, their favorite prey, had exploded. The wolves were migrants, not hopeful reintroductions of rare species by human hands but a natural event. And they had begun to multiply, splitting off into new packs as their numbers grew.

Most Upper Peninsulans have welcomed the return of the wolf as well as the fisher, the big martenlike weasel now legally trapped for its fur. Eagles abound. Young moose now wander through downtowns and have to be shooed back into the woods. The cougar is back, too, many Yoopers will tell you, although the DNR steadfastly denies its presence in Upper Michigan. It's too easy, say the rangers, to mistake a fleeting sight of another animal, perhaps a lynx, for the big tawny cat. Still, most folks who say they have seen them don't strike me as the kind to be fooled easily.

All the same, the return of once vanished animals warms the hearts of people who love the wilderness and all its wonders, as it does mine. More than once I've spotted one or two wolves trotting along highway verges. I have pulled off the road to watch them, and they have stopped, turned and stared at me confidently, as to say, "Keep out of our way, and we'll keep out of yours." They're beautiful, proud animals, and, like any Ojibwa or Lakota, I'm happy to share the territory with them. They call out to me from the heart of a land they lived in for many millennia before human beings arrived. "We were Native Americans long before you," their piercing golden eyes seem to say, "and we belong to this country as much as you do."

But in some places, Johnny-come-lately wolf haters are almost as plentiful as wolf lovers. Driven by emotion and irrationality, they condemn the animals as wasteful and indiscriminate, preying on domestic dogs and cattle and killing for sport, not for survival. The nuttier among them claim anti-hunting organizations have encouraged government efforts to reintroduce the wolf, even though it has come back on its own, absolutely unaided by humans. They say elderly berry pickers can no longer walk the woods confidently, for the wolves will kill them and drag them to their lairs for supper. The very nuttiest perceive wolves as a sign of the Devil, as if their fur were emblazoned with the number "666."

Sam Williamson is one of those, and no amount of argument from the opposite side would sway him as wolf sightings increased in the last few months. No wild wolf has ever attacked a human in the entire state of Michigan. Wolves do take the occasional calf, but the Michigan Department of Natural Resources reimburses farmers for their losses. Wolves do prey on deer, but prefer old, sick and catchable specimens, leaving more browse available for strong bucks and does. Wolves do kill dogs running loose as well as those tied out overnight in their owners' yards. A breeder of Karelian bear dogs had been repeatedly warned by the Forest Service not to release his animals in a particular stretch of the Ottawa National Forest where a wolf pack had been sighted, but scoffed and did so anyway. In a single day the pack killed all four of his dogs, and the breeder shouted that his right to use public lands had been violated.

Sam, who is an educated man—he grew up in Porcupine County, graduated from the University of Michigan, and spent forty years as a certified public accountant in Lansing before retiring to his home county— took up the breeder's case, writing furious letters to the *Porcupine County Herald* that spurred furious counter-letters. For weeks the letters-to-the-editor page roiled with rage, and readers couldn't wait for *The Herald* to appear in the supermarkets on Wednesday morning to see who had taken up the cudgels.

Steve Turner was one of these, and though he had the facts on his side so far as I was concerned, he was as hotheaded as Sam, who had been his closest friend in high school. Like Sam, Steve had left home after high school, made a living as a plumber in the Chicago area and, when he reached retirement age, had come back to Porcupine County to live. Not for nothing do some Porkies call their home the world's largest retirement village.

Twice Steve and Sam had been thrown out of Hobbs' Bar, Grill and Northwoods Museum downtown after coming to blows over the subject of wolves, and the second time I arrested them, drove them to jail, and clapped them into separate cells to sleep it off. The next morning we didn't bother with charges — if we did that we'd have to triple the size of the jail to accommodate all the drunken Saturday-night score-settlers we pick up — but the undersheriff had threatened to skin them and nail their hides to his wall if they went at it again.

Gil's tough love had done no good. Slowly the dispute had escalated. Now Sam had threatened to take his rifle from his cabin in the woods off Norwich Road — he is an expert deer hunter, like Steve — and kill every wolf he could find, and Steve had vowed to shoot him before he could carry out his threat.

"They're liquored up, too," Joe cut in, almost as an afterthought. Surprise.

If Porcupine County had been a big city, SWAT teams swiftly would have been called out and the subjects immediately isolated and perhaps picked off by black-clad sharpshooters before they could threaten the lives of others. There is a plan for sheriff's departments and state police posts to come to the aid of any Upper Michigan jurisdiction that needs such a show of force, but Sam and Steve were likely to kill each other before reinforcements could arrive.

I keyed the radio. "Chad?" I asked.

"On the way," he replied immediately. "I'm at Matchwood. I can be at Sam's cabin in ten minutes." That was on State Highway M-28, the main east-west road in the southern part of the county, about seven miles south of Sam's cabin on Norwich Road. Though Chad's voice was brisk and professional, that did not make me feel better. Inexperience often trumps courage. Though Chad hardly lacked grit, he had almost no seasoning.

"Trooper with you," crackled the gravelly voice of Sergeant Alex Kolehmainen. "I'm at Ewen." That was five miles southwest of Matchwood on M-28. If Alex and I started now, we both knew, we'd get to Sam's about the same time. Chad, being closest, would arrive first, and I hoped he wouldn't do anything stupid and heroic.

"Chad?"

"Yes, Steve?"

"When you get there, wait for us."

"Yes sir!"

I perform my highway patrols in the department's Explorer. Much of my work takes me into the woods on old logging tracks, and a sturdy four-wheel-drive is much better than the old Ford police cruisers the other deputies use. The Explorer is fast enough, but it still took nearly fifteen minutes to slalom around the potholes down Norwich Road to Sam's cabin. When I pulled up, Chad's cruiser and a beefed-up state police Tahoe Alex had lately been driving stood cheek by jowl on what passed for Sam's lawn. They had come in silently, as I had, without siren or flashers. No reason to announce our arrival with fanfare and spook our targets into wasting bullets in our direction.

"They're not here," Alex said. "Neighbor said Sam ran into the woods with his rifle and Steve followed. They've gone north."

Alex glanced at me. Though we shared the jurisdiction, troopers outrank deputies. But Alex is not a rank-puller. And he respected me and I him. Slowly our relationship had become collegial, then friendly. He knows forensics better than I do, I know nature better than he does, and we divide tasks according to our talents.

"What think?" he said.

I pulled out a topographical hiker's map and pointed to a faint dashed line representing the North Country Trail.

That's a little-known transcontinental work-in-progress nominally headed by the National Park Service but administered by local hiker's groups. Some seventeen hundred miles of a planned four-thousand-mile trail so far has been carved from east to west across the United States. The existing path stretches from the Appalachian Trail in eastern New York State to the middle of North Dakota. It is not unbroken, but the gaps are slowly being filled in. In western Upper Michigan, the trail has been well established with blazes, wooden footbridges, lean-tos and campgrounds for 140 miles from Baraga to the Wolverines, and it draws hundreds of serious hikers every summer. The rugged track is gorgeous, traversing hardwood and conifer forests, lakes, bogs, rivers, beaver ponds, waterfalls, and high cliffs with spectacular views. Ginny and I had trekked much of it one October when the bugs lay dormant and the nip of oncoming winter rustled the falling leaves.

"See where the trail crosses Norwich Road and enters the woods, right there? Sam and Steve probably took it. They're old guys and they won't be moving fast. They'll stop now and then to fire at each other and keep at it until one hits the other or they run out of ammo."

As if to punctuate my words a muffled rifle shot rang through the woods, followed by another, not quite as loud. Sam and Steve both were packing powerful rifles that could easily drop a deer or a man. I hoped we could catch up to them before one did in the other. I also hoped drink would spoil their aim.

"Maybe we should split up," I suggested. "One of us can follow the trail while the other two go through the woods twenty or thirty yards away on either side and a little bit behind. We'll be able to cover each other better that way. And if Sam or Steve uses us for targets, we won't be bunched up."

"Good idea," Alex said. He had been in the military, too, and knew infantry tactics. "You take the lead, Steve, and Chad and I will cover the flanks."

We set off, each armed according to our preference. Chad and Alex carried lightweight AR-15 military rifles, and I a police riot shotgun, an excellent weapon for close combat. I hoped mightily that none of us would need to use them. While neither Sam nor Steve was a particular friend of mine, neither were they truly bad guys, only impassioned hotheads who had suddenly lost what remained of their good sense, if they ever had any in the first place. That's what's tough about law enforcement in this part of the world. We're not dealing with simple clashes between good and evil, but the petty imperfections of human beings. Big-city cops separate themselves from the people they arrest by calling most of them "assholes," but we country deputies just call ours "idiots."

That part of Porcupine County is world-class rugged, the rocky trail dipping into bramble-choked gullies and climbing up bare, slippery escarpments. The going was slow. The temperature had climbed into the nineties, as it often does in late August. Blackflies and no-see-ums assaulted every square inch of bare skin. I tried to breathe shallowly, hoping not to inhale the fiery midges. And, following the trail, I had the best of it. Chad and Alex had to fight their way through the brush. Neither man made much noise, except now and then the crack of a dry twig or the scrabble of loose rock.

A shot rang out nearby, immediately followed by an answer. If they were still trading gunfire, Sam and Steve had not killed each other yet. At such moments I grasp for the obvious.

"Steve!" Chad yelled. He crouched only a few yards west of me, but I couldn't see him through the brush.

"Which one?" I yelled back. A common name can be most inconvenient when both hunter and hunted share it.

"You! Not him!"

"Well, thanks!" I shouted. "Call me Martinez, for Chrissake!"

"Martinez! Turner's coming your way!"

At the same moment I spotted the other Steve twenty yards up the trail, shambling toward me in a crouch. He wore hunting camouflage and no signal orange to announce his presence in the woods. That was evidence of premeditation. It might mean a rap for attempted murder.

Turner whirled, knelt and fired in the opposite direction. A heavier report answered, and a bullet neatly decapitated an inch-thick sapling six feet from my head. I dropped to my belly and thrust the riot gun in front of me, taking a bead on Turner's broad back. At this range a spread of buckshot couldn't miss. It probably wouldn't be fatal, but the heavy shot would tear him up some.

"Turner!" I yelled. "Police! Drop the rifle right now!"

He had the good sense to stop in his tracks, toss the rifle to the side, and fall to both knees, his hands up.

"Don't let Sam shoot me!" he called. "I'm out of ammo!"

"Well, shit," Williamson shouted whiskily from behind a stump on higher ground. "So am I! Ain't this your lucky day?"

"Shut up, Sam," Alex called.

"Steve, lie down on your belly and put your hands behind your back!"

"Who zat?" Sam said.

"Sheriff's department," I called back. "State police. We've taken Turner. Put your rifle down and walk toward us slowly and keep your hands in sight."

Slowly Sam lurched into view, grinning sheepishly.

"The son of a bitch tried to kill me," he said righteously.

"Yes, yes," I said. "Never mind. You're coming with us till we get this all sorted out."

Alex stepped out from the shelter of a thick tree trunk and swiftly cuffed Sam's hands behind him. Sam did not protest. All the vinegar had whooshed out of him, whether from the exertion of the chase or the sudden realization that his cause had very nearly gotten him killed, I didn't know.

As Alex covered Turner, facedown in the leaves, I knelt, one knee in the small of his back, and clapped my own set of cuffs on him, wrinkling my nose against a cloud of cheap rye. Before I pulled him to his feet I fished the Miranda card from my shirt pocket and read him his rights.

Almost before I finished, a crackle of branches and a thud echoed from close by "Shit! Damn!" Chad bellowed.

"Chad, are you all right?"

"Yeah. Slipped down a creek bank. I'm okay. . . . Holy Mary, mother of God!"

"What's wrong?" I shouted.

"Aagh," he replied.

In a moment Chad had climbed back up the muddy bank, his uniform stained with mud, his face white. With a trembling hand he held toward me what appeared to be a small brown horseshoe.

It was a human mandible.

EIGHTEEN

The jaw, stained by decades in the muddy bank of the forest creek, looked almost ancient, maybe a century old. Yellowed teeth still clung to its sockets.

We scrambled down the bank, rising the height of a man above the pebbly trickle of a creek, and braced our feet on roots jutting from the ground. As he skidded down the steep slope, Chad had reached out to catch himself, and his hand had unwittingly plucked the mandible out of the moist earth. The skull to which it had once been attached protruded from the rocky loam.

"This," said Alex, "is a crime scene."

"How?"

"See that?" He pointed a latex-clad finger at the large triangular hole on the back of the skull. "Dollars to doughnuts that was made with a miner's pickaxe."

We had frog-marched the two woozy miscreants back to Sam's cabin, where Undersheriff O'Brien and Sheriff Garrow had rolled up shortly before in the sheriff's nearly new Crown Victoria cruiser, the one a jailhouse trusty washed once a day and waxed once a week. They and Chad had transported Sam and Steve to the lockup at Porcupine City, where Sam faced a stern lecture from the undersheriff and Steve a felony charge that probably would send him to prison long enough to douse his political fires. Afterward Gil, his ranks always understaffed, had ordered Chad back on patrol. I wished he were still on the scene. Like the aftermath of the discovery of Frank Saarinen's body, what happened next would have been instructive for a green young police officer.

Alex opened his crime-scene kit, fished out his digital camera and examined the bare creek bank before him. "That's a hand," he said. "And there's a boot."

The body protruded from the bank a good four feet below the surface of the forest floor. It had been buried away from the creek, which over the decades had slowly carved its way through the earth toward the body until its bones lay exposed.

Carefully Alex troweled out every bone and bit of moldered clothing he could find after photographing it *in situ*. The job took several hours because the stained skeleton was mostly disarticulated, though a few remaining thews and sinews bound together an arm and a hand here, the spine and pelvis there. Alex lay everything on a plastic tarp in more or less the same arrangement it had enjoyed in life.

"Good thing the anthropologists aren't here," Alex said halfway through. "They'd want to do things their way, and that'd take days and even weeks."

University scientists set up tents over their sites and uncover artifacts layer by layer, pebble by pebble, capturing everything as it lies, amassing mountains of data to sort out in their labs and workrooms. Cops have crooks to catch and prosecute and just don't have the time to enjoy the details of history. This is not to say that good cops are careless about their crime scenes. They try hard to preserve and record anything and everything that might convict a perp.

"But this is no archaeological dig," Alex continued. The scene isn't that old."

"Yeah."

"Steve, this guy was probably a miner. It's not just the hole in the skull. Look at that boot."

The thick rubber sole dangling from a crushed ankle-high boot, its leather falling in tatters, was the sort miners of a hundred years ago favored to cushion their feet against the rocky floors of mine drifts.

"Figures," I said. "We're almost on the site of the old Norwich mine, and the Venture is just a couple of miles away."

"Aha!" Alex said as he troweled a greenish round lump from beneath a tattered leather belt. "Here's a pocket watch!" With a paintbrush he whisked away the damp soil. "Look."

The legend A. CARMICHAEL 1889 loomed faintly through the mold and verdigris.

"This is probably the name of our victim," Alex said, unconsciously adopting the tone of a schoolmaster, as he usually does in such situations. "And what else does that tell you?"

"That he most likely wasn't killed in a robbery," I said. "The perp or perps would've taken everything, even a cheap two-dollar brass pocket watch from a general store."

"Right," Alex said. Those conclusions were obvious to both of us, but voicing them put them out in the open where we could use them as a point of departure.

"Whoever killed this guy didn't want him to be found," Alex added. "Even with six inches or so of new leaf mold laid down over seventy-five or a hundred years, this grave was at least three feet deep. That would've kept animals from getting at the body."

"And if it had been an honest burial, which it wasn't," I said, "the hole would have been the traditional six feet deep. There always have been plenty of cemeteries around here. No reason to bury a loved one alone in the woods." Like most rural people, Upper Michiganders favor community for death as well as survival.

Alex daintily fished a rusty clasp knife from the grave. "Look, there are a few coins, too. Here's a silver dollar."

Finished, Alex folded the tarp carefully around its contents and clambered up the bank.

"I'll ship this stuff to Lansing," he said, "but we may never hear a thing about it. The forensic guys have enough to do without worrying about a murder so old the perps are long gone."

"I'll see if I can find out who A. Carmichael was," I said.

"Why bother?"

"Never can tell."

"Suit yourself," Alex said with a grunt, but his tone wasn't derisive. He knew a little dogwork in old archives could sometimes turn up surprising clues. Like me, he'd solved crimes that way. And like me, he took a deep interest in the history of his jurisdiction. In the Upper Peninsula of Michigan, one can sometimes find motives for latter-day murder in resentments buried so long and so deep that everyone but victim and villain have forgotten them.

"Let's take a look around," I said. "Cover a bit of ground, see what we can turn up."

We trudged along the North Country Trail over the creek and through the woods west along the ridge that, I knew from my study of old maps, marked the limit of the Norwich Mine. Over a rise we heard the grinding hum of a wood chipper, and in a few moments we entered a large clearing in the forest. On one side rose a ridge four hundred feet high. On the opposite side of the ridge lay the Venture Mine.

Two eighteen-wheelers with big open box vans stood on a gravel road along the ridge. The steel spout of a wood chipper, its machinery turned off, curved high into the top of one of the trailers. A nearly new galvanized steel building, thirty feet by forty, fetched up against the ridge. Before it stood three men, rough and unshaven woods types clad in soiled canvas jackets and pants. They stared at us suspiciously as we emerged from the brush. One held a rifle loosely in his hands.

"Why the weapon?" I said, hand on my holster.

The man relaxed slightly and glanced away. He was a stranger, as were the other two. "Heard shots a couple hours ago," he said laconically. "Didn't know what was going on. Just wanted to be careful."

I wondered if he ever used the first person singular.

People who avoid "I" usually avoid your eyes, too. They're a little short on personality.

"Well, it's okay now," I said. "You can put that away."

Carefully he cranked back the rifle's bolt, extracted the cartridge from its chamber, and laid the weapon against the chipper, but his stony expression remained.

"Just a couple of drunks shooting at each other," Alex said, reducing a complex story to a sentence fragment. "We sorted that out. Nobody hurt here, right?"

They nodded silently, still tense. That was odd. Most woodsmen would have relaxed visibly, maybe made a little joke.

"Who you working for?" I asked, nodding at the chipper.

"Weinstein," said the oldest of the three.

"Ah, yeah," I said. "This is Venture Mine property." Morrie Weinstein liked to maximize his income, even though the money his property earned from the sale of shredded pulpwood couldn't have covered much more than the cost of its labor. "Where do you sell the chips?" I asked, just to be conversational.

"Wisconsin."

I didn't ask "Where in Wisconsin?" because there was no reason to. But I did think it curious that Morrie, who was such a Porcupine County booster, wasn't selling the chips to the paper mill in his adopted hometown. I grunted.

Alex had picked up on my suspicion. "Let's have a look at the trucks," he said.

The three men stiffened. But they didn't protest as Alex swung up the ladder on the side of one open trailer box and peered inside.

"Looks full," he said. "You must be ready to make tracks."

"Yeah," said the oldest of the men.

None of them had anything to add, and neither did we.

"Take care," Alex said. "Stay out of trouble." He was

subtly warning the men that the cops had their eye on them. Law-abiding citizens will resent such a suggestion, but you can sometimes get a rise out of crooked ones with it.

Both Alex and I spotted the quick, furtive glances the men shot at each other.

We disappeared into the woods and made our way through whippy saplings and grasping underbrush back to the old trail. Out of earshot Alex stopped and turned.

"Those guys are up to no good. Those wood chips were almost pure aspen. No hardwood at all." Paper mills prefer hardwood chips, which bring a much greater yield of pulp per cord—a ton and a half per cord—than aspen at eighty-five hundredths of a ton. No real woodsman, unless he were desperate, would cut only aspen. He would also throw in as much low-quality scrub hardwood as he could find, leaving the good stuff to grow, as the law demanded. Otherwise the return for his heavy labor would be absurdly low, like collecting thousands of soda and beer cans for the nickel deposit.

"Agreed," I said. "But what?"

"I don't know," he said. "What's there for criminals to do out here in the woods? Poach? Maybe they have some deer carcasses buried in those chips."

"Nah. There are easier ways to transport poached deer."

"Maybe they're just idiots."

"Probably."

Neither of us really thought so.

NINETEEN

Less than forty-eight hours had elapsed since the unpleasant scene on my beach, and I was missing Ginny mightily. The whole town now knew that the quiet pool of our relationship had been roiled by a huge rock, although no one had any idea of the stone's shape or size. At the sheriff's department that morning, nobody offered a word to me but carefully made sure not to cross my path. Even Gil, a martinet born to stare daggers through underlings, avoided my gaze. Only the gossipy Joe Koski, who had never in his life been at a loss for words, said anything.

The dumpy little dispatcher slipped off the stool at his counter in the front of the office and patted me on the shoulder. "Want to talk about it?" he asked solicitously. Everyone's jaw dropped in astonishment. Even for Joe, a man who had absolutely no self-awareness, that was presumptuous. Gil scurried into his office and shut his door. Chad clapped on his hat and shambled out the door, his big hip catching an oak swivel chair and spinning it madly. Riley Pearson, another deputy at his desk, found something to do in the lockup. Only Joe and I were left in the room.

I sighed. Joe is really a good fellow, even if he matches Chad's gorilla-in-a-china-shop clumsiness with folks' feelings.

"I don't think so, Joe," I said, trying not to sound irritated but failing.

"It'll be okay," he replied confidently. "Uncle Joe knows." He patted my shoulder.

"See you, Joe," I said. "I'm heading for the archives to see if I can identify that body we found yesterday."

I quickly thrust back my chair and stalked out, winning the battle against slamming the door as I departed.

On the short drive to the courthouse, where the county's archives are stored, I realized that the chances of discovering the identity of A. Carmichael were not open and shut. The watch presumably had come into his possession in 1889, but the sheriff's department had burned to the ground in 1896, when a forest fire from the south ignited nearly the entire village of Porcupine City, the holocaust fueled by the super dry tinder of the Diamond Match Company mill in the center of town. If Carmichael had been killed before then, no official trace of him might exist. After the great Porcupine City fire, however, the county had carefully stored its records in the most fireproof manner it could, and today's nearly new courthouse was a shining example.

I wasn't a stranger to the records department, and Julie Boudreau, the birdlike little French Canadian clerk in charge, seemed to think me one of her more interesting patrons. Ginny's eager tales about Porcupine County had whetted my curiosity about the place's history, and once I had asked Julie to help me research famous old murders in Porcupine County for a little slide lecture for a dinner meeting of the historical society.

But the interest Julie showed that day had nothing to do with smoking out obscure old facts. She looked up with sad, concerned eyes from her desk and said simply, "Hello, Steve." I was glad she neither offered condolences nor pretended perkily that everything was fine and isn't it a nice day.

"Need the sheriff's archive beginning in 1896," I said.

"Trying to identify the body you found yesterday?" Julie said. "I've already got the boxes lined up."

I wasn't the least bit surprised. News travels fast even in these parts, over the forest telegraph network—CB and police radios, scanners, cell phones and landlines, even e-mail and the Web. When a county's lifeblood is slowly leaking away, the survivors stay afloat by paying close attention to each other, as if lashing together their life rings. That's annoying and gratifying at the same time. You can't change your brand of toothpaste without everyone knowing about it. And mounting a quiet investigation out of sight and out of mind? Ho-ho.

Julie led me to the back of the fireproof storeroom, its walls constructed of painted concrete blocks, and sat me at a long low table among a dozen large white cardboard boxes. She removed the lid to the box marked "1896-97" and handed me a pair of soft cotton gloves. The records, I knew, would be of considerable historical value someday, and Julie was taking very good care of them.

"Be real careful, Steve," Julie said.

"Will," I said.

As she turned to leave, she solicitously patted me on the back. I sighed.

The old sheriffs, I saw, had been meticulous at their recordkeeping. The closed cases were arranged in separate files marked ascending order of gravity—"Incidents," "Papers served," "Misdemeanors" and various felonies all the way up to "Homicides." But it was the open case files I was looking for, and in a few moments of rummaging I fished out the "Disappearances" folder for the pertinent years. It was surprisingly thick.

In those days many men disappeared every year into the forest or out onto the lake. The late nineteenth century was a violent time in Upper Michigan, for the territory marked the northern frontier of the United States. It didn't have cowboys and horses, but it had tough, rowdy, hard-drinking miners and loggers. From time to time, as the years rolled by through the files, I'd spot a dry, brown and crumbling "Missing" or "Information Sought" clipping from the Porcupine County Herald attached to a missing-persons sheet. Arthur Kempainen, Toivo Karttunen, Michael Welch, Ronald Aho, William Mazurek, Guy Paulsen and John Kucinich all were being hunted by their wives and sometimes their children, too. Some of them had wandered drunkenly out of gin mills and passed out in the woods or out on the frozen lake, and in the spring a few bodies would turn up in the forest or wash up on the shore. For the most part nothing ever was heard again about the men (and a few women) who had vanished.

And then, in the box marked "1909," I finally found what I was looking for — the sheet headed with the name of my quarry and a cutting of a classified ad, just a few lines in the "Personals," in *The Herald* of April 12, 1909:

MISSING

Information sought on the whereabouts of Andrew Carmichael of Porcupine City, last seen at his place of employment at the Venture Mine, Norwich Road, Porcupine County, last March 6. Reward. Write Mrs. Mary Carmichael, 312 Lead Street, Porcupine City. Your wife and children long for your return.

A faded photograph of a square-jawed, heavy-browed man was clipped to the missing-persons sheet, together with a description of the clothes Carmichael had been wearing and the possessions he had been known to carry — including a "brass Parker & Ives pocket watch engraved with the subject's name and the date 1889."

That nailed it. I'd send copies of the sheet, the clipping and the photo to the state police forensics lab in Marquette, and if the pathologists had time — which I doubted — they'd compare the photo to the skull and officially identify the bones in the folded blue tarp. Probably the case would get shunted aside, victim of tight budgets and more pressing latter-day investigations. I kept on reading to see if there had been a follow-up, perhaps an obituary or a death notice, though I didn't expect to see a funeral announcement for a body that had never been found — until yesterday.

A shadow loomed over my shoulder. "What do you got, Stevie boy?" it said.

He was Horace Wright, *The Herald*'s only reporter, a retired Milwaukee newspaperman who ten years before had moved to the Upper Peninsula and gone to work part-time as a proofreader for the weekly. Slowly the job had expanded and he had returned to his old street-reporter specialty full-time. It kept Horace, now pushing eighty, alert and active. He was the only man in Porcupine County who, day in and day out, wore a suit and bow tie, usually with deliberately clashing color and design, underneath a wild gray walrus mustache that set off his plump, reddish face. "Got to be noticed some way," he once had confided. All that was missing was a fedora with a press card in the hatband. Horace usually went hatless, except when the winter wind chill approached absolute zero. Then he'd don a bright red plaid woolen Elmer Fudd hat, carefully tying the earflaps under his chin.

I marveled at the broad ground Horace covered in the Herald every week, reporting on the meetings of the village commission, the county board and a score more official bodies. Horace's reports on governmental meetings were narratives, not news stories that presented the important stuff first and worked their way down through lesser details to trivialities. Like official minutes, every one of them began at the beginning, following Robert's Rules of Order from first gavel and the reading of old business and including every parliamentary detail, comment, aside, and, I could swear, fart and burp. This method made for long, long articles, but Herald readers are not busy-busy urban types and have plenty of time to devote to them. Horace said he believed in letting his readers make up their own minds about the importance of items of county business, not filtered through the biased brain of a journalist. From time to time, however, he would let drop a jaundiced editorial aside if he felt strongly about a subject. "Horacisms," we called them, and we could recognize them for what they were, although some readers resented Horace's interjection of opinion in news stories.

Horace also exercised his considerable prose skills in the pungent right-wing opinion pieces he "contributed" to the Herald in the guise of letters to the editor. During Bill

Clinton's presidency he had expounded almost weekly on the character flaws of "Slick Willie," and the discovery of Monica's semen-stained dress had brought forth stern and doom-laden flourishes that startled even the most ardent conservatives of Porcupine County. A couple of evangelical preachers had asked Horace to tone things down. But enthusiastic demonization was the mark of a true Horacism, and he continued to load his pen with vitriol. Lately he had been teeing off on "the homosexuals" and was calling for a constitutional amendment against not only gay marriage but also civil partnership.

Liberal readers—and there are quite a few of them in this conservative but not monolithic rural county—may have scorned Horace's political ideas, but they still liked the man. Although cops and reporters are natural enemies, I respected Horace. He was nosy and noisy, but he was also bright, quick and mostly accurate. I liked the guy, too. He was cordial company at the dinners of the Historical Society, full of rollicking cop stories from his younger days in Madison and Milwaukee. And, despite his printed fulminations against "alternative lifestyles," Horace included Billy Bissell, a large, muscular and flamboyantly gay local plumber, among his poker-table friends. "Hate the sin, love the sinner," Horace said grandiloquently when anyone pointed out this apparent contradiction. Billy was good-natured and forgiving enough to put up with Horace's unconscious patronizing.

"You know perfectly well what I've got, Horace," I said. I shot a resigned glance at Julie, who was trying hard to look studious and innocent at her desk across the room. I knew she had called Horace as soon as she saw I had found what I was looking for. She was one of his best sources. He took her out to dinner frequently.

"May I see?"

They were public records and as a citizen Horace had a perfect right to examine and copy them.

"Okay," I said without rancor, standing back as Horace donned cotton gloves. Horace can be a colorful writer, and I have to admit I looked forward to the story and photo that would appear on the Herald's front page the following Wednesday. I wouldn't be surprised if Horace also turned up a Carmichael descendant or two for comment. He had once been an investigative reporter, and he was as much a digger as he was a political bomb-thrower.

"Would you say Carmichael had been murdered?" Horace asked.

"Fishing for a headline, are you, Horace?" I said with a laugh. "No, I won't. It's not my job to do that. But you can draw your own conclusions."

Horace grinned.

"Julie, can you scan in this stuff and print out three copies of it?" I asked. "One for me, one for Horace and one for the forensics lab?"

"Sure thing." Swiftly Julie ran the documents and photograph through her scanner, producing the results on a big laser printer and slipping them into three folders.

"Don't forget to bill The Herald for Horace's copies," I said. The cost was trivial, two dollars a sheet, a dollar for the folder, but economy is economy, especially in Porcupine County.

"Cheapskate," Horace shot back as he sauntered out with his folder.

Afterward I pushed back the chair and sank into a cloud of contemplation. Frank Saarinen, Roy Schweikert, and now Andrew Carmichael. Three dead men, all employees of the Venture Mine. Add a perhaps overly chummy Venture Mine owner, his creepy yacht skipper, and an unfriendly trio of woodsmen near the mine. What did all that mean?

Maybe something. Maybe nothing.

TWENTY

"What do you think?" I asked Alex a day later in Anthony's, a diner at Bergland at the junction of Highways M-64 and M-28 in the southwest corner of the county, hard by Lake Gogebic and its first-class walleye fishing. I'd asked him to meet me for a late lunch there, and we sat at a booth in the back, well away from curious ears.

Donna, the overstuffed and overcurious owner-baker-waitress who presided over Anthony's the way Gil O'Brien directed the sheriff's department, tried to find things to do at nearby tables, but Alex and I just stopped talking as she approached and gave her big toothy smiles to encourage her to go away and let us be. She waddled back to the front, mopped the counter and shot furious "you're-up-to-something-and-I-have-a-right-to-know-what-it-is" glances at us. But Alex and I were adamant. That pay phone on the wall behind Donna was a direct link to the rest of Porcupine County.

"I hate to admit it," said Alex, "but I think you're right. Something is going on around the Venture. Those three guys in the clearing yesterday sure had pickles up their asses. There's more going on than having just a hard-on against cops. I sure would like to know what they're up to. As for Saarinen and Schweikert and that old corpse, that's *probably* just coincidence."

The stress on the word said Alex, for all his doubts, was keeping an open mind on the facts.

"We can't just go poke around in back of the mine and that building without a warrant," I said. To mount a legal search, we needed the owner's consent, or probable cause that a crime was being committed or had been committed, and that evidence of said crime would be found there. A puzzling encounter with three silent and hostile woodsmen with two truckloads of almost pure aspen pulpwood wasn't probable cause. If we simply traipsed around on private property looking for evidence, found the loggers up to no good and busted them, Judge Rantala would throw out the case. That's what Eli and Gil would tell me if I informed them of my suspicions. And they'd also tell me to lay off the Venture. Don't piss off Morrie, they'd say. He's too important to the county. Go serve subpoenas, douse domestic fires and catch speeders. That's your job.

They'd be right. And Alex's superiors would tell him much the same thing. They don't like independent investigations. Brass hats everywhere hate loose-cannon cops who operate on their own.

But we will anyway if we think we can get away with it. And sometimes we do.

"I have an idea," I said. "Can you get hold of a night-vision video camera? Without the brass asking questions?"

"Sure," Alex said, his dark eyebrows rising at the prospect of performing old-fashioned police work with cutting-edge tools. A wide smile suddenly enlivened his narrow, mournful and blue-jawed face. He looked almost handsome in his ugliness, like a young Abraham Lincoln. For some reason I cannot understand, women find that attractive—even Ginny does—and Alex, a confirmed and dedicated bachelor, makes the most of it. "I can call in a marker at the aviation division. I'm going downstate tomorrow anyway. What have you got in mind?"

For drug-hunting over vast rural expanses, wooded and open, the Michigan State Police headquarters at Lansing equips its helicopters with night eyes and infrared heat-seeking equipment so sensitive it can spot a live Bunsen burner in a meth lab deep inside somebody's basement, although the Supreme Court has ruled that an illegal search. Night-vision gear is too expensive for a country sheriff's department. Our application for a federal grant for some hadn't yet been approved. I often wish we had a pair of goggles or two for night searches in the sheriff's old four-seater Cessna, but those things have to be left to the big boys with bigger budgets.

"A night flight," I said. "We can't go in and look on the ground, but we can go over and look from the air," I said. "Whatever we find, if we find anything, we can always say we were hunting for drugs. And who knows, maybe we'll find some." Search-and-seizure laws are written to protect a citizen's privacy, but sometimes are much harsher where drugs are concerned.

"Right you are!" A smile wreathed Alex's face as the idea sank in.

"How long will it take you to get the stuff?"

"Two, three days," Alex said. "This isn't the sort of equipment you can just put in a overnight chit for. But I'll get it."

"Great." We got up to leave. Donna stirred crankily by the cash register, still miffed at having been shut out of our conversation.

"But." Alex's expression had suddenly turned dubious.

"But what?"

"Won't they hear us?" The roar from airplane engines carries at night, and even a small single-engine Cessna can be heard from miles away.

"You leave that to me. How much do you weigh?"

"One-eighty-two. Why?"

"You'll see."

"I'm afraid I will."

TWENTY-ONE

Even throttled back to idle, the single 160-horsepower engine of a vintage Cessna 172 burbles loudly enough to be heard from more than a thousand feet up, and the still air of a quiet summer night would magnify the noise. But I knew there was a way around that obstacle—a kind of poor man's stealth technology. Basically, Alex and I would take the sheriff's airplane to an altitude high enough and far enough away from the clearing where we had met the three suspicious characters so that I could turn off the engine, kill the airplane's lights, and glide invisibly and noiselessly—or almost so— until we were upon the target we wanted to reconnoiter. Then we'd peer down at the clearing through night-vision equipment, seeing whatever there was to see.

That sounds like a no-brainer, but the details of the plan would need to be carefully thought out and rehearsed, for gliding without power at night over a dark forest is not a casual stroll in the woods. Most pilots like to know exactly where they are over the ground so that if anything goes wrong with the engine they can glide to a safe landing in a field or on a highway if they can't reach an airport. And when they can't see the ground in the dark of night, they get nervous. Still it could be done, and I was confident Alex and I could get away with the stunt.

First, I'd have to work out a plan on paper, drawing a course from Point A to Point B over the midsection of Porcupine County. Then I'd have to roll out the sheriff's airplane and make a casual daylight flight to scope out the course and locate the waypoints I'd need to mark on the chart to tell me where I was. I'd traverse the county at an altitude high enough so that nobody on the ground would think I was on a search, whether for malefactors or the missing.

Back at my cabin I unfolded a topographical hiker's

chart and spread it on the dining table. All of Porcupine County, and much of the rest of western Upper Michigan, is visible on the chart, whose scale is about three miles to the inch, detail sufficient for my purpose. First I drew a straight line from the Bergland lookout tower on a bearing of 095 degrees to the ridge in whose shadow the Venture Mine nestled, the clearing I wanted to reconnoiter lying on the other side of the hill. I measured the line with a ruler, then compared it with the map's scale. Almost exactly ten miles from Point A to Point B.

Then I started on the calculations. A fully loaded Cessna 172, engine at idle, set up for its best glide speed — 70 miles per hour — glides for slightly more than a mile and a quarter while losing 1,000 feet of altitude. Let's see now. The top of the Venture Mine hill is 1,100 feet above sea level. I'd need to arrive above the hill about 500 feet higher. That'd put me on a collision course for the 1,600-foot Norwich lookout tower directly ahead, a little too close for comfort. Hmm. Tinker, tinker, mutter, mutter. Don't forget the drag of a stopped propeller. Better allow for a little wind in either direction. Night air isn't always still. I filled several sheets of paper with scratched-out sums.

At last I had a plan. I'd climb to 8,000 feet above sea level right over Point A, the U.S. Forest Service lookout tower at Bergland, ten miles from the clearing. Then I'd point the plane slightly east by southeast, cut the engine, douse the navigation and strobe lights, and put the nose down until the airspeed indicator read 120 miles per hour. She'd glide almost noiselessly, the rush of wind over her wings and tail barely audible on the ground. Those with sharp ears directly under the flight path might think they'd heard an eagle or a large owl after its prey. The plane would steadily lose altitude over that 10 miles until it reached 1,400 feet above sea level, just 500 feet above the ground at Point B, a little to the left of the clearing Alex and I had our eye on. The course would carry the plane well clear of the Norwich lookout tower.

As we swept by the clearing, we could take a look through night eyes at the place, then sneak away unheard as I lifted the plane's nose and turned southeast, turning the extra glide speed into a few hundred feet of altitude and giving me a couple of miles' room to soar out of earshot before I restarted the engine. Whoever was committing anything naughty on the ground would have no idea that they'd been spied upon.

But we were going to do this in the black of night, without lights or power. If I couldn't restart the engine at the end of the run, we would be in deep diddly indeed. In my mind's ear Ginny berated me for risking my beloved neck.

Beloved? Maybe not any more. A pang shot through my heart. I missed her, more than I could say. Forming the plan had helped make my loss more bearable, but again blood oozed from the cut of my loneliness.

I shook my head against the heartsickness. I'd have to practice by day, to make sure my calculations were accurate and to see if there wasn't something I hadn't thought of. Unexpected events can spoil a pilot's day.

One of my tasks as a deputy with a pilot's certificate is to fly the sheriff's airplane for an hour once a week, to keep the engine rust-free, the control systems limber, and everything ready for business. It would be easy to camouflage my trial run in the logbooks by declaring it a maintenance hop and writing in the real trip as a training flight to maintain my night proficiency. I make a night flight every three months to satisfy Federal Aviation Administration requirements.

And so two afternoons later I pulled up in my Jeep at the ramshackle hangar at Porcupine County Airport where we stored the old Cessna. A breeze blowing no more than three miles an hour wisped up from the south. It wouldn't throw off my figures by much. After preflighting the plane, checking to make sure all parts were present and accounted for and that they worked as intended, I measured the level of gas in the tanks, then at the pumps added a few gallons more fuel to reach the one-quarter mark I had calculated I needed for the flight. To the weight of the gas I added that of Alex. Bang on. To stretch the long power-off glide I proposed to make, I didn't want to carry any more weight than necessary. And, in case we got into trouble, I wanted an emergency reserve of a little more gas than I had calculated the Cessna would burn on the entire flight. The FAA wants forty-five minutes of reserve fuel, but I settled for fifteen minutes. I had had enough experience in the air to know exactly how many gallons that engine would burn under a variety of conditions. Good pilots leave as little to chance as they can. And I tried hard to be a good pilot. There are old pilots, the saying goes, and there are bold pilots, but there are no old, bold pilots.

After warmup I took off on the northbound runway, clearing the tall birches at the far end with plenty of room to spare, and arched out over the bright blue lake before banking left and heading fourteen miles southwest to Norwich lookout tower, which guarded the Ottawa National Forest against wildfires. The Cessna knifed smoothly through the air, soaring upward through light, almost imperceptible turbulence, the song of its Lycoming engine filling my ears. In flight I feel most connected to my Lakota ancestors, for they, too, must have soared with eagles as their war ponies raced into battle. Climbing away is an exultant time. Ask any pilot — not just an Indian one.

At three thousand feet I leveled off. In a few minutes the sights I was looking for came into view below — the Norwich tower, the Venture Mine hoist house against the high ridge, and finally the clearing beyond it. I banked the plane right and peered at the clearing with seven-by-fifty Bushnells, marking its location on my handheld GPS. That would be my aiming point on the money flight. Two eighteen-wheelers sat in the center, not at the edge, of the clearing. If those were the same trucks Alex and I had seen, they should have left for

Wisconsin days before. Men — at least six of them — lolled about on crates and tarps. There seemed to be no activity. And that was curious all by itself. I wanted to circle a thousand feet lower to get a better view. I was too high for them to identify the airplane, and Cessna 172s are ubiquitous everywhere, the Chevrolets of the sky. But if I went in low and circled, they might wonder why and take a hard look at the Cessna, noting its registration number, looking it up on the Internet and making it as the sheriff's airplane.

So I banked to the left, heading southeast, and examined the terrain. It was mostly thick second-growth forest, hundred-year-old white pines beginning to tower over copses of birch and aspen and singleton hardwood trees, but here and there old gravel logging roads, their verges cut back several yards on either side, appeared. Having driven them in my Jeep many times, I knew they would make adequate emergency landing strips. I was leaving nothing to chance. I marked their locations on the GPS. If need be, I could steer to them with the GPS and locate them even in pitch dark. But it wasn't necessarily going to be pitch dark. There might even be what pilots used to call a bomber's moon, a bright, full moon that enabled attacking aircrews of the Second World War to follow unfamiliar terrain on night flights to their targets.

One more task to do before making the dry run from Bergland Tower: see if I could restart the airplane's engine after turning it off. Some aero engines are difficult to restart when hot after an hour or so of flight. A bit of fussing with throttle and primer — and anywhere from a few minutes to half an hour of patience — often is necessary to get the cylinders firing again. I'd been temporarily stranded on an airport many times after refueling, waiting for the engine to cool down enough to get started again. But never in the sheriff's 172. Its sturdy four-cylinder Lycoming always roared to life on the first crank of the starter, no matter how little time had elapsed since it had been shut down. At any rate, high up the rush of cooling air past the engine would hurry its temperature down to a tractable level.

Just to be safe I arrived over the Porcupine City airport at a point three thousand feet above the ground, giving me plenty of maneuvering altitude for a dead-stick landing in case the engine failed to catch. First looking all about for traffic—even if there are only a few small airplanes in the far north, they always seem to blunder into your airspace when other things occupy your attention—I snaked back the throttle and the mixture knob. Quickly the engine, starved of fuel, coughed and died. The propeller stopped.

As I expected, the propeller, at first stationary but then spinning slowly as the airspeed increased, caused a great deal of drag, steepening the airplane's angle of glide. In barely three minutes the Cessna lost a thousand feet of altitude, at which point I closed the mixture, opened the throttle and turned the ignition key. Immediately and without a cough the engine burst into song and the whirling propeller swiftly carried the airplane away from the airport. I set course for Bergland tower, climbing all the way.

The airplane spiraled upward above the tower until it had reached the target altitude of eight thousand feet. Then I again killed the engine and banked eastward at a diving glide at 120 miles an hour onto a course that would take me within half a mile of the clearing, but far enough away to make it unlikely I would be seen and heard. Slowly the airplane dropped until, just abeam the clearing, I checked the altimeter. One hundred feet too low, but not bad. I pulled back the yoke gently. The plane rose almost five hundred feet until the altimeter needle stopped, a good two miles southeast of the clearing. Quickly I started the engine and went home.

It was a workable plan. Plans are always workable when you rehearse them.

TWENTY-TWO

In my cabin that evening I sat alone at the dining table picking at a pasty I'd bought at the supermarket on my way home. Normally I have to ration myself with that Upper Michigan specialty, a portable pot pie stuffed with diced beef, potatoes, carrots, rutabagas and onions. About the size and shape of a softball and four times heavier, the pasty was brought to America by miners from Cornwall who unwrapped theirs and lunched on them deep in the copper mines, still hot inside their thick pastry hides. Pasties are as caloric as they're tasty, and for the sake of my arteries I don't have them more than once a week.

But loneliness had taken the edge off my appetite. It had been a week since Ginny had disappeared.

The phone rang.

"Steve?" said a familiar voice. "Nancy Aho."

The kindly docent at the Historical Society. I sat upright so quickly the silverware rattled. "Yes?"

"Ginny's back. She arrived from Detroit this afternoon and went right into her office."

"Is she all right?" I blurted.

"Yes. But something's on her mind. She's been furiously digging into boxes in the back room. She asked that we hold all her calls."

"I'll go over right away," I said, forgetting that this was none of Nancy's business and that she had no good reason to call me. But I was glad she had. The human concern country people often show for each other sometimes can match their nosiness, and this was one of those times.

"I wouldn't," Nancy said, her voice full of warning. "She still needs time."

Something told me that Nancy knew exactly what she was talking about. Embarrassed at the public nature of my predicament, gratified that Nancy cared enough to try to help and annoyed that she had, I fell silent.

"Come around in a couple of days," Nancy said helpfully. "She might not see you at home but she has to open her office door to the authorities."

I closed my eyes. This was too much. "Yes, Mom," I said, trying to sound sarcastic but failing. Nancy was right.

She chuckled. "Everything will be okay. You be patient."

The sweet little old busybody hung up.

I sat slumped in the chair, wrestling with my emotions. Ginny was home. She was safe. She was back at work. And she still hated my guts.

As much to forget my predicament, I reached for the phone and dialed Alex at home.

"Commence," he said briskly. No "hello" or "howdy" or even "yeah?" for Alex Kolehmainen is a superefficient man who hates to waste words, even to identify himself on the phone.

"Hello, Mr. Clements," I said. "Could you put Sergeant Kolehmainen on?"

Alex recognized my voice and grunted.

"That's why you're still a bachelor," I said nastily. "You don't know the meaning of foreplay."

"What's on your mind, Steve?" Alex was unruffled.

"Got the night vision stuff?"

"Yeah."

"Tomorrow good for you? The forecast's for a clear sky with a full moon."

"Sure," Alex said. "Time to ride!"

His voice wasn't as enthusiastic as his words. Alex hates flying and always stiffens into a bundle of tension the minute he boards even a jumbo jet. Small planes and helicopters greatly spook him. But he is a brave and tenacious fellow, and even makes fun of his own fear, calling the state police's aviation fleet "the Michigan White Knuckle Airways." He calls the sheriff's battered old Cessna "that piece of flying crap."

"Midnight at the airport?" I asked.

"Sure." I could hear Alex's mainspring commencing to wind tight.

"See you then."

TWENTY-THREE

Before dawn the next morning I drove into Porcupine City, passing the Historical Society on River Street, the main drag, on my way to the cop shop. Though first light was only just beginning to fill the sky, Ginny's van already occupied its slot in the parking lot. The sight both gladdened and saddened me. So close, yet so far. I carried my maudlin mood into the sheriff's department. As usual, everyone looked my way and then away, but this time their unspoken curiosity clouded the air like blood thirst at a dogfight. They all knew Ginny had returned and something was soon to happen. It doesn't take much to entertain Yoopers.

I spent the day at my usual routine, chasing speeders on M-64, lurking in driveways just out of sight with the radar gun switched on. Almost all the drivers I busted were from outside the county and in my grey mood I didn't give any of them a break, such as knocking a few miles an hour off the actual offense and reducing the fine they'd pay.

Only once did I let someone off with a warning. He was a familiar face, an old-timer with a weak bladder. He was doing eighty miles an hour in his ancient pickup, whose color was that of overcooked asparagus shot through with rust, twenty-five miles an hour over the limit and twenty more than was reasonably safe in such a wobbly old beater.

"Deputy, I've got to go real bad," he wailed as I walked up alongside.

"Give me your license and registration and proof of insurance and go off into the bushes while I check them out."

Gratefully he opened the pickup door and skittered into the woods. His license and record were clean. I was sterner than I needed to be but let him off just the same. Old men can't help it. When they need to go, they need to go.

And then just outside Porcupine City, a nearly new Grand Cherokee pulling out of the marina on the opposite side of the highway had slowed almost imperceptibly, its driver swiveling his head to check for traffic, before blowing the stop sign and accelerating toward town. I flicked on siren and flashers, swung the Explorer around and in a few hundred yards pulled the offender to a stop like a cowboy roping a calf. I parked behind the Cherokee and, as I always do, radioed the location and plate number to Joe Koski before I dismounted and walked up to the vehicle, hand on gun butt, a precautionary act for any traffic stop. No telling what a driver will do.

But this one kept both hands on the wheel where I could see them. On his left bicep, bared by a sleeveless T-shirt, was tattooed a large fouled anchor. As I saw his hooded eyes I recognized him as the skipper of the *Lucky Six.*

"Good afternoon, Mr. Anderson," I said gravely. "License, registration and proof of insurance, please." A traffic bust is an official event, and I use formal address with the busted.

Slowly, as I watched, Anderson reached into the glove compartment and fished out the vehicle's Michigan registration card.

"License in my wallet," he said. He was no stranger to traffic stops. I nodded for him to reach behind and pull the wallet from his hip. Slowly he did so. As he proffered the Illinois driver's license I relaxed.

"What did I do, Steve?" They are all *so* disingenuous.

"That was quite a California stop you pulled back there at the stop sign."

"I thought I slowed enough."

"No," I said. "The law says *full* stop."

"Oh. I didn't know." They are all *so* shameless.

"Sit there. I'll be right back."

Back in the Explorer I copied the license and registration numbers and radioed Joe again. I heard the clacking of his keyboard as he plugged his computer into LEIN, the Law Enforcement Intelligence Network, linked to all fifty states and Canada. If I had been a big-city cop or a state trooper, I could have done the job myself from a laptop attached to the dash, but that equipment is too expensive for a boondocks sheriff's department on a tight budget. Within seconds Joe had the answers. The Cherokee hadn't been used in a crime, nor had it been reported stolen. Owner, Morris Weinstein, 2 Hazel Street, Porcupine City, Michigan. No surprise there.

As for Michael Anderson, 1440 North Lake Shore Drive, Chicago, Illinois — my eyebrows rose at the upscale address on Chicago's Gold Coast — he had a perfect driving record, with two years to go before his license needed renewal. A poster child for a warning ticket for a violation that wasn't terribly reckless. I made a decision.

I wrote out a citation for a moving violation and walked back to the Cherokee. Anderson gazed without expression at me, like a motionless stone lizard taking in the summer sun. I kept my voice civil and professional.

"Mr. Anderson, you have a clean record. I saw you slow down and I saw you look for traffic, so you might argue that your violation isn't necessarily a dangerous one. But you need to obey the law. I'm going to give you this citation. You may pay the fine by mail. The amount is ninety dollars. Maybe this will help you to remember to come to a full stop at every stop sign in Porcupine County."

"All right, *Steve.*" He spoke quietly, almost lazily, but did not glance away from my eyes. He held my gaze almost insolently. I stifled my irritation at his deliberate use of my first name. Familiarity with a cop isn't a violation of the law, although in this case it was a small but definite challenge of my authority. For that reason I had jotted down not only Anderson's address but also his Social Security number. You never know when those things might come in handy, and I have notebooks full of them.

"Be careful now." I walked back to the Explorer and Anderson drove away.

I have to admit it. I had given him the ticket not only because he gave me the creeps but because he had pissed me off.

TWENTY-FOUR

An hour before midnight I rolled off the couch after a brief sleep and turned on my laptop. The thick web of the Internet sprawls even way up here in the North Woods. Some homes along the highway even enjoy fast broadband service—cable television arrived in the Upper Peninsula long ago—but a deputy sheriff's pay won't finance more than a dialup connection. It didn't matter. The weather forecast service funded by the FAA wasn't bandwidth-heavy with fancy graphics. I punched up the service and typed away. No need to feed in the information for a flight plan. It wasn't required, and in any case I didn't want anybody knowing what I was up to, not only to keep things quiet but also because I would be breaking a goodly number of federal aviation regulations.

In a few seconds the data from the closest weather station, at Houghton fifty miles to the northeast, unrolled down the PC screen. I skimmed the lines of code until I found the important stuff: 36003KT 10 SM CLR. That, in aviation weather parlance, meant that right now the wind was blowing from magnetic north at a gentle three knots, and that I'd be able to see at least 10 statute miles ahead in clear weather. The forecast for the next three hours was FM 0600 VRB03KT P6SM CLR. Decoded, the line told me that from 0600 hours Zulu—two o'clock in the morning Eastern Daylight Time—the wind would continue to swirl about at a negligible three knots, with the visibility six miles plus, and the skies cloudless and clear. Finally, the winds aloft at 3,000 and 6,000 feet were reported at "9900," meaning no wind at all. I wouldn't have to redo my figures.

"It doesn't get better than that," I exulted to myself as I hopped into the Jeep and headed for the airport.

Alex was waiting by the sheriff's hangar when I

arrived. Like me, he was dressed in civvies, Michigan State sweatshirt over faded jeans. If anyone was around, we'd just be a couple of old buddies going for a night flight. But even by light of day the Porcupine County airport is usually deserted. In the summer a few wealthy pilots bring their Bonanzas and Mooneys up from Detroit, Chicago, and Milwaukee, and a local farmer's half-century-old Piper Tri-Pacer, its fabric covering streaked and faded, occupies a ramp tie-down all year round. But most of the time I encounter only Doc Miller, chief of medicine at the Porcupine County Hospital, in his hangar working on the cranky engine of his Bird Dog, a Korean War-vintage spotter plane a little bigger than the sheriff's Cessna. At midnight he was home in bed, like every sensible pilot I knew.

"Got the thing?" I asked.

Alex held up the trophy of his expedition to Lansing. It looked like a super-8 video camera with a few extra lumps and knobs. "Gallium arsenide!" he chortled. "Generation three image intensifier, mil-spec stuff. Ten power zoom. Four gigs of digital memory."

"Could you put that into English?"

"All you need to know is that with this baby you can spot an ant at a thousand yards in starlight, and capture it forever. It's cutting edge, the very latest thing. The Army hasn't deployed it yet, but the DEA and the flying coppers are already having fun with it."

Swiftly I reviewed the plan with Alex.

"I've detached the stop bracket on the passenger side window," I said, showing Alex. "When it comes time to point the camera out of the plane, you unlatch the window carefully and keep hold of the handle until the slipstream pulls the window up underneath the wing. The air pressure will hold it there no-hands."

Then I came to the money issue.

"You're going to turn off the *engine*?" he said, his grimace etched in horror.

"Yup. Practiced it the other day. Should work fine."

"If you say so." He looked more than dubious.

"All right, let's saddle up."

Together we rolled the Cessna out of the hangar and I swiftly completed the preflight ritual. Alex folded his skinny frame into the right seat and I climbed into the left.

"Steve." Alex sat rigidly, staring forward. His voice was desperate. His anti-aviation funk had enveloped him.

"Is this going to be *safe*?"

"As houses."

"You sure?"

"Trust me."

"Okay," he said resignedly. "Let's get it done."

"One thing."

"Yes?"

"Would you mind removing your feet from the rudder pedals? I can't drive the airplane that way."

"Oh, sorry." Alex unlocked his rigid legs and stepped away from the pedals. I hoped he wouldn't freeze in panic on the controls once we were in the air.

"I'll be all right," he said, as if reading my mind.

He sat quietly, hands cradling the camera, as I started the engine, fiddled with knobs and switches and dials and checked the magnetos during the run-up before takeoff.

"Ready?"

"As I'll ever be," his voice crackled through the intercom. At least he kept a sense of humor. That meant he was in control of himself.

"Away we go then."

After climbout I set course for the Bergland fire tower, its coordinates captured on my GPS, but the light from the new moon was so bright that I saw the dim outline of the tower on its rocky knob miles before flying over the spot and banking into a gentle upward spiral.

Just as the plane leveled out at 8,500 feet—I decided to

add a little more height, just to be sure — I decided that a little hackneyed pilot humor might relax Alex and help him to get through the ordeal of the next ten minutes.

"Know what a propeller is for?"

"What?"

"To keep the passengers cool."

"You're kidding."

"No. Turn it off and watch 'em sweat." I chuckled.

Alex shot me a dirty look. "All right, all right."

Pointing the nose of the airplane toward Norwich Tower, I pulled back the throttle, then the mixture knob, and switched off the ignition key. That turned out to be a mistake.

The engine choked and died and the propeller stopped. I flicked off the airplane's navigation lights and strobe. We now swooped silent and dark through the night, like a great horned owl on the prowl.

The rush of wind increased as I dropped the nose slightly until the airspeed indicator needle touched the 120 miles per hour mark. The propeller began to windmill slowly. My ears popped and Alex gulped audibly, pinching his nose and blowing slightly to clear the pressure. The good old Valsalva maneuver.

"Open the window," I said. "We'll be over the spot in three and a half minutes."

Ahead I could see the line of ridges snaking across the midsection of Porcupine County like the backbone of a great gray sea monster. Every few seconds I checked airspeed and altimeter and made tiny, almost imperceptible course and speed corrections. As the high ridge under Norwich Tower appeared ahead, I turned slightly to the left, so that Alex would have a clear view of our target clearing just below and to the right.

"There it is!" I said.

"Got it!" Alex said as he opened the window on his side and let the slipstream press it up against the wing. Wind roared into the cockpit and swirled small bits of paper and dust around our heads. Alex bent to the camera's eyepiece. I banked the plane slightly to the right to give him a better view of the clearing. Suddenly we were alongside our target.

"Buncha guys," Alex said. "Two trucks. They're carrying stuff from the building to the trucks."

Then we shot away from the clearing and I gently pulled back the yoke, zooming the airplane upward and away from the tower, at the same time banking to the right. On the other side of the ridge I'd have a thousand feet of altitude to restart the engine.

"They see us?" I asked as I reached for the ignition key.

"No. They never looked up. We got clean away."

There was no key in the ignition. *Damn. It must have fallen on the floor.* Quickly I unhooked my shoulder belt, bent over and groped around on the floor. Nothing.

"Looks like we'll have to go to Plan B," I said, trying to keep my voice calm. We were losing altitude rapidly, though the airplane was gliding at optimum speed, seventy miles an hour.

I didn't need the GPS to locate the road below that I'd reconnoitered two days earlier. It loomed ahead, a long tan stripe against the dark forest.

"I'll put her down just up there."

I snapped on the landing lights just to be sure I had seen what I thought I had, then turned them off again to save the battery.

"Why'd you do that?"

"If you don't know what's under you," I said, keeping my voice as casual as I could, "you turn on the landing lights. If you don't like what you see, you turn 'em off." Another hoary old pilot joke.

"*Shit.*" Alex wasn't amused.

We were a little high. To bleed off speed, I put the airplane into a slip—a maneuver in which the pilot banks the airplane in one direction while turning the rudder the other way. The plane crabs forward, one wing low, nose pointing to the side, increasing drag as the side of the fuselage meets the airflow. A slip helps an airplane lose altitude quickly. It's one of the first maneuvers a student pilot learns. But slips scare hell out of uninformed passengers. They think the plane is falling out of control.

"*Son of a bitch!*" Alex cried.

"Relax. We'll be down in a second."

I turned the landing lights back on. The road rushed up at us. The old Cessna's wheels gently kissed the ruts, then bounced sharply over the uneven gravel and within fifteen seconds rolled to a stop. Just to be safe, immediately before touchdown I had killed all the electric switches and closed the fuel valves as well.

We sat silently for a moment as our adrenaline levels sank back to normal. I took a deep breath. I didn't tell Alex that was the first time I'd ever made a genuine emergency landing at night, though I'd done plenty of simulated ones. I took a Maglite from its clip and played it around on the floor of the cockpit. "Where the hell is that key?" I said.

"It's hanging from your sleeve," Alex said, pointing.

A cuff button on my shirt had come partly undone, dangling just enough to snag the large ring hanging from the ignition key and pull it out as I maneuvered the airplane in the darkness.

"Well well well," I said. "Let that be a lesson to me. Never hang up an airplane ignition key on a ring that could catch on anything. In my two thousand hours of flying, that's never happened before."

I kicked myself mentally. I didn't tell Alex, but a pilot does not need to turn the ignition key to OFF to kill his engine. Simply cutting off the mixture does the job. Had I left the key turned to ON, it would have been locked in the ignition and ready to be turned to the right for the restart, like that of an automobile.

"That's nice to know," Alex said. His sarcasm meant he

had come back down to earth in more ways than one. "Now how are we going to get home? And aren't you going to radio for help?"

"We're not going to let anybody know we're here," I said. "With the key the engine will start just fine. We'll take off at dawn."

"Why wait until then?"

"Don't want to risk a takeoff down an unfamiliar road in the dark. That wouldn't be safe."

"*Safe? Safe?*" Alex yelled. "What the hell, do you think what we just did was safe? You said it was going to be safe!"

I looked at him pityingly. "We got down, didn't we? Have we got a scratch on us?" Sometimes cops bicker like old couples. After a moment of silence I patted the night-vision camera in Alex's hands and added, "Now, what have we got?"

Alex stopped grumbling and opened the camera's folding video screen.

"Later we'll look at this on a big monitor," he said, "but I think this will show us all we need to know." He flicked a switch.

Dim green shapes materialized on the tiny screen, then sharpened into absolute clarity, as if we were watching the scene in broad daylight. Half a dozen men moved about, one driving a forklift piled high with unidentifiable flat boxes. The wide door to the building stood open, as did the rear doors of the trucks. Scurrying green figures hoisted boxes into the empty interiors. But the open tops showed full loads of pulpwood chips. In a few seconds the picture was gone. None of the men glanced up at the airplane as it ghosted by.

"Got away with it!" Alex chortled. "Clever, no? False tops under a shallow layer of wood chips. I don't know what's inside those trucks but I'm willing to bet you next year's salary it's illegal. Why, it might even be . . . drugs."

We looked happily at each other. We now had probable

cause, reason enough to go to the prosecuting attorney for a warrant to present to Judge Rantala, requesting permission to enter private property and open up that steel building to see what was inside. Whatever it was, the possibility, however slim, that narcotics were involved would instantly unlimber the stern judge's pen.

Alex and I dozed in our seats the rest of the night, awkwardly elbowing each other like an old couple in a tiny guest-room bed. Just before dawn I climbed out of the airplane and brewed coffee from its small survival kit. We sat silently on logs, shivering against the morning chill and munching chunks of the *korppu* I had tucked into my flight bag, washing it down with the coffee.

As daylight broke we climbed back aboard. This time the engine started smoothly, and in a few minutes we lifted off the gravel road. No one, I felt sure, saw our takeoff.

At the airport no one saw us land, either. After I had pulled down the hangar door, I extended my hand to Alex. "We done good, sarge," I said.

"By God," Alex said, relaxing for the first time in seven hours. "Fighting crime is fun."

TWENTY-FIVE

"And so, at my request, Deputy Martinez made the department's aircraft and himself available for the search," Alex said in a lofty tone. During the meeting in the sheriff's office, in which we had screened the video from our previous night's mission, he had pointedly and frequently reminded us that as a state police sergeant he perched above sheriffs, undersheriffs and deputies on the law enforcement totem pole. "I congratulate your department on its excellent co-operation."

Eli, who really had no idea what we had done, beamed. Gil, who did, grimaced. "That was a risky thing to do, wasn't it?" the undersheriff asked, a skeptical eye on me. I tried hard to look innocent and nonchalant, leaning back in the chair and hooking my feet around the legs.

"Not at all," Alex said. "Deputy Martinez is an outstanding pilot and at no time during the flight did I have any doubt of the outcome." I stifled a chuckle.

We had not told Eli or Gil of the night emergency landing, nor had I committed it to either my pilot's logbook or deputy's daily report. Why ask for trouble?

"All right," Gil said, unable to keep the disbelief out of his voice. "The state police, of course, will reimburse the county for the cost of the flight."

"Send me the chit," Alex said. "I'll make sure Lansing gets it."

I smiled inwardly. Alex would simply make sure the request for reimbursement—just a couple of hundred dollars—got lost, and sooner or later Gil would give up asking about it. As undersheriff he may have to pinch pennies, but he knows when a cause is futile. And Alex's lieutenant would remain blissfully unaware of his sergeant's unauthorized mission. Everybody wins.

"Eli, to save time I'd like to ask you to join me in requesting a search warrant from Judge Rantala so that we may go back to that clearing today and toss that building for drugs," Alex said. "It'll take another few hours if we make the request from the state police post at Wakefield. And I'd also like to request that Deputy Martinez accompany me on the search. Is that all right?"

"Yes, sir," Eli said, ever the helpful old pol. "Steve's your man."

Gil raised a finger. "Please be careful. We can't afford any errors."

Cops do make mistakes. When evidence is circumstantial and causes are vague, fixating on one idea at the expense of others is dangerous, and that single-mindedness often grips police and prosecutors. If we can't admit we might be wrong, our judgment becomes cloudy. We exaggerate soft evidence and ignore harder facts. Too often the innocent are punished, in extreme cases sometimes by execution, and the guilty escape. Things are a little easier in Michigan, which has no death penalty.

Exactly the opposite had seized my mind about Morrie Weinstein. I just could not believe that he was something I very much wanted him not to be. But nagging clues, like three dead men, kept getting in the way. I couldn't write him off until I'd found out more. But the time had arrived to take the case to my bosses before it turned into a rogue investigation. I had thought that maybe with their superior experience they'd view the situation through different eyes.

At the beginning of the meeting they hadn't wanted to see it at all.

"Jesus Christ, Steve," the sheriff had moaned when Alex told him who we were investigating. "Morrie Weinstein is the second biggest employer in Porcupine County. We can't go after him with what you've got!"

"Can you spell 'c-i-r-c-u-m-s-t-a-n-t-i-a-l'?" said Gil

nastily.

But now that we had laid out what we had seen the night before, Eli and Gil admitted that very likely something was going on.

"We'll be very careful," Alex promised.

"How are you going to conduct the search?"

"We'll drive to the site, proffer our identifications if we see anyone, and request that the building be opened. If there is any resistance, we'll show the subject or subjects the warrant. If no one is there, we'll open the door and effect a search." When he wants to, Alex can speak police bureaucratese with the best of them.

We, in other words, would do things by the book. Except we wouldn't.

As we drove to the courthouse in the Explorer I turned and said admiringly, "Alex, you are full of shit."

"It's all that summer stock I've done." Two years before, Alex had played a supernumerary in a single performance of "The Mikado" at the Ironwood Playhouse when a cast member fell ill. His dramatic role had been to shut up, sit still, and look scenic.

"You do all the talking," Alex said as we climbed out at the courthouse. "It's mostly your case anyway. I'll back you up."

That surprised me. Alex was not the sort to hide his light under a bushel. He had done a good job of intimidating Eli and Gil in the sheriff's office. Why should he suddenly take on the role of second fiddle? Before I could ask him to explain, we had arrived in the office of Garner Armstrong, the county prosecutor.

Garner is the nephew of Geoffrey Armstrong, the Upper Peninsula's longtime and only congressman, and is as different from his uncle as can be. Geoffrey is a caricature of a politician, a man who bends with the wind more than he needs to in order to stay in office. I can't stand him. But I like and respect Garner, a tall, skinny and handsome fellow who looks like James Stewart and has something of that actor's deceptively diffident personality. But Garner is highly ambitious, and sooner or later, everyone thinks, he will oppose his uncle at the polls. He is the unchallenged leader of the Democratic Party in Porcupine County. Few argue with him when he has made up his mind.

Garner listened carefully as I presented the case, Alex nodding sagely as I made each point.

"Okay," the prosecutor said without hesitation or questioning. "Let's do it." He called in his secretary and in a few minutes she had typed up the warrant.

"Walk with me," Garner said.

Down the hall we strode to the chambers of the district judge, General Rantala, a bald-headed, big-eared squirt of a man with all the prickly personality of Judge Judy, the television figure. Judge Rantala's first name really is General, inflicted upon him (or so the rumor goes) by a father embittered by his failure to rise higher than buck private in the Army during World War II. Every time the judge makes a restaurant reservation in a city where he isn't known he says in a commanding tone, "This is General Rantala. I'd like your best table at eight o'clock. Carry on." And the maitre d' always replies, "Yes, *sir!*" The snap of a salute is almost audible.

Behind his back we call the judge "The General," although he never rose higher than second lieutenant as a motor pool commander in the National Guard. He is stern and authoritarian, the DEA's best ally in all of Upper Michigan. He complained mightily when the legislature relaxed the state's minimum sentencing laws for drug offenses—once the toughest in the nation—and gave judges more leeway to be lenient. In my opinion, mandatory sentences of twenty years for simple possession were cruel, unusual, and harmful to society, and I would have held the judge in pitying contempt if he had not otherwise handled his courtroom expertly and fairly. Prosecutors and defense attorneys alike always appear before him as well prepared as they can be. His cases are rarely overturned on appeal.

The judge read the warrant carefully and without asking questions, and almost as soon as he encountered the first mention of drugs, he picked up a pen and quickly signed it with a flourish.

"Bring them to me," he growled. "I'll throw their ass in jail. If they're guilty, of course."

"Thank you, Your Honor," Alex and I said simultaneously, bringing a small smile to Garner's face.

As we left the judge's office Garner leaned toward me and said quietly, "You going to be home tonight, Steve?"

"Yes," I said, surprised.

"Mind if I come by for a minute or two? I'd like to talk to you about something."

"Well, sure," I said, utterly puzzled. What private business would the county prosecutor want to lay upon a lowly deputy sheriff?

As Garner returned to his own office I stole a glance at Alex.

"What do you suppose that's all about?"

A cherubic smile played around the corners of his mouth. "Beats me." He shrugged, a little too elaborately. Then he said, "Let's ride."

We headed through town — yes, Ginny's van occupied its space outside the Historical Society, sending a dagger through my chest — and out Norwich Road. Halfway there Alex said, "We going to drive all the way to that clearing, Steve?"

"Nah."

"Nah," Alex echoed.

We were simply employing good military tactics. First reconnoiter in the air, then on the ground, then destroy the target — if the intelligence supports an attack. If anything was going on, we'd surprise our quarry in the act. If not, we'd withdraw and regroup.

We parked Alex's cruiser off a Forest Service track a mile from the clearing and the mine. "In the old days," Alex said, "snipers would put on war paint and gillie suits and go in on their bellies. We're too old for that now." While I was herding captured Iraqi prisoners in the first Gulf war, Alex had been an Abrams tank commander chasing the enemy toward Baghdad.

At that "war paint" I shot a suspicious glance at him but he meant camouflage greasepaint, not Indian ochre. Relax, I told myself.

With sidearms and binoculars we set off through the woods on a deer track I knew skirted the mine from the west and climbed the ridge in back of it. The going was rugged, as it always is in this part of Porcupine County, and the bugs didn't help. Mosquitoes slithered under my uniform collar and probed through my epidermis, taking deep draughts of my being. As soon as I slapped one, another came to take its place. Deerflies buzzed around our heads and now and then one bit painfully, sometimes on the exposed backs of our necks and sometimes on the exposed backs of our hands. Wherever skin showed, it was assaulted. Bug dope, the industrial-strength insect repellent Yoopers use in the woods, barely slowed the creatures.

As he swatted the bugs Alex issued a faint growl, barely audible, that would have reminded me of the soft chant of a Lakota war chief but for the words: "Shit . . . goddam . . . shit . . . shit . . . little bastards . . . shitassratfuck," over and over. Maybe, I wondered, that's what the warriors said in Lakota when they went into battle. Maybe the bugs drove them nuts, too.

"Soft white man," I whispered. "What a wuss."

"Why did I ever let you rope me into this?" Alex whined.

"Shh. There it is."

We emerged onto a shelf of bare rock overlooking the clearing, fifty yards away and the same distance below. With two fingers Alex pointed to his eyes, then with one finger pointed to the clearing. Crouching out of sight, we slowly traversed the scree down to the forest floor, careful to place our feet on solid rock. A small avalanche of pebbles would spook anyone in the clearing.

In a few minutes Alex and I squatted at the edge of the clearing, five or six feet inside the tree line, screened by leaves and branches. Two men, one holding a heavy military rifle loosely on his chest, hand on trigger, muzzle downward, emerged from the steel structure. As one swung the heavy door shut and clapped a softball-sized padlock on its hasp, the rifleman scanned the tree line all across the clearing. I unlimbered my Bushnells and peered at him.

The reptilian eyes of Mike Anderson met mine, seeming to hold them for an instant, then swept away toward the other side of the clearing.

The two men took another quick look around, then climbed into a dusty Expedition and bounced away down the gravel track that led to Norwich Road. As the big SUV disappeared, I turned to Alex and said, "I recognized the guy with the rifle. He's the captain of Morrie Weinstein's boat."

Alex's eyes widened. "Five will get you ten Morrie is involved in this, too," he said.

"Whatever it is," I said.

"Yes. Well, maybe something inside that building will tell us."

We crept around the edge of the clearing, staying carefully inside the tree and brush line, concealing ourselves from any sentry who might spot us from the ridge above. At the front of the galvanized steel building we examined the lock. Large as it was, it was an old hollow barn padlock that wasn't as strong as it looked.

"Easy to break," I said, "but do we want the bad guys

knowing we were here?"

"Easier to pick," replied Alex, fishing from his shirt pocket a small plastic box and opening it. "Here, hold this."

He selected a thin steel rod with angled ends from the assortment of lock picks. In a few seconds Alex swung free the hasp.

"Where'd you learn that?" I said, astonished.

"Once I escorted a second-story man to prison on a train from New Jersey to Lansing. To pass the time he taught me to pick locks. Never forgot how."

The door swung open noiselessly on well-oiled hinges. Inside the windowless, cavernous building, its interior warmed by the sun steadily beating down on the steel roof, was strewn a shambles of chainsaws, axes, shovels, sawhorses and lumber peaveys — the typical equipage of woodsmen who make a living in the forest any way they can. In the corners lay a big wood- chipping machine, an old Farmall tractor missing a wheel, and the forklift we had seen from the air. In one corner squatted a chemical toilet. I opened the lid. Yuck. My eyes stung.

I played my flashlight around the single room. The building had been constructed right up against the escarpment. A wide latticework of steel shelving spanned half the back wall from top to bottom, a few hand tools occupying part of one shelf, but the rest lay utterly bare. I waved my hand over the empty shelves.

"What's all this for?"

"Beats me," Alex said.

We had half expected to find the paraphernalia of a meth or cat lab inside, but everything we saw suggested a much older and more rugged way of making a living. It didn't make sense. What was being loaded onto those trucks in the dead of night?

For nearly an hour we carefully examined everything we could see, returning every item to its place exactly as it had been. Alex snapped photo after photo with a digital camera. In all that time we turned up nothing interesting except a small Baggie of pot, hardly worth busting anyone for. Alex pocketed it.

" I'll take this bag to the lab," Alex said. "Otherwise we're skunked."

"Maybe not. Let's see where Mike Anderson's trail leads us."

Alex and I glanced at each other at the same instant. Great minds and all that.

"Didn't you say the *Lucky Six* was in Lake Huron when we found that stiff on the beach last month?" Alex said.

"Yeah."

"I've got an old buddy in Customs at the Soo who owes me one. Let me drop a dime on him, see if I can find out the dates the boat went through the locks."

"You do that. I've got Anderson's numbers. I'll run them down in Chicago. I busted him the other day for running a stop sign."

We replaced the lock on the shed door and hiked back to the cruiser, rousting a cloud of no-see-ums and releasing another round of soft invective from Alex, and drove back to Porcupine City.

"Call you tomorrow," Alex said when we pulled up at the cop shop. It was way past quitting time, but I stopped inside before picking up the Explorer to report to Gil what we had found — or, rather, hadn't found.

"All that trouble for a goose egg?" said Gil, who hates wasting time and effort, let alone meager resources.

"Something's going on," I said. "We just haven't found it yet."

Gil grunted. "Will you ever?"

I didn't tell him about Mike Anderson. It wasn't time yet.

When I drove through town on the way home, Ginny's van still stood in its spot outside the Historical Society. I started to turn into the lot, then caught myself.

For that it wasn't time yet, either. It was time to withdraw and regroup.

TWENTY-SIX

I had just washed the single dish I'd used to nuke a
Lean Cuisine—convenience food doesn't thrill my taste buds,
but I also dislike cooking only for myself—when Garner
Armstrong's Grand Cherokee rolled into the driveway, Alex's
Chevy pickup close behind. Riding with Garner was Jack
Kemppainen, the wispy True Value hardware store proprietor
who was chairman of the county commissioners. Shoulder to
shoulder they strode onto my porch and knocked. I opened
the door.

"Hello, gentlemen," I said, baffled. What could they
want with me?

"Isn't it a splendid evening?" Garner said. "Shall we go
sit out on the beach and enjoy it?"

I don't have much patience with social foreplay, but
one doesn't get shirty when two powerful county politicians
and a state police sergeant come to call.

"Beer?" I asked.

The three nodded, and we carried our Molsons and
folding chairs out to the beach. It *was* a splendid evening, the
temperature hanging in the comfortable low eighties, a light
bugsweeper of a breeze clearing the sand. Wispy stratus
wreathed the sun, still high in the western sky. It would be
more than an hour before it settled into the lake, and the thin
clouds promised another spectacularly multicolored sunset.

After a few minutes of idle North Woods chitchat about
deer and bear and fishing, I could control myself no longer.
"Why are you guys here?" I demanded as politely as I could.

Garner chuckled. "Softening you up," he said.

"For what?"

Jack patted me on the shoulder. "You know, Steve," he
said gravely, "Eli is getting on in years, and it's time for him to

retire."

"But he said just the other day he planned to file for re-election," I said.

"Yes," Jack said. "We asked him not to. But he's a proud and stubborn old bastard."

Eli Garrow had once been as good a sheriff as Porcupine County ever had. He had come up through the ranks as a sworn deputy and served as undersheriff before running against and beating the incumbent in his first election. Short and bald, Eli is in his seventies, a sawed-off big man whose luxuriant handlebar mustache, accompanied by an unfeigned folksiness, delights widows and small children. Women find him charming and men like him instantly. Once I did, too, and worried for him when he hired his own wife as jail matron and used a brand-new all-terrain vehicle belonging to the county for deer hunting, much to the outrage of Porkies who couldn't afford that kind of useful but expensive tool. But that was as far as scandal ever colored his long career.

But now Eli had become more of a self-serving politician, devoted more to keeping himself in office than doing his job as a hardworking public servant. He held forth on the rubber-chicken circuit as amusingly as ever, but he rarely showed up at the office, preferring to let Gil O'Brien run things while he tooled around in the department's newest cruiser, the only expensive, purpose-built beefed-up Ford police car it owned. And Eli's behavior was growing ever more worrisome. He was drinking more than he should, and he was starting to become forgetful.

Late one snowy night the previous winter, returning from a liquid evening at a friend's house, he had spun out at speed on a patch of ice, his cruiser ending up in a ditch along M-64. Fortunately, a short while later while driving home from Ginny's, I spotted the vehicle before the snow covered it and blended it into the background. Immediately I stopped and pulled Eli, unhurt but confused and reeking of Wild Turkey, from his cruiser and put him into my Jeep. I drove him home and called Bill Gleason, a local mechanic, who winched the cruiser out of the ditch and towed it to his garage to repair a broken tie rod and replace the smashed muffler. I swore Bill to secrecy—not very difficult, since he owed me a couple of favors—and at my suggestion he had sent the bill to Garner, who paid it out of petty cash instead of submitting it to a vote of the commissioners at an open meeting, where Eli's folly would have been revealed. Thus scandal was avoided and no one ever heard what had happened.

Eli never thanked me for saving his hide. In fact, he had never acknowledged the incident in any way. I suspected he simply did not remember it, that he had suffered an alcoholic blackout. He was guzzling that much about once a week, though most of the time he could hold his liquor without seeming drunk.

"I understand what you mean," I told Jack. "But isn't Gil next in line?"

Traditionally, when a Porcupine County sheriff retires, the undersheriff—if he has the stomach for politics—runs for his boss' old office. Occasionally, as Eli had, he even runs against his boss.

"Gil is a great undersheriff," Grant said, popping his second Molson's, "but he's no politician. Just hasn't got the temperament. Can you imagine him kissing babies?"

As an administrator Gil O'Brien was superefficient, running a tight ship, holding down costs—important in a county whose straitened finances had been stretched even tighter by the loss of federal funds, thanks to a parsimonious White House—and handling arrestees and prisoners so meticulously that judges and juries rarely found Porcupine County law enforcement at fault.

But this transplant from Nebraska, a decorated veteran of two hitches in the Army, was a dour and irascible man who held to the Hobbesian view that life was nasty, brutish and short and that all men were irredeemable sinners, most

416

particularly the deputies who worked for him. He was unmarried, lived alone in a small house in town, and seemed to have no private life of any kind. No one had ever seen him smile. Joe Koski claimed to have spotted a grin once, but I thought the dispatcher was just putting us on. I could not imagine Gil campaigning for office of any kind.

Up here in the wilderness, local politics is low-key. Compared to the nasty knock-down-drag-out campaigns in most of the rest of the United States, Porcupine County political warfare tends to be outwardly genteel, the candidates publicly stressing their own positives rather than focusing on the negatives of their rivals. No matter what hopefuls might say privately about their opposition, they keep their public comments clean.

And they run their campaigns on a shoestring. They press the flesh at church suppers, display their faces at every public event they can, buy and post signs, walk door to door, hand out buttons and brochures and buy ads in *The Herald*. If their modest war chests — fed by meager donations — are large enough, they might purchase a little airtime on the local radio station. On Election Day they'll also work the polling places just outside the one-hundred-foot boundary, campaigning to the very last minute. They have to. They're not millionaires who can spend their way into office like wealthy Chicagoans and New Yorkers and wait out the events of Election Day in swanky hotel rooms.

The Democratic Party all but owns the Upper Peninsula, so Republicans rarely bother to field a candidate. Often there's no competition for clerk, treasurer or prosecutor, but once in a while two names will run for sheriff. The only other candidate for sheriff besides Eli in recent years had been Benny Kramer, a "Finndian" — half Finnish, half Ojibwa — who had been a Porcupine County deputy, but after Eli's landslide victory quit the department and became a tribal cop on the Lac Vieux Desert reservation at Watersmeet in Gogebic County, just to the south.

Our pols are not necessarily saintlier than others — it's just that Porcupine County is so poor and budget-strained every nickel is accounted for and voted upon at the county board meetings. There's nothing to loot, no extra money for nest-feathering. Our political scandals run on human frailty, not corruption.

Still, behind the scenes of any contested campaign, even in Porcupine County, a certain amount of sniping and logrolling goes on. During the campaign when Eli first won the sheriff's office, the incumbent attempted to intimidate the then nonunionized deputies into supporting him publicly, threatening to fire them if they refused. Things were tense in the sheriff's department when both candidates occupied their offices off the squadroom — the incumbent refused to speak to his challenger or even acknowledge him in any way — and the deputies found reasons to be elsewhere.

The man Eli vanquished had taken his defeat personally, refusing to come to the office even once during the eight weeks between Election Day and the swearing in of the new sheriff. But when the old sheriff belatedly discovered that he was a couple of weeks short of qualifying for a full pension, Eli magnanimously hired him as a desk officer for the few shifts he needed. People noticed that.

The idea of running for office in Porcupine County did not exactly repel me now that the subject had been broached. But I had never thought much about it, having preferred to consign that event, like fatherhood, to some vague time in the future. And now that prospect, as fatherhood had been just a short time ago, had suddenly been dropped in my lap. Again I didn't know if I could handle it.

"Is Gil going to run?" I asked.

"Don't know," Garner said. "We haven't approached him and we don't plan to."

"But what makes you think I can beat Eli? He may not be what he used to be, but he's still very popular with the voters."

"So are you, Steve. You're a personable guy. People like you. And they respect you, too. We know you're a first-class cop. You have a hell of a record."

"But I'm only a deputy," I protested. "What makes you think I can run a whole department?"

"Let's not hide behind false modesty," Garner said. "You were a first lieutenant in charge of a military police company during Desert Storm. That's good enough for us."

"What if Gil runs?"

"That could be a problem. He wouldn't stand a chance against Eli alone in the primary. But if you and Gil both run against Eli, Eli would be likely to get a plurality while you and Gil divided up the rest of the votes. If it's you against Eli alone, you've got a good chance. And if it's you against Gil alone, the people will vote for the more likeable guy, and we both know who that is."

"But I'm an Indian."

"Is that a liability?"

"It could be. I'm not saying that Porkies as a whole are prejudiced, but there are more than a few who don't care for people who look like me. They might make the difference in a tight election."

"Only one way to find out," Jack said.

"Look," I said. "I've just lost my girlfriend, and I'm not sure I can handle a campaign on top of that." That public admission of vulnerability discomfited me, but it didn't seem to surprise the three other men on the beach.

"Those things have a way of working themselves out," Garner said. "I wouldn't worry about that. Every man here has been in that fix at some time in his life."

I sighed. "Could I get back to you on this? I've got some crooks to catch first."

"And a girlfriend to make up with," Jack said.

I didn't bother to shoot him a none-of-your-business look. The truth is that the men's proposal had affected me deeply. In spite of having been a Porky for a decade, in spite of setting down roots at the cabin I owned, in spite of having fallen in love with a native, I had always carried a burden of unease — a feeling of not quite belonging. Being half one thing and half another will do that to a guy. But Garner and Jack, in suggesting I run for office, were telling me they considered me a true Porky, and I was not going to argue.

"Can you wait for an answer?" I asked.

"Take your time. Still got months to file the petition." Garner and Jack stood up and gravely shook my hand. They folded their chairs and as we walked through the sand back to my cabin I realized that Alex had not said a word during the entire evening.

"What's Alex got to do with all this?" I said.

"Oh, not much," Garner said, chuckling. "He put us up to it. It was his idea. And a very good one, I might add."

"You bastard," I told Alex.

"Yup," Alex said, laying a long arm across my shoulders. "That I am."

Grant and Jack grinned. And so did I, for the first time in a week.

TWENTY-SEVEN

The next morning I phoned the building manager at 1440 North Lake Shore Drive in Chicago. I called from home, not wanting Joe or Gil to know — yet — that I was trying to scare up dirt on an employee of Morris Weinstein. For all our labors, Alex and I hadn't yet come up with persuasive evidence of wrongdoing at the Venture Mine, and the undersheriff would have taken a dim view of a uniformed loose cannon rolling around gundecks he didn't belong on. But sometimes poking a pile of clothes with a stick stirs up something useful.

"Not here," the building manager said brusquely.

"Moved, maybe?"

"Never heard of a Mike or Michael Anderson at this address. And I've been here thirty years."

"Thanks anyway," I said. Then I dialed the Chicago Police Department.

"Criminal records."

I identified myself and gave my star number. A flurry of keyclicks and the clerk had my bona fides. "What can we do for you, Deputy?"

"Hunting a suspect." I offered name, address, driver's license number and Social Security number, all jotted down the day I stopped Anderson on the highway outside the marina.

"We have no sheet on a Michael Anderson with that Social Security number. The Secretary of State driver's license records does show that name at that address."

"Apparently a fake."

"Not surprising. This is Illinois, after all. Driver's licenses are bought and sold every day." Her voice was weary and cynical. The State of Illinois' driver's license system is notorious for corruption. A former governor who had been secretary of state in charge of the system had recently been indicted by the feds.

"Mm. Thanks all the same." I hung up and pondered my next move. Aboard the *Lucky Six*, Anderson had said he'd learned his seamanship in the navy. I thought of calling Joe Koski and asking him to look up the number of the Naval Criminal Investigative Service in Washington. He'd find it in a trice in the computer directories. But Joe would wonder aloud, no doubt with Gil in earshot, why a country deputy was calling the feds.

I snapped my fingers. The Internet. Everybody's on the Internet, including the NCIS. In a couple of seconds I fished half a dozen hotline numbers from its Web site, and called the one reserved for naval affairs. A clerk answered, and after a couple of handoffs, I reached the records office.

"Senior Chief Tom Clark here. What can I do for you?" The voice was professional and polite.

"Deputy Steve Martinez, sheriff's department, Porcupine County, Michigan," I said. "I'm investigating a possible drug case." Then I took a deep breath and added, "Not sure, but homicide might be involved, too." There. For the first time I'd expressed my suspicions aloud.

A few swift keyclicks later the chief responded. "Okay, Deputy, what can you tell me?"

Name, address, Social Security number.

Tap-tap-tap.

"We don't have anyone by that name or address in our system. But we do have the Social Security number."

"Who owns it?"

"Algis Petrauskas. P-E-T-R-A-U-S-K-A-S. He's a former sailor."

"He have a record?"

"Does he ever."

"Can you share it with me?"

"There seems to be a Chicago mob connection, though

it was never proved in court," the chief said. "Otherwise a clean record there. But Petrauskas did five years at Naval Consolidated Brig Miramar for smuggling several kilos of marijuana from Tijuana and selling it in the naval barracks on the base at San Diego. Beat a couple of charges of aggravated assault. He was a mean one with a knife. Suspected of having killed a fellow prisoner in Miramar. But nobody would testify. The guards were damned glad to see him go."

"Physical description?"

"Five-five, hundred forty-five pounds. Six-inch fouled anchor tattooed on his left arm. Pretty ugly guy, too, judging by his photo."

"Sounds like my man. Can you scan his jacket and email it to me?"

"Sure. It'll take just half an hour."

"One more thing. Why do you suppose he didn't change his Social Security number to a fake one when he took the alias of Michael Anderson? He could have had the number left off his driver's license. Illinois allows that option to help people protect their privacy."

"You never can tell with criminals, even the smart ones," the chief said. "In the back of their minds a lot of 'em think keeping a Social Security number means they'll eventually get a full pension from the government. They buy and sell drugs for hundreds of thousands of bucks on the street, and they're worried about chicken feed in their old age? Go figure. As for the option of omitting the number from the Illinois license, either the guy got careless or it's a fake number."

Thirty-three minutes later my computer beeped. I opened the message and scanned the contents. The flattened, snakelike muzzle of the man I knew as Mike Anderson stared out at me from the photograph on the computer screen.

Before his drug arrest, conviction and incarceration in one of the military's toughest maximum-security prisons, Algis Petrauskas had served a three-year hitch aboard the frigate USS *McClusky,* rising to petty officer third class as a bosun's mate as well as earning a commendation for skillful small boat handling. He had been busted back to seaman twice, once for a barroom brawl on shore in Seattle and again for three days' absence without leave after too enthusiastic a liberty at San Diego. Needless to say, after serving his sentence he had been sent packing with a dishonorable discharge.

It was his hometown that intrigued me the most. Petrauskas had grown up in Winnetka, Illinois, and had graduated from New Trier High School. That wealthy lake shore suburb of Chicago, with its famous high school, is not the kind of place the usual violent thug comes from. Mary Ellen Garrigan lived in Winnetka during the winter. Just a coincidence? Maybe not.

I dialed Alex.

"Commence."

"I don't want Clements," I said for the tenth time. "I want Sergeant Kolehmainen."

Alex whooped.

"Got something," I told him. "Mike Anderson, Weinstein's boat skipper, one of the guys we saw in that spot behind the mine yesterday? He's got a heavy record." I spelled it out for Alex. "Navy says there seems to be a Chicago mob connection, too."

"Doesn't surprise me a bit," he said. "Got something for you, too. This morning I called that friend in Customs at the Soo Locks. Asked him to check the transit records back in June and see when the *Lucky Six* sailed through from Huron. He gave me a little la-de-da about national security but I just blackmailed him. Never mind what I had on him. It was good enough."

"Don't keep me on tenterhooks."

"The *Lucky Six* cleared the Soo and entered Lake Superior on June 18. That was five days before the stiff washed up on the beach."

"Aha!" I said.

"Weinstein lied. The *Lucky Six* wasn't in Lake Huron when he said it was."

A boat whose captain had a drug conviction and maybe was connected to the Chicago mob. A dead Chicago hood who had been a drug runner. The link wasn't open and shut, but only an idiot couldn't see its potential. "This sure is worth following up on," I said unnecessarily.

Everything we had still was circumstantial, nowhere near enough to pick up Anderson and interrogate him, let alone call his boss on the carpet. Morrie Weinstein was still a hot potato we'd have to handle carefully. We needed to scare up one or two more solid leads before informing Eli and Gil and Lieutenant Jim Card, Alex's boss at the Wakefield post, of what we had found so far, and maybe really getting down to business.

"Go to it," said Alex.

I drummed my fingers on the kitchen table. But where could I start?

TWENTY-EIGHT

Mary Ellen Garrigan. Algis Petrauskas alias Mike Anderson. I'd shake that tree and see what fell out. And the best place to start was Chad Garrow, who, so far as I knew, was as familiar with Mary Ellen — in more than one way — as well as anybody else in Porcupine County.

After patrol the following day, as we turned in our traffic stop copies, summons sheets and other products of the paperless society at the sheriff's department, I stopped Chad on the way out. "Buy you a beer at Hobbs'?" I offered.

Chad didn't hesitate. In my experience, next to newspaper journalists, cops are the easiest people on earth to seduce with a freebie. But I knew I'd have to play him carefully, partly out of respect for a brother officer and partly to avoid spooking a naïve young man infatuated with an older woman.

For a while at the tavern, full of quitting-time drinkers, we talked about everything and nothing: the girls' high-school basketball team, the peewee hockey teams, the cost of grooming snowmobile trails, whether Eli would stand for re-election, whether Gil might challenge him, the relative merits of Winchester and Browning shotguns, which restaurant had the best pasties, the Farmers' Almanac snow depth prediction for the following winter, whether the flashing red light at the intersection of U.S. 45 and M-64 ought to be replaced with a true stoplight, the Vikings and the Packers, the hot young kindergarten teacher, what would become of the abandoned boat works and half a hundred more everyday topics that occupy the minds of working Porkies. Two Buds had disappeared down Chad's commodious gullet and thoroughly relaxed him before I made my move.

"Speaking of women," I said casually, nibbling on a

bartop pretzel, "that Mary Ellen Garrigan is a knockout, isn't she?" I carefully watched Chad's expression. It did not change. That meant no one knew what had happened on my beach the week before. Only Ginny had witnessed the tail end of the encounter, and she was not the sort to confide such details to her friends—only her lawyer, and I wondered if she had done even that.

Chad's brows rose, his eyes widened and a stupid grin crept up his chubby cheeks. I had to stifle my own smile. But the lad offered no details of intimate activities, as many immature and self-absorbed louts eagerly would have in order to pump up their reputations among the boys. Young as he was, green as he was, clumsy—even oafish—as he could be, Chad Garrow respected women.

He straightened, his smile giving way to a grave expression. "You know, Steve, she's a little older'n me." A *little?* Chad, I knew, had just turned twenty-four, and Mary Ellen had to be in her mid-forties, though the miracle of cosmetic surgery had shaved a decade off the truth. "I'm not sure she's right for me."

"Well, I don't think the time you've spent with her has been wasted," I said. "She's an interesting person, isn't she?"

"Damn right. Interested, too. Allus wants to know what we do up here in the sheriff's department. Loves all the yarns about crooks and weirdoes and stuff. So easy to talk to. So different from the girls up here. Always wants to know what I'm doing."

Like many backwoods Yoopers, Chad often speaks a foreshortened language of sentence fragments, and sometimes a listener needs to guess at their subjects, though the verbs and objects are perfectly clear.

Mary Ellen sounded like a cop groupie, I thought. I'd had experience with those.

"She must be a bright lady," I said encouragingly

"Yeah." Chad's eyes widened again.

"Where's she from?" I knew that already.

"Winnetka, Illinois. Real rich town near Chicago."

No kidding. Even up here we knew about upscale suburbs.

"What does she do down there?" I asked

"Don't really know," Chad said, "but maybe charity work and stuff, whatever those rich ladies do." Probably, I thought, more stuff than charity work.

"She's divorced, isn't she? Who's her ex?"

"Big auto dealer named Bill Garrigan."

Even north woods cops knew about Garrigan Motors, a Chicago dealership empire that peddled Hummers, Acuras, Caddies, Land-Rovers, Mercedeses and BMWs to social underachievers who bought their status with expensive cars. Along M-64 I'd stopped quite a few costly SUVs with Illinois plates and GARRIGAN MOTORS affixed to their rear decks. Bill Garrigan had built up the empire from the single dealership he had inherited from his father, handed down in turn by *his* father, Nevil Garrigan, a pioneering Cadillac dealer. In the 1920s and 1930s Nevil had sold Caddys to Al Capone, Machine Gun Jack McGurn and other mobsters of his era. And Morrie Weinstein's father had been a Caddy dealer.

"Mm. Wonder what broke up that marriage."

"Ready for this, Steve? Morrie Weinstein."

I nearly knocked over my beer. "Morrie Weinstein?"

"Yeah. Mary Ellen said they had an affair ten years ago and Bill Garrigan threw her out." Chad's scruples against kiss-and-tell didn't extend outside the bedroom.

"She must have done okay in the divorce settlement."

"Sure did. Helluva house she's got on the beach."

I decided to plunge in as far as I could. "Tell me, how did you meet ?"

"In Frank's. Stopped in for a pasty and right by the produce stand she told me she liked my uniform. Got to talking and I guess we just hit it off. She invited me for dinner."

And dessert, I thought. "Even in the country the supermarket's a great place to meet chicks," I said unnecessarily. "Then you started seeing her regularly?"

"Couple, three times a week."

I shook my head admiringly, encouraging him. "Quite a looker she is."

"Yeah." He brightened even more. Pride of possession was written all over his face. He started in on his third beer. I hoped that would be his last. Big as he was, he could handle three brews without hitting the gong on the Breathalyzer, but not more than that.

"Hey, when we went fishing a couple of weeks ago, did Morrie invite you or did she?"

"She did."

"Cool. Surprising they still get along, considering their thing's all over."

"Oh, yeah. Said Morrie brought her up here and she just fell in love with the beach and Morrie helped her find a contractor to get that house built."

"Know much about her family? She ever talk about them?"

"Came over from Lithuania after World War II. Her dad was an auto mechanic and worked for Morrie's father. She was born here."

"The American dream," I said as I took another sip of Molson's. "What was her maiden name?"

"Pet-something, pet-rah—"

"Petrauskas?"

"That's it." He looked at me wonderingly.

"Very common Lithuanian name."

"I guess."

"Brothers? Sisters? Maybe she's got a knockout of a sister?"

"No, but she did mention a brother."

"He in the auto business too?"

Chad's brow furrowed. "Think she said he was in the

Navy. No, he's out now."

Bingo.

"Hey, why you so interested in Mary Ellen?" Chad suddenly asked.

He was slow, but he wasn't dumb. I shrugged, then nudged him in the ribs and winked. "Two good reasons."

"Yeah, they're great," Chad said dreamily. Then he blushed.

Better change the subject. "Think the county will cough up for new cruisers?" The two older Fords had racked up more than 200,000 miles in just two years, and none of us thought they'd make it through a third.

"Beats me," Chad said, "but we gotta get 'em." The driver's seat of his cruiser was badly rump-sprung, thanks to the almost daily abuse of his two hundred eighty pounds, and the engine needed another ring job.

A little more everything and nothing, and we called it an evening. As we rolled out of Hobbs,' I was glad to see that Chad stopped after three brews. And he did not drive, but walked the two blocks home to the bachelor room he occupied on the third floor of Eli's house. This was a young man learning how to control himself. There's hope for him yet, I thought.

As I drove out the highway to my cabin, a knot of worry began to form at the back of my mind. There was more to Mary Ellen Garrigan, *née* Petrauskas, I was certain. Neither she nor Mike Anderson — Algis Petrauskas — had mentioned their kinship during our morning out on the *Lucky Six*. Wouldn't a brother and sister normally have done that? Nor had either she or Morrie Weinstein given a hint of their previous relationship, not that it was anybody's business. I decided to make it mine.

As soon as I arrived, I picked up the phone and called the Chicago Police Department. In a few moments I reached the sergeant on duty in Organized Crime, and told him what I was looking for. In a few minutes he returned to the phone.

"We do have a sheet on Morris Weinstein. No arrests, no convictions, but he runs with the mob. Often seen in company with Two Ton Tony Cella, he's a major capo, in restaurants and at racetracks, and out on his own fishing boat. Weinstein's father was a made man, provided Caddies to the gangsters before he sold his dealership to Francis Garrigan, also a hood."

"Francis' relationship to Bill Garrigan?"

"Father."

"Anything else?"

"Weinstein hasn't been seen in town for quite a while. Rumor is he moved up to your jurisdiction."

"He did."

"You have anything on him?" I could hear the sergeant clicking his keyboard.

"Not yet. Soon, probably."

"Keep us informed."

"I'll do that."

TWENTY-NINE

At my cabin late the next evening the doorbell rang through the steady thrum of driving rain on the roof. Momentous things had been happening at my cabin in the evenings quite a bit lately, and this occasion was no different.

Ginny stood in a voluminous yellow slicker on the deck clutching a large leather dispatch case, her expression set and unsmiling, as lightning crackled out over the lake and rain puddled around her. My mouth fell open. "Ah . . . ah . . . ," I said. Good thing the reservation orphanage hadn't named me Stevie Silvertongue. Finally I found my voice.

"Ginny, am I ever glad to see you! I've missed you so very much. I . . . I . . . There's a reason for what happened."

"I'm sure there is, Deputy," she said flatly, "but I'm not here about that."

"What?"

"Are you going to let me in or do I have to stand out here in the rain?"

Dumbly I stood aside and made little waving motions to usher her inside. "Ah . . . sit down. I'll make coffee."

With careful deliberation, avoiding my eyes, she removed her slicker, hung it on a kitchen hook, and strode to the dining table, placing the case upon it. "Never mind, thanks."

"Ginny, I . . ."

"We're not going to talk about it, I said. I'm here to see you as a law enforcement officer. I have some important information for you."

Her tone was stern, flat, and businesslike. She kept her eyes on the dispatch case. She pulled out a chair and sat down at the table, hands in her lap, spine straight, gaze fixed downward as if waiting for the host to say grace so that everyone could dig in. She reminded me of a balled-up porcupine, quills spread in self-protection.

Inwardly I sighed. So beautiful, so close, and yet so far. I pulled myself together. "What is it?" I said.

Like a Horace Wright county board report in the Herald, a Ginny Fitzgerald story does not unfold in big-city newspaper fashion, first giving the most important facts and then filling in the tale with subordinate details that grow less important the longer the story runs. She believes in beginning at the beginning in once-upon-a-time fashion, telling her story chronologically and letting the subtleties of narrative fill in the blanks. This is not a bad way to present an event, although impatient listeners, wanting to get to the meat of a tale quickly, might squirm and fuss and miss important nuances. With people like her I learned long ago to sit back and let their stories unroll. Maybe the patience is in the genes, generations of my ancestors having listened to Lakota storytellers spin yarns this way, refusing to hurry even when enemies lurked in the night outside the corral getting ready to steal the horses. But I really didn't know. I'm not much of a Lakota.

"It's about the Venture Mine." She opened the dispatch case and carefully removed a sheaf of yellowed old papers and envelopes, neatly stacked and tied with ribbon.

I skidded back a chair on the bare maple planks and sat down opposite Ginny. "Yes?"

"Last week I saw Horace's story about Andrew Carmichael in *The Herald*."

It had been a humdinger even for Horace, covering nearly a quarter of the bedsheet-sized front page with several photographs. Violence may be common but murder is rare in Porcupine County, and *Herald* readers snapped up stories about even century-old homicides. As I had thought he would, Horace had found a couple of Carmichael great-grandchildren living in Wisconsin and plumbed their thoughts about the discovery of the body of an ancestor neither had known and only one of them had ever heard of.

They expressed only surprised banalities so commonplace that even Horace couldn't sweeten their quotes. But that still gave Horace the opportunity to make a few lugubrious editorial remarks about the fleeting nature of life and memory. He would have made a first-class true-crime author. The very end of the story gave details about a funeral and burial to be held in the home town of one of the survivors. I felt sure Horace had shamed them into paying for the services.

"And that reminded me about something I'd almost forgotten," Ginny said. "The day after I started the job at the Historical Society a few years ago, Edna Holderman came into my office staggering under a wooden box of papers almost as big as she."

"Edna Holderman?"

"You have the memory of a colander. Edna Holderman, the daughter of Gordon Holderman, late owner of the Venture Mine. Morrie Weinstein's mother."

I slapped the table. "Now I remember. Please go on." I had nearly forgotten my anguish over Ginny's unreachable presence.

"She said she was clearing out her house, getting ready to move into a retirement village in California, and she wanted her husband's papers to be preserved for future historians. 'They're just mining records and stuff like that,' she said. 'Nothing exciting, nothing we need now, but I want to give it to the society before it's thrown out in the trash.' I stuffed the box into a back room with a hundred other boxes at the society and simply forgot about it."

Ginny took a deep breath. "Then I saw Horace's story, and I suddenly remembered that box."

"What's in it?" I asked.

Having embarked on her careful narrative, Ginny would not be derailed from it. "It took me an hour to find the box," she said, "and then I had to vacuum maybe ninety years' worth of dust and grime out of the inside — the box was very old and had no top. It had been left open all the time the Holdermans had it. Much of the paper is brittle and I had to handle it carefully."

Ginny donned white cotton gloves and handed me a pair. Then she fished a portfolio out of the dispatch case, opened it and slowly and deliberately spread out the documents it contained, placing them gently on the table.

"Most of this stuff is just ore and assay reports, how many tons were brought up from the various drifts and sold for whatever price and so on, interesting only to an economic historian who specializes in mining." Her voice was brisk, that of the academic lecturer leading a seminar. She, too, had forgotten the awkwardness of our initial encounter and now had entered deep into her professional self. When she is like that I just sit back in admiration and take it all in. This time I had no choice.

"And here's a map of the mine in 1905. That was during its height, two years before prices collapsed and Gordon Holderman started managing the place as a tribute mine." Carefully she unfolded the yellowing paper, trying to keep it from cracking and disintegrating, and spread it on the table. The map took up nearly all the heavy maple table, four feet by six feet even without the two leaves I had never used.

The mine chart was almost identical to the smaller one I had seen on the wall of Morrie Weinstein's office. Like it, the old map showed seven drifts, each of them a good deal shorter than the ones on the modern chart.

"Um," I said, wondering where Ginny's presentation was going.

"Now here's a different map. It's dated 1920." She spread it over the older drawing. This one was smaller and cruder, its lines clearly hand-drawn in pencil, then traced over in ink. It was headed CONFIDENTIAL in large bold letters. Under that lay the legend EXTENSION BEGUN 1908 COMPLETED 1914. The map bore no Township and Range surveyor's coordinates to mark the mine's location on the surface of the earth. It had been drawn from memory, not to scale. It showed a modest mine of three horizontal drifts attached to a long vertical shaft. The lowest drift was marked 1,089 FEET. Unlike the others, this bottom drift was not closed at one end but open, leading off toward the west on the left side of the map, the two inked lines that outlined its dimensions fading into short broken lines. On the other side of the map, the eastern side, a small X at the end of the lowest drift bore the legend SILVER LODE.

I looked up at Ginny, my mouth open. "Silver?"

"Yes."

"Wow." Silver is often found in very small quantities with copper ore, mostly as tiny flecks in the rock, but late in the nineteenth century, rumors erupted that a large lode of mass silver had been found deep in what is now the Wolverine Mountains Wilderness State Park. Thousands of miners flooded in from all over the nation to seek their fortune, just as the Forty-Niners had during the California gold rush of 1849. The town of Silverton had grown up at the mouth of the Iron River to serve them, and had hung on to this day, even after the strike turned out to be a will-o'-the-wisp. Still, for more than a hundred years old-timers had related legends about a lost silver lode in Porcupine County.

"Where is this mine?" I asked. "Does anyone know?"

"I'm coming to that," Ginny said, pulling out a six-inch stack of pamphlets. I recognized them as old composition books made of cheap pulp paper, each page lined for handwriting. Most elementary and high schools used them well into the twentieth century for examinations, and some still did. As a small-town schoolboy myself I'd written countless quizzes and essays on them. Like the other documents in the dispatch case, their edges were yellow and cracked, but the wide blue fabric ribbon binding them was new. I said so.

"Yes," Ginny replied. "The old ribbon deteriorated as soon as I undid the knot. Can't use rubber bands to hold these old chapbooks together — that would just crush the paper. There are a dozen stacks like these. I found them along with the maps inside a steel strongbox at the bottom of the wooden one. It was locked. I had to take the box to a garage to have the lock drilled out."

She took the top book off the first stack and slid it under my eyes, turning it so I could read the legend on the cover, in faded brown but still elegant Palmer Method handwriting:

JOURNAL
OF
GORDON HOLDERMAN
VOLUME ONE
1904-

I opened the first page. It was written in the same neat copperplate, in ink from a metal nib. "January the first in the Year of Our Lord 1904. Here begins the record of the life of Gordon Holderman, age 38, of Porcupine County, Michigan. On this day nine tons of ore were taken from the Venture Mine . . ." On I leafed, marveling as the everyday details of life of a foreman inside and outside a copper mine piled up on the pages. Holderman wrote a faintly fusty Victorian English, for the most part simple and serviceable but occasionally with a long, ornate sentence that was so gingerly balanced, like a round-bottomed boat with a high superstructure, that if it had been bumped at one end it would never have stopped rolling. He was extraordinarily painstaking with his grammar and spelling, frequently crossing out a misspelled word and sometimes substituting another. He must have been an excruciatingly slow writer.

No detail was too small to commit to paper. A cable was beginning to fray and by the end of the week the hoist would have to be shut down several hours for repairs. The men were grumbling about the rotted condition of the shoring in the Level Two drift and carpenters would have to be hired at great expense and sent down to fix the ceilings. Only two tons of ore was extracted January 10. A blizzard raged above ground, piling the snow too deep and sending the temperature too low — twelve degrees below zero Fahrenheit — for the horse teams to drag the crushed ore to the tram line two miles away where it would be hauled to the smelter at the Minesota Mine. Travel was so difficult that miners huddled in the bunkhouse rather than going home after work. Complaints about the cookhouse food were mounting. "Two men injured in a rock fall on Level Three. One will lose his leg, the surgeon says." There was no expression of regret or concern. Mining was a hard life, and miners were hard men.

"Does it go on like this?" I asked Ginny.

"More or less." She fished out another beribboned stack of composition books. New pink paper slips researchers used for placeholders instead of Post-Its, whose adhesive might harm delicate historical documents, peeked from some of its pages. "Take a look at this one."

Its cover was similar to the first, but the year was 1908. "You remember that Holderman became manager in 1907 and ran the Venture as a tribute mine?"

I did.

"Open to the first pink slip, please."

On "the twelfth of April in the year 1908," Holderman had written, "the air in the seventh level has begun to grow foul." Work would have to be stopped while a new air shaft was drilled. The surveyors had determined that the best place to start the vertical shaft lay half a mile northwest from the main shaft, where the rocky knob overlooking the Venture again met level ground. A half-mile-long horizontal shaft, six feet high by six feet wide, would have to be drilled from the farthest edge of the seventh level to meet the new vertical shaft. Fans atop the vertical shaft would pump air down and across into the mine proper.

"I think that might be the tunnel Morrie took me into when I visited the mine," I said. I shuddered when I recalled the panic that had welled into me when he turned off the lights. "But it's all fallen in now."

"Don't think so," Ginny said, leafing to another pink slip. "Read this."

"The second of November 1908." At almost the point where vertical met horizontal shaft, Holderman had written, flecks of pure silver had appeared in the rubble. Tunneling a bit further revealed a vein of silver the thickness of a man's thigh. "I have sworn foreman Peterson and miner Carmichael to secrecy," Holderman wrote. "We have discovered this strike by our own honest sweat and justice demands we be those to profit from it. We shall not inform New York of our discovery."

And so began the conspiracy to cheat the owners of the Venture Mine.

In mounting excitement I leafed quickly through the rest of the chapbook, stopping now and then to read as carefully as I could the passages Ginny had set off with pink placeholders. Over the next year the three men and a dozen trusted and well-paid miners extracted the silver, at first carrying it through the horizontal air shaft and up and out of the mine with the copper ore, shipping the silver-bearing rocks aboard a lake steamer from Porcupine County to a smelter at the Soo where the foremen could be bribed to keep quiet. During this whole time the mine owners and stockholders stayed utterly unaware of the conspiracy. Within a few months the conspirators had cleared nearly seventy-five thousand dollars in profit, a huge sum for the time. So well were things going that the cabal decided to enlarge the vertical air shaft to six feet square, enough to admit a small skip capable of hoisting two tons.

In the next chapbook Ginny pointed to the Post-It marking the entry for the sixth of March, 1909. "Unfortunately Andrew Carmichael has become untrustworthy," Holderman wrote in characteristically flat and neutral language, "and it was decided he had to be dealt with." This, I saw immediately, was the historical version of a smoking gun. If it had been discovered at the time it would have sent Holderman to the gallows.

He offered no further details about Carmichael's offense—who made the decision to dispatch him, or how it was carried out. In my mind's eye I filled in the missing facts. There was a brief meeting outside the shaft entrance. Harsh words, then pleading ones, a scuffle, and finally the sickening moist thunk of pickax against skull. The killers dragged Carmichael's body a quarter of a mile through tall white pines that had not yet met the logger's ax to a creek embankment where the still warm corpse was thrown, the contents of its clothing undisturbed, into a shallow grave. There it would lie for nearly a century before three cops chasing a couple of drunks through the woods in comic-opera fashion happened upon it.

And that galvanized steel building two of the officers had searched just the week before very likely concealed the entrance to that old shaft in the rock face behind. It did not take a genius to guess what was going on in the drifts far below. Expensive designer coca plants, poppy bushes, marijuana and God knows what else were being grown and harvested and maybe even refined in a lost section of the Venture Mine nobody knew about except Morris Weinstein and his gang. And I would have bet my snug little cabin on the lake, the home I loved and had sunk deep roots into, that Weinstein and his thugs had killed Frank Saarinen, Roy Schweikert and—yes, Danny Impellitteri, the hoodlum whose body had washed up on the beach. They had probably died because, one way or another, they knew too much.

"Exactly, Steve," Ginny said as I looked up at her. It was the first time all evening that she had addressed me familiarly. I took a deep breath.

"There's nothing to connect this drawing with the other, is there?" I asked, pointing at the maps of the Venture Mine and the extension.

"Nothing," Ginny said, "except that the extension map was lying on top of the main map in one envelope inside that strongbox. And, of course, the statements in Holderman's journal."

"Do you think Edna Holderman was aware of these maps and that journal?"

"Probably not. She wouldn't have given that box to the historical society if she had known."

"I recall you said Gordon died in 1956. Morrie is in his late forties, almost fifty maybe. If he was born before 1956, then Gordon could have willed the information in some form to his infant grandson, perhaps to be given to Morrie when he came of age."

Ginny nodded.

"However Morrie discovered his grandfather's—ah—adventure, it's pretty obvious he knows all about it. And he knows more than we do. That's what makes him dangerous."

"What are you going to do now?"

I thought a moment. "Consult with the allies. Bring in reinforcements. Alex and I can't do this alone, and in any case our bosses aren't going to let us. But now I think we may have almost enough evidence to plan a raid in force. I'll have to talk to the prosecutor."

Ginny looked into my eyes for the first time since she turned up on the doorstep. "Steve, please be careful," she said, concern coloring her voice.

"I will. Now can we talk about—"

"No!" She shook her head firmly, reached for her jacket, and was out the door before I could say anything more.

She left behind the journals and the maps. That was a message of a sort. I wanted to believe it was.

THIRTY

Two days later the better part of Porcupine County's law-enforcement establishment, plus a few outside troops, crowded into the county commissioners' chambers at the courthouse. Garner Armstrong, as prosecutor and the highest-ranking official present, chaired the meeting with his usual gentle but brisk authority at the head of a long, heavy oak table I suspected was left over from the cookhouse at a nineteenth century logging camp. The modern Porcupine County Courthouse is full of such stray heirlooms, most of them hand-me-down, government-issue items that nobody thought were valuable until a Chicago antiques dealer paying a speeding fine in the 1960s offered to quintuple it if he could have the county magistrate's massive maple roll-top desk. The magistrate, who knew something about turnip trucks, declined. Judge Rantala still uses it.

Eli and Gil sat as far apart from each other as they could, and gazed at each other and at me with barely concealed hostility. "They've both filed for sheriff," Joe Koski had whispered from behind his counter when I arrived that morning, "and they're both afraid of you."

Word had got out in the sheriff's department that Garner had approached me—I suspected from Garner himself. He is a canny politician who knows the value of a leak at stirring up action. But I was sorry that Gil had filed. He had done so, I thought, just to preserve his job with the county, not because he actually wanted to be sheriff. I suspected he worried that if I won the election I'd send him packing, for undersheriffs serve at the pleasure of the sheriff. I had no intention of canning Gil because I hadn't made a decision to run. But, I mused, if I did run—and win—I'd have to think hard about the undersheriff's job. Gil is superb in it, but could we get along? We are like night and day, alpha and omega, in our respective approaches to police work. And, needless to say, in our personalities.

Carelessly tilted in his chair against the far wall sat Chad Garrow, who had no idea what had been going on with the Venture Mine during the last few weeks but was about to find out. The night-shift deputies, portly Jim Haas and buxom Betty Allen, had been called in as well. Joe was manning the department's desk. We'd clue him in later. Lieutenant Jim Card, commander of the state police post at Wakefield, sat next to Alex. By rights Garner should have invited an investigator from the Drug Enforcement Administration, but like me, he can't stand the officious twits. Like federal agents everywhere, DEA guys always want to run the investigations, even in jurisdictions they know nothing about. Garner would inform the DEA only when he had to, and that would be at the very last minute before an operation began. We hoped it would end before the feds could bull their way in and piss everybody off.

"Alex, you're the ranking investigator in this case," Garner said. "Please bring us up to speed."

"I'll defer to Deputy Martinez, who knows more about this than I do."

Garner nodded to me. He, Alex and I had briefly rehearsed the opening of the proceedings before the meeting. Eli and Gil looked at me in surprise.

"Somebody dim the lights, please."

I turned on the digital projector — another of the many grant-writing trophies that made Gil such a valuable undersheriff — and the prosecutor's laptop, on which I had scanned all the facts and maps into PowerPoint. Up here in the North Woods we enjoy not only hot and cold running water and flush toilets but also all the modern electronic conveniences of the big city. We in Porcupine County government may not enjoy state-of-the-art technology in every department, but neither do we write with crayons.

First I projected on a blank white wall photographs of Morris Weinstein, Algis Petrauskas (alias Mike Anderson), and Mary Ellen Garrigan, explaining what I had learned about their relationships. When Mary Ellen's photo snapped on the wall, Chad gulped audibly and looked at me in consternation.

"Later," I mouthed to him, and put up the historical facts about the Venture Mine as well as the maps Ginny had given me. The whole presentation took fifteen minutes. I left nothing out, including my encounters with Mary Ellen at George's and on the beach, although I was careful to edit the more salacious details while leaving in Ginny's role in the events. At that everyone else in the room except Alex, in whom I had already confided, glanced at each other in sudden understanding.

When I turned off the projector and the lights came on, Eli swiftly bounded to his feet and said, "Very good, Steve, that was brilliant and really, really helpful. Now here's what we're going to do—"

Garner immediately thrust out long arm like a traffic policeman. "*I* am in charge here, Eli. Deputy Martinez has developed this case. He knows more about it than any of us except possibly Detective Sergeant Kolehmainen. I am going to give Martinez full field command, with the sergeant his backup, if that's all right with Lieutenant Card. And what's more, I will take strategic command myself."

I looked up in mock astonishment, as if surprised by Garner's words. Having a junior deputy run the whole show in the field was all but unheard of in law enforcement circles, even in Porcupine County. But Garner knew what he was doing. He was telling Eli Garrow that his day was done and new blood soon would be in charge of the department. Garner glanced at Lieutenant Card, who, having been informed of the prosecutor's intentions before the meeting along with Alex and me, nodded. Alex shot me a casual sidewise smile. Eli glowered. Gil smoldered. Chad gaped.

"Okay, Steve, it's all yours," Garner said. "Now what?"

"Alex?" I said.

The big detective leaned forward on the table. "This morning the forensics came back from Marquette on that Baggie of pot we found in the building at the clearing," he said. "Almost fifteen per cent tetrahydrocannabinol."

Everyone's eyebrows shot up.

"Exact same proportion as in the marijuana we found on the body of Danny Impellitteri, the Chicago hood whose body washed up on the beach in June. But we don't know that it's the same, and we don't know for sure that it came out of the mine. It probably did, but we have no proof. It could have been brought from elsewhere and dropped there accidentally, of course. Steve?"

"We know something's going on in that mine," I said "We don't know exactly what. We have pretty strong evidence to connect the two separate parts of the mine, and those also to the suspicious actions Sergeant Kolehmainen and I witnessed at that clearing. But that pot doesn't constitute a smoking gun. Not just yet."

"Agreed," Garner said. "We're so close. But we can't move against Weinstein right now. The chances are that we're right, but what if we're wrong? We would not only damage the reputation of one of the county's most important employers but we would all look pretty stupid."

The prosecutor turned to me. "What next, Steve?"

"For the next week or so I'll find a reason to fly over that clearing every day. We don't know how often the trucks come. But if we spot them from the air or perhaps from the road, we can put an officer on stakeout at Matchwood and when the trucks come out, we can flag them down on the highway and check their loads. We'll get the General — excuse me, Judge Rantala — to sign an open warrant ahead of time."

Everyone knew the tactic. A cop could ask to see a truck's load, and if the driver refused, detain him until backup arrived with a warrant. A prepared warrant saves time and bother.

Alex spoke for the first time. "Of course we'll have backup — at least three other units — when we stop the trucks. We'll be ready to go as soon as we get word of the stakeout."

"Yes," I said. "And we have to remember that we likely will have only about twenty-four hours, probably less, before Weinstein finds out that his load hasn't arrived wherever it's going. If the load turns out to be what we think it is, we'll have to mount the raid on the mine immediately."

"I'll have all my troopers equipped and ready to go," Lieutenant Card said. "Alex, see to it."

"Yes sirree," Alex said, eagerly cracking his knuckles. The old soldier loved action.

"Let's stress the importance of security," I said. "We don't want Weinstein and his gang to find out anything if we can possibly help it."

For the first time Gil spoke. "Yes. We can work out a code so any officers can report what they find when they find it without anybody else knowing." His oblique reference was to the forest telegraph. And cell phone coverage up here is still too spotty to be reliable. Only the landline is reasonably secure, but there are precious few call boxes out on the lonely highways.

In a few minutes we had drawn up an order of battle for our first wave of fourteen sworn officers — Eli, Gil, the department's five deputies, and eight troopers from Wakefield, including three who lived close by in Porcupine County. Within two hours we could bring in another couple of dozen reinforcements if we needed them — deputies from adjoining Gogebic, Iron, Baraga and Houghton counties, tribal policemen from the Lac Vieux Desert reservation, and several more troopers.

"Eli, we'll need you to stay at the department and help Joe with communications and liaison," Garner said.

"All right," Eli said grumpily. He clearly wanted to be

part of the on-scene action, but he knew his enemies were at last trying to ease him out of the job he had held for almost twenty years. His shoulders slumped in defeat. I felt sorry for the man. But I knew he wouldn't go down without a struggle at the ballot box.

"Gil and I will lead three deputies and four troopers over the road to the mine entrance from Norwich Road," I said, carefully including the undersheriff in the chain of command. No use angering him by treating him as an underling. "Alex, will you take Chad and three troopers and wait by the clearing on the other side of the ridge for the rabbits to bolt from their hole? Chad, you know that area as well as anyone here, and I'd like you to help Alex."

"Whatever you say, Steve," Alex said. Chad, still looking astonished and upset at the events of the last half hour, nodded.

"And, Garner, wouldn't the start of the raid be the best time to notify the DEA? By the time they arrive things might be all over."

Garner beamed. "Just what I was thinking, Steve," he said.

The meeting broke up. On his way out Eli leaned toward me and hissed quietly, "Watch it, kid. You're in way over your head."

I didn't answer but looked at him sadly. It was just a defiant roar from an aging lion, and not the last one, either.

Gil didn't even glance my way, but stared stonily ahead as he stalked out of the room.

I caught Chad before he could leave and pulled him back by his massive elbow. When everyone else had left and we were finally alone, I said as gently as I could, "Chad, I'm sorry to lay all this stuff on you. And I'm sorry to have kept it from you all this time. But I had to."

"The bitch was using me, Steve," he said.

I took a deep breath. I would not have to worry about Chad Garrow's loyalties. I decided to cement them firmly.

"She tried to use me, too," I told him.

Chad straightened and squared his jaw.

"Why?" he said. "Why would she do that?"

"I think she was acting at Morrie's request. I think he hoped to stay one boat-length ahead of us if we cottoned on to what he was doing in the mine. I think she was his spy."

"*Shit*," Chad said. He now understood completely. I could see him searching his mind, trying to remember if he'd revealed any sensitive details about the operation of the sheriff's department during his pillow talks with Mary Ellen.

"I'm going to ask you to do something difficult," I said.

"Anything."

"Until the raid starts, stay in touch with Mary Ellen. Do your usual thing, don't let her know anything might be up. We want to keep her in the dark as long as possible."

A small but wicked smile played on Chad's face. "I can do that."

I didn't ask the details.

THIRTY-ONE

Each afternoon for four consecutive days, I rolled out the Cessna and flew surveillance flights past the mine and the clearing beyond it, careful to stay 2,500 to 3,000 feet above the ground and on varying courses, never coming near my target more than once a day. I did not want anyone below suspecting that a lone aircraft was conducting a search. But the seven-by-fifty Bushnells closed the distance well enough. I couldn't make out anyone on the ground, but I certainly could spot eighteen-wheeler trucks. But each day I was skunked. The clearing remained empty.

Before I could take off on the fifth day, a radio call came in just before noon from a trooper at Matchwood, a semi-ghost town where Highway M-28 intersects Norwich Road on the way to the mine and the clearing. "Three boys heading for the barn," he said. For all anyone outside the law enforcement community knew, he was just talking about three troopers going off duty. But we in the task force knew the trooper had seen three big semis on their way north toward the clearing. As planned, he would follow the trucks in his unmarked cruiser, staying just out of sight, watching to make sure they turned off on the track to the clearing.

Ten minutes later I had my answer from the trooper. "The boys are home. Going off duty."

I called Alex on the landline. He had already heard.

"Steve, I'm putting on the stakeout at Matchwood now." Four troopers would rotate the twenty-four-hour job, carefully planned so nobody at the mine or clearing would be tipped off. Matchwood, an old logging town deserted long ago but for a few homes on its outskirts, is barely a bump in the road. Any cruiser, even an unmark, parked along the highway would stand out like a pink bullfrog on a lily pad. Luckily an old barn, half its roof collapsed, overlooks the intersection of M-28 and Norwich Road, and Alex had hidden a cruiser inside the barn with a clear view of the highway. We had figured the bad guys would want to load up and get away as soon as possible, probably within twenty-four hours, and so Alex's first man would take up the duty immediately.

I walked into Gil's office. "The trucks have arrived, sir," I said. "Shall we get things moving?"

He wasn't fooled by my deference — Garner had made it especially clear to him that I was in unquestioned tactical command of the operation — but this former Army drill instructor is a self-disciplined man. However he felt about an underling placed over him to run things, he was going to cooperate to the hilt. He nodded. "I'll send the word out now," he said evenly.

I felt better, much better, knowing that Gil O'Brien had my back.

Gil strode into the squadroom. "Joe," he said, "radio Chad and tell him to get ready. I'll phone Jim and Betty."

Joe keyed his mike. "Chad? Joe. Your package has arrived. Pick it up after your shift."

Everything was now set, each officer in the task force ready to go, with weapons and fresh ammunition, Kevlar vests — which most of us never bothered to wear on duty, despite the rules — at hand. I loosened my tie and flopped on a bunk in an open cell in the adjoining lockup. Gil did the same.

The hours ticked by. I lay awake, adrenaline coursing through my system. Finally, just before midnight, I fell asleep.

The call, from a tap in the landline along the highway from the hidden troopers at Matchwood, came just before four. "They're on the move," Alex said. "Three trucks heading east on M-28. I'm following with another unit behind me. Four officers total."

"We'll nail them on 45," I said. "Keep 'em in sight. Radio silence as much as possible."

In an instant Gil and I rolled out to his cruiser. "Shall I

drive, sir?" I asked. The junior deputy always does the driving, unless his superior chooses to.

"Suit yourself."

I took the wheel and we took off, headlights on but flashers dark and siren silent, and soon reached ninety miles an hour on U.S. 45 heading to Rockland ten miles south. At that hour the highway was deserted, and I slowed to sixty for the ninety-degree eastward curve just south of Rockland, the rear end of the cruiser skidding through the tight turn. One mile farther east the highway took a sharp right to the south, and after negotiating it I eased the cruiser up to ninety-five. In a few minutes we had bombed through darkened Bruce Crossing thirteen miles south, where M-28 intersects U.S. 45.

"Alex?" I called on the radio.

"With you. It's naptime. My undies are in a bunch."

That meant the convoy of trucks had reached Sleepy Hollow Road just north of Paulding, a hamlet seven miles south of Bruce Crossing. Four more miles and they'd be out of my jurisdiction, but Alex, as a state trooper, would make the official stop and arrest. And the trucks were running close together, like elephants in a parade, instead of spread out down the highway — which would make the stop easier.

"Natives?"

"Roger twice." That meant two Lac Vieux Desert Tribal Police cars from the reservation at Watersmeet three and a half miles south of the county line in Gogebic County were at the ready if needed to pinch off the trucks before they could escape. If not, they'd lend a hand in other ways.

"Ready?" I asked.

"On the move," Alex said.

When we were still two miles north of the trooper, I saw his flashers suddenly wink on, then the faint howl of his siren. I killed my headlights. In a few minutes Gil and I ghosted up behind a trooper's cruiser parked just behind the last truck, its blinding flashers camouflaging our arrival. Alex had stopped his unit in front of the first truck, blocking its escape. Six officers on the scene now.

I strode forward to the first eighteen-wheeler. Alex stood by the driver's door, seemingly relaxed as he examined the manifest. The two men inside sat quietly, with resigned expressions suggesting irritation at once again being harassed unjustly by law enforcement. I recognized neither of them. They were roughly dressed and unshaven, but they did not look like typical woods Yoopers. Their jackets did not bear the scrapes and stains genuine lumbermen's clothes would suffer from close encounters with branches, logs, and sticky pine pitch.

"Just a routine random check, Deputy," Alex said elaborately, milking the pecking-order scene for all it was worth. "They're carrying wood chips bound for Rhinelander. You know what those are, right?" I had to stifle a grin at Alex's studied theatricality.

I looked back down the line of trucks. Alex's fellow troopers stood by their drivers' doors, chatting unconcernedly with the trucks' occupants, no doubt commiserating with them about such routine harassment at such an early hour.

"Yes, sir," I said, ladling on the servility. "I do know. But perhaps it might be a good idea to take a look at the loads?"

"Well now," Alex said. "You've been going to school, haven't you?" He looked up at the men in the cab and rolled his eyes. They grinned. Alex is a magnificent ham.

"Do you mind if I take a look, sir?" he asked the driver, a dumpy, bearded fellow in greasy overalls. There was no edge of tension to Alex's courtesy. He *could* have done well in summer stock.

"No," the driver said, "but you'll have to climb up the side."

"Okay, but would you guys get out and stand by the cab while I check the load? Hate to ask you do that, but it's just routine." It is, but the crew's presence on the ground would keep them away from their CB radios and a panicky call to Morris Weinstein. We had not heard any CB activity as we pulled up behind the trucks.

Alex scrambled up the ladder and peered over the side. "Yep, wood chips, matches the manifest," he said, dropping from the last step lightly to the pavement, like a cat, making no sound.

"Wood chips," called the troopers from the other trucks. Like Alex, they had asked the two-man crews to step down and stand by the cabs while they checked the loads.

"Well now, guys, I think we're done here except for one thing. Hey, what's this?"

The two tribal police units from Watersmeet coasted to a stop on the opposite side of the highway, sirens silent but flashers full awake, dazzling the scene with the other cruisers like a rock disco at midnight. Cops keep flashers on at scenes not only to warn away oncoming traffic but also for psychological reasons, to intimidate and confuse, to keep their subjects off balance. It's hard to react belligerently when the night is lit up in blue, white and red fireworks.

"Hidy ho, Steve, Alex," said Sergeant Camilo Hernandez, the first of the four tribal officers to emerge from the cars. "What's up?" Camilo is not Ojibwa but a Tex-Mex *mestizo* from El Paso, "mostly Apache but with a little Spanish grandee thrown in," he likes to say. His Indian genes led the Lac Vieux Desert Ojibwa to hire him. He is a veteran cop and one of the odd ducks, like me, who washed up in the Upper Peninsula for reasons of his own. His partner was Benny Kramer, the "Finndian" who had once run for sheriff in Porcupine County.

"You missed all the fun, Camilo," said Alex. "We're just wrapping up here."

Camilo smiled and leaned against the truck's fender with one hand, the other casually at his waist. The other officers had wandered down to the second two trucks to chat with the troopers by the cabs.

"Uh, let me think," Alex said. "Oh, yes, now I remember."

He turned to the driver. "Mind if we open the trailer doors, sir?" he asked. "Just want to be sure."

Camilo and I slowly turned so that the truck's crew could not see our armed sides and unclipped our holsters. The officers at the other trucks, I knew, had done the same thing.

"You can't do that!" the driver said in astonishment. "The chips will just spill out!"

"Well, yeah," Alex said, "*if* they're chips."

"They *are*."

"You gonna open the door?" Alex's tone had shifted from crisp politeness to a soft menace.

"I can't."

"Then I will."

"It's not legal. You *can't*."

"Oh yes it is and oh yes I can. Here's my warrant. Give me the padlock key."

The driver turned and tried to bolt into the woods, but ran right into the muzzle of Camilo's Beretta, one inch from his nose. Swiftly I covered the other man with my .357.

"Hit the ground, all of you," Alex said. "Put your arms in front of you and spread your legs. You know the drill."

The six men all sullenly complied. They weren't dumb. They were outnumbered and outgunned. I quickly frisked the two in front of me, relieving both of them of Glock pistols and Buck knives concealed under their jackets and one of a snub-nosed .32 in an ankle holster. Then I cuffed them, hands behind their backs.

"The key?" Alex asked again.

The driver shook his head.

"Very well." Alex strode around to the rear of the trailer with a crowbar and hefted it, examining the padlock.

"Not going to pick it?" I asked.

"No need for finesse." Alex threaded the crowbar

through the hasp of the padlock and twisted sharply. With a cry of torn metal it sprang open. The six men leaning against their trucks jumped, but the clack of pistols being cocked squelched any intention they might have had of departing the vicinity.

"Showtime," Alex said. He threw open the doors and we played our Maglites on the interior.

"Wow," I said.

"Wow indeed."

Foot-high plants in flats sat stacked seven feet high along the sides of the van box. I recognized poppies and coca and marijuana but most of the rest eluded me. The pot plants bore huge iridescent blue-green leaves of a size that I'd seen only on mature eight-foot-tall bushes. A few cacti, six inches high, occupied one shelf. Peyote, most likely. But it was several large plastic bags of white powder at the front of the trailer that most interested us.

"Coke, probably," Alex said. "Heroin, too. Doubtless pure and uncut. This stuff would bring in a couple of million bucks wholesale, let alone on the street, and never mind the plants. Hands down this truck alone adds up to the largest dope haul ever made in Upper Michigan. And there are *two* more trucks behind us."

"And our adventure isn't over yet," I said.

"No, indeed."

Quickly the tribal police Mirandized the six suspects, then bundled them into their squads for the ride to the jail at Porcupine City, where they'd be kept on ice until the raid was finished. The tribal cops' own lockup at Watersmeet has only two holding cells and isn't state certified for holding prisoners for off-reservation arrests. Three tribal cops remained behind to drive the trucks to the police lot on the reservation, where they'd be guarded until the contents were moved to an evidence room at the Marquette state police post. It was the only one in the western Upper Peninsula big enough to store the haul in the three trailers.

Back at the cruiser Gil radioed Joe.

"Horses in the stable," he said. "Weigh the jockeys." That meant we had made the stop and identified the suspect cargo as illegal, and for all officers in the task force to meet at the sheriff's department in Porcupine City.

We climbed in and dashed north at ninety-five miles an hour, followed by the two state police cars. It was only five-thirty in the morning, and sunup was still more than an hour away.

THIRTY-TWO

At six-thirty we headed out of town and rolled in a three-vehicle convoy south on Norwich Road, flashers off, sirens silent and headlights out, proceeding slowly and as quietly as we could. I felt tense yet exhilarated, like a Lakota warrior embarking on a night raid against a Cheyenne village. A favorite tactic of the Lakota was to hobble their horses outside an enemy encampment, creep on their bellies among the tepees and fall silently upon their sleeping antagonists, quietly slaughtering them before they awoke. The Lakota would have understood the plan Gil and I had worked out at the sheriff's department, although they might have been puzzled by our intention to shed as little blood as possible. A dead enemy, they would have pointed out reasonably, is no longer a dangerous one. Times have changed.

Enough light from the fading moon and the false dawn outlined the faint asphalt ribbon through the trees so that we could navigate it safely at twenty-five miles an hour, but I worried that a deer or two would leap in front of the oncoming cruisers. Like most back-country Upper Peninsula tracks, even the paved ones, Norwich Road has no verge to speak of. The high and thick tree line crowds the shoulder, a dark curtain concealing large animals that seem almost eager to throw themselves before automobiles, like Southern Californians seeking an easy payday in fat insurance settlements. Norwich Road plays host to the largest number of deer-vehicle collisions in all of Porcupine County and, I suspect, all of Upper Michigan. The accidents are supposed to be reported to the local authorities, but drivers of old junkers don't bother. Only owners of newer cars who want the insurance payments go to the trouble of filing reports. Many drivers of both kinds keep their freezers stocked with choice cuts of fresh roadkill. Less paperwork for everybody. I don't mind, and even Gil doesn't.

But we were in luck. No bucks, does or fawns chose to commit suicide that morning, and at the Venture Mine turnoff, Gil and I and our squad of two other deputies and a pair of troopers rolled off onto the road leading to the mine. Alex and his crew headed farther south to the track that led to the clearing and the secret shaft hidden by the steel shack. A quarter of a mile short of the mine we stopped and parked our vehicles in the bushes beyond the verges, armed ourselves with riot guns and rifles, then hiked the rest of the way, whispering. In a few minutes, as the lights of the mine buildings came into view, we fell silent. At that hour only a skeleton night shift would be working the mine—the legitimate greenhouse mine, that is—maybe three or four caretakers. We had no idea how many Weinstein henchmen were about, nor whether they had gone to ground or where. But we were taking no chances.

Swiftly we separated into pairs and tiptoed around the edges of the mine property, concealing ourselves behind piles of lumber and darkened outbuildings. At the hoist house a lamp inside outlined the greasy ground-floor windows of the office. Silently pulling myself up to one window, I peeked inside and saw two middle-aged men. Both were known to me as longtime Porkies, hard workers and upright men, if a few cups short of a tea party. Ken Towers hid his long bearded face in a tattered old Motor Trend and Ralph Otwell slept at his desk, head thrown back, mouth open in that unconscious, fly-catching posture that always looks stupid and embarrassing when one is caught at it.

Neither man appeared to be a threat, but no cop ever takes that for granted—until after the subjects have been searched and salted away safely, to be sorted out later. I looked at Gil. He nodded and silently took up his prearranged station a few feet opposite the door. If it were locked, he would kick it in with a shower of splinters and I would roll into the room, riot gun at the ready.

But the door wasn't bolted. Gently I turned the knob, then slowly and silently swung open the door into the room. The sleeping man did not wake. The other kept his head in his magazine. When he saw my shadow on the floor, cast by the light behind me, Towers grunted, "Hiya, Denny."

"It's not Denny," I said, keeping my voice low, "it's the sheriff's department." I trained the riot gun on Towers while Gil covered Otwell.

Towers choked and Otwell nearly fell out of his chair.

"Sh!" I said sharply but as quietly as I could. "Keep your mouths shut! Get up and get against the wall!"

"But, Steve—what? What's going on?" Towers said as he quickly complied. Otwell followed. Both men looked stunned and scared. I knew they weren't the bad guys we wanted, but I didn't have time to explain.

"Something's going on," I said in a whisper as I searched Towers and Gil the other man, "but I can't tell you just yet. Please be patient with us. We just can't take a chance. We are not arresting you, but for your own safety we are going to put you in restraints until we find the people we're looking for. Then we'll release you and you can go home. Will you work with us?"

Poleaxed expressions still clouding their faces, the two men nodded. Swiftly Gil bound their wrists with plastic handcuffs and gently but firmly sat them in chairs along the wall.

"Please stay there till you're told to go," I said, glancing out the window. Three troopers squatted in the shadows just outside the entrance to the hoist house. "Who else is here?" I asked Otwell, the senior man.

"Denny Britton," he said. "He's down on Level Five watering the tobacco. Us three's the whole night crew."

"Call him up here—no, no, don't call him," I said. "We'll go down and get him. Anyone else?"

"I don't think so. The boss came in last night about ten

with a woman and went down into the mine, giving her the tour, I guess. But I didn't see them leave."

He turned around in his chair and peered out the window into the slowly lightening morning. "His car's still in the yard."

"The boss?"

"Mr. Weinstein."

"Did you know the woman?"

"Yeah. Mrs. Garrigan, that knockout blonde who's around here all the time with the boss."

I glanced at Gil. He raised an eyebrow.

"Is Weinstein often here at night?" I asked Otwell.

"No, not really. He's usually here for the eight-to-five shift. I see him coming in for the day when I knock off work."

"Anything seem unusual to you?"

"The boss was het up, worried about something. He didn't stop to chew the fat like he usually does when he goes down into the mine."

"Mrs. Garrigan?"

"She acted like she was scared about something. I don't know what."

Gil cut in. "They know we're here, Steve."

THIRTY-THREE

I thought we had achieved perfect surprise. Now we were going to have to hunt Weinstein and his men like terriers after rats, and that was a dangerous game, for they knew the tunnels and warrens of their burrow far better than we did. I stood back and took a deep breath.

Gil grasped my arm with a powerful hand. "You okay, Steve?" he asked, locking his eyes with mine. "Can you handle this?"

"Yes. Thanks." I took another deep breath. "We'll have to go to Plan B."

That scheme presumed an alerted Weinstein and his gang would try to make their escape through the old horizontal air shaft to the old silver mine and the secret entrance Gordon Holderman had had drilled through the earth from the other side of the ridge.

"I don't see any reason to think Weinstein knows we know about that part of the mine," I said. "Do you?"

"No," Gil said. "Those boys in the trucks never got off a transmission. Joe was monitoring the CB band on his scanner the whole time. And Weinstein doesn't know we saw those documents Ginny found at the Historical Society. Or does he?"

"No, I don't think so. I hope not. I don't know," I said.

"It doesn't matter," Gil said calmly. "He knows we're here. One way or another, he's going to try to bolt from his other hole if we chase him. And we've got a welcoming party just outside it, whether or not he knows it."

I felt a quick flash of gratitude for Gil's crisp levelheadedness. However he felt about me as a rival, this veteran cop wasn't going to let me down — or allow me to let myself down.

"Right. Let's get going."

Gil stepped out and with his hand-held radio raised Alex. "The moles know," he said. "Bar the door."

I doubted Weinstein and his gang could listen in from deep in the earth. If they did, it didn't matter, but I hoped Alex would achieve at least a measure of surprise.

"Copy," Alex replied.

"Let's leave the two deputies out here to watch the hoist house entrance and the road in," I said to Gil. "You, I and two smokeys will go down into the mine. The troopers will clear the first six levels and you and I will take the seventh and the air shaft. Then the troopers can follow us. Sound okay to you?" I wasn't just currying favor with Gil, but making grateful use of his long experience as a lawman. In police work as in anything else, two heads are often better than one.

"Roger. Sounds good. I'll be right behind you."

We left the room and crept into the cavernous hoist house, stuffing dark goggles into our pockets. Before we could reach the opening to the vertical shaft, the giant electric winch groaned and began to roll, its thick cables slowly hoisting the skip up from far below. LEVEL 5, the electric signboard proclaimed, then LEVEL 4 and LEVEL 3 . . . This was no speedster of an Otis skyscraper elevator but a copper-mine slowpoke, however modernized it may have been. The wait seemed interminable.

At last SURFACE flashed on the signboard, and the cage enclosing the skip rose into view. Gil and I trained our shotguns on Denny Britton as the hard-hatted nurseryman emerged from the cage, lunch pail in hand. He blanched as he saw our drawn weapons. "What the . . ." he spluttered.

In thirty seconds we had Britton politely cuffed, warned and seated in the office with Otwell and Towers, by now grumbling at their treatment but resigned to cooperation until the excitement had passed. If any of them ever had entertained suspicions that something they didn't know about was going on in the mine, such misgivings weren't visible in their resigned expressions. They were no threat to our backs.

"See anyone down there?" I asked Britton.

"No."

"Weinstein or anyone else?"

"No. I'm almost always alone all night except when Ralph or Ken's working in the other drifts."

"So the skip's been going up and down all night?"

"Pretty much. Like it always does."

"Thanks." I beckoned to Gil and the two troopers, and we returned to the hoist house.

"We'll all go down together," I told the troopers. "We'll drop you off at Level One. While you're checking it out, Gil and I will head on down to Level Seven. We'll send the skip back up to One, and you can sweep Levels Two through Six while Gil and I do our thing. Then you come down to Seven and back us up. If you hear gunfire or we call you on the PA system, you come right away. Okay?" They nodded, their faces grim. They had both been combat infantrymen in Iraq at the same time I was there. That gave me confidence that whatever happened, our backup would be there.

We donned miner's helmets, climbed aboard the skip and began our long descent into the bowels of the earth.

THIRTY-FOUR

In a few minutes we reached Level One and the troopers stepped out into the drift, Maglites at the ready and extra batteries in their pockets, although the long tunnels to the chambers were brightly lighted with bare bulbs hanging from cables stapled to the rough shoring that reinforced the rough rock ceiling. That was a good sign. If Morrie Weinstein and Mary Ellen were hiding in the old copper mine, they'd very likely have killed the lights in order to let searchers betray their presence with flashlight beams, the better to pick them off with gunfire. But I doubted that they had holed up in any of the seven drifts, all closed at their ends so far as I knew—except perhaps for the bottom one. The door at the end of it might be concealing the old air shaft that led to the secret part of the mine. Rats don't go to ground unless there's a way to get out. But we still had to search the drifts, just to be certain our quarry wasn't hiding somewhere, ready to make their escape upward once we had passed on to the levels below.

"Good luck, boys," I said, slapping the troopers on their broad backs. Then I pressed the LEVEL 7 button on the skip's control board and the cage slowly started downward again. As the rock wall unrolled upwards before my eyes, I fretted. What if an armed welcoming committee waited for us at the bottom? Gil and I would be bunched up inside the skip, unprotected by anything except our Kevlar vests, easy meat for bad guys armed with automatic weapons. I wished we had brought along slabs of armor plate to hide behind.

Past Level Two, as brightly lighted as Level One, then Three, Four, Five, Six . . . and with a soft mechanical clunk we ghosted to a stop at Seven. The drift was also illuminated. Dead quiet, not a soul in sight. Swiftly Gil and I donned the dark goggles we had brought down with us, exited the skip and dashed into the open drift, checking all the rooms, finding nothing except rows and rows of plants of every identifiable species on earth and then some. At the farthest room we fetched up against the heavy iron door marked DANGER. DO NOT ENTER. It was padlocked. I peered at it. "What the hell?" I said. "Another locked room mystery?"

If Weinstein and Mary Ellen had passed this way through the tunnel to the hidden silver mine, they could not have locked themselves in from the outside. A confederate would have had to do that, then make his escape up the skip shaft and out of the mine, but the caretakers would have been tipped off by the noise of the lift's machinery. But we had found no one on the seventh level. And on closer examination I noticed a thin and uniform layer of dust on the padlock. It had not been handled for many days, possibly weeks.

"Look at this," I said. Gil bent close and straightened up.

"They didn't go this way," he said. "Where then?"

I stared at the lock with pursed lips for several seconds. Then a light dawned in my brain as I remembered something I'd seen when Weinstein took me on the mine tour a few weeks before.

"I think there's an eighth level in this mine. Let's backtrack to the skip."

In a moment we reached the vertical shaft. The troopers above us had called the skip back up to descend to the second level, and the shaft lay open. We trained our Maglites down it. Water glimmered on the bottom about fifty feet below. The thick electrical cable I had seen on the tour snaked down for about thirty feet, then disappeared under a slight overhang. A rusty steel ladder firmly bolted to the rock wall descended just a short way past the cable. It was almost invisible from the seventh level. I wouldn't have noticed it unless I had been looking for it. Droplets of water sparkled on the rungs.

Nodding to Gil, I carefully climbed down the ladder

and, thirty feet below the seventh level, a gentle breeze kissed my face. I switched on the Maglite and illuminated the opening to a long and darkened horizontal tunnel curving upward from the entry at a slight angle. I played the light on the damp rock floor. Two sets of fresh tracks, one large, one small, disappeared into the dark.

I called up to Gil in a harsh whisper. "Someone's been down here recently. I'll bet Weinstein and Garrigan came this way. This has got to be where Grant Holderman's old air shaft to the secret part of the mine starts. That steel door up on the seventh level probably just shuts off a collapsed part of the drift, like Weinstein said. This cable has to feed all the juice the secret part of the mine uses. Alex and I didn't see any outside electrical lines over the ridge into that clearing."

Gil nodded. "Ready when you are."

I climbed back up to the seventh level and rang the internal telephone attached to the cables running down the shaft. "First four drifts clear," the trooper said.

I told him what Gil and I had found. "Seven is clear. After you do Five and Six, come on down and follow us through the horizontal shaft I just found."

Gil clambered down right behind me as I descended the ladder for the second time. At the level of the air shaft, I swung out slightly to the left to step down onto the solid rock of the shaft floor. A few boards — pressure-treated pine of recent vintage — bridged the rocky footing of the tunnel. Its ceiling hung low, in places only five feet high, the breadth scarcely four feet. This was not a heavily traveled passageway for the transport of ore dug from a drift far ahead, but a true air shaft drilled to carry ventilation up through the mine. It was black as the inside of a bat.

"Mind your head," I told Gil. "If we see light ahead, we'll douse our flashlights."

Gil nodded silently. All the while we had been underground, the undersheriff had followed my lead, once in a while stopping me with a tap on the shoulder if he thought he had heard or seen something odd. Maybe he resented the elevation of an underling to a position of command above his, but he did not show it. He was being the consummate professional, and I appreciated that mightily.

For long minutes we hiked, sometimes at a crouch under low ceilings, into the slowly increasing breeze. Twice my foot slipped on a wet rock but I caught myself, and once Gil's strong hand kept me from lurching into the jagged walls of the shaft. The long bore was not straight and true but took several slight jogs right and left as well as up and down, course corrections made by the miners drilling from the opposite end nearly a century ago as they drew closer to the original vertical shaft of the mine. Several times I thought I heard a faint scrabbling ahead, perhaps the scrape of a foot, and we stopped to listen carefully. That noise—if it was indeed a noise and not a figment of our imaginations— couldn't have been made by an animal, for the shaft was far too deep for even tunnel rats to find food.

After about half a mile of slow creeping I spotted a tiny glimmer of light ahead. Gil and I stopped, shut off our Maglites, and waited for our eyes to adjust to the darkness. Redoubling our efforts to stay quiet, we crept forward. After five or six minutes of silent progress, we fetched up against a sharp turn to the left, a bright light streaming onto the tunnel walls. I dropped to the ground, donned dark goggles and slowly peered into the light.

It was a large growing room, its rocky walls brightly whitewashed, fluorescent grow lights dangling from the ceiling like those I had seen back in the seventh level of the old mine. Rows and rows of two-foot-high marijuana plants, bushy and thick-leaved like the ones we had seen earlier that morning in the trucks we had stopped on U.S. 45, marched six abreast for twenty-five yards. Red poppy bushes lined the walls. No one was in sight.

"Cover me," I told Gil, and inched into the room, riot

gun cocked and at the ready. Slowly and silently I crept forward, heading for the far end of the room, where an entrance tunnel no doubt led to either another open room or the vertical shaft. Remembering the map I had seen, I guessed we still stood at the far end of the drift and another open room or more lay ahead.

In a few seconds I reached the entrance to the tunnel. A ragged line of naked incandescent bulbs marched along the top of the tunnel—a short one, not more than ten yards long. Squatting, I motioned to Gil to come up behind me. "Stay here till I'm through the tunnel," I whispered. "No use us both getting caught like fish in a barrel." He nodded.

Again goggled, I peered into the room. It was just like the other one—empty, except for the lush greenery of narcotic plants. I waved Gil forward, covering him from threats ahead as he crept up behind me. As we stepped into the room together, Gil a step to the rear, a switch clicked somewhere ahead and pitch darkness enveloped the room, sucking the light out of our eyes like a black hole in space.

THIRTY-FIVE

Morris Weinstein chuckled savagely. "How does it feel, Steve?" he called from somewhere ahead. I opened my eyes as wide as I could, trying to draw in whatever stray electrons of light might have remained in the drift. "You're trapped like a rat, and millions of tons of rock's just waiting to drop on your head!"

I gripped Gil's arm behind me. Keep quiet, I fiercely willed him to understand. Stay quiet. Keep your Maglite off. Don't give Weinstein a target.

Gil patted my back reassuringly. He didn't need to be told those things. He was smart and experienced enough to know not to give a shooter even a muzzle flash to aim at in the dark. Wait for Weinstein to make the next move, then react.

"Getting nervous, huh, Steve?" Morrie called. "I bet you've already pissed your pants!" I did not, however, feel the slightest pang of claustrophobia. Maybe I would have done so under normal circumstances, but the tension of imminent combat kept me focused. Nothing engages the mind like the prospect of a gun battle.

Minutes passed. They felt like hours. Whenever fear edged into my heightened consciousness, I forced myself to think about the Big Water, its fish, the birds, the animals, the glory of life on the surface. The happy mental pictures I conjured thrust the terror of blackness out of my head. I breathed slowly and deeply. I can do this, I thought, and so can Gil.

More time passed.

Weinstein lost patience first. He fired a short burst from a MAC-10, the bullets ricocheting madly off the rocky walls, the frantic bedsheet-ripping roar of the heavy .45 caliber machine pistol reverberating throughout the grow room. Before decapitated branches and leaves could sigh and rustle to the floor, Gil and I each stood and fired a load of Double-0 at Weinstein's muzzle flash. We rolled to opposite sides of the room as he answered, the bullets gouging up sparks and shards of rock as they struck the spot where we had crouched. I nearly sprained my sphincter trying to present the tiniest possible target, for a .45 slug can take off an arm or a leg. My ears rang. I wished we'd had the foresight to bring along pistol-range earplugs. Gunfire in enclosed spaces can damage eardrums.

"Assholes!" Weinstein shouted. "Suckers! I can stay here for days and starve you out!" That meant he had plenty of food, water and ammunition. It also meant he was unaware of the welcoming party high above. Sooner or later Alex and his fellows would pick off Weinstein's henchmen and search the mine. Then we'd have him pinched between two parties of lawmen.

"Weinstein!" I called. "Do you have any idea what's going on on top? We've got officers surrounding the entry to the air shaft. We've got your trucks. Do yourself a favor and throw down that weapon, and I'll see what I can do for you."

"Fuck you!" Weinstein shouted as he ripped off another burst.

"Stay down!" hissed a trooper just behind us at almost the same time both answered with a double salvo from their riot guns. The heavy shot ricocheted wildly from wall to wall and ceiling to floor at the other end of the room, and my eardrums took another pummeling.

Now that the troopers had caught up to us, we had the advantage in manpower if not quite in firepower. But Double-0 buckshot isn't a bad close-quarters load, especially if you can't see your target.

"Aah!" Weinstein groaned in pain, then emptied his MAC-10 magazine in our direction. We heard the scritch and snick of another clip driven home, then silence fell in the drift. At that distance individual buckshot pellets wouldn't have done much damage, but they'd at least get him bleeding, maybe sap his energy.

A minute passed, then another. Down the drift echoed a faint sound of gunfire from up above.

"Last chance, Weinstein!" I called. "Drop it, or we'll catch you in a crossfire!"

"Ha!" Weinstein shouted defiantly. "So long, suckers!"

One more burst from his MAC-10, then we heard him scrabbling away down the tunnel. Before we could return fire, another fusillade of bullets hammered past us. They were from a different automatic weapon. To my ear it sounded like an MP-5, a short-barreled military machine pistol that's another favorite of drug runners.

"Come on, Algis!" Weinstein shouted. The scrabbling resumed.

Petrauskas. There were two of them, one to cover the other. We'd have to be careful. In the black we inched forward on our bellies, twice ducking behind rocky outcrops when Weinstein and Petrauskas took turns stopping to lay down bursts of suppressive fire. For the interminable span of perhaps five minutes, silence reigned in the tunnel, broken only by the soft clink of loose rock underfoot as our quarry made their way toward the skip that would take them up to daylight and into the sights of Alex Kolehmainen and his crew.

Once the noise of their footfalls had faded we rose and gave chase, Maglites pointing the way, stopping only to clear the view ahead of jogs in the tunnels. On we ran for a quarter of a mile. And then we fetched up at the old vertical air shaft, watching the skip recede upward and away from us, carrying Weinstein and Petrauskas.

I keyed the hand radio, hoping the vertical shaft would carry the transmission up to the troopers waiting above. "Alex? Steve. We're at the bottom of the shaft. Where are you? What's happening?"

"Steve!" Alex almost crooned, relief palpable in his

voice. "You okay? We're at the top of the shaft. Everything's secured up here. Three subjects down, four captured. One bad guy dead. One trooper wounded but he'll be okay."

"Alex, Weinstein and Petrauskas are coming up in the skip now. They've got automatic weapons. Be ready."

"Gotcha."

"Steve," Gil said, tapping me on the shoulder. He played his Maglite on the wooden planking underfoot, where a few droplets of fresh blood glittered. "Pinked him, but probably not badly."

We waited while the whining hoist hauled the skip to the surface. It stopped.

"Steve?" Alex's voice crackled on the radio. "They're not on the skip."

"Oh hell," I said. "They got off the skip at either the first or the second drift."

"Which one?" Gil said.

"Beats me."

"We'll have to flush him out."

Quickly I radioed Alex. In a few minutes two troopers, armored with loose steel plates they had found in the outbuilding, rode the skip to the first drift. They dismounted and sent the skip down to the third drift, where Gil, our two troopers, and I awaited. In a few minutes we emerged onto the second drift and searched. Nothing except rows and rows of Colombian and Huanaco coca plants and some other greenery we couldn't identify. Damp fog billowed out of misters hanging over the coca, mimicking the rainy season that spurred the plants to high-speed growth. My shirt began to stick to my back.

We radioed the first drift.

"Nothing, Steve," said one of the troopers. "But look what we found."

We rode the skip to the first drift and dismounted. The huge room on the first level — bigger than the ones in the second and third drifts—contained a small-scale but complete drug laboratory for refining cocaine, with vessels and retorts, extractors and purifiers, cans of potassium permanganate, ether, acetone and hydrochloric acid, and copper piping. But first things first. Where the hell could Weinstein have gone?

"Look," Gil said.

A droplet of blood glistened in the dust on the floorboards.

"Is there a trail?"

"Here's another." The second droplet lay four feet from the first.

"And another."

The last speck of blood sat in front of a wooden skid, six feet by six feet, leaning against the rock wall next to the mouth of a large wall fan. Quickly we swept aside the skid, revealing a rough hole in the rock wall. A galvanized steel duct—obviously the vent for gases from the lab—occupied half the low straight tunnel, leaving just enough room for a man to scrabble through on hands and knees. Fifty feet on, daylight poured into the tunnel.

"He must of come this way," a trooper said unnecessarily.

With .357 in hand I crept through the tunnel and emerged into daylight, shouldering aside a bush, its leaves dried brown from the lab's exhaust gases, concealing the mouth of the bore. It lay in a low valley on the far side of the ridge, in view of the Venture hoist house just a few hundred yards away. Trampled grass showed Weinstein and Petrauskas' path directly to a Forest Service rut with fresh tire marks in the damp earth. Exhaust fumes still hung in the windless morning air.

"Damn," I said.

"Steve," Alex said, so close behind me I jumped. "He's after Ginny."

"*Ginny?*"

"Garrigan is singing. Just after we caught her coming

out of the shaft, she started babbling. She said you destroyed Weinstein's dream, and now he's going to destroy yours."

"Jesus! Who's closest to Ginny's house?"

"Chad. I just sent him back to town for a couple of hazmat suits."

"Raise him, willya, and tell him to go straight to Ginny's. It may not be too late."

I broke into a dead run for the Venture yard and my Explorer, Alex and Gil close behind, radioing Chad on the run. We leaped into the vehicle and took off, scattering gravel.

"Talk to me," I told Alex as I wrestled the Explorer onto Norwich Road. Both he and I were panting from the sprint.

"Garrigan said Weinstein had a call yesterday from a mobbed-up mole in the Chicago police department who said the law in Porcupine City had been asking questions about him. Last night he decided to hole up in the old silver mine— he had no idea we knew about it—until he could make his getaway after the last load of trucks had been sent out. It wasn't until he spotted you and Gil coming through the vent tunnel that he finally cottoned on to the plan. By then, of course, we were in position in the clearing. One thug came out first, shooting with an AK, and we nailed him in a crossfire. Garrigan and the rest came out with their hands up. She's been talking to us ever since."

I barely heard him. "Ginny," I said. "Son of a bitch!" I pounded the steering wheel. We had reached the lakefront highway, but were still a mile from her house.

"Chad?" I called. No answer. "Chad?"

Just as I wrested the Explorer onto Ginny's driveway, Chad's voice crackled on the radio.

"It's over," he said.

THIRTY-SIX

"Ginny!" I shouted as I leaped, .357 in hand, from the Explorer, halted behind Chad's cruiser — I couldn't miss the neat row of .45 caliber holes stitched across its hood and through the starred windshield — and a muddy old Blazer. On a dead run Alex and I rounded the side of the house.

Ginny sat on a bench behind her kitchen, her .30-30 deer carbine held loosely in her hands. Chad stood beside her, riot gun in one meaty hand. Ten yards away, on the wooden steps to Ginny's deck, sprawled the body of Morris Weinstein, MAC-10 still in his right hand, the back of his head a grisly pudding. A neat round hole punctured the middle of his forehead.

Just above Ginny's head the door frame dangled, splintered by bullets.

"What happened?" I asked.

"Saw the whole thing," Chad said. "Weinstein got here just before I did, and as I got out of the cruiser he fired a burst at Ginny's door. I ducked behind the car and yelled, and he turned around and shot it up. But just as he turned to aim back at Ginny, she stepped out the door and fired. It all happened in two seconds."

I was surprised. But I should not have been. As a teenager Ginny had killed her first deer. She is as comfortable with rifles as I am, and she has a cool head in a crisis. It probably didn't matter that Chad had momentarily deflected Weinstein's attention. Ginny had the high ground on her deck and concealment behind the heavy logs of her house. She very likely would have used her advantage against Weinstein's superior firepower and won. He had no chance against this gutsy and very competent woman.

Ginny's shoulders slumped, a bleakness clouding her face, as she sat mired in the emotional shock that always accompanies such a terrible event. She had killed a man. Never mind self-defense, the taking of a human life, however justified, always forever alters the comfortable selfhood of a person. Any combat infantryman will tell you that. I had experienced it myself.

"It was a righteous shooting," I said, squatting next to her. "I'm sorry."

I did not touch her, but kept my physical distance, fervently willing an emotional closeness toward her. I was sorry not only for what she had just been through and what she still would have to go through, but also what had happened to us. But this wasn't the time or place to bring that up.

"Do you have somebody to stay with you until this is over?" I asked.

"I'll call Nancy Aho," she said. Calmly though a little shakily, Ginny stood and walked back into the house to phone Nancy. I wished very much that Ginny had asked me to be with her through the next hours and days. But the historical society docent was a strong, grandmotherly sort, the kind of person people naturally leaned on, and I knew Ginny would have a firm shoulder of support for the days to come. Police would interview and reinterview her, and print reporters and blow-dried cable television media creatures would yammer for sound-bite quotes. She would have to tell her story over and over again. It would be a long time before her life returned to normal—if it ever did. I hoped the press never discovered Ginny's secret life as Porcupine County's financial benefactor.

Meanwhile Alex had spread a tarp over Weinstein's ruined body. For the next half hour sheriff's cars, trooper's cruisers, DEA Hummers, and an ambulance rolled into Ginny's driveway while the authorities did their various things. Out of concern for Ginny, Alex asked all the officers to douse their vehicles' flashing lights—there was no need to intimidate or distract anyone — and when an arrogant DEA agent demurred, Gil quietly but vehemently threatened to stuff the fed's head up his nether region. The agent complied.

Alex and I were standing in the driveway when the thought struck us at the same time. *"Where's Petrauskas?"* we both shouted.

THIRTY-SEVEN

"Good God!" I cried. "What's the matter with us?"

"Simply forgot all about him," Alex said grimly. "Shit happens. We've just gotta clean it up now."

As we raced toward Porcupine City in the sheriff's Explorer, lights flashing, Alex raised the Porcupine River bridge tender on the radio. "Has the *Lucky Six* left harbor today?" he asked.

"She cleared the bridge forty-six minutes ago," replied the tender, who keeps careful score of all vessels' comings and goings. "It was going like a bat outta hell through the channel, too. Went straight out into the lake and headed due north."

Alex and I looked at each other. Weinstein must have dropped Petrauskas off at the marina on his way to Ginny's. Probably their plan had been for Petrauskas to pick up Weinstein in the shallow water off Ginny's cabin after he had killed her, and make their escape together aboard the *Lucky Six*. Somehow Petrauskas discovered things had gone wrong and was bolting off by himself. Maybe Weinstein was to have phoned him at the marina from Ginny's to coordinate the pickup, and when there was no call, Petrauskas had figured things out.

"We'll have to take to the air," Alex said as he turned to me. I looked at him. No sign of the fearful small-plane hater in his resolute expression.

"You bet. Let's go."

In ten minutes we took off in the sheriff's Cessna, heading north into the teeth of a stiff wind from Canada. To save time I had done the most cursory preflight examination of the airplane, checking only the oil and fuel and praying everything else was present and accounted for. We had plenty of fuel for a four-hour search if it came to that, for I had topped off the tanks after my last flight.

"Petrauskas won't be heading for the Soo or anyplace else on the American shore," I said. "He'll be aware that there's a BOL out for him." What other jurisdictions call APBs, or All Points Bulletins, we call BOLs, or Be on the Lookouts.

"Where's he going, ya think?" Alex asked.

"Canada. Straight north into the teeth of that oncoming gale. He'll hope to get lost in it and make landfall on a deserted shore somewhere during the storm and abandon the boat before the Ontario provincial police can get to him." Much of the Canadian shore of Lake Superior is unbroken wilderness even more isolated than Porcupine County, and it would be easy for a fugitive to conceal himself in the woods.

A long low front was rolling in from Canada, Flight Service had said on the radio, with heavy rain, low cloud, high winds, seven- to nine-foot waves and a good prospect of lightning. Already the plane was bouncing heavily in gusty turbulence as it shouldered through scattered low clouds, and we were still a good hour or so away from the oncoming front. I gazed down at the roiling whitecaps below, marching south under the wind in scattered but powerful ranks. A dangerous Lake Superior storm was building, and we were flying directly into it.

"He won't be making more than ten knots in that stuff," I said. "Any faster and he'd batter the boat to pieces against the waves. Let's see, it's been an hour now, and he'll be no farther than ten or so nautical miles out. We'll head due north and look for boats."

I throttled the Cessna's airspeed back to 110 miles per hour to reduce the impact of the bumps, and we droned out onto the lonely lake—so lonely that we saw only two boats, one a cruiser and one a sailboat, making their way toward Porcupine City Harbor as fast as they could, pushed along by the heavy chop. Alex busied himself arranging loaded 9mm magazines under his thighs, eight of them so far as I could see. He didn't want the clips to get loose and fall on the cockpit floor, perhaps jamming the rudder pedals. At the clearing he had relieved one of Weinstein's thugs of his Uzi and a knapsack of ammunition, carrying both down into the mine and then to Ginny's.

"I thank the sun, moon and stars that you had the foresight to bring that Uzi along," I told Alex.

"Weinstein had that MAC," Alex said, "and the Uzi just seemed like a useful equalizer. I thought we'd need it at Ginny's."

"Petrauskas probably has an automatic weapon of some kind, too. I know he's got a .30-'06 rifle in that boat."

"What for?"

I told him.

"Pirates," Alex repeated in soft amazement. "But now he's the one flying the Jolly Roger."

On the way I'd explained to Alex what we'd do. The passenger-window stop bracket was still detached from our night flight across Porcupine County, and again Alex could fold the window up where the airflow would hold it flat against the underside of the wing, allowing him to bring the muzzle of the Uzi to bear against a target abeam the plane. He'd have to loosen his seat belt, twist his body in the cramped space and fire left-handed, but it could be done. "You'll have a pretty good field of fire," I said, "but for godsake please don't hit the wing strut." With that shot away, the right wing would just fold up and we'd spin down to a watery grave.

"Won't," Alex promised. "Just give me a steady gunnery platform."

"I'll do my best," I said, "but there's a lot of turbulence."

A Cessna 172 does not make the world's best police aircraft, but the smokeys' helicopters all were hangared in Lansing, 320 air miles to the southeast, and the nearest Coast Guard chopper lay at Traverse City 230 miles distant. In the

Upper Peninsula, we make do with whatever we've got.

"How're we going to do this?" Alex asked. "I haven't got a loud-hailer to tell Petrauskas to turn back and surrender."

"That'd be futile." A thug fleeing a possible rap for conspiracy to commit murder and possibly Murder One itself isn't going to cooperate with the coppers, but desperately try to escape.

Ten minutes went by, then fifteen. The wind against us grew stronger and stronger, slowing the plane's forward progress over the water to a mere eighty miles per hour. At the point the GPS told me was ten nautical miles from shore, I banked left. We'd fly for five minutes to the southwest parallel to the Upper Michigan shore, searching all the way, and if we saw nothing we'd just turn one hundred eighty degrees, retrace our route and head ten minutes to the northwest. On and on the plane droned.

Alex said, "This reminds me of the movie *Tora! Tora! Tora!* Those lonely search planes way, way out over the wide, wide sea, and noplace to land."

"Don't get all uptight on me now," I said.

"I'm okay. Never mind. Just making an observation."

At almost the fifth minute past our initial turn Alex shouted "Sail ho!" as if we had been searching for a windjammer. "Or whatever it is sailors say!"

I spotted the vessel ahead, throttled back and guided the Cessna down through the growing turbulence to five hundred feet above the waves, keeping its nose pointed at the boat, itself bouncing madly as it shouldered its way through the heavy chop. Alex peered at it through my Bushnells.

"Looks like a big cruiser," he said. "Tall flying bridge near the stern."

"That's the *Lucky Six*, I'm sure. We'll have to do a flyby to make certain, and order the skipper to return to port. Just wave your arm out the window and point back to shore. Okay, battle stations."

Alex opened the window and folded it against the wing as the tempest of a slipstream raised a dust storm inside the plane. He loosened his seat belt and arranged his lanky body so that he could bring the Uzi to bear, but kept the weapon in his lap.

Down to three hundred feet we bounced, then two hundred, approaching the cruiser from astern. We could see a figure in the cockpit looking up at us. As we began to draw abreast, Alex leaned out the window and made a sweeping gesture, pointing back to land. The man turned, one hand on the wheel, and aimed a short-barreled weapon at us, trying to keep the barrel steady as the boat pounded and rolled in the surf.

"It's Petrauskas, all right. He's firing," said Alex. "I can see the muzzle flashes."

Whang! Whang! Two bullets struck the airplane's fuselage behind us and passed through.

"That's the *Lucky Six* for sure," I said, breaking off the approach before Alex could return fire. "I don't think we're badly damaged. The bullets didn't hit the control cables or anything else important." I tested the yoke and rudder pedals to be sure of that. The plane responded as it should. I took a deep breath.

"That's it," I said. "An armed subject resisting arrest. That's the second time he's tried to kill us. We have good cause to use lethal force."

"Uh," said Alex. "Look." He pointed across me and out the pilot window. A stream of aviation gasoline gushed out of a hole in the bottom of the wing. Petrauskas had pinked us. Immediately I reached down and turned the fuel selector switch from BOTH to RIGHT, isolating the left wing tank. We'd lose no more fuel than the sixteen or so gallons remaining in that tank.

"Damn," I said. "Lucky hit. But now we have only about two hours of flying left. That ought to be enough for what we need to do." I hoped very much that it was.

"How we gonna do this?" Alex said.

"We'll approach him from ahead," I said. "He's got to conn the boat, and that's a big, wide windshield in front of him. He won't be able to fire around it and drive the boat at the same time, especially in such heavy seas. He'll have to wait until we're going right past him, and that's a full-deflection shot, the hardest one to make. Likely the bullets will just pass behind us."

"Right," Alex said. "Let's do it."

I gunned the Cessna well ahead of the boat, and at a range of half a mile wrestled the airplane around through the chop. Throttling back to a hundred ten miles an hour, I dropped the airplane to less than a hundred feet above the waves and headed directly for the *Lucky Six*, bouncing and rolling wildly in the mounting surf. We had the advantage. Turbulence or not, the plane held fairly steady between gusts while the boat pounded ahead, breakers crashing over its bow.

Then we were upon the *Lucky Six*. Alex fired burst after burst, pieces flying off the boat's superstructure as the bullets chewed it up, tall splashes bracketing hits as a ragged line of 9mm bullets walked through the hull. The Uzi's roar reverberated throughout the airplane, ejected shell casings ricocheting off the aluminum bulkheads. My ears rang even though, like Alex, I was wearing a noise-attenuating radio headset. Coupled with the painful noise of gunfire in a small enclosed space deep inside the mine, this was going to affect my hearing for days.

The figure at the wheel of the *Lucky Six* ducked, turned, and fired wildly as we swept past. His bullets, as I expected, passed harmlessly through our track way aft.

"Another approach," I said, "and then I'm going to circle the boat while you pour fire into it."

"Gotcha," said Alex, reloading the Uzi.

The oncoming front had almost reached the site of the

air-sea battle, low scattered clouds almost obscuring our view of the boat. A steady rain began to fall.

Again we flew through the ragged scud toward the approaching bow of the boat, and when the Cessna drew abreast of it I banked the airplane into a tight circle, fighting to keep the arc of the turn snug and true against the increasing wind. Holding the plane steady in the turbulence was like trying to break a recalcitrant horse, and Alex found it no easier to aim the Uzi. But although scores of bullets splattered the water wildly, he managed to pour clip after clip of nine-millimeter fire into the *Lucky Six*. Suddenly she slowed to a halt, rolling drunkenly against the building waves.

"Got him!" Alex shouted.

Petrauskas lay slumped and unmoving in the cockpit well of the cruiser as we circled. Alex looked at him through the Bushnells.

"Lot of blood," Alex said. I couldn't see that, but I could spot water pouring into the cockpit as the cruiser broached, its starboard side overwhelmed by the oncoming waves. The boat began to settle by the stern. Bullets, probably a score or more, had also holed the fiberglass hull. The *Lucky Six* clearly could not remain afloat for long before the Big Water claimed it forever.

The sky suddenly darkened as the full fury of the front rolled over upon us, nearby lightning flooding the cockpit.

"We're getting the hell out of here," I said, firewalling the throttle and pointing the airplane due south. The scattered clouds had formed into heavy unbroken scud, the ceiling barely 300 feet above the waves, driving rain cutting visibility to half a mile or less. I was now flying on instruments, keeping a careful eye on the altimeter and the wings level with the attitude indicator as I put the Cessna into a gentle climb through solid cloud, the airplane bouncing madly. Within seven minutes the clouds suddenly lightened and the airplane broke through into sunlight and smoother air. I set course for Porcupine City and in a short while, just as the fuel gauge needles were bouncing against the EMPTY mark, we landed.

Alex and I rolled the airplane into its hangar just as the storm broke wildly over the shore, lightning shattering the tops of pine snags and the wind-driven rain drilling painfully into our faces.

"Think they'll ever find Petrauskas?" Alex asked as we climbed into the Explorer.

"His corpse might wash up on the beach somewhere east of here," I said, "and wreckage from the *Lucky Six* is bound to, but you know what they say."

"Lake Superior never gives up its dead," Alex said.

THIRTY-EIGHT

Later the same day, prisoners and bodies having been sorted out and salted away and both ends of the Venture Mine sealed as a crime scene, Prosecutor Garner Armstrong, DEA Agent William Underhill (the arrogant one), Undersheriff Gil O'Brien, State Police Sergeant Alex Kolehmainen and lowly Deputy Sheriff Steve Martinez (no longer tactical commander of the Venture Mine investigation), interviewed Mary Ellen Garrigan, resident of Winnetka, New Trier Township, Cook County, Illinois, in the county commissioners' chambers at the Porcupine County courthouse. The sheriff's tiny interrogation room being too small and too intimidating for the task, Gil had suggested the capacious chambers. "She's willing to talk," he said reasonably, "and let's make her comfortable." We drew the blinds against the yammering press and the bright television lights outside in the parking lot and got to work. It was an easy job, because Mary Ellen had waived her rights to a lawyer. She knew she faced hard time as a principal in a conspiracy involving illegal drug manufacture and sale as well as homicide, and wanted to make things as easy for herself as she could.

"I hope you Mirandized her before she started talking at the mine," I said before the interview began.

"Barely had the chance," Alex replied. "We had no more snapped the cuffs on her when she let loose with everything she knew. Chad actually had to clap a hand over her mouth before he could read from his card."

By common assent Gil, who is very good at interrogation, was in charge of the interview, Garner assisting. Chad set up the video camera and tape recorder and we began by noting date and time of day and the names of those present.

"Do you waive your right to remain silent?" Gil asked in a surprisingly gentle voice. He is a tough and efficient law-enforcement bureaucrat, and he has the personality of a dyspeptic crocodile, but he is not a bully. "Do you waive your right to a lawyer? Do you understand that everything you say in this room may be used against you at trial?"

"I do," Mary Ellen replied with quivering lips. Without jewels and makeup and clad in shapeless orange jailhouse coveralls, she had aged twenty years. No longer was she the glamorous and arrogant suburbanite, but a frightened felony suspect facing a prison term, a substantial one even if she cooperated to the hilt.

She signed and initialed the waiver forms and noted the date and time. At trial a defense lawyer wouldn't be able to claim she wasn't properly read her rights.

"What is your relationship with Morris Weinstein?" Gil began, still in a soft voice. I had seen him interrogate suspects many times, and knew that at any moment whenever he thought he was being lied to his gentle whisper could suddenly turn caustic enough to peel wallpaper off a ballroom. Fearsomeness was his natural disposition.

"I was his lover for six years. After my divorce we remained good friends."

"What is your connection with the Venture Mine drug operation?"

"He asked me to invest the cash settlement from the divorce in the Venture Mine—the legal operation, that is—so that he could show on the books that it was a going concern."

"He being Morris Weinstein?" Gil left nothing to chance.

"Yes."

"Was it a going concern, as you said?"

Not at first, she replied, although in the last few months the losses had dwindled to the point where the prospect of black ink seemed visible not far down the road. During the three years the nursery had been in operation, Weinstein had worked hard to build a brand name and goodwill among garden centers in the Milwaukee and Chicago areas, and, Mary Ellen said, he had taken great pride in the results. I wouldn't have argued with that.

"So the nursery was not just a front for the drug operation?" Garner asked.

"At first it was. All the time Morrie was building up the business, his main profits came from the bioengineered narcotic plants. But as time went on Morrie saw himself as a savior of Porcupine County. He loved the place and he liked the people. He was not completely a bad guy. I think that if the nursery became really successful he would have shut down the drug operation and gone completely legitimate."

Alex and I looked at each other. Under pressure from the feds, many Chicago mobsters had over the years invested their soiled money in clean enterprises. Mobsters being mobsters, however, their business methods tended to stay dirty. I doubted that even if part of his heart were pure, Morris Weinstein ever would have become much of an angel.

"What was Weinstein's connection to the Chicago crime syndicate?" Gil continued.

"He was a made man," Mary Ellen said. "As was his father."

"And your former husband, William Garrigan?"

"Him too. He was a big investor in Morrie's businesses. Including the Venture Mine."

The DEA guy looked up. "Let's take a short break," he said.

During the interval the agent called his superiors in Chicago to tip them off about Bill Garrigan's financial involvement. As he was making the call I quietly told him of the mole in the Chicago cops' organized crime unit, and suggested he and his bosses avoid any contact with it. When we returned, Gil asked Mary Ellen about the trucks we had stopped that morning, and their load.

The coca and poppy bushes, she said, were genetically engineered high-potency plants Weinstein intended to ship to growers in Peru and Colombia. The pot was on its way to northern California. All the greenery was trucked to a warehouse in a small Wisconsin town just over the Illinois state line called Wilmot, where it was divided and transshipped in vans to seaports, chiefly Corpus Christi and Los Angeles, to take ship for South America. Nobody in authority had yet cottoned on to this reverse flow of drugs out of the United States.

So much for biosecurity. Weinstein's benevolence extended only to legitimate crops.

"Those bags of white powder you saw in the trucks were just samples to demonstrate the potency of the plants to the buyers," Mary Ellen said. "That lab's not big enough to turn out much product. It's just a test kitchen."

"Tell us about the other men in the operation," Gil said. "Let's start with Algis Petrauskas, also known as Michael Anderson."

"My brother." Mary Ellen stifled a sob.

"I'm sorry for your loss. How'd he get involved?"

"It's a long story."

"That's okay, Mrs. Garrigan," Gil said almost languidly. "We have plenty of time."

Algis, four years Mary Ellen's junior, had followed her to New Trier High School in Winnetka. She had been one of the popular girls, a cheerleader and like nearly all her classmates college-bound for the University of Illinois, but Algis had been a square peg in a round hole. Tormented because of his ugliness, he lived up to his looks and became a vicious troublemaker and a thief, graduating from schoolyard bully to a thorough embarrassment to Mary Ellen's upper-middle-class family in the wealthy suburb. Their father, a prosperous banker, had washed his hands of his son after he was convicted of burglary as a juvenile at age sixteen and sent to St. Charles, the tough state reformatory for delinquents.

When Algis turned eighteen he agreed to continue his so-called rehabilitation by joining the navy. After her brother's release from the naval prison, Mary Ellen persuaded Weinstein—still the wealthy and connected entrepreneur she had met while buying a Mercedes—to take Algis on as a gofer. At first Algis labored as an enforcer in Weinstein's loan-shark enterprise, softening up marks who couldn't come up with the vigorish, but Weinstein soon discovered Algis' small-boat expertise and made him the skipper of his yacht. Together they took fellow hoods as well as charter parties fishing.

"Did he take Danny Impellitteri for a cruise?" Garner asked. I perked up. This was the corpse that had washed up on the beach at the beginning of the case.

"Yes."

"What happened on that cruise?"

Impellitteri had been one of Weinstein's go-betweens with the South American drug lords, Mary Ellen said, and he had demanded a greater cut of the proceeds. Outraged, Weinstein ordered Petrauskas to dispose of Impellitteri in Lake Superior while the *Lucky Six* purportedly was in Lake Michigan. One foggy night Petrauskas suddenly caught Impellitteri unaware, pushing him overboard and immediately putting a bullet into the man's chest as he struggled in the water. No wonder, I thought, that Petrauskas had tried so desperately to escape. He was looking at life without parole.

"How do you know this?" Gil said.

"Morrie told me everything. He never kept anything from me. He loved to boast about what he did to people who crossed him."

"Tell us about Roy Schweikert and Frank Saarinen."

Schweikert, she said, had been a hit man before he discovered horticulture—even mobsters can have green thumbs—and killed Frank Saarinen. Frank had discovered the hidden mine, she didn't know quite how, and Weinstein tried to buy him off by enlisting him in the secret operation. But Frank's conscience interfered and Weinstein told Schweikert to get rid of him. Schweikert had followed Frank into the woods on the opening day of deer season and put a bullet into his head.

"What happened to Schweikert?"

"Bad attitude," Mary Ellen said. "He forgot who was boss and tried to run the dope growing operation the way he thought it should be. Morrie warned him several times to do it his way but Roy wouldn't listen."

One winter afternoon Weinstein and Schweikert went out on a "snowmobile monkey drunk" — that's when snowmobilers swing from trailside bar to trailside bar, in between snootfuls barreling across the wintry landscape at high speed. Weinstein induced Schweikert to get blind staggering drunk, put him on his snowmobile and pointed the machine at the thin ice of a nearby creek. As the alcohol-addled Schweikert struggled to gain his feet in the shallow water, Weinstein waded in and held him underwater until he drowned. The Gogebic County deputies wrote it up as still another snowmobile death. In that county that winter alone, seven snowmobilers had gone drinking, driving and dying.

"Mrs. Garrigan," I cut in, mindful of the fate of Andrew Carmichael almost a hundred years earlier, "were there any other homicides Morris Weinstein boasted about?"

"Yes," she said. "As I said, he loved to talk about killing his enemies. But they were all done years ago before he came up to Porcupine County."

The Chicago police, I was sure, would like to talk to Mary Ellen. Not that they could bring charges against a dead man, but they would be happy to clear a few cold cases.

"That's it for now," Gil said. Two hours had passed and Mary Ellen was visibly tiring. "We'll pick it up later."

"Just one more question?" I said.

"All right."

"Mrs. Garrigan, did you or Weinstein wonder how law

enforcement discovered the secret part of the mine?"

"Yes. How did you do that?"

"Never mind."

I did not want Ginny's role in uncovering the drug operation made public unless it was absolutely necessary to achieve convictions, and that did not seem likely. Mary Ellen was cooperating and Garner would present only enough evidence for the General to accept her guilty plea. With luck the Venture Mine Murders soon would be forgotten as the yammering reporters outside the courthouse fastened upon another crime du jour, the media circus pulling up stakes and moving to another town in search of circulation and ratings. Ginny's secret as the loving benefactress of Porcupine County would never be discovered.

The interrogation ended, Mary Ellen was returned to her cell, and the better part of law enforcement in the western reaches of Upper Michigan departed for their homes and families, if they had any. I headed for the door, too.

"Deputy," Gil said sharply. "I'll expect your report by tomorrow night."

I had to smile. He was back in command, and he was letting me know it.

"Afterwards, take a week off, will you?" he said in an only slightly softer voice. "That's an order. Besides, you've earned it."

"Yes sir, boss," I said.

THIRTY-NINE

Two evenings later I was relaxing in a canvas chair on the beach, squidging holes with my toes in the cool damp sand and belching softly as the westering sun descended redly through a clear sky into the lake. Alex and I had just put away porterhouses the size of hubcaps at George's while reliving the happenings of the last few weeks. He had not complimented me on my role in those events. Like Gil O'Brien, Alex does not think people should be praised for performing the jobs they were hired for — but he quietly worked on me to go to the courthouse and start the paperwork to run for sheriff. I said I'd think about it.

"Think long and deep," Alex had said in farewell. "But say yes. Say yes now so that before the local primary next August the whole county will have got used to the idea that it needs a new sheriff."

Sometimes the idea of the long-distance political campaign puts down roots even in the boondocks. The idea of running had been growing on me, but I didn't know whether I had the stomach for almost a year of campaigning. Still, as Alex said, all of Porcupine County now knew who had led the mission against the Venture Mine, and who had not. If I threw my hat into the ring, Alex said, with Garner's help Eli would be shunted farther and farther into the background over the next few months, keeping him — and the sheriff's department — out of trouble. With luck Eli would become the lamest of lame ducks while Gil, who actually ran the department anyway, kept on doing his job. But, I objected, with Eli out of the picture that would mean unbearable tension in the department between the undersheriff and me if I chose to run against him for sheriff.

A soft footfall sighed on the deck behind me. Every hair on the back of my neck alerted. These days momentous things tend to happen at my cabin, either with a knock on the door or a footstep on the floorboards, especially in the evenings. I turned and looked back.

It was Ginny with a soft smile on her face and an overnight bag in her hand.

She strode down the path and sat on the sand beside me before I could offer her the chair. I was dumbstruck.

"What brings you here, Mrs. Fitzgerald?" I said, trying to keep my voice even, but failing at the job. My voice cracked like a fourteen-year-old boy's.

"I'm here on another mission, *Steve*," she said, applying a slight spin to my name. It was only the second time she had used it since the day Mary Ellen Garrigan came between us.

I nodded dumbly.

Ginny gazed out over the Big Water, scanning the horizon and crinkling her eyes against the sun, the slight crow's feet I loved to kiss sending chills up my spine. Best to let her speak in her own good time. And, being Ginny, she took her own good time, starting at the beginning.

"I had a couple of visitors today," she finally said.

"Mm. Who?"

"The first one was Chad Garrow."

"Is he in trouble again?"

"Not with me." She looked down at the sand, a smile growing at the corners of her mouth.

"What did he want?"

"He said he didn't want me to think less of him because of his former relationship with Mary Ellen. He wanted to explain how he became involved with her and how ashamed he was of himself."

I knew the basics but didn't mind hearing the details. I nodded. "How did it happen?"

"You're the closest deputy to her house," Ginny said. "One morning a few weeks ago she waited until she heard on the radio that you were going to be out of the county, and then she called the sheriff's department to report that she thought someone had been trying to break into her house the night before. Naturally Chad was covering your beat and Joe Koski dispatched him.

"Chad said that when he arrived she was wearing a housecoat. She showed him a screwdriver mark on a window sill — Chad thinks she made it herself — and then told him she found him, in his words, 'absolutely fascinating.' He had such a stupid grin on his face when he told me that. But he had the grace to shake his head ruefully."

The silvery tinkle of Ginny's laughter broke the moment. "Now he didn't go into graphic details — he's both too shy and too much of a gentleman for that — but he did say that after a while she suddenly lost her housecoat. Of course she wasn't wearing anything underneath."

I had to smile, too, at the mental picture of Chad's testosterone-fueled consternation at Mary Ellen's display and the consequences, as logical as they were biological. Very, very few young men in good health could have had the fortitude to resist such an offer. Who could blame him?

But then Ginny frowned. "It grew from there. Chad visited her house almost every day after work. For quite a while, Chad admitted, Mary Ellen pumped him for information about the daily operations in the sheriff's department. And he told her. He said he didn't think anything he said was sensitive. He thought she just wanted to hear cop stories."

"He told me the same thing, too," I said. "But I don't think he spilled anything about the moves we made on Weinstein. He couldn't have, anyway. He didn't know about the investigation until the last minute, when we planned the raid. One thing, though. I asked him to keep on his visits to Mary Ellen even on the last day so she wouldn't suspect something was going on. He said he sure would. I wonder what he did. I don't think he'll tell me. Did he tell you?"

Ginny grinned wickedly. "Yes, he did. And I'm not

going to betray a confidence."

"Hmph. All right."

"There was one other thing Chad told me that I *can* tell you."

I leaned forward on the chair, my expression intent.

"He told me what you had told him about that afternoon with Mary Ellen on the beach."

"I'm so sorry about that," I said. "I'm so *damned* sorry."

"So am I. I saw what I saw. I don't think you can blame me for reaching the conclusion I did."

"But it wasn't the right one."

"I realize that now."

"You do?"

"Yes, Steve."

"But how do you know I wasn't feeding Chad a line of bull?" I could have kicked myself for saying that. But I'm a cop. I think like a cop, which means I can't take anything at face value without checking it out—even anything I say myself—and it sometimes gets me in trouble.

"Because whatever else you are, Stevie Two Crow, you are not a liar." She calls me "Stevie Two Crow" only in highly sentimental moments. And her eyes were glistening. She placed her hand on mine.

Nothing more needed to be said. I took her in my arms, and she took me in hers, and we held each other tightly for an interminable time, so tightly that we both became breathless. We did not want the moment to end. We had been deprived of each other for so long. But I interrupted the proceedings.

"Why do you think Mary Ellen put the moves on me?" I asked. "Was she going to pump my brains for Weinstein the way she did Chad's, or did she just want to score her first Indian?"

"Sometimes a piece of ass is just a piece of ass," Ginny said.

"Your choice of words surprises me," I said primly.

496

"How else would you put it?"

I avoided the question. "Maybe she wanted all three —
inside information, a boy in blue, and a lark with a Lakota."

"How uncharacteristically poetic of you!" Ginny
chuckled.

I changed the subject. "You said you had two visitors
today," I said. "Who was the second one?"

Ginny unwound herself from me, but not completely.
"Gil O'Brien."

"Finishing up the proceedings?" I asked. Gil had
conducted the formal interview with Ginny on her shooting of
Weinstein. Nobody had had to tell me to stand aside because I
was personally involved.

"Yes. He brought an amended statement for me to sign.
The coroner had ruled self-defense, he said, and he wanted to
tell me that the state and county will have no further reason to
deal with me in the matter. I won't have to testify when Mary
Ellen is tried. She's going to plead guilty to conspiracy and
accept her sentence."

It had surprised me, I said, that Mary Ellen had rolled
over and given up so quickly. "I wonder why."

"I went to school with lots of people like her," Ginny
said. "They always play to the main chance. She married Bill
Garrigan because he represented money and power, and she
had an affair with Morris Weinstein because he represented
not only money and power but also excitement. She knew
from the beginning that if Weinstein was ever caught, her
financial involvement in the mine would come out, and the
best way for her to avoid a maximum sentence would be to
cooperate with the police, to betray her friends. She uses
people and she uses circumstances."

I sighed. "I wonder what's going to happen to the mine
now."

After the drugs and narcotic plants had been removed
and trucked to the state police post in Wakefield to be held as
evidence, the mine had been shuttered, its doors and gates

padlocked, the legal crops abandoned deep below the ground to wither and rot. Morrie Weinstein had left neither survivors nor will. If any distant family member came come forward to claim ownership of the mine, the DEA would just seize the mine under drug crime forfeiture laws. I doubted that it would bother, preferring to let the county condemn the property for tax arrears and take it over. Workers would dismantle and carry away whatever could be sold, then the forest would be left slowly to creep back over the years and decades, concealing the mine and its history as it had so many other abandoned copper mines in Upper Michigan.

More than fifty people had lost their jobs, jobs that very likely never would be replaced. Some of them would leave the county for better opportunities elsewhere, as so many Porkies had done over the decades, shrinking the population even more. But many would remain, hanging on by the skin of their teeth, refusing to leave the land they loved, surviving any way they could.

Ginny broke my reverie. "There's more about Gil," she said.

"Hmm?"

"We talked about next year's election. Gil said Eli isn't going to give up without a fight, that he's going to run hard on his record. That's his right."

"Yes. He'll win if Gil runs against him. Eli has done too many things for too many people for them to turn against him easily. And if Gil should by some miracle win the Democratic primary, Eli will run as a Republican."

"But this is a Democratic county. You can't split tickets in the primary. I can't think many Democrats would cross over to the Republicans just to vote for Eli. Would he really be able to win as a Republican?"

"Maybe. Gil's no glad-handing pol. He's just not easy to like. He scares people."

Ginny nodded. "And if you run against Gil, you and he

will just split the anti-Eli vote and Eli will win even bigger."

"How the hell did you know they'd asked me to run? I thought that hadn't got out of the sheriff's department yet."

"Garner came to me about a week before Mary Ellen tried to put the moves on you at the beach and asked me what I thought," Ginny said sweetly.

I was outraged, but only momentarily. "All you guys were ganging up on me," I said, but without much conviction.

"How do you think Garner got to where he is as a politician?" Ginny said. "He knows that the whole family runs for office, not just one person."

"Family?" I was dumbfounded.

"Yes. And that's one reason why I told you I wanted to adopt a child. It's about time we became a family, whether or not you realize it."

"I have news for you, young lady. I *do* realize it." And then I told her what had been going through my mind that day on the beach, what I had been planning on telling her at dinner before Mary Ellen Garrigan spoiled the whole thing. I left out no detail.

Ginny moved toward me, and it was another while before we came up for air.

"Oh, there's one more thing," she said.

"What?"

"Gil asked me whether I thought you'd fire him if you happened to win the election."

The undersheriff serves at the pleasure of the sheriff. He can be let go any time and for any reason.

"Jeez, no," I said. "I couldn't possibly get along without him."

"Then why don't you tell him that?"

"How? I'd rather run naked through a patch of nettles than let my hair down with that guy."

Ginny sighed. "You idiots are so macho."

"I'll show you macho."

"All right, let's see what you got." She giggled.

And that was it for the rest of the evening, and far into the night.

FORTY

The next morning I drove to the department in jeans and sweatshirt, for I was still on leave. I walked in, sat at my desk and rummaged whistling through the drawers, pretending to look for something. All I could turn up was a withered apple core that must have been two deputies old and a ballpoint pen Joe Koski had given me for Christmas three years before. Its transparent barrel displayed a cartoon of a pretty girl in a bikini that slid off when you turned the pen upside down.

"I thought I told you to take a week off," Gil growled from his office across the squadroom.

I took a deep breath, stood and strode resolutely into his office, quietly closing the door behind me as the intensely curious eyes of Joe, Chad and two other deputies followed me in.

"What do you want?" The undersheriff did not raise his head but directed his gaze upward at me through hooded eyes, like a cantankerous eagle that had just missed a leaping trout in mid-snatch.

I scratched my head and shuffled my feet. "Um . . ." I said.

"I'm busy, goddam it. What is it?"

"Well, Undersheriff, I'd like to ask you a hypothetical question."

"Ask away."

"Suppose a guy decided to run for sheriff and another guy also decided to run for sheriff, too, because he didn't want to lose his job?"

Gil folded his arms, leaned back in his chair and drilled his laser glare directly into me.

"And the first guy told the second guy that no way would he lose his job if the first guy won because the first guy knew that he couldn't possibly get along without the second guy?"

"You're not making a lot of sense."

"Well, ah, what I'm trying to say is . . ."

"Deputy Martinez, you do what you have to do. I will do what I have to do." Gil slammed his desk drawer. He nodded curtly in dismissal.

"All right."

"But before you go, would you be ever so kind as to sign these reports you failed to sign before you decided to go goof off?" Abruptly he threw a folder on his desk. I opened it, stifled the urge to tell him that he had ordered me to take the furlough, and hurriedly scribbled my name on the sheets. It was as if we had never shared a couple of hours under fire, each of us depending on the other to cover his back. There is no stronger bonding experience among men than combat against a common enemy.

Just as I opened the front door, Gil called from his office. "Where are you going?" he demanded sharply.

"The courthouse," I said. "I'm going to pick up a petition for the election." The first step in running for a county office in Porcupine County is to submit to the county clerk a petition signed by a sufficient number of registered voters attesting that they support the petitioner's candidacy. In a place as sparsely populated as Porcupine County, only three to eight signatures are needed.

"Not so fast. I'll go with you."

He slid back his chair and stood, still gazing at me, reached for his garrison cap, and buckled on his equipment belt as if he was going out on patrol. "I'm going to withdraw mine," he added almost casually. "For the good of the county."

He did not smile. But I thought I saw the beginning of a crinkle at the corner of one eye. Or maybe Gil was just relaxing his gimlet gaze at me by a hair. It was hard to tell.

As Gil and I departed, not exactly shoulder to shoulder but with a full two feet of daylight separating us, I glanced back to see a beaming Joe Koski reaching for the mike with one hand and the phone with the other.

"It's happening," I heard him say.

Jeez.

Cache of Corpses

First published in hardcover by Forge Books, 2007
First published as an e-book, 2011

For Melody and Annie

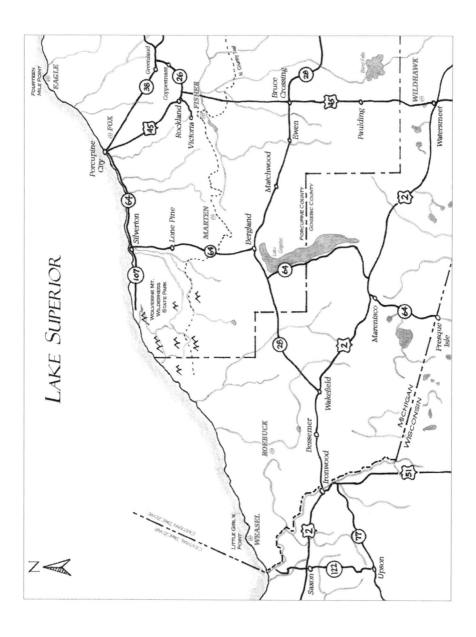

ONE

"It's in the Dying Room," Jenny Besonen said, voice strained, ample chest heaving. "And it has no head."

Billy Ciric, her boyfriend, sat disconsolately next to her on a bench in the Poor Farm courtyard, staring at the breakfast he had splashed on the rusty flank of Amos Hoskinen's tractor.

"*What's* up in the Dying Room?" I asked. I was a bit breathless myself, having been yanked a few minutes earlier out of the Porcupine City Health Center, where I had been pumping a stationary bike for nearly an hour, and dispatched in the sheriff's department's Explorer out to the scene on State Highway M-38 three miles southeast of town.

"The *body*." Jenny glanced at me almost accusingly, as if I should magically have known the reason for her distress.

"The body?"

"It's a lady. She's wrapped in plastic. And she has no head." Jenny took a deep breath, mending her tattered composure.

"Go on."

"We'd been exploring, and—" Jenny glanced away and hesitated. She wasn't telling the truth. Seventeen-year-old kids are still too immature and transparent to lie convincingly. But it wasn't yet time to insist on the facts, young lady, nothing but the facts.

"Anything else?"

"No . . . Ah . . . I don't know."

"Wait here, okay? I'll have a look. Amos, would you keep an eye on Jenny and Billy?"

"Sure," Amos said. He had not moved from the seat of his tractor, but had kept his phlegmatic calm ever since Jenny and Billy had scrambled, screaming in terror, out the front door of the Poor Farm and told him what they had stumbled

507

across up in the Dying Room. Immediately Amos had relayed their discovery to the sheriff's department on his cell phone — luckily, the Poor Farm lay within the spotty cellular coverage of Porcupine County — and I, the nearest deputy within the dispatcher's grasp, had been hauled to work early and sent to the scene.

A tall, rawboned farmer and stable keeper, Amos was the latest in a succession of owners of the sprawling property once officially known as the Porcupine County Poor Farm and still called that. Looking almost like a brooding red-brick Victorian mansion gingerbreaded with cupolas and turrets — "Hogwarts West," the local children say — the Poor Farm still catches the eye of motorists speeding by on the highway a hundred yards away.

More than a century ago Porcupine County built the Poor Farm to shelter two dozen or so indigents who worked the rocky, deforested fields in exchange for their survival. For poorhouses of the age, this one wasn't so bad. Daily life there, I knew from the lecture the director of the Porcupine County Historical Society had given a year or so ago, was rugged but not cruel. The unfortunates were expected to help work the land if they could and do chores inside if they couldn't. The Poor Farm had been no Dickensian horror but a lighthouse of modest respite in an unforgiving land where harsh winters arrive early, dig in deeply, and stay long.

From the highway, the place looked sturdy enough to be rehabilitated someday. Closer in, however, a visitor could see that splintered plywood shrouded half the Poor Farm's windows while the glass in the other half simply had gone missing. Doors dangled askew from sprung hinges. Frayed blue plastic tarps, lashed loosely over holes in the roof, snapped in the wind.

The two-foot-thick masonry, however, remained solid and mostly unblemished except for the faded five-foot-tall "EaT *more* BeeF" sign whitewashed by a shaky hand on the highway side. The notice had doubtless been posted by some desperate long-ago cattle farmer, perhaps the one who had bought and worked the house and its lands when the state took over care of the poor after the Second World War.

Inside, a large warm kitchen and a commodious parlor once had made up most of the now empty and cavernous ground floor. Shreds of straw left by the hay bales stored there in later years now shared the oaken planks with decades of rodent droppings. Upstairs, men had slept in a large dormitory room at one end, women in another across the wide hall, its door guarded by a stern Cerberus of a nurse. Children had occupied bunks on half the third floor, the highway side. A series of small rooms, used mostly for storage, separated them from the Dying Room, whose face was turned to the fields on the other side of the house.

The Dying Room was where the deathly ill awaited their fate, the thick walls insulating their cries and screams from the rest of the house. The arms of two tall men could have spanned the width of the room and almost its length. It had space for just two narrow beds, whose utilitarian steel frames and springs, now broken and rusted, still stood on the floor. Just off the room lay another chamber, little more than a closet, according to legend the coldest enclosure in the house during the winter. There plain wooden coffins and their contents were stored until the April thaw, when they could be discreetly smuggled down a back stairway and carted to potter's field, where they were often buried in the presence of just two mourners, the gravedigger and a minister hired by the county to speed the souls on their way.

Carefully I mounted the front stairs to the third floor, brushing away decades of cobwebs as splintered oaken treads creaked in annoyance. I stepped over the dusty threshold of the Dying Room.

That was the perfect name, for the place itself looked bound for the boneyard. A jagged fissure gaped between the ruined walls and stained ceiling, sagging like a double bed in a cheap motel. Shattered lath grinned from lightning-shaped cracks in the plaster walls. Most of the elaborately carved oaken frieze molding had been pried out and salvaged decades ago.

On one of the bedsprings lay the sight that had so upset Jenny and Billy. A rectangular shroud of thick plastic sheeting, sealed all around to form a transparent but airtight container, encased a yellowish-green corpse. The plastic bulged slightly from gas emitted by slow decomposition. A thick scrim of moisture clouded the inside of the soiled plastic, like a dirty shower curtain in a humid bathroom, blanketing a clear view of the contents. I could see enough of the shape within to tell that it was the nude body of a woman, probably young judging by the firmness of the breasts and tightness of the thighs. It had neither head nor hands. Instead of looking like a once living body, it resembled a mutilated life-size statue toppled off its pedestal in a ruined Greek temple.

I stood, picked my way back through the third floor and down the rickety stairs, and strode out into the courtyard. Deputy Chad Garrow, whose patrol area encompasses the Poor Farm, stood talking to Jenny, Billy and Amos. Chad had been writing a traffic ticket twenty minutes south on U.S. 45, hence I had been called in early to investigate. I quickly filled him in on what I had seen in the Dying Room.

"Shall I radio Alex?" Chad asked. Detective Sergeant Alex Kolehmainen was the local state police forensics investigator and the authority we almost always called in to investigate suspicious deaths. The state police are better equipped for that than are tight-budgeted sheriff's departments in rural counties whose population—and tax base—shrinks by ten per cent every decade. And this at first looked like a homicide, although doubts were beginning to seep into my head.

"Do that," I said in a whisper. "Then talk to the kids. Soften 'em up."

After radioing Alex from his cruiser, Chad quietly chatted with Jenny and Billy, still sitting on the bench in the warm noonday sun outside the manor house. They were both high school seniors, and I knew them. Billy was tall, black-haired in a modified Marine crew cut, good-looking and muscular. A star football player at Porcupine City High School, Billy was a tight end promising enough for a football scholarship to half a dozen universities. His black sleeveless T-shirt set off his well-cut biceps. Only a bent nose, the product of a hard check into the goal on a hockey rink, marred his sculpted features.

Jenny, the oldest daughter of a dairy farmer, was a sturdy and slightly chubby but winsome and pretty blonde whose loose chambray work shirt, denim overalls and swampers — rubber-bottomed leather boots — couldn't conceal her abundant womanliness. Her arms and shoulders had been built up by years of farm work, many of them with the heifers that always scored well in the 4-H division at the county fair. Doubtless she had been mucking out stalls that morning, for she smelled cowy, a homey aroma of sweet milk and stale dung whose familiarity comforts rather than repels the country dweller.

Both were nice, hard-working, intelligent kids who applied themselves in school, and both were headed to college, Billy to the University of Michigan and Jenny to Michigan Tech. He wanted to follow his dad into law and she was hoping to become a veterinarian. I thought both would achieve their dreams — and after graduation probably would leave Porcupine County for good. Jobs are hard to get in a land where the mines have long closed and where most of the tall pines and cedars were cut down more than a century ago, and what jobs still remain don't pay much. I just hoped Billy wouldn't get Jenny pregnant, as happened so often in rural America. Young dreams are so easily ruined by careless rolls in the hay.

Jenny and Billy laughed with Chad, as if the kids had

forgotten the unpleasant sight in the Dying Room. I was not surprised. Chad, as amiable as he was large, knew how to get witnesses to relax, even to let down their guards so they would tell the truth while being interrogated. He was the perfect good cop who made witnesses and suspects alike think he was on their side.

And now playing tough cop was my job. Jenny and Billy, after all, had found the body, and even in the most remote reaches of the Upper Peninsula of Michigan, those who find bodies are always the first to be questioned, if only to be quickly eliminated as suspects. Despite the astronomical odds against kids like Jenny and Billy having anything to do with the presence of that corpse, I decided to approach them as if they might have. You never know.

I beckoned Billy over to the Explorer, ushering him out of Jenny's earshot so that their stories would be independent of each other's.

"Hop in," I said. "We might as well make ourselves comfortable while we sort this out." I looked back at Jenny, giggling as the beaming Chad, easily ten years her elder, flirted shamelessly with her.

"Okay," Billy said, his expression earnest and helpful.

"Let's start at the beginning," I said. "How did you come to be on the Poor Farm?"

"We were exploring," he said, looking at me with a steady gaze, "and — "

"Exploring?" I interrupted. "Really?" That's what Jenny had said, too, but I didn't believe Billy, either.

"Um — "

"Billy, tell the truth. If you're straight with me and you're in the clear, I'm not going to tell anybody what you were really doing." I was better at playing stern uncle than bad cop.

The kid blushed. "Okay, Mr. Martinez." He looked off into the distance.

"Steve's fine."

"Steve." He slowly tried out the word, as if being asked to call a figure of authority by his given name was another step into adulthood. The invitation was a favorite ploy of mine. Some cops insist on maintaining a dominating distance from those they are interrogating, encouraging a little fear to get them to talk. But casual friendliness often encourages subjects to join me on a mutual path toward the truth. I wasn't chummy like Chad, but I kept the door open.

I waited.

"Well," Billy said tentatively, "Jenny and I wanted to make out, and we thought the Poor Farm would be a good place to do it. Nobody ever comes here. Nobody would see us."

"Billy," I said, "I know as well as you do that there must be a million places in Porcupine County where a boy and a girl can go to *make out* without anybody catching them." I stressed the term to tell him I knew exactly what he meant by it. "Why the Poor Farm, really?"

Billy glanced at me half nervously and half slyly. "Because Jenny and I done it in a million places already," he said.

I had to stifle a smile. But Billy wasn't boasting or playing the smartass, just being matter-of-fact. Kids these days approach sex casually, as if it has all the significance of a good breakfast before school.

"We thought the Poor Farm would be exciting. Especially the Dying Room." That he knew the place's history wasn't surprising. Every kid as well as adult in the county did, thanks to the bloodcurdling stories their parents told them every Halloween about the ghosts of the lost and abandoned that wafted out of the Dying Room.

"Did you bring protection?" I asked.

Billy bristled. "You're not my dad."

"No," I said as gently as I could. "But did you?"

"Yes."

"Let's see."

After a moment's hesitation he pulled a foil-wrapped Trojan from his shirt pocket. That the condom was in his pocket, not his wallet, told me he had planned to use it right away, that his intention in trespassing upon the Poor Farm was exactly what he said it was. Besides, I reflected idly, what was there to steal or trash in such a godforsaken place?

"Okay, Billy. I believe you. Put it away." With only a little prompting he related the rest of the story. Shortly after noon he and Jenny had parked her pickup on the disused dirt road that marked the eastern boundary of the Poor Farm property a quarter of a mile away. They then crept across the meadow, tiptoeing carefully through a minefield of cow patties, to the back of the manor house. They entered it through a doorway whose door was long gone, and enough daylight filtered through the ruined windows to show them the way up the creaking back stairs, festooned with cobwebs, to the Dying Room.

"With some of the seniors at Porky High," Billy finally said, "it's a kind of a game to do it in cool places. We try to top each other. A couple of my friends did it in the district courtroom one night. We did it at high noon on the hardware store roof during the Fourth of July parade, and another time somebody used the cab of the pumper in the fire station. We all used the old shipyard building at the end of Main Street."

I remembered that one. In one of the smaller rooms earlier in the year, a caretaker had discovered a mattress, an old microwave oven, a small television and a DVD player, and a couple of porn videos. How long it had been a love nest for teen-agers was anybody's guess.

"Once me and Jen used the bridge tender's shelter. The door was open."

I whistled. That tiny cubbyhole atop the State Highway M-64 swing bridge over the Porcupine River must be tighter than the backseat of a Volkswagen Bug. Then I had a thought.

"The lighthouse?" I asked. The previous week someone had broken into the old Coast Guard structure, now owned by the historical society, jimmying a window and leaving screwdriver marks, but had disturbed nothing else.

Billy blushed. "Yes. They did it right on top of the pedestal where the lens used to be."

I shook my head, covering a chuckle by saying sternly, "That could be a dangerous game. That was breaking and entering, a misdemeanor meaning ninety-three days in jail and a five-hundred-dollar fine. If they had done anything else illegally at the same time, like swiping something or drinking underage, they could have been charged with a felony—and given a stretch in state prison."

"Yeah, but—"

I didn't tell Billy that Garner Armstrong, the county prosecutor and a man vastly experienced in the thoughtless stupidities of youth, most likely would offer the lighthouse miscreants a plea bargain for unlawful entry of an unoccupied building and a light sentence of a few months on probation and community service. If nothing was stolen or wrecked, Garner wouldn't apply the heavy lumber. To him it wasn't a matter of giving a youngster a sentimental break. He hated to ruin young lives with felony records. Good thing, too. Kids liked to break into deer camps deep in the woods for beer parties and "making out." Usually they were smart enough to clean up after themselves, and only when they left a mess or did damage did the sheriff's department apply its scarce manpower to an investigation.

"So you take each other's word that you've really, uh, *done it* in the places you claim?" I asked.

"No, we prove it with pictures from a digital camera." I closed my eyes. *Oh, Billy, Billy, Billy.* I tried to keep the disapproval out of my voice, but failed.

"That's dangerous. What if the wrong people get hold of the pictures?"

"They won't. We don't make prints. We keep them on

our computers and upload them to each other by email."

"That's not such a good idea."

"Why?"

"Somebody else could get at them. Your parents. Your little brothers or sisters. Believe me, it happens."

"Well ..."

"I think you and your friends had better think carefully about this game. It could have consequences you never imagined."

I decided to go no further with the lecture. Too much censure might make Billy clam up. "All right, go on with your story."

Only mildly chastened, Billy related how he and Jenny climbed the back stairs to the third floor, opened the door to the Dying Room and found the corpse. The gruesome sight, of course, deflated their excited lust. Screaming, they half-stumbled, half-ran across the third floor, down the front stairs and out into the front courtyard, where, I knew, Billy had vomited on Amos' tractor, barely missing the astonished farmer in the John Deere's seat. Jenny, being the daughter of a farmer and used to the less pleasant sights of animal husbandry, kept her cool — or most of it. In many ways the females of the human species in Upper Michigan are tougher than the males.

Immediately, Billy said — he delicately avoided mention of decorating Amos' tractor — he and Jenny told the farmer what they had seen, and they dutifully remained on the scene while the farmer called the sheriff's department. Teenagers can be both reckless and responsible.

"You never saw that body before?" I asked.

Billy glanced sharply at me. "Of course not."

"Dumb question," I said. "But it always has to be asked. All right. I'm done with you. I'm going to talk to Jenny now, and if what she says backs up what you said, that will be all I need from you, and you can go home. I think you were straight with me, and I'll keep your secret." Billy nodded, his confidence returning. I could see that he believed Jenny would back him up in the smallest detail.

And so she did, although she displayed absolutely no embarrassment when she told me what she and Billy had intended to do in the Dying Room. She had also brought protection.

"You can't always expect a boy to do the smart thing," Jenny said.

"You think breaking into the Poor Farm was a smart thing to do?" I said, trying to stifle an amused tone.

"You sound like an old fart, Mr. Martinez," she said. "Weren't you young once?"

I didn't take offense. Her words were smart-ass but her tone wasn't. It was just the way many of today's kids spoke, respectful of their elders but not deferential toward them. They had grown up with a directness my generation hadn't.

"All right, you have me there," I said. "I do agree that being prepared is a smart idea."

Conservative pastors in the Upper Peninsula, especially the evangelicals, preach abstinence, which is a perfectly sensible thing to practice but in my opinion hasn't a prayer against the raging hormones of the teen-age years. Youngsters in the Michigan backwoods are just as sexually active as those in the cities and suburbs. In the Great White North there isn't much for kids to do in their off hours besides play sports, smoke dope and make whoopee while waiting until they're old enough to depart for the bright lights.

While I was talking to Jenny, Alex had arrived in his cruiser, returned my wave, was quickly filled in by Chad, and had mounted the stairs with his forensics kit to the Dying Room.

"Stay here a while," I said to Jenny and Billy, and followed the trooper into the manor house.

"This stiff was meant to be found," Alex announced heartily as I entered the Dying Room and found him squatting by the body. "But not to be identified."

The lanky trooper rose to his feet like a folding wooden carpenter's rule, rearranging the angles of his knees and elbows until he stood straight, and surveyed the scene. What he said made sense. The plastic-shrouded corpse had been laid carefully on the bedspring, only the closed door hiding it from the rest of the house. But why? Few people braved the place. I suspected months, maybe a year or even two, went by before anyone—usually Amos—opened the door to that room.

"Deputy Sheriff," Alex said presently, addressing me with the exaggerated formality he always adopted when he wanted to insert the needle, which was every other day, "what do you think? If you are capable of thought."

Long ago I had learned not to rise to the bait. Alex is my second closest friend in Porcupine County. Number one is Virginia Anttila Fitzgerald, a gorgeous native daughter and the historical society director who had given the Poor Farm lecture I had attended. Alex is a master of irony and indirection as well as the owner of an impish sense of humor. We worked together easily, partly because he never lorded it over me like some state troopers who like to treat county deputies like not-too-bright lackeys and gofers, and partly because our investigative skills had complemented each other's through several knotty cases.

"Detective Sergeant," I said with equal gravity, "I am not sure we are looking at a homicide."

"And why is that?"

"This body looks pickled."

"What makes you think so?"

"Same color as the embalmed casualties I saw in Kuwait." I had been an Army lieutenant after college and criminal justice school, commanding a company of military police during Desert Storm. Now and then my tasks took me to the Graves Registration mortuary outside Riyadh where dead American soldiers were prepared for the sad journey home. "No blood at the points of amputation. Unless I miss my guess, those cuts on the abdomen were made by a mortician's trocar."

"Hmm." Alex's eyes rose in mock surprise. He knows even more than I do about corpses. On his way to detective sergeant he had been trained thoroughly in forensics and evidence gathering. He still often did double duty as the evidence technician he once was, for the tight-fisted Wakefield state police post commander hated to pay overtime to his two busy crime scene techs.

"How long do you think this has been here?" I asked.

"Hard to tell. In a place like this the dust isn't often disturbed to swirl around and settle on things. But there's only a fine layer, almost invisible, on this plastic. My guess is probably a month, six weeks tops."

"Shall we open the — uh — shroud and take a look?" I was kidding.

"No, no, no!" said Alex. "Let the white coats at Marquette do that. Besides, we didn't bring hazmat suits." The laboratory investigators did most of their work at the state police crime lab in Marquette, 120 miles to the southeast. Carefully Alex photographed the scene and its grisly contents. "Let's turn her over," he said after a while. We did so, careful not to tear the plastic shroud on the broken bedsprings. "Looky this," he said, pointing to a soiled white computer label, an inch high by three inches wide, neatly affixed to one corner of the plastic. On it was imprinted a bar code.

"Hmm, I don't see a sell-by date." Alex's sense of humor is sometimes questionable. He photographed the label.

"Maybe it'll tell us where the body came from," I said. "Although I don't think undertakers put bar codes on their handiwork."

"Why not?" said Alex. "It'd speed the bodies through the celestial cash register." I winced and shook my head. But I knew that Alex's lighthearted remarks were just a veteran cop's way of coping with unpleasant sights. Police officers may sound callous and hard-hearted, but the truth is that we are as moved as anyone else by the sight of human death.

"Just a sec," he said. He reached under the bedsprings and fished out a quarter and a penny. "These don't look all that old."

"Dates?" I said.

"Nineteen ninety-two on the quarter, twenty-oh-one on the penny."

"Not so old," I agreed. " 'Ninety-two quarters are still in common circulation."

"What do they mean?" Alex said. "Perp drop them accidentally?"

"Probably. Took something out of his pocket, the coins followed."

For a couple of beats, we fell silent. Then Alex said, "Let me show you the back stairs."

We left the Dying Room and walked down the narrow hall to the stairs, carefully keeping to the sides where the joists better supported the rickety floorboards. Alex played his big Maglite on the dust shrouding the topmost treads of the narrow stairway.

"See the tracks in the dust? Three different people came up this way very recently."

"And two of them were Jenny and Billy."

"Who're they?"

"The kids outside with Chad and Amos." I told Alex what they had said, keeping the story brief but frank.

"Hmm," he replied. "Every generation invents its own excitement, I guess."

"What was yours?"

"Oh, the usual kind, beer and cigarettes. We weren't terribly adventurous."

"Speak for yourself." He and I were the same age.

"Here, take this footprint kit and make impressions of the kids' shoes, will ya? That'll eliminate two sets of tracks.

That means the third could have been left by the perp. Not that his tracks are likely to hang him, but you never know."

I did so, and in the courtyard half an hour later Alex said, "We're done here. I'll call the meat wagon."

Afterward we sent Billy and Jenny on their way, and with Chad's help, Alex and I carried the gruesome package down the front stairs, carefully keeping it clear of rusty nail heads and jutting lath, and zipped it into a body bag. That wasn't necessary to protect the vehicle from the corpse, for the clear plastic shroud was far stronger than a body bag, but we didn't want anyone to have to see what was inside. Then we rolled it into a hearse from the Beninghaus Funeral Home for the trip to Marquette. When it had gone, Alex turned to me and said, "Soon's I hear from Marquette forensics, I'll give you a call."

He didn't have to, but I knew he would. In the small world of Upper Michigan police work, Alex and I are a comfortable old crime-fighting couple. We bust perps together, drink together, hunt together, play golf together, take our women out together, and in general behave like buddies—all activities that many county sheriffs and state police brass disapprove of, because they think deputies and troopers should remain carefully separated in their assigned slots in the pecking order of law enforcement. Hierarchy has its uses.

And, in what passes for Upper Michigan politics, Alex is my campaign manager. Self-appointed and unofficial, of course.

TWO

"Want to help post campaign signs for Steve?" Alex had asked Chad in the squad room of the sheriff's department the day before, deliberately—and a little cruelly—putting the big deputy on the spot. Chad is the nephew of my rival for the office of sheriff of Porcupine County, the incumbent Eli Garrow, and got his job partly because of nepotism. Chad is large and friendly, clumsy and eager, but he is no longer a greenhorn with a badge. He has proven his competency more than once, although I try not to get in his way when he's shambling through the office. The cliché is that big men— Chad is six-six and pushing three hundred pounds—often are remarkably delicate with their hands and light on their feet. Not Chad. Just being in his general neighborhood can get you knocked off your feet. In high school his classmates had called him "Lurch" for his clumsiness, but his speed as well as heft as a center on the football team had won him more than cursory glances from college recruiters. He'd gone to Michigan Tech for two years before joining the sheriff's department.

"He reminds me of a St. Bernard puppy," Ginny once said fondly, "all huge paws and head." She likes him as much as I do even though, like all women in Porcupine County who have experienced his social graces, she hides the antique chairs when he drops in.

Politically speaking, however, Chad is caught between the devil and the deep blue. I think he secretly hoped I would win the election, but he was also loyal to his kinsman. Alex and I never criticized Eli in front of Chad, though Eli certainly deserved criticism, especially of late. Hiring his own wife as jail matron was bad enough and so was using the department's newest snowmobile as his personal playtoy, but those peccadilloes have been long forgotten. In the poor counties of Upper Michigan, that's as far as political scandal ever gets, and while such niggardly nest-feathering could cost a politician an election, it's not worth an indictment.

For a long time, Eli was a first-rate sheriff, but as he aged in the job, he began to treat it as a sinecure, doing less and less work in his office while hanging out in taverns and veterans' halls and deer camps and restaurants with other powerful county old-timers. These days he was bragging too much and drinking too much, often driving with a snootful, and sometimes patting a female constituent farther down her back than was appropriate. Gil O'Brien, a first-rate if overly stern undersheriff, really ran the department, and he tacitly supported my candidacy although he'd never admit it in public. Eli hadn't been in the office since I filed for a spot next to his name on the Democratic primary ballot many weeks ago. Only Chad represented the family, and when he was in the squad room he and the rest of us avoided the topic of the election as if it were a turd on the doorstep.

But the county's prosecutor and commissioners considered Eli an increasing embarrassment, and they had asked him to stand down for a new sheriff. They'd promised him a big retirement dinner at the best restaurant in the county with fulsome speeches of praise, but Eli refused the bait. As soon as he learned that I had filed a nominating petition for sheriff, he stormed out of his office, slammed the door and said he was taking a few days off for a rest. That few days had grown to several weeks, then months. In the beginning he had called in now and then to consult with Gil over departmental matters, but for quite a while he hadn't bothered.

Gil is as competent an administrator as he is a cop. He could have run for sheriff, but having neither taste nor talent for politicking, had stood aside when Garner Armstrong, aided and abetted by Alex and Ginny as well as a couple of the commissioners, tapped me for the task. Why I accepted the challenge, I'm sometimes not sure. Though I was still a deputy in my early forties, I loved the job as much as I love Porcupine County, where I washed up long ago, another stick of human driftwood, after a broken romance. Being a deputy was never dull. It got me out both among people and into the woods. But to complete his life a man needs a little ambition, a willingness to use his talents to the fullest. I'd had some luck solving a couple of celebrated cases, but now maybe I needed to move on.

Still, politics complicates a life. Unlike Eli, I wasn't born to be a pol. For one thing, I am shy. I'd rather have an ingrown toenail removed than get up before a crowd to talk. Pressing the flesh at church suppers and the VFW Hall got old the first day I tried it. I like talking with individual folks at length on the sidelines, getting to know them, not exchanging a face every few seconds for another as a temporary center of attention. The self-aggrandizing insincerity of professional politicians nauseates and repulses me. If I can't be candid, I tend to shut up, and taciturnity is fatal for an office seeker.

But somehow I had persuaded myself that Porcupine County needed me. In the middle of the night, at the tiny hour when a man lies naked to his deepest secrets, I have to admit that holding such an idea is an act of ego. That was not easy. For one thing, although I was adopted as an infant from the Lakota Sioux reservation in South Dakota by a visiting missionary and raised in upper New York State as a good white Methodist, I still retained an Indian tendency to hide my light under a bushel. Indians hate to make a fuss, which historically has hurt them with politicians, who tend to grease the squeakiest wheels. Modesty is a cultural imperative for Indians brought up in their own traditions. But the roots of my diffidence might also lie in my white upbringing. My adoptive father, a devout and strong-willed preacher, had raised me to be humble and polite. Which the chicken and which the egg? Which the wound and which the bow? It didn't matter. I am what I am, never mind how I got to be that way.

But my Indianness definitely colored the campaign. People in these parts are annoyed by what they consider the double-dipping of Ojibwa from Upper Michigan reservations into casino money *and* government welfare. Why them and not us? the whites ask. We're poor, too, and nobody's looking out for us. Three hundred years of nearly genocidal history doesn't matter much to anybody, white or otherwise, struggling to survive in the here and now. True, I'm Lakota and not Ojibwa. To the majority culture, however, members of minorities look alike, and they tend to lump Indians together. I won't say Porkies are bigoted any more than rural Americans anywhere, but some of them are, and in a tight race their votes can make the difference.

The trouble with all this is that I'm a cop as well as an Indian. Is a citizen's averted gaze or hesitant handshake evidence of deep-seated prejudice against Native Americans or merely the usual citizen's skittishness in the presence of the law? Who can tell?

Politics is always complicated. Not only was Eli Garrow a likable fellow and a superb campaigner, but his family all but owns the southern reaches of Porcupine County. The Garrows arrived from Cornwall and set up camp on the shore of Lake Superior during the copper boom of the 1850s. They went forth and multiplied, intermarrying with the Irish, Croatians and fellow Cornish who followed, then with the Finns in the early twentieth century. Half the South Porkies, it sometimes seems, are descended from Obadiah Garrow, a mining engineer who wrested a fortune in high-grade copper ore from a mine, now long shuttered, deep in the Trap Hills, which bisect the two halves of the county. And the rest of the population seem to be close cousins. Some mean-spirited folks claim incestuous relationships among certain Garrows, but I don't know about that. Every Garrow I have ever met has just five fingers on each hand. All the same, I could swear the eyes of some of them are set suspiciously close together.

Porcupine City, on Lake Superior, holds more than half the county's population, and since I was so visible in town — my daily beat covers the north and west of the county, Chad's the south and east — I was strongest there, Alex thought. The farther away from Porcupine City I stood, the less appeal my name held for voters.

"Maybe that's because townspeople are more sophisticated than country dwellers?" I once asked him.

Alex shook his head. "Not in the Upper Peninsula. Yoopers are Yoopers."

But our very rough polling technique — casual questions asked of a few passersby — suggested I wouldn't do better than 60 percent in town. If Eli had 80 percent of the smaller number of people in the south, he'd beat me in the primary.

Unlike many other states, Michigan holds its primaries the first Tuesday of August, three months before the general elections in November. Eli and I were both running as Democrats, unchallenged by any Republican. Upper Michigan is solidly Democratic so far as voting is concerned, although many — possibly most — Yooper voters are deeply conservative in cultural matters. They favor hunting and gun rights, are family-oriented, anti-abortion and suspicious of gays and lesbians — but often they depend on financial subsidies from the state for their daily survival. Hence they send Democrats to the state house as well as the U.S. Congress and Senate, although they often split their tickets and vote for a Republican president.

For the most part, however, personality, not political ideology, drives local elections in Porcupine County. That's what made running for office such an uphill climb for the likes of me.

"You've got to go campaign outside town, especially in the south," Alex declared, and he was right.

And so on my off hours I'd drive to Ewen, Bruce Crossing, Trout Creek, Paulding, Paynesville, and Coppermass, saying a shy hello at the Elks and American Legion wiener roasts and speaking a few words if I was invited to the microphone, which wasn't often. I fared no better at the church suppers, except for the Catholic potlucks. Thanks to the Black Robes, the French Jesuits who had explored the region in the seventeenth century, most Indians in these parts are Catholic when they are not traditional, and evangelical congregations tend to look askance at Catholics. The evangelicals probably thought I used to be a papist, although I was brought up Protestant, and, like so many preacher's kids, I left the church in a youthful act of rebellion. To many born-again southern Porkies, faithlessness was worse than being Indian and heathen. But I wasn't about to join a congregation and become a campaign Christian, like so many politicians. I dislike in-your-face religiosity from the sincere and cannot abide it in the insincere.

On the way to an event, I'd stop by a few roadside homes and walk up, uniform cap in hand, to ask if I could post a campaign sign in the front yard. "Sorry, we're Eli people," most home owners said, although a few — Porcupine County residents are not rude — did invite me in and hand me a glass of lemonade. Some of them even said, "Sure thing, be our guest." I had a lot of campaign signs, most of them financed by a couple of benefit dinners Alex had organized, as well as by a couple of friendly county commissioners and Garner Armstrong, the district attorney. My political war chest, however, was probably one-tenth the size of Eli's. His cousins contributed en masse, partly because Eli was shameless in using his influence to find them jobs with the county and the state. And he saved money by reusing his campaign posters from several previous elections, while I had to start from scratch.

And now he was rubbing my nose in my tiny budget by buying full-page ads in the Herald, the county's weekly newspaper, almost every week, even though the primary election lay two months away. I could barely afford a four-inch-high notice in the paper once a month. What's more, Eli was now engaging in what passes for hardball politics in Porcupine County, dealing in subtle innuendo.

"ELI GARROW FOR SHERIFF," today's full-pager said. "BORN AND RAISED IN PORCUPINE COUNTY." That was Eli's way of saying "Steve Martinez is an outsider," and no local could miss the point. I arrived in Porcupine County shortly after Desert Storm and had been a resident and a property owner for only a decade and a half, a blink of the eye in the long memories of homegrown Porkies whose roots often go back four and even five generations.

"A CHURCHGOER ALL HIS LIFE." That appeal to the religious underscored the fact that I am "unchurched," as the Episcopalians politely say. Many people in the Upper Peninsula measure a man's character by his public as well as private commitment to the Lord.

"MARRIED 47 YEARS." I had been keeping company with Ginny Fitzgerald, the Porcupine County Historical Society's director, for three years. Until very recently we had been happy in our arrangement, choosing to put off the topic of permanence until some vague time in the future. Though we often shared the nights, we lived in separate homes, I in a rustic cabin on the lake shore six miles west of Porcupine City, Ginny in a log home she'd financed with an inheritance so considerable nobody knew about it but me. But some voters, especially elderly women with nothing more important to condemn and even less to keep themselves occupied, considered such an arrangement "living in sin," and occasionally told me so.

"A FAMILY MAN." Eli and Dorothy had had seven children, who themselves had large broods, and the photograph displayed forty-seven Garrows of three generations at the family's umpteenth reunion last month.

And those didn't count the hundreds, maybe even thousands, of first cousins, second cousins, cousins once removed and cousins by marriage, who also showed up at the VFW Hall. And me? I was a bachelor without a family. Bachelors are always suspect. We haven't put down biological roots, sowed our seed in the land. We could pull up stakes at any time and disappear for greener pastures. We haven't committed. We're untrustworthy.

"ONE OF US," said the headline next to a large photograph of Eli beaming before a knot of maybe three dozen Porcupine Countians, every last one of whom was white. Unsubtle. "Eli's getting desperate," Alex had said after the latest ad had appeared. I wasn't so sure. It felt more like getting piled on by the entire defensive line of the Packers. All I am is a good cop with a decent record.

And that arrangement with Ginny had arrived at a crossroads.

THREE

"Hello, Mr. Martinez," said Tommy Standing Bear with grave courtesy, gazing without blinking into my eyes as I arrived at Ginny's place the morning after the incident at the Poor Farm. Tommy was twelve years old, mahogany skinned and black haired like me. Ginny had become his foster mother just two weeks before. He had been a ward of the tribe on the Ojibwa reservation at Baraga.

Tommy had had a hell of a life. His parents had been unemployed alcoholics, and they had both died the previous year when their pickup spun off the highway south of Baraga and struck a tree. Edgar Standing Bear had been driving under the influence. An unmarried uncle who was a logger and a sergeant in the National Guard had agreed to take Tommy into his care, but was deployed to Iraq before the paperwork could be completed. The boy had been shunted into the reservation's foster home system until his uncle could return.

I had felt an uneasy sense of déjà vu when Ginny introduced me to Tommy. My birth parents on the reservation at Pine Ridge had died of alcoholism and a drunken driver had killed my adoptive mother and father. My heart had immediately gone out to the lad, but Tommy still wrapped himself in a carapace of subtle mistrust. Not outright hostility, for he was too polite for that.

It would take a while to get through to him. But we Indians are nothing if not patient. Patience is one of the few weapons we still have, whether we are traditionals or steeped in white culture.

"Hi, Tommy," I said. "Where's Ginny?"

"Kitchen, Mr. Martinez," he said. Ginny was too warm and loving to want to be called "Mrs. Fitzgerald" and too realistic to suggest that he call her "Mom," a term frowned upon for a foster mother anyway, for the foster relationship always begins with the understanding that it is temporary. She hoped that he would, in time, call her something more than "Ginny" if she showed him lots of love—and patience. White people need to have patience, too, and Ginny had more than her share. Maybe it came from hanging out with an Indian, rubbing off from me. That's what I once told her, anyway. She just chuckled and waved away the notion. She doesn't think Indians are much different from white people, although I do my damnedest to persuade her otherwise.

In the last few months I had paid several visits with her to Baraga to do the paperwork, to be vetted by the state children's services social workers and lawyer, and to meet Tommy. Ginny was the sole foster parent, but I went along to lend moral support and to help persuade the social workers of Ginny's moral probity and financial responsibility.

"Wear your uniform," Ginny had said. "That makes you look respectable."

"I don't look respectable in civilian clothes?" I had demanded.

"Oh, you do," she had said hastily, "but the star on your chest speaks multitudes."

I had thought Ginny would be given an infant or, at most, a two-year-old, but the social workers had other ideas. There were just too many older children needing temporary homes. When we arrived, Tommy had stood up from his chair in that gravely polite fashion Indians have with strangers and had gazed at her with an unsettling calm. In its own way it was love at first sight, at least on Ginny's side, and I have to admit I was struck by a similar feeling.

"He's got that indefinable something," she said, "just like you."

"Me?" I said in puzzlement. "What's so indefinable about me?"

"You'll never know," she said with a giggle.

"Indefinable is indefinable."

In the middle of my woolgathering in Ginny's living room Tommy returned to his computer to surf the Internet, looking for songs to download and transfer to the iPod Ginny had given him as an offering of welcome when he arrived at her house. Tommy is an intelligent lad, a whiz at math, scoring several grades ahead of his age in tests at the Baraga reservation school. As soon as he arrived in early June, Ginny enrolled him in a special summer algebra class. Summer school had long been a thing of the past in cash-poor Porcupine City, but so many freshmen had flunked algebra that winter that the school board decided to offer the course to meet the requirements of the No Child Left Behind Act. Partly to make retaking the course less embarrassing to the flunkees, it was opened to any interested kid.

"It'll give him something to do," she said, "and it'll give him a chance to make some friends before school starts in the fall."

Tommy was also mature beyond his age. He was not sullen and uncommunicative, as are so many adoptees from troubled backgrounds, just quiet, polite and guarded. He could laugh, especially at a joke, but he still kept everyone at an emotional arm's length, including Ginny. He was still sizing us up, determining how we would fit into his world and how he would fit into ours. That is a very adult thing to do, and I felt deeply sorry that Tommy had been robbed of the carefree childhood all youngsters deserve.

He was slowly making friends among the kids in town. Small for his age, he was still quick, wiry, and athletic, and though he could barely hit the ball out of the infield, he did so with remarkable consistence. Porcupine City's Little League team was happy to have a dependable new leadoff batter and second baseman. When school started in the fall, I felt sure, this Indian boy would mix well with the third- and fourth-generation Finns, Irish and Croatians, descendants of the miners and woodsmen who had settled this remote land. People up here are almost entirely white, with maybe one or two African Americans and Mexicans wanly peppering the salt, and though like large white majorities everywhere they tend to be suspicious of people who do not look like them, they are still familiar with Indians. Their children tend not to care so much about human differences. Even in the boonies, diversity today finds a better reception among the young than it does among their elders. Ginny worried that Tommy's size and skin color might lead to a confrontation with a schoolyard bully, but I told her I didn't think there were enough kids in Porcupine County anymore for that to be common. Early on they all learn to look out for their neighbors, just like their parents. It means survival in a harsh land.

"You're just being sentimental," Ginny said. "There are bullies everywhere, even here." I didn't argue. She's a native Porky and I'm not.

When Tommy and I met at the orphanage, he looked me in the eye and said candidly, "You're Lakota. You used to be enemies of the Ojibwa." The Ojibwa of Baraga evidently knew all about the Native American lawman in the next county.

"Yes," I said, "but that was a long time ago." Almost three centuries, in fact. But today Indian kids on the reservation learn their tribal histories early. That had been denied them for a long time by the missionaries and the Bureau of Indian Affairs, who for more than a century had wanted them to worship the white man's god and practice the white man's ways.

"Yes," Tommy said with a shrug. "It doesn't matter anymore."

"No. Times change."

He nodded. Ever since that day, he had continued to treat me with cool formality whenever I dropped by, still calling me "Mister" even though Ginny encouraged him to call me "Steve." He was just beginning to call her "Ginny" instead of "Mrs. Fitzgerald." I couldn't understand why he hadn't fallen in love with her at first sight, as I had. Or maybe he had but didn't want anybody to know. As for me, I didn't know whether he was cool because I was a stranger, because I was a rival for his foster mother's heart, or because I was a Lakota. Sometimes you just can't read the wandering trail a kid's mind takes. Sometimes he can't either.

I was still learning to read Ginny's, even though we had been lovers for a long time. Originally Ginny, who had been feeling the biological imperative, had wanted to adopt outright. As a woman in her forties she had not wanted to risk the potential complications of having a child naturally. When she first brought up the idea of adoption, I had thought she was peremptorily nailing the banns of marriage to my forehead, and that scared me for a bit. But I came around, as does just about every man sooner or later, to the idea of commitment. Still, Ginny wanted a child for herself. "I hope you'll be in the picture, Steve," she said. "Every child needs a father. But I'm going to start my family whether or not you're ready. The door is always open. You know that."

But Ginny hadn't walked through that door just yet herself. For a single person, adoption is difficult, for social services prefer families with two parents, not one. So she decided to test her maternal skills first by fostering a child.

And God knows I couldn't enter that door of parenthood, foster or otherwise, just then. Running a political campaign had taken up almost all my free time, as I had known it would. For Tommy, I decided, being his foster mother's busy and often absent boyfriend was better than being a busy and often absent foster father. A boyfriend has fewer obligations to a child, and the child knows that. But at some point after the election I intended to go to Ginny and Tommy, hat in hand, and ask to be formally sworn into the partnership. I told Ginny more or less as much, without quite using the word "marriage" — that word, for some reason I can't explain, frightens me—and she nodded and said calmly, "All in good time."

That's not just patience. That's forbearance. That's one reason why I'm nuts about her. There are so many reasons. She is a very wealthy woman, but lives modestly though tastefully. She does not lord it over the people of Porcupine County, nor does she play Lady Bountiful, but shares her considerable fortune with them in absolute secrecy. She knows very well that money alters the way people look at a person and she does not want anyone to know she has it. As a trained historian she is a gifted researcher, able to smoke out the most obscure facts about the most ordinary people, and that is a boon to a boyfriend who is a law enforcement officer. She is sweet and funny. And, by the way, she is also very well-shaped and good-looking in her early forties. She is, in short, a hell of a redhead.

I walked into the kitchen, grasped Ginny about her slim waist as she stood at the sink, and breathed in the scent of her hair. As I picked up a dish towel, feeling loving and helpful, the phone rang. Ginny, her hands full, leaned over and elbowed a button on the speakerphone. She likes to chat while cooking and doing the dishes.

"It's Alex," the voice said. "I'm calling from Marquette."

FOUR

"Tewk?" Alex said.

"Tewk?" I echoed.

"Short for Two Crow."

"That's not gonna fly. My name is Steve, goddammit."

But I wasn't really pissed off. Alex is comfortable enough with my Indianness to make genial fun of it now and then. He thinks I'm oversensitive. I guess I am. But I know Alex hasn't a malicious bone in his body.

The smart-ass preamble surprised me, though. On the phone Alex is usually peremptory, not bothering with the polite noises of social lubrication. I don't think he's picked up a receiver and said "Hello" for decades. Ginny blames his long bachelorhood.

"It's a cadaver," he said.

"Yes, I know," I said, thinking Alex was again setting me up for a one-liner. Through the doorway I could see Tommy gazing at the screen of his iMac, hands unmoving over the keyboard, head cocked toward me, listening. Kids don't pay attention to their elders when you want them to, but they always do when you'd rather their interest lie elsewhere. Nothing escapes a kid. Especially Tommy, I was learning rapidly, and he also knows how to think about what he hears. I tried to be discreet whenever he was within earshot, especially when talking about police matters. Hard as I tried, I usually failed.

And on this occasion I failed big time. I completely forgot Alex and I were on a speakerphone. Brain fart.

"No, a *cadaver* cadaver," Alex said. "You're right. It was embalmed. But not for burial."

"What, then?"

"Medical school, probably, the forensics guys said. It

contained industrial-strength quantities of phenol, formaldehyde, alcohol, and glycerine. The hands and head had been removed with surgical saws. The entrails had been sucked out."

"So I was right about the trocar cuts." Embalmers use trocars, sharp-pointed hollow needles an inch or so wide, to vacuum out the innards of the corpses they prepare, either for medical study or for funerals. The absence of gas-producing entrails slows down decomposition and keeps the body fresh for a longer time. "But what about the hands and head?"

"Harvested. These days the majority of medical cadavers aren't dissected as entire specimens in anatomy classes but are cut apart and the pieces distributed for specialist study. Sometimes the harvested items aren't embalmed but kept fresh on ice for transplants. Plastic surgeons practice on heads and hand surgeons on hands. I suppose belly button specialists—"

"Enough, please, Alex," I said, trying not to gag. "I haven't had lunch yet."

"Well, that shoots down my idea that the hands and head were cut off to prevent identification."

"It does. Convenient, though, isn't it?" I said. "What about that label with the bar code?"

" 'Frank's,' " it said. " 'One dollar and seventy-nine cents a pound. Sell by December 31.' " Frank's is the local supermarket.

"You're disgusting."

"Aren't I? Anyway, we came up empty on the code. The numbers and letters resemble no commercial bar code anybody's ever seen."

"Could it be a private code?"

"Could be."

I sighed. "What's forensics going to do with the case?"

"Ice twice."

"Come again?"

"Put it in both the cooler and the cold case file."

I winced. "Aren't we clever?"

"Aren't we?" Alex can be so smug. "Eventually they'll just cremate the remains. No point in keeping them around."

Ginny, who had been listening to both ends of the conversation, slammed the silverware drawer. "You're creeping me out!" she declared. "Tommy, let's go out on the beach and hunt agates and leave the policemen to their business."

The lad stood up obediently from his computer and strode with Ginny out the back door, but not before shooting me a speculative look. I was sorry I hadn't kept the conversation with Alex more private. Kids don't need to hear that kind of stuff. *I* don't need to hear that kind of stuff, either.

"Well, I'm glad we're not looking at a homicide," I said presently. Alex and I do enjoy the thrill of chasing a killer now and then—a rarity in the sparsely populated Upper Peninsula, where murders are few and far between—but, like most U.P. lawmen, we really prefer the comfortable routine of police work, burglaries and thefts and traffic stops and the like. Routine is easier on the head as well as the emotions. You get more sleep that way, too. "What charges, exactly, are we looking at?"

"Illegal transport of human remains. A felony."

"That's all? What about desecration?"

"If the amputations were done legally, by licensed embalmers for a legitimate reason, it's not desecration."

"Hmm. Probably a worker in a mortuary or cadaver lab sold the body to whoever planted it in the Dying Room," I said. "What's the penalty for that?"

"Up to ten years in prison and a five thousand dollar fine."

"What about the guy who carried it away and dumped it?"

"Same ten years and five thousand. I looked it up. Michigan is one of the few states that by law limits the privilege of the final disposition of human remains to funeral directors."

"Yeah. The Tom Rooney case." Three years before, a farmer in Coppermass had wanted to bury his dead mother in the family backyard without the intervention of a funeral director and had fought round after round in the courts with the State of Michigan, the stories about the dispute entertaining readers in the Herald all winter. His mother had requested the unusual means of final disposition in her will and he had suffered sticker shock at the funeral home. The law is the law, the judge said. Tom was adamant, standing on principle and even refusing a local mortician's offer of free services. For months, Mama languished in the Porcupine County Hospital refrigerator. Finally, when the judge ordered the hospital to hand over the body to an undertaker for burial in potter's field, Tom caved in.

"The Full Employment for Michigan Funeral Directors Law," Alex said with a contemptuous growl.

I fell silent, thinking. Why would anyone *want* a cadaver in the first place?

"Alex."

"Yes?"

"No sexual evidence?" I had never read Krafft-Ebing's *Psychopathia Sexualis* but I knew about necrophilia, as every police officer does, and perhaps some of the kinkier necros liked to use medical cadavers for their jollies. I said as much.

"No sexual evidence," Alex echoed. "Nothing at all. It wouldn't matter anyway. Michigan isn't one of the eleven states that criminalize necrophilia. In fact, Tewkie boy, it's so rare that it wasn't illegal anywhere until 1965, when a female Oregon funeral home worker got caught serially abusing the customers and the press had a field day with it."

"My name, goddam it again, is Steve. And your deep knowledge of the weird and obscure never fails to amaze me."

"It's just the company I keep," he said. "Breakfast chat at the Marquette morgue, you know. Pathologists and forensics investigators like to talk about their work. You ought to hear them on Halloween."

I returned to the subject. "But why?" I asked. "What was the perp doing with a body missing its head and hands? Why would he go to the trouble of sealing it in heavy plastic and depositing it in an old house where it was bound to be discovered sooner or later? Why not just bury it in the backyard?"

"Or perps?" Alex said. "Maybe it took more than one person to hump that stiff up the stairs to the Dying Room. Even without head and hands it and that plastic sack still weighed a hundred thirty pounds."

"I don't know. A fellow in good shape could have done it. Remember all those ten-mile marches with seventy-pound packs in Army training?"

"All right. Then where did they, or he, get the cadaver?"

"Coulda been anywhere." Alex was right. Whether they are disassembled or not, there are never enough cadavers to feed the demand in medical schools and transplant hospitals, and so there's a thriving black market in fresh new bodies. A crooked crematory worker might fob off an urn of animal ashes on the bereaved and sell the human corpse to a broker, or a hospital morgue attendant might pass an unclaimed body to a trusted ambulance driver to peddle to a cadaver lab, no questions asked, and doctor the record to hide the transaction. Cadaver labs, too, aren't always careful with the stream of corpses that flowed in every day from hospitals and big-city morgues. Sometimes there was a bit of shrinkage in the warehouse.

"Illegal trafficking in organ transplants?" I suggested. In a celebrated case recently, a bodysnatcher working for a shady New Jersey tissue-harvesting lab had strip-mined the corpse of Alistair Cooke for his bones, even though the cancer that had killed the television personality had spread to his skeleton. Cancerous transplants can cause malignancies.

"Don't think so," Alex said. "Far as I know, they're not transplanting whole heads and hands and feet. And nothing else was taken. All the organs were intact."

"Yeah," I said. "And you would think ghouls like that would make sure today that the corpses were cremated afterwards. Gets rid of the evidence." In the New Jersey case, a buried body had been exhumed and discovered to be missing half its organs even though the former owner had never given permission for harvesting.

I could hear Alex rubbing his stubbly jaw.

"It still doesn't make sense," I added.

"Everything will make sense when we know the facts."

"A brilliant remark. So where do we start?"

"Beats me."

"*Should* we start?"

Alex grunted.

By simultaneous but unspoken acclamation we trundled the Poor Farm Corpse into our mental cold case file and rolled it shut. Why bother? Sometimes a mystery is best left a mystery. Especially in these remote and budget-conscious parts where the law is stretched thin. We do that all the time. We have to.

"See you tomorrow," I said.

"You've forgotten," Alex said, sharp accusation in his voice.

"Forgotten what?"

"The open wedding dance."

"What?"

"Not yours, numb nuts."

"Whose?"

"Jerry Muskat and Adela McLaughlin."

I groaned. Now I remembered.

"Duty calls."

"Damn."

FIVE

In much of backwoods America and especially in the Upper Peninsula of Michigan, people often celebrate weddings and anniversaries and birthdays that end in a zero by renting a hall, buying a keg or two, then publishing an ad in the local weekly newspaper inviting all and sundry to come share their happiness, even if they might be strangers or merely passing through town. Open celebrations are one way the members of a dwindling population hang on to one another. Attendees often bring potluck dishes to pass around on folding tables lined up along one side of the hall, for the party givers are usually too pinched to afford much more than the communal beer and the small fees charged by the operators of the halls, who make their profits at the cash bars.

These blowouts foster a sense of community, a feeling of we're-all-in-this-together, and showing up is a way of saying, "Here we are. We exist. Appreciate me, and I'll appreciate you, for we may not be here tomorrow."

I enjoy these shindigs immensely. Once in an off-duty while I will work an event as the lone hired security, wearing my deputy's uniform although usually not my revolver, unless a township official requests it. I'm not out to arrest people, just calm them down and make sure they're not driving if they've had a snootful. Often they have, and the trick is to judge when a fellow is just having a hell of a good time or is about to cross the line into noxious behavior. When that happens, I quietly usher them to the nearest door and tell them to find somebody to take them home. Often I have to ask, sometimes all but order, someone to volunteer for the task, and they usually say okay.

On the few occasions when someone gets pig drunk and belligerent, there's always an off-duty deputy or state cop in civvies to help frogmarch the lout to a patrol car for a ride to the sheriff's department lockup, where we'll allow him to post bond or spring him loose in the morning with a headache and a lecture. In either case, when the court date rolls around the prosecutor will usually drop the charges as not worth the county's time. Of course, if someone throws a punch and it connects, that's misdemeanor battery and we'll ask the connectee if he wants to press charges against the connector. Usually he doesn't, and often he can't remember the connection anyway.

Most of the time I attend these hoedowns not as security but as a member of the crowd. I like to stay on the sidelines, nursing a beer, chatting with friends and dancing with Ginny, who is indefatigable on the dance floor and wears out half the male population of Porcupine City, young and old, before she calls it a night. At Jerry and Adela's celebration, however, I had to be present as a political candidate, and I didn't look forward to that. At all. Ginny sent her regrets—she was taking Tommy to a movie in Houghton—and I knew I'd miss her.

I wore civilian clothes, jeans and a new Packers sweatshirt. Ginny thought I should wear my deputy's uniform, reminding people of what I was running for, but I was in a contrary mood. As I parked my battered Jeep in the lot of the cavernous old clapboard-sided town hall of Coppermass on the eastern side of Porcupine County, I walked by a brand-new cherry-red BMW two-seater bearing a City of Chicago sticker and the Illinois vanity plate REBEMER. That must be a pun of some kind, I thought, although the car easily cost fifty thousand dollars and needed no fancy plates to set it apart from the muddy pickups and SUVs in the lot, sporting mostly dented Michigan plates.

Out of long habit, I fished a notebook from my shirt pocket and jotted down the Beemer's plate. Doubtless the car's owner was a rich summer person from the big city slumming with the rubes, but I liked to make notes of unusual sights.

You never know if they might come in handy someday. Both my glove compartment and my desk at the sheriff's department squad room are stuffed with dusty, stained notebooks that go back years to my rookie days.

"Hiya, Camilo," I said as I approached the Town Hall door, "how's it going?" I stuck my hand out. Sergeant Camilo Hernandez looked at it in surprise. He is a tribal police officer for the Lac Vieux Desert Band of the Ojibwa Nation at Watersmeet in Gogebic County, and Jerry and Adela had hired him as security for the party. It didn't matter that Camilo was well out of his jurisdiction, though he wore full uniform except for his sidearm. Enough Porcupine County deputies and Michigan state policemen attended these things as civilians to make official arrests if needed. Those were rare when Camilo was doing security. He almost never needed our help, for he is a persuasive fellow.

Camilo is a Tex-Mex mestizo who hails from El Paso and is mostly Apache. I know him well, regularly losing part of my paycheck to him at poker. We don't need to shake hands any more than one would shake hands with one's spouse in the morning. He is short, wiry, bowlegged and fast as a rattlesnake, but full of smiling good humor. I have seen him take down large and powerful drunks with only a nightstick and without losing his grin. They never see what's coming.

"Ah," Camilo sighed in sudden understanding. "Politicking, eh?" He grasped my hand and shook it elaborately. "You have my vote," he said in a voice meant to carry. People looked at us and I colored. Everybody knows Camilo doesn't vote in Porcupine County, but in Gogebic County.

"Get your ass in there, Steve," Camilo said. "Pat people on the back and shake their hand and ask about the family. That's what Eli does and it works for him."

"All right, all right, I'll do my best."

Just as I entered the doorway I turned back to Camilo. "See who was driving that red Beemer?" I asked. BMWs are rare in Upper Michigan.

"Yeah." With his chin, Camilo pointed inside at a tall, slim and dark-haired young man. I couldn't have told you the name of his tailor, but I knew he was expensive. So was his barber. The sleeves of his Hugo Boss shirt were rolled up, the better, I thought, to display the Rolex on his tanned left wrist. The young man stood talking quietly with a knot of others along one wall, all of them Porkies in their twenties well known to me. He shifted from side to side on his feet, glancing about nervously to see if people were watching. I noticed that his conversations were brief, one or two words with locals who showed little interest in him. There was nothing arrogant about him, just the shyness of wanting to belong. He looked utterly out of place, and he knew it.

I was not surprised. Many of the well-educated, well-to-do young Chicago suburbanites who summer at their parents' expensive vacation homes on the Lake Superior shore are swaggering, supercilious young punks who like to lord it over the rubes, insulting waitresses with paltry tips. "FIBs," the waitresses call them. "Fucking Illinois bastards."

But some of them, often misfits and loners at home, seek acceptance among Porkies of the same age, admiring the locals' skills with their hands and their craft in the woods. If a young Porky thinks a city boy means well, he'll take the greenhorn under his wing. That happens with older summer residents, too. We don't mind summer people so long as they treat us with respect. Those are the best kind, for sometimes they fall so much in love with the people and the country of the Upper Peninsula that they move up here permanently, often to retire, and they modestly expand the suffering local economy.

Not so long ago I had experienced the lad's feeling myself. I turned away but not without sympathy. It's always tough to be an outsider.

I steeled myself and went into campaign mode, working the outskirts of the crowd. "Hi," I said to everyone whose attention I could catch. "I'm Steve Martinez and I'm running for sheriff. Here's my card. Call me if you'd like to talk about it. I'm hoping for your vote."

Scores of people, perhaps a hundred, sat at folding picnic tables, scarfing potluck barbecued pork, butter-slathered corn on the cob, fruit Jell-O and Finnish cakes and pastries while the speakers at the edge of the rickety stage played soft rock tunes. When sober, Porkies are polite and deferential. Gravely most of the men shook my hand noncommittally, took the card I proffered and quickly lost themselves in the crowd. A few looked me in the eye and turned away. Some made sure they weren't in my path as I approached. Several smiled, grasped my hand warmly and whispered into my ear, "You've got my vote, Steve. Go get 'em."

They whispered because they didn't want to get on the wrong side of Eli Garrow, who had arrived and was glaring at me from the far corner of the room. Unlike me, Eli was resplendent in full uniform, including brilliant white shirt, gold-encrusted garrison cap and Glock automatic pistol at his waist. Behind his back we called him "The Target," because his bright finery would have attracted the bad guys' bullets if he ever got into a firefight, an unlikely prospect in quiet Porcupine County. I caught Eli's eye, nodded and waved politely. "Defer to him," Alex had said during one of our campaign skull sessions. "He's the boss, after all. Be courteous and respectful. It'll piss him off." And so it did. I bowed slightly and saluted Eli, who turned away, a dark cloud wreathing his face.

The speakers in the corners suddenly boomed with the voice of Charlie Yarema, the mechanic at Syl's Garage in Coppermass who moonlighted as a disk jockey. "Yo, gang," he crooned. "Let's start with everybody's favorite!" The unmistakable piano introduction to Bob Seger's "Old Time Rock and Roll" washed over the growing crowd, and couples twirled from the supper tables to the dance floor. Spectators, including me, swayed and snapped to the music, and I had to remind myself I was on a mission. For the next hour I worked the crowd, keeping mostly to its outskirts but now and then plunging in to the edge of the dance floor when I spotted somebody whose hand I hadn't yet shaken.

I stopped once to watch Camilo skillfully edging a boisterous logger out the door, one hand in the small of his much bigger subject's back and the other gripping an elbow right at the painful pressure point we called the "come-along nerve." So swift and efficient was the smiling Camilo that the overserved lumberman barely had time to protest before the door shut on him.

The place jumped. Everybody was having a noisy good time, especially when Charlie put BTO's "Takin' Care of Business" on the player, and half the crowd fell laughing to the floor to dance the alligator, limbs flailing. Then it was time for a couple of polkas — Charlie always made sure the older folks enjoyed their favorites — followed by "Proud Mary" by Creedence Clearwater Revival, the band Yoopers most adore.

"Dollar dance!" Charlie shouted over the din.

One by one the celebrants popped a dollar bill into a hat Charlie held, then danced with bride or groom for a few seconds before the DJ motioned in the next. The lines were long for Adela McLaughlin, a cute freckled redhead who waitressed at O-Kun-de-Kun Restaurant in Lone Pine, and her new husband Jerry Muskat, the M-64 bridge tender. As the noise level rose out of sight, so did inhibitions, and soon women were dancing with Adela and men with Jerry. The hat overflowed and Charlie had to stuff bills into his shirt pockets. Afterward, the purse would go to Jerry and Adela, defraying many of the costs of the evening. I thought they might even make a small profit.

I felt a hand on my shoulder. It was Alex, dressed in a

cowboy outfit. His tooled leather Western boots and fringed buckskin jacket would have made a Houston oilman jealous. Alex loved country-and-western music.

"Havin' a good time?" the trooper shouted over the din.

"Nobody can hear me," I shouted back. "I'm just shaking hands now!" Alex grinned, then grunted as he bumped into Eli Garrow, who had been working his way through the crowd from the opposite end of the room.

"Didn't know you were working security," Alex yelled to Eli, nodding toward his uniform. "Times are that hard, eh?"

"Fuck you, Kolehmainen," the sheriff growled, loudly enough for heads within a ten-foot circle to turn and stare at Eli's angry red face and clenched fists.

"Tsk." Alex turned away, grinning. One more second and Eli, old and slow as he is, might have tried to throw a punch. Alex not only is a master of the needle, but he also knows just how far to thrust it before provoking his opponent into violence. Had Eli exploded, not even Camilo could have stopped the brawl that would have ensued — and Coppermass being Garrow territory, Alex and I would have come out a very poor second best. Besides, cops aren't supposed to get into fights. We moved away before hostilities could escalate.

Soon Charlie took a break, and the din settled down to a dull roar as people left the floor and fell upon the desserts. I had just taken a bite of nisu, the sweet Finnish pastry, when a heavy hand landed on my back and a drunken "Hello!" burst into my ear. I turned to see who it was. It was Harold Garrow, a ne'er-do-well and sometime beneficiary of his brother Eli's nepotism. Eli had steered a couple of county road patching contracts to Harold, who screwed up the jobs so badly they had to be redone. Among other things, Harold was suspected of having impregnated a niece, who left the state and was never heard from again. He looked just like Eli. Both men were short and broad, bullet-headed and mustachioed. Harold was not one of my favorite people. And he was loaded.

"God, Shteve, I'm happy to know ya!" he drawled through a cloud of peppermint schnapps, wavering on his feet and thrusting his ham-sized hand in my general direction. I grasped it. It was wet and greasy. God knows where it had been.

"Ya really done ya people proud!"

Here it comes again, I thought, the patronizing. Some folks just don't believe Indians can solve crimes all by themselves. After a recent drug case in which Alex and I pooled our talents to catch a bunch of dangerous felons, the whispering started in certain hostile quarters: The Injun was only fronting for white brains. He was Garner Armstrong's boy and did what the prosecutor told him to.

"But ya know, ya had help from that trooper. He really ran things, didn't he?"

I held my temper. "We work as a team, Mr. Garrow," I said.

"*Sure* you did," he said. "Ya know, when Eli wins you're gonna hafta find another job. I can always use a strong back on my trucks."

Harold spoke without irony. He was technically wrong. I was a union member and couldn't be fired for political activity. But if Eli won, he could make life miserable enough for me to look for another job somewhere.

Bile rose into my throat, but I held my tongue, took a deep breath, and said evenly, "Nice to see you, Mr. Garrow. Excuse me." As he lurched away I turned on my heel and nearly knocked down the tribal police.

"Want me to shoot him?" inquired Camilo, who had heard the exchange. He was still smiling, but his grin bore a ragged edge, like a knife sharpened with rocks. He doesn't like Harold, either.

"No," I said quietly, "but feel free to cut his heart out and feed it to the wolves."

"Tsk. You Lakota are *so* bloodthirsty."

"Bullshit," I said. "We both know what Apaches did with fire ants."

"Yeah," said Camilo. "But you have to admit that didn't leave so much mess."

"Like hell." I was chuckling now. Camilo always makes me feel better.

By this time the party was beginning to wind down, the crowd slowly trickling out to the parking lot and departing in cars and pickups, only half of which, I suspected, had designated drivers. Jerry and Adela saw them all off, friends and strangers alike, hugging and kissing, shaking hands and waving. It had been a happy evening for everyone. Almost everyone.

I needed to pee, and strode back inside, looking for the men's. I opened the wrong door, the one to a storeroom, and walked in on a couple in the throes of passion. His slacks were down, her denim skirt was up, and they were coupled together over a countertop like a locomotive pushing a caboose uphill. He was the young man who had arrived in the BMW, and he was lost between the billowing thighs of a beefy blonde filling station attendant from Lone Pine easily ten years his senior. They both looked ecstatic, oblivious to the world around them. They did not even glance my way.

"Excuse me," I whispered needlessly, swiftly closing the door.

It looked as if tonight the lad had found a big welcome in this part of Porcupine County. I was glad one of us had.

SIX

Gazing into the bathroom mirror, I fretted over the premature bags under my eyes that Ginny says make me look like a younger Iron Eyes Cody, the imitation Hollywood Indian who wasn't born a Cree/Cherokee, as he had claimed, but was actually the son of Italian immigrants. But my hair is still genuinely thick and black, with the beginnings of gunmetal gray at the temples. Indians, thank goodness, generally don't get bald unless there's a honky in the woodpile, nor do most of us need to shave. Our cheeks just don't grow hair. Speeds up the morning toilette. Then a few loose ends that had been pricking the back of my brain wormed their way into the foreground of my thoughts.

Loose ends bother me, as they do any conscientious cop. One reason we become cops is that we want to know the answers to everything, no matter how trivial. Were those fresh screwdriver marks on the garage window jamb left by someone trying to break in? Or was a home owner just trying to get the window open so he could paint it—and did he simply forget a few weeks later that he'd tried, and called the sheriff when he noticed the gouges? It happens more often than you think, especially if the home owner is elderly and beginning to lose his short-term memory.

Of course police officers can't afford to spend much time thinking about such minutiae. We have real crimes to solve and crooks to catch. Still, that cadaver at the Poor Farm had been bothering me. Some kind of misbegotten prank? Probably. Was a crime committed? Obviously. It's against the law to leave dead bodies lying around. But was anyone injured or even offended? Probably not, except for that amorphous and abstract lump we call Justice. Sooner or later the Poor Farm cadaver would slide of its own accord to the back of my mental cold case drawer, perhaps to be resurrected sometime in the distant future as a fleeting wisp of memory. But it still lay fresh in my mind, poking insistently at my consciousness.

Later that morning the curtains slowly began to part. The first break was the sort of coincidence you can't believe when it happens in second-rate mystery novels but to a real-life cop is a vital part of solving crime. Investigations are full of coincidences. The trick is discriminating between the trivial and the significant. This one came two weeks after Jenny Besonen and Billy Ciric had sneaked up to the Dying Room for a little extreme whoopee. I had just come from lunch at Merle's Cafe on River Street, the main drag of Porcupine City, when I saw Phil Wilson across the road, descending a short slope underneath the big wooden sign that said, "BEGINNING OF U.S. 45: PORCUPINE CITY TO MOBILE, ALABAMA."

Phil, a big, beefy fellow in his late fifties who sports a lush white Santa Claus beard, was the co-owner of Wilson & Simon's Ace Hardware on River Street. His people go back several generations in Porcupine County, Ginny had once told me, to the earliest days of the copper mines. A grandfather had been mayor of Porcupine City and his father had founded the hardware emporium. Phil grasped one of the six-by-six legs of the sign, bent down, and retrieved a tiny object from the gravel where the six-by-six plunged into the ground. He straightened up, examined the object, and made a prying motion on its top. Out of it he drew a long coil of what appeared to be film. Curiosity got the better of me.

"What in the world are you up to, Phil?" I called.

He didn't answer.

"Phil?"

"Geocaching," he called back.

"Geo-what?"

"Caching."

"Oh yes," I said as I walked up to the sign. "I've heard of that. Orienteering with a GPS, isn't it?" Hand-held Global

Positioning Satellite receivers are everywhere these days. I use one while flying the sheriff's airplane and often carry it with me into the woods to pinpoint the precise geographic locations of crime scenes. Knowing roughly where you are is pretty, but knowing *exactly* where you are is gorgeous. That makes it much easier to dispatch a rescue squad to an injured hiker or a recovery team to a crime scene, or just return to a lovely spot you discovered in the woods.

"Sort of," Phil said, his face reddening as he spoke. For him, conversation took a major effort. Vietnam had changed him. The once ebullient boy had become painfully shy. He never married, never attended social events, and ran his store from inside his tiny office, allowing his clerks to wait on customers. When he had to interact with others, he treated them with polite deference and with as few words as possible, never looking them in the eye. They liked him all the same. They remembered what he had been and were sorry about what war had done to him.

"Tell me," I coaxed.

"This here's a minicache." He held up a plastic thirty-five-millimeter photo film can painted the same color as the signpost, a tightly wound roll of paper and a tiny nub of a pencil.

"Yeah?" I said.

Suddenly the old Phil poked through the fog and the words tumbled out. "See, Steve, people who locate the cache with their GPSs write their name and the date to prove they've found it, then put everything back like it was. Couple days ago, the twenty-second name appeared. Not too bad for a cache that's only six months old."

He bent down and replaced the film can at the foot of the post. "There," he said. "You'd never spot it."

Talking about a private passion sometimes parts the curtains of hurt, and what Phil said interested me for its own sake. I had to admire the handiwork, too. From ten feet away the film can looked like the head of a bolt holding the post to its concrete base. As Phil said, unless you were looking for it, you'd never notice it.

"You put it there six months ago?"

"Right."

"And how do people know it's there? What do you do, put an ad in the paper with the latitude and longitude of the spot?"

The words flooded out. "No, I post the information on the Internet. There's a bunch of websites devoted to the sport, and I used www.geotreasure.com. People see the name of the cache and a clue to what it's all about—this one is called 'Where the Road Begins'—and the coordinates, and go hunt it up and sign their names. This is an easy one. I designed it for beginners."

I stood up and smiled. If the game of geocaching could bring a little happiness to this sad man, I approved of it.

"OK, Phil, that's fascinating. Have a good day." And I strode to the sheriff's Explorer to return to patrol. As I got in, I looked back. Phil was watching me, his eyes on mine. He raised a hand in goodbye. I wouldn't say he smiled, but he looked a little less melancholy. I waved back, my heart lightened by the encounter. We cops serve and protect in unusual ways sometimes.

On my way west to Silverton on M-64 the idea slowly began to grow in my mind: Could that corpse in the Dying Room be somebody's idea of a geocache? Maybe that was only a coincidence, but it fit. The body was put where it could be found, but you had to know where it was to find it. Swiftly I wheeled around the Explorer and headed for Ginny's a few miles back toward Porcupine City.

SEVEN

"What do you know about geocaching?" I called as I swept into Ginny's sprawling log home on the lake and nearly tripped over an Oriental rug that hadn't been in the foyer before. Genuine Persian, I could see at a glance, for I hadn't washed down my idle hours in the bars of officer's clubs in Kuwait and Saudi Arabia, but had gone out into the markets and learned a little about the fine carpets and jewelry of the Middle East.

Ginny doesn't live flashily — like most women in Upper Michigan, she wears shorts and a T-shirt in the summer, Levi's and Pendletons in the winter — but she furnishes her roomy log home with the elegance of a woman fortunate enough to be tasteful as well as educated and wealthy, although she chooses not to show that side of her life to anyone except a handful of trusted friends. She has truly returned home to Porcupine County, where she was born in more than modest circumstances as the daughter of a university-educated mining engineer who believed his children ought to earn their places in society and respect others who also had. She never lost that legacy of modesty and regard for others, even at Wellesley and later as the bride of a wealthy businessman who left her his considerable fortune when he died. She is a well-respected and well-liked citizen of Porcupine County, and that sense of belonging, not her money, her house, or its furnishings, is her most beloved possession.

"For goodness' sake, Steve, can't you say hello first?" Ginny called as she skipped down the stairs past a pair of Helen Frankenthaler drawings on the landing wall. I knew they were not prints, but originals. "Haven't you ever heard of foreplay?"

I blushed, because Tommy Standing Bear was gazing at

us from the kitchen where he was doing his homework at the counter while watching MTV, a form of multitasking I have never been able to understand. He looked at me shrewdly. You never can tell what's going on in a youngster's mind, but I was sure a lot was going on in his. I knew from his small smile that he had not only heard what Ginny had said but also knew what it meant. Kids learn so early these days about intimate relations between the sexes. Among them, too.

"Hi, Tommy," I said.

"Mr. Martinez," he replied with his usual courteous nod, the smile still on his face.

"Steve," Ginny prompted for the umpteenth time. "He likes being called Steve."

I didn't say anything. "Mr. Martinez" was better than "Tewk."

Tommy just nodded politely. I knew he demurred, but he was too circumspect to argue. I admire that in anyone, especially a kid. Smart kids like to challenge adults on the spot. Very smart kids know how to bide their time. Tommy is one of those.

"You said something about geocaching?" Ginny said.

"Yes," I said, and, in my eagerness having forgotten about the boy, told her about Phil Wilson's little cache, his sudden blossoming, and the "Eureka!" moment it had spurred in the Explorer. "I think that corpse at the Poor Farm may have been left there by geocachers."

Too late I remembered Tommy's presence. At the kitchen table, his eyebrows had risen.

So had Ginny's. "Now that sounds like a possibility," she said. "Let me see what I can find out about geocaching."

The sources of Ginny's gifts as a historian are twofold. One, she never forgets a fact, but can pluck it in an instant out of the high-speed memory chips of her mind. Two, she is an expert researcher, especially in library databases and on the Internet. I loved her for many things, including her warm heart and shapely person, but it was her nimble mind that was most invaluable to a boyfriend who works as an underpaid law enforcement officer in an impoverished rural county.

She stepped over to the computer she kept in an office nook off the kitchen. It was, I knew, connected to the high-speed network that ran along the lake from Porcupine City to Silverton thirteen miles west. I have my laptop hooked to a slow dial-up connection, all I could afford on a deputy sheriff's salary. Ginny, however, never settles for anything but cutting-edge technology. "Saves time," she often said. As a girl, she learned that good tools were always worth their cost.

Tommy had followed and was standing behind her as she logged on.

"Let's see what Google tells us," she said. "Ah, it's a biggie. More than a million hits. Let me winnow them down."

A few minutes passed as Ginny, Tommy helping by pointing to likely sites, worked her way through the World Wide Web.

"Found a site that explains it simply," she said. "You ready?"

"Sure," I said.

"Quote. 'On May first in the year 2000, the military stopped degrading the accuracy of the GPS navigation system, a series of two dozen satellites in low Earth orbit that continuously broadcast their positions, allowing receivers to triangulate on the signals and determine their location on the surface of the Earth. Suddenly hand-held GPS receivers were accurate to within thirty feet instead of three hundred feet. On that day the game called geocaching was born.

" 'The concept of geocaching is really quite simple. Someone hides a stash—usually a Tupperware container filled with assorted small trinkets, such as Monopoly game pieces—in an interesting, out-of-the-way place, and records the exact geographical coordinates with a GPS receiver. These coordinates, along with a few helpful hints, are posted on one of several geocaching Web sites. The stash seekers then use their GPS receivers to find the treasure. Each person who locates the container adds an entry to a logbook included within, takes a trinket and replaces it with one of his own, then puts the container back where he found it. Sometimes a cache includes a disposable camera so that the finders can take photos of themselves for the cacher to put on a Web page.' Unquote."

"That's it?" I said. "Somebody would pay two or three hundred bucks for a GPS receiver just to trade a few trinkets? Sounds like a bunch of gadget heads hunting for each other's junk." For a moment I forgot what the game had done for Phil Wilson.

"There's more to it than that," Ginny said. Listen to this: 'Knowing the location of a cache is only part of the goal. Getting there often is an adventure. You might hike for miles through the woods toward a cache, only to discover that a deep chasm lies between it and you. There's always more than one way to approach a cache.'

"And besides," she said, "what's wrong with promoting a little exercise in the fresh air?"

"What else?" I asked.

"Quote. 'Geocaching has its roots in the nineteenth century British orienteering sport called letterboxing,' Ginny continued. 'Its practitioners secreted a container with a one-of-a-kind rubber stamp inside it somewhere on a moor or a heath, then posted in the local newspaper a PERSONALS notice giving either the location's map coordinates or a coded message telling how to find it. Those who found the container used the rubber stamp to mark logbooks they carried with them. Sometimes the containers held clues to other containers located elsewhere, and often letterboxers spent days and even weeks hunting down the next treasure trove.' End of quote."

"Are there rules to this game?" I asked.

"Oh, yes," Ginny said. "Just a couple. The first rule is to trust everyone. Not only do cachers trust finders to put everything back as it was, they also trust people who happen upon the caches by accident not to plunder them."

"And the second?"

"No drugs, explosives, ammunition, pornography or food," she said. "Kids might find them or animals might dig them up."

"Anything else?"

"There are all kinds of caches. Microcaches, like the one you saw in town today. Multicaches, in which the cache seeker is sent from location to location until he finds the final cache. Offset caches, in which the posted coordinates take the hunter to a location where he must continue by using map and compass to find the container. There are event caches, where a whole bunch of people get together in a park to find stuff, like a high-tech Easter egg hunt. And there are virtual caches that aren't really caches at all but a spot on Earth where you can stand and look for something, like an unusual road sign, and report back to the cacher on a Web site what you saw. Those are popular in national parks where the rangers don't want people trampling sensitive areas."

"I'll be damned," I said. "I had no idea that geocaching was such a big deal."

"There's more," Ginny said. "The caches are rated for difficulty. Some, like the one you saw in town today, are really easy, little more than a Sunday stroll in the park. Then there's extreme geocaching, in which you need to be a rock climber to find a cache at the bottom of a ravine or be rich enough to afford a helicopter to reach the summit of a steep peak. One cacher put a container on the bottom of the Red Sea."

"That's it?"

"Not quite. Here's a reference to 'rogue geocaching.' That's putting caches in places people shouldn't go—sewer systems, abandoned mine shafts, fences at maximum-security prisons, the White House lawn, et cetera. Or putting things in caches that shouldn't be there, like rusty nails or moonshine."

"Or cadavers," I said. "Yeah. That's what we've got.

Can you print out all that stuff for me?"

"Sure. Tommy, would you take care of it?" Eagerly the lad filled the printer with paper and began the job. *Wise of Ginny*, I thought. Nothing reaches a youngster's heart more than a simple gesture that tells him he is of value.

"May I borrow your phone?" I asked Ginny.

She nodded. I dialed Alex's cell number.

He listened. "Be right over," he said.

"Ask him if he'd like to stay to dinner," Ginny said.

I did. The answer was as I expected.

EIGHT

I don't believe Alex has ever had supper all by his lonesome. As a bachelor with a host of female friends, he never lacks for invitations. One reason he is so popular is that when he calls on a woman, he leaves his smartass self at home. Rather than scoring points off her tender sensibility, the way he does with mine, he solicitously asks how she's feeling and offers approving comments on a new hairdo, piece of jewelry or sweatshirt. A new embroidered sweatshirt often passes for haute couture in the Upper Peninsula, where harsh weather dictates fashion. Woolriches are far more common than Donna Karans and Timberlands outnumber Manolo Blahniks.

Alex always amazes me. He's quick to spot the smallest alteration in a woman's appearance or the slightest change in her emotions and casually mention it. Ginny once claimed that's because he's genuinely sensitive and observant, a true gentleman, but I replied that the truth is nothing more than that he's a smart detective highly trained to spot things other police officers might miss.

"You have no imagination, Steve," she had retorted.

Maybe not, but I learned long ago never to argue with her assessments of my mental capacity, which usually were generous when she wasn't herself trying to score a point off my hide. After a round of Molsons and cheese curds on Ritz crackers, a common Yooper hors d'oeuvre, I turned the conversation to business.

"You think that cadaver is somebody's idea of a cutting-edge geocache?" Alex asked, disbelief in his voice.

"What else have we managed to come up with?"

"I guess you may be right," said Alex. "But I can't imagine a corpse as the object of a high-tech scavenger hunt. Why do people do the things they do?"

Alex is very good with women and hard evidence but less imaginative when it comes to motive.

"Look at 'Folsom Prison Blues,'" I said, "Johnny Cash sings that he'd 'shoot a man in Reno just to watch him die.'"

"What's that mean?"

"Just what it says. People do the damnedest things for the damnedest reasons."

"If you say so." Alex didn't sound convinced.

"Why'd Hillary climb Everest?" I asked.

"Because it was there."

"Exactly."

Alex's dubious expression didn't change. I decided to try another tack. "What'd the forensics guys make of that bar-coded label on the plastic shroud around that cadaver?"

"Not a lot. They ran it through a standard bar-code reader and got this." Alex pulled out a typewritten sheet. It said:

JDGIJIH2GJAIAFD1

"A cryptogram?"

"Maybe," Alex said. "We thought it might be a simple substitution code, letters for numbers, the kind amateurs think of. To start with, we assigned the letter A to mean the numeral 1 and B to mean 2 and C to mean 3 and so on. We came up with" — and Alex wrote the following on a sheet of printer paper:

0479098?7019164?

"We don't know what the numbers 1 and 2 in the original alphanumeric sequence would stand for, though," he added. "That's why the question marks."

"Maybe North and West?" I asked. "See, there are enough alphanumeric digits in that line to add up to a geographical location. For instance, right here on my GPS" — I took out from my knapsack the hand-held Garmin I used on both the ground and the air — "the coordinates where Quarterline Creek next door enters the lake are N 46 50.631 W

89 26.682. That's 46 degrees 50.631 minutes North latitude, 89 degrees 26.682 minutes West longitude. Sixteen characters, leaving out the decimal points. That sixteen-character bar code could be a geographical location."

"Looks like it might be," Alex said.

"But what we've got doesn't look like one," I said. "Break that line in half and assign the letters N and W to the halves, and finally put in the periods. Now we've got 04 70.098 N, for latitude, and 70 19.164 W, for longitude. See, the N and W letters follow the numbers in the old way geographers used, rather than preceding them in the modern manner.

"But this doesn't work. If those numbers 7 and 0 after the first question mark mean degrees West, sure, that could be a longitude reading, but we have a problem with the latitude numbers. North 4 degrees is okay, but 79.098 minutes is impossible. Minutes don't go higher than 60. And even if that was actually 59.098 minutes, the coordinates would put us in eastern Colombia."

We stared at the sheets of paper for many minutes, hoping the key to the code would leap out at us. But neither Alex nor I are professional cryptographers, though both of us have worked simple newspaper cryptograms.

It took a twelve-year-old Ojibwa math whiz to divine the meaning.

"Try looking at the numbers backwards," Tommy said.

Alex and I jumped. So concentrated had we been on the sheets of paper before us we hadn't noticed that Tommy had come downstairs and was standing by us at the table.

"Uh, Tommy," Alex said with a gentle but firm tone, "this is humdrum police work. It's not very interesting. I think you'd find something more fun on television or on the computer." Alex may be an ace with women, but not with kids.

Tommy Standing Bear may have been only twelve, but he knew when he was being patronized. He shot Alex a wounded glance.

But suddenly Alex shouted, "The boy is right! Look!" With a pencil he laboriously wrote, in reverse order, all the digits taken from the letters on the bar code:

? 4 6 1 9 1 0 7 ? 8 9 0 0 7 4 0

"If the first question mark stands for longitude and the second for latitude," Alex said in an excited voice, "and we apply North to the first and West to the second, we get North 46 degrees 19.107 minutes and West 89 degrees 09.740 minutes. Ginny, where's your map of the U.P.?"

Ginny—who had come in from the kitchen where she was fixing a pilaf from raisins, almonds and wild rice, her Upper Michigan variation on an old recipe she had brought home from a visit to Pakistan with her late husband—pulled a rolled topographical chart from a cabinet drawer and handed it to Alex. He spread it open on the dining table and with a ruler pinpointed the location.

"Five miles northeast of Watersmeet! We're in business! Dollars to doughnuts the corpse in the Dying Room was a— what did you call it?—a multicache? When one cache sends the finder to another?" Alex had suddenly become a believer.

"Damn right," I said. I turned to the boy and said, "Tommy, thank you very much. We apologize for doubting you." I glanced at Alex and held his gaze. "We" meant "he," not "me."

A grin began to curl at the corners of Tommy's mouth. "That's okay, Mr. Martinez," he said.

I stuck out my hand. Immediately, Tommy grasped it and shook it gravely.

That moment was, I would recall much later, the real beginning of the bond between Tommy and me.

"Ginny," he said, "maybe I could have a GPS for my birthday?"

She looked at me and we both nodded. A simple but capable hiker's GPS costs a hundred dollars on Internet retailers and can be had used for less than half that on eBay. Such a device would be a more than suitable gift for an intelligent twelve-year-old who lived in the country.

"Let's call Camilo," I said presently, looking back at the map on the dining room table. "That spot near Watersmeet is in his bailiwick." The tribal police, who were cross-deputized as Gogebic County peace officers with full privileges of arrest, covered mostly the eastern reaches of the county although their jurisdiction extended all over it. Sometimes speeders on U.S. 45 were startled to be pulled over by a tribal police cruiser and handed a ticket from a mahogany-skinned officer well away from the tiny Lac Vieux Desert reservation. Camilo's polite but stern cop manner cowed almost all of them, but once in a while an out-of-state driver would protest, "We're off the reservation! You have no jurisdiction!"

"Want to bet?" Camilo would say, removing his Serengetis and flashing his victim a shark's smile. "Double or nothing on the fine?"

They always gave in.

Speaking of Camilo, he wasn't in, or on duty. Gone to Rhinelander for dinner, the dispatcher said. That was more than an hour southwest of Watersmeet, but the Upper Peninsula has so few decent restaurants that Yoopers think nothing of driving sixty or a hundred miles into Wisconsin for a good meal. Camilo would overnight there, the dispatcher added, and return sometime the next day.

"Time to hit the air," I told Alex. "We'll fly over that spot with my GPS and see what there is to see from above."

"Hold your horses, Steve!" Ginny said firmly. "Time for *dinner*. And let's not talk about this subject at the table, shall we?"

We didn't. The pilaf, superb even for Ginny's sophisticated kitchen, kept our minds off cadavers. And we didn't have to drive a hundred miles for it.

NINE

The Porcupine County Sheriff's Department Aviation Division—that's me—operates a new Cessna 182 Skylane, a trade-up from a threadbare old 160-horsepower Cessna 172 Skyhawk the county once owned. Actually, the Skylane isn't exactly new, having been manufactured in 1981, but it's in much better shape than the smaller and older Skyhawk, with an almost new paint job, a freshly overhauled engine, and a refurbished interior. It carries four people, like the 172, but the 230-horsepower engine of the 182 enables the department to ferry the pilot, an oversized prisoner, and a large escort deputy all the way to Lansing at better than 150 miles per hour with a full load of fuel, and its big wing tanks allow us to loiter miles out on Lake Superior during long searches for overturned boats. As the chief pilot—actually, the only pilot—of the Aviation Division, whose decidedly unluxurious six-by-ten-foot office occupies one greasy, cluttered corner of the communal county hangar at Porcupine County Airport, I count among my tasks the job of exercising the Skylane for an hour once a week to keep engine and controls limber and corrosion free. I earned a pilot's license on weekends in the Army and as soon as he discovered that, Undersheriff O'Brien, a master at manipulating grants for expensive police equipment, fished for and landed the Skyhawk. That airplane served us well for several years, but when it eventually proved less than adequate for some tasks, Gil wheedled and lobbied and pulled strings until the State of Michigan agreed to finance the Skylane. However, the 182 being considerably more expensive to operate than the 172, Gil made me justify every drop of fuel the larger plane burned. I wouldn't think of going lollygagging in her, boring aimless holes in the sky like a weekend pilot.

But when I took the airplane up on official duties, I secretly shed my land-bound self and became my middle name, Two Crow, mounted Lakota warrior at one with the hawks and eagles, married to sun and wind. I never told anybody about that. My friends wouldn't have understood, except maybe Camilo and a traditional Ojibwa or two. One of these days, I vowed, I would take Tommy Standing Bear up in a rental airplane from Land O' Lakes and introduce him to the exhilaration of soaring with the birds. He, I thought, would not only understand my feeling but also embrace it. I was beginning to feel proprietary toward him, ready to share with him the tiny link I occupied in the great chain of being.

Today I was alone. Alex had other duties, and I suspected he was secretly delighted. Alex hates small planes, although he is brave enough to swallow his fear of them when duty calls. He makes a terrible passenger, sweating and clenching his teeth and fists and yipping in consternation whenever the airplane hits a patch of mild turbulence. I have to keep up a steady stream of soothing chatter to placate his white-knuckled demons.

Doc Miller, one of the internists at Porcupine County Hospital and my personal physician, waved from the hangar where he kept his Cessna Bird Dog, a lovingly restored Korean War-era Army spotter plane the same size as the Skylane. "A warbird on the cheap," he called the meticulously maintained old airplane, but I knew that keeping half-century-old aircraft flying is anything but cheap. And Doc, as a physician in the boonies of Upper Michigan, is not handsomely paid. But he is a bachelor with only one expensive obsession, that Bird Dog, and nobody gainsays the money he spent on it, often taking children for rides in the sky. And I was glad for his frequent help during air searches for lost hikers and overturned boaters.

As the Skylane roared skyward from the runway, I gently banked her into a climbing turn south toward Watersmeet, a crossroads town of a thousand people fifty-six miles south of Porcupine City at the junction of U.S. 2 and U.S. 45. In less than thirty seconds the plane had clawed its way to five hundred feet above the treetops. I leveled off, set the throttle and manifold pressure for cruising speed, and watched the numbers unroll on the screen of the handheld GPS receiver I had Velcroed to the instrument panel. Southern Porcupine County is mostly second-growth forest interspersed with open land, some of it cropped by cattle but most slowly being overrun by brush and scrub. Dirt roads still used by pulp loggers snake across the landscape, now and then disappearing under the forest canopy that in many places grows higher and thicker with every passing year. Soon the rocky outcrops of the copper-bearing Trap Hills and the Victoria Dam and Impoundment on the Porcupine River passed below, as did the crossroads of Bruce Crossing, and the open, flat, forest-and-lake lands of Gogebic County approached through the whirling propeller. Ecologically, this area of the southern Upper Peninsula looks like neighboring northern Wisconsin, sparkling ponds and lakes scattered across the dark forest like diamonds on jeweler's velvet.

At almost the precise spot reported on the bar code tag stuck to the shroud of the Poor Farm corpse, I looked directly below. A tiny, almost circular clearing of tanned grass and low brush not more than seventy yards wide, a small pond in its center, appeared in the forest canopy. *It figures*, I thought. Tree cover blankets and fuzzes the line-of-sight transmissions from the GPS satellites far out in space, and it would make sense for a geocacher to stash a treasure at the edge of a clearing where a hand-held GPS can lock on to several satellites for an accurate fix. I dropped down further to two hundred feet above the treetops, holding the Cessna in a tight circle above the clearing. Through the edges of the trees I could see the twin ruts of a Forest Service dirt road leading to U.S. 45 three miles to the southwest. It would be easy to hop in a SUV or Jeep to reach N 46 19.107 W 89 09.740, and I knew exactly what we would find there.

TEN

"Almost the same," Alex said as he, Camilo and I gazed with distaste at the plastic-wrapped, naked torso that lay behind and under a downed log five feet thick, just a hop, skip, and jump through the brush off the Forest Service track through a corner of the tiny Lac Vieux Desert reservation and out onto public land just outside the national forest. It had taken us ten full minutes to locate the corpse after stopping at the exact coordinates given by the tag on the Poor Farm cadaver. A GPS may be accurate within twenty or thirty feet of a given point, but in heavy brush a circle of twenty or thirty feet in diameter can conceal a lot. Ten minutes seemed like hours in humid ninety-degree July heat with no-see-ums and blackflies buzzing around our heads, swathed in beekeeper's muslin, and Alex kept up a running mutter of salty terms, mostly variations on "fucking bugs," as he stumbled into trees and over brambles, head down as he watched the numbers unroll on his GPS. Had we been searching for a geocache in the city, he would have walked into a lamppost.

I cussed a few times myself. Camilo, who had spent much of his professional life searching for clues through tropical heat in thick East Texas brush, chuckled at our discomfiture.

It was a clever place for a geocache. From the Forest Service track the log was barely visible in the tall grass and brambles, and only when the searcher was standing directly on top of it could he see the shallow depression slightly behind and under. From every other angle the geocache couldn't be seen.

Like the Poor Farm cadaver, the body was missing its head and both hands. This time, however, putrefaction was well established, the gases of decay plumping the plastic shroud seemingly to the bursting point.

"Almost the same," I echoed. "But not quite."

"Not quite how?" said Camilo, who had not seen the corpse at the Poor Farm.

"The body at the Poor Farm was a well-embalmed medical cadaver," I said. "I don't think this one is."

"And this one is old," Alex pointed out. "See the wrinkled skin, the gray pubic hair? The one we found at the Poor Farm was young."

"So?" Camilo said.

"Many people think medical cadavers are almost always of the young or early middle-aged and are in good physical condition," Alex said. "They think medical students need to learn about anatomy from those and that specialists need to practice on the healthy. Not true. Most dead people are old people, after all. This is one of those, probably sick, full of arthritis and prostate cancer and God knows what else."

"But just look at the decomposition," I said. "I'll bet my next paycheck this body was embalmed for a funeral, not for study, as the first one probably was."

Morticians, I knew, prepare corpses to look fresh only for a few days, just to last through the end of a funeral service and make it to the cemetery in time. Anything more would be gilding the lily, wasting talent and materials. Funeral directors appreciate economic efficiency as much as any other businessmen.

"Then why would the perp cut off the head and hands?" asked Alex. He knew the answer, but somebody had to say it, and I did.

"To prevent identification," I said. "In this case, only that."

"Come again?" Camilo asked.

I explained how the Poor Farm cadaver's head and hands probably had been harvested for specialist study, but not this one.

Camilo nodded in understanding. "But if you're right and this stiff was embalmed for a funeral, wouldn't an undertaker somewhere be short a customer?" he asked. "Wouldn't he report it missing — and couldn't we identify it that way?"

"Yes," I said, "but it could have been earmarked for cremation after the funeral, not before. If the mortician was crooked, he could easily have sold the corpse to our perps and delivered an urn of dog ashes to the mourners."

"God," Camilo said.

"Jeez," Alex said.

Both men were offended, not by what I had said but by its implications. Cheating the bereaved is high on the average cop's scale of evildoing, not quite in the league of homicide but not far from it either.

"What do you make of the coins?" Alex asked after a while.

Five American coins — a dollar, a half dollar, a quarter, a dime and a penny — sat on the plastic-encased chest of the corpse. So did a shilling coin.

"My best guess," I said, remembering Ginny's lecture on geocaching, "is that these are tokens left by the geocachers who found the location, left to prove they were here. Each geocacher would have a coin assigned to himself."

"Or herself," said Camilo, not so much in political correctness as in keeping an open mind about the perp or perps.

"Does that mean one of our suspects is a Brit?" Alex asked.

"Maybe," I said, "but not necessarily. There are six coins in common American circulation, and if more than six geocache hunters are involved in this, they'd need some other coins to identify all of them."

"There were a quarter and a penny at the Poor Farm cache," Alex said. "But not the others."

"There's no nickel here," Camilo said, voicing what we all had noticed.

"Gentlemen," I said, "maybe that means that Mr. or Ms. Nickel hasn't found this cache yet."

"Could be," Alex said thoughtfully.

"We oughta get to the bottom of this," Camilo said. "Once is a stunt but twice is a crime."

"Ya think?" Alex said dubiously.

"Yeah," I said.

"We could set up a stakeout here," Camilo said. The tribal police's resources, augmented by the federal Bureau of Indian Affairs, are modest but still far greater than Porcupine County's. "I can deputize a bunch of reliable guys to sit in a car all day and all night on U.S. 45 and report every vehicle or person who goes up this road. Not many do. We can check them out pretty easy."

"All right," Alex said. "Your catch for now, Camilo, but when things happen the state police will be happy to help."

By that Alex meant that the troopers were ready to take over if the case turned out to be too much for a tribal force or county sheriff's department to handle, or if the crime spanned more than one jurisdiction. In a murder case on an Indian reservation the FBI would take ultimate responsibility, although these days the Feds were slow to do so, being up to their ears in antiterrorism chores. Often the FBI would ask the state police and sheriff to investigate as far as they could, and the G-men would take over the case when the bulk of the work, sometimes all of it, had been done.

But though the tribal cops were in charge for the moment, the clearing wasn't part of the Lac Vieux Desert reservation. No need to notify either the FBI or the U.S. Forest Service police, who would have been called in if the corpse had been on national forest land.

"All right, let's turn him over and see what's underneath," Alex said.

Gingerly, careful not to tear the plastic, we rolled the

body over on its front. And saw nothing on the underside. Not even a bar code.

"Hmm," I said. "Maybe this was the last cache in a series of them, and maybe the one we found at the Poor Farm was the first—or even the second or third or God knows what."

"Lordamighty," Alex said. "This *is* a puzzle. It makes my head hurt."

"Let's look around," I said. "Maybe there's some other kind of clue." An hour's search turned up an old fishing creel and a few tattered twelve-gauge shotgun shells.

"Ain't nothing here," Camilo said, "other than a few tire ruts, and we've already taken casts of them."

I believed him. Apaches made some of the world's best trackers. Nothing escaped their notice.

"All right, we're done here," Alex said. "Let's call a taxi to take this fellow to Marquette."

The taxi turned out to be a muddy Chevy Suburban belonging to the state police, and Alex turned out to be the reluctant cabbie.

ELEVEN

I was sipping coffee at my desk under the grimy green concrete block walls at the Sheriff's Department and chasing overdue paperwork around a cracked china mug emblazoned "TAKE A MYSTERY AUTHOR TO BED TONIGHT" when Alex called, jolting me from my reverie about the source of the mug. It had come from an itinerant wannabe whodunit writer from Chicago who had stopped in one day to check a few facts about police work and was never heard from again, at least not at the department. I wonder if he had ever managed to publish a book.

"Just as we thought," Alex said. "Yesterday's stiff definitely was a short-term embalming, the pathologist said. A quick dip in the juice and a bit of makeup to look good in church."

"Just as *I* thought, you mean," I said. Sometimes Alex needed to be reminded who came up with some of the brilliant ideas.

"All right, all right. Well, the pathologist also said the hands and head were hacked off with a cleaver or an axe, not surgically removed. The bone ends were shattered, not sawn."

"You know what that means," I said.

"You tell me."

I sighed. Alex likes to play dumb. "That means it wasn't a professional who did the dismembering," I said. "I think a pro would insist that head and hands be removed before he sold a corpse — if it ever was identified it'd get back to him — but he probably watched while the guy he sold it to did the job, just to make sure it was actually done and the buyer didn't take the parts along with him. The pro probably saw to it that the head and hands were cremated along with a dead deer or whatever was available, so there would be enough weight to the urn and the family wouldn't suspect a thing." Car-deer accidents are so plentiful in Upper Michigan and northern Wisconsin that a crooked crematory worker on his way to the office could easily gather a carcass from the side of the road and throw it into the back of his car or pickup.

"Yeah," Alex said. "So we can add desecration of a human body to the charges when we catch the assholes."

"*If* we catch them," I said.

"You don't sound so confident."

"I think these perps are smart people. And I think they're playing with us. I think they're from outside somewhere, and they think we're a bunch of Barney Fifes, and that's why they've picked us for their game."

"From outside?" Alex said. "Why?"

"I don't know. Fooling around with dead bodies doesn't seem to be the sort of thing a Yooper would do. It's such a . . . a . . . a *jaded* thing to do." There it was. I just didn't want to believe anybody in my adopted bailiwick was so bored with life that he was capable of playing sports with corpses.

"Hey, Yoopers have committed all the other crimes in the book," Alex said. "Why not this one? Besides, it's so unlikely that a casual visitor would've known about either of those two places where we found the bodies. It's probably a whole bunch of people playing this game, and one or more of them could be local."

"Don't forget the Internet," I said.

"Internet?"

"Yes. You would be surprised what Web sites can tell you. There's a Web site for every county in Michigan, and the one for Porcupine County has a page on the Poor Farm. In fact, Google brought up no fewer than forty-six hits on it. If I were looking for a place to stash something like a cadaver, I'd start with the Web."

"Now what?"

"I guess we wait and see if anybody shows up at the

stakeout."

"Right."

I hung up and pursued another form around my desk.

"Deputy Martinez!" Gil's gravelly voice thundered from his office.

"Sir?"

"Come in and sit down!"

I relaxed. The invitation to plant my butt in a chair meant the undersheriff wasn't going to grill me about the cost of the latest oil change on the Cessna. He did his chewing out while his victims stood before his desk at attention, sweating. Gil liked to do things the military way. He had been a drill instructor in the Army for four hitches before deciding upon a new career of tormenting rural deputies.

"Shut the door!"

I did.

"Have you seen this?" He shoved a Herald across the desk at me and thrust a massive index finger at a front-page article. "CHANGES NEEDED IN SHERIFF'S DEPARTMENT," the headline said. It was an "interview" of Sheriff Eli Garrow — actually, it was an op-ed column he had written himself in third-person format and disguised as a news story. I could tell Eli's voice by the awkwardly folksy language — the kind a cop uses when he doesn't want to sound like a cop — as well as shaky grammar and questionable spelling. The Herald would print just about anything handed to it, and often did so without the polish of an editor's pencil. That gave the letters and amateur-contributed articles a certain just-folks authenticity, but sometimes the authenticity was so great the result was nearly incomprehensible. That was, I thought, unnecessarily cruel to the writers. Semiliterate doesn't necessarily mean stupid. People who can barely read and write are often smart in other ways.

"Can you believe this shit?" Gil demanded.

Among other things, Eli wrote, if he were re-elected, the department would keep two deputies on road patrol twenty-four hours a day, seven days a week, in addition to the dispatcher. These days, with cutbacks in state and federal funding, we'd had to furlough two of our nine sworn deputies and spread the rest thin. Only during daylight hours did we have two officers on patrol, and at night we had one based at the office to be sent out as needed. On Friday and Saturday nights we had one or two other deputies on call if barroom disputes escalated beyond the duty officer's ability to handle them. It wasn't a great way to police a big county in the middle of the wilderness, but it was all we could do with our scarce resources. Grants could bring in new equipment, but we had to pay our personnel with funds from the increasingly undernourished county coffers.

"Where's Eli going to get the money for that?" I asked.

"Doesn't say," Gil grunted. "Pie in the sky."

We stared at the newspaper for a few minutes. Then what passed for a smile distorted Gil's face, usually as composed as a pressure cooker just short of the bursting point.

"The only way Eli could do that," he said, "would be to talk the county into raising taxes. A lot."

In Upper Michigan, economic times are never good—they're just variations on bad and worse. The voters are sensible. In the last elections they voted Yes on a proposal to raise the millage just a tad for the county public library and the county public transit, both highly popular services. But two or three more full-time deputies and their benefits would cost a lot more than that.

"Deputy Martinez. You are hereby ordered to campaign on the fact that Eli's proposals would hike our taxes. Is that clear?"

"You can't order me to do that!" Gil may be the boss of me as a deputy, but he's not the boss of me as a politician.

"Of course not," he said, in a tone about as placating as he ever gets. "But be sensible. Eli thinks he's gonna fool the voters, but they're gonna realize what he'll cost them. You've got to point that out to them."

"Yeah. But I'll be damned if I do it Eli's way."

"You don't have to. Just go out there and shake hands and let them know what happens if you don't get elected."

"All right."

"Now get out of my office." Gil turned to the file cabinets behind him in dismissal.

In encouraging me, he was committing an act of insubordination. Eli was still the sheriff in name, though he hadn't been in the office for weeks, ever since Garner Armstrong told him his days were numbered. The undersheriff's first loyalty is always to his boss. If it ever got out that Gil was giving me campaign advice, Eli would fire him on the spot, for the undersheriff serves at the sheriff's pleasure and is not protected by a union, as we deputies are. And that would kick up an enormous fuss in Porcupine County, for Gil is a highly respected if not exactly cuddly police officer.

I'd keep my mouth shut. But I could see my task clear: to commit dirty politics, or what passed for dirty politics in Upper Michigan. I had to. My opponent was doing so—in more ways than one.

Shutting my desk drawer and grabbing my ball cap from the hat rack, I started for the door.

"Stick around a bit," said Joe Koski from his dispatcher's desk. "Chad's coming in with an interesting pinch."

"What? Who?"

"You'll see."

When I was halfway through my second cup of coffee the big deputy rolled in, pushing two grizzled and unkempt men in their forties ahead of him like a monstrous border collie nipping at the heels of a couple of raggedy sheep.

"What do we got?" asked Joe, the booking officer as well as dispatcher and town gossip. Soon all of Porcupine County would know what we got.

"Caught 'em pulling up and trashing campaign signs," Chad said, "from both public and private property. They had a couple dozen signs in their car trunk, too."

I blinked. Gil came out of his office and glared at Chad. Messing with campaign signs was a third-class misdemeanor, about as serious as public drunkenness or disorderly conduct. The fines would barely pay for the deputies' labor. Some laws are just not worth enforcing. Had I been in Chad's shoes, I'd just have read the riot act and made the perps put the signs back.

Chad saw my blink. "Just doing my job, Steve," he said, calmly and not at all defensively.

Joe asked the question we all wanted answered. "Whose signs were they?"

"Martinez's," Chad said.

"Mine?"

"Just doing my job," Chad said again. Gil turned on his heel and without a word strode back into his office.

"Names?" Joe asked.

"Jim and John McCulloch," Chad said. "Residence, Two-thirty-three Stover Road, Bergland." I recognized the names. McCullochs are first cousins to the Garrows.

"Eli put you up to this?" Joe asked.

Neither of the unshaven men responded.

"Eh?" Joe asked again. Both men just glowered.

"Stay right here," Joe told them. "Chad, let's talk." The two deputies walked into the empty sheriff's office and conferred for a couple of minutes. Then they returned unsmiling to the squadroom.

"We're booking you on misdemeanor malicious destruction of property," Joe told the men. "We'll send you a court date in the mail. Meanwhile, sign here, and we'll release you on your own recognizance."

I shot a glance at Gil in his office. His head bobbed slightly in approval. Fifty-dollar fines wouldn't begin to pay for the labors of the deputy, the dispatcher and the magistrate as well as the paperwork, but they'd send a clear message to the forces of Eli Garrow.

As for Chad Garrow, I now knew where his loyalty lay. Not to Eli, not to me, but to his badge and to the law. That was enough for any man to ask.

I got up once more to leave, and Gil stuck his head out of his office again. "Deputies," he said, "henceforth we will enforce the campaign sign laws. For *everyone*." He shot me a glance. I could have sworn he winked, but with Gil that was not only unlikely but probably physically impossible.

In Porcupine County, as in just about any Michigan locality, campaign sign ordinances usually are honored in the breach. Cops have more important things to do than pounce on technical infractions of the election ordinances. But now I'd have to look sharply at my own signs. At least three I could think of were maybe five or six feet too close to the road. But that was all. I didn't have one-third the number of signs Eli set out. Couldn't afford them.

"Put it on the order board for everyone to carry tape measures on patrol," Gil told Joe. "Make sure those signs are at least sixty-six feet from the center lines of all two-lane highways and that the sight lines at all road intersections are clear. And if any campaign signs violate the law *in any way*, confiscate 'em."

I couldn't keep my eyebrows from shooting up. That meant maybe half of Eli Garrow's signs were technically illegal, not just because they were posted where they weren't allowed, but also because they didn't clearly state who had paid for the sign, as the law required. The Ewen graphics shop Eli used for most of his signs didn't have the proper equipment to do small-size lettering, and so left off "The Committee to Re-elect Eli Garrow" from their products. Most everyone in the county had noticed the omission, and a few had even clucked in disapproval, but the infraction not having the gravity of, say, bank robbery, we all had forgotten about it.

As I passed by Gil's office he looked up at me from his desk.

"Just doing my job," he said. He did not smile.

TWELVE

Sure enough, by midafternoon, the entire county knew what had happened that morning at the sheriff's department. Joe Koski had gone out to lunch at Merle's and told a few folks, who told a few folks, and soon the news had been carried far and wide. Out of habit, Joe had also broadcast the order to all cars, even though both deputies on patrol that day—Chad and I—had been in the office. Up until that spring the Porcupine County Bush Telegraph would have picked up his transmission. That was the old unofficial network of radio scanners most everyone kept on the kitchen table and many illegally carried in their cars and pickups, tuning them to the various government bands—police, fire, ambulance, hospital, highway, even the bridge over M-64—keeping track of what went on in the county. That way the news would have spread instantly throughout coffee shops, garages and taverns all over Upper Michigan.

But the bush telegraph had suffered a heavy blow when the new eight hundred megahertz radio system was adopted by all the Upper Peninsula police forces as well as the state police. For technical reasons scanners tuned to the police frequency have a hard time picking up broadcasts, so no longer did everyone in the county know when Joe dispatches an order to the deputies in the field. The new system not only allows us to keep a better handle on security, but at last it covers the many dead spots all over the county that the old line-of-sight radio technology couldn't reach. No longer do we have to try our cell phones—themselves hobbled by huge dead spots—or stop at someone's house and ask to use their landline phone.

Also, I knew that as soon as I left the squadroom Joe would call Horace Wright, *The Herald*'s only reporter, and the next Wednesday a small front-page story would appear about the arrest of two Bergland residents for malicious destruction of campaign signs. *The Herald* wouldn't mention their names, not until sentence had been passed—if it ever was, because the district judge often dismissed trivial offenses as not being worth the court's time. But Joe, who spent half his off hours at Merle's Cafe, would make sure those names got out into the sunlight where everyone could hear them. Rough justice, but justice nonetheless.

Before Joe had had time to spread the gossip, I was on my way out of town on M-64, heading west to start my patrol by delivering a civil court summons, when I decided to stop in at Ginny's for a quick hello and a cup of her first-rate Colombian coffee. I knocked, she called "Come in!" and I found her sitting at the kitchen table gazing gloomily at Tommy, whose head was bowed so that I couldn't see it.

"Good morning," I said cheerily to both.

Ginny nodded, but Tommy didn't look up.

"S'matter?"

"Tommy was in an altercation after school yesterday," Ginny said. "He doesn't want to tell me about it."

Altercation? What's wrong with "fistfight"? Women are so dainty with words, as if a prettier one softened reality.

"That so?" I asked Tommy.

He looked up. A large mouse discolored his left eye socket and his upper lip lay split and swollen over the lower.

"Who did that to you?"

Tommy shook his head.

"I'm talking to you as a friend, Tommy, not as a cop."

Tommy nodded but kept mum.

"May I see your hands?"

Slowly he brought them out from under the table. Cuts and bruises lathered with antiseptic ointment covered his knuckles.

"Looks like you gave as good as you got."

Tommy nodded.

"What was it about?"

"Nothing."

"That's a lot of something on your face and hands for nothing," I said.

"Tommy, talk to me," Ginny said. "Maybe I can help."

"Thanks, but I don't need help." Tommy said the words politely, without rancor or sullenness. His calmness unsettled me.

I looked at Ginny and nodded. She shrugged, as if what was happening at her kitchen table was a hopelessly male thing and utterly beyond her power to understand, let alone influence.

"If you do," I said, "let us know, okay?"

"All right, Mr. Martinez."

"The bus is almost here, Tommy," Ginny said. "Better run." Visibly relieved to be let off the spot, the lad grabbed his book bag and dashed out the door, sprinting up the short distance to the highway. Through the trees I could see the flashing strobe light atop the approaching school bus. He'd just make it.

"What do you suppose the fight was about?"

"I don't know," Ginny said. "I'm afraid some bully attacked him."

Ice knifed into my heart. Was it because Tommy is an Indian?

"Maybe it was just a bully," I said. "Maybe not. Boys get into fights for all sorts of reasons."

"I don't know," she said, hugging herself. "But he came home last night bleeding and barely able to see out of that eye. He let me give him first aid but he refused to say what happened. He went to bed right away."

"Hmm. How's he doing in algebra?" The summer class had begun three weeks earlier.

"Quite well," Ginny said. "Jack Queeney said he's picked up algebra so fast he's actually helping teach the class."

"Hmm. Lots of remedial students in it, aren't there?"

"Most are from the high school."

"Wonder if some thug resents a smaller kid being smarter than him." Smarter, maybe with a different color of skin, who knew?

"I don't know. Maybe."

"I have an idea."

"What?"

"I'll find a reason to be at the school when the class lets out later this morning. I'll see if there's another kid with battle scars."

"Don't push it too hard, Steve. Tommy is a very proud boy. I wouldn't want him to think we were going to come running every time he had a problem. He needs to be independent."

"He *wants* to be independent," I said. "There's a difference."

"You'll be careful?"

"I'll just do my job."

At one minute before noon I stopped by the junior high to consult with Jack Queeney, who coached the Little League team and taught math at the high school, including algebra and the summer class. The new baseball jerseys we deputies had chipped in to buy had arrived at the sheriff's department, and it was the perfect excuse to pay Jack a visit.

As the bell rang I waved to Jack and strode into his room with an armful of uniforms while the two dozen pupils filed out. I nodded to Tommy, who looked at me quizzically, and said hi to a few of the youngsters I knew. One of the last boys to file out was a big, overstuffed towhead with scuffs and bruises on his chubby cheeks and a lip even fatter than Tommy's. He outweighed Tommy by at least twenty pounds, maybe thirty. He had the weight and the reach but not, I thought, the speed.

"Who's that kid?" I asked Jack when they had gone.

"Teddy Garrow, from Matchwood. He's fourteen, and

it's his second time around in this class. He'll never pass."

If Jack had noticed that two of his students bore the fresh marks of a fight, he didn't let on, and I didn't mention it. But it looked as if the campaign for sheriff might be trickling down into places where it didn't belong. I hoped not.

THIRTEEN

As I was broiling on the big kettle grill a freshly thawed walleye I'd caught a few weeks earlier in Lake Gogebic, the phone rang.

"Steve? Camilo."

"What's happening?"

"We just had a visitor at that stakeout. Remember that rich young guy in the red Beemer at the dance last week? That was him. He turns in and parks just out of sight of the highway, looks around behind him, goes up the road. Billy Bones saw him from his pickup and followed him in on foot."

Billy — actually William Bonham — was an Ojibwa, a retired tribal police officer in his mid-seventies, who often filled in at the shop when Lac Vieux Desert cops called in sick or went on vacation. Billy had been getting forgetful lately, and one of the things that often slipped his mind was his concealed carry permit for his huge and old-fashioned Colt Peacemaker .45. Issued long ago when he first joined the force and renewed regularly since, the permit wasn't good outside Michigan. The tribal police and the Gogebic sheriff's deputies often had to rescue Billy from indignant Wisconsin and Minnesota law enforcement officers who had been alarmed by the bulge in his windbreaker. Amazingly, no one had confiscated the weapon. It was only professional courtesy, but I thought sometimes that can be taken too far.

Still Billy was a peaceable and competent unofficial reserve officer, a man of widely known reliability, and had been one of the first Camilo had enlisted for stakeout duty at the Watersmeet cache.

"The Beemer guy didn't see Billy?"

"Steve, Billy's an *Indian*. What do you expect?"

"Not all Indians know how to hide in the woods

anymore."

"That's all Columbus' fault, you know." Camilo, who could become one angry Native American on the subject of the manifold sins of the white man, would orate at the drop of a hat on the incompetency of the European explorer "who didn't know what he'd found but wrecked the neighborhood anyway." Then he would start in on Coronado and Pizarro and De Soto and the rest of the Spanish invaders who despoiled the Southwest looking for El Dorado, and we always had to stop him before he had worked up too much of a froth. We'd heard it all anyway, and even if we agreed with him — as I did — there wasn't much we could do about it. Way too many conquistadors and cavalrymen.

"Never mind, Camilo. Go on."

He sighed in irritation, thwarted from his soapbox. "The subject was carrying a GPS and at about the spot where we found the corpse, he stopped and tramped around for ten or fifteen minutes searching for something. When he didn't find what he was looking for, he cursed loudly enough for Billy to hear him, then ran back to his car and took off south on 45. Billy not only got his plate but also his face with a telephoto."

"Excellent."

"What now? Alex is downstate in Lansing." The case had begun in my bailiwick, and Camilo was deferring to me as the unofficial senior investigator. Such deliberate politeness was how cops in differing jurisdictions got along, and we in the U.P. were especially careful about it. We needed each other.

"What was that license plate?"

"Illinois. One of those cutesy vanity things. 'REBEMER,' all capital letters. Whatever that means. Also a City of Chicago sticker and a neighborhood parking permit."

"Camilo, we're in business," I said. "If you'll contact the Illinois DMV for the owner of those plates, I'll pay a young lady a visit."

"What young lady?"

I told Camilo what I'd seen in the storeroom of the Coppermass Town Hall at the wedding dance of Jerry Muskat and Adela McLaughlin, mildly editing the story in the interest of PG-rated decency.

"Hoo boy," Camilo said delightedly, slapping his thigh. "Dead bodies and sex. We haven't had such a combination in years."

It *was* a break in the routine.

"Pervert," I said primly.

"Sure."

"Camilo, let's not tip the guy off too soon. There are probably others involved in this and we don't want to spook them just yet. Let's just find out what we can about him from Illinois and Chicago law enforcement."

"All right, call you later."

As the sun sank into Lake Superior an hour later I pulled up at the Mobil filling station and convenience store on M-64 just north of Lone Pine in the western reaches of the county. Luck was with me.

The beefy blonde I had seen locked in embrace with the Beemer guy was on duty. Two suspiciously young men strode out to a pickup as I entered, calling as they left, "S'long, Sharon." They carried a couple of six-packs of Bud, but I decided they were old enough and left them alone. Other things occupied my mind.

"Aren't you a handsome one now, Deputy?" Sharon said lightly as I took a Slim-Jim from a rack and plunked down a five-dollar bill. She wore extreme low-rider Diesel jeans and a yellow T-shirt two sizes too small. The effect would have been knockout sexy had she weighed twenty pounds fewer and had her heavy perfume come from elsewhere than the Dollar Store. As she placed the change in my hand she stroked my palm with long fingernails. I gently pulled it away and said just as lightly, "Sorry, honey, I'm spoken for."

"Well, ain't that my tough luck?" She spoke flirtatiously and without anger, but there was a wistful note in her voice. Many single young women in rural northern Wisconsin and the Upper Peninsula are like her, high school dropouts who grow up there or drift in from elsewhere to work in dead-end minimum-wage jobs, barely keeping their heads above water, until they become single mothers supported by the state. Many of their sisters depart for the big cities aboard Greyhounds and are snared by enterprising pimps shadowing the bus stations for new blood. In the country, a surprising lot of these young women have no families and only a tiny circle of friends. With them they spend their equally tiny disposable incomes in bars on the weekends, often waking up with a hellacious hangover next to a man they met the previous night. They eat a cheap, high-carb diet and turn to fat rapidly, often shedding teeth but never seeing a dentist.

Sharon, I thought, probably had been pretty when she was a teen-ager, but hard lines had settled into her face and a roll of fat had started above her hips. Within a year or two she would cross the line into obesity and flirt with diabetes.

"Maybe it's *my* tough luck," I said. I leaned my forearms flat on the counter, hunching my shoulders and ducking my head, and looked up from under the brim of my ball cap with an encouraging crinkle of my eyes. Ginny once called that a devastatingly irresistible posture, and it does seem to work with women and small children.

"Sharon, isn't it?" I asked.

She nodded hopefully.

"Sharon what?"

"Sharon Shoemaker."

"I'm Steve Martinez."

"I know, Deputy. Seen you around lots of times." She had a faraway expression on her face, as if she was trying to remember if she had ever slept with me, and if she had, whether I had been any good.

"Actually, Sharon, I'm here for another reason. There's a guy I'm interested in, and maybe you can tell me something about him."

"Who?"

"Don't know his name. But I saw you with him a few nights ago at that party for Jerry and Adela at the Coppermass Town Hall."

"Huh?"

I looked at Sharon carefully. It did seem that she was honestly drawing a blank. So many men, so many nights, who could keep track?

"Tall, rich looking. Drove a Beemer."

The light of recognition dawned on her face. "Yeah," she said as a slow smile that spoke of remembered delight crept up her lips. It must have been good, really good, that encounter in the storeroom.

Then her grin faded. "Did he do something bad?"

"I'm not sure," I said truthfully. "Trying to find out. What was his name?"

"Artie. Arthur. Clyde, no, Kein, no, *Klein*," Sharon said. "He said he was from Chicago."

"What happened afterward?" I said. "I'm sorry, but I have to ask. Did you go home with him that night?"

"Oh, *no!*" she said with mostly mock indignation. "I'm not that kind of girl!"

"Didn't say you were. But do you remember anything about him?"

"Not much. He didn't call after."

So there were limits to Artie Klein's acceptance by the community—limits he himself had drawn. I was not surprised. A rich kid from Chicago might help himself to a little ice cream, but he wasn't going to take over the freezer. A classic one-nighter—and maybe not even that.

"Did he say what he was doing up here in Porcupine

County?"

"I'm trying to remember," she said. "Yeah. He said he was looking at property on the lake, maybe going to buy it."

"Did he say what he did for a living?"

"Some kind of investor."

"Did he say what company he worked for?"

"Fiddler something."

"Fidelity?" A shot in the dark.

"Yeah! That's it!"

"He give you an address, a phone number?"

"He wrote down a number. But it turned out to be a laundry, a dry cleaner's. Yeah, I called it."

"What'd he write the phone number on?"

"A business card he got out of his wallet."

"Do you still have it?"

She hesitated a moment, then said, "Yeah, I think so." She turned and squatted to pick up her purse, hidden behind a filing cabinet. Her short T-shirt rode up and her low-riding jeans rode down, and just atop the cleft of her doughy buttocks peeked a small tattoo of a Teutonic cross. Maybe she had once been a biker bimbo. Germanic symbols are popular in that culture.

She rummaged in her purse and found the card. "It's not his, just an old one he used to write the number on the back."

I took the expensive pearl-colored pasteboard. BEAR STEARNS AND COMPANY, it said in raised copperplate engraving. ANDREW MONAGHAN. Under that, the phone number, with a 201 prefix—Manhattan. Nothing else. Not even an address. Utter simplicity, as bespoke the card of an employee of one of the country's richest investment firms. On the back was scrawled a phone number.

"Did you call this number too?" I asked, tapping the front of the card.

She hesitated almost imperceptibly, then shook her head. I let it go. A blind phone call from an unknown woman

593

in the middle of nowhere never would get past a secretary at a New York investment house. Very likely she didn't want to admit she'd been rebuffed. People have their pride.

"May I keep this?" I asked. As it had for Sharon, the card probably would lead to a dead end for me, but then it might not. Possibly Mr. Andrew Monaghan was just an acquaintance in the industry, but it was equally possible that he was keeping nefarious company with Mr. Arthur Klein. You never know. You always have to check.

"Sure," Sharon said. "It ain't doing me any good." Then, a beat later, she finally asked the obvious question: "What did he do?"

"That I can't tell you at this time," I said. "We're not sure. We're still investigating." That was the truth.

"Oh."

"Thanks for your help, honey," I said, flashing her my most winning smile. "Bye for now."

"Uh, Steve," she said as I turned to walk out.

"Yes?"

"If you find out anything about him, could you let me know?" The fretful expression on her face suggested she remembered something else. Perhaps Artie hadn't used protection during their unscripted encounter and she worried that she was pregnant.

"If I can, I sure will. Thanks again for your help."

"Thanks." She came out of her station behind the counter and stood in the doorway, the pool of light from a single bare bulb above outlining her sad and lonely face as I drove away into the night.

FOURTEEN

I had just moved one of my own roadside campaign signs two feet further into legal territory when the radio call came from Joe Koski.

"Steve, we got another," he said.

"Another what?" I asked, wearily knowing the answer.

"Stiff. Looks like it may be a homicide this time," Jerry said. "Hiker called in and said he found a body in a cave just off the North Country Trail about two miles west of Norwich Road. Says it's real ripe, just lying there uncovered. I took his statement about an hour ago."

"Alex back from Lansing yet?"

"He's on his way, but won't be here till tonight."

"All right. I'll swing by and get the bug and safe kits and a body bag." I had been sent to Lansing not long before to be trained in the basics of forensic-evidence gathering on the rare occasion when a state trooper with those skills wasn't available, and Gil had used his grant-writing skills to promote a bit of sophisticated crime-scene equipment, including a forensic entomology outfit and a couple of personal protection kits for cases involving hazardous materials. "Call Chad and tell him to meet me at the parking spot by the trail at Norwich," I added. "Have him bring a stretcher. Where's that hiker?"

"Right here in the department."

"I'll take him along to show us. Is he okay?"

"Sure. A little green around the gills, but willing."

Thank goodness for concerned citizens.

"I meant did you check out his story?"

"Yes," said Joe. "He's clean. So is his gal. I've got their particulars in case we need to talk to them again."

After I'd gathered the bulky kits and the hiker and we were on our way, I asked him to talk to me. He was in his early thirties, tall and athletic, sporting an outdoorsman's stubble, and was dressed in sensible but not in-your-face-expensive outdoor gear.

"Can I see some ID?" I asked.

He showed me a Wisconsin commercial license that entitled him to drive eighteen-wheelers. I handed it back.

"What were you doing on the North Country Trail?"

"I already told the deputy at the department," he said. "Do you need to hear it, too?"

"The deputy hasn't had time to fill me in," I said. "Do you mind going through it all again?" If what he told me matched what he told Joe down to the last detail, chances were he was on the side of the angels and could be scratched off the suspect list.

"Oh, nope," he said. "Let's see. I'm from Green Bay. My name's Dan Kowalczyk. Me and Katie, she's my girlfriend, we drove up yesterday to walk the North Country Trail and do a little camping."

"Where's Katie?"

"In the Porcupine City Motel," he said. "She ain't feeling so good. Not after what she saw."

"We might need to talk to her later, but we can do that when she's feeling better. Go on."

"We parked our car at Victoria yesterday and pitched our tent at a campsite near there last night and were making good time on the trail this morning when I had to take a dump. I decided to climb down into a ravine below the trail and go behind a tree. When I got down there I smelled something awful. I recognized that smell. I was in the Army in Iraq."

No soldier who has ever crossed a fresh battlefield can forget the cloying odor of human putrefaction. There is nothing else like it in the world. It sticks to your clothes, it sticks to your skin, and it sticks to your soul.

"Yeah, I know," I said. I'd experienced it a little more

than a decade before, in the same part of the world.

"I looked around a little, and found a shallow cave under an overhang. Right inside it there was this body, all bloated and purple and stinking. It had no head and it had no hands. The noise from the flies was awful."

"What did you do then?"

"Me and Katie walked back up the trail to Norwich Road and waved down a car. It was almost an hour before one came along. The driver brought us to town. I put Katie in the motel and went to the sheriff's office."

"Thank you, Dan. You did exactly the right things."

"I hope so." He took a deep breath.

So did I. "Do you have a GPS?" I said.

"No," he said calmly. "I don't get lost in the woods very much. Maybe sometime I'll get one. I know they're handy and can save your life, but I don't need one, and anyway it's more fun to do things the old-fashioned way, with a map and compass."

"Bet you drive a stick shift, too."

"How'd you know that?"

"I'm kinda retro myself. Prefer the good old tools, like this revolver." I patted the .357 at my waist and chuckled.

Dan smiled wryly but didn't laugh. He wasn't one of our geocachers.

Presently we arrived at the almost hidden entry to the North Country Trail on Norwich Road. A wooden U.S. Forest Service sign marked it, but if you weren't watching you'd speed right past the small hole in the forest wall. Chad was waiting on the verge of the road with his equipment, and we changed into heavy canvas brush clothing before starting off with Dan. I filled Chad in as we began the hour's hike west along the ridges of the Trap Hills. It was slow going. The North Country Trail is not a well-tended national park path pounded flat by hundreds of thousands of feet a year, but a sometimes all-but-invisible track land-mined with roots, loose rocks and mud holes. In spots, only the metal blazes nailed to the trees, their paint fading under the elements, showed us the way. The faint path took us through heavy brush, down rocky screes and up steep slopes. Often we had to climb over dead trees that had fallen over the trail. Blackflies and brambles plucked at us everywhere, and in spots the humming clouds of no-see-ums were so thick we had to tie bandanas across our faces to avoid breathing in the tiny insects. We sweated piggishly.

Fortunately, before starting back to Norwich Road, Dan had had the presence of mind to mark the spot where he had stepped off the trail for his call of nature. He had tied a red handkerchief around a branch overhanging the trail. He must have been a competent soldier, I thought, probably a noncom.

I recognized the niche in the rock where the body lay. It wasn't a natural cavern, but one of many mine entrances in the high ridges that were started but never finished during the first frantic copper boom of the nineteenth century. Prospectors had hacked away at the rock for a few weeks before giving up on their hope of finding a vein of copper, leaving behind man-tall gouges six or eight feet deep and ten or so feet wide. This one, just above a pretty brook bubbling at the foot of the ravine, had been a favorite spot of campers for a long time before the Forest Service set up a string of official campsites along the trail. Once, during a cloudburst on a weekend hike, Ginny and I had taken shelter at that very spot.

The smell staggered me, causing bile to lurch up my gullet and my eyes to water. Chad gagged, stepped off the trail and vomited. Quickly he wiped his mouth and returned.

"Shouldn't have had that anchovy pizza for lunch," he said calmly. Tender tummy and all, Chad was not a wuss.

"It's right there," Dan said, pointing.

I stepped over a log and saw it through a buzzing cloud of flies.

Even with the gaseous distortion and discoloration I could see that it was the body of a young woman. As Dan had said, there was no head and no hands. The body lay mostly inside a torn plastic shroud much like the others we had found, but made of a much thinner material. Animals had been feeding on one leg.

"Dan, if you want, you can move up the trail to a spot where the air's not quite so foul. But I'd appreciate it if you stuck around for a while. We might need you to answer questions."

The ex-soldier nodded quietly. He knew his duty.

"Chad, let's dress up." Up the ravine at a healthy distance away from the corpse, we broke open the hazmat kits and donned disposable Tyvek coveralls, hoods and booties, thin neoprene gloves and respirators. It was a warm afternoon, and I began to sweat as soon as I took the first step toward the corpse, but the respirators cut the stink to almost nothing. There wasn't much we could do about the swarms of flies.

For two hours Chad and I worked, first photographing the corpse in situ from several angles. Multiple knife marks on the torso, both shallow slashes and deep stabs, suggested the cause of death. There was no blood, meaning that the woman had been killed elsewhere and her body cleaned before it was carried down the North Country Trail. Both her nipples and her navel were pierced by silver rings an inch in diameter.

"Look at those needle tracks, Steve," Chad said. "She was a junkie."

A trail of purplish punctures surrounded by bruised flesh walked up the inside of the body's left elbow.

"Might have been a prostitute," I said. "If semen's present and the medical examiner finds the DNA of several sexual partners in it, that'll all but clinch it. Hey, look at the bone ends. They're crushed and splintered, not cleanly sawn. This lady wasn't dismembered by a mortician, like the Poor Farm corpse. She was butchered, like the one near Watersmeet. If embalming fluid was used at all, the job was botched. This is the work of an amateur."

We plucked maggots from the teeming flesh of the corpse as well as the soil around it and popped them into specimen jars. Those might help the forensic entomologist at the central state police crime lab in Lansing to pinpoint the time of death. Flies frequently lay eggs on a corpse within an hour after its owner is killed, and the times of the developmental stages of the resulting maggots, even their internal temperatures, can be measured accurately.

"We're done, Chad. Let's zip her up."

Gently we slid the body into the bag and onto the aluminum stretcher. With a roll of duct tape I sealed the zipper, hoping the smell wouldn't leak from the bag but knowing it would.

"Hold it," Chad said. He bent down, scratched in the gravel where the body had lain, and pointed. "Look."

A shiny nickel, head facing up, glittered from the dust.

"Stand aside," I said, stepping forward to photograph the coin where it lay. Then I scooped it up, examined it carefully and dropped it into a ziplock bag. "That wasn't there before the body was laid on top of it. It's brand new, right from the mint. No weathering at all."

"What's it mean?" Chad asked. He hadn't been with Alex and Camilo and me down by Watersmeet, where we had discovered the array of coins atop the cached corpse.

"Maybe nothing," I said. "But it might be a link to the other two bodies."

I explained what Alex and I had speculated about the existence of coins at the cache sites. Skepticism and puzzlement wreathed Chad's face.

"Let's get going," I said.

"Give you a hand?" Dan called from up the hill. I nodded.

It took two hours for the three of us to make our way back with the bagged body down the rocky, winding trail to Norwich Road, and I was grateful for Dan's help. When we arrived we slid the stretcher half crosswise into the back of the sheriff's Explorer, over the folded rear seats. We drove back to Porcupine City with all the windows open and the intake fan on high against the noisome mess in the back.

After dropping Dan at the motel and telling him we might need to be in touch again, Chad and I drove the two hours to the lab at Marquette and delivered the corpse and the evidence we had gathered, but FedExing the maggots to Lansing. At my cabin that night I showered for twenty minutes, lathering up heavily and scrubbing vigorously, then fell into bed and into a fitful sleep, the stench of corruption still heavy in my nostrils.

FIFTEEN

Two days later we held a war council in the sheriff's squad room. Garner Armstrong, as prosecutor and chief law officer of Porcupine County, presided. Gil, Chad and I were present as duty officers on shift, Alex represented the state police, and Camilo Hernandez drove up from Watersmeet for consultation since one of the bodies had been found in his bailiwick. Joe Koski took notes.

"Here's what we have," Garner said. "Three bodies. One a fully prepared medical cadaver, one an old guy embalmed just enough to last through his funeral, and one a woman, probably a prostitute, stabbed to death elsewhere and left to rot in our county." In the last case, the medical examiner had confirmed the cause of death and discovered the DNA of four different men in semen samples taken from her vagina. The victim had been a longtime heroin addict, common among urban streetwalkers. The entomological evidence showed that she had been dead for eight days. Embalming fluid, but not enough to have done much good, leaked from her tissues. As for the other two bodies, the forensic experts' best guess was that they had been stowed away for three to six weeks. More tests were needed to narrow down the times of death, although knowing those probably wouldn't help in the first two cases, for they weren't homicides.

"So what ties them together?" He answered his own question. "GPS coordinates link the second one to the first. A nickel links the third to the second — maybe. That could just be a coincidence. But all three are missing their heads and their hands. Maybe in the case of the medical cadaver there's a good reason for that, but not in the other two."

For the record Gil said the painfully obvious: "Those

bodies were meant never to be identified."

"But they were also meant to be found," Camilo said. "Maybe even by us. They were hidden in plain sight, if you know what I mean."

"Kind of like a message in a bottle," I said, surprising myself.

"Explain," Garner said.

"You know," I said. "You write a message with your name and address and put it into a bottle and throw it into the lake. Then you wait for somebody to find it and write you that it was found. There could be a million reasons to do that. Maybe a young couple is just curious about the chances for a reply. Maybe a teenage girl sends a message she hopes a boy will find. Maybe a church lady puts in a passage from the Bible and hopes it will touch somebody's soul. Maybe somebody's shipwrecked and wants to say 'Help me.' "

"We looking for a freak?" Alex said. "Or freaks?"

The room fell silent. Then Chad spoke. "What about missing persons?"

"Nobody's reported either a lost cadaver or a missing body prepared for burial so far as we can find out," Alex said. "And who's going to report a missing hooker, especially a junkie? They come and they go, and nobody cares. What's more, the hooker being a homicide victim may have nothing to do with her being a cached corpse. Maybe she was just the closest thing on the shelf at a funeral home, hadn't been embalmed yet, and was sold as is to the guy or guys who cached her."

"DNA?" Chad persisted. He may be ignorant about some things, but he knows how to educate himself. He's not afraid of asking questions some people might consider inane — he thinks the only stupid question is the unasked one.

"The examiner took tissue samples from the vic for that possibility, but he's not going to run a full DNA test unless there's some DNA to compare it with, like a relative's," Alex said. "Complete DNA tests are too expensive and take too long unless there's a good chance of getting a match. And when nobody's reported a relative missing, what's there to compare DNA with?"

Chad wasn't satisfied. "What about the DNA in the sperm?" he said. "Possibly her last john killed her. That would link killer and victim."

"Yes," Gil said patiently, "but the mere presence of sperm doesn't mean the owner of the sperm did the vic, just that they had a business relationship."

"It's circumstantial," Chad said, "but it *is* evidence." We all looked at him. The lad was learning fast.

"Again, what do we have?" Garner cut in. "Three dumped bodies. One of them clearly a homicide, but probably committed elsewhere before being brought to Porcupine County. Why 'probably'? For one thing, we don't have heavy-duty professional hookers like that up here. Not enough customers. She's got to be from one of the big cities. And she isn't exactly the kind of victim most police departments want to break their backs for." He sighed deeply.

Garner was just being honest. Like the rest of us in that room, he values human life and wants whoever had the evil effrontery to take it to pay for the crime. But he is also a practical man and knows that the resources of a financially pinched county would have to be allocated where they could do some good. We are forced to practice a kind of legal triage.

"So what can we do?" he asked.

"We can go deeper on that guy with the Beemer," I said.

"You have his name," Garner said.

"Arthur Kling," Camilo said, checking his notebook. I nodded. That was close enough to Klein, the name Sharon had given me during our tete-a-tete at the Lone Pine convenience store. She had had a snootful and couldn't remember clearly.

"Illinois DMV gives his address as Twenty-two ten North Remington Avenue in Chicago," Camilo continued.

"That's a gentrified old neighborhood, the Chicago cops tell me, full of rehabbed condos popular with young professionals getting ready to settle down and raise families. But the cops have no sheet on him. He's clean."

"And all we have him on is being present at a place where we had found a body earlier."

"Not quite enough," Garner said. "We don't know that he'd ever been there at the same time the body was. Matter of fact, he probably hadn't, not if he was looking for a geocache. Only way to find out is to ask him."

"Yes, but grabbing him up for questioning might spook the other perps," I said, "so we've decided to move slowly on him."

"You sure there are others?" said the prosecutor.

"I think there has to be at least one other," I replied. "Those bodies are heavy. And there might be as many as seven perps, if those coins left on the body at Watersmeet mean what they might mean."

"Be that as it may," Alex said, "one of the perps just has to be local. I just know it. Yeah, it's possible to Google good hiding spots on the Internet, but even with that the Poor Farm isn't the sort of place outsiders are likely to know about. That one is probably an inside job. Hell, it's got to be."

"So what now?" Garner leaned back in his oaken swivel chair. It squeaked.

"I'll go talk to Phil Wilson," I said. "Maybe he knows other geocaching fans in the county. Maybe one of them is our guy."

"I can check out Arthur Kling," Alex said. I'll call in a marker at Chicago Homicide." The Chicago police automatically would send an investigator to question Kling if we asked, but a detective who owed a favor would try harder on an out-of-town request.

"You know any profilers, Alex?" I said. "If these are freaks we're dealing with, maybe a profiler can help us figure out what's going on in their heads."

The others glanced at me dubiously. Criminal psychological profilers are favorites of pulp fiction writers and television dramas, but many detectives in the field have doubts about them. They're not often much help catching perps, although they're terrific at shrinking their brains afterward. True, they have had successes, like psychics who divine where a body is buried. Cynical cops, however, argue that profilers and psychics come to their conclusions only after other people have done all the shoe-leather work, eliminating the impossibilities and leaving nuggets of truth for the shrinks and mediums to divine. I kept an open mind about them. So did Alex.

He nodded. "I'll talk to a good friend at Lansing who's a profiler. She's a pretty good psychologist and might have some ideas for us."

"Okay," said Garner. "We'll meet back here when somebody has something solid."

As the gathering broke up, Alex cornered me on the way out.

"Ten days to go," he said.

"To what?" I was just playing dumb, but Alex missed the joke.

"The *primary*, you idiot."

SIXTEEN

The moment of truth—at least the one about the election—was almost upon me.

"In Bergland last night," Alex said, "Eli was holding forth on WPRC"—the local FM station, devoted to country and talk—"about the three bodies that've turned up in Porcupine County that the deputies can't seem to identify. He said that if he was in charge that wouldn't have happened."

"The bodies or the identification?" I asked.

"He didn't say. He didn't have to."

"Not good."

"Not good."

"So you're going to have to tell Horace why Eli's wrong." With his chin Alex pointed to the Herald reporter, sitting patiently outside the sheriff's squadroom, notebook in hand. "Good luck."

As Alex left I beckoned Horace into the squadroom and sat him in a chair next to my desk.

"What's on your mind?" I asked the reporter.

"You know perfectly well what's on my mind, Steve," said Horace, who actually is quite friendly toward me and never misses a chance to make me look good. Eli has offended him several times, more than once in a humiliating way. Horace is a dapper fellow, affecting suits and colorful bow ties in a place where they are worn primarily to funerals. Horace also fulminates against gays in the right-wing editorials he writes, but his dress once caused Eli to call him an "old queen" on a radio show. Whether or not Horace, a retired Milwaukee newspaperman, is that or just flamboyant I don't know and don't care. He tries hard to be unbiased in his reporting and sometimes succeeds, but I am glad that when he fails it is usually in my favor. But he had not endorsed me for sheriff in the colorful and highly conservative op-ed columns he writes when his dander is up. He knew that if Eli won, he'd have to get along with the old sheriff, so he tried not to offend him needlessly.

I did know what was on Horace's mind, but I played it coy. "Tell me," I said.

"Those bodies. You know. Last night Sheriff Garrow all but said you were incompetent."

Eli hadn't, not quite. Election etiquette in Upper Michigan doesn't permit direct attacks of that kind. But he had left the possibility dangling unsaid on the air where everybody could hear it. And Horace was running with that possibility, like the good reporter he is.

"Well, Mr. Wright," I said—I call him Horace most of the time but "Mr. Wright" when we're dealing with each other professionally—"you know very well I can't comment on an ongoing investigation. All I can tell you is that we have discovered three human bodies where they should not have been."

"I've heard they've been mutilated. How?"

Joe Koski may be a gossip, but he is a careful one. Most likely the information had come from a blabbermouth at the crime lab in Marquette. It happens. But the exact details hadn't gotten out.

"That will have to remain confidential for legal reasons," I said. That could be true, but the most important reason was that we didn't want the perps knowing we knew what we knew.

"Name one."

"*Mr. Wright!*" I had to laugh. Horace was a persistent cuss.

"All right, all right."

"But I can tell you that we believe that although the bodies were dumped in Porcupine and Gogebic Counties, the deaths took place elsewhere."

"So it is not a murder investigation?"

"I can't comment on that."

"Can you comment on what Sheriff Garrow said last night in Bergland?"

"Exactly what did he say?"

"Quote. 'If they hadn't run me off I'd have got to the bottom of this long ago.' Unquote."

"All I will say about that is I'm surprised Sheriff Garrow thinks he was run off. He said he was taking a few days off a few months ago after the prosecutor asked him to stand aside and let somebody else run for the office, and he never bothered to come back. The rest of us go to work every day and do our jobs."

"Thanks, Steve," Horace said delightedly. "There's my lead." All I had voiced were facts that everyone knew — but facts neither candidate had articulated up to now.

And Horace's would be a good story, I was sure. He is an old pro. People would be clucking with excitement when the front-page leader was published the following Wednesday. What I had said was Porcupine County's version of a savage political counterpunch. It might even win me a few votes.

As Horace left Joe Koski looked up, grinning, and gave me the thumbs-up sign.

SEVENTEEN

Ginny and I were sitting in her kitchen that evening when Tommy bounced downstairs from his room in his Pony League uniform.

"Hello, Mr. Martinez," Tommy said gravely.

"Evening, Tommy. What've you been doing?"

"Surfing on the *wiinindibmakakoons.*"

"And that is?" I said.

"*Ojibwemowin* for computer. Means 'little brain box.' "

Ojibwemowin is the language of the Anishinaabe, the Ojibwa word for themselves. Anishinaabe means "Original People."

"I've heard something like that," I said. "An Ojibwa medicine man who once visited my cabin called my laptop a *windibaanens* and said that meant 'little brain machine.' I guess that means *Ojibwemowin* has more than one word for many things, just like English."

Tommy shot me one of those "maybe-the-old-guy-isn't-as-dumb-as-I-thought-he-was" looks the young of any culture often display when surprised by their elders.

"Find anything interesting?" I asked.

"Yes, an Anishinaabe story." Like most large surviving Native American tribes, the Ojibwa have committed much of their history and their culture to the World Wide Web. "It's the story about how the dog came to the Anishinaabe."

"Tell us."

Tommy scratched back a chair on the kitchen floor and sat down at the table. This would be a long story. Ginny and I sat down, too.

"Two Anishinaabe in a canoe got lost in a storm on the lake and were blown onto a strange beach," Tommy began, with the same faraway look I had seen in the eyes of all kinds of Indian storytellers. He recited from memory, not from a computer printout. This lad had been taught the traditions of his people and he knew how to repeat a narrative. His voice had subtly changed from a boy's to an Ojibwa storyteller's, almost a singsong, with inflections and colorations that added subtle meanings to nouns and verbs. Back on the reservation, he must have listened to the old ones tell the ancient tales, and their style clearly had made an impression on him. Maybe he would become a storyteller himself, one in much demand at powwows. I began to feel both envy and pleasure at his rootedness. An orphan Tommy may be, but he has a greater sense of belonging than I did. His links to his origins have never been broken.

"When they saw huge footprints on the beach they were frightened," Tommy continued. "Soon a giant with a caribou hanging from his belt like a rabbit came walking down the beach. The giant told the Anishinaabe he was a friend and to come home with him. They were tired and hungry and had lost their weapons in the storm, so they followed the giant to his lodge.

"That night a *windigo* snuck into the lodge and told the Anishinaabe the giant had hidden other men away to eat them. The *windigo* pretended to be their friend, but he was actually the eater of people."

A *windigo,* I knew, was an evil spirit analogous to the demons of Christian teaching.

"But the giant would not give him the two men and grew angry. He took a big stick and turned over a big bowl with it. Out jumped an animal the Anishinaabe had never seen before. It looked like a wolf, but the giant called it 'Dog' and told it to kill the evil windigo. Dog shook himself, and began to grow huge and fierce. He sprang at the windigo and killed him. Then Dog shrank down and crept back under the bowl.

"The Anishinaabe were so happy with what happened that the giant gave Dog to them, although he was his old buddy. He said Dog would take them home. They went to the beach and the giant gave Dog a command. Dog grew bigger and bigger until he was almost as big as a horse. The Anishinaabe held tight to the back of Dog as he ran into the water and hung on while he swam and swam for a long time.

Many days later Dog saw a part of the coast the Anishinaabe knew, so he headed for shore. As they came close to the beach Dog shrank back to his normal size so the Anishinaabe had to swim the rest of the way.

"When they reached shore Dog disappeared into the forest. When the Anishinaabe told their tribe what had happened, the people thought the men were lying. 'Show us your little mystery animal,' the chief said, 'and we'll believe you.'

"A few moons rose and fell, and then one morning Dog returned to the two Anishinaabe. It allowed them to pet it and took food from their hands. The tribe was surprised to see the creature, and pleased. And Dog stayed with them.

"And that, as the Anishinaabe say, is how the dog came to the Earth to live with man."

"I love that story!" Ginny said, looking a bit confused. "What's the moral, though?"

"North American Indian stories don't necessarily have obvious morals, or even points, in the sense that Western European stories do," I said, unable to keep a touch of academic loftiness out of my voice. "But they're rich in irony. You have to think about them, let them sink into you."

Tommy nodded and glanced at me with another you're-not-as-stupid-as-I-thought expression. He was, I thought, putting me through some kind of a test. Or maybe the spirits were using him to send me a message about the growing mystery of the three corpses. There was a lot more to this lad than met the eye.

"I'm sure the Lakota have a story very much like that," I said. "Maybe someday you can show me how to find it on the computer."

"Sure," Tommy said, and smiled. He was smiling at me more and more these days. I thought I was getting somewhere with him.

"Almost time for the ball game," Ginny said as a honk resounded from the driveway.

"See ya later!" Tommy said, suddenly a little boy again, and dashed out the door to his ride.

When he was gone I turned to Ginny and said, "There was a reason he told that story, but I don't know what it is. I had the distinct feeling I was being sent an important message."

"You are so dense, Stevie Two Crow, but I love you anyway."

"Huh?"

"Steve, Tommy was just telling us he wants a dog."

EIGHTEEN

Two days later, after the usual conversation between a
youngster and the adults in his life about responsibility for the
dog's care, we came home from the Porcupine County Animal
Shelter with a scrawny yellow Labrador mix someone had
abandoned on the baseball diamond with a water bowl, a
name tag that said "Hogan" and a paper sign around his neck
that read "Free to a good home." Hogan, who the vet said was
about three years old and weighed a rib-revealing sixty-five
pounds, had the graceful, alert conformation of a Lab and
from a distance could be mistaken for a purebred. But the vet
said his deep-set teeth, broad chest, narrow waist, slim tail,
basketball head and steam-shovel chops suggested pit bull
somewhere in his ancestry and probably not far back, either.

I had owned a couple of pitties as a boy, and I knew
that the breed's reputation for viciousness was largely myth
fostered by unscrupulous personal injury lawyers, lazy cops
and a gullible and often cynical press that knew headlines
such as "PIT BULL ATTACKS CHILD" sold newspapers. Cops, I
knew, will often identify any rogue dog as a pit bull, even if it
may have so little of that breed in it that it bears no
resemblance to the real thing, for "pit bull" is easier to spell on
a report sheet than "Viszla." Pitties were originally bred to
fight other dogs, not people, and their noisy combativeness is
almost always directed at fellow members of their species. It's
true that drug dealers and other such lowlifes train pit bulls as
attack dogs, but just about any breed can be cruelly goaded
into such aggressiveness. Pitties' natural instinct is to cherish
people, and treated with kindness, they make great family
dogs. I'd rather have a pit bull than a cocker spaniel, the breed
that any vet will tell you bites people more often than any
other.

From the first Hogan was friendly enough with Ginny and me, but Tommy was clearly his main man. At home, boy and dog immediately became inseparable. Hogan lay under the desk while Tommy worked, under the table while Tommy ate, and by his bed while Tommy slept. Out on the beach, they played for hours, chasing each other up and down in great explosions of sand. Despite his Labrador genes Hogan showed absolutely no interest in swimming and just gazed at Tommy in puzzlement when he threw a stick for the dog to fetch. Instead, Hogan displayed the pit bull's propensity for dashing about in happy abandon, butt tucked underneath, eyes rolling, ears flying. Everywhere and all the time he insisted on being petted, a task Tommy enjoyed, and would sharply lever his massive muzzle up under our hands if we neglected his loving. "Grubbing," Tommy called it. Hogan was "the Grubber." He had both the Lab's sweet, clumsy nature and the pittie's unbridled, tail-wagging exuberance — a singular and sometimes dangerous combination for delicate objects on the coffee table, especially since he quickly filled out, soon reaching a solid eighty-five pounds of muscle and bone. When asked if he wanted to go for a walk or to be fed, Hogan would suddenly burst into an excited little dance Ginny called "the pit bull two-step," his claws drumming an Irish dancer's *rat-tat-tat* on the wooden floor. Tommy, I was coming to learn, was his own boy and Hogan in turn was his own dog.

Ginny was pleased by the turn of events. "Tommy's an orphan," she said, "and Hogan's an orphan, and because of that they take care of each other in ways we can't even begin to imagine."

"Does it need to be as deep as that?" I asked. "Maybe they're just a boy and his dog."

"You could be right, Steve. But I don't think so. You always simplify things that can't be simplified and complicate things that don't need to be complicated."

I didn't argue.

NINETEEN

"I've got bad news, Steve," Alex said without preamble on the phone from his office in Wakefield. "Arthur Kling seems to have taken a powder."

"Hmm?"

"About a week ago, my source in Chicago said, a neighbor saw him pack his car with camping gear and drive away. His boss at the Fidelity office in the Loop says he didn't put in for time off and just left."

"Anyone report him missing?"

"The boss. After two days he got worried and called the Chicago police. That was about the same time my guy started looking for him."

"The neighbor or anybody else have any ideas where he might have gone?"

"Not a clue. He didn't tell anyone in his apartment complex where he was going, and when the cops got in they found nothing that would suggest he wasn't coming back. It looked quite normal. He left clothes, possessions, fresh food in the fridge, all the sort of stuff anybody would come home to."

"What did the boss say about his behavior?"

"He said Kling's a good investment analyst, but shy and nervous, and in the last few weeks his mind seemed to be elsewhere. He's not the kind who makes friends in the office and he didn't tell anybody what was going on in his life, so far as the boss knows."

"So he didn't know anything about Kling's hobbies?"

"Nothing, except that Kling seemed to be an outdoors type, a hiker. On casual Fridays he'd wear stuff from L.L. Bean, Lands' End, Cabela's, those stores. And a couple of times he left a phone number where he could be reached on weekends."

"What was it?"

"The Evergreen Lodge." That was a small lakefront Mom-and-Pop motel on M-64 close to the Wolverine Mountains Wilderness State Park in the western reaches of the county. A gentle elderly couple, the Lemppainens, owned and operated it.

"Check it out already?"

"Did I roll off the turnip wagon yesterday?" Alex said in irritation.

"Who knows?"

"He's not there."

"The Lemppainens have anything to say?" I asked.

"Not much. Kling was quiet, polite, kept to himself, was gone most of the time. Paid cash, though he reserved the rooms with a credit card. The Lemppainens didn't save the number and don't remember the bank."

"Damn. No other paper trail?"

"No. I got Garner to subpoena his Visa and Master Card billings. Lots of mail-order, local Chicago stuff, but no meals, motels or gas stations north of the Illinois-Wisconsin state line. He thinks he's a smart cookie, but he's not that clever if he left the Lemppainens' number with his boss. That puts him up here."

"And he's been seen by locals," I pointed out. "Slept with, too."

"Hmm. Maybe he wanted to establish his presence up here at a certain time, and hide it at other times. But why?"

I thought for a moment. "Did the Chicago cops find his computer?" Often a hard drive yields clues to the computer owner's plans. People confide things to their computers they'd never trust to a human being.

"No computer in the apartment," Alex said.

"Could've been a laptop," I said. "Maybe he took it along."

"But where would he go?"

"He's up here in the U.P. now," I said. "I'm almost

certain of it."

"Why?"

"You know that returning to the scene of the crime is the most common thing perps do. It's their way of hoarding their own crap, of staying connected to the stuff that's important to them."

"Crap as in—oh, never mind."

"If we can find his car," I continued, "we'll likely find his computer, and I think it might tell us everything we need to know."

"Why are you so sure about that computer?" Alex asked. "Why are you so sure he even has one?"

"A talk I had with Phil Wilson the other day." I had dropped by the Ace Hardware and engaged its owner in conversation about geocaching. After a bit of isn't-it-a-nice-day to-and-froing I asked Phil if he knew of any other geocaching fans in Porcupine County.

"Some," he had said tersely without looking at me. He rarely even glanced at the people he spoke to.

"Who are they?" I asked, and pulled a chair into Phil's small office. This was going to take a while, and the pickings turned out to be slim.

He didn't know their names, he said. Most geocachers identify themselves on the Internet with pseudonyms. That's because they want to keep the focus on the sport, not on the participants. Besides, they also give themselves email addresses on Yahoo.com or Hotmail under invented names so that their personal addresses don't get choked by spam. So much for subpoenaing the membership lists of geocaching Web sites.

Phil said he had met a few fellow geocachers on the trails, and they were friendly enough, but they identified themselves only by their geocaching names. (Phil said his was "Trailboss.") He did know of one other local geocacher by his real name—Willie Kemp, a young garage mechanic, husband of a checker in the supermarket and the father of a little girl. I knew Willie, and while I wouldn't dismiss him entirely as a potential suspect—I learned not to do that years ago—I knew him well enough to doubt that he'd get involved in such a crime as we were investigating. And Phil himself was simple and guileless.

"If these guys who have been strewing bodies over the landscape have their own private Web site," I told Alex, "we'll find clues to it and its members on a computer. Maybe this Kling brought his laptop up here."

"*If* he has a laptop," Alex said.

"True."

"What now?"

"We go hunting for Kling. There's a BOL out for a red BMW, isn't there?" What other jurisdictions call All Points Bulletins, or APBs, we in the Upper Peninsula call Be on the Lookouts, or BOLs.

"First thing I did," Alex said.

"I'll go check with Sharon, that convenience-store clerk Kling got it on with at the dance in Coppermass. Possibly he's contacted her, although from what she said I doubt they'd ever hook up again."

"Do that."

I hung up, grabbed my cap and walked out to the Explorer.

Twenty minutes later I rolled up to the convenience store near Lone Pine, parked and strode inside. The store's owner, an irascible old ex-miner named Mort Johnson, stood behind the counter. Sharon was nowhere in sight.

"Sharon?"

"She don't work here no more."

"Since when?"

"Since yesterday. She didn't come in for her eight-to-five shift and she didn't come in today neither. She won't never work here again."

"She give any notice?"

"None. Just disappeared. God damn it, my arthritis is killing me. I can't cover for airhead bimbo employees no more. I just can't work two jobs at the same time."

He was whining now.

"What do you know about her?" I said.

"She said she came up here from La Crosse and had tended bar down there."

"You check that out? References?"

"Not really." Lazy bastard. I wondered if she invited Mort into the sack from time to time to keep her job.

"She ever say anything about herself?"

"Once when we were in—Once she said her parents were dead and she had no family."

"No photos of her?"

"No." Johnson looked at the floor, at the wall, everywhere but at me. I knew he was lying. Probably he had photographed or taped himself in bed with her. Without a warrant, though, I was helpless to search the place.

Suddenly a chill ran through my veins. Maybe Arthur Kling had returned to Porcupine County intending to make Sharon Shoemaker his newest geocache.

TWENTY

No sooner had I called Alex to ask him to add Sharon to the BOL than I suddenly recalled another election task to perform that very evening: to go up against Eli in a town meeting debate. Nobody in the county could remember the last time there had been such a to-and-fro among the candidates for sheriff. There usually isn't, because in recent decades most offices haven't been contested. But because he had nothing to lose, Eli had suggested going head-to-head, and Jenny Tompkins, the village clerk, had been enchanted with the idea. Not me.

I don't think Eli had ever had formal debate training, but I knew I faced a formidable adversary on the podium. For all his advanced age and often pickled condition, the sheriff was quick on his mental toes, and in front of a crowd exuded friendliness and confidence. As for me, I'm the kind of slow-thinking fellow who comes up with the perfect devastating retort hours after the best time to deliver it.

I feared taking a beating, especially since the ground rules Jenny had laid down said: "No personal attacks. Stick to the issues." Exactly what constituted a personal attack I wasn't sure, but I didn't think pointing out Eli's latter-day failings would please the good people of Porcupine County. Most of them thought of him fondly, and many were unaware of his recent peccadilloes. I would have to tread carefully. Politics in a small Upper Michigan town are pursued with considerably more civility than those on the state and national stages. That's because candidates and voters run into each other every day in the hardware store, at the supermarket and in church. One just doesn't foul one's own nest with casual invective.

I dressed in my best uniform, because I knew Eli would be resplendent in gold braid and all the shiny emblems of membership in various organizations in the county and state he had joined purely for political reasons, never bothering to attend a meeting. He looks the part much more than I do, and if I hadn't known about his faults, I'd have been impressed, too.

Some three hundred people sat wall to wall in folding chairs in the American Legion Hall, hoping for blood, for this was as close to a dogfight as Porcupine County ever got. As the challenger I strode onto the raised stage first, to a chorus of cheers and clapping from — I hoped — at least half the audience. Few boos, and what there were got shushed by indignation. Porkies are much too polite for overt contempt of that kind. When Eli climbed onstage, his decorations twinkling in the lights, at least as many clapped and cheered. We shook hands, then everyone settled down.

Horace Wright, as the county's foremost (and only) political reporter, had been tapped as moderator. He sat at a small table, back to the audience, as Eli and I stood at lecterns a dozen feet apart. Horace opened the proceedings with all the relish of an announcer at a boxing match.

"In this corner," he boomed over the mike, "weighing about two hundred and ten pounds . . . "

The audience chuckled.

" . . . stands Deputy Stephen Two Crow Martinez, candidate for sheriff of Porcupine County. At the other lectern is Sheriff Elias Anthony Garrow, candidate for reelection to the same office. Everyone knows them both. I'm just stating this for the record."

I drew myself up to my full six feet two — Horace had exaggerated my weight by only about ten pounds — and nodded bashfully at the audience. Eli beamed grandly. He did have a dazzling smile.

"Let me just state the qualifications of each candidate," Horace said, fingering a couple of index cards. "First, Deputy Martinez. Forty-four years old. Born in Pine Ridge, South

Dakota, and raised in Troy, New York. A graduate of Cornell University and the criminal justice school at City University of New York. A veteran of three years in the military police of the United States Army, including service in Kuwait and Iraq during Desert Storm, rising to the rank of first lieutenant. A deputy sheriff in Porcupine County for almost a dozen years. A member of the Porcupine County Rod and Gun Club, the Porcupine County Historical Society, and the Friends of the Wolverine Mountains." He turned over the card, looking for more memberships. There weren't any. I've never been much of a joiner.

"And now Sheriff Garrow. Seventy-four years old. Born in Porcupine City and raised in Bruce Crossing. Attended Michigan Tech. Two years in the United States Army, rising to the rank of sergeant. A Vietnam veteran. Forty-seven years of service in Upper Michigan law enforcement, including twenty-four years as sheriff of Porcupine County. Married for forty-seven years. Seven children, nineteen grandchildren. A member of St. Matthew's Episcopal Church in Porcupine City, the American Legion, the Veterans of Foreign Wars, the Michigan Sheriffs Association . . ." Listing all of Eli's mostly specious memberships took seemingly a full minute.

"Here's how we're going to do this," Horace said when he finally came up for air. "I'll ask one question of each candidate, who will have two minutes to answer the question. The other candidate will have one minute to rebut. Then I'll throw the floor open to questions from the audience. Same rules, two minutes to answer, one to rebut. That okay with you both?"

Eli and I nodded.

"Now then. We all know that in the last few years, state and federal funds for rural law enforcement have been drastically cut. How do you think the Porcupine County Sheriff's Department should deal with this? Deputy Martinez, you first."

I took a deep breath. This was the biggest question on

everybody's mind, and Gil and I had gone over my answer carefully. Whatever I said, I was to propose *no new taxes*.

"In the last year the department has had to let two vacancies for deputies go unfilled and spread the work of the rest around as much as it can to cover the gaps," I said. "Everyone knows that. We had no choice."

I looked over at Eli. He nodded. This had happened on his watch, but it wasn't his fault.

"So we've had five deputies cover the eight-to-four and four-to-midnight watches, two on each watch," I said. "We pulled the single deputy off the midnight-to-eight watch during the week, because nothing much ever happens after midnight, except on weekends, of course. There's always a dispatcher, who also works as jailer, on each of the three watches. Two of us are always on call if we're needed. But with two deputies short, there's little coverage for vacations or sickness. We have to put in a lot of overtime. Until we get more money, I don't see this pattern as changing. But we're managing."

I nodded to Horace, yielding the floor.

"Eli?" Horace said.

"The deputy is right," he said, jabbing his finger toward me and then toward the audience, "but there's a solution. It's to be more aggressive in seeking grant money for personnel. I promise that if I'm re-elected we'll find enough money to field a full complement of deputies, and that we'll always have two deputies out on patrol twenty-four hours a day, seven days a week. The safety of Porcupine County is our number one priority. I promise you that."

Much of the audience clapped. They didn't know that thanks to draconian federal belt-tightening, grant money for police personnel had all but dried up all over the state of Michigan. I should have mentioned that in my answer, but I'm not a debater. I should have pointed out that Sheriff Eli Garrow had plenty of time to write grants but hadn't been in the office for weeks to do so, but I'm not a debater. I think of all this stuff too late, for I'm not a debater. And so Eli took the first round on points.

"Thank you," Horace said. "Now, Sheriff, here is my question for you. What do you think is the most important task of the sheriff of Porcupine County?"

I was appalled. That was practically a gift, the kind of question that could be answered easily with ringing campaign slogans. But Horace was smarter than that.

Eli rose to the bait. "Why, to make Porcupine Countians feel safe!" he declared. "To have law enforcement on the job twenty-four seven. And the best way to do that is to have a sheriff who's been in the county all his life, who's raised a family here, who goes to church here, who's one of us!" He beamed a triumphal smile out over the audience, a good part of which broke into applause.

"Deputy Martinez, your rebuttal?" I could have sworn Horace winked at me as he fed me the ball like a quarterback at the line of scrimmage. And I didn't drop it.

I looked directly at Eli and said, "The most important task of a sheriff is to be on the job twenty-four seven, to be in his office every day doing administrative work so that his undersheriff and his deputies can be out there attending to the safety of all residents of Porcupine County. For reasons you will have to ask him about, the current sheriff has not been seen in his office for almost five months. The undersheriff has been doing the job instead, and so have the deputies. This is not an accusation of anything. This is a simple statement of fact."

The entire audience gasped. Chairs skidded back and both my cheering section and Eli's roared. The sheriff blanched. Horace pounded his table with the gavel until everyone had settled down. Round two to me.

"All right then," Horace said. "Now we will entertain questions from the audience."

A sea of hands shot up. Horace pointed to a small,

gray-haired woman in the front row. "Peggy Toivonen," he said, "what's your question?"

Most of the audience winced. Peggy Toivonen was an irascible octogenarian who lived alone in a little house on Norwich Road, and like so many of her age, she thought the world revolved about her and looked at local, national and world issues entirely in their capacity to affect her personally. And she didn't disappoint our expectations. Peggy levered herself to her feet with her cane and demanded, "When's the county going to fix my driveway? The highway plows carved it up last winter and nobody's come out to fix it!"

"Now, Peggy," said Horace, "that's a matter for the road department, not the sheriff."

"Let me answer!" Eli bellowed. "Mrs. Toivonen, I'll make sure it gets fixed. You go home and get a good night's sleep. I'll take care of everything."

Horace looked hopefully at me for the rebuttal.

"Horace is right," I said. "Road repairs are properly the job of the road department. I can't imagine the sheriff having anything to do with that. We've got crime to fight."

"Hey —" Eli tried to cut in.

"Sorry, Sheriff," Horace said. "You had your two minutes. Other questions?" Hands shot up. Horace chose one. "Will Brenner, what's on your mind?" I darted a glance at Horace. Brenner, a retired Bergland contractor, was a Garrow cousin, a hostile. But Horace knew what he was doing.

"This question is for Deputy Martinez. Can you give me a rundown of the changes in crime rates in Porcupine County over the last ten years?" I could see the setup coming, but I was ready for it.

"Yes. Burglaries are down seven per cent, petty larceny eight per cent, general misdemeanors nine per cent," I said, enumerating a dozen classifications. "I'd anticipated the question and had looked up the figures that morning. "There were just four murders, same as in the previous ten years.

Things have gotten quieter."

"And that all happened on my watch!" Eli interrupted with perfect timing. Cheers broke out.

Horace went to work with his gavel. "You're out of order, Eli!"

"I'm not finished, Sheriff," I said. "The crime rates are down across the board in Porcupine County because the population fell almost ten per cent in those ten years. There are just fewer of us to commit offenses. Actually, when the drop in population is factored in, the rate of offenses is about the same as it was a decade ago. People have pretty much stayed the same."

Horace turned to the sheriff. "Eli?"

"No answer," Eli said, quietly fuming. Round three to the deputy.

Hands shot up again, and Horace chose one. "What's yours, Emily Hahn?" he asked.

"This is for Sheriff Garrow," said the middle-aged housewife from Green. "We know that three bodies have been found in Porcupine County in the last few weeks. All we have heard is that the sheriff's department thinks they died outside the county and were just dumped there. What's going on?"

That the question had been addressed to Eli and not me suggested that Emily, and probably many other voters, didn't get it: Eli was sheriff in name only. He wouldn't know what was going on, not if he didn't come into the office for briefings. And his answer proved his ignorance, although I wasn't sure Emily understood.

"If I'm reelected, Emily," Eli said with a broad smile, "people won't be dumping bodies in our wonderful county. You can count on that."

"That's not an answer!" shouted someone in the audience.

"They're dumping 'em *now* and you're the sheriff!" shouted another. Not all of the audience bought Eli's smoke screens. Horace pounded his gavel.

When the room settled down Horace turned to me and said, "Care to rebut, Deputy?"

"I'm sorry, everyone," I said, and echoed my words to Horace a few days before. His story was scheduled to appear the following morning. "I cannot comment on an ongoing investigation. I can tell you, however, that the investigation has reached a sensitive phase. I can assure you all that when we are finished we will give you all the facts."

That was a slick evasion, though all of it was true, and it surprised me that I had the wit to come up with that meaningless "sensitive phase." Maybe I had been hanging around Eli Garrow too much. Maybe I was turning into a politician. Round four to me, though.

The questions resumed. "Where do you stand on abortion?" Father Jim Sweet wanted to know. Even at the lowly county level, candidates all around the United States these days are always asked where they stand on hot cultural issues. For many voters a candidate's character is more important than his actions, and they measure that character by how close the candidate's publicly announced beliefs on the issues of the day are to their own, no matter how irrelevant they may be to the office he is seeking.

"I am sworn to uphold the law," I said, "and uphold the law I will." The priest sat back down, clearly annoyed at the rope-a-dope answer.

"I'm against abortion," Eli said in rebuttal, "but the law's the law. I can't do anything until the law's changed. I'll do everything I can to change the law."

Several members of the audience snickered. How a lowly county sheriff in an obscure corner of the Upper Midwest was going to present an argument to the United States Supreme Court to overturn Roe v. Wade beggared the imagination.

"How about ho-mo-sex-u-al marriage?" someone in the crowd shouted. Michigan had outlawed that in the state in the last election but many Michiganders wanted an amendment to the United States Constitution as well.

"You're out of order!" said Horace, banging his gavel. He pointed at another man in the back. "Your question?"

"How about it, then, Eli? How about homosexual marriage?"

"An abomination," Eli said. "It'll never happen while I'm sheriff." He fulminated on, warning against the dangers to the American family of unwitting incest, unbridled public sodomy and the rest of the bogeymen the subject tends to bring up in people who feel strongly about the issue.

"Deputy?" Horace prompted.

"Edna?" I called. Edna Juntunen was the longtime county clerk and the issuer of marriage licenses. I had spotted her while walking into the hall.

"Yes, Steve?" She stood up in the middle of the audience, an upright little woman everyone respected, for she never acted as if she thought her job was a right although she certainly considered it a duty.

"Edna, how many gay or lesbian couples have come to you in the last ten years asking for marriage licenses?"

"None. No sirree. Not one."

"I have to congratulate the sheriff," I said. "It all happened on his watch."

The place rang with laughter and Eli looked poleaxed.

The appointed ending hour having arrived, Horace gaveled the meeting to a close as the audience stirred restlessly, people squabbling among themselves. As we left the stage, Horace beamed at me, as if I'd been the winner by a TKO.

At the door Edna patted my hand. "You done good, Steve."

"I hope so."

"I know so," said. "You showed up that old blowhard for what he is. A lot of people had their eyes opened tonight."

I went home feeling pretty good about the events of the

day, so good I forgot all about Sharon Shoemaker until the next morning.

TWENTY-ONE

Stewing at my desk the next day, baffled and frustrated by the three corpses and worried about the fate of Sharon Shoemaker, I had an idea. To get a feel for the sport, I'd go geocaching and hide a treasure in the woods myself. Maybe that'd give me some insight into our perps' modus operandi— how they chose their sites, for instance. It was time to get aggressive instead of just reacting to events. The smart lawman tries to head the bad guys off at the pass, not chase them through it.

Besides, I didn't know what else to do.

And so on my day off the following Saturday, I stopped by Ginny's to pick up a rucksack and raid her refrigerator for a bit of lunch before starting off into the woods.

"And where are we going?" Ginny said, her eyes widening as I constructed a towering sandwich out of salami, lettuce, tomatoes, mustard and slices from a loaf of Russian black bread she had scored the previous day in Rhinelander. "That looks good."

"We?"

"The editorial we, I mean. I have things to do at the historical society this afternoon."

"Bummer. You'd have fun."

At that, the front door opened and Tommy marched in, Hogan lolloping by his side and bouncing off my legs.

"Why don't you take him along?" Ginny said.

"Well . . . "

"Take me along where?"

What the hell. I could use the company. "The woods," I said. "I'm going to try this geocaching thing."

"Cool," Tommy said. "Now I can see if my new GPS works."

"Oh, it does, I'm sure," I said. Ginny had bought Tommy an inexpensive used GPS, a simple hiker's model, during a previous shopping foray to Rhinelander . With it the delighted lad had taken so many waypoint fixes along the beach that the unit ran out of room to store them and he had to purge the memory for new ones. Now he could go into the woods and fix some fresh new waypoints.

"Can Hogan go, too?"

"I don't see how I can prevent that from happening," I said as the dog companionably leaned his bulk against my leg and licked my hand.

"Double cool. What are you going to cache?"

"Uh . . . I hadn't thought about that yet."

Tommy clearly had. "Ginny, can I have a bowl?" he said. "One of those things with a plastic lid?"

From a kitchen cabinet she fished a squarish Tupperware cake container with a lid, ten inches long by eight inches wide and three inches deep. "Will this do?"

"Yes!" Tommy said. "It'll be great."

"What are we going to put in it?" I asked.

"Toys," he said. "A notebook and a couple of pencils."

He rummaged in a kitchen drawer and came up with a couple of spools, a rubber bathtub duckie, a STP key ring, a folding corkscrew from a Paris hotel, a couple of Heineken coasters, a two-year-old road map of Michigan, a blank CD, two dime-store earrings, a tiny screwdriver, a comb, a Schoolhouse Rock children's book, two Hot Stuff balloons, a bag of ore pellets from a mine in Ishpeming, three refrigerator magnets, a roll of Velcro tape, and finally a spiral notepad and two golf pencils.

With a felt-tip pen he wrote on a note card:

THIS IS A GEOCACHE.
The name of the cache is TallBear's Cache.
If you do not play, please put the box back where you found it. Thank you.

If you play, take something but leave something. Write down in the notebook your name and the date. Write down what you took and what you left. Then put the box back. Then go to TallBear's Cache on www.cache-it.com and write that you found it.

Thank you. TallBear.

"Is that your caching nickname?" I said.

"Yup." Tommy taped the card to the underside of the container lid and sealed the box. "There," he said. "Once we've hidden it we'll take down the GPS waypoint coordinates and then put them on the Web site."

"You sure seem to know what you're doing," I said.

"I read up on it on the Internet," he replied.

Ginny smiled proudly. This boy did not lead a life of cultural isolation, as did so many youngsters on Indian reservations. His connections extended into the now and the future as well as the past. Tommy was a thoroughly modern American kid.

"All right. Let's go. Bring Hogan's leash."

We drove east to Porcupine City and south on U.S. 45 to Bruce Crossing, then headed west on M-28. Half an hour after leaving Ginny's home, we stopped at the well-marked entry to a snowmobile trail that led deep into the Ottawa National Forest. In the summers the path was used by hikers and four-wheeler all-terrain vehicles, and at any time of the year it carved an easily visible trail through the woods and brush.

As Tommy clipped Hogan's leash to his collar, I reached into the glove box and fished my .357 Combat Magnum out of its leather holster. Checking the cartridges, I slipped the revolver into my fanny pack. We set off northward on the snowmobile/ATV trail, Tommy checking our progress on a hiker's topographical map with his hand-held GPS as we strode in tandem atop the flat and level dirt track that plunged into the brush ahead. I carried my GPS, too, but let Tommy do the trailblazing. The boy quickly picked up the trick of finding our spot on Earth by comparing the GPS readout with the latitude and longitude ticks on the edges of the map. I grasped one end of Hogan's leash, but the dog trotted ahead alongside Tommy, as if they had been joined at the hip. From time to time, just to be companionable, he clumsily bumped against Tommy, throwing the boy off his stride, but Tommy didn't mind and rumpled Hogan's ears whenever that happened.

"Heads up, Tommy!" I said just before the lad, his head down as he watched the numbers change on his GPS, crashed into a sapling that had fallen over the track. "Gotta watch where you're going, too!"

He grinned, amused and embarrassed at the same time. Smart, and can laugh at himself, too.

After a while we hove alongside a clump of aspen I knew well. "Tommy, can you see what's in there?"

"Yeah. What's that?" Through the aspen we could see a rusty metal standard, ten feet high, atop which was bolted a splintered wooden V that once had been painted white, one arm of the V broken off halfway.

"An old railroad whistle post," I said. "This trail was a logging railroad a hundred years ago, and the engineers blew their locomotive whistles as they passed by the post so that people down the tracks would know a train was coming. Somehow, when the railroad was abandoned long ago and the tracks and signs were torn up, the salvagers missed the post. And everybody who walks along this trail never sees it, because you've got to be looking for it to see it. Only a few people know about it, and now you're one of them."

For a moment Tommy didn't answer. He was, I knew, contemplating the small gift I had bestowed upon him: I had entrusted him with special knowledge. Then he turned to me, smiled, reached out a hand and touched my sleeve. It was, I knew, his silent way of saying "Thanks." For Indians, gestures are as important as words and sometimes say more.

Hogan looked up at us both and wagged his tail.

"Let's press on," I said.

Forty-five minutes after setting out, we reached a clearing where the trail dipped as it forded the west branch of the Porcupine River, really a narrow but deep creek this far upstream. A steep rapids had carved its way between two low ridges, part of the Trap Hills, and the water gurgled as it pirouetted, corkscrewed and stair-stepped over basalt boulders and sandstone slabs.

"This looks like a good place to hide the cache," I said. "A GPS antenna would have a pretty clear view of the sky. But where's a good spot? What about here?" I pointed under a low overhang a dozen feet from the water.

"Too low," Tommy said. That surprised me.

"How do you know?" I asked.

"Look at the mark up there on the ridge. The water gets up to there in the spring when the creek floods."

He was right. Tommy Standing Bear had been born to the forest. Someone had taught him woodcraft, maybe his father, maybe the uncle who was waiting to take him in.

"So where's a better spot?" I asked.

"Let's look around."

"Under that downed tree?" I said. Just like the cache near Watersmeet.

"Too easy," Tommy said. "That'd be the first place anybody would look. Got to make it harder."

"You've been studying up on this, haven't you?"

"Yup."

Hiding something in plain sight is an art. The trick is to find a spot the normal eye would quickly pass over at first, but one that, upon finally being found, turns out to be the most logical and obvious hiding place yet causes the finder to marvel at the cleverness of the hider. And Tommy found it.

It was a twenty-foot by ten-foot level stretch of broken shale, flat gray rock that had been part of the original streambed millions of years ago. The shale had been shattered by weathering into irregular pieces ranging from the size of a pie plate to a manhole cover. Deep potholes pocked the gaps between the pieces. The shale stood well above the high-water mark.

"This looks about right," said Tommy, who fell to his knees and pulled the Tupperware container from his rucksack. He placed it into a pothole of sufficient depth and dragged a nearby slab of shale over it, strewing a few more pieces around.

"It's perfect, Tommy. Nobody's going to find it unless they're looking hard for it, and it'll take 'em a while. There's no trampled grass or packed down dirt to give away the spot."

"Yeah!" The lad's smile was the broadest I'd seen yet on his handsome little face.

"All right, let's measure a waypoint."

Tommy stood atop the cache with his GPS and called out the coordinates showing on the device's screen as I wrote them on a notepad. He walked a hundred feet south, stopped, then returned to the original spot, again calling out the coordinates he read from the GPS. He repeated the procedure, walking a hundred feet west, then north, then south. We looked at the four coordinates I had recorded. All of them showed numbers identical to the second decimal place, but varying slightly over the third. A possible twenty-foot error, quite accurate for a hiker's GPS.

With pencil and paper Tommy averaged the coordinates. Finally he levered up the slab, pulled the container out and wrote the final coordinates on the note card taped to the inside of the lid. Then he replaced container and slab and smoothed his handiwork.

"Easy to get to," I said, "but not so easy to find."

"Not so easy to find," Tommy said agreeably.

"Okay, let's start back."

We had not gone a hundred yards when Tommy again plucked at my sleeve.

"Steve!" he said in a harsh whisper. It was the first time he had called me by my first name. "Look!"

Four adult gray wolves gazed down at us from scarcely a hundred feet away at the top of a high ridge. They were beautiful specimens, their coats thick and healthy, their almond-shaped yellow eyes fixed on ours. They made no sound. We made no sound. They did not move. We did not move. Humans and animals held each other's stares for long seconds. Hogan, who had neither seen nor smelled the wolves, sat unconcernedly on his haunches, gazing into the creek below. Then slowly I reached into my fanny pack and pulled out the .357.

Most Porkies never bother to carry weapons into the woods unless they're actively hunting, and I don't either, but this trip was different, for we had Hogan with us. Gray wolves have returned to the Upper Peninsula and have established so many new packs that the federal government wants to remove them from the protected species list in order to control their numbers by hunting. Wolves will attack any dogs they encounter, for they consider their fellow canines competitors for food and territory. The .357 was simple insurance that any such meeting would not end unhappily.

Pointing the .357 downward, I said in a low whisper, "Let's go, Tommy. Keep your eye on the wolves and don't run. Walk slowly."

We moved away down the track. The wolves trotted silently along the ridge, watching and following us as we passed below. One of the animals split away and ran farther down the outcropping ahead of us, as if to set up an ambush.

Then the wind shifted and Hogan caught their scent. First his hackles rose all along his back, then he emitted a low growl, followed by a growing snarl full of rocks and nails, and finally a heavy bark, like the backfire of a dump truck. The wolves answered with vicious snarls, baring yellow teeth. Hogan strained at his leash and I had to set my feet against his powerful pull. He was ready to rumble.

Some of his ancestors had been bred for fighting, and he was all muscle and sinew, with powerful jaws. Possibly he could acquit himself well against a lone wolf—but not a pack of them. Two or more operating in tandem would make short work of the biggest and strongest domestic dog.

And that is why I had brought the .357. Not to save Tommy and me, for wolves rarely attack human beings, but to protect Hogan.

"Stand back, Tommy," I said. "Cover your ears."

Into soft ground a few feet away I fired two rapid shots, the heavy cough of the Magnum shattering the silence and reverberating throughout the woods. The wolves quickly turned tail and fled, the curtains of the forest swiftly closing behind them as if they had never been there.

Hogan, I noticed, alerted at the shots but did not spook, as most dogs would have. He had almost certainly spent his puppyhood in a household with guns, probably a hunter's. There was so much we didn't know about him. But what we did know was encouraging.

Quickly I ejected the two spent cartridges from the revolver's cylinder and replaced them with fresh loads. We wouldn't need the weapon again that day, I thought, but better be safe than sorry.

I looked at Tommy. He stood calmly, no fear on his face, no relief at having survived what many non-Indians would have considered a potentially dangerous encounter with powerful wild beasts. Instead he gazed at me with that unreadable expression I had grown used to in his presence.

"Think I did the right thing?" I said.

He didn't hesitate. "Yeah. No point killing them. They did what they're supposed to do. They checked us out and then they left."

I was silently impressed. This boy knew how to live with his fellow creatures. He had been taught well. He was a native of the forest, at one with his environment, an existence I was often painfully conscious of not sharing.

"Let's head back now, Tommy," I said. "We've done what we set out to do."

We trudged back to my Jeep, the Magnum in my right hand and pointing downward, ready if the wolves backtracked and attacked—which I doubted they would. That species may be fearless but it is not stupid. From time to time Hogan stopped, looked back and growled a soft warning. But the wolves did not reappear.

TWENTY-TWO

On the Sunday two days before the primary election I went hunting—hunting for speeders. I didn't have to look far, either. Like ducks to a gunner in a blind, they flew to me in the sheriff's Explorer, parked on a dirt road screened from the highway by high bushes, my radar tracking them as they sped by. The speeders, mostly from Minneapolis, Milwaukee and Chicago and used to driving thirty miles an hour over the limit on the interstates around those cities, ignored the fifty-five-miles-per-hour limit on the broad but still two-lane M-64 and tromped their accelerators. I ignored the drivers doing sixty-five and seventy as not worth the trouble and concentrated on those zooming along at eighty and eighty-five, where the fines were in three figures and would help Porcupine County's lean coffers the most. After nailing one driver, I drove back, and almost before I had parked the radar chirped as another sped past at better than eighty. If duck hunting were like this, I thought, I'd be up to the tops of my hip boots in mallards before the day was out.

I cut slack for none of the drivers, either. If they gave me lip I asked politely if they were looking for a citation for failure to cooperate with a police officer. There's no such offense. The real one is obstruction of an officer in the performance of his duties, but pissing and moaning is just bad manners. Only the lawyers among them knew that, and up here in the wild North they were fortunately few and far between. If the offenders were polite and contrite, I'd sometimes knock five miles per hour off the citation, especially if they were residents of Porcupine County.

Two were a couple of local teen-agers seeing how fast their old but freshly tuned pickup could go, and I not only wrote them up for every mile per hour they had gone over the limit but also laid upon them my well-practiced Dutch-uncle speech, which I had polished with the hides of hundreds, maybe thousands, of young men and women over the years. It had mostly to do with endangering not only their own lives but also those of innocents, and I drove home the point by showing them several grisly eight-by-ten color photographs of accident victims I carried in the Explorer's glove compartment, winding up my little talk by saying, "See, you wouldn't want to be decapitated or disemboweled like them, would you now?" Sometimes they staggered off to the bushes and lost their lunches, but most of the time they just sat in their seats, pale and shaking. Rarely did I ever have to stop them again.

I had just cited the fourteenth offender of the morning when the radio crackled. "Steve, car fire at Page Falls," Joe Koski said. "Silverton's on the way." That meant the single wheezing pumper that constituted the entire equipage of the Silverton Volunteer Fire Department had already trundled out of its tumbledown garage and departed for the scene, and I quickly swung the Explorer onto M-64 and accelerated west at ninety, siren keening and strobes flashing. Drivers ahead of me hit their brakes and pulled off onto the verge, guilty expressions on their faces as I sped by.

Within ten minutes I pulled up at the dirt road that dead-ends at the falls a few miles west of southbound M-64 six miles south of Silverton. The latest "TO PAGE FALLS" highway sign was gone, as I expected. They never last more than a few days before being uprooted and carried away by a furious Porky. Page Falls, a breathtakingly beautiful glade on the Agate River flowing northward through the Wolverine Mountains Wilderness State Park and eventually Lake Superior, is a place Porkies cherish as their very own secret.

For approximately three hundred yards through an opening in the forest canopy, the Agate winds and tumbles down three layers of prehistoric shale, dropping nineteen feet to a broad trout pool full of fat brookies we mostly leave alone, for fear strange anglers that follow us might discover the gorgeous glen. Spray from the falls wreathes the place in mist, and through it the setting sun on a summer's evening intensifies and saturates the colors of the forest, turning Page Falls into what we consider the nearest thing to heaven on earth.

It is true that Porcupine County's increasingly shaky economy depends heavily on tourism—campers and hikers in the summer and skiers and snowmobilers in the winter—and we are eager to share our natural beauties with them. But there are some special places whose locations we never reveal to outsiders, and Page Falls is one of them. It is such a beautiful wonder of nature and so ecologically delicate that the unspoken and longstanding rule is never to congregate there in large numbers for fear of damaging its glories. We Porkies visit the falls alone or in twos, limiting the numbers of our visits to one or two a year, and rarely encounter others there.

I had lived in Porcupine County for almost ten years before Ginny vouchsafed the secret to me after making me swear on my parents' graves that I would never reveal its location to anyone except a true Porky. The state highway department, however, brooks no such home-grown sentimentality and regularly erects a new sign directing M-64 traffic to the falls. The road guys, most of whom live outside the county, complain bitterly that law enforcement in Porcupine County deliberately refuses to hunt down the sign thieves. It's true that we don't try very hard, but we just tell the highway boys we're doing our best.

It takes a good ten minutes to bounce over the rocky two miles from M-64 to the falls, and the odor of burning automobile, an amalgam of charred metal, melted plastic and smoldering rubber, grew stronger the farther I drove. By the time I pulled up in the Make-out Meadow, as we called the narrow verge of grass and gravel between the dirt road and the river just below the falls where Porky teen-agers occasionally parked to neck and pet, the Silverton firefighters had struck the blaze. Heavy, sooty black smoke had given way to billows of white vapor, itself dwindling under the onslaught of water from the pumper, asthmatically inhaling its supply from a hose dropped into the river.

The hulk of the automobile stood squarely in the center of the single-lane track off the verge, its passenger side parallel to the river. It clearly had not been parked before the fire started.

Peggy Strauch, the Pine Yard Inn's owner and captain of the fire volunteers, stepped over to me, streaks of soot around her eyes giving her the look of a cute raccoon. "Looks like it was set, Steve," she said. "Much too hot to have been an engine fire. I'm sure we'll find accelerant."

"Like what?"

"Gasoline, probably."

"Think it's an insurance scam?" People who can't make the installments on expensive automobile loans sometimes destroy the vehicles, by fire as well as other means, so that the insurance covers the payments.

"No."

I looked at Peggy. Sweet as she is, she's one of those people who are naturally stingy with their words. She's perfectly forthcoming, but you have to ask questions to get answers. She won't volunteer them.

"All right. Why?"

"There's a body in the driver's seat."

"Jeez. Couldn't you have let me know that first?"

"You didn't ask."

"Well, damn. What make of car?"

"Beemer."

Immediately I strode over to the still smoldering car. Enough paint remained near the sills to show that it had once been cherry-red, and the distinctive BMW grille had not burned away.

"Plates?" I asked.

With a gloved hand Peggy wiped soot and ash off the front license tag, careful not to burn herself. The car was still hot.

REBEMER.

"I know this car," I said. "Belongs to a guy we've been looking for."

"Maybe he's the cinder behind the wheel," Peggy said neutrally. I wasn't surprised by her studied nonchalance. She had seen more than her share of ugly death as an emergency medical technician in the Minneapolis Fire Department before moving to the Upper Peninsula. EMTs, like cops, hide their emotions behind a veneer of cynicism to help them get through the night.

"Let's take a look." I peered into the window of the driver's side, holding my breath against the smell of burnt flesh.

Indeed it was a cinder. The body behind the melted steering wheel had nearly been incinerated. Fire had shrunk it to almost half its size. It leaned to the left, against the driver's door jamb and the left window sill. The eyeless head, now not much bigger than a softball, faced out from the car at a forty-five-degree angle. I took a closer look at the face. Lips and nose had been burned away, but enough probably remained of the teeth for dental identification. It was impossible to identify the sex of the corpse.

Stepping to the other side of the car, I played my Maglite on the corpse. Much of the back of the head had been reduced to coals, but a large scooped-out indentation suggested that a projectile, probably a rifle-caliber bullet, had carried away some of the occiput before the fire. On a line with the angled position of the head, one of the charred headrest supports had been broken—maybe by the same bullet that possibly had killed the driver.

I straightened up. "I don't know who this is yet," I told

Peggy, "but I think we're looking at murder."

Back at the Explorer I radioed Joe Koski.

"Joe? Steve. I'm at the car fire. It's a Beemer. And there's a corpse behind the wheel. Please call the staties at Wakefield and raise Sergeant Kolehmainen. We need him. Looks like homicide."

"Yeah. Just a sec."

I waited.

Barely sixty seconds later Joe radioed back. "Alex's on his way."

"Thanks. Now would you send Chad out here? We need a block at the junction of M-64 and the road to Page Falls." No use letting gapers near the crime scene to gum up the works and slow us down.

Forty minutes later Alex arrived in his Ford Police Interceptor, escorted by a state police Suburban carrying two other troopers.

"What's doing?"

I told him.

"Hmm."

Two hours passed as Alex and his comrades meticulously did their thing, I watching closely as the troopers carefully combed the area in a hundred-yard radius.

"I think you're right," Alex said presently, holding up a shapeless lump of copper with a pair of tweezers. "This is likely the bullet that killed the vic before the perp torched the car. Found it in what's left of the back seat. Too bad it's melted. That'll prevent us from matching it to a weapon. But maybe the forensics guys can find traces of copper from the bullet in the body. At least that'll be a start."

"Male or female?" I asked Alex, fearing the answer.

"Male. Enough pelvis remains to tell us that."

I breathed a sigh of relief. Not Sharon Shoemaker, then.

"Arthur Kling?"

"Most likely. A stiff behind the wheel is usually the owner of the car. The teeth'll clinch it, but here's a pretty good preliminary ID."

Alex held up the charred, partly melted remains of a Rolex. "Found this on the floor between the driver's seat and the window. Look on the back."

"A.K. 8-17-95," said the engraving.

"Fits. Kling was wearing a Rolex at Jerry and Adela's party."

We looked at the watch in silence. Then I spoke for both of us. "Um. Then who? And why?"

"Hell if I have any idea," Alex said. "We're back at square one."

"See where the car is," I said. "The driver never parked it on the verge. If you ask me, he had just driven in. The driver's-side window's rolled down. That suggests to me that someone stepped out of the woods to the left and a little in front and hailed the driver, who stopped the car and rolled down the window to answer him. And when the perp came close enough, he put a bullet through Kling's — the victim's, 'scuse me — head from that oblique angle as the driver was looking toward him."

Alex nodded. "Makes sense."

"What's more," I said, "either the shooter was local or a local was with him. He, or they, must have told the vic — if he indeed is Kling, he's an outsider — about Page Falls and invited him here for a meeting or something. Maybe to cache another body."

Alex looked at me. "No sign of a cache."

"Maybe Kling, if that's him, was meant to be the cache and something went wrong."

"I'm not able to connect the fire with that," Alex said. "Nobody was out here. The killer could have done the job with plenty of time and privacy if this guy was meant to be a cache."

"I think you're right. Maybe there had been a falling out elsewhere and this was where the shooter wanted to end it. That would work for someone who stepped out of the trees as the car arrived and fired quickly."

"But why Page Falls?" Alex said. "There have got to be thousands of other secluded spots in Porcupine County that are better suited to bumping off people."

"Let me think out loud some more. Maybe the killer and the vic agreed that Page Falls was going to be the next site of a cached corpse, and the vic arrived thinking the killer would already have a corpse ready for caching, but the killer really intended to get rid of him instead."

"I don't know," Alex said. "It would take a real Porky to know about Page Falls, but would a real Porky use this place for a cache and risk outsiders finding out about it? I doubt that."

"Yeah."

"Maybe the killer's car made one of the tire tracks we've casted," Alex said. "But judging from what we've got, there were at least two dozen cars in here in the last week since it rained and softened the dirt enough to capture a tire tread. I'm not sure that's going to lead anywhere."

We looked at the car for a long time, shaking our heads, but we could come up with nothing else. As dusk fell and the state police Suburban crept away with the body and the tow truck with the charred hulk, Alex and I stripped off our latex gloves.

"This can't be good for you," Alex said.

"Why?"

"Too close to the election. Once Eli gets wind of this, he's going to blame it all on you."

"Oof. The October Surprise, but this one has come in August."

"Huh?"

"The last-minute event that throws an election up for grabs."

"Oh, yeah."

My radio crackled. "Steve? Joe."

"What's up?"

"The word's out, and you-know-who's making hay."

"See?" Alex said with a grim smile "Already."

TWENTY-THREE

"I suggested to Gil that he relieve you for a day," Garner Armstrong said on the phone that night. He sounded worried, and Garner, a man of unshakable equanimity, never sounds worried, even when everyone around him is frantically losing his mind and running around in little circles.

"Why?"

The prosecutor sighed. "Steve, the sheriff is calling everybody he knows and telling them this homicide proves that you and I and Alex and everybody else don't know what we're doing. Eli is poisoning the wells. You've got to go campaign all day tomorrow. There's just one day left before the primary."

"All right."

"Steve?"

"Yes?"

"Wear your best uniform."

"But I won't be on duty." I've always avoided wearing a deputy's browns when I'm not working. It's less intimidating.

"Doesn't matter. You know Eli will be turned out in all his glory."

"All right."

And so on the day before the election I arrived in my Jeep at Merle's Cafe in downtown Porcupine City for ham and eggs and as many hands as I could shake.

"Never rains but it pours," said the proprietor, Merle Lahtinen, heartily grasping my paw and holding it against her ample chest a little too long for propriety. She must be pushing eighty, but she still flirts shamelessly with her customers. The food at Merle's is okay, just okay—it used to be unbeatable, especially her meat pasties, but time and age had dulled her skills at the grill. Still Porkies flock to Merle's just to bask in her mildly libidinous Auntie Mame charm.

For a couple of minutes I chased hard egg yolks around the plate with a corner of soggy toast, thinking about Merle's words, a veiled but still crystal-clear reference to the events at Page Falls the day before. Then I wiped my mouth, laid a five-dollar bill on the table, breathed in a deep sigh and started politicking.

"Boys," I said to a table of four burly loggers, "tomorrow's Election Day, and I hope I can count on your votes."

"Yeah, Steve," chorused three of the loggers.

"I ain't registered," said the fourth. The other three turned and glared at him. He shrank into his seat, at least as much as a logger with yard-wide shoulders could shrink. This was a major transgression in Porcupine County, where civic duty is a given. After the quartet left Merle's, his mates would abuse him thoroughly.

"Why?" one of them said, jumping the gun.

"Didn't want to have to do jury duty."

"Dummy! They pick people for juries from driver license lists, not the voter rolls!"

"Oh." The logger's hangdog expression deepened.

Then followed one of those disapproving silences as uncomfortable as they are brief.

"Next election, then?" I said lightly.

The unregistered logger nodded quickly under the gimlet gaze of his companions.

I worked table after table, shaking as many hands as I could, glad there were no babies to kiss but receiving swift hugs from women young and old. Some of those embraces surprised me, for by nature most folks keep policemen at arm's length. What's more, I am not a member of the loose clan of whites that makes up more than ninety per cent of the Upper Peninsula's population. And even though I've lived in Porcupine County for going on a dozen years, I'm from elsewhere and I'm still, in many eyes, an outsider.

Maybe, I mused, it takes running for office to get accepted as a true Porky. With the next thought I rejected that notion. From time to time someone, often a summer person from a big city, decides Porcupine County is where he has always wanted to live and moves in, soon deciding to volunteer for something, to become a closer part of the community. If that person is willing to start at the bottom and humbly learn while expending lots of sweat, native Porkies will encourage the labor and sooner or later accept it as a ticket to anointing the newcomer as one of their own.

The arrogant and overeager, however, will meet a brick wall. More than once someone who had been a high-powered professional in the city, perhaps an attorney or accountant, had moved in and quickly let it be known to the rubes that they were doing everything wrong and should adopt more modern methods. Some of them even ran for office and invariably were beaten badly at the polls.

From a place like Merle's, word travels fast. In the half hour since I arrived, customers had jammed all the booths and stools, and dozens packed the foyer up front. They had come not to eat but to see the candidate at the eleventh hour. "Speech! Speech!" they cried.

There was nothing I could do except make one. At Merle's nod of consent I stood atop a chair.

"Friends," I began. "That is, if you *are* friends . . ."

"We are!" the crowd chorused.

I had not really prepared a stump speech, but one had been forming in the back of my mind, thanks to all those appearances at church suppers and the like. And to my own surprise I delivered it, without too many hems and haws.

"Tomorrow we go to the polls," I said, "and I hope you'll all do the right thing: Vote."

"For you!" shouted a highway engineer from the back of the room.

"Yeah!" echoed most of the crowd.

"As you all know, we've got a tough case on our hands right now," I said. "The investigation is still going on. But I am sure we'll get to the bottom of it, as we did at the Venture Mine."

Chortles and knee slaps greeted the joke. There were also thoughtful nods at the reference to the celebrated case of the year before in which the sheriff's department, the state police, and the tribal police joined to break up a murderous drug-growing ring that had been operating under our noses for a couple of years. I had been the tactical commander of the effort, and near the end of it Garner Armstrong asked me to put my hat in the ring for sheriff.

"And don't forget the Paul Passoja case." With Ginny's help a couple of years before, I had caught the killer of Porcupine County's most powerful business leader and shadow politician.

"Yay!"

I blushed. I was not used to heralding my own accomplishments. My adoptive father had taught me never to boast, and in any case Indians are not given to self-congratulation. But if I was going to be a successful politician I had to learn to let my light shine from under the bushel.

"What's more," I said, "my fellow Porcupine County deputies and I have been going to the office every day and putting in a full day of work. It may take us some time to break the case everybody knows we're working on, but I promise you that sooner or later we'll do it. Staying home out of spite isn't going to do the job."

The assembled Porkies knew exactly what—and who— I was talking about. "Yeah!" some shouted. "Vote Eli out!" others called.

Now that his name had been mentioned I could afford to be magnanimous.

"Eli Garrow was a great sheriff," I said, "and he's still a great guy. We should respect him and what he has done for the county. More than once he has put his life on the line, and for a long time he has helped to keep the county a law-abiding one. But time and age take their toll. We all get old and less effective, and, to be honest, some day I will, too. But right now Eli has, and so it's time for him to pass his star on to someone else. He's done it proud and I hope to do it just as proud. Thank you."

Amid the cheers, I stood down and strode out of Merle's under a shower of backslaps. Then I drove to Frank's, parked the Jeep and stood by the entrance to the supermarket as shoppers trickled in and out, shaking their hands, even hugging some of the ladies. I'd swear I was getting almost as good as Eli at that kind of thing.

Soon a large knot of onlookers formed. I climbed atop a bench under the store canopy and began, "Tomorrow we all go to the polls, and I hope you'll do the right thing . . ."

And that was my whole day, with stops in Silverton, Bergland, Matchwood, Coppermass and Bruce Crossing, meeting and greeting outside gas stations, taverns, cafes and wherever I could find more than three people together. Maybe I was only kidding myself, but I thought the reception in the southern reaches of Porcupine County was warmer than it had been earlier in the campaign. Only a few catcalls broke the benignity. And, as luck had it, I did not run into Eli or his far-flung kinsmen. Later I discovered they were essentially following in my tracks, stopping where I had stumped and trying to quench enthusiasm for me.

That night I stayed at Ginny's after putting away the better part of her signature pot roast and wild rice at dinner, Tommy matching me forkful for forkful. In the presence of superior cuisine, Indians have always displayed excellent appetites, and we were not about to insult the traditions of our ancestors, let alone the talents of our hostess.

"This was a good day," I said as Ginny and I snuggled under the coverlet of her huge oaken bed upstairs, Tommy having fallen asleep in his room at the other end of the house.

"And it's not over yet," she said with a giggle. "Come here."

TWENTY-FOUR

I woke up on primary day fretting, as usual, about those cached bodies. They were not ordinary victims of crime. Except for the hooker's homicide—which might not even have been committed in Michigan—the offenses against them had been done after their demise, not before. Victims of violent crime have histories and personalities, and good cops painstakingly try to learn them for clues to the perps, because crimes are often committed by people who know their victims. But these corpses had no past, no selves, that we could discover. They were just nameless shells their former occupants weren't using anymore. They would lead us nowhere. All we had to go on was Arthur Kling.

In a black mood I rolled out of bed, knowing that Eli would work the hustings all day, buttonholing incoming voters at just the legal distance outside the polling places while election judges watched him with narrowed eyes. I chose to do my job instead. I'd done my best the day before, I figured, and anything more would only be wasteful. Besides, campaigning on primary day was, I thought, an act of desperation. I wanted to seem cool and confident. Of course I was anything but.

One way or the other, this was going to be a life change. Running for office means putting yourself out on the line in the most public way, where people can poke and prod you like a side of beef and tell you whether you make the grade or not. If you do—if you win—you are forever a public figure and a piece of you belongs to other people. If you lose, you can look forward to a lifetime of pitying handshakes and snickering whispers. I do not understand how candidates who lose an election can find the strength to run again, but then I am not a professional politician and hope never to be one.

For much of the morning I inventoried my bare desk,

desultorily shoving reports from one side to the other, lining up pencils, dusting the bulb in the gooseneck lamp and stewing. Stewing about the election and stewing about Sharon Shoemaker, that burned-out BMW and its grisly contents, and those three plastic-wrapped corpses. Finally I thumped the desk and stood up.

"Go out on road patrol?" I finally asked Gil, who that morning had assigned me to paperwork, a task I didn't object to.

"In a pig's eye," he said severely. "What if you pinch somebody on his way to the polls? You stay right here."

"Yes sir."

Idle minutes passed.

To kill time I opened the growing case folder I'd jocularly labeled "Cache of Corpses." The small calling card Arthur Kling had given Sharon Shoemaker tumbled out. Might as well start there. I called the number scrawled on the back.

"Hong Sing Cleaners," the voice said, in a thick Cantonese accent.

I identified myself. "Do you know an Arthur Kling?"

"Shirts long time ready. Pick up today?"

"Is that a yes?"

"Yes."

"How long have they been ready?"

"Many, many days. Pick up today?"

"I'll send someone. Thank you." I'd tip off the Chicago police. Maybe there'd be a clue in those shirts. Perhaps a bloodstain ordinary washing couldn't get out. Perhaps a clue in the label on the collar. But we — I, mostly — had been reduced to shots in the dark.

I looked on the other side of the card. ANDREW MONAGHAN. BEAR STEARNS AND COMPANY. Another arrow worth shooting into the night. People picked up calling cards for all sorts of reasons. Kling might have met Monaghan at some investment function and pocketed the proffered card automatically, like a piece of lint, and probably had. But calling the number wouldn't hurt. I dialed.

"Bear Stearns." The female voice was haughty and impatient in that inimitable New Yorkish I don't-want-to-be-bothered-with-you-but-I-have-to-because-it's-my-job fashion. "Mr. Monaghan's office."

"This is Deputy Sheriff Stephen Martinez, Porcupine County, Michigan," I said, mustering the sternest police-officer tone I could. "May I speak to Mr. Monaghan, please?"

"About what, may I ask?" she said icily. "Mr. Monaghan is very busy."

"Police business."

You had to give the woman credit for tenacity. You could almost hear her spike heels dig into the carpet. "I am his personal administrative assistant," she said, turning up the haughtiness. "You can tell me whatever you need to say to Mr. Monaghan."

She tried to cover the receiver, but I could hear the tag end of her whisper to someone else in the office. ". . . Michigan cop," she breathed.

"What is the nature of the police business?" she asked, still starchy.

"It's a homicide investigation. Please put Mr. Monaghan on."

She couldn't stifle a small gasp. "Just a moment, please."

An electronic click. Then a male voice. "Monaghan here. What's this all about?"

"Good morning, Mr. Monaghan," I said, then identified myself as a deputy sheriff in Porcupine County, Michigan. "I'm calling about an unexplained death here." I waited for Monaghan's reaction.

It was swift. "I've never been to Upper Michigan in my life," he said. "What's going on there?"

My eyebrows rose. I hadn't said Porcupine County was

in Upper Michigan. Either Monaghan was dissembling, or he had a remarkable knowledge about the state.

"I have a calling card here with your name and number on it. It had been in the possession of the deceased."

"Who?"

"His name is Arthur Kling. He lived in Chicago. He was an investment counselor. Worked for Fidelity."

A short silence. "Don't know him, I'm afraid. I give out business cards every day to lots of people. Might have met him at a meeting somewhere." Monaghan's voice was even and smooth — too even and smooth, I thought. Maybe he'd practiced this response. But his statement was perfectly logical, maybe even true, and I had no reason to challenge it.

"Well, thanks anyway, Mr. Monaghan. I'll give you my number so that you can call if you remember anything." I did so.

"Okay. Anything else?" That old Manhattan impatience.

"Nope."

"Good-bye then." Click.

I took a deep breath. Monaghan had not asked how Kling had died, let alone when or where. Ninety-nine people out of a hundred would have. That's just normal human concern and curiosity. There was, I thought, a good deal more to Andrew Monaghan than met the eye.

I riffled through my Rolodex — unlike some of my law enforcement brethren, I still use horse-and-buggy paper databases — and found the number of a NYPD Vice Enforcement detective who'd been a friend at criminal justice school at City University a decade and a half ago. I could have called the NYPD Detective Bureau, but the cops there are extraordinarily busy and likely wouldn't want to waste time helping out a boondocks deputy grasping for straws in a case far from their jurisdiction.

"Dick?" I said. "Steve Martinez."

"God, it's been years. How the hell are ya?" Dick Franciscus' voice was genuinely friendly, and I was grateful. We *had* been good buddies. You never really know the true depth of a friendship until years later, when a need arises.

I explained in some detail, finishing up with my phone call to Bear Stearns.

"Now that's a strange one, all right," Dick said. "You want me to check out this Monaghan?"

"I'd be in your debt," I said. "Whatever you can find out might help."

"Gimme half an hour."

I went back to my game of file-folder hockey.

"Bearing up okay?" asked Joe Koski from his counter.

"Yeah, but I'll be glad when the day's over." It would be a long day. The polls in Porcupine County close at eight in the evening, and while Porcupine City's voting machines are automated and the results tabulated immediately, every other precinct in the county uses paper ballots that must be stuffed into locked boxes and driven to the courthouse for hand scanning. It would not be until well past midnight that we had the results.

My phone rang.

"It's Dick," the voice said.

"Tell me."

"Be careful. Be *damn* careful."

"Why?"

"Monaghan's connected."

"Connected? The mob?"

"Not the mob. Politically."

"How?"

"Uncle's the mayor's right-hand man."

"Yeah?"

"Gotta take it easy here, ya see?" Dick said. "Tread on the wrong toes and I'll be back walking a beat in the projects."

I sighed. "Anything else?"

"Yale grad, twenty-four years old, not married, typical

young professional about town, travels a lot, nothing unusual. He's pretty much clean."

"Pretty much?"

"Half a dozen unpaid parking tickets, everybody has those, and a juvenile arrest on suspicion of killing and mutilating a dog. He was fifteen. Not the dog, the boy."

"What was the outcome?"

"Doesn't say."

"How'd you find that out? Aren't juvenile arrest records expunged from the computer?"

"They're supposed to be." I could almost hear Dick wink. "But this one wasn't. It happens."

"That could be a useful bit of information."

"Yeah, but don't tell anybody where you got it, okay?"

"Thanks for the facts," I said. "Now what do you really know? The unofficial stuff?"

"You really want to know?"

"You bet."

"Poster child for tougher inheritance taxes. He's a trust-fund parasite. Great-grandpa got filthy rich by owning Irish sweatshops in the garment district at the end of the nineteenth century, exploiting his own people. Grandpa and papa never worked a day but lived off the family fortune, and the kid got his job through pull and doesn't seem to do much on his own."

"Ah. We have some of those out here, too." The wealthy — among them the idle rich — from Chicago, Minneapolis and Milwaukee have been buying up choice Lake Superior beachfront property in Porcupine County, sometimes for sprawling summer homes, sometimes for long-term investments. All too often these people contribute little to the county, choosing to import labor from northern Wisconsin to build and maintain their houses, and alienating the locals with their arrogance and overweening sense of entitlement.

"There's more. Couple of vice dicks who grabbed him

up in a hooker sweep—of course Uncle pulled strings and got the record expunged—say he's a piece of work. Arrogant puppy. Didn't seem to give a shit when he was pinched and all he cared about was the cuffs didn't dirty his shirt. Pushed the hookers around some. Propositioned a female vice cop right in the station. Laughed all the time."

"That's a lot for a couple of vice detectives to turn up in one prostitution sweep."

"I didn't say there was only one. There have been three arrests, all swept under the rug on orders from above. Mr. Monaghan likes to buy his jollies."

"Well, this is an education. Thanks."

"Call me if you need more," Dick said. "I'll do what I can. This one sounds interesting."

A few more pleasantries and we hung up.

I leaned back in my swivel chair and gazed up at the ceiling. The North Country Trail victim was a prostitute. Andrew Monaghan consorted with prostitutes. Was there a connection? Maybe. But a little pasteboard card wasn't much of one. The whole thing could be a coincidence. Coincidences can be important, though.

More time passed, and in the late afternoon my fingers began drumming on the desk. Gil heard the soft noise.

"Deputy!" he called from his office. When he is irritated with me, which thankfully is not often, he calls me by my rank, not by my name.

"Undersheriff?" I do the same thing.

Gil harrumphed. "Think you can deliver this summons to this guy in Bergland without getting into trouble?"

"Of course!" I was glad for the chance to get out of the office and into the fresh air. Gil handed me the papers and turned back to his office.

"Be good," he said as I left. That was about as close to humor as he ever got.

Half an hour later, I handed the summons to a concrete contractor who was being sued by the county for shoddy work. The expression on his face suggested not only dismay at having been handed the papers but also by a candidate he hadn't voted for that morning. I didn't ask.

I was driving back to Porcupine City when Joe Koski called on the radio.

"Deer-car accident on M-64 five and a half miles south of M-28," he said. "Driver called. New Caddy."

"On my way," I replied.

TWENTY-FIVE

In the Upper Peninsula, suicidal deer throw themselves into the paths of oncoming cars with alarming regularity. The beasts always come off second best, the drivers of the old beaters that hit them not bothering to report the accidents and often scooping up the carcasses to butcher for the freezer. Sometimes they just drive off, leaving injured deer suffering by the roadside, and it's the deputies' sad task to euthanize the animals.

But deer are big and can smash good-sized dents into automobile grilles and fenders. Owners of newer cars who want to collect the insurance do report the accidents, and several times a week a Porcupine County deputy is called out to view the damage, do the paperwork and call the road commission to send a truck to dispose of the carcass.

The Cadillac in question—almost brand new—was parked on the verge of the highway, a few feet north of the sign that said "WELCOME TO GOGEBIC COUNTY." A bloody brown heap, a large doe, lay in the middle of the road squarely atop the double yellow line a good twenty feet from Porcupine County. The Caddy had Minnesota plates, and its owner, a middle-aged woman in smartly fitted blue slacks and matching jacket with a simple strand of pearls around her neck, stared in dismay at the crumpled left fender, smeared with deer dung. *Urban culture meets rural in a nexus of violence*, I thought absently as I parked the Explorer behind the Cadillac, my blues-and-reds flashing to warn oncoming traffic.

"You okay?" I said. "Nobody hurt?"

"Nobody but my new car," the woman said. "I know all about deer on the road, but I never thought it'd happen to me."

"It does."

"I saw the first deer and managed to avoid it," she said,

"but I never saw the second."

"Par for the course," I said, shaking my head in sympathy. "Is the car drivable?"

"I think so."

"I'll write a report," I said, "and give you a copy, and then you can send it to your insurance company."

"I've got a five hundred dollar deductible," she said in a forlorn voice.

"I've got good news for you. Deer-car strikes are *comprehensive* claims. The deductible won't apply. If you'd swerved to miss a deer and hit the guard rail, then that would have been a chargeable accident that goes under the collision coverage of your insurance policy, and you'd have to pay the deductible to get the damage fixed. But not if you hit the deer."

"All right." She sighed, but she didn't look as if she felt better.

I didn't tell her that some drivers who accidentally mash a fender against the garage try to avoid paying the deductible by claiming the incident as a deer-car strike, planting deer hair and turds—easily obtainable in the U.P.—over the crumpled metal and radiator. They rarely get away with it, for the damage to a car caused by a deer is distinctive and almost impossible to fake.

At that moment a big red Dodge extended-cab pickup from the Gogebic County Sheriff's Department stopped behind the dead doe and flicked on its own flashers to warn off traffic from the other direction. A burly, redheaded deputy sporting a Sir Francis Drake goatee alighted and strode up.

"Hiya, Dan," I called. Dan Roane was a veteran North Woods lawman who had worked every police job in Gogebic County during a career that spanned more than two decades, and was now the county's animal control officer. In fact, he was the only certified police animal control officer in the entire Upper Peninsula. Dead deer, stray dogs, feral cats, animal abuse and wildlife complaints in general were his bailiwick. He wore his uniform trousers bloused inside old-fashioned lace-up boots like a Mountie, justifying his departure from the Gogebic sheriff's rigorous dress code by saying it made sense for an officer who had to chase animals through heavy brush every day. The sheriff didn't argue.

Dan was full of stories about his job, and the ones he liked to tell the most involved successful rescues of distressed animals. Once he and a Department of Natural Resources officer had to get a deer out of a manhole it had fallen into in downtown Bessemer. They sedated the deer with a shot of tranquilizer from a dart gun borrowed from a local veterinarian, then a city crew tenderly hauled it up in a sling and nestled it in Dan's pickup to be taken to the woods, where it revived and was released to high fives all around.

"Looks like this is going to be a border dispute," Dan said with mock gravity. "Car hit the deer in your jurisdiction and it ended up in mine. Who's going to catch the carcass?"

"Rock, scissors or paper?" I replied.

The woman stared at us both in consternation.

"Just a little cop humor, ma'am," I said.

"What *will* become of the deer?" I gazed at her with new respect. She cared about the animal. She was sorry her car had killed it.

"Inasmuch as the deer's in Gogebic County," Dan said, "I'll carry it to a sand pit in the woods west of here where it'll become food for eagles, wolves and coyotes."

"At least it won't go to waste," the lady said.

"Nope. That sand pit's one reason why our eagles are so fat and happy," Dan said. "I've seen as many as twenty of them feeding there."

The paperwork completed, the Minnesotan drove off, and Dan and I heaved the carcass into his truck bed.

"Come along for a bit?" Dan said. "Want to see our zoo?"

"Why not?" I said. Porcupine County had a similar site

for disposal of animal remains, but it was about time for a break, and I enjoyed Dan's company. It turned out to be a serendipitous decision.

I radioed Joe to let him know I'd be out of the jurisdiction briefly, and half an hour later we arrived at the Gogebic County Gravel Pit in Ironwood Township. Right away the place creeped me out. It looked like an outdoor charnel house, a football-field-sized wound of reddish earth scraped from the hide of the green forest, dried white rib cages, spines and bones scattered all around by picnicking scavengers. The man-made pit, first scooped out of a prehistoric dune deep in the forest by bulldozers decades ago and kept open with front-end loaders, provided sand and gravel for the highway department. The high walls of the pit also made a perfect backstop for a shooting range, and not only did the county's deputies perform their monthly weapons qualifications there, local civilian shooters also used it to keep up their skills. Animal carcasses were tossed over a berm to one side, and today half a dozen eagles and a couple of osprey were contesting loudly for possession, their skreeks and squawks reverberating from the trees. The eagles were both young dark brown specimens and fully grown ones with brilliant white heads. Two scruffy coyotes lunged at the birds, trying to drive them away from their dinner, but the eagles held their ground, snapping their beaks and flashing their talons.

A pair of turkey vultures perched on a low pile of foot-thick pulpwood logs at the far edge of the pit, alternately watching the eagles and scratching with beaks and claws at the topmost logs, as if trying to move them to one side.

"That's odd," Dan said. "Something's going on over there."

"Have a look?"

"Yeah."

I followed Dan around the perimeter of the pit and up

the shallow sides, our boots scrabbling in the gravel, to the log pile. The logs, all cut to the same ten-foot lengths in proper U.P. lumbermen's fashion, had been laid on top of and parallel to each other in a neat pile. Dan waved his arms at the buzzards. The huge, ugly birds slowly flapped out of range, grumbling loudly, and alighted on the ground, watching us with their piercing eyes.

Dan peered into the pile.

"Hey, look at this," he said.

I followed his gaze. Dew glinted on cloudy plastic two layers of logs into the pile.

"Jeez," I said. "Not again."

"Yeah?"

"I think I know what's in there. We'll need to take off some of the logs."

Dan took one end of a log and I the other and with a mighty whoof we tried to muscle it up enough to roll down its neighbors to the ground. It wouldn't budge.

"Just a sec," Dan said. He walked over to his truck and returned with a homemade "rabies stick," a hollow steel pole five feet long through which was threaded a plastic-clad steel cable ending in a noose. With it Dan controlled obstreperous biting animals. With only a small grunt he used the pole to lever the log up over its cousins and it thumped to the sand. Three more logs and our quarry lay open to daylight.

It was an oblong plastic package nearly identical to the one we had found at the Poor Farm. But its yellow-green contents were male, youthful and unmarked except for the missing head and hands.

"Another one," Dan said unnecessarily. I strode to my Explorer and picked up the mike.

Two hours later Alex and his assistants finished the job and sent the corpse to Marquette.

"A cadaver for sure," he said. "The lab'll back us up."

"That's five," I said "Two cadavers, a burial and two homicides. How many more are we going to find? And how many of them are going to be homicides?"

"I don't know," said Alex. "But I have this awful feeling that the homicides aren't over."

Alex got into his cruiser and I into my Explorer.

"Bearing up okay?" Dan called back from his truck just before we all pulled out.

"What?"

"The election. Hope you win."

"It's going to be close."

The polls were still open, and the word about the fresh corpse was already out, thanks to a couple of riflemen who had driven to the pit for a little target practice. *I could lose this thing*, I thought, as I headed back to the sheriff's department.

TWENTY-SIX

At six P.M. I signed out and drove to Ginny's for supper. A knot of half a dozen cars and pickups clogged her driveway, including a state police cruiser.

"What are you guys doing here?" I demanded as I opened the door. "I didn't tell anybody I was coming!"

"Now, now," Garner Armstrong said from behind an enormous Old Fashioned. "It's election night and we're your crew and we'll see you through." He laughed at his own rhyme.

"Hear, hear," Alex chortled.

Joe Koski stood smiling in a corner as Tommy handed him a plate of crackers and cheese. Even Gil was there, looking about as relaxed as a man with a fist for a face could, patting Hogan on the head, rumpling his floppy ears. The dog's tail thumped the floor in greeting.

"Evening," Horace Wright said. "Stopped in for a bit, then I have to go to Eli's, of course, and then the courthouse. But I'll have some of Mrs. Fitzgerald's leg of lamb, if I may."

"Typical newsie," Alex hooted. "Freeloader!"

"Sergeant!" Horace said with mock severity. "That's no way to talk about the Fourth Estate!"

The banter rolled back and forth all during dinner. Although a certain imposing case of cached corpses and allied homicides squatted like a great gray toad in the backs of everyone's minds, nobody mentioned it, as if to do so might hex the outcome of the election. As the hour for the closing of the polls approached, eyes glanced nervously at the clock and the conversation grew strained. Another thing I hate about election night is waiting for the shoe to drop, like the blade of a guillotine.

At five minutes past eight the phone rang and everyone jumped, the chatter instantly cut off. Ginny answered.

"It's the county clerk's office. The polls have closed and Edna's about to call the results for Porcupine City," she said. "We'll have them in a couple of minutes."

Dead silence fell around the dinner table. Minutes ticked away on the tall walnut grandfather clock in Ginny's hallway. Not even Alex could break the hush with a wisecrack.

The phone rang again. Ginny picked it up.

"Martinez, one thousand, two hundred twenty-eight votes," Ginny said. "Garrow, seven hundred forty-three."

"Mr. Martinez's ahead by four hundred eighty-five," Tommy, the human calculator, said almost instantly.

"Not too bad," said Alex, who earlier had predicted that I'd need to be ahead of Eli by well over five hundred votes in Porcupine City to stay a boat-length ahead of the sheriff while the ballots trickled in from the rest of the county. But Alex didn't look confident.

"Let's have another piece of that coconut cream pie," said Garner calmly. He's a man with a sound sense of proportion about life. We tucked in and Ginny served the coffee.

Just before nine the phone rang again, and we all jumped. "The ballots have arrived from Rockland and Silverton," Ginny said. Those are the two towns closest to Porcupine City in the northern reaches of the county, where I was strongest.

At nine-fourteen their ballots had been scanned and the results reported via Ma Bell. "Martinez, one hundred ninety-eight," Ginny said. "Garrow, one hundred sixty-six."

No surprise there, and I was grateful that my lead had been padded by thirty-two votes. I'd need them all.

For as the results slowly trickled in from the rest of the county, that opening 517-vote lead began to shrink, and it steadily shriveled as the hours ticked away toward midnight.

"Bergland," Ginny said. "Martinez, two hundred two.

Garrow, two hundred eighty-three."

That brought an uneasy stirring around the dinner table. We'd hoped to break almost even there.

"Matchwood. Martinez, nine. Garrow, eighty-two."

Unsurprising, for that was the heart of Eli's power base.

It wasn't until half past eleven that the results arrived from Lone Pine, Ewen, Trout Creek, Paulding and Bruce Crossing, whittling my lead to 181 votes. Just two more towns to hear from—Coppermass and Greenland in the eastern portion of the county, both of which we thought would favor Eli but not by much.

At almost midnight, as we began to nod, those two towns were heard from. As the grandfather clock struck 12:18, we all jumped as the phone rang. The mistress of the house answered, as she had all evening. A slow smile spread over her face.

"Final results," Ginny said. "Martinez, two thousand two. Garrow, one thousand eight hundred ninety-four."

I had never dreamed a sobersided county prosecutor could whoop so loudly. Garner enfolded me in his arms two seconds before Ginny planted a wet kiss on my lips. Alex hoisted a Molson's in my direction and Gil gravely shook my hand, maybe the first time he had ever done so. A happy grin spread over Tommy's face. Hogan added a flurry of barks to the excitement.

But it had been close.

"A hundred eight votes," Garner said. "Eli won't demand a recount. If it had been less than a hundred, I'm sure he would have."

Edna Juntunen, we all knew, is so meticulous in the counting of votes that her results have never been challenged.

The phone rang again.

"It's for you," Ginny said, handing me the receiver. "It's Eli."

"Hi" was all I could think of to say. I am not Stevie Silvertongue and never will be.

"My congratulations, Deputy Martinez," the sheriff said, in a tightly controlled voice. He clearly did not want to appear bitter.

"Thank you. You ran a fine campaign," I said, not meaning it at all.

"It's not over."

"Hmm?"

"You'll be surprised."

Eli hung up. Silence fell around the table as everyone took in my grim expression.

" 'It's not over,' he said. What's he mean by that?"

Shrugs all around. "Sore loser," Alex said dismissively. Nobody wanted my victory spoiled. But a more pressing matter took hold of my thoughts.

TWENTY-SEVEN

Two days after the primary we held another war council, as an increasingly frustrated Garner Armstrong was calling our conferences about those damned corpses, at the Porcupine County Courthouse. Alex reported the crime lab's findings on the Gogebic Sand Pit corpse. A cadaver, sure enough. I reported my phone calls to Andrew Monaghan and Dick Franciscus.

"Monaghan sounds like a slim possibility," said the prosecutor. "But awfully slim. We'll need a lot more than a vague circumstantial feeling that he's involved with these corpses to go after him. And I think Detective Franciscus is right—one has to be careful with the politically connected. Not only Franciscus but his sergeant, his lieutenant, his captain, his watch commander—hell, his *commissioner* — wouldn't want to get their balls in a vise with a powerful mayoral assistant in New York City. If we do anything we'd better have a lot of ammunition."

"I've got an idea," I said. "How about a subpoena for his credit card records for the last year or so? We can keep that quiet."

"What good would that do?" Alex said. "If he was in this thing with Kling, he'd likely have been careful not to leave a paper trail, too."

"Maybe not," I said. "Even brilliant crooks get careless. Anyway, it won't hurt."

"All right," Garner said. "I'll get the subpoena and you get those records."

It took forty-eight hours and some shin-kicking of both the legal and quasilegal type—I had to threaten an officious young lawyer at one credit card company with a contempt charge—but the fax in the squadroom finally began to spit out the records from Visa, Master Card, Discover and American

Express. After a couple of hours I gathered up all the sheets and examined them.

The American Express card was a platinum one. The young men who carried them thought they'd impress waiters and auto rental clerks as well as their girl friends, but the merchants who took the cards knew their holders were suckers enough to pay four hundred dollars a year just for the prestige of flashing one and maxing it out to a ridiculous sum. Andrew Monaghan had an indiscriminating ego, and maybe that could be a weak point.

Immediately a few patterns emerged from the lists of charges. In New York, Monaghan used the Amex card almost exclusively to pay for restaurant meals and retail purchases. He wanted other New Yorkers to think he was rich. But when he went out of state he used the Visa, Master Card and Discover almost exclusively — and his forays took him to Minnesota and Detroit, though not the Upper Peninsula. If he had ever been in Upper Michigan in the last year, his credit trail didn't show that at all.

But I noticed something. Seven times in the past year he had flown to Minneapolis, then upstate to Duluth, often staying overnight in the small city at the western edge of Lake Superior. Ten days or two weeks later he had turned in a rental car in Detroit and flown back to New York, sometimes overnighting in the Motor City. He alternated among the three credit cards to pay his air fare and car rentals. One set of sheets might not show much of a repetitive pattern, but taken together, all three did. There were no charges for meals or lodging other than at Duluth the day he arrived and Detroit the night before he left — no charges *at all,* meaning he did not use the credit cards at all for periods of seven to nine days. He was paying cash. And why?

And where did Monaghan go in that rental car between Duluth and Detroit? The shortest distance between those cities was along U.S. 2 to the Straits of Mackinac — straight through the entire length of Upper Michigan — then south on Interstate 75 to Detroit, a total of 699 miles. The route via Chicago added up to 760 miles, plus clotted bumper-to-bumper traffic around the south end of Lake Michigan. The Chicago route easily would have taken two hours longer to drive, maybe three. I was now certain, although I couldn't prove it, that Andrew Monaghan had spent a good deal of time in Upper Michigan that spring and summer, and that he had been lying when he said he had never been in these parts.

As for those airline tickets, he was probably buying round trips and tossing away the return portion. Another subpoena of ticket records would prove that, if we needed the additional evidence.

Not so smart a guy. It's what a paper trail doesn't say as well as what it says that can convict a perp. Of course, what I had was still circumstantial in the extreme, but I was now certain Andrew Monaghan was our guy — or, rather, one of our guys. Or people, I could hear the scrupulous Camilo saying.

I picked up the phone and dialed Dick Franciscus' number.

"Dick? Steve Martinez."

"Argh."

"Argh?"

"You're calling about Monaghan again, aren't you?"

"Yup."

"What now?"

I told him.

"Hmm. You're getting somewhere, but I can't grab him up on just that."

"I'm not asking you to. What I'm asking is can you get me a photo of him, a clear head-and-shoulders shot?"

"Who am I, fucking Ansel Adams?"

"I was thinking Weegee."

"Weegee? Shitkickers don't know about him."

"This one does." Arthur "Weegee" Fellig had been a

famous Manhattan crime photographer in the 1930s and 1940s who specialized in crooks, thugs, and other lowlifes, some of them society matrons. His dark and malevolent stuff hangs in art museums today.

"Smart guy," Dick said, but his tone was admiring, not disdainful.

"If you could get a photo from the drivers' license people, I'd appreciate it. I could do it myself but it'll be faster if the request comes from a New York detective."

"All right. But I don't remember liking you that much back at CUNY."

"You didn't care for my cooking, as I recall."

Dick laughed. "Now *that* I remember."

"It's improved since."

"It couldn't have gotten any worse."

Two hours later I had a fax photograph of Andrew Monaghan. Drivers' license photos normally make the subjects look either stupid or dyspeptic. I decided Monaghan's made him look cruel and unscrupulous. He had slicked-back dark hair and those saturnine eyebrows that made the urbane television newsman Edwin Newman look like the devil's consigliere. Drivers' license photos are usually several years old and don't account for weight changes and facial hair, but Monaghan had renewed his license just the year before and the photo clearly was of a handsome young man in his midtwenties.

I made several copies and faxed them to the state police and sheriff's departments in the Upper Michigan counties surrounding Porcupine County. Monaghan wasn't wanted, I said in the accompanying notes, but was a "person of interest" in the recent case involving three corpses discovered in Porcupine and Gogebic Counties, and I'd appreciate it if fellow officers would discreetly ask restaurateurs and motelkeepers if they recognized the face, and if they did, to let me know.

Detail of the cache locations

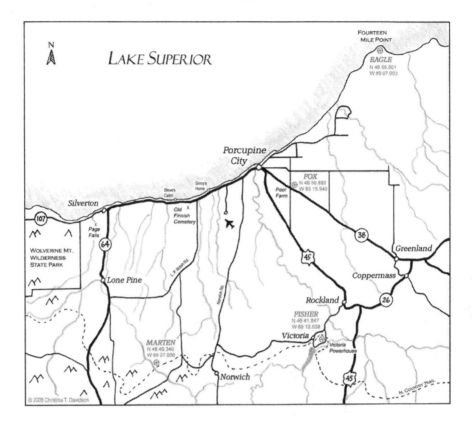

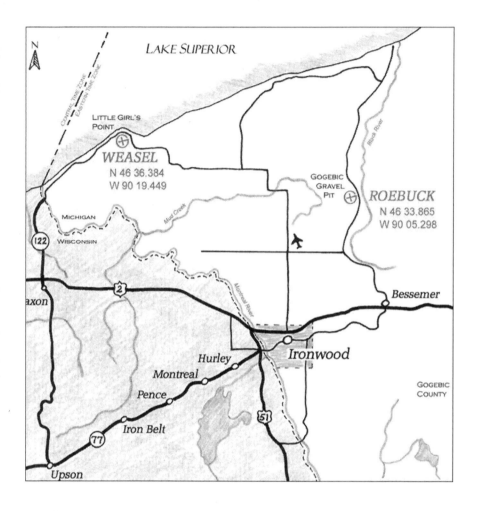

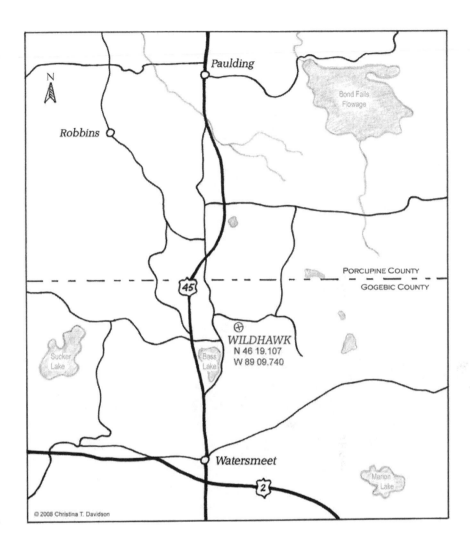

TWENTY-EIGHT

A week later, we finally caught another break. A motel owner in Bessemer at the west end of Gogebic County called the state police when a guest, who had paid cash for two weeks in advance, did not show up at the end of the rental period to collect his belongings. In fact, the motelkeeper said, he had not seen the guest since he checked in. A team of troopers, led by Sergeant Alex Kolehmainen, arrived and examined the room and the clothing and luggage it contained. There were no names, no identifying marks of any kind except laundry tags on the shirts. The address the guest had given was false, and the Master Card number he had proffered to hold the reservation was bogus. So were the numbers on the Illinois license plate he had given the motelkeeper. So many of them, including clerks at big chain motels, let alone the Ma and Pa ones, never check out those things until it's too late. It's understandable. There are so many tasks to get done around a motel and so few hours in the day.

But the two items the troopers found behind the ironing board in the closet were real enough. One was a nearly brand-new Bushmaster AR-15 rifle, a heavily modified version—with a powerful long-range scope—of the military M16. The other was a Toshiba laptop computer. If rifle and laptop weren't stolen, their serial numbers could lead to the person who had left them there. That might not be absolutely necessary, for the motelkeeper made a definite identification of the Illinois driver's license photograph the troopers showed him. The photo was of Arthur Kling. And the Chicago laundryman, shown a fax of the tags on the shirts from Kling's luggage, identified them as belonging to our man.

"The laptop's passworded," Alex said, "but we've got a pretty good hacker here at the post. Come on down and we'll wait for you before we open it. Bring your case files, too."

Less than an hour later I pulled up at the red-brick state police post in Wakefield, parked, and strode into the squad room. Alex, a young trooper named Willie Hanson, and a tall and trim, blonde and attractive woman were awaiting. Alex performed the introductions, carefully stating that I was the lead investigator in the case, the first corpse having turned up in my jurisdiction.

Sergeant Susan Hemb was a criminal psychological profiler for the state police who had driven in from Lansing that morning. She gave me a polite handshake and smile. She wore a smart black-and-white business outfit and heels, like a lawyer or businesswoman. Only the shield at her belt revealed that she was in law enforcement. I pegged her age at close to forty. If she was a sergeant she had to have been with the staties at least a decade.

"Sergeant," I said.

"Sue."

"Steve."

"Right." I relaxed. She wasn't going to be severe and officious and overbearing toward a lowly deputy sheriff. And maybe she could help.

"May I have the case files?" she said without preamble. No wonder she was a chum of Alex. Wasted no time, like him. Absolutely no-nonsense. They must have had quite a thing together once. I pushed the alarming picture out of my mind and handed over the folders.

"If it's all right with you," she said, "I'll read these and do my job while you guys do yours. I'll listen in."

"Okay," Alex told Willie, sitting at a long low folding table, the Toshiba open before him. "Let's break in."

Willie, who had minored in computer science at Michigan Tech, answered with a flurry of keyclicks.

"Piece of cake," he said. "Passworded only on the Windows level."

"What's there?"

"The usual stuff. Internet Explorer, Outlook Express, bunch of financial software—this thing probably belonged to somebody in the investment business."

"We already knew that," Alex said. "What else?"

"Something called MapSource—one word, capital M, capital S."

"That's GPS tracking software," I said. "I use it myself."

"The MapSource data folder is encrypted," the young trooper said. "So are a couple of Word folders. It might take a little work to find the passwords to open those folders."

Alex and I huddled around the coffeepot at one corner of the squad room.

"What do you make of this rifle?" Alex said, handing me the AR-15 the troopers had found in the motel.

"I don't know," I said. "It's a specialized varmint rig, isn't it?"

That particular Bushmaster model, with a heavy twelve-power scope and a folding bipod to support the muzzle, shot a .223-caliber high-velocity bullet over long distances, three or four hundred yards. Gunners would lie patiently on rises at the edges of meadows and wait for woodchucks and other small animals considered vermin to amble into view. Varmint shooting wasn't a kind of hunting I particularly cared for. Woodchucks do dig holes in meadows that might break the legs of horses and cows, but those who hunt varmints hunt mostly for the joy of killing, not to put meat on the table. Killing for its own sake is not a pastime I approve of, but it is legal, and I generally keep my mouth shut when I see a varmint hunter on property that is not his to protect. Varmint hunters almost never are Indians, whose cultural taboo against the unnecessary slaughter of animals is so deeply ingrained that even the most modern of them shun the practice.

"From what we've been able to find out about Kling," Alex said, "he wasn't a hunter of any kind. At least his neighbors didn't seem to think so. So what was he doing with this rifle?"

"Maybe it wasn't intended for varmints of the furry kind," I said.

"If somebody wanted to do Arthur Kling in," Alex said, "maybe Arthur Kling wanted to do somebody in."

"And got done in first."

"Looks like it. This rifle's brand-new. I'm not sure it's ever been fired. Barrel's clean, action's immaculate."

"I'm in!" Willie called.

Alex and I crowded behind him in front of the laptop screen. Sue looked up from her desk.

"What do you see?" I asked.

"Let me call this up. It's the GPS program."

A few taps of the keys and a click of the mouse brought up a topographical map of the western Upper Peninsula of Michigan.

"Looky this," Alex said. Seven tiny red flags speckled the map. Five of them lay inside the boundaries of Porcupine County, two in Gogebic County.

"Put your cursor on this one," I said, pointing to a flag that looked as if it had been pasted on the map at a point five miles northeast of Watersmeet.

The young trooper did so.

"Now click on it."

Right next to the flag a small box suddenly appeared, with the legend WILDHAWK in tiny letters inside it.

On the left side of the screen lay a large box headed WAYPOINTS. Inside the box appeared seven names: ROEBUCK, FISHER, WEASEL, WILDHAWK, EAGLE, MARTEN and FOX.

"Click on WILDHAWK," I said.

The trooper did so. Another box opened. In it lay the legend N 46 19.107 W 89 09.740.

"Sue, let me see the file a minute," I said. She handed it to me, and I riffled through the contents until I found the page

I wanted, and checked the numbers on the computer screen against those we'd decoded from the bar code tag on the Poor Farm corpse. They matched down to the last decimal place.

"Bingo," I said. "That WILDHAWK waypoint's where we found the corpse near Watersmeet."

"What's a waypoint?" Sue said.

"It's the name GPS users give a spot on the earth whose coordinates have been marked with a receiver. Those flags show waypoints."

"Look at MARTEN," Alex said. "Bet that's right on the North Country Trail where you found the third stiff."

"Not to mention FOX," I said. "That's the Poor Farm cache."

"And ROEBUCK. The Gogebic County sand pit."

"What about FISHER, WEASEL and EAGLE?" asked Sue. She had been paying careful attention to us while studying the case file. I admire people who can multitask.

"What do we think those are?" Alex asked rhetorically.

"More corpses?" Willie interjected.

"Have you ever bet on a sure thing, son?"

Willie sat silent for several beats. Then he spoke.

"Seven cached bodies, one of them a homicide, plus a car homicide and a missing person? Are we dealing with a serial killer?"

"Possibly," Sue said. She was a little more than half through the thick file we had assembled. "Maybe. Probably. I don't know. We won't know till those other three corpses are found, and maybe not even then. Right now I'd say we've got a serial weirdo of some kind. Got to keep plowing through this stuff."

"Weirdo?" I said. "Is that what you shrinks call them?"

"Among other things," she said. "And I'm not a shrink, I'm a psychologist." Her tone was amused.

"Or serial weirdos," Alex said.

"Indeed," Sue said. "That's why I'm here. We're

usually called in for serial homicides."

"Before we go look for those other three bodies," I said, "let's figure out what we're going to do when we find them. I don't think we should scoop 'em up right away."

"Why not?" asked the young trooper, who didn't yet know all the details.

"We don't want to tip off the perps that we've got this laptop," Alex said. "We don't know who they are yet. For now we're going to treat those caches as bait for the cachers."

"Right," I said. "Let's clue in Andy."

Andy Messner was Gogebic County's longtime sheriff. He knew all about the corpses at Watersmeet and the sand pit and was letting Dan and Camilo handle those headaches. In fifteen minutes, Andy arrived from his headquarters at Bessemer, four miles west of Wakefield on U.S. 2, and quickly we told him all the details. In outraged disbelief he shook his massive, bejowled head, wattles flapping — he looks like a Shar-Pei although he's as tenacious as a fox terrier — and said only one word: an appalled "God." People just did not do that kind of thing in *his* jurisdiction.

Half an hour later deputies and troopers had been dispatched with GPSs and coordinates to locate the three undiscovered corpses and instructions to leave them untouched exactly where they were as they were, but to photograph them as much as possible in situ.

"What else we got on that 'puter?" Alex asked Willie, who had further explored the contents of the laptop while Alex, Andy and I worked on the manpower.

"Quite a bit. The encryption code was kid stuff. There was just one password for everything."

"Talk to us."

"Okay, first we got an Excel expense spreadsheet with motels and meals and gas and stuff. Started four months ago and ended ten days ago. Dates and places, they're all there."

"Can you print everything out?" I asked.

"Sure," Willie said, hooking a cable to the laptop. In a

moment the office laser printer began coughing out evidence.

"Now we got this Word file, and I think you'll find it *very* interesting."

"What is it?"

"It's kind of a diary."

"Print it, too."

Alex collected the printouts and he, Sue and I sat down to examine them.

"MAY 1. FOX placed by PLUMBER at coordinates N 46 50.889 W 89 15.940. Clue: Bar code."

Under that, "MAY 18. Found by FIREMAN. Comment: "Great cache, easy to locate, hard to find. Took two hours of searching."

Then, "MAY 18. Found by BROKER. Comment: Took him three tries." And so on later in the summer, by ACTUARY, MEDIC and CLERK.

The FOX paragraphs were followed by six neat entries for the other caches, again listing when they had been found and by whom. Their cachings spanned the early summer, the last one having been cached on July 10. Not all caches had been found by all participants in the scheme. Only two caches, FISHER and WEASEL, were followed by all six names plus the one who had done the caching. FISHER, judging from its map coordinates, was located close to the powerhouse just below Victoria Dam, an impoundment on the Porcupine River in the high Trap Hills twelve miles south of Porcupine City. A mile-long concrete flume carried the river down from the dam to the powerhouse, which provided considerable megawattage to the Upper Peninsula power grid. The pool just below the powerhouse was a favorite Porky fishing spot, and I'd caught bass and bluegill there. Scattered around the area were lots of copses and rocky outcrops perfect for stashing a large cache.

We found the laptop's coordinates for the cache called WEASEL spang in the middle of a Gogebic County campground at Little Girl's Point on Lake Superior. Interstate tourists rarely visited that remote but beautiful shore, popular with locals as a site for weekend partying as well as camping.

And EAGLE? Quick work with a topographical map placed that cache squarely on Fourteen Mile Point, an outcropping of beach fourteen miles northeast of Porcupine City along the lakeshore. A ruined old lighthouse stood there.

Andy threw up his hands in frustration. "This is too damn complicated for my poor simple brain," he said. "Waypoints, caches, code names, dates, corpses, all that shit. Put it up on the blackboard, willya?"

The blackboard covered nearly an entire wall of the Wakefield post's squadroom. In ten minutes Alex and the young trooper had posted almost all we knew about the case, listing the facts according to the site of the cache, the name of the cache, and the map coordinates:

POOR FARM: "FOX," N 46 50.889 W 89 15.940.
Placed May 1 by PLUMBER. Found by FIREMAN May 18, BROKER May 18, ACTUARY May 20, MEDIC June 10, CLERK June 13.

Discovered June 20 by local youths. Sent to MSP Crime Lab Marquette for analysis. Fully embalmed medical cadaver, good condition, slight decomposition, head and hands missing.

WATERSMEET: "WILDHAWK," N 46 19.107 W 89 09.740.
Placed May 18 by BROKER. Found by ACTUARY May 22, MEDIC May 28, CLERK June 3, BARTENDER June 14, FIREMAN June 15, PLUMBER June 18.

Discovered June 25 by PCSD deputy and LVDTP officer. Sent to MSP Crime Lab Marquette for analysis. Funerary embalming only, head and hands missing, decomposition begun. Suspect (Arthur Kling) observed on site July 3 by LVDTP auxiliary.

"Look at that," I said. "All six of the cachers who were looking had found WILDHAWK. Why would Kling come back to the site if he'd already been there, stashed the corpse there?"

"Beats me," Alex said.

"Maybe he was BROKER, the guy who placed the cache? Checking up on it?"

"Wait a minute," Willie said. "How come PLUMBER knew what to put on that bar code on FOX if he didn't know where BROKER was going to cache WILDHAWK? PLUMBER didn't even know BROKER personally, did he? They knew of each other only on the Internet." We mulled that one a while in silence. Then it came to me.

"Maybe, instead of posting the location of WILDHAWK on the Internet," I said, BROKER affixed that bar code to FOX when he found it, thus making it a multicache."

"Multicache?" Willie and Andy asked simultaneously.

I explained how a clue at a multicache sent the seeker to another cache.

"That's a possibility," Alex said. "Let's look at the rest."

N. COUNTRY TRAIL: "MARTEN," N 46 40.340 W 89 27.036.

Placed July 2 by ACTUARY. Found by MEDIC July 5, CLERK July 9, FIREMAN July 10, BROKER July 17.

Discovered by hikers July 20. Sent to MSP Marquette for analysis. Stabbed to death. Head and hands missing. Well decomposed, weak attempt at embalming.

GOGEBIC GRAVEL PIT: "ROEBUCK," N 46 33.865 W 90 05.298.

Placed June 17 by BARTENDER. Found by CLERK June 26, BROKER July 14, PLUMBER July 21, MEDIC July 24.

Discovered Aug. 3 by GCSD and PCSD deputies. Sent to Marquette. Fully embalmed medical cadaver, good condition, head and hands missing.

LITTLE GIRL'S POINT: "WEASEL," N 46 36.384 W 90 19.449

Placed May 22 by MEDIC. Found by ACTUARY May 30, CLERK June 7, BROKER June 11, PLUMBER June 15, FIREMAN June 19, BARTENDER June 22.

Not yet located.

VICTORIA POWERHOUSE: "FISHER," N 46 41.847 W 89 12.508

Placed June 5 by CLERK. Found by BROKER June 10, PLUMBER June 12, BARTENDER June 14, FIREMAN June 27, MEDIC July 7, ACTUARY July 22.
Not yet located.

FOURTEEN MILE POINT: "EAGLE," N 46 59.501 W 89 07.003

Placed July 10 by FIREMAN. Found by PLUMBER July 25.
Not yet located.

I stepped to the blackboard. "We're forgetting a couple of things," I said, quickly scrawling them in:

PAGE FALLS

Car fire and homicide August 2. Victim: Arthur Kling. Shot to death.

UNDETERMINED LOCATION

Missing person of interest: Sharon Shoemaker. Last seen July 28. Possible homicide victim?

We stared at the blackboard for a while, taking it all in, trying to establish patterns and trying to perceive questions that needed to be answered.

"How'd they stay in touch with each other?" Alex suddenly said.

"Easy," Willie said. "Email. This stuff suggests they may all have used the same Yahoo email address, each of them adding a few lines to a single stored message without ever actually sending it out over the Internet. That's a common dodge with criminals who worry about leaving an electronic trail for Internet snoopers to pick up."

"Can we find out who owns that email address?" Alex asked, not very hopefully.

"Naw. We could subpoena the records but the guy who

set up the address would never have used his real name when he registered, probably from a stolen computer or a public one in a hotel lobby. Take it from me, this stuff is untraceable."

"But *who* are these people?" Alex said. "Surely they didn't use their jobs for their code names? That would be too easy."

"Maybe *former* jobs," Sue said. We all looked at her in surprise. She held up another page from the file. "Arthur Kling started his career as a stockbroker."

"And Sharon Shoemaker used to be a bartender," I said. "But I don't think she's that one. That's probably a coincidence. She didn't strike me as having a geocacher's kind of intelligence. Much too simple a person. But I have no idea where she is, and I hope she's not one of those three caches we haven't found yet."

"What about Andrew Monaghan?" Alex said. "If he's in the financial business, too, he might've been an actuary once."

"It'll take me a few minutes to find out," I said. "Alex, your phone?"

"Be my guest."

I called Dick Franciscus at Manhattan Vice. He answered immediately, unsurprised that I was calling. I explained briefly why I was on the line, telling Dick that Monaghan may have had the code name ACTUARY.

"A bit ahead of you," he said. "I knew you'd call again. I've done a little more digging. Monaghan did begin his career after Yale with Penn Mutual Life as an intern in the actuarial department. He moved to Bear Stearns after three years."

I whistled.

"What now?" Dick said.

"Nothing for the moment. We've got to put together a strategy."

"At your service. This is more interesting than hookers and druggies."

That reminded me. "The slashed-up body we found at the site on the North Country Trail called MARTEN, which the laptop credited to ACTUARY, almost certainly was a prostitute. She had needle tracks and the semen of four different men. Hmm. You missing any hookers?"

"Around here they come and go and nobody takes any notice. Once in a while somebody, usually a relative or friend, reports a disappearance. I can check. But don't expect anything. This'll be true anywhere."

"Thanks. It's a long shot, but maybe we can identify her by DNA and tie her to somebody."

I turned to Alex, Willie and Andy. "We seem to be getting somewhere, don't we?" I said.

"Why would the perps use such obvious names as former jobs?" Willie said. "They're such easy clues."

"Maybe they weren't so obvious to them," Andy said. "In-joke, maybe. Those names are easy to remember, at any rate."

"Or they thought they were putting one over on us."

"That happens once in a blue moon," Alex said. "But it's not going to happen in this case."

I snapped my fingers.

"PLUMBER," I said. "Phil Wilson! He's a geocacher and he used to be a plumber."

"*Phil Wilson*?" Alex, Andy and Willie said almost simultaneously. "Oh, no, not Phil."

"Tell me about him," Sue said. I told her all about the Phil I knew. Quiet, shy, lonely, kept to himself, Vietnam vet, apparent post-traumatic stress disorder. A respected citizen, however, a native-born Porky, a successful businessman in a place where simple survival was the greatest mark of success. The last person on earth you'd think would get involved in a scheme like this.

"I don't know," I said, grasping for straws. "Maybe some people like to lead secret lives. Maybe it's a way of getting a little excitement into their lives."

"Yeah, but *Phil*?" Alex said.

"It's hard to say right now," Sue said, closing the case file and placing it on the table directly in front of her, gazing at it as if it were a crystal ball. "But in Mr. Wilson we could be looking at a kind of depression. Often reclusive people with low self-esteem become obsessed with Internet chat groups. They give them a sense of belonging, for the need of human beings for community is powerful.

"Chat groups also give many lonely people a sense of participating in something unique. They feel helpless and hopeless and are easily enticed into irrational acts by people with magnetic personalities. Lonely women who really ought to know better hook up with men they meet in chat rooms who just want quick sex and sometimes the woman's bank account. Once in a while she gets murdered.

"At the other extreme, in Japan hundreds of young people suffering from clinical depression have died in suicide pacts put together on the Web. That almost happened here. Just last year a charismatic drifter in Oregon was charged with trying to talk almost three dozen lonely and depressed housewives from all over the country and Canada into coming to Klamath Falls on Valentine's Day and having sex with him, then hanging themselves naked from a beam in his house afterwards. And remember Jim Jones and all those people he talked into drinking cyanide-laced Kool-Aid?"

Alex, Andy, Willie and I stared at one another.

"Something analogous to that could be happening here with these geocaching enthusiasts," Sue added. "I agree that you ought to talk to Mr. Wilson. And to Mr. Monaghan. He could be another Jim Jones. Or Charlie Manson. Or Ted Bundy."

"How's that?" I said.

"That report from Detective Franciscus in New York. The vice cops' description of Monaghan suggests he's glib, charming, emotionless, deceitful, affects an air of boredom, has a sense of grandiose self-worth and is probably a pathological liar. The childhood arrest for cruelty to animals is a classic early marker. And the car fire after the killing of Kling might be pyromania, not just intent to get rid of the evidence. Those are all classic traits of a sociopath."

"Motive?" I asked.

"Power," Sue said. "Not sex or money or revenge, but lording it over his followers, enticing them into committing an act that society considers one of the most forbidden of taboos. In enticing people to cache human bodies, he may have beaten down whatever weak objections they may have had about respect for the dead by arguing that no living person was being injured by their game."

"Could some of them be necrophiliacs?" I asked.

Sue took a deep breath. "Death and sex go together like apple and pie," she said. "That's why after a funeral, everybody goes home and makes babies. And it's well known that sex can be made more exciting by games that simulate danger and pain, games that come close to death.

"But in this case I don't think the cachers want to have sex with a dead body. You know Erich Fromm, the psychoanalyst and philosopher? He argued that attraction to human corpses wasn't necessarily sexual, that it was just an attraction to that which is dead, therefore totally under the person's control. Dead people are not people—just objects, things that can be dealt with. That includes being hidden under logs in the forest."

"In other words," Willie said, "they're all sick fucks."

"Not a term I'd use," Sue said with feigned primness, "but it'll do for now."

TWENTY-NINE

Phil Wilson was certainly sick but in no way a fuck, I felt certain as I entered his hardware store the next morning. At my hello he looked up from stocking shelves with Black & Decker power tools, the favorite weapons of weekend woodworkers. "Need a word with you." I said. "Somewhere we can talk in private?"

"My office." He stood and walked toward it.

Although he did not look me in the eye, his gait was calm and unperturbed, his voice even, his hands steady. Either he was a very good actor, I thought, or he didn't have a damned thing to do with the case.

"Do ya for?" he said, gazing at the wall as he settled into a scarred but still valuable antique oak swivel chair behind a small table camouflaged with piles and piles of invoices. Phil had been offered as much as a thousand dollars for it on the spot by antique dealers who dropped in to buy a screwdriver and discovered a treasure. Up to then I thought Phil had liked it too much to let it go, and that he was not an avaricious man. Now I was beginning to think he just didn't care.

I took a plastic lawn chair from a pile beside the door, pulled it into the office, closed the door and faced Phil. Maybe a frontal assault would jolt him into dropping his guard, if his calmness indeed were a guard he had put up against me.

"Phil," I said, "we have information that suggests you are involved with those embalmed corpses we've found around the county in the last couple of months."

I wasn't prepared for his answer.

"Knew you'd find out sooner or later," he said, looking me in the eye for the first time, maintaining his composure. "I tried to tell the others we couldn't get away with it for long."

I stared at him. Phil *Wilson*? It had been my idea that he might be involved in this appalling game, but I still couldn't believe the truth. For a few moments he returned my silent gaze.

"Phil, I think you'd better come down to the department and make a statement," I said. "This is pretty serious and it could take a while."

"Can I bring my lawyer?"

"That's your right. Tell him to meet us there."

"I'll call him now."

He did so while I stood sentinel outside his office, watching him through the glass door, mindful of lawyer-client confidentiality. The conversation was short. Phil rose from his chair and nodded.

"Ready?"

"Yup. Let's go."

He shrugged into his jacket and stood facing me, hands slightly forward, as if anticipating being cuffed.

"Am I under arrest?" he asked.

"Not at this moment. You're cooperating in our investigation. But I'd like you to ride with me." I wasn't letting him out of my sight until we'd got to the bottom of this matter.

"All right," he said unconcernedly, his expression morose. In another suspect it would have appeared that of the situation at last were beginning to sink in, chipping at his armor. But Phil was beyond caring what happened to him.

At the sheriff's department Grady Craig was waiting for us. Like those increasing numbers of summer outsiders from the cities who had fallen in love with Porcupine County and moved here, the skinny, bearded lawyer had retired early, in his fifties, from his job as a veteran assistant state's attorney in Peoria, Illinois, and set up a general legal practice in Porcupine City. It wasn't often that a criminal case broke up the daily and not very busy country grind of wills, probates, land deeds and other civil matters. I liked him. I thought he was a reasonable fellow. Maybe that was because he usually saw things my way, but he also knew how to do his best for his clients without needlessly pissing off the other side. That was the mark of a good advocate.

"Conference with my client?" Grady said.

I let them have the interrogation room to themselves while I called Alex and filled him in. Their chat lasted less than a minute. That told me Phil probably had already informed Grady of his involvement and they had discussed the best course to follow.

I sat across the small table from Phil and Grady.

"Steve, before you turn on the recorder," Grady said, "I'd like to say that my client has agreed to speak freely in exchange for immunity from prosecution. He had planned to come forward, anyway."

"I can't promise immunity. You know that. I'll have to talk to the prosecutor first and see what he says. I can't say what the charges will be. I think he'll give Phil every consideration, though, if he agrees to be open and frank with us."

"That's all right," Grady said. He knew the ropes and was just going through the motions. "Phil has agreed to talk no matter what."

I looked at Phil. He nodded.

"Go ahead," Grady said, "Turn on the recorder."

I delivered the usual warnings and Phil gave the usual response that he had been instructed and was speaking of his own free will.

"Shall I begin at the beginning?" he asked emotionlessly, his eyes on the desk in front of him.

"Please do."

And he did, the flood of words suggesting that he was at last beginning to emerge from the lonely darkness that had so long enveloped him.

A little more than a year before, Phil said woodenly, he

had been cruising an Internet chat room devoted to geocaching when the discussion suddenly turned jokingly to extreme forms of the sport. Most of the talk was absurd, such as suggesting hiding a handgun somewhere on the grounds of a high-security prison or caching a tin full of cookies at the top of Mount Everest. LOL. :-). Et cetera.

Then someone suggested digging up a grave and caching the contents in another cemetery.

"Everybody said 'Yuck,' Phil said in a monotone. 'Then somebody said, 'This is going too far. We really shouldn't be talking this way.' He was right. Geocachers know the rules of the sport have to be obeyed or somebody's going to ruin it for everybody.

"It was at that point I got a private instant message from a geocacher in the room who had been calling himself MONEYBAGS. He'd been cruising the chat rooms for a couple of weeks."

I kept my expression neutral.

"He said, 'Hey, that gives me an idea. You can't beat dead bodies as a cache, can you? How about getting together a few guys for a private group caching game, each of us to hide one in the woods somewhere for the others to find?'

For a brief moment animation entered Phil's voice and he reached across the table, touching my sleeve. I did not pull back.

"I've got to tell you, Steve, that blew my mind. The idea's not only awful but it goes against everything in the rules of geocaching. But when MONEYBAGS invited me to a private chat room to talk about it I couldn't resist. He was so smooth and persuasive. 'Nobody's ever done this before,' he said. 'We'll be pioneers. We'll be the only geocachers on earth who've ever used bodies as caches. That'll set us apart from everybody else.' The great thing about it, he said, was that nobody would get hurt, because nobody would ever know. He said what we'd do is use medical cadavers, bodies that nobody would miss. Cadavers are easy to get, he said. He'd help us with that. And the bribes wouldn't need to be very big. Piece of cake.

"There were seven of us in that room, and everybody but one said okay. He said 'Not for me, sorry,' and clicked off. MONEYBAGS then said that to protect ourselves we all should use new names for this particular round of caching, and suggested we take them from old jobs we'd once done. He said he would call himself ACTUARY. I used to be a plumber, so I became PLUMBER. The others were BROKER, CLERK, FIREMAN, MEDIC and BARTENDER."

Now I had no doubt that Phil was telling the truth.

"Okay. Go on."

"Part of the deal was we would never meet each other. We would know absolutely nothing about each other — only our code names. We didn't know what the others did for a living, or even where they lived, let alone what their real names were. That would protect the rest of us if one got caught. MONEYBAGS — ACTUARY, actually — said part of the fun would in be not getting caught, and if anyone was, it'd be his own fault."

The conspirators then decided they'd all cache their treasures in the same general region, to make traveling simpler and finding the caches easier. "I suggested the western Upper Peninsula because there are so many good places to cache things," Phil said. "And I volunteered to do the first cache, while BROKER agreed to be the coordinator of information. He set up an untraceable email address on Yahoo for us all to use."

Phil took a deep breath and shuddered.

"Where did you find your cadaver?" I said.

"ACTUARY gave me a cell number to call in Duluth. The guy said he had a body whose head and hands had been harvested and was waiting for orders for more parts, but he could let me have it for fifteen hundred bucks, that he could easily doctor the records. The guy met me with a van down by the docks with the package, already wrapped in clear plastic. I put it in my truck and brought it back that night."

Where'd you get the fifteen hundred?" I asked. That was a considerable sum in Porcupine County for even a successful small businessman to spend on a whimsy, even if it had turned into an obsession.

"Savings bond I'd had since high school. It was a graduation present."

"Oh," I said. "So you didn't have the head and hands removed to prevent identification?"

"No. That was just a convenient extra. I told the others about it right away, and they all agreed they'd make sure their caches didn't have hands or heads, too. It would be more protection for everybody."

"Where and when did you place that first cache?"

"May first, at the Poor Farm."

"Why the Poor Farm?"

"Nobody would ever think of going to that room in the house. Nobody had been there in maybe years. You see, the idea was that once everybody had located a cache, the guy who put it there would carry it away and bury it deep in the woods somewhere where it never would be found. And so we'd be safe."

"Did you give the cache a code name?" I asked.

"Yes. FOX. We decided to use the names of forest animals. It seemed to be appropriate to the Upper Peninsula."

Again that matched the information we had found on Kling's computer.

"Did everybody find FOX?"

"I don't think so. FIREMAN and BARTENDER said they hadn't found it yet. But I don't know. It's been a couple of weeks since our email drop was updated."

"Email drop?"

"We all use the same Yahoo email address, adding to the single message there and not sending it out."

"Yeah, I understand that."

"How'd you know?"

Phil was cooperating. Everything he had told me corresponded exactly to what we had learned from Arthur Kling's laptop. I decided to cooperate, too, to tell him some of what I knew so that he would be encouraged to keep on talking.

"We found a laptop, and we think BROKER was using it. It had the locations of all the caches on it as well as all the participants in the game. Did you find all the locations yourself?" That was a trick question, for I already knew the answer. Phil didn't disappoint me.

"No. I didn't find MARTEN. I hadn't looked for it yet when the word got out that you guys had found a corpse on the North Country Trail. I knew from the email site that ACTUARY had put one in that area. That's when I started to get scared. I knew you guys would find me sooner or later. ACTUARY said you were dumb but I know you're not.

"Wish you'd done that earlier, Phil," I said. "Would've saved us a lot of trouble."

"Yes, I'm sorry," he said, genuine contrition in his voice. He looked up. "Did you find BROKER, the guy with the laptop?"

"Yes."

"Where's he now? Is he under arrest?"

I stared at Phil's guileless face. He had not made the connection to the homicide in the burned Beemer. Yes, he was being honest. No reason for him not to be.

"Phil, he's dead. Murdered. He was that guy in the car fire at Page Falls."

Both Phil and Grady gasped audibly.

"Yes, Phil, this is a homicide investigation now," I said.

He buried his hands in his face and said in a quavering voice, "I was afraid this whole thing would go too far, that somebody would fuck up. I'm so stupid. Stupid, stupid, *stupid!* We all fucked up the day we decided to do this thing."

We all three sat silent for a while. Then I said, "Hang on a moment. I'll be right back."

At my desk I called the prosecutor and told him what I had learned. "Garner, I don't want to move on Phil right away, if that's okay with you. To detain him right now would take him out of circulation on the Internet, and that might tip off the other perps that we've cottoned on to their game and might insure we'll never be able to catch them. Can you postpone your interview with Phil for a day or two?"

"Sure," Garner replied. He is one prosecutor who knows the value of patience in a criminal investigation.

Back in the interrogation room I said, "Phil, I'll probably want to talk to you some more. I'm not going to charge you now. I'm going to let you walk out of here a free man. What I want you to do is go about your business as if nothing has happened, and to say absolutely nothing to anybody about this. Can you do that?"

He nodded dumbly.

"If you feel you have to talk to somebody, go see Grady. Or come to me."

I glanced at the lawyer. He nodded. He understood perfectly well.

On the way out I gripped Phil's shoulder. "I'm sorry," I said. "Soldier to soldier."

He began to weep.

THIRTY

I called Alex at Wakefield and quickly filled him in. He did the same for me.

"FISHER and WEASEL are gone," he said. "There's no WEASEL, as far as the Gogebic deputies could find, at Little Girls Point. They did find a scooped-out spot in the sand that looked as if it had been disturbed recently. It was under a downed pine, four feet thick, just below a bluff right at the tree line of the beach. Anything put there would've been well out of sight from the beach and the woods. They found a quarter and a dime at the bottom of the depression."

"That's good enough for me," I said. "We can chalk off WEASEL."

"And right at the coordinates the laptop gave for FISHER just below the Victoria powerhouse, we found a broken cairn of rocks that was big enough to easily have covered a human cache. The rocks had been scattered very recently. The earth was disturbed and it was raw."

"That should pretty well clinch it," I said. "Phil said when everybody found a cache it'd be removed and disposed of. That leaves just one we haven't found: EAGLE, at Fourteen Mile Point."

"Correction. Chad just called. He found it. Right inside the open wall of the old lighthouse at exactly the waypoint he was looking for. Another clean cadaver in heavy plastic, the usual M.O., no head or hands."

We sat silent for a moment. "Now what?" Alex said.

"Let's backtrack a bit and add things up. If Phil didn't know Kling had been killed, that probably means most of the others don't know, either."

"Except the guy who killed him."

"Right."

"So that leaves five geocachers we haven't found."

"Remind me," Alex said. "How many of the other caches haven't been found by everybody yet, according to that laptop?"

"WEASEL and FISHER seem to have been the only ones everybody found. That leaves five."

"Stakeout time for the remaining five caches," Alex said. "Stake 'em out till somebody shows up."

"That's a lot of guys for five stakeouts," I protested. "Two twelve-hour shifts each. That's ten guys."

"Look, it's already out that four corpses have been found by the cops. Maybe the five surviving cachers all know the story. They've already all located WEASEL and FISHER. Maybe they know we've found FOX, WILDHAWK, MARTEN and ROEBUCK. If they do, that would leaves only one cache that really needs staking out: EAGLE, at Fourteen Mile Point."

"But you're assuming that all the cachers read the newspapers. Maybe they don't. And I don't think the case has become a national story yet. If any of the cachers live outside the Midwest, maybe it hasn't been in their papers. I've checked the Internet, and it's still only a regional story."

I could hear Alex riffling the pages of the printouts from the laptop.

"You may be right," he said. "But I think with our manpower shortage we ought to stake out just one cache right now, the one at Fourteen Mile Point."

"That's gonna take some pretty hard camping."

"That's what Chad said."

"He already figured on a stakeout?" I said.

"Yup. He's learning."

"What say we give him the first couple of days?"

"That's cruel."

"He's younger than either you or me. He'll hold up better."

"Speak for yourself, old man."

I chuckled. "I'll give him a call right now and get him

going out there. The sooner we have that covered the better. I have a feeling we're going to make our big pinch there."

"Something else you ought to know," Alex said.

"Yes?"

"Eli's not giving up. This morning he announced in a full-page ad in the Globe that he was starting a write-in campaign for November."

"Oh, damn. That's what he meant when he said it wasn't over."

Alex and I both knew the implications. A lame duck who won't stay lame can complicate life for a sheriff's department. I'd have to keep campaigning for three more months, for I couldn't afford to relax. It's true that write-in campaigns rarely if ever win an election anywhere, but this was not the usual anywhere, nor was it a run-of-the-mill election. The citizens of Porcupine County are veteran ticket-splitters and quite capable of write-in voting en masse. Moreover, Eli was still determined, powerful and dangerous, perfectly capable of running the kind of intense campaign that turned things to his advantage.

And I wondered where he'd got the money for that ad. The *Ironwood Globe* is a daily with a circulation of several thousand, not a weekly seen by a thousand or so. Full-page ads are costly. Someone must be supporting him. But who and why? I had no idea about the first, but entertained some suspicions about the second. Some people in the far North, even at the beginning of the twenty-first century, didn't care for the idea of a nonwhite person in a position of authority over them. And perhaps Eli was in somebody's pocket, although Porcupine County is so poor that the fruits of official corruption would be so thin and starved that they were hardly worth the bother.

I sighed and called Chad. He was all ready to go and only needed the order.

THIRTY-ONE

At the sheriff's department the next morning I made up an excuse to drive to Matchwood and pay a call on my erstwhile and still titular boss.

He was not friendly. As I dismounted from the Explorer, his glowering face appeared inside the screen door, and as I walked up the flagstone path to his modest frame house set into a clearing just off a dirt road fronting onto Highway M-28, he opened the door and stepped out onto the porch, bristling so fiercely that I looked carefully to make sure he was not holding a weapon. He wasn't.

"Martinez, you have some nerve coming here," he said, his sun-ruddied cheeks quivering with anger.

"Yeah, sheriff, but I have to talk to you. Departmental business."

He glared, and we stood awkwardly on the porch for a moment, eyeing each other like roosters at a cockfight. Then he said, "You'd better come in," and held the door open.

"Sit anywhere," he said, sweeping his arm around the small living room. It was modestly furnished with a clean but threadbare sofa and easy chair, battered walnut coffee table, crazed yellow china lamps that probably had come from St. Vincent de Paul's, and a brand-new fake Oriental rug of Wal-Mart quality. One wall almost sagged with the weight of scores of family photographs in cheap metal frames. Chintz curtains dressed the windows and an aged golden retriever lying on the rug thumped his tail in lazy greeting. This was not the house of a politician on the take, not that I had ever thought Eli might be. He was the kind of pol who did questionable favors for people because either they were relatives or he just liked them.

Dorothy came in from the kitchen, followed by the aroma of baking bread. Ever polite and welcoming even in the most awkward social situations, she said, "Coffee, Steve?"

"He won't be here that—," Eli started to say before his wife's iron stare cut him short. Dorothy takes no crap from her husband. She will not allow her hospitality to be compromised.

"Yes, please. Black with one lump, please," I said.

When Dorothy returned to the kitchen Eli heaved a deep sigh and said resignedly, "All right, Martinez, what's on your mind?"

"A lot of things."

"What's the first?"

"Why are you still running for sheriff, Eli? I beat you fair and square in the primary. You haven't got much chance as a write-in."

"Maybe not," Eli said, his gaze drilling through me, "but it's still a chance."

"The talk is you spent all your money in the primary. Where's the dough coming from for those full-pagers in the Globe?"

"None of your business."

"It's the people's business. You and I both know that." Election laws everywhere require full disclosure of political donations over a nominal sum.

"Yeah, I'll file the info when it's required." Eli's tone was only slightly conciliatory.

"But that doesn't explain why you're doing this. You're risking all your assets as well as your reputation on this . . . this . . . this wild-goose chase." I wanted to say "Thermopylae," where in 480 B.C. Leonidas, the hopelessly outnumbered Spartan king, made his last stand against the Persian army, but I didn't think Eli, hardly an educated man, would recognize the classical allusion.

"You don't have to know."

"Maybe not, but, goddammit, I want to. I care. I care about this county and I care about who I work for."

"Used to work for," Eli said dismissively.

"Still do."

Eli grunted.

Dorothy swept in with a tray, a carafe of coffee, three cups, cream and sugar, and sat down in an armchair next to Eli's. I looked at her.

"Anything we say she can hear," Eli said. "From all over the house. She might as well be here. I don't keep stuff from her anyways."

It struck me that he might have wanted a witness to anything that ensued, whatever it might be.

"No problem," I said. "Thanks for the coffee, Dorothy."

She nodded. I had always been on first-name terms with her and there was no reason to change.

I looked at Eli. "We were talking about why you were still running."

"No Garrow has ever backed down from a fight. We've always been in it to the last."

"Why?"

"We care. Like you, we care. We care about the county and we care about the job. And we care about history."

"History as in?"

"History as in how it'll remember me." Eli's voice quavered slightly and his ruddy cheeks colored even more deeply. I had never heard that from him before, not even at the cop funerals where he often spoke, and he is not an unsentimental man. But for the first time that morning Eli looked old, as if he had finally realized that he was no longer the vigorous lawman he had been in his prime. The color suddenly faded from his face, leaving it gray and almost sunken.

I made a decision. "I'm going to tell you something, Sheriff."

"What?"

"What's been going on with all those bodies. You have a right to know."

"All right." He sat up straight and fixed his gaze on me, awaiting his deputy's report. He almost looked like the old Eli again.

I filled him in, leaving nothing out, making sure he understood the fine points of geocaching and outlining Sergeant Sue Hemb's hypotheses. He listened attentively, nodding in all the right places and shaking his head in all the right places too.

"It's hard to believe that anybody could be talked into doing something this weird, joining a game to plant bodies in the woods for somebody else to find," Eli said. "That isn't a game, it's . . . it's evil. It's a *perversion.*"

"Yes," I said. "But I think Sergeant Hemb is right. In an Internet chat room, psychologically susceptible people can be manipulated into doing things they'd never even think about out in the light of day. Think how easy it'd be for a psychopath to mesmerize a bunch of mentally ill people into playing around with the illegal transport of human remains."

"God." Eli's eyebrows shot up disbelievingly. "I don't know anybody who'd bite."

"But you do." When I told him about Phil Wilson his eyebrows rose even higher and he said "*Phil?*"

"That's what we said, too."

"I'll be damned. But . . . I see what you mean." Eli knew Phil well, too.

"And so we're keeping a lid on the case," I finished.

For a few moments we sat silently as Eli digested my story.

"That stiff at Fourteen Mile Point," he finally said. "That wasn't humped in by any stranger. Those old logging trails were grown over long ago. It had to have been carried there by boat and by somebody who knew the place." The only other ways to reach the lighthouse there are to hike the fourteen rugged miles of lake shore from Porcupine City, or, in the winter, go by snowmobile.

"The other geocachers had to have come in by boat, too," I said. "And if any if them don't yet know we've found some of their caches, they'll come in from the lake as well."

"Should be easy to stake out," Eli said. "Haul the camping gear in with the department's Whaler, hide the boat up the first creek east of the lighthouse, pitch a tent inside the tree line and keep an eye on the beach. If it takes more than a few days before we make a bust we could borrow a couple of old Indians from the tribal police, give them the tent and a wanagan of grub for the duration."

Eli, once again the veteran cop, had anticipated exactly what Alex and I had done.

"Yes," I said. "Chad's gone out already."

"Anything more?" said Eli, his tone still commanding.

"No, that's it," I said. "You know everything."

"I'll let you know if I think of anything else."

"Yes, sir," I said, keeping my tone deferential.

Eli stood up. "Thanks for coming," he said. He did not hold out his hand.

I put on my ball cap and turned to leave.

"Steve, I'm not going to quit," he said. "I'm going to run. And I'm going to beat you." Leonidas, defiant as ever, facing the hordes of Xerxes. Leonidas was a stubborn old son of a bitch, too.

"It'll be a contest," I said noncommittally, and stepped out the door.

As I started the Explorer it finally struck me: Eli had called me "Steve." Not "Martinez." Not "Deputy."

"What's in a name?" Shakespeare's Juliet asked. She didn't know the half of it. "Everything" — that's the real answer.

THIRTY-TWO

True to his word, Eli campaigned hard. But, for a change, he campaigned cleanly. From the day of our meeting at his house, his ads and his words focused on his record and his proposals, not on innuendo about the perceived shortcomings of his opponent. In fact, he barely mentioned me at all, and he said absolutely nothing about the case that had so frustrated four police forces for weeks. Yes, he was cranky and contrary and stubborn and self-involved, but under all that old man's blather, his essential decency was emerging again. You can't despise a man for caring.

Voters talked about the change. The political junkies took it as a shrewd new tack taken by a candidate for whom negative campaigning hadn't worked. The broad Garrow fan base treated it as something they'd known about all along. The Steve Martinez brain trust worried about it. "I've never heard of a write-in winning any office in Porcupine County," Garner Armstrong declared, "but there's going to be a first time, and this could be it."

I changed my own campaigning in the same way, avoiding the subject of Eli's absence from office and never mentioning the issue of age. Instead — at Garner's insistence — I uneasily focused on my education, experience and accomplishments. I didn't want to rub my master's degree under people's hides in a region where high school and maybe a year or two at a community college was as much formal education as most people had. Nor did I want to talk about having been an Army officer to people whose sons and daughters had been enlistees. All that sounded too elitist.

I had less trouble telling people about tracking down the murderer of Paul Passoja, who had been the most powerful citizen of Porcupine County when he was killed in an act of revenge concocted by a female deputy sheriff he had sexually abused when she was a girl. Nor did I hesitate to mention catching a big-city drug lord who had grown world-class narcotic plants deep inside an abandoned copper mine and shipped them to South America. To my surprise, the slightest hint of those cases drew cheers during my campaign stops, temporarily banishing growls of dismay over the vexing case of the corpses strewn around the countryside. Maybe mentioning the earlier victories raised hopes that the new case would also be solved.

I was beginning to have doubts, although we were making progress.

On my day off a few days after I went to see Eli, I got a phone call at home from Dan Roane. "We caught one of the geocachers this morning," he said.

"Tell me."

"It's FIREMAN. His name's Ted Wilt. He's a Wal-Mart superstore manager in Minneapolis, and a summer resident here. He has a cottage on Lake Gogebic. I busted him myself at the sand pit. He drove into the pit and was poking about with his GPS when I rolled up behind his car with a couple of deer carcasses in my truck. Caught him right at the cache site, levering the logs aside. He's scared and he's talking, but he's not telling us much we don't already know. He says he's never met any of the other players except on the Internet."

"Where'd he get his corpse?"

"Duluth," Dan said. "A cell phone connection ACTUARY gave him. Just like the other guy's."

I whistled. This case was getting ever deeper.

"What about Fourteen Mile Point?" I said. "Did he admit caching there?"

"Yes."

"Doesn't surprise me that he's the one. I always thought some of these places had to have been picked by people who knew this country. What's he like?"

"Very cooperative. Quiet, mild-mannered, nerdy,

baldish, dumpy, lives alone—poster boy for Sergeant Hemb's theory. He seemed shocked when we told him that homicide was involved and he wanted to know exactly how. When I told him about the car fire he said he hadn't heard anything about that because he'd been back in Minneapolis. He also said he'd been there most of the summer and had no idea we'd found any of the caches. He didn't seem to be trying to hide anything. I believe him."

"Maybe that's a good thing he didn't know about the fire or that we'd found the caches," I said. "Maybe our killer doesn't know we know, either. Dan, can you keep this guy on ice for a day or two?"

"I'll charge him with the dead-body felony and get the judge to set the bond high enough to keep him in jail until Monday. I'll tip the press then."

"Good."

A moment of silence while a radio crackled in the background, then Dan said, "Shit. Got another deer-car call. That's the third one today."

"The eagles love you, don't they? You're their best buddy."

"Ha. Later, Steve."

Almost as soon as I hung up, the phone rang. It was Ginny.

"Could you stop by?" she said. "I need a favor."

"Sure. What is it?"

"Tell you when you get here."

I hung up and walked out to the Jeep, whistling. Two geocachers down—actually, three down, if we included the dead Arthur Kling—and four to go. At Ginny's I'd wheedle a little lunch out of her in return for that favor, whatever it was. I pulled into her driveway still in a good mood, thinking that at last the assembled law enforcement community of the western Upper Peninsula was getting closer to a resolution of the vexing Case of the Cached Corpses. Of course we were, but unknown to me another rock was about to be thrown into the machinery of my life.

A black Rollaboard stood just inside Ginny's front door as I walked in. Small as it was, it held at least a couple of changes of clothes. Ginny knew how to travel light and still make the most of what she took along.

"Going somewhere, Ginny?" I called.

"Yes," she replied from upstairs. "Thanks for coming by. I have to go to New York today. Would you take Tommy for a few days?"

"Sure, but what's happening in New York?"

She swept downstairs in a smart gray executive suit I'd seen her in only once before, when her lawyers visited her to discuss foundation matters. Neutral hose and heels and a faint spray of Vol de Nuit completed the ensemble. When she wanted to, she could dress in the trappings of power and wealth. She knew exactly how to present herself.

"Sit down."

I groaned inwardly. Whenever she told me to sit down, I knew heavy news was about to be laid upon me. "All right."

"Steve, Malcolm called me last night."

"Malcolm Benson?" He was the gold-digger who had very nearly persuaded the wealthy young widow Virginia Fitzgerald to marry him so that he could plunder her fortune to support the Baptist international refugee agency he ran. He had been married five times, Ginny discovered just in the nick of time, soaking every one of his wives for most of their assets before they threw him out of the house and consulted a divorce lawyer. Ginny's heart had been slashed and bruised, and it had taken her a long time to learn to trust a man again.

"Yes. He's dying of cancer at Memorial Sloan-Kettering. He wants to see me before he goes."

I took a deep breath. "Is he really?" I said skeptically. "Or is this another scam he's running?"

Ginny's green eyes flashed, as they did every time I called her judgment into question. Whenever this happened I was usually wrong, but not always.

"I've had my lawyers check out the situation," she said. "They said it's true, that he hasn't long to live."

I nodded. Ginny's Detroit law firm, though small, was one of that city's shrewdest and most powerful. It handled the foundation through which she secretly supported much of Porcupine County. It was very, very competent.

"Why is he reaching out to you after all these years and after what he tried to do to you?"

"He wants to apologize, to make peace with those he has wronged," she said. Not "He says he wants to . . . ," the words a cop would have used. Cops are careful. Cops expect the worst and are surprised at the best.

"Born again, huh?" Cops are cynical. Deathbed and death row conversions are as common as baptisms, but the newly saved are still guilty as hell. Salvation doesn't always change their behavior towards others, either. They were born sinners and they will die sinners. "Being sorry doesn't change history," I said.

Ginny glared. I winced. I shouldn't have said that. I should have gathered her into my arms and whispered words of support and assent. But I can't help it. A cop is a cop. Cops can be dumb. Even smart ones.

"I'm sorry. Flying out of Houghton? Want me to drive you to the airport?" I said quickly in a futile attempt to cover my tactlessness. She'd take a little commuter jet to Detroit, then a Northwest 737 to LaGuardia.

"Thank you, but no," she said coldly. "I'll drive myself. Thank you for taking Tommy. He's packing upstairs."

She did let me carry her Rollaboard out, and she coolly held up her cheek to be pecked before getting into her minivan.

"When will you be back?" I asked.

"Don't know," she said. "A few days. Maybe a week."

She drove away, her face still set in granite.

Tommy appeared on the doorstep, gazing at me sadly. He had heard everything. I could have sworn he shook his head slightly, as if to say, "You've blown it."

I took a deep breath. "Let's go."

He whistled and Hogan bounded out the door. Suitcase, backpack, dog gear and dog in the back seat, we drove to my cabin a few miles west down the lake shore. When we arrived, I said, "Tommy, I've got some errands to run in town. Can you keep yourself busy?"

"Sure," he said. "I'd like to take Hogan and put a little geocache in the woods. Can I?"

"Where?"

"Just off Town Line Road near the old Finn cemetery," he said. That was just a quarter of a mile up a lightly traveled asphalt road through the woods. The place was fairly close to civilization. Plenty of houses kept watch along the road. And Tommy knew how to handle himself in the woods.

"Okay," I said. "Be back by six and we'll have a steak for dinner, okay?"

"Sure thing! Thanks!"

I was in the doghouse, but there was hope if Ginny had entrusted me with Tommy. I wouldn't let her down, either, I thought as I got back into my Jeep and drove to Porcupine City.

THIRTY-THREE

Tommy hadn't returned from his mission when I arrived at my cabin shortly after four. I wasn't worried. The kid was twelve, knew his way around the woods, and carried a GPS. Hogan was with him, but that wasn't worrisome either, for wolves hadn't yet been seen so close to civilization. So far they'd stuck to the most remote wilderness in the county, many miles south and west of the Finnish cemetery.

Five o'clock arrived. Tommy is a lad with seemingly inexhaustible curiosity, the kind who, like a cop, carries plastic Baggies in his backpack—not for evidence but for specimens. When I was growing up, we collected interesting bugs, plants and garter snakes in screw-top jars for later examination, sometimes forgetting our stashes until our mothers' screams announced their discovery of strange creatures slithering down the stairs into the living room. The invention of the zip-top Baggie has brought considerable modern convenience to the young backyard explorer, and when the backyard is as big as Porcupine County, those baggies pile up in the kids' bedrooms. Sometimes Ginny has to remind Tommy to either feed his menagerie or let it loose—outside, of course.

Five-thirty. Tommy must be loading down his backpack with lots of weird critters. I hoped none of them were the biting kind.

Five forty-five. Looks like the lad planned to use all the allowed hours of his freedom. I'd done the same as a kid, walking into the house at almost the last minute while Mother glanced suspiciously at the clock. Dad's concept of time was a lot looser. So long as I got in before dark, he didn't mind. He understood the need of boys for adventure. "Don't upset your mother," was all he'd ever say, and if she heard that she was always upset—with him, not with me.

Six o'clock and no Tommy. I stood up from reading Google News on my laptop and looked out the kitchen window onto the driveway, hoping to see his small figure trudging toward the cabin. I sighed. Ginny hadn't ever complained that Tommy abused the privileges of the clock. Maybe, having come to crash with me for a few days away from his foster mother, he was seeing how far he could stretch the envelope. Or maybe he'd just lost track of time, would suddenly glance at his watch, shout guiltily, and hotfoot it for my cabin at flank speed.

Six-fifteen. The first stirrings of irritation. Another glance out the window. A lecture about time and reliability awaited that young man unless he had a good excuse.

Six-thirty. Maybe Hogan had had a run-in with a skunk or maybe Tommy had twisted an ankle and was hobbling slowly home.

Seven. An hour late. Where could that boy be? Now I was beginning to get worried.

At seven-thirty I threw on my denim jacket — mid-September brings cool evenings and chilly nights — and took my Jeep south on Town Line Road, stopping at every house to inquire if they'd seen a small boy, brown-skinned like me, with a dog. Three housewives had, and Mrs. Peters, the widow who lived almost across from the Finnish cemetery, said she'd had a brief chat with Tommy at about three in the afternoon before he crossed the graveyard with his dog and disappeared into the forest on a deer trail. "Nice kid," she said. "Ginny must be delighted with him."

"*I* am not," I said. "Not right now."

I walked to the deer trail and shouted, "Tommy! Tommy!"

No reply. I didn't really expect one.

After five minutes on the trail I decided to turn back. In places the thick leaves blanketing the trail had been disturbed, and a couple of twigs had been stepped on and broken. I may be an Indian, but I'm not a tracker, and I had no idea whether the sign had been left by Tommy, a deer, or something else. And dusk was beginning to fall. It'd be dark a bit after nine, in less than an hour. Nightfall comes late in this part of the Upper Peninsula. Porcupine County lies farther west than Chicago, but we're on Eastern time, not Central as Chicagoans are.

It was time to raise the hue and cry.

I walked back to the Jeep and keyed the new eight-hundred-megahertz handheld radio the department had issued to all deputies for their personal vehicles.

"Twelve-year-old boy missing in the woods," I told Joe Koski, working the night shift this week. "We need a search team out at the Finnish cemetery on Town Line Road. He was last seen there about three this afternoon."

"Who's the boy?"

"Tommy Standing Bear. Ginny Fitzgerald's foster son. He's staying with me while she's out of town."

"Good Lord."

I don't mean to imply that Porcupine County's search-and-rescue squad, made up of law enforcement, firefighters and civilian volunteers, wouldn't give its all to hunt a complete stranger lost in the woods. We're professionals at what we do, and if we sometimes seem a little reticent about showing our feelings, that doesn't mean we don't care. Cool detachment means we can think straight and consider every angle carefully without the baggage of emotion nudging us down a dangerous path. But when one of ours in the law enforcement community is killed, hurt or just missing, we unconsciously try a little harder. Family is family. And though he had no official connection to Deputy Stephen Two Crow Martinez, Tommy Standing Bear was linked to me through my liaison with Virginia Fitzgerald. He was one of ours. He was one of *mine*.

Within the hour every deputy in the county, on duty and off, the better part of the Porcupine City Volunteer Fire

Department, Doc Miller from the hospital, several emergency medical technicians from local ambulance companies and half a dozen loggers—all of them experienced woodsmen—had gathered at the Finnish cemetery. There Gil was setting up a command post.

"You stand down, Steve," Gil immediately barked when he arrived. "That's the rule." He was right. An emotionally involved officer might take unreasonable chances and endanger himself and others, therefore must be removed from the case. This is standard operating procedure in law enforcement departments everywhere.

"But who's going to fly the plane?" I asked. An air search for someone lost in the woods is also SOP.

"Yeah, you'll have to," Gil said. "But not tonight. New moon. Overcast. No starlight."

"Yeah. If Tommy doesn't turn up tonight I'll launch at daybreak. There'll be low cloud but high enough for a low-level search."

"Tell me what you know about Tommy."

I told him, not forgetting to include Tommy's Ojibwa education in the woods, and wound up with Mrs. Peters's conversation with the boy before he disappeared into the forest.

"Think he went to the old Hawthorn Hill Farm?" Gil said.

"Possibly. He said he was going into the woods here, and there's a trail to the farm that branches south a hundred yards or so into the trees."

The Hawthorn Hill Farm, or rather what remains of it, is an abandoned, overgrown ruin, mostly crumbling stone foundations but with a few almost fallen sheds still leaning askew, just south of the Finnish cemetery. During the nineteen-twenties one of the county's lumber magnates, a man who adored the Upper Peninsula—unlike so many of the plutocrats who raped the land and abandoned it to the tax man—decided to do something with the countryside his loggers had denuded, instead of walking away from it. He started Hawthorn Hill as a model farm, first laboriously destumping a hundred acres and then stocking it with the best bulls, cows and pigs he could find in the United States. He had flyers distributed far and wide, including northern Europe and Finland, and advertised in major city papers, touting Hawthorn Hill as a showplace for the land of opportunity for immigrant farmers. Unfortunately the meager provender they were able to produce in the harsh climate couldn't compete with the animals and crops of more temperate Ohio and Indiana, Illinois and the Plains to the south. The immigrants had to scratch out a living in other ways.

Hawthorn Hill today is mostly older second-growth pulpwood, much of it aspen, and some of the most godawful brambles to be found in the North. Few people go there except firewood gatherers from the immediate vicinity and now and then a hopeful fellow with a few marijuana plants. And it was exactly the kind of place an adventurous kid like Tommy might explore, looking for early-twentieth-century farm artifacts abandoned in odd corners.

"How was Tommy dressed?" Gil said.

"A light warmup jacket, blue, with a red Cubs emblem, jeans, Nikes."

"Not enough for a cold night." The temperature often drops below 40 degrees after midnight in September this far north.

"No. But I think he'll have the sense to hole up somewhere, break off boughs, cover himself to stay warm. And he has the big dog."

"That's good to know," Gil said. "But the subject could be injured and need immediate medical aid and we'll have to send a few search teams into the woods now."

"The subject . . . immediate medical aid." Gil was thinking like the professional he is, and I was grateful for that.

"Why don't you go home?" Gil said, as gently as he ever does. "You'll need your rest for the flight tomorrow if the subject doesn't turn up tonight."

I looked at my watch. Ten-thirty. Fifteen searchers dressed in hunter's orange for visibility and carrying powerful flashlights, a couple of them with night-vision scopes mounted on military helmets, stood ready for orders.

"In a minute," I said.

"All right."

Gil turned to the group. "Gonna sound the alarm," he said.

As we covered our ears he reached into his cruiser and flicked a switch. For several seconds the *ooh-ah-ee-ah-ee* of the vehicle's powerful siren knifed into the screen of trees.

"Tommy!" everyone called.

Not a whisper of a reply, nor did anyone expect one.

But the searchers had to start somewhere. At least there had been no howling from wolves in response.

Men began moving up the trail, the beams from their big flashlights bobbing and weaving on the thick foliage as they stepped over roots. At intervals pairs of searchers would split off the trail, calling Tommy's name as they headed southwest, following not only the path to Hawthorn Hill but also the low ridges and valleys of the creeks that ran northward into Lake Superior. Only five miles separated Town Line Road from the vast moonscape of copper tailings from the Lone Pine Mine to the west, but the trails and ridges ran south for nearly ten miles to the L.P. Walsh Road. That was fifty square miles, which does not sound like a lot but is almost all thick forest interspersed with a few small clearings. It is full of deer and bear and coyotes and maybe—I hoped not—wolves. Over the decades scores of people, many of them drunken hunters, have vanished into that country and never turned up again, not even as scattered bones. I did not think the searchers would locate Tommy in the dark. I hoped he and Hogan had gone safely to ground somewhere for the night.

"I'll be by in the morning," I told Gil just as the clouds opened and a steady rain began to fall. He nodded silently and turned back to his cruiser, listening to the steady hum of the searchers as they reported on their progress and complained about the wet.

Back at my cabin I took a deep breath. Time to call Ginny and break the news that her foster son was missing in the woods on a dark and rainy night.

There was no answer. Her cell phone was switched off. She had not told me where she was staying in Manhattan. It was too late in the day to call her lawyers in Detroit and see if they knew.

I slept badly, frequently waking to feelings of overwhelming guilt. I should have had the sense not to allow a minor given into my care to enter the woods alone even in the middle of the day, no matter how good a woodsman he might have been, no matter if he was an Indian who had grown up with the Indian skills I did not have, no matter how doughty a companion animal was with him, no matter if boys of all ages in Porcupine County have gone into the woods since time immemorial. Tommy Standing Bear was only twelve years old.

Each time I awoke I tried Ginny again. No answer.

THIRTY-FOUR

After scarcely five hours of sleep I returned to the command post at the cemetery an hour before first light, my head logy, running on guilt and adrenaline. Taking just a splash of coffee from the big urn Mrs. Peters seemingly had kept filled all night—a pilot who may be aloft four or five hours without a place to relieve himself cannot afford more than a few sips of diuretic—I stepped over to Gil's cruiser, where the undersheriff slept across the backseat. I nudged him, and he instantly snapped awake ready for action, the product of years as a soldier. Other searchers stirred in their cars.

"Brought back the guys at two a.m.," Gil said. "We didn't find a thing. They'll be ready to go at daybreak. Mrs. Peters is bringing over some breakfast."

I could smell the bacon frying across the road. I wondered where she kept the rations to feed two dozen men, one of whom, I noticed, was Chad Garrow, who with Fred Kohut, a retired tribal policeman, had been pulled from the stakeout at Fourteen Mile Point to join in the search. Fred had gone home to the reservation to attend to an ailing wife, but big Chad could eat as much as two ordinary men himself. Part of me was unhappy that the stakeout had been left unmanned, but a more important issue flooded my heart: Tommy was missing.

"Andy Messner's sending up his search-and-rescue crew from Bessemer by ten a.m. If we don't find Tommy by then," Gil said. "Alex asked if we needed the troopers from the Wakefield post. I told him not just yet."

I knew the drill. In an area of this size, if the subject of a search was not found within a few hours of daylight reconnaissance, a line of men twenty feet apart would begin traversing the forest from the cemetery in a broad skirmish line, examining every tree, hollow, downed branch, rock and bush along the way. They would be looking for a body or bodies.

"Okay. I'll be in the air as soon as I can see the end of the runway."

"Take Joe with you."

The dispatcher, who had also spent most of the night sleeping in his pickup, nodded. Two pairs of eyes are much better than one in an air search, especially if one pair was Joe's. He'd flown shotgun with me several times during hunts out on the lake for lost boaters and sweeps of the woods for lost hikers, and on every occasion he spotted our target before I did. So much for the keen eagle vision of an Indian.

"Can't beat a Finn's eyes," Joe often said. His grandfather had emigrated from Helsinki to the Upper Peninsula in the early twentieth century along with many thousands of farmers and woodsmen seeking a new life in a bountiful land. I wonder if he had bought clear-cut land from Hawthorn Hill's founder and destumped it. But Einar Koski, I knew, had died a miner in an accident at Lone Pine, the Upper Peninsula's last copper mine.

After I had preflighted the Skylane and we had strapped ourselves in it, I started the engine, throttling back to low RPMs and holding the plane on the ramp to warm up. It had been a chilly night, the temperature dropping to thirty-eight degrees. I hoped Tommy had been able to stay warm. In ten minutes the Skylane's oil temperature needle had climbed over 200 degrees into the green arc, just as the eastern sky began to bloom a reddish gray with the approaching sun, illuminating the trees at the south end of the runway. I released the brakes and taxied down to the south threshold for a takeoff northward into the soft but increasing breeze off Lake Superior.

A few minutes later we arrived over the Finnish cemetery, where the few members of the search party left at the command post waved as we flew by at seventy knots scarcely two hundred feet above the ground. The rain clouds had cleared out and daylight had just started to outline the wet hills and trees below, but I wanted Tommy to hear the airplane as early as possible so that he would know we were looking for him. I set course for the south over Hawthorn Hill, aiming to fly a pattern of parallel north-south tracks, each one a couple of hundred yards farther west, so that Joe and I could scour every square foot of ground below. As the sun rose and the details of the ground below emerged into high relief, I could see the dark shapes of the searchers fanning out along the ridges and valleys.

For twenty minutes we flew between M-64 and the southern boundary of L.P. Walsh Road, working our way west. Suddenly Joe slapped my shoulder and pointed ahead and slightly to the right. A growing tendril of smoke from a smudge fire crept upward from a small clearing. As we reached the clearing I throttled back to just above minimum controllable speed, lowered two notches of flaps and put the Skylane into a tightly banked circle above the clearing.

"It's him!" Joe shouted through the intercom as at the same instant we saw a small figure wrapped in an olive drab blanket emerge waving with both arms from the tree line into the tall grass, followed by a big yellow dog.

I am not a religious man, but silently, tears brimming in my eyes, I thanked God, the Great Spirit, all the angels of the heavens and all the manitous of the forest for Tommy's deliverance.

Joe keyed the mike. "We've got him!" he called, passing the coordinates of the clearing on his hand-held GPS to the searchers below.

"This is Chad," came the first reply. "We're just half a mile east and are proceeding directly to the spot."

"Write a message to Tommy," I told Joe. "Tell him to stay where he is and the rescuers will arrive in a few minutes. Put it in this backpack and tie this banner to it."

The banner was the four-foot-long signal orange streamer reading "REMOVE BEFORE FLIGHT" that plugged the airplane's pitot tube against mud dauber wasps on the ground. It would make the backpack more visible to Tommy. A small plastic canteen of water and a few granola bars gave the backpack some heft. Joe opened his window and latched it up under the high wing.

This early in the morning there was little breeze, so I didn't have to allow for the wind. Still in the tight circle, I increased the bank slightly, to place the right wing almost on Tommy's head in my field of view, and shouted, "Drop it!"

Joe tossed out the backpack and streamer. The package hurtled down and in three seconds bounced off a hillock not ten yards from the boy and the dog, who both scampered for it at top speed—an exultant sight for me, for it meant Tommy wasn't hurt. Hogan reached the backpack first and carried it to Tommy in his mouth—the first time I had ever seen the dog retrieve anything, half Lab or not.

Tommy pulled out the note, read it, and waved to us as he and Hogan sat on the hillock to eat their impromptu breakfast. Joe and I kept circling until three searchers emerged into the clearing and made their way to Tommy.

"He's fine," Chad radioed. "But hungry."

"Yee-haa!" shouted another voice I couldn't recognize over the slight static.

"Who's that?" I said.

"Garner. I'm at the command post. Everybody's celebrating."

"Yep," I said, the lump still in my throat. "Heading back to the airport now."

In less than half an hour the Skylane was back in its hangar and Joe and I had returned to the cemetery. Grinning searchers still trickled back from the woods, slapping each other on the back. Garner gave me a high-five as I got out of my Jeep. To my surprise Eli was there, having driven up from his home during the air search, and he nodded to me.

"Well done," he said in his old genial but authoritative voice, as if the history of the last few months had never happened. Whether he was actually back in command could have been debated, but he wasn't forcing the issue. It didn't matter. As undersheriff Gil had tactical command over the search operation. Even in old times. Eli wouldn't have second-guessed Gil or tried to override his orders. But everyone at the cemetery noted Eli's presence. It meant things were changing, maybe for the good.

"Tommy back yet?" I asked Gil, whose preternaturally sour expression hadn't softened a smidgen. He knew that I was at fault for letting Tommy go into the woods by himself, but he wasn't going to say a word. He knew that I blamed myself, and that I faced much worse than he could lay upon me when Ginny found out what had happened.

"Just heard from Deputy Garrow," Gil said, ever the professional. "They're still about an hour south. The going is tough."

I nodded.

"That's a smart boy," Gil said. "Deputy Garrow reported the boy stated that he found himself in thick woods when the batteries in his GPS ran out. He tried to backtrack, but couldn't find the right trail. When night began to fall he remembered a hunting camp he had passed on the way in. He forced a window open and found a couple of cots and Army blankets inside. He built a small fire in the wood stove and he and the dog stayed warm all night."

"What's his condition?"

"Excellent. Good color, plenty of energy, just a little hungry, Deputy Garrow said. He had a couple of candy bars for supper. He's walking home with the team. Wouldn't let them carry him."

"Good," Eli cut in. "Did he say why he went so deeply into the woods?"

"He said he spotted a red fox and followed it down a

trail and lost track of both time and location," Gil said, professional deference to a superior in his voice. Eli had returned, sure enough.

"I believe that," Eli said, and I agreed. Many times I had seen Tommy on the beach and in Ginny's back yard, rapt in thought and oblivious to the world as he contemplated the newest natural wonder he had found. He was smart, but he was, after all, only twelve.

We heard Chad and Tommy chatting and laughing before we saw them stride out of the forest. Tommy had the presence of mind to put on a somber face when he saw me standing with Gil, and he walked directly to us, unbidden.

"We'll talk about this later, Tommy," I said. "But I'm very glad to see you again."

"Yes sir, Mr. Martinez," he said, gazing at the ground.

"Steve's okay," I reminded him for the thousandth time.

I wanted to hug the lad but felt awkward. I stuck out my hand instead and Tommy quickly took it.

Gil studied the tops of the trees intently. Eli beamed avuncularly, as if he had been in charge all along and we had all loyally done his bidding. But he still did not behave as if he were the boss and we his underlings, although that had just been silently established by Gil's deference.

"Be sure to thank everyone who went out looking for you, okay?" I added.

Tommy strode around and shook everyone's hands, including Eli's, accepting their hair-tousles and congratulations. Doc Miller, who could accurately assess a kid's health with one glance, listened to Tommy's chest, took his temperature, peered into his eyes and patted him on the back. Mrs. Peters, who was cleaning up after the enormous breakfast she had served—she would accept no payment for doing her part in the search—grasped the blushing boy to her enormous bosom. There is no greater satisfaction for wilderness law enforcement and its civilian friends than the successful rescue of a lost child, and everybody grinned widely, our laughter heartfelt.

THIRTY-FIVE

"Tommy, it's not my place to chew you out for last night," I said quietly when we had returned to my cabin. "That belongs to your foster mother. But maybe we can talk about what happened and maybe we can make sure it doesn't happen again. Does that make sense to you?"

"Yes, it does," Tommy said, looking directly into my eyes. He was neither defiant nor defensive, just a kid who knew he'd made a mistake and was bravely ready to take his medicine.

"What do you think is the most important lesson you learned from last night?" I asked, expecting Tommy to say the obvious — to keep track of the time, especially the remaining daylight.

"Never go into the woods without fresh batteries for the GPS."

"Well . . . yes," I said. "And maybe don't forget how to use a compass. You didn't have one, did you?"

"No, I was using the GPS for a compass." When its batteries died, the device didn't know which way north lay. No hiker or pilot can afford to be without a magnetic compass as a backup.

"I think you're right about the batteries, Tommy, but sometimes the signals from the satellites in orbit can fail, and people who are navigating by GPS can get in deep trouble if they don't have a backup of some kind." Countless pilots of small planes had become so dependent on their hand-held or panel-mounted GPSs that a battery or electrical system failure, or the disappearance of the signals, caused them to panic and fly frantically in circles, their hearts pounding, trying to get their bearings from their aviation charts. More than one had run out of fuel not far from an airport that way, sometimes with fatal results. Against such an event I practiced constantly not only with a compass but also the old-fashioned direction-finding radio equipment in the sheriff's aircraft—and I regularly checked my position on a chart, making sure I could recognize where I was from landmarks. GPSs are wonderful tools, but when you let down your guard they can bite you.

"I didn't think about that," Tommy said forthrightly. "I'm going to get me a compass."

"And maybe a hiker's map or two," I said.

For a few minutes we sat lost in thought.

"You did do some things very well," I said. "Making that smudge fire was very smart. So was finding a camp and spending the night inside. It got pretty cold. How did you get in?"

"The door was locked with a padlock, but a window was loose, and Hogan and I were able to squeeze inside."

"Were you frightened?"

"Yes, a little, when the wolves came."

"*Wolves*?" A chill coursed through my stomach.

"Yeah. Two of them took down a deer right by the cabin before dark came. Hogan smelled them and started barking."

"What did they do?"

"They growled and snarled and threw themselves against the door. But it was locked tight. When they'd finished eating they moved away into the forest."

My stomach dropped into my knees and I stifled a gulp. That was the first time I had heard of wolves ranging so close to the northern part of the county, where the human population was heaviest. While Tommy himself probably had been in no danger of a direct attack from the animals, he very likely would have tried to go to his dog's aid, and in the melee the slashing predators might not have discriminated between boy and dog. Now the full force of my error in letting even an accomplished woodsman like Tommy go into the forest alone struck me. We had been very, very lucky.

For the rest of the afternoon Tommy and I went about our respective businesses, he catching up with the homework he hadn't done the night before and I repairing a few rotted boards in the woodshed next to my cabin. At about four the phone rang. It was Ginny.

"I'm at Houghton airport," she said. "Malcolm died last night. If you tried to reach me I turned my phone off so I could sit with him without being disturbed."

"I'm very sorry, Ginny," I said, only partly meaning it. Malcolm had hurt her badly and I resented that.

"It was a hard death. It was prostate cancer. He was in a lot of pain. Nobody should have to endure that. Especially alone. That's why I went to him, despite everything. He needed somebody. He had no one else."

I'll admit it. Ginny is a better human being than I am. She is comfortable with the grace of forgiveness, while I can never seem to let go of a grudge.

"How's everything?" she continued. "How's Tommy? Was he a good boy? Was Hogan a good dog? Were they any problem?"

"Uh, no, not at all," I said. "We did have an exciting time but I'll tell you about it when you get home."

"What's for supper?"

"Hmm, how about spaghetti?" My meat sauce is justly famous in the Upper Peninsula, at least among those who have sampled it, and there aren't all that many.

"Perfect. I'll be by about six. Bye for now."

She sounded a lot friendlier than she had the morning before, but she was not going to be happy when Tommy and I told her about the events of the last twenty-four hours. An iceberg of dread coursed through my stomach and settled in my entrails. To keep my mind off the impending ordeal I called Joe Koski.

"Ginny'll be home tonight," I said, "and I'll be able to take over the stakeout at Fourteen Mile Point tomorrow morning."

"Good," Joe said. "No point in Chad going back now. He's due for his rotation back to regular duty anyway. The stakeout will have been unmanned only twenty-four hours— what could happen in such a short time?"

I didn't want to think about that. I called Alex instead.

"News for you," he said. "On a hunch, Sue called a contact in the New Jersey State Police an hour ago and asked about Monaghan. His name turned up in the records of that case about the illegal organ transplant harvesting. For a while he was a person of interest. He was suspected of money laundering for the harvesting ring. But that lead went nowhere."

"Enough probable cause right there," I said. "I'll call Dick Franciscus."

A few minutes later, after a bit of thought, the New York detective agreed to move on the case.

"It's my neck," Dick said, "but it's my gut, too."

"Come again?"

"The commissioner could chop off my head if you're wrong, but my stomach tells me you're right. I'll take some guys and visit Monaghan in the morning for a little talk."

"Thanks, Dick," I said with feeling, and hung up.

While waiting for Ginny to arrive I put together my camping kit—a goose-down sleeping bag, an Ensolite ground pad, a canteen, coffee and a few military-issue dried Meals, Ready to Eat that Gil somehow had scrounged from the state police. Chad and Fred had left a cooking kit inside a forest green two-man nylon backpacker's tent pitched inside the tree line, well hidden from both the beach and the human geocache at Fourteen Mile Point. To my gear I added my hiker's GPS and the new novel by one of my favorite crime writers, P. D. James. After all the huggermugger of the last day and night, I looked forward to the quiet of the stakeout and two days in the woods with a fellow Indian. With Camilo's assent, Gil had recruited Billy Bones, the retired Lac

Vieux Desert tribal cop, to keep me company. I would need two days, anyway, to heal the welts and cuts Ginny's forthcoming eruption most likely would inflict on my hide.

And it was not long in coming. She arrived hungry and after hugging Tommy fiercely and me warmly — a lot more warmly than I had expected or even thought I deserved — she tucked into the spaghetti while Tommy and I sat mostly silent, stirring now and then to say something trivial. As she slurped away — she is usually a dainty eater, but not where pasta is concerned — I asked if she wanted to talk about New York.

"Some other time, Steve," she said. "It was tough and revisiting it is going to be tough, too."

"All right. But I'm here whenever you need to unload."

She put her hand on mine. "Thank you," she said. I was forgiven. For a while.

Presently, stifling a belch in ladylike fashion, she pushed her chair back. "I always know," she said, drilling her eyes into both Tommy and me, "when you've got something to tell me. Give."

We gave. She listened, her expression unchanging but her eyes smoldering, as we told our story. Tommy related the events as he had seen them — including the encounter with the wolves, which I'd hoped he would save for a later day — and I told my side. When we were done Ginny took in a deep breath.

"Go upstairs, Tommy," she said calmly. "I have things to talk about with Steve."

"Uh . . . there isn't an upstairs here," he said. My modest four-room cabin occupies all of one story.

"The bedroom then."

"Yes'm." He shot me a look full of remorse and sympathy.

When he had closed the door Ginny directed her full gaze upon me.

"What. Were. You. Thinking?" she said slowly and

evenly, as if each word were a complete sentence, without raising her voice a notch or changing her iron expression. I hate that. I can deal with frenzied yelling and screaming — a professional lifetime of dealing with domestic disputes involving sometimes armed combatants gives a cop that capacity — but calm, measured anger is a lot tougher. She did not cast ugly aspersions on my ancestry, one of the most ordinary forms of a thorough bawling out, but concentrated on the inadequacy of my intelligence and judgment. For the next ten minutes I quietly absorbed my drubbing, which involved weighty and completely deserved abstractions such as "what if?" and "stupidity" and "irresponsibility" and "idiocy."

I did not try to mitigate my guilt by bringing up Ginny's own words about her childhood next door to the forest. "We country kids *lived* in the woods," she had said over dinner several years before. "I'd go there on expeditions, gathering wildflowers, looking for birds, hunting treasures like old bottle tops and cans. Maybe we'd get lucky and find a hundred-year-old garbage dump in a gully where people threw things they couldn't burn, like broken dishes and patent medicine bottles. There were old foundations and maybe an abandoned shack.

"If I had a friend with me, we'd take a lunch and a jar of Kool-Aid. We'd make little shacks in the woods, perhaps finding a downed tree to make one wall and dragging branches over to make the rest. They were our forts. We were at home in the woods as much as we were in our own houses."

But Ginny, I knew, had changed. She had grown up and become a parent. Parents look at things differently from those who aren't parents.

When Ginny's batteries finally ran down she sat silently in the deathly calm she had maintained the while, her fiery green eyes lasering holes through my soul. I sat in a puddle of sweat.

"You're right, honey," I said. "I completely screwed up. I am so very sorry." That was all I could think of to say.

"Don't honey me!" she said.

I spread my hands in supplication. She ignored them.

"Tommy," she called. "Let's go home." As they walked out to her van, her arm around him lovingly, I knew she wouldn't lambaste him with what she'd lambasted me. He was only a boy. I was a grown man and should have known better.

THIRTY-SIX

The next morning I woke up still feeling bruised and prepared to suffer, at least in spirit, for quite a while. Ginny is not often stirred to anger, but when she is, she holds on to her mad for a long and thoroughly satisfying time until she is certain the object of her fury has truly repented of his sins. I'd been there before.

But now an urgent task awaited me. Thanks to the search for Tommy, Fourteen Mile Point had gone unwatched for nearly twenty-four hours and needed to be staked out quickly again if we ever were to catch the subject of our hunt—a subject who most likely was a psychopath and a killer. I threw on my clothes, gulped a bachelor's breakfast of toast and coffee, and headed for the marina. Dawn was sunny and already warming, the temperature climbing into the sixties, a balmy day for the middle of September in the Upper Peninsula. But a sharp breeze tousled the still green tall grass along Highway M-64 to the Porcupine City Marina. A cool front was blowing in from the north and would stir up the lake.

On the way to the marina I radioed the sheriff's department to tell the dispatcher I was on my way to Fourteen Mile Point.

"Billy Bones there yet?" I asked Joe.

"Can't make it till noon," he said. "Has a teacher conference with his granddaughter." Billy, I knew, was the only caregiver for his three grandchildren.

"Damn," I said. "I don't want to leave that stakeout unattended a minute longer than we have to."

"We won't have to," Eli cut in on the radio. My eyebrows rose.

"Back at the shop?" I asked needlessly. Most of me was delighted that Eli had gone back to work, but part of me—the political candidate part—was dismayed all the same. Maybe he was just playing figurehead and still relying on Gil to administer the department, but the voters wouldn't know the difference

"Yeah. I'll go with you in the Whaler. Billy can come out in my boat as soon as he gets here this afternoon. When he arrives at Fourteen Mile I'll come back in it." Eli often went out for lake trout from the marina in his sixteen-foot runabout.

"Yes sir."

"That way we'll be on the job but you won't be without backup."

"Yes sir."

I had to smile at that "we."

The sheriff's search boat, a workaday eighteen-foot Boston Whaler powered by a 150-horsepower Evinrude, is not the fastest or most comfortable craft on Lake Superior but still is a sturdy fiberglass hull that can hold its own in a rough seaway. I threw my gear on its well deck and stowed in a seat locker a waterproof plastic case containing my holstered .357 and the military-issue M16 light assault rifle we deputies preferred for open country rather than the short-barreled riot shotguns we carried in our cruisers for close-quarters combat. Eli arrived shortly later at the marina, lunch pail in hand and Glock holstered at his waist, warmly but lightly dressed in white uniform shirt and sheriff's windbreaker because he would be returning to base while the sun was still high. It was not lost on me that a Kevlar vest, which he rarely wore, added a couple of inches to his already considerable bulk. Eli had come back on the job and had dressed the part.

"Great day for police work," he said amiably. "Ready to go?"

"Yup." I waved to Paul Betty, the septuagenarian harbormaster, who during boating season lived in a small shack next to the docks and missed nothing.

"Seen anything go out yesterday?" I called. "Any

strangers?"

"Naw," he said. "Just a couple of locals. They came back yesterday evening." I felt better — the Porcupine City Marina is the largest and best-equipped harbor for a hundred miles along the lakeshore — but there are other ways to launch a boat onto the lake, such as the public access ramps at Silverton and the Wolverine Mountains Wilderness State Park thirteen and fourteen miles west of Porcupine City. There are also rough, rarely used skids — little more than loose wooden boards — on the beaches near summer cabins for scores of miles in both directions. I hoped nobody we were looking for had taken advantage of those.

"Heads-up, guys," the harbormaster called as Eli pulled in the dock lines and I started the outboard. "The lake's running a bit high today. Four-footers."

I waved in acknowledgment and pulled away into the channel. The breeze wasn't a gale, but it wasn't going to be an easy ride northeast over the fourteen miles of shoreline, long stretches of it uninhabited, that gave Fourteen Mile Point its name. The Whaler had an enclosed steering cuddy big enough to shelter two people, and that, I hoped, would keep us mostly dry from spray as the boat pounded its way over the heavy chop through the harbor channel to the open lake. But my knees would take a pounding, for I stood at the wheel, the better to see where I was going, while Eli sat upon a couple of cushions. He could have taken the wheel, being the senior officer, but senior officers are used to their juniors doing the driving, and so I did.

Once out into the lake I had to throttle back to six miles per hour so that the Whaler could shoulder safely over the quartering swells, its high freeboard keeping the crashing waves out of the cockpit. The spray, however, dampened me thoroughly. I grumbled. We'd have to dry our clothes over a fire as soon as we reached Fourteen Mile Point. The afternoon would be warm, in the mid-sixties, but by nightfall would have dropped to forty degrees or less. This wasn't going to be a luau in the tropics.

Eli and I exchanged few words, partly because of the roar of the outboard and the thumping of the boat's hull on the waves, but mostly because we were a little uncomfortable in each other's presence. We were still political rivals, after all. We were polite, but hardly chummy.

Still, when I thanked Eli for coming with me, he replied, "No problem, Steve. Thanks for coming out to my house to see me."

Ten minutes into the voyage the radio under the cockpit coaming crackled.

"Steve? Alex. Dick Franciscus and his squad tried to pick up Monaghan at his condo this morning, but he wasn't there. His secretary said he left on vacation the other day. He's been taking a lot of vacations, she said. Goes to Minneapolis, she said. Be careful. Be damn careful."

"Thanks."

Over the next several minutes I brought Eli up to speed on the latest developments in the case, and in soundless response the sheriff drew his Glock and checked the magazine. We both patted our armored vests.

Fourteen Mile Point is easy to spot even from a low boat running two miles offshore. Eli and I had decided to pass the lighthouse to the east as if we were just a couple of fishermen heading to Houghton, then turn the boat inshore around the point, out of sight of the lighthouse. If anyone had arrived there in the last twenty-four hours, we reckoned, they would have come from the east and maybe we could land unnoticed.

The ruins of the massive light station, built late in the nineteenth century, still tower over the forest, and the station's big fog signal building still squats on the shore. The lighthouse had been manned until it was automated in 1940, and the light was finally extinguished in 1945 when radio-beacon navigation rendered it obsolete. A few years later the place was sold to a private owner, and in 1984 vandals torched the main structure, burning everything combustible. The fog building escaped the torch, although its two ten-inch whistles, designed to throw an ear-shattering noise miles across the lake to provide a bearing to blinded vessels during fog and storms, will never scream again.

Decades ago the lighthouse keepers had brought in equipment and provisions over a rough dirt track, four miles long, leading to a gravel road that originally had been a logging trail. But, as Eli had pointed out, it was long grown over and had become impenetrable, and now the only reasonable way to reach Fourteen Mile Point is by boat, a long, rugged shoreline hike past several streams, or by snowmobile in the winter. The remoteness of the place made it the most challenging of the caches we had found.

Chad and Fred had discovered the cached cadaver, like all the others headless and handless but apparently well embalmed in plastic, tucked between the double walls of the ruined keeper's quarters, right where the waypoint on Arthur Kling's laptop said it would be. The deputies had left it there for the duration of the stakeout. After we'd caught our perps or given up on the attempt Alex would come in and do his thing, then we'd move the corpse to Marquette.

Meanwhile, the Whaler chugged slowly past Fourteen Mile Point as I squinted at the beach still more than a mile away through binoculars, searching for signs of human presence. A boat beached while the stakeout was unmanned or a tendril of smoke from a campfire might have betrayed human presence. Nothing. A bald eagle rose majestically from a tall snag on the low granite outcropping that marked the point and soared out low above the waves, seemingly to greet the boat passing by. A traditional Indian might have said that the eagle was acknowledging the presence of another who shared its existence on earth. But I knew the bird was ignoring me, that my arrival had nothing to do with its stirring, that it was scanning the waves below hoping a fat fish would rise into the shallows to be snatched with sharp talons.

I checked the GPS, looked up and immediately spotted directly onshore the sandy bluff we sought. There was no sand beach in front of the lighthouse, only rocky shallows, but a small stream lay under a low bluff half a mile east of the lighthouse, emptying onto a sandy bottom. There, as we had planned during the trip out from Porcupine City, Eli and I could winch the boat over the shallow inlet and hide it in the creek a few yards in behind the grassy dunes, where it couldn't be seen either from the lake or by anybody walking along the beach. Chad had made camp just inside the tree line, where the tent would also be invisible. It would be my home for the next two days.

"Ready now," I said, yielding the wheel to Eli. I gathered up a sixty-foot nylon line and took up position on the coaming at the port side while Eli swung the Whaler so its stern faced the waves. He opened the throttle to drive the boat into the inlet as far as it could go before grounding on the sand. At just the right moment Eli killed the motor and yanked its propeller out of the water before it churned into the bottom. I leaped over the side with the nylon line and strode over the sandbar into waist-high water along the creek bank, ready to tie one end to a tree ten yards in so that Eli could operate the bow winch, pulling the boat off the sandy bottom and into the creek.

I was reaching up to secure the line to a stout birch when a woman yelled "It's a cop!" from just inside the tree line fifty yards to the west. I knew that voice. It belonged to Sharon Shoemaker.

"Where?" a strange male voice called from farther away.

"The guy in front of that boat!"

"Oh, shit." He sounded irritated, not anxious—like a man who had prepared himself for any eventuality, including the unwelcome but not unexpected arrival of the law.

My blood curdled. My revolver and rifle lay zipped inside that waterproof bag at the bottom of the Whaler, thirty feet away.

I motioned to Eli to stay down. They hadn't seen him yet. The sheriff nodded and crouched out of sight in the cuddy, his Glock drawn, but I stood unarmed out in the open, a perfect target for a man with a gun. I am forever getting caught this way, with a lot of open space between me and my weapons. This time, I told myself futilely, it wasn't so much poor judgment as it is the accident of circumstance. In this instance I could hardly be expected to carry a revolver at my waist when wading through deep water up a creek. Could I? Shit.

"Let me try to jolly them along," I whispered to Eli.

"Okay," the sheriff whispered back. "Be careful."

I tried to play it cool. "Hello!" I shouted. "Didn't expect to find anybody so far from civilization!" But I knew they knew why I was there.

"It's Deputy Martinez!" Sharon called.

The man stepped out from the tree line and raised a rifle. He was tall and handsome, with arrogantly flaring nostrils and a sardonic, contemptuous smile, and outfitted in expensive outdoor clothing he no doubt had paid for with a platinum American Express card at the original Abercrombie & Fitch store on Water Street in Manhattan. I recognized Andrew Monaghan immediately, having seen his photograph.

"Sorry about this, cop," he said calmly. With a swift twist and click he snaked the rifle bolt back, loaded a cartridge into the chamber, and drove it home. Even at this distance I could see that it was a costly Weatherby Magnum, the kind of rifle wealthy captains of finance bought for guided antelope hunts on game ranches in Texas. I didn't know what caliber the rifle was, but knew it was capable of blowing a very large hole in me.

"He's armed," I whispered to Eli. "Rifle." I heard a soft click from inside the cuddy, where Eli had quietly pulled back the receiver on his Glock, charging the chamber with a cartridge.

Don't!" the woman called to Monaghan. She emerged from the tree line halfway between Monaghan and me, but well out of his line of fire.

"Haven't seen you for a while, Sharon," I said, trying to keep my voice conversational and my hands down, as if I hadn't noticed that a loaded and cocked rifle was pointed at me.

"Shut up!" Monaghan said. He raised the rifle to his cheek and sighted through the scope as Sharon Shoemaker's jaw dropped in dismay.

"Monaghan, don't shoot!" I called.

He lowered the rifle, his smile slowly disappearing. "How do you know my name?" he demanded.

"I'm the deputy who talked to you on the phone last month," I said. "Remember? We know all about you, Monaghan, my department, a bunch of others and the state police of Michigan, New York and New Jersey. The New York Police Department, too. Think, man! I'm a cop. If you kill me, you'll be hunted down. And you know what cops do to people who kill cops. Drop the rifle."

Instead he returned it to his shoulder and took another bead. I took a deep breath.

"We all know you're ACTUARY, that you cached the body of a murdered prostitute on the North Country Trail and that you killed Arthur Kling and torched his car. We know all about the geocaching game and where you guys planted all those bodies."

"How the hell did you find that out?" he said, looking up from the scope, his expression wreathed in unbelieving fury.

That amounted to a confession, but fat lot of good it would do me if Monaghan made Eli and me his second and third victims — third and fourth, if he had killed that prostitute. And, I thought absently, Sharon would be his fifth.

"Come on, drop the rifle. You know Michigan and Minnesota don't have the death penalty. You can spend the rest of your life in prison. But if you kill me, I can assure you that a cop will see to it that you die, too. And I guarantee you it'll be a painful, *painful* death."

Whether or not that was true I didn't really know — nor was I sure Camilo Hernandez was capable of torture — but I couldn't think of anything else to say. Monaghan kept the rifle at his shoulder.

"You're not as dumb as I thought," he said. "Gotta give you that." The cheerless smile returned to his face.

"Why'd you do it?" I said, as much to buy time as anything else, to keep him talking.

"If you have to ask, cop," he said, "you're not as smart as you think." He sighted through the scope, the muzzle steady, pointing directly at my head. At this range it would be impossible to miss.

But Monaghan wasn't as smart as *he* thought, not if he refused to consider the possible consequences to himself. He was so caught up in his own game, so possessed by his own magnetic personality, that he could see no way out except more killing.

Just before he squeezed the trigger I dived to the side, toward the boat, making a large splash in the shallow water of the inlet and spoiling his aim. But just before I reached the Whaler the bullet caught me in the last rib in my left flank just below the armor that had hiked up my torso as I dived. The round whined out into the lake.

In the movies the winged lawman holds his side with one hand and with the other resolutely raises his weapon and takes aim, drilling the bad guy squarely between the eyes. In real life it doesn't work that way. Getting shot, even by a bullet that glances off bone, is a powerful insult to the human body. The first shock usually incapacitates the victim, allowing the shooter to take his time with the coup de grace.

But I had dived into the cold, cold water of Lake Superior, and within two seconds my head had cleared and, my side screaming with pain, I had splashed around the port side of the boat and huddled behind the steel mass of the big Mercury outboard, groping for the gun case in the stern well. Monaghan still hadn't seen Eli, a good thing because the quarter inch of fiberglass that made up the walls of the cuddy couldn't have stopped a .22 bullet, let alone a Weatherby Magnum round.

Eli still crouched out of sight, waiting to make his move. "You okay, Steve?" he hissed.

"I'm hit," I whispered back from behind the motor, "but stay down. He'll cut you to pieces."

Monaghan loosed three more shots at me, one striking the water a foot away and ricocheting way out into the lake, another splattering against the cast steel of the motor and possibly cracking its case, and the third punching through four layers of fiberglass hull, entering at the bow and exiting at the stern a foot from my head. That Weatherby was a small-caliber cannon.

While Monaghan reloaded I reached around the motor and snaked the rifle case out of the well. Quickly I wrested the M16 and a couple of loaded thirty-shot magazines out of the case, drove home one of the magazines and cocked the action. I had the advantage in firepower now. Although the M16's lightweight 5.56 millimeter bullet is nowhere near as heavy as even a small-bore Weatherby Magnum, the military rifle can fire three-cartridge bursts of automatic fire as well as accurate single shots.

But Monaghan had the advantage of higher ground as well as stout pines and birches to hide behind. I had only the small mass of the Evinrude to protect me, and could not move away from the boat without exposing myself. I was losing blood, too, growing weaker by the minute. If Monaghan took his time, another of his bullets eventually would find me.

Whang! Another Weatherby bullet slammed through the hull and ricocheted off the lower unit of the Evinrude, the wind of its passage ruffling the hair on my exposed neck. In blind reaction I stood and fired two bursts at the gap in the trees where I had seen Monaghan last, the rounds ripping flinders of bark from the trunk of a hemlock. Just as I ducked back down, I caught a glimpse of Monaghan aiming his rifle from around a tree a good dozen feet from the spot I had shot up. I ducked to the right of the outboard and the bullet punched a ragged hole through the stern exactly where I had been.

This couldn't go on much longer.

Suddenly Eli's pistol barked from the other side of the boat. I glanced around the stern. A few feet away, resplendent in brass-bedecked white shirt and garrison cap, stood the sheriff, Glock cradled in both hands and aimed at the tree line, coughing every three seconds in careful timed fire as he waded through the water and strode up the sand in a gunfighter's crouch. Despite his arthritic bulk he had quickly rolled over the side of the Whaler into the shallow water while Monaghan was reloading.

"Get into the woods, Steve!" Eli yelled. "I'll cover you!" It took every ounce of my remaining strength to stagger out of the water and across the sand, spraying the woods behind the beach with the M16 as I stumbled up behind a screen of heavy logs atop a low dune, thinking that this must have been what it was like for the Marines hunkering on the beaches of Tarawa, pinned down by deadly Japanese fire.

Eli continued to advance, firing.

"Run!" I yelled, ready to cover Eli. His Glock wasn't very accurate at a fifty-yard range, but his bullets were striking close, forcing Monaghan to whip around from behind a thick white pine and snap off wild shots. Eli's ancient legs responded, breaking into a trot that was little more than a fast shuffle. Ten yards from the hummock that sheltered me, his emptied and he stopped for a second to dump the magazine and ram home a new one. It was a fatal pause.

The Magnum bullet struck Eli squarely in the center of his Kevlar vest and punched through and through in a spray of blood. The sheriff fell on his back onto the sand, his arms and legs flung out. The armored police vests worn under a roomy uniform shirt will stop a pistol bullet, but a high-velocity rifle load just keeps going. Only heavy tactical vests with steel rifle plates will stop such a slug, and those are normally worn by SWAT teams outside their uniforms.

"Whoooo!" yelled Monaghan in his moment of victory, stepping out from the tree line onto the beach. That was *his* fatal mistake.

Groaning in pain, I rose from behind the hummock, took a quick bead, and pumped two bursts into Monaghan's chest. He staggered, then fell to his knees and collapsed on his face, blood from his tattered lungs pouring from his mouth.

Then I fainted.

I wasn't out long. I came to with a female form leaning over me, her hands binding a rough compress made of my ripped-up shirt around my ruined side.

"Ginny?" I very much wanted to see her lovely face.

"No. It's Sharon."

"Why?"

"Long story, Deputy. And it's not my fault. But nobody's going to believe me. I'm sorry, but I have to go. When I get out of the woods I'll phone the police and tell them where you are."

"Don't do that. There's no trail out of here anymore. Stay here. I'll put in a good word."

"Sorry, Steve. I'm leaving. But help's coming." With that, Sharon sprinted west down the beach, stumbling over logs and rocks as she ran, once falling to her knees on the unsteady sand.

She was unarmed. She could have taken my M16, still with a dozen cartridges in its magazine, with her. But she did not. That counted for something. I passed out again.

Presently I awoke to the thrum of outboard motors, rose on one elbow and peered out onto the lake. Two boats bounced through the surf. Before he assaulted the beach, Eli must have radioed the sheriff's department and told Joe what was going on at Fourteen Mile Point.

Five minutes later the boats beached on the flat rocks offshore and four deputies, including Gil and Chad, leaped over the side and waded through the water.

"The sheriff's down," I called weakly as they approached. "So's the shooter. It's Monaghan. I think he's dead. Sharon Shoemaker was with him and she's gone west on the beach. She's not armed, though. Try to grab her, not shoot her. She likely knows the whole story."

A deputy knelt at Eli's side and searched for a pulse. When he looked up and shook his head Gil shoved Chad away before he could approach his fallen uncle. "Stand down," Gil said. "You're off the case. But tend to Steve."

Chad, who knew the rules, turned and gazed forlornly out over the lake for a few seconds, then shook his massive head, stifled a sob and knelt at my side. As he applied a gauze dressing to my shattered rib Gil barked a few words into his hand-held radio.

"Troopers on the way," he said when he was finished. "They'll drive in to a cabin three miles west on the beach and head this way to cut Shoemaker off. Now let's get you to the hospital."

As Chad brought up the folding litter we kept in the Whaler, I passed out for the third time.

THIRTY-SEVEN

"I can't trust you to go out alone, either, can I?" said Ginny as I struggled out of the fog of anesthesia in a bed at Porcupine County Hospital. But she said the words softly and lovingly, with a cool hand on my cheek.

"It was supposed to be just a stakeout," I said weakly, still in defensive mode after her reaming-out the other day.

We'd taken a chance, a dangerous one, I knew. We had hoped Fourteen Mile Point would still be deserted after Chad and Fred had left the stakeout to join the search for Tommy. What could possibly happen in twenty-four hours if it had taken the cachers nearly all summer to locate their quarries? There is a corollary of Murphy's Law that deals with this kind of situation, and I tried to put it into words, but failed.

"Shush," Ginny said, kissing my forehead.

Night had fallen outside. I tried to sit up and fell back, groaning from the lightning in my side.

"You'll have to come live with me until I can nurse you back to health," Ginny said.

"I can think of worse places to be," I said. Actually, there was nowhere I'd rather be than Ginny's house, and often I'd spend a night or two there. I had to be tough, though, or maybe I was just playing the macho game in a cloud of Vicodin. "But I can't impose on you."

"Nonsense," she said, stroking my cheek. "Maybe you'll get used to living with me. Think of it as practice, maybe." Her eyes twinkled and a small smile played at the edges of her mouth.

Tommy, who was standing on the other side of the bed, suddenly turned and looked out the window, his face a study in suppressed consternation. Indians embarrass so easily, I thought, or maybe it's just because he's a kid. I chuckled and gasped as my ribs shot me a painful reminder.

"Take it easy, Steve," said Doc Miller from the foot of the bed. "You're gonna be fine, but you're gonna hurt for a while. That bullet took out a hunk of one rib and cracked two others. I had to dig around in there and put in seventeen stitches to hold you together. You pay attention to Ginny, you hear? If you stay with her you'll save the county a bunch of money in nursing home bills." Ever the practical man, Doc was.

Ginny bent and kissed me again. "The authorities want to talk to you," she said. "Tommy and I will be back tomorrow to take you home."

Her home. Not mine. I'm fond of my cabin, but Ginny was right. I could get used to her place very easily. I squeezed her hand and she and Tommy stepped out the door, to be replaced by the much less attractive countenance of the undersheriff.

"Did they get Shoemaker?" I asked.

"You bet," Gil said. "She just walked up to the troopers and gave in without a fight. She's talking. And how."

"How'd Shoemaker and Monaghan get to Fourteen Mile?"

"He and the girl drove out to a cabin four miles past the light, parked their car and hiked down the beach."

"That's what I was afraid of," I said. "Anyway, what's the rest of the story?"

"Oh, it's quite a story," Gil said. "Stay right there. Don't move. I'll tell you all about it."

I was beginning to feel woozy again, and Doc Miller stepped in.

"Can it wait, Undersheriff?" he said. "The patient needs rest."

"Oh, sure," Gil said. "Nobody's going anywhere anyway. See you tomorrow, Deputy."

I passed out for the fourth time that day.

THIRTY-EIGHT

The next afternoon my side still ached, even with Vicodin, but my head was clearer after a brief but loving visit from Ginny and Tommy. I had just put away a decent lunch when Gil knocked. Alex and Sergeant Sue Hemb followed him into the room, and the three pulled up chairs around my bed.

"Ready, Deputy?" the undersheriff said without preamble.

"Given the circumstances," I said, "maybe you could call me Steve."

Gil's expression remained set. Alex and Sue exchanged amused glances.

"That corpse on the North Country Trail?" Gil said. "Yeah, Monaghan cached it there, Shoemaker said. This is where things get really interesting. She said Monaghan had told her he and Kling had been roommates at Yale — we checked and she was right. All the way back at college, Monaghan had been the leader, Kling the follower. Sue?"

Sergeant Hemb nodded. "It's a common phenomenon with antisocial personality disorders," she said. "The mastermind and his loyal servant work together, until the mastermind decides the servant is no longer useful and does away with him."

"Yeah," Alex cut in, opening his notebook. "In the last couple of years Monaghan and Klein had helped bankroll a couple of mortuaries, one in Jersey — that's the one that got busted last year — and one in Duluth. They both specialized in medical cadavers and harvested body parts for the legitimate market. At the Duluth mortuary, they got a crooked diener to cut out and sell illegal organs and alter the paperwork. Monaghan was the brains and Klein the bagman."

"Diener?" I asked.

"That's a mortuary worker responsible for handling, cleaning and moving bodies. Sometimes he helps harvest organs."

"Go on."

"When the cops busted that ring in Jersey last year, Monaghan nearly got caught in the backwash. He and Kling decided to lie doggo with the Minnesota operation for a while until the heat blew over, but they had had so much fun, and made so much money, with harvesting cadavers in Minnesota that after a few months they decided to start up again—but with the geocaching game."

"Whatever for?" I said.

"Just to keep their hand in," Gil said. "And we think they hoped to keep the diener happy by letting him make a few bucks selling the cadavers to the geocachers. It was probably just something to do until they could start peddling illegal organs and making big money again."

"Did Monaghan kill that hooker?"

"Shoemaker says he said he did."

"Just because he could?"

"Don't think so. The Duluth mortuary—it was raided and shut down last night—just didn't have a handy prepared cadaver that day for Monaghan to take. The diener is talking, by the way.

"Shoemaker also says Monaghan told her that he went out that night in Duluth, found a hooker, took her back to his motel room, had sex with her, then strangled her. Shoemaker said Monaghan told her in great detail how he stashed the body in his car, drove east into Wisconsin, cut her up in the woods and tried to embalm her with formalin and a syringe. He buried the head and hands and carried the rest to the cache in Michigan."

"Alone?"

"Probably. Monaghan kept himself buff working out at a Bally's and had the beef to carry a heavy torso on his back two miles into the woods. What's more, Shoemaker said Monaghan told her he was doing the world a favor by ridding it of someone it would never miss."

"That's cold," I said.

"It's typical," Sergeant Hemb said.

"According to Shoemaker," Gil said, "that's what Arthur Kling told Monaghan, too, when he found the cache on the trail. It was stinking, and Kling guessed it wasn't a cadaver, but a vic done just to be a geocache. He called Monaghan in New York to complain that murder wasn't part of the game. Monaghan said he'd come out and meet Kling and talk over the matter. They agreed to meet at Page Falls at three p.m. August first. Shoemaker had told Kling about the place and even taken him there for a little sex.

"But now, if Shoemaker's story is right, Kling was badly worried. Somebody had been killed. He could be charged as an accessory to murder. But if he got rid of Monaghan, there would be no witness, either, that Kling was involved. That's what Shoemaker says he said."

"That explains why he had that varmint rifle in the motel," I said. "But why didn't he take it to Page Falls?"

"Bad timing. Shoemaker says Kling wanted to wait till after the meeting so he could hear Monaghan's side. He knew Monaghan hadn't yet been to the Fourteen Mile Point cache and was going to pick him off there and bury both Monaghan and the cache there in the woods. But Monaghan was waiting with a gun at Page Falls and got him first, then torched the car."

"Wait a minute," I said. "How come Sharon knows all this stuff? Why would Monaghan tell her anything?"

"If I may," Sue said quietly. Gil nodded.

"Sociopaths like to tell their victims all about their crimes, to impress them with how brilliant they are," she said. "Then they kill the people to whom they have allowed this knowledge, and in doing so, they symbolically bury the truth.

It's how they live with themselves. And then they do it again and again."

"I'll be damned," I said.

"No, Steve," Gil growled. "*Monaghan* be damned."

I looked up at the use of my first name but Gil's glower didn't change.

"Did Sharon say how she came to hook up with Monaghan?"

"She got into it with him when Kling wrote that fake phone number on Monaghan's business card after their, ah, encounter during Jerry and Adela's wedding dance. When Kling stopped calling and the phone number he gave her turned out to be bogus, she called Monaghan at his number on that business card to see if he knew where Kling might be. He told her he couldn't remember Kling, like he told you. But he got her phone number and after she gave you the card, he called her back."

"What for?" I asked.

"A little whoopee while he was out here hunting for caches and peddling corpses," Gil said. "Sharon decided she liked Monaghan better than Kling. He was rich and connected—and *quote*, masterly, *unquote*. And he was, *quote*, great in the sack, *unquote*. She hoped he would take her away from this, *quote*, stupid backwater, *unquote*." Gil unnecessarily pronounced "quote" and "unquote" in precise italics to make sure we knew they were her words, not his. The undersheriff never overestimated anybody's intelligence, least of all mine.

"Where was she when Monaghan did Kling?"

"Right there at Page Falls, watching from the woods. She said Monaghan stepped out when Kling drove up, said 'Artie?' and when Kling said 'Yes,' just popped him."

"That makes her an accessory."

"Right."

"What did she say she felt when that happened?"

"Glad," Gil said. "She said she hated Kling for running out on her."

"What's even worse is what Monaghan most likely planned to do with Sharon," I said. "Does she have any idea?"

"Not yet," the undersheriff said. "She says she thinks he planned to take her to New York with him."

I tried and failed to get my mind around the picture of a young urban sophisticate plunking a poor, uneducated and unpolished woman from the backwoods into the drawing rooms of Wall Street society.

"Do you believe that?" I asked Sue.

"Not at all," she said. "When it was all over Sharon would have become his third victim. I'm certain of it."

"How can any woman be that dumb?" I said.

"Bad boys attract women," Sue said. "Very bad boys attract stupid women."

At that we all fell silent for a few beats.

"But something doesn't make sense," I finally said. "Monaghan must have known we were on to the geocaching scheme. He must have known we knew the corpse on the North Country Trail was a homicide, not a cadaver. And why did he come back to look for the last cache at Fourteen Mile?"

"In the simplest possible terms," Sue said, "sociopaths like to finish what they start. In shrink jargon, they're anal."

Alex snorted. "He probably thought he could get away with it. He probably thought a bunch of hayseed cops could never catch him."

"That's always their mistake, isn't it?" I said.

"Always," Sue said. "The sociopathic personality thinks he's figured out all the angles, but in reality he always leaves an important stone unturned. That's how we catch him."

Suddenly I groaned as pain knifed through the Vicodin and laid open my side. Doc Miller stepped back into the room. "We're wearing Steve out," he said. "Let's give him the rest of the day off."

All night I tossed and turned.

THIRTY-NINE

The second morning in the hospital I awakened still weary, but at last was beginning to feel that I would survive my wound. I ate all the breakfast the nurse brought and was on my second cup of coffee when Gil again stuck his head in the door.

"I need your statement on what happened at Fourteen Mile Point," he said briskly, without even the customary how-are-you-feeling hello. "I'll tape it, type it up, and bring it for you to sign."

I took him through the events on the beach. Gil asked no questions, but simply listened carefully. When I was finished he observed mildly, "What would you have done different if you were to do it all over again?" This is part of every postmortem discussion of a significant piece of police work.

"First, we should've assumed that somebody might have gotten to Fourteen Mile during those twenty-four hours Chad and Fred were away," I said. "We'd have beached the boat much farther down the shore from Fourteen Mile and walked to the lighthouse inside the tree line, staying out of sight. They wouldn't have gotten the drop on us that way."

"Right," Gil said. "You weren't thinking, were you?" His tone was gentle, not accusatory. He is a realist, but he is not cruel.

"No," I had to admit. "Nor was Eli, I guess. Our minds were on other things." The election. Our rivalry.

"That was *my* mistake," Gil said. "Somebody else should have gone on that stakeout."

I nodded. No argument with that.

"Second," I wouldn't have put my revolver in the rifle case. I'd have wrapped it in a plastic grocery bag and kept it in my holster on my belt."

"Would that have done any good?" Gil said skeptically. "The range was fifty yards. You'd have had a handgun, but he had a rifle with a scope."

"Yes, well," I said. "But I might have got lucky."

"You *did* get lucky, didn't you? You're alive."

"Yeah," I said.

"Thanks to Eli."

"May God bless his soul," Gil said with feeling. I looked up in open-mouthed astonishment. I had never before heard the undersheriff express a sentiment of any kind. He was full of surprises.

Gil stood and opened the door. Then he whirled back on his heel. "By the way, Steve, you're the sheriff now. The county board's voted to appoint you to the remainder of Eli's term, even though you're shot."

I looked up. "Does that mean you have to call me 'sir'?"

"Not right now. You haven't been sworn in yet." I could have declared that Gil smiled, but the grimace on his creased face, like a baby's, might have just been from gas.

In a few minutes Ginny swept in, filling the room with the scent of the Vol de Nuit I loved but which she wore only on special occasions.

"Let's go home," she said.

FORTY

Five days later, we buried Eli in grand style.

More than a hundred cops drove in from all over Upper Michigan, Wisconsin, Minnesota and even Iowa, Illinois and Canada to pay their respects to one of their own who had fallen in the line of duty. Eli had been a sheriff for a long time and had been on speaking terms with just about every other law enforcement officer in five states and two Canadian provinces. He had been a good lawman and was now a renowned one.

All night at the Jones Funeral Chapel in downtown Porcupine City, an honor guard of four officers, one at each corner of the casket, had stood gravely at attention as mourners passed in review. Every fifteen minutes the guard rotated, beginning with Porcupine County deputies and ending with Ontario Provincial Policemen.

I had stood my turn at watch, moving as gingerly as I could, unable to salute as briskly as my brother officers. Ginny had not wanted me to serve on the honor guard—she pushed me to rest another day at her home, where I'd gone after Doc Miller sprung me from the hospital two days after the shootout at Fourteen Mile Point. But standing sentinel over Eli's casket for a measly quarter of an hour was the least anybody could do for someone who had saved his hide. Tommy stood in the back of the room at the funeral parlor, ready to bring his foster mother to the rescue if I faltered. I didn't.

Those three quiet autumn days at Ginny's, spooning with her by night under the warm quilt of her huge oaken bed and resting across from her by day in the leather recliner in her great room, carving the venison at dinner and quizzing Tommy on his homework, was the closest I had ever come to domesticity. It wasn't so bad, either. I was beginning to think I could get used to being an official part of a nuclear family.

The next morning Eli's casket was driven to St. Matthew's Episcopal Church in downtown Porcupine City, and another honor guard took up its position in the church.

I had been to a dozen police funerals, most of them for retired cops who had died in their beds, but a few for those who had fallen on duty. With Ginny on my left and Tommy on my right, I took up my position in a front pew. Dorothy Garrow, who knew the healing power of a magnanimous gesture, had asked for our presence there. By rights I should have been one of the pallbearers—all of them were Porcupine County deputies, including Gil O'Brien—but my wound kept me from that honor.

The interior of St. Matthew's looked and smelled as if every florist within fifty miles of Porcupine City had been cleaned out for the occasion. Lilies and carnations flooded the altar and every corner of the church. Seemingly every police force in a radius of five hundred miles had sent a floral arrangement.

Dorothy, followed by a dozen of her children and grandchildren, walked slowly, chin held high, from the vestry and took her seat in the pew across from mine. Gil stepped away from the casket, snapped to attention before Dorothy and gave her a smart white-gloved salute. Stooping, he gently folded into her hands Eli's six-pointed sheriff's star so that she would have a part of her husband to hold during the service, and whispered something into her ear. She nodded, looked at her lap and dabbed at her eyes with a handkerchief. My eyes widened and Ginny and I glanced at each other. *Gil* had a tender side?

As the opening hymn ended in a hush, Father Ted McGillicuddy, St. Matthew's veteran rector and an immigrant Scot, mounted the pulpit. "Elias Anthony Garrow is dead," Father Ted began somberly in his soft burr. "The law enforcement community has lost a brother officer and

Porcupine County has lost a fine citizen and protector."

Father Ted, a theatrical sort who affected scarlet vests and tartan slacks around town, liked to scatter little rhetorical surprises in his eulogies as well as his homilies and sermons. "But we will all see our beloved sheriff again some day," he said happily. "This is really a going-home party for Eli."

Even Dorothy smiled at that one.

"Let us celebrate his life."

Briskly Ted took the congregation through the highlights of Eli's colorful career as a law enforcement officer, a husband, and a father—there were a remarkable lot of them, too—while skimming over the peccadilloes. No need to spell them out. But Father Ted was too honest not to acknowledge Eli's humanity.

"We don't shy away from the bad times," Father Ted said, "because as fragile and sinful human beings we make mistakes, we hurt each other, and we don't do things right all the time. We are not perfect. Neither was Eli. In God, it is never too late to ask for forgiveness of those who have gone before us. In God, it is never too late to forgive."

Whatever human flaws Eli had displayed during his long life, I was perfectly willing to agree, were small and easily excused, considering the manner in which he'd left that life.

And that expensive ad in the Ironwood Globe after I'd defeated him in the primary? There was nothing dark and threatening about that, as I had presumed. Eli, Dorothy said, had simply cashed in a couple of government bonds he'd squirreled away as a small cushion under what would have been a modest county pension.

"He just cared too much about being sheriff," Dorothy had said during our long conversation when I'd phoned her to offer my condolences. "I tried to talk him out of using that money. He was just too proud."

At the end Father Ted said what we all expected him to say. We would have been indignant had he not said it. "Eli

Garrow was a hero. In saving the life of another officer, he made the ultimate sacrifice."

The hush in the church deepened into dead silence as Father Ted continued.

"Eli Garrow has died. None of us has ever come back from the dead to tell the tale. And the Bible and the church — indeed, all the religions of mankind — are not very consistent when it comes to defining exactly what it is we enter into at death. And even if they were consistent, they still would convey only matters of faith, rather than scientific proof. I too have no proof. All I can offer is hope."

A few more words followed by communion, then we all stood for the Lord's Prayer and Ralph's benediction. A bagpiper — George Haskell, who owned an ambulance service in Ironwood and had played at the funeral of every cop in three counties for decades — piped a mournful tune while the pallbearers bore the coffin out of the church past two lines of white-gloved officers standing at attention, holding their salute rigidly until Eli was placed gently into the hearse.

The procession to the cemetery, led by more than sixty police vehicles, was the longest in Porcupine County anybody could remember. Ginny, Tommy and I, driven by Chad in a freshly washed cruiser just behind several limousines bearing the Garrow family and just ahead of those carrying Garner and the county commissioners, rolled slowly down U.S. 45 to the cemetery three miles south of town. Uniformed officers guarding every corner held salutes as the hearse passed by. So lengthy was the procession that the first vehicles arrived at the cemetery before the last ones had pulled out of the church parking lot and from the side streets surrounding it.

As we drove, I thought about the events of the day before. Alex had dropped by Ginny's to fill me in on the loose ends the investigative team had been able to tie up. All the remaining corpses had been recovered from their caches and transported to the Marquette lab for sampling in case a DNA match could be made some time in the future, if ever. The police in Duluth said no prostitute had been reported missing, the homicide commander adding that he doubted one ever would be. Eventually the headless and handless bodies would be laid to rest in a potter's field, just like all those indigents from the Poor Farm so long ago.

"As for the other geocachers," Alex said, "we may never know who they are, either. We got four of them — Monaghan, Kling, Wilson and Wilt — but the other three probably will never turn up. If they have any sense they'll never set foot in Porcupine County again."

Because they had cooperated with us, I thought, Wilson and Wilt would receive light sentences — a year in county jail with time off for good behavior, perhaps a bit of community service afterward. Considering their crimes, I thought snarkily, a few hundred hours of picking up litter and mowing the lawns of county cemeteries would be appropriate. But neither man was a hardened criminal, just another lost and damaged soul who had fallen under the spell of a murderous Svengali. Having tried to cover his trail, Kling had been a harder case, but Monaghan was purely and simply evil. I wished I had learned more about him, what horrible events of his childhood had transformed him into an unredeemable sociopath. I felt no guilt over having relieved society of his presence, but the act of killing a fellow human being would stay with me for years to come, as had all the others.

Sharon Shoemaker would do time in state prison as an accessory to murder, although her sentence also would be lightened because she had cooperated. I didn't see much of a future for her after prison.

We'd keep the case open for a year or so, then, no new facts coming to light, the file would be moved from a cabinet in the sheriff's squadroom to a dusty cardboard box in a dark corner of the archives at the Porcupine County Courthouse. And that would be that.

"Monaghan's uncle literally screamed bloody murder when word got to City Hall in Manhattan," Alex continued. "He said his nephew could never have done what we said he had, and he wanted the police commissioner to find and fire anybody on the New York City force who had helped us. The commish stood behind Franciscus. Rumor is that he's in line for a lieutenancy. And when the uncle told Garner he'd demand an official investigation into misconduct in the Porcupine County Sheriff's Department, Garner told him to go take a flying—"

"A flying what?" Ginny had said disingenuously as she walked in on us, causing Alex to blush violently and splutter. He can be *so* old-fashioned.

We arrived at the cemetery. With Ginny's cool palm in my left hand and Tommy's in my right, I strode to the grave, flinching as the wound in my side reminded me of its presence. I am not ashamed to admit that I hid behind the wince, for it camouflaged the emotions I felt. Despite my unchurchedness, funerals touch me deeply, and funerals for brother officers are almost unbearable. More than any other human rite, saying farewell to the dead is an ingathering of community, an acknowledgment of social kinship, a way of reaching out to others. We are all in this together, the ceremony declares, and together we shall survive even as some of us die.

Two hundred years ago we Lakota constructed open-air scaffolds on which to place our dead and leave them to become one with the eagles and vultures, a rite that was every bit as holy and reverential as that performed today for a Christian burial. I doubted that any Lakota shaman would have found fault with Father Ted's closing words when it came time to scatter earth on the casket.

"We commend to Almighty God our brother Eli, and we commit his body to the ground; earth to earth, ashes to ashes, dust to dust. The Lord bless him and keep him; the

Lord make his face to shine upon him and be gracious unto him, the Lord lift up his countenance upon him and give him peace. Amen."

As an Army veteran Eli was entitled to a military salute, and a team from the local Veterans of Foreign Wars raised their rifles, barking a rapid volley into the sky as we all twitched.

"In an important way," my pastor father had once told me, "the military salute is a reminder for the living of God's wrath."

The VFW tenderly handed its flag to Dorothy, then Garner stepped forward. "On behalf of a grateful county and state," he said, "we present you with this flag in remembrance of the ultimate sacrifice Eli made serving the residents of Porcupine County."

On his bagpipe George Haskell skirled "Amazing Grace," the moment in a police funeral during which absolutely no eye can remain dry. Mine sure didn't. Ginny and Tommy both sobbed quietly beside me. As the last notes drifted into the sky, all the mourners burst into "Sheltered in the Arms of God" and loosed brightly colored balloons to float up into the sky, a singular touch I had been seeing at more and more Upper Peninsula funerals.

Gil spoke quietly into a hand-held radio. We looked up past the slowly rising balloons as the drone of aircraft engines intruded on the hush. Four small planes approached from the north at a thousand feet in tight finger-four formation.

At the Number Two position, just behind a state police Bonanza from Lansing, Doc Miller flew his Bird Dog. Numbers Three and Four were Cessnas from the Civil Air Patrol at Ironwood.

Just before the formation passed over the cemetery, the Bird Dog lifted skyward, climbing away in the classic Missing Man maneuver. The gesture had been my idea. Eli deserved it and Dorothy had welcomed it.

"I thought that was only for pilots," she had said.

"For one very important moment in my life, Dorothy," I had replied with feeling, "Eli was my wingman."

"He now guards the heavens," said Father Ted, who always comes up with just the right thing to say, as we all watched the Bird Dog ascend into the clouds. As the airplane disappeared into the mist it was transfigured, in my Lakota mind's eye, into an eagle.

A Note to Geocachers

All the geographic waypoints given in this novel are real spots on Earth. But if you choose to go looking for these locations with your GPS, be aware that their surroundings are fictional.

THE AUTHOR

About the Author

Henry Kisor is the author of five Steve Martinez mysteries, *Season's Revenge, A Venture into Murder, Cache of Corpses, Hang Fire,* and *Tracking the Beast.* A sixth, *The Riddle of Billy Gibbs,* is forthcoming.

He and his wife Debby spend half the year in Evanston, Illinois, and the other half in a log cabin on the shore of Lake Superior in Ontonagon County, Michigan, the prototype of Porcupine County.

He is also the author of three nonfiction books, *What's That Pig Outdoors: A Memoir of Deafness; Zephyr: Tracking a Dream Across America,* and *Flight of the Gin Fizz: Midlife at 4,500 Feet.*

He retired in 2006 after thirty-three years as an editor and critic for the old *Chicago Daily News* and the *Chicago Sun-Times.* In 1981 he was a nominated finalist for the Pulitzer Prize in criticism.

Made in the USA
San Bernardino, CA
11 March 2015